Short Stories
of the Sea

Short Stories of the Sea

Selected and Arranged by
George C. Solley and Eric Steinbaugh
with Introductions and Biographies by
David O. Tomlinson

Naval Institute Press
Annapolis, Maryland

Copyright © 1984
by the United States Naval Institute
Annapolis, Maryland
Third printing hardcover, 1990
First printing paperback, 1990

Library of Congress Cataloging in Publication Data
Main entry under title:

Short stories of the sea.

1. Sea stories, English. 2. Sea stories, American.
I. Solley, George C., 1946–   . II. Steinbaugh, Eric.
PR1309.S4S48   1984   823′.01′0832162   84–9823
ISBN 0–87021–650–3
ISBN 0–87021–786–0 (Ppbk)

Printed in the United States of America on acid-free paper ♾

Contents

Preface

Even as we were putting the finishing touches on our anthology of sea poetry, *Moods of the Sea,* we knew that this book would be our next project. We had talked about the need for a collection of the best short stories of the sea; we had discussed what it should and should not contain; and we had outlined just how we would go about searching for and selecting the stories for such a book. Many excuses arose not to commit ourselves so soon after the publication of the poetry anthology to another such venture. But the new book would not be denied, and so we set aside other business to begin working on what was to become the volume that is now before you.

The material was collected with the understanding that it would include only short stories. Thus the reader will not find here any works by such renowned writers of sea literature as Marryat, Cooper, Smollett, Nordhoff, or Hall for the very simple reason that they were novelists and not short story writers. Even with these exclusions, though, we assembled enough sea stories of literary merit to fill a volume the size of an unabridged dictionary, and we had to face the reality of the anthologist's remora—limited space. Only about a quarter of the stories we had collected could be printed, and the selection process was difficult, frustrating, sometimes even painful. We were forced to use other criteria for inclusion besides the initial one we had in mind of merit: It would have been easy to compile a volume consisting only of stories by Melville and Conrad, but in addition to those stories of the sea that have become classics of the genre, we wanted to present the best sea tales of major literary figures and a well-balanced cross section of the works of lesser-known authors. Although we sought the opinions of others in helping us select the stories, we alone are responsible for the final choices, and in some cases the only defense that can be offered for a particular selection is that it represents the editors' whim.

In arranging the selections, we were first tempted to place them in chronological sequence, partly because the reader could then gain a sense of the genre's development and partly because of the difficulty of organizing such a diverse collection in groups. In the end, however, an arrangement was worked out by sections based on subject, setting and theme: There are stories of the land and sea; sea legends; accounts of adventures at sea; tales of storm and shipwreck; and stories whose greatness gives them a special place in literature over and above their claim as part of the genre of sea fiction.

As always in a project of this sort, there are many people who deserve recognition. We wish to thank our colleagues in the Department of English at the U. S. Naval Academy for their advice and suggestions. A special debt of gratitude is owed to Professor David O. Tomlinson, who gave up his valuable time to write section introductions and authors' biographies. We are indebted once again to the staff of the Naval Institute Press for supplying the editorial and design expertise required to transform a manuscript into a book. Finally, we want to thank Meg and Billy Solley and Leif and Kyle Steinbaugh for helping us rediscover the simple wonders of literature with their unyielding and urgent requests for a bedtime story.

GEORGE C. SOLLEY
ERIC STEINBAUGH

Short Stories
of the Sea

Sea and Shore

THE SEA EXERCISES a mysterious, mesmerizing power over man. Many of the great stories trade on one aspect of this power—the fortunate or fateful attraction that draws a young man to sea at some decisive moment in his life. The sea also holds sway over those who have left her and those who have never done more than tread her shores or settle near them. She is a schemer who likes to bewitch those who have hired cabins in a modern liner to insulate themselves from her. With or without our consent she will touch us all.

It is by virtue of this power of hers that the sea shapes lives and elicits responses from writers. Sometimes these responses are in the form of meditations. In the case of Nathaniel Hawthorne's "Foot-prints on the Sea-shore," the sea presents puzzles to the mind of the narrator and fires his imagination. John Masefield's two pieces, "Being Ashore" and "On Growing Old," are reflections on how the sea shapes those who are no longer with her but cannot forget her. The first is an adventure recalled; the second, a remembrance of bygone years spent exploring the world.

Sometimes the responses are more violent and direct. The sea, like God, is omnipotent: what she gives to man one day she can take away the next. In "Malachi's Cove," Anthony Trollope tells of a place where people gather and sell the seaweed that the ocean coughs up daily, where they risk their lives for this pittance, and where their bodies are broken and finally their spirits mended by the sea.

Sarah Orne Jewett, in "All My Sad Captains," relates the story of Mrs. Peter Lunn, a woman who never went to sea but whose life has been shaped by one man who did and who died. In "Red," master storyteller Somerset Maugham shows how the ocean brings two people together in an idyllic South Sea setting, how it separates them, and how the memory of their relationship destroys another human being.

A storm is sometimes at sea, sometimes on shore. In Fitzgerald's "The Rough Crossing," the passengers of an ocean liner see turbulent emotions which have never emerged before erupt in response to the anger of a tempestuous sea. John Thomason's "Meeting" portrays the violence that meets the crew of the loyal ship *Kaiser* when they dare come ashore during the German naval uprising of 1918.

John Updike plays with language in "Lifeguard." He tells the story from the viewpoint of a theological student who earns money in the summer as a lifeguard at the beach. The man's theology is given substance by his experience on the shore, and his job as lifeguard is fortified by his religious reverence.

Foot-prints on the Sea-shore

BY NATHANIEL HAWTHORNE

IT MUST BE a spirit much unlike my own, which can keep itself in health and vigor without sometimes stealing from the sultry sunshine of the world, to plunge into the cool bath of solitude. At intervals, and not infrequent ones, the forest and the ocean summon me—one with the roar of its waves, the other with the murmur of its boughs—forth from the haunts of men. But I must wander many a mile, ere I could stand beneath the shadow of even one primeval tree, much less be lost among the multitude of hoary trunks, and hidden from earth and sky by the mystery of darksome foliage. Nothing is within my daily reach more like a forest than the acre or two of woodland near some suburban farm-house. When, therefore, the yearning for seclusion becomes a necessity within me, I am drawn to the sea-shore, which extends its line of rude rocks and seldom-trodden sands, for leagues around our bay. Setting forth, at my last ramble, on a September morning, I bound myself with a hermit's vow, to interchange no thoughts with man or woman, to share no social pleasure, but to derive all that day's enjoyment from shore, and sea, and sky,—from my soul's communion with these, and from fantasies, and recollections, or anticipated realities. Surely here is enough to feed a human spirit for a single day. Farewell, then, busy world! Till your evening lights shall shine along the street—till they gleam upon my sea-flushed face, as I tread homeward—free me from your ties, and let me be a peaceful outlaw.

Highways and cross-paths are hastily traversed; and, clambering down a crag, I find myself at the extremity of a long beach. How gladly does the spirit leap forth, and suddenly enlarge its sense of being to the full extent of the broad, blue, sunny deep! A greeting and a homage to the Sea! I descend over its margin, and dip my hand into the wave that meets me, and bathe my brow. That far-resounding roar is Ocean's voice of welcome. His salt breath brings a blessing along with it. Now let us pace together—the reader's fancy arm in arm with mine—this noble beach, which extends a mile or more from that craggy promontory to yonder rampart of broken rocks. In front, the sea; in the rear, a precipitous bank, the grassy verge of which is breaking away, year after year, and flings down its tufts of verdure upon the barrenness below. The beach itself is a broad space of sand, brown and sparkling, with hardly any pebbles intermixed. Near the water's edge there is a wet margin, which glistens brightly in the sunshine, and reflects objects like a mirror; and as we tread along the glistening border, a dry spot flashes around each footstep, but grows moist again, as we lift our feet. In some spots, the sand receives a complete impression of the sole—square toe and all; elsewhere, it is of such marble firmness, that we must stamp heavily to leave a print even of the iron-shod heel. Along the whole of this extensive beach gambols the surf-wave; now it makes a feint of dashing onward in a fury, yet dies away with a meek murmur, and does but kiss the strand; now, after many such abortive efforts, it rears itself up in an unbroken line, heightening as it advances, without a speck of foam on its green crest. With how fierce a roar it flings itself forward, and rushes far up the beach!

As I threw my eyes along the edge of the surf, I remember that I was startled, as Robinson Crusoe might have been, by the sense that human life was within the magic circle of my solitude. Afar off in the remote distance of the beach, appearing like sea-nymphs, or some airier things, such as might tread upon the feathery spray, was a group of girls. Hardly had I beheld them, when they passed into the shadow of the rocks and vanished. To comfort myself—for truly I would fain have gazed a while longer—I made acquaintance with a flock of beach-birds. These little citizens of the sea and air preceded me by about a stone's-throw along the strand, seeking, I suppose, for food upon its margin. Yet, with a philosophy which mankind would do well to imitate, they drew a continual pleasure from their toil for a subsistence. The sea was each little bird's great playmate. They chased it downward as it swept back, and again ran up swiftly before the impending wave, which sometimes overtook them and bore them off their feet. But they floated as lightly as one of their own feathers on the breaking crest. In their airy flutterings, they seemed to rest on the evanescent spray. Their images,—long-legged little figures, with grey backs and snowy bosoms,—were seen as distinctly as the realities in the mirror of the glistening strand. As I advanced, they flew a score or two of yards, and, again alighting, re-commenced their dalliance with the surf-wave; and thus they bore me company along the beach, the types of pleasant fantasies, till, at its extremity, they took wing over the ocean, and were gone. After forming a friendship with these small surf-spirits, it is really worth a sigh, to find no memorial of them save their multitudinous little tracks in the sand.

When we have paced the length of the beach, it is pleasant, and not un-profitable, to retrace our steps, and recall the whole mood and occupation of the mind during the former passage. Our tracks, being all discernible, will guide us with an observing consciousness through every unconscious wan-dering of thought and fancy. Here we followed the surf in its reflux, to pick up a shell which the sea seemed loth to relinquish. Here we found a seaweed, with an immense brown leaf, and trailed it behind us by its long snake-like stalk. Here we seized a live horse-shoe by the tail, and counted the many claws of that queer monster. Here we dug into the sand for pebbles, and skipped them upon the surface of the water. Here we wet our feet while examining a jelly-fish, which the waves, having just tossed it up, now sought to snatch away again. Here we trod along the brink of a fresh-water brooklet, which flows across the beach, becoming shallower and more shallow, till at last it sinks into the sand, and perishes in the effort to bear its little tribute to the main. Here some vagary appears to have bewildered us; for our tracks go round and round, and are confusedly intermingled, as if we had found a labyrinth upon the level beach. And here, amid our idle pastime, we sat down upon almost the only stone that breaks the surface of the sand, and were lost in an unlooked-for and overpowering conception of the majesty and awfulness of the great deep. Thus, by tracking our foot-prints in the sand, we track our own nature in its wayward course, and steal a glance upon it, when it never dreams of being so observed. Such glances always make us wiser.

This extensive beach affords room for another pleasant pastime. With your staff, you may write verses—love-verses, if they please you best— and consecrate them with a woman's name. Here, too, may be inscribed thoughts, feelings, desires, warm outgushings from the heart's secret places, which you would not pour upon the sand without the certainty that, almost ere the sky has looked upon them, the sea will wash them out. Stir not hence, till the record be effaced. Now—for there is room enough on your canvas—draw huge faces—huge as that of the Sphynx on Egyptian sands—and fit them with bodies of corresponding immensity, and legs which might stride half-way to yonder island. Child's play becomes magnificent on so grand a scale. But, after all, the most fascinating employment is simply to write your name in the sand. Draw the letters gigantic, so that two strides may barely measure them, and three for the long strokes! Cut deep, that the record may be permanent! Statesmen, and warriors, and poets, have spent their strength in no better cause than this. Is it accomplished? Return, then, in an hour or two, and seek for this mighty record of a name. The sea will have swept over it, even as time rolls its effacing waves over the names of statesmen, and warriors, and poets. Hark, the surf-wave laughs at you!

Passing from the beach, I begin to clamber over the crags, making my difficult way among the ruins of a rampart, shattered and broken by the assaults of a fierce enemy. The rocks rise in every variety of attitude; some of them have their feet in the foam, and are shagged half-way upward with sea-weed; some have been hollowed almost into caverns by the unwearied toil of the sea, which can afford to spend centuries in wearing away a rock, or even polishing a pebble. One huge rock ascends in monumental shape, with a face like a giant's tombstone, on which the veins resemble inscriptions, but in an unknown tongue. We will fancy them the forgotten characters of an antediluvian race; or else that nature's own hand has here recorded a mystery, which, could I read her language, would make mankind the wiser and the happier. How many a thing has troubled me with that same idea! Pass on, and leave it unexplained. Here is a narrow avenue, which might seem to have been hewn through the very heart of an enormous crag, affording passage for the rising sea to thunder back and forth, filling it with tumultuous foam, and then leaving its floor of black pebbles bare and glistening. In this chasm there was once an intersecting vein of softer stone, which the waves have gnawed away piecemeal, while the granite walls remain entire on either side. How sharply, and with what harsh clamor, does the sea rake back the pebbles, as it momentarily withdraws into its own depths! At intervals, the floor of the chasm is left nearly dry; but anon, at the outlet, two or three great waves are seen struggling to get in at once; two hit the walls athwart, while one rushes straight through, and all three thunder, as if with rage and triumph. They heap the chasm with a snow-drift of foam and spray. While watching this scene, I can never rid myself of the idea, that a monster, endowed with life and fierce energy, is striving to burst his way through the narrow pass. And what a contrast, to look through the stormy chasm, and catch a glimpse of the calm bright sea beyond!

Many interesting discoveries may be made among these broken cliffs. Once, for example, I found a dead seal, which a recent tempest had tossed into a nook of the rocks, where his shaggy carcass lay rolled in a heap of eel-grass, as if the sea-monster sought to hide himself from my eye. Another time, a shark seemed on the point of leaping from the surf to swallow me; nor did I, wholly without dread, approach near enough to ascertain that the man-eater had already met his own death from some fisherman in the bay. In the same ramble, I encountered a bird—a large grey bird—but whether a loon, or a wild goose, or the identical albatross of the Ancient Mariner, was beyond my ornithology to decide. It reposed so naturally on a bed of dry sea-weed, with its head beside its wing, that I almost fancied it alive, and trod softly lest it should suddenly spread its wings skyward. But the sea-bird would soar among the clouds no more, nor ride upon its native waves; so I drew near, and pulled out one of its mottled tail-feathers for a remembrance. Another day, I discovered an immense bone, wedged into a chasm of the rocks; it was at least ten feet long, curved like a scimetar, bejewelled with barnacles and small shell-fish, and partly covered with a growth of sea-weed. Some leviathan of former ages had used this ponderous mass as a jaw-bone. Curiosities of a minuter order may be observed in a deep reservoir, which is replenished with water at every tide, but becomes a lake among the crags, save when the sea is at its height. At the bottom of this rocky basin grow marine plants, some of which tower high beneath the water, and cast a shadow in the sunshine. Small fishes dart to and fro, and hide themselves among the sea-weed; there is also a solitary crab, who appears to lead the life of a hermit, communing with none of the other denizens of the place; and likewise several five-fingers—for I know no other name than that which children give them. If your imagination be at all accustomed to such freaks, you may look down into the depths of this pool, and fancy it the mysterious depth of ocean. But where are the hulks and scattered timbers of sunken ships?—where the treasures that old Ocean hoards?—where the corroded cannon?—where the corpses and skeletons of seamen, who went down in storm and battle?

On the day of my last ramble, (it was a September day, yet as warm as summer,) what should I behold as I approached the above described basin but three girls sitting on its margin, and—yes, it is veritably so—laving their snowy feet in the sunny water! These, these are the warm realities of those three visionary shapes that flitted from me on the beach. Hark! their merry voices, as they toss up the water with their feet! They have not seen me. I must shrink behind this rock, and steal away again.

In honest truth, vowed to solitude as I am, there is something in the encounter that makes the heart flutter with a strangely pleasant sensation. I know these girls to be realities of flesh and blood, yet, glancing at them so briefly, they mingle like kindred creatures with the ideal beings of my mind. It is pleasant, likewise, to gaze down from some high crag, and watch a group of children, gathering pebbles and pearly shells, and playing with the surf, as with old Ocean's hoary beard. Nor does it infringe upon my seclusion, to see yonder boat at anchor off the shore, swinging dreamily to and fro, and rising and sinking with the alternate swell; while the crew—four gentlemen in round-about jackets—are busy with their fishing-lines. But, with an inward antipathy and a headlong flight, do I eschew the presence of any meditative stroller like myself, known by his pilgrim staff, his sauntering step, his shy demeanour, his observant yet abstracted eye. From such a man, as if another self had scared me, I scramble hastily over the rocks and take refuge in a nook which many a secret hour has given me a right to call my own. I would do battle for it even with the churl that should produce the title-deeds. Have not my musings melted into its rocky walls and sandy floor, and made them a portion of myself?

It is a recess in the line of cliffs, walled round by a rough, high precipice, which almost encircles and shuts in a little space of sand. In front, the sea appears as between the pillars of a portal. In the rear, the precipice is broken and intermixed with earth, which gives nourishment not only to clinging and twining shrubs, but to trees, that gripe the rock with their naked roots, and seem to struggle hard for footing and for soil enough to live upon. These are fir trees; but oaks hang their heavy branches from above, and throw down acorns on the beach, and shed their withering foliage upon the waves. At this autumnal season, the precipice is decked with variegated splendor; trailing wreaths of scarlet flaunt from the summit downward; tufts of yellow-flowering shrubs, and rose bushes, with their reddened leaves and glossy seed-berries, sprout from each crevice; at every glance, I detect some new light or shade of beauty, all contrasting with the stern, grey rock. A rill of water trickles down the cliff and fills a little cistern near the base. I drain it at a draught, and find it fresh and pure. This recess shall be my dining-hall. And what the feast? A few biscuits, made savory by soaking them in sea-water, a tuft of samphire gathered from the beach, and an apple for the dessert. By this time, the little rill has filled its reservoir again; and, as I quaff it, I thank God more heartily than for a civic banquet, that He gives me the healthful appetite to make a feast of bread and water.

Dinner being over, I throw myself at length upon the sand, and basking in the sunshine, let my mind disport itself at will. The walls of this my hermitage have no tongue to tell my follies, though I sometimes fancy that they have ears to hear them, and a soul to sympathize. There is a magic in this spot. Dreams haunt its precincts, and flit around me in broad sunlight, nor require that sleep shall blindfold me to real objects, ere these be visible. Here can I frame a story of two lovers, and make their shadows live before me, and be mirrored in the tranquil water, as they tread along the sand, leaving no foot-prints. Here, should I will it, I can summon up a single shade, and be myself her lover. Yes, dreamer,—but your lonely heart will be the colder for such fancies. Sometimes, too, the Past comes back, and finds me here, and in her train come faces which were gladsome, when I knew them, yet seem not gladsome now. Would that my hiding place were lonelier, so that the Past might not find me! Get ye all gone, old friends, and let me listen to the murmur of the sea,—a melancholy voice, but less sad than yours. Of what mysteries is it telling? Of sunken ships, and whereabouts they lie? Of islands afar and undiscovered, whose tawny children are unconscious of other islands and of continents, and deem the stars of heaven their nearest neighbours? Nothing of all this. What then? Has it talked for so many ages, and meant nothing all the while? No; for those ages find utterance in the sea's unchanging voice, and warn the listener to withdraw his interest from mortal vicissitudes, and let the infinite idea of eternity pervade his soul. This is wisdom; and, therefore, will I spend the next half-hour in shaping little boats of drift-wood, and launching them on voyages across the cove, with the feather of a sea-gull for a sail. If the voice of ages tell me true, this is as wise an occupation as to build ships of five hundred tons, and launch them forth upon the main, bound to 'far Cathay.' Yet, how would the merchant sneer at me!

And, after all, can such philosophy be true? Methinks I could find a thousand arguments against it. Well, then, let yonder shaggy rock, mid-deep in the surf—see! he is somewhat wrathful,—he rages and roars and foams—let that tall rock be my antagonist, and let me exercise my oratory like him of Athens, who bandied words with an angry sea and got the victory. My maiden speech is a triumphant one; for the gentleman in sea-weed has nothing to offer in reply, save an immitigable roaring. His voice, indeed, will be heard a long while after mine is hushed. Once more I shout, and the cliffs reverberate the sound. Oh, what joy for a shy man to feel himself so solitary, that he may lift his voice to its highest pitch without hazard of a listener! But, hush!—be silent, my good friend!—whence comes that stifled laughter? It was musical,—but how should there be such music in my solitude? Looking upwards, I catch a glimpse of three faces, peeping from the summit of the cliff, like angels between me and their native sky. Ah, fair girls, you may make yourselves merry at my eloquence,—but it was my turn to smile when I saw your white feet in the pool! Let us keep each other's secrets.

The sunshine has now passed from my hermitage, except a gleam upon the sand just where it meets the sea. A crowd of gloomy fantasies will come and haunt me, if I tarry longer here, in the darkening twilight of these grey rocks. This is a dismal place in some moods of the mind. Climb we, therefore, the precipice, and pause a moment on the brink, gazing down into that hollow chamber by the deep, where we have been, what few can be, sufficient to our own pastime—yes, say the word outright!—self-sufficient to our own happiness. How lonesome looks the recess now, and dreary too,—like all other spots where happiness has been! There lies my shadow in the departing sunshine with its head upon the sea. I will pelt it with pebbles. A hit! a hit! I clap my hands in triumph, and see my shadow clapping its unreal hands, and claiming the triumph for itself. What a simpleton must I have been all day, since my own shadow makes a mock of my fooleries!

Homeward! homeward! It is time to hasten home. It is time; it is time; for as the sun sinks over the western wave, the sea grows melancholy, and the surf has a saddened tone. The distant sails appear astray, and not of earth, in their remoteness amid the desolate waste. My spirit wanders forth afar, but finds no resting place, and comes shivering back. It is time that I were hence. But grudge me not the day that has been spent in seclusion, which yet was not solitude, since the great sea has been my companion, and the little sea-birds my friends, and the wind has told me his secrets, and airy shapes have flitted around me in my hermitage. Such companionship works an effect upon a man's character, as if he had been admitted to the society of creatures that are not mortal. And when, at noontide, I tread the crowded streets, the influence of this day will still be felt; so that I shall walk among men kindly and as a brother, with affection and sympathy, but yet shall not melt into the indistinguishable mass of human kind. I shall think my own thoughts, and feel my own emotions, and possess my individuality unviolated.

But it is good, at the eve of such a day, to feel and know that there are men and women in the world. That feeling and that knowledge are mine, at this moment; for, on the shore, far below me, the fishing-party have landed from their skiff, and are cooking their scaly prey by a fire of drift-wood, kindled in the angle of two rude rocks. The three visionary girls are likewise there. In the deepening twilight, while the surf is dashing near their hearth, the ruddy gleam of the fire throws a strange air of comfort over the wild cove, bestrewn as it is with pebbles and sea-weed, and exposed to the 'melancholy main.' Moreover, as the smoke climbs up the precipice, it brings with it a savory smell from a pan of fried fish, and a black kettle of chowder, and reminds me that my dinner was nothing but bread and water, and a tuft of samphire, and an apple. Methinks the party might find room for another guest, at that flat rock which serves them for a table; and if spoons be scarce, I could pick up a clam-shell on the beach. They see me now; and—the blessing of a hungry man upon him!—one of them sends up a hospitable shout—halloo, Sir Solitary! come down and sup with us! The ladies wave their handkerchiefs. Can I decline? No; and be it owned, after all my solitary joys, that this is the sweetest moment of a Day by the Sea-Shore.

NATHANIEL HAWTHORNE
1804–64

While Nathaniel Hawthorne was still a youth his father, a sea captain, died on a Caribbean voyage. The boy was raised in Salem, Massachusetts, by a reclusive mother, though he spent time in Maine with unmarried aunts and uncles. A lonely childhood ended when he went to Bowdoin College, where Henry Wadsworth Longfellow and Franklin Pierce, later fourteenth president of the United States, were his classmates.

After graduation in 1825, young Hawthorne returned to Salem to live with his mother and spend time reading and writing. His first novel, *Fanshawe* (1828), which recounted his college experiences, was printed at his own expense. It was a failure, and Hawthorne subsequently tried to destroy all copies of the book.

In 1832 his stories began appearing in gift books and magazines; in 1837 they were published in a volume, *Twice-Told Tales*, which a few discerning critics recognized as an artistic triumph. Critical success was not popular success, however, and Hawthorne had to work in the Boston customhouse to support himself. Later he spent seven months in a utopian community at Brook Farm, a place where he hoped to find the means of supporting himself with little effort through cooperative farming so that most of his time could be spent writing. The experiment was a failure for him. He became productive again only after his marriage to Sophia Peabody in 1842. The couple settled down in Concord, Massachusetts, in Ralph Waldo Emerson's ancestral home. In their three years there, Hawthorne wrote a number of stories which were published in periodicals and then as a volume, *Mosses From An Old Manse* (1846).

In 1845 the Hawthornes returned to Salem. After working for a few years at the Salem customhouse, Hawthorne was catapulted to fame and financial success with the publication of *The Scarlet Letter* (1850). Next he wrote *The House of the Seven Gables* (1851) and *The Blithedale Romance* (1852) as well as short stories—*The Snow-Image and Other Twice-Told Tales* (1851), *A Wonder-Book for Girls and Boys* (1852), and *Tanglewood Tales for Girls and Boys* (1853).

Hawthorne's campaign biography of Franklin Pierce secured him an appointment as U.S. consul in Liverpool when Pierce won the presidency. *The Marble Faun* (1860) was written while the Hawthornes were still in Europe.

"Foot-prints on the Sea-shore" appeared in the second edition of *Twice-Told Tales* (1842).

Malachi's Cove

BY ANTHONY TROLLOPE

ON THE NORTHERN COAST of Cornwall, between Tintagel and Bossiney, down on the very margin of the sea, there lived not long since an old man who got his living by saving seaweed from the waves, and selling it for manure. The cliffs there are bold and fine, and the sea beats in upon them from the north with a grand violence. I doubt whether it be not the finest morsel of cliff scenery in England, though it is beaten by many portions of the west coast of Ireland, and perhaps also by spots in Wales and Scotland. Cliffs should be nearly precipitous, they should be broken in their outlines, and should barely admit here and there of an insecure passage from their summit to the sand at their feet. The sea should come, if not up to them, at least very near to them, and then, above all things, the water below them should be blue, and not of that dead leaden colour which is so familiar to us in England. At Tintagel all these requisites are there, except that bright blue colour which is so lovely. But the cliffs themselves are bold and well broken, and the margin of sand at high water is very narrow—so narrow that at spring-tides there is barely a footing there.

Close upon this margin was the cottage, or hovel, of Malachi Trenglos, the old man of whom I have spoken. But Malachi, or old Glos, as he was commonly called by the people around him, had not built his house absolutely upon the sand. There was a fissure in the rock so great that at the top if formed a narrow ravine, and so complete from the summit to the base that it afforded an opening for a steep and rugged track from the top of the rock to the bottom. This fissure was so wide at the bottom that it had afforded space for Trenglos to fix his habitation on a foundation of rock, and here he had lived for many years. It was told of him that in the early days of his trade he had always carried the weed in a basket on his back to the top, but latterly he had been possessed of a donkey which had been trained to go up and down the steep track with a single pannier over his loins, for the rocks would not admit of panniers hanging by his side; and for this assistant he had built a shed adjoining his own, and almost as large as that in which he himself resided.

But, as years went on, old Glos procured other assistance than that of the donkey, or, as I should rather say, Providence supplied him with other help;

and, indeed, had it not been so, the old man must have given up his cabin and his independence and gone into the workhouse at Camelford. For rheumatism had afflicted him, old age had bowed him till he was nearly double, and by degrees he became unable to attend the donkey on its upward passage to the world above, or even to assist in rescuing the coveted weed from the waves.

At the time to which our story refers, Trenglos had not been up the cliff for twelve months, and for the last six months he had done nothing towards the furtherance of his trade, except to take the money and keep it, if any of it was kept, and occasionally to shake down a bundle of fodder for the donkey. The real work of the business was done altogether by Mahala Trenglos, his granddaughter.

Mally Trenglos was known to all the farmers round the coast, and to all the small tradespeople in Camelford. She was a wild-looking, almost unearthly creature, with wild-flowing, black, uncombed hair, small in stature, with small hands and bright, black eyes; but people said that she was very strong, and the children around declared that she worked day and night, and knew nothing of fatigue. As to her age there were many doubts. Some said she was ten, and others five-and-twenty, but the reader may be allowed to know that at this time she had in truth passed her twentieth birthday. The old people spoke well of Mally, because she was so good to her grandfather; and it was said of her that though she carried to him a little gin and tobacco almost daily, she bought nothing for herself;—and as to the gin, no one who looked at her would accuse her of meddling with that. But she had no friends, and but few acquaintances among people of her own age. They said that she was fierce and ill-natured, that she had not a good word for anyone, and that she was, complete at all points, a thorough little vixen. The young men did not care for her; for, as regards dress, all days were alike with her. She never made herself smart on Sundays. She was generally without stockings, and seemed to care not at all to exercise any of those feminine attractions which might have been hers had she studied to attain them. All days were the same to her in regard to dress; and, indeed, till lately, all days had, I fear, been the same to her in other respects. Old Malachi had never been seen inside a place of worship since he had taken to live under the cliff.

But within the last two years Mally had submitted herself to the teaching of the clergyman at Tintagel, and had appeared at church on Sundays, if not absolutely with punctuality, at any rate so often that no one who knew the peculiarity of her residence was disposed to quarrel with her on that subject. But she made no difference in her dress on these occasions. She took her place on a low stone seat just inside the church door, clothed as usual in her thick, red serge petticoat and loose, brown serge jacket, such being the apparel which she had found to be best adapted for her hard and perilous

work among the waters. She had pleaded to the clergyman when he attacked her on the subject of church attendance with vigour that she had got
no churchgoing clothes. He had explained to her that she would be received
there without distinction to her clothing. Mally had taken him at his word,
and had gone, with a courage which certainly deserved admiration, though
I doubt whether there was not mingled with it an obstinacy which was less
admirable.

For people said that old Glos was rich, and that Mally might have proper
clothes if she chose to buy them. Mr. Polwarth, the clergyman, who, as the
old man could not come to him, went down the rocks to the old man, did
make some hint on the matter in Mally's absence. But old Glos, who had
been patient with him on other matters, turned upon him so angrily when
he made an allusion to money, that Mr. Polwarth found himself obliged
to give that matter up, and Mally continued to sit upon the stone bench in
her short serge petticoat, with her long hair streaming down her face. She
did so far sacrifice to decency as on such occasions to tie up her back hair
with an old shoestring. So tied it would remain through the Monday and
Tuesday, but by Wednesday afternoon Mally's hair had generally managed
to escape.

As to Mally's indefatigable industry there could be no manner of doubt,
for the quantity of seaweed which she and the donkey amassed between
them was very surprising. Old Glos, it was declared, had never collected
half what Mally gathered together; but then the article was becoming
cheaper, and it was necessary that the exertion should be greater. So Mally
and the donkey toiled and toiled, and the seaweed came up in heaps which
surprised those who looked at her little hands and light form. Was there not
someone who helped her at nights, some fairy, or demon, or the like? Mally
was so snappish in her answers to people that she had no right to be surprised if ill-natured things were said of her.

No one ever heard Mally Trenglos complain of her work, but about this
time she was heard to make great and loud complaints of the treatment she
received from some of her neighbours. It was known that she went with her
plaints to Mr. Polwarth; and when he could not help her, or did not give her
such instant help as she needed, she went—ah, so foolishly! to the office of a
certain attorney at Camelford, who was not likely to prove himself a better
friend than Mr. Polwarth.

Now the nature of her injury was as follows: The place in which she
collected her seaweed was a little cove; the people had come to call it Malachi's Cove from the name of the old man who lived there;—which was so
formed, that the margin of the sea therein could only be reached by the
passage from the top down to Trenglos's hut. The breadth of the cove when
the sea was out might perhaps be two hundred yards, and on each side the

rocks ran out in such a way that both from north and south the domain of
Trenglos was guarded from intruders. And this locality had been well
chosen for its intended purpose.

There was a rush of the sea into the cove, which carried there large, drifting masses of seaweed, leaving them among the rocks when the tide was
out. During the equinoctial winds of the spring and autumn the supply
would never fail; and even when the sea was calm, the long, soft, salt-
bedewed, trailing masses of the weed could be gathered there when they
could not be found elsewhere for miles along the coast. The task of getting
the weed from the breakers was often difficult and dangerous—so difficult
that much of it was left to be carried away by the next incoming tide.

Mally doubtless did not gather half the crop that was there at her feet.
What was taken by the returning waves she did not regret; but when inter-
lopers came upon her cove, and gathered her wealth,—her grandfather's
wealth, beneath her eyes, then her heart was broken. It was this interloping,
this intrusion, that drove poor Mally to the Camelford attorney. But, alas,
though the Camelford attorney took Mally's money, he could do nothing for
her, and her heart was broken!

She had an idea, in which no doubt her grandfather shared, that the path
to the cove was, at any rate, their property. When she was told that the cove,
and sea running into the cove, were not the freeholds of her grandfather, she
understood that the statement might be true. But what then as to the use of
the path? Who had made the path what it was? Had she not painfully,
wearily, with exceeding toil, carried up bits of rock with her own little
hands, that her grandfather's donkey might have footing for his feet? Had
she not scraped together crumbs of earth along the face of the cliff that she
might make easier to the animal the track of that rugged way? And now,
when she saw big farmers' lads coming down with other donkeys,—and,
indeed, there was one who came with a pony; no boy, but a young man, old
enough to know better than rob a poor old man and a young girl,—she
reviled the whole human race, and swore that the Camelford attorney was
a fool.

Any attempt to explain to her that there was still weed enough for her
was worse than useless. Was it not all hers and his, or, at any rate, was not
the sole way to it his and hers? And was not her trade stopped and im-
peded? Had she not been forced to back her laden donkey down, twenty
yards she said, but it had, in truth, been five, because Farmer Gunliffe's son
had been in the way with his thieving pony? Farmer Gunliffe had wanted
to buy her weed at his own price, and because she had refused he had set on
his thieving son to destroy her in this wicked way.

"I'll hamstring the beast the next time as he's down here!" said Mally to
old Glos, while the angry fire literally streamed from her eyes.

Farmer Gunliffe's small homestead—he held about fifty acres of land—
was close by the village of Tintagel, and not a mile from the cliff. The sea-
wrack, as they call it, was pretty well the only manure within his reach, and
no doubt he thought it hard that he should be kept from using it by Mally
Trenglos and her obstinacy.

"There's heaps of other coves, Barty," said Mally to Barty Gunliffe, the
farmer's son.

"But none so nigh, Mally, nor yet none that fills 'emselves as this place."

Then he explained to her that he would not take the weed that came up
close to hand. He was bigger than she was, and stronger, and would get it
from the outer rocks, with which she never meddled. Then, with scorn in
her eye, she swore that she could get it where he durst not venture, and
repeated her threat of hamstringing the pony. Barty laughed at her wrath,
jeered her because of her wild hair, and called her a mermaid.

"I'll mermaid you!" she cried. "Mermaid, indeed! I wouldn't be a man to
come and rob a poor girl and an old cripple. But you're no man, Barty
Gunliffe! You're not half a man."

Nevertheless, Bartholomew Gunliffe was a very fine young fellow, as far
as the eye went. He was about five feet eight inches high, with strong arms
and legs, with light, curly brown hair and blue eyes. His father was but in a
small way as a farmer, but, nevertheless, Barty Gunliffe was well thought of
among the girls around. Everybody liked Barty—excepting only Mally
Trenglos, and she hated him like poison.

Barty, when he was asked why so good-natured a lad as he persecuted a
poor girl and an old man, threw himself upon the justice of the thing. It
wouldn't do at all, according to his view, that any single person should take
upon himself to own that which God Almighty sent as the common property of all. He would do Mally no harm, and so he had told her. But Mally
was a vixen—a wicked little vixen; and she must be taught to have a civil
tongue in her head. When once Mally would speak him civil as he went for
weed, he would get his father to pay the old man some sort of toll for the
use of the path.

"Speak him civil?" said Mally. "Never; not while I have a tongue in my
mouth!" And I fear old Glos encouraged her rather than otherwise in her
view of the matter.

But her grandfather did not encourage her to hamstring the pony. Hamstringing a pony would be a serious thing, and old Glos thought it might be
very awkward for both of them if Mally were put into prison. He suggested,
therefore, that all manner of impediments should be put in the way of the
pony's feet, surmising that the well-trained donkey might be able to work in
spite of them. And Barty Gunliffe, on his next descent, did find the passage
very awkward when he came near to Malachi's hut, but he made his way

down, and poor Mally saw the lumps of rock at which she had laboured so hard pushed on one side or rolled out of the way with a steady persistency of injury towards herself that almost drove her frantic.

"Well, Barty, you're a nice boy," said old Glos, sitting in the doorway of the hut, as he watched the intruder.

"I ain't a-doing no harm to none as doesn't harm me," said Barty. "The sea's free to all, Malachi."

"And the sky's free to all, but I mustn't get up on the top of your big barn to look at it," said Mally, who was standing among the rocks with a long hook in her hand. The long hook was the tool with which she worked in dragging the weed from the waves. "But you ain't got no justice nor yet no spirit, or you wouldn't come here to vex an old man like he."

"I didn't want to vex him, nor yet to vex you, Mally. You let me be for a while, and we'll be friends yet."

"Friends!" exclaimed Mally. "Who'd have the likes of you for a friend? What are you moving them stones for? Them stones belongs to grandfather." And in her wrath she made a movement as though she were going to fly at him.

"Let him be, Mally," said the old man; "let him be. He'll get his punishment. He'll come to be drowned some day if he comes down here when the wind is in shore."

"That he may be drowned then!" said Mally, in her anger. "If he was in the big hole there among the rocks, and the sea running in at half tide, I wouldn't lift a hand to help him out."

"Yes, you would, Mally; you'd fish me up with your hook like a big stick of seaweed."

She turned from him with scorn as he said this, and went into the hut. It was time for her to get ready for her work, and one of the great injuries done her lay in this,—that such a one as Barty Gunliffe should come and look at her during her toil among the breakers.

It was an afternoon in April, and the hour was something after four o'clock. There had been a heavy wind from the north-west all the morning, with gusts of rain, and the sea-gulls had been in and out of the cove all the day, which was a sure sign to Mally that the incoming tide would cover the rocks with weed.

The quick waves were now returning with wonderful celerity over the low reefs, and the time had come at which the treasure must be seized, if it was to be garnered on that day. By seven o'clock it would be growing dark, at nine it would be high water, and before daylight the crop would be carried out again if not collected. All this Mally understood very well, and some of this Barty was beginning to understand also.

As Mally came down with her bare feet, bearing her long hook in her hand, she saw Barty's pony standing patiently on the sand, and in her heart she longed to attack the brute. Barty at this moment, with a common three-pronged fork in his hand, was standing down on a large rock, gazing forth towards the waters. He had declared that he would gather the weed only at places which were inaccessible to Mally, and he was looking out that he might settle where he would begin.

"Let 'un be, let 'un be," shouted the old man to Mally, as he saw her take a step towards the beast, which she hated almost as much as she hated the man.

Hearing her grandfather's voice through the wind, she desisted from her purpose, if any purpose she had had, and went forth to her work. As she passed down the cove, and scrambled in among the rocks, she saw Barty still standing on his perch; out beyond, the white-curling waves were cresting and breaking themselves with violence, and the wind was howling among the caverns and abutments of the cliff.

Every now and then there came a squall of rain, and though there was sufficient light, the heavens were black with clouds. A scene more beautiful might hardly be found by those who love the glories of the coast. The light for such objects was perfect. Nothing could exceed the grandeur of the colours,—the blue of the open sea, the white of the breaking waves, the yellow sands, or the streaks of red and brown which gave such richness to the cliff.

But neither Mally nor Barty were thinking of such things as these. Indeed, they were hardly thinking of their trade after its ordinary forms. Barty was meditating how he might best accomplish his purpose of working beyond the reach of Mally's feminine powers, and Mally was resolving that wherever Barty went she would go farther.

And, in many respects, Mally had the advantage. She knew every rock in the spot, and was sure of those which gave a good foothold, and sure also of those which did not. And then her activity had been made perfect by practice for the purpose to which it was to be devoted. Barty, no doubt, was stronger than she, and quite as active. But Barty could not jump among the waves from one stone to another as she could do, nor was he as yet able to get aid in his work from the very force of the water as she could get it. She had been hunting seaweed in that cove since she had been an urchin of six years old, and she knew every hole and corner and every spot of vantage. The waves were her friends, and she could use them. She could measure their strength, and knew when and where it would cease.

Mally was great down in the salt pools of her own cove,—great, and very fearless. As she watched Barty make his way forward from rock to rock, she told herself, gleefully, that he was going astray. The curl of the wind as it blew into the cove would not carry the weed up to the northern buttresses of the cove; and then there was the great hole just there—the great hole of which she had spoken when she wished him evil.

And now she went to work, hooking up the dishevelled hairs of the ocean, and landing many a cargo on the extreme margin of the sand, from whence she would be able in the evening to drag it back before the invading waters would return to reclaim the spoil.

And on his side also Barty made his heap up against the northern buttresses of which I have spoken. Barty's heap became big and still bigger, so that he knew, let the pony work as he might, he could not take it all up that evening. But still it was not as large as Mally's heap. Mally's hook was better than his fork, and Mally's skill was better than his strength. And when he failed in some haul Mally would jeer him with a wild, weird laughter, and shriek to him through the wind that he was not half a man. At first he answered her with laughing words, but before long, as she boasted of her success and pointed to his failure, he became angry, and then he answered her no more. He became angry with himself, in that he missed so much of the plunder before him.

The broken sea was full of the long straggling growth which the waves had torn up from the bottom of the ocean, but the masses were carried past him, away from him,—nay, once or twice over him; and then Mally's weird voice would sound in his ear, jeering him. The gloom among the rocks was now becoming thicker and thicker, the tide was beating in with increased strength, and the gusts of wind came with quicker and greater violence. But still he worked on. While Mally worked he would work, and he would work for some time after she was driven in. He would not be beaten by a girl.

The great hole was now full of water, but of water which seemed to be boiling as though in a pot. And the pot was full of floating masses,—large treasures of seaweed which were thrown to and fro upon its surface, but lying there so thick that one would seem almost able to rest upon it without sinking.

Mally knew well how useless it was to attempt to rescue aught from the fury of that boiling cauldron. The hole went in under the rocks, and the side of it towards the shore lay high, slippery, and steep. The hole, even at low water, was never empty; and Mally believed that there was no bottom to it. Fish thrown in there could escape out to the ocean, miles away,—so Mally in her softer moods would tell the visitors to the cove. She knew the hole well. Poulnadioul she was accustomed to call it; which was supposed, when translated, to mean that this was the hole of the Evil One. Never did Mally attempt to make her own the weed which had found its way into that pot.

But Barty Gunliffe knew no better, and she watched him as he endeavoured to steady himself on the treacherously slippery edge of the pool. He fixed himself there and made a haul, with some small success. How he managed it she hardly knew, but she stood still for a while watching him anxiously, and then she saw him slip. He slipped, and recovered himself;—slipped again, and again recovered himself.

"Barty, you fool!" she screamed; "if you get yourself pitched in there, you'll never come out no more."

Whether she simply wished to frighten him, or whether her heart relented and she had thought of his danger with dismay, who shall say? She could not have told herself. She hated him as much as ever,—but she could hardly have wished to see him drowned before her eyes.

"You go on, and don't mind me," said he, speaking in a hoarse, angry tone.

"Mind you!—who minds you?" retorted the girl. And then she again prepared herself for her work.

But as she went down over the rocks with her long hook balanced in her hands, she suddenly heard a splash, and, turning quickly round, saw the body of her enemy tumbling amidst the eddying waves in the pool. The tide had now come up so far that every succeeding wave washed into it and over it from the side nearest to the sea, and then ran down again back from the rocks, as the rolling wave receded, with a noise like the fall of a cataract. And then, when the surplus water had retreated for a moment, the surface of the pool would be partly calm, though the fretting bubbles would still boil up and down, and there was ever a simmer on the surface, as though, in truth, the cauldron were heated. But this time of comparative rest was but a moment, for the succeeding breaker would come up almost as soon as the foam of the preceding one had gone, and then again the waters would be dashed upon the rocks, and the sides would echo with the roar of the angry wave.

Instantly Mally hurried across to the edge of the pool, crouching down upon her hands and knees for security as she did so. As a wave receded, Barty's head and face was carried round near to her, and she could see that his forehead was covered with blood. Whether he were alive or dead she did not know. She had seen nothing but his blood, and the light-coloured hair of his head lying amidst the foam. Then his body was drawn along by the suction of the retreating wave; but the mass of water that escaped was not on this occasion large enough to carry the man out with it.

Instantly Mally was at work with her hook, and getting it fixed into his coat, dragged him towards the spot on which she was kneeling. During the half minute of repose she got him so close that she could touch his shoulder. Straining herself down, laying herself over the long bending handle of the hook, she strove to grasp him with her right hand. But she could not do it; she could only touch him.

Then came the next breaker, forcing itself on with a roar, looking to Mally as though it must certainly knock her from her resting-place, and destroy them both. But she had nothing for it but to kneel, and hold by her hook.

What prayer passed through her mind at that moment for herself or for him, or for that old man who was sitting unconsciously up at the cabin, who can say? The great wave came and rushed over her as she lay almost prostrate, and when the water was gone from her eyes, and the tumult of the foam, and the violence of the roaring breaker had passed by her, she found herself at her length upon the rock, while his body had been lifted up, free from her hook, and was lying upon the slippery ledge, half in the water and half out of it. As she looked at him, in that instant, she could see that his eyes were open and that he was struggling with his hands.

"Hold by the hook, Barty," she cried, pushing the stick of it before him, while she seized the collar of his coat in her hands.

Had he been her brother, her lover, her father, she could not have clung to him with more of the energy of despair. He did contrive to hold by the stick which she had given him, and when the succeeding wave had passed by, he was still on the ledge. In the next moment she was seated a yard or two above the hole, in comparative safety, while Barty lay upon the rocks with his still bleeding head resting upon her lap.

What could she do now? She could not carry him; and in fifteen minutes the sea would be up where she was sitting. He was quite insensible and very pale, and the blood was coming slowly,—very slowly,—from the wound on his forehead. Ever so gently she put her hand upon his hair to move it back from his face; and then she bent over his mouth to see if he breathed, and as she looked at him she knew that he was beautiful.

What would she not give that he might live? Nothing now was so precious to her as his life,—as this life which she had so far rescued from the waters. But what could she do? Her grandfather could scarcely get himself down over the rocks, if indeed he could succeed in doing so much as that. Could she drag the wounded man backwards, if it were only a few feet, so that he might lie above the reach of the waves till further assistance could be procured?

She set herself to work and she moved him, almost lifting him. As she did so she wondered at her own strength, but she was very strong at that moment. Slowly, tenderly, falling on the rocks herself so that he might fall on her, she got him back to the margin of the sand, to a spot which the waters would not reach for the next two hours.

Here her grandfather met them, having seen at last what had happened from the door.

"Dada," she said, "he fell into the pool yonder, and was battered against the rocks. See there at his forehead."

"Mally, I'm thinking that he's dead already," said old Glos, peering down over the body.

"No, dada; he is not dead; but mayhap he's dying. But I'll go at once up to the farm."

"Mally," said the old man, "look at his head. They'll say we murdered him."

"Who'll say so? Who'll lie like that? Didn't I pull him out of the hole?"

"What matters that? His father'll say we killed him."

It was manifest to Mally that whatever anyone might say hereafter, her present course was plain before her. She must run up the path to Gunliffe's farm and get necessary assistance. If the world were as bad as her grandfather said, it would be so bad that she would not care to live longer in it. But be that as it might, there was no doubt as to what she must do now.

So away she went as fast as her naked feet could carry her up the cliff. When at the top she looked round to see if any person might be within ken, but she saw no one. So she ran with all her speed along the headland of the corn-field which led in the direction of old Gunliffe's house, and as she drew near to the homestead she saw that Barty's mother was leaning on the gate. As she approached, she attempted to call, but her breath failed her for any purpose of loud speech, so she ran on till she was able to grasp Mrs. Gunliffe by the arm.

"Where's himself?" she said, holding her hand upon her beating heart that she might husband her breath.

"Who is it you mean?" said Mrs. Gunliffe, who participated in the family feud against Trenglos and his granddaughter. "What does the girl clutch me for in that way?"

"He's dying then, that's all."

"Who is dying? Is it old Malachi? If the old man's bad, we'll send some-one down."

"It ain't dada, it's Barty! Where's himself? Where's the master?"

But by this time Mrs. Gunliffe was in an agony of despair, and was calling out for assistance lustily. Happily Gunliffe, the father, was at hand, and with him a man from the neighbouring village.

"Will you not send for the doctor?" said Mally. "Oh, man, you should send for the doctor!"

Whether any orders were given for the doctor she did not know, but in a very few minutes she was hurrying across the field again towards the path to the cove, and Gunliffe with the other man and his wife were following her.

As Mally went along she recovered her voice, for their step was not so quick as hers, and that which to them was a hurried movement, allowed her to get her breath again. And as she went she tried to explain to the father what had happened, saying but little, however, of her own doings in the matter. The wife hung behind listening, exclaiming every now and again that her boy was killed, and then asking wild questions as to his being yet alive. The father, as he went, said little. He was known as a silent, sober man, well spoken of for diligence and general conduct, but supposed to be stern and very hard when angered.

As they drew near to the top of the path, the other man whispered something to him, and then he turned round upon Mally and stopped her.

"If he has come by his death between you, your blood shall be taken for his," said he.

Then the wife shrieked out that her child had been murdered, and Mally, looking round into the faces of the three, saw that her grandfather's words had come true. They suspected her of having taken the life, in saving which she had nearly lost her own.

She looked round at them with awe in her face, and then, without saying a word, preceded them down the path. What had she to answer when such a charge as that was made against her? If they chose to say that she pushed him into the pool, and hit him with her hook as he lay amidst the waters, how could she show that it was not so?

Poor Mally knew little of the law of evidence, and it seemed to her that she was in their hands. But as she went down the steep track with a hurried step,—a step so quick that they could not keep up with her,—her heart was very full,—very full and very high. She had striven for the man's life as though he had been her brother. The blood was yet not dry on her own legs and arms, where she had torn them in his service. At one moment she had felt sure that she would die with him in that pool. And now they said that she had murdered him! It may be that he was not dead, and what would he say if ever he should speak again? Then she thought of that moment when his eyes had opened, and he had seemed to see her. She had no fear for herself, for her heart was very high. But it was full also,—full of scorn, disdain, and wrath.

When she had reached the bottom, she stood close to the door of the hut waiting for them, so that they might precede her to the other group, which was there in front of them, at a little distance on the sand.

"He is there, and dada is with him. Go and look at him," said Mally.

The father and mother ran on stumbling over the stones, but Mally remained behind by the door of the hut.

Barty Gunliffe was lying on the sand where Mally had left him, and old Malachi Trenglos was standing over him, resting himself with difficulty upon a stick.

"Not a move he's moved since she left him," said he, "not a move. I put his head on the old rug as you see, and I tried 'un with a drop of gin, but he wouldn't take it,—he wouldn't take it."

"Oh, my boy! my boy!" said the mother, throwing herself beside her son upon the sand.

"Haud your tongue, woman," said the father, kneeling down slowly by the lad's head, "whimpering that way will do 'un no good."

Then having gazed for a minute or two upon the pale face beneath him, he looked up sternly into that of Malachi Trenglos.

The old man hardly knew how to bear this terrible inquisition.

"He would come," said Malachi; "he brought it all upon hisself."

"Who was it struck him?" said the father.

"Sure he struck hisself, as he fell among the breakers."

"Liar!" said the father, looking up at the old man.

"They have murdered him!—They have murdered him!" shrieked the mother.

"Haud your peace, woman!" said the husband again. "They shall give us blood for blood."

Mally, leaning against the corner of the hovel, heard it all, but did not stir. They might say what they liked. They might make it out to be murder. They might drag her and her grandfather to Camelford Gaol, and then to Bodmin, and the gallows; but they could not take from her the conscious feeling that was her own. She had done her best to save him,—her very best. And she had saved him!

She remembered her threat to him before they had gone down on the rocks together, and her evil wish. Those words had been very wicked; but since that she had risked her life to save his. They might say what they pleased of her, and do what they pleased. She knew what she knew.

Then the father raised his son's head and shoulders in his arms, and called on the others to assist him in carrying Barty towards the path. They raised him between them carefully and tenderly, and lifted their burden on towards the spot at which Mally was standing. She never moved, but watched them at their work; and the old man followed them, hobbling after them with his crutch.

When they had reached the end of the hut she looked upon Barty's face, and saw that it was very pale. There was no longer blood upon the forehead, but the great gash was to be seen there plainly, with its jagged cut, and the skin livid and blue round the orifice. His light brown hair was hanging back, as she had made it to hang when she had gathered it with her hand after the big wave had passed over them. Ah, how beautiful he was in Mally's eyes with that pale face, and the sad scar upon his brow! She turned her face away, that they might not see her tears; but she did not move, nor did she speak.

But now, when they had passed the end of the hut, shuffling along with their burden, she heard a sound which stirred her. She roused herself quickly from her leaning posture, and stretched forth her head as though to listen; then she moved to follow them. Yes, they had stopped at the bottom of the path, and had again laid the body on the rocks. She heard that sound again, as of a long, long sigh, and then, regardless of any of them, she ran to the wounded man's head.

"He is not dead," she said. "There; he is not dead."

As she spoke Barty's eyes opened, and he looked about him.

"Barty, my boy, speak to me," said the mother.

Barty turned his face upon his mother, smiled, and then stared about him wildly.

"How is it with thee, lad?" said his father.

Then Barty turned his face again to the latter voice, and as he did so his eyes fell upon Mally. ·

"Mally!" he said. "Mally!"

It could have wanted nothing further to any of those present to teach them that, according to Barty's own view of the case, Mally had not been his enemy; and, in truth, Mally herself wanted no further triumph. That word had vindicated her, and she withdrew back to the hut.

"Dada," she said, "Barty is not dead, and I'm thinking they won't say anything more about our hurting him."

Old Glos shook his head. He was glad the lad hadn't met his death there; he didn't want the young man's blood, but he knew what folk would say. The poorer he was the more sure the world would be to trample on him. Mally said what she could to comfort him, being full of comfort herself.

She would have crept up to the farm if she dared, to ask how Barty was. But her courage failed her when she thought of that, so she went to work again, dragging back the weed she had saved to the spot at which on the morrow she would load the donkey. As she did this she saw Barty's pony still standing patiently under the rock, so she got a lock of fodder and threw it down before the beast.

It had become dark down in the cove, but she was still dragging back the seaweed, when she saw the glimmer of a lantern coming down the pathway. It was a most unusual sight, for lanterns were not common down in Malachi's Cove. Down came the lantern rather slowly,—much more slowly than she was in the habit of descending, and then through the gloom she saw the figure of a man standing at the bottom of the path. She went up to him, and saw that it was Mr. Gunliffe, the father.

"Is that Mally?" said Gunliffe.

"Yes, it is Mally; and how is Barty, Mr. Gunliffe?"

"You must come to 'un yourself, now at once," said the farmer. "He won't sleep a wink till he's seed you. You must not say but you'll come."

"Sure I'll come if I'm wanted," said Mally.

Gunliffe waited a moment, thinking that Mally might have to prepare herself, but Mally needed no preparation. She was dripping with salt water from the weed which she had been dragging, and her elfin locks were streaming wildly from her head; but, such as she was, she was ready.

"Dada's in bed," she said, "and I can go now if you please."

Then Gunliffe turned round and followed her up the path, wondering at the life which this girl led so far away from all her sex. It was now dark night, and he had found her working at the very edge of the rolling waves by herself, in the darkness, while the only human being who might seem to be her protector had already gone to his bed.

When they were at the top of the cliff Gunliffe took her by her hand, and led her along. She did not comprehend this, but she made no attempt to take her hand from his. Something he said about falling on the cliffs, but it was muttered so lowly that Mally hardly understood him. But, in truth, the man knew that she had saved his boy's life, and that he had injured her instead of thanking her. He was now taking her to his heart, and as words were wanting to him, he was showing his love after this silent fashion. He held her by the hand as though she were a child, and Mally tripped along at his side asking him no questions.

When they were at the farm-yard gate, he stopped for a moment.

"Mally, my girl," he said, "he'll not be content till he sees thee, but thou must not stay long wi' him, lass. Doctor says he's weak like, and wants sleep badly."

Mally merely nodded her head, and then they entered the house. Mally had never been within it before, and looked about with wondering eyes at the furniture of the big kitchen. Did any idea of her future destiny flash upon her then, I wonder? But she did not pause here a moment, but was led up to the bedroom above stairs, where Barty was lying on his mother's bed.

"Is it Mally herself?" said the voice of the weak youth.

"It's Mally herself," said the mother, "so now you can say what you please."

"Mally," said he, "Mally, it's along of you that I'm alive this moment."

"I'll not forget it on her," said the father, with his eyes turned away from her. "I'll never forget it on her."

"We hadn't a one but only him," said the mother, with her apron up to her face.

"Mally, you'll be friends with me now?" said Barty.

To have been made lady of the manor of the cove for ever, Mally couldn't have spoken a word now. It was not only that the words and presence of the people there cowed her and made her speechless, but the big bed, and the looking-glass, and the unheard-of wonders of the chamber, made her feel her own insignificance. But she crept up to Barty's side, and put her hand upon his.

"I'll come and get the weed, Mally; but it shall all be for you," said Barty.

"Indeed, you won't then, Barty dear," said the mother; "you'll never go near the awesome place again. What would we do if you were took from us?"

"He mustn't go near the hole if he does," said Mally, speaking at last in a solemn voice, and imparting the knowledge which she had kept to herself while Barty was her enemy; "'specially not if the wind's any way from the nor'ard."

"She'd better go down now," said the father.

Barty kissed the hand which he held, and Mally, looking at him as he did so, thought that he was like an angel.

"You'll come and see us to-morrow, Mally," said he.

To this she made no answer, but followed Mrs. Gunliffe out of the room. When they were down in the kitchen, the mother had tea for her, and thick milk, and a hot cake,—all the delicacies which the farm could afford. I don't know that Mally cared much for the eating and drinking that night, but she began to think that the Gunliffes were good people,—very good people. It was better thus, at any rate, than being accused of murder and carried off to Camelford prison.

"I'll never forget it on her—never," the father had said.

Those words stuck to her from that moment, and seemed to sound in her ears all the night. How glad she was that Barty had come down to the cove,—oh, yes, how glad! There was no question of his dying now, and as for the blow on his forehead, what harm was that to a lad like him?

"But father shall go with you," said Mrs. Gunliffe, when Mally prepared to start for the cove by herself.

Mally, however, would not hear of this. She could find her way to the cove whether it was light or dark.

"Mally, thou art my child now, and I shall think of thee so," said the mother, as the girl went off by herself.

Mally thought of this, too, as she walked home. How could she become Mrs. Gunliffe's child; ah, how?

I need not, I think, tell the tale any further. That Mally did become Mrs. Gunliffe's child, and how she became so the reader will understand; and in process of time the big kitchen and all the wonders of the farmhouse were her own. The people said that Barty Gunliffe had married a mermaid out of the sea; but when it was said in Mally's hearing I doubt whether she liked it; and when Barty himself would call her a mermaid she would frown at him, and throw about her black hair, and pretend to cuff him with her little hand.

Old Glos was brought up to the top of the cliff, and lived his few remaining days under the roof of Mr. Gunliffe's house; and as for the cove and the right of seaweed, from that time forth all that has been supposed to attach itself to Gunliffe's farm, and I do not know that any of the neighbours are prepared to dispute the right.

ANTHONY TROLLOPE
1815–82

Anthony Trollope spent much of his English boyhood in the miserable embarrassment of his family's financial ruin. His father, a barrister with a difficult temperament and little ability to order his affairs, gradually failed in his legal practice and engaged in a series of disastrous money-making schemes. Trollope, sent as a day boy to Harrow at age seven, attended Winchester at twelve. When accumulated bills could not be paid, he was removed from there, but not before his classmates had begun to taunt him because of his family's difficulties. In a state of disgrace he returned to Harrow, where he was ostracized. His father's bankruptcy ended that embarrassment. The Trollope family moved to Belgium in 1834, when his mother, Frances Trollope, began to support the family by writing. She had published forty-one books by the time she died at eighty-three.

Family friends obtained a position for Trollope in Britain's post office when he was nineteen. Because of his lack of punctuality and his penchant for getting into trouble, he maintained the job with some difficulty. What transformed him into a more diligent civil servant was being sent to Ireland to work as an inspector. He became a more stable, happy man, married, and began to write. His sojourn in Ireland continued until 1859; his service with the post office, until 1867.

Trollope's first novels—*The MacDermots of Ballycloran* (1847), *The Kellys and O'Kellys: A Tale of Irish Life* (1848), and *La Vendée* (1850)—were artistic failures, but with *The Warden* (1855) he displayed his particular talent for characterization. This novel initiated the "Barsetshire Chronicles," a series of books on morality and the Anglican clergy which has become the cornerstone of Trollope's achievement. *Barchester Towers* (1857), *Doctor Thorne* (1858), *Framley Parsonage* (1861), *The Small House at Allington* (1864), and *The Last Chronicle of Barset* (1867) all belong to this heralded series. Of the forty-seven novels Trollope penned, those that comprise his other series, the "Parliamentary series," rival the Barsetshire novels in importance. Beginning with *Phineas Finn* (1869), it includes *The Irish Member* (1869), *The Eustace Diamonds* (1873), *Phineas Redux* (1874), *The Prime Minister* (1876), and *The Duke's Children* (1880).

Two other novels that deserve attention are *The Claverings* (1867) and *The Way We Live Now* (1873)—the first for its distinctive style, the second for its savage satire.

"Malachi's Cove" was first collected in *Lotta Schmidt and Other Stories* (1867).

All My Sad Captains

BY SARAH ORNE JEWETT

I.

MRS. PETER LUNN was a plump little woman who bobbed her head like a
pigeon when she walked. Her best dress was a handsome, if not new, black
silk which Captain Lunn, her lamented husband, had bought many years
before in the port of Bristol. The decline of shipping interests had cost this
worthy shipmaster not only the better part of his small fortune, but also his
health and spirits; and he had died a poor man at last, after a long and
trying illness. Such a lingering disorder, with its hopes and despairs, rarely
affords the same poor compensations to a man that it does to a woman; the
claims upon public interest and consideration, the dignity of being assailed
by any ailment out of the common course—all these things are to a man but
the details of his general ignominy and impatience.

Captain Peter Lunn may have indulged in no sense of his own consequence and uniqueness as an invalid; but his wife bore herself as a woman
should who was the heroine in so sad a drama, and she went and came
across the provincial stage, knowing that her audience was made up of
nearly the whole population of that little seaside town. When the curtain
had fallen at last, and the old friends—seafaring men and others and their
wives—had come home from Captain Lunn's funeral, and had spoken their
friendly thoughts, and reviewed his symptoms for what seemed to them to
be the last time, everybody was conscious of a real anxiety. The future of the
captain's widow was sadly uncertain, for every one was aware that Mrs.
Lunn could now depend upon only a scant provision. She was much
younger than her husband, having been a second wife, and she was thrifty
and ingenious; but her outlook was acknowledged to be anything but cheerful. In truth, the honest grief that she displayed in the early days of her loss
was sure to be better understood with the ancient proverb in mind, that a
lean sorrow is hardest to bear.

To everybody's surprise, however, this able woman succeeded in keeping
the old Lunn house painted to the proper perfection of whiteness; there
never were any loose bricks to be seen on the tops of her chimneys. The
relics of the days of her prosperity kept an air of comfortable continuance in
the days of her adversity. The best black silk held its own nobly, and the

shining roundness of its handsome folds aided her in looking prosperous and fit for all social occasions. She lived alone, and was a busy and un-procrastinating housekeeper. She may have made less raspberry jam than in her earlier days, but it was always pound for pound; while her sponge-cake was never degraded in its ingredients from the royal standard of twelve eggs. The honest English and French stuffs that had been used in the fur-nishing of the captain's house so many years before faded a little as the years passed by, but they never wore out. Yet one cannot keep the same money in one's purse, if one is never so thrifty, and so Mrs. Lunn came at last to feel heavy at heart and deeply troubled. To use the common phrase of her neigh-bors, it was high time for her to make a change. She had now been living alone for four years, and it must be confessed that all those friends who had admired her self-respect and self-dependence began to take a keener inter-est than ever in her plans and behavior.

The first indication of Mrs. Lunn's new purpose in life was her mournful allusion to those responsibilities which so severely tax the incompetence of a lone woman. She felt obliged to ask advice of a friend; in fact, she asked the advice of three friends, and each responded with a cordiality delightful to describe. It happened that there were no less than three retired shipmasters in the old seaport town of Longport who felt the justice of our heroine's claims upon society. She was not only an extremely pleasing person, but she had the wisdom to conceal from Captain Asa Shaw that she had taken any one for an intimate counselor but himself; and the same secrecy was ob-served out of deference to the feelings and pride of Captain Crowe and Cap-tain Witherspoon. The deplored necessity of re-shingling her roof was the great case in which she threw herself upon their advice and assistance.

Now, if it had been the new planking of a deck, or the selection and stepping of a mast, the counsel of two of these captains would have been more likely to avail a helpless lady. They were elderly men, and had spent so much of their lives at sea that they were not very well informed about shing-ling their own houses, having left this to their wives, or agents, or some other land-fast persons. They recognized the truth that it would not do to let the project be publicly known, for fear of undue advantage being taken over an unprotected woman; but each found his opportunity to acquire in-formation, and to impart it in secret to Mrs. Lunn. It sometimes occurred to the good woman that she had been unwise in setting all her captains upon the same course, especially as she really thought that the old cedar shingles might last, with judicious patching, for two or three years more. But, in spite of this weakness of tactics, she was equal to her small campaign.

It now becomes necessary that the reader should have some closer ac-quaintance with the captains themselves: and to that end confession must be made of the author's belief in a theory of psychological misfits, or the occasional occupation of large-sized material bodies by small-sized spiritual tenants, and the opposite of this, by which small shapes of clay are sometimes animated in the noblest way by lofty souls. This was the case with Captain Witherspoon, who, not being much above five feet in height, bore himself like a giant, and carried a cane that was far too tall for him. Not so Captain Crowe, who, being considerably over six feet, was small-voiced and easily embarrassed, besides being so unconscious of the strength and size of his great body that he usually bore the mark of a blow on his forehead, to show that he had lately attempted to go through a door that was too low. He accounted for himself only as far as his eyes, and in groping between decks, or under garret or storehouse eaves, the poor man was constantly exposing the superfluous portion of his frame to severe usage. His hats were always more or less damaged. He was altogether unaware of the natural dignity of his appearance, and bore himself with great honesty and simplicity, as became a small and timid person. But little Captain Witherspoon had a heart of fire. He spoke in a loud and hearty voice. He was called "The Captain" by his townsfolk, while other shipmasters, active or retired, were given their full and distinctive names of Captain Crowe, Captain Eli Proudfit, or Captain Asa Shaw, as the case might be.

Captain Asa Shaw was another aspirant for the hand of Mrs. Maria Lunn. He had a great deal more money than his rivals, and was the owner of a tugboat, which brought a good addition to his income, since Longport was at the mouth of a river on which there was still considerable traffic. He lacked the dignity and elegance of leisure which belonged to Captains Crowe and Witherspoon, but the fact was patent that he was a younger man than they by half a dozen years. He was not a member of one of the old Longport families, and belonged to a less eminent social level. His straightforwardness of behavior and excellent business position were his chief claims, besides the fact that he was not only rich, but growing richer every day. His drawbacks were the carping relatives of his late wife, and his four unruly children. Captain Crowe felt himself assured of success in his suit, because he was by no means a poor man, and because he owned the best house in town, over which any woman might be proud to reign as mistress; but he had the defect of owing a home to two maiden sisters who were envious and uneasy at the very suggestion of his marrying again. They constantly deplored the loss of their sister-in-law, and paid assiduous and open respect to her memory in every possible way. It seemed certain that as long as they could continue the captain's habit of visiting her grave, in their company, on pleasant Sundays, he was in little danger of providing a successor to reign over them. They had been very critical and hard-hearted to the meek little woman while she was alive, and their later conduct may possibly have been moved by repentance.

As for the third admirer of Mrs. Lunn, Captain Witherspoon, he was an unencumbered bachelor who had always dreamed of marrying, but had never wished to marry any one in particular until Maria Lunn had engaged his late-blossoming affections. He had only a slender estate, but was sure that if they had been able to get along apart, they could get on all the better together. His lonely habitation was with a deaf, widowed cousin; his hopes were great that he was near to having that happy home of his own of which he had dreamed on land and sea ever since he was a boy. He was young at heart, and an ardent lover, this red-faced little old captain, who walked in the Longport streets as if he were another Lord Nelson, afraid of nobody, and equal to his fortunes.

To him, who had long admired her in secret, Maria Lunn's confidence in regard to the renewing of her cedar shingles had been a golden joy. He could hardly help singing as he walked, at this proof of her confidence and esteem, and the mellowing effect of an eleven o'clock glass of refreshment put his willing tongue in daily danger of telling his hopes to a mixed but assuredly interested company. As he walked by the Lunn house, on his way to and from the harbor side, he looked at it with a feeling of relationship and love; he admired the clean white curtains at the windows, he envied the plump tortoise-shell cat on the side doorstep; if he saw the composed and pleasant face of Maria glancing up from her sewing, he swept his hat through the air with as gallant a bow as Longport had ever seen, and blushed with joy and pride. Maria Lunn owned to herself that she liked him best, as far as he himself was concerned; while she invariably settled it with her judicious affections that she must never think of encouraging the captain, who, like herself, was too poor already. Put to the final test, he was found wanting; he was no man of business, and had lost both his own patrimony and early savings in disastrous shipping enterprises, and still liked to throw down his money to any one who was willing to pick it up. But sometimes, when she saw him pass with a little troop of children at his heels, on their happy way to the candy-shop at the corner, she could not forbear a sigh, or to say to herself, with a smile, that the little man was good-hearted, or that there was nobody who made himself better company; perhaps he would stop in for a minute as he came up the street again at noon. Her sewing was not making, but mending, in these days; and the more she had to mend, the more she sat by one of her front windows, where the light was good.

II.

One evening toward the end of summer there came a loud rap at the knocker of Mrs. Lunn's front door. It was the summons of Captain Asa Shaw, who sought a quiet haven from the discomforts of the society of his sisters-in-law and his notoriously ill-bred children. Captain Shaw was prosperous, if not happy; he had been figuring up accounts that rainy afternoon, and found himself in good case. He looked burly and commonplace and insistent as he stood on the front doorstep, and thought Mrs. Lunn was long in coming. At the same moment when she had just made her appearance with a set smile, and a little extra color in her cheeks, from having hastily taken off her apron and tossed it into the sitting-room closet, and smoothed her satin-like black hair on the way, there was another loud rap on the smaller side-door knocker.

"There must be somebody wanting to speak with me on an errand," she prettily apologized, as she offered Captain Shaw the best rocking-chair. The side door opened into a tiny entry-way at the other end of the room, and she unfastened the bolt impatiently. "Oh, walk right in, Cap'n Crowe!" she was presently heard to exclaim; but there was a note of embarrassment in her tone, and a look of provocation on her face, as the big shipmaster lumbered after her into the sitting-room. Captain Shaw had taken the large chair, and the newcomer was but poorly accommodated on a smaller one with a cane seat. The walls of the old Lunn house were low, and his head seemed in danger of knocking itself; he was clumsier and bigger than ever in this moment of dismay. His sisters had worn his patience past endurance, and he had it in mind to come to a distinct understanding with Mrs. Lunn that very night.

Captain Shaw was in his every-day clothes, which lost him a point in Mrs. Lunn's observant eyes; but Captain Crowe had paid her the honor of putting on his best coat for this evening visit. She thought at first that he had even changed his shirt, but upon reflection remembered that this could not be taken as a special recognition of her charms, it being Wednesday night. On the wharves, or in a down-town office, the two men were by way of being good friends, but at this moment great Captain Crowe openly despised his social inferior, and after a formal recognition of his unwelcome presence ignored him with unusual bravery, and addressed Mrs. Lunn with grave politeness. He was dimly conscious of the younger and lesser man's being for some unexplainable reason a formidable rival, and tried blunderingly to show the degree of intimacy which existed between himself and the lady.

"I just looked in to report about our little matter of business. I've got the estimates with me, but 'twill do just as well another time," said the big mariner in his disapproving, soft voice.

Captain Shaw instinctively scuffed his feet at the sound, and even felt for his account-book in an inside pocket to reassure himself of his financial standing. "I could buy him an' sell him twice over," he muttered angrily, as loud as he dared.

Mrs. Lunn rose to a command of the occasion at once; there was no sense in men of their age behaving like schoolboys. "Oh, my, yes!" she hastened to say, as she rose with a simpering smile. "'Tain't as if 'twas any kind o' consequence, you know; not but what I'm just as much obliged."

Captain Crowe scowled now; this was still the affair of the shingles, and it had been of enough consequence two days before to protract a conversation through two long hours. He had wished ever since that he had thought then to tell Mrs. Lunn that if she would just say the word, she never need think of those shingles again, nor of the cost of them. It would have been a pretty way to convey the state of his feelings toward her; but he had lost the opportunity, it might be forever. To use his own expression, he now put about and steered a new course.

"I come by your house just now," he said to Captain Shaw, who still glowered from the rocking-chair. "Your young folks seemed to be havin' a great time. Well, I like to see young folks happy. They generally be," he chuckled maliciously; "'tis we old ones have the worst of it, soon as they begin to want to have everything their way."

"I don't allow no trouble for'ard when I'm on deck," said Shipmaster Shaw more cheerfully; he hardly recognized the covert allusion to his drawbacks as a suitor. "I like to give 'em their liberty. To-night they were bound on some sort of a racket—they got some other young folks in; but gen'ally they do pretty well. I'm goin' to take my oldest boy right into the office, first o' January—put him right to business. I need more help; I've got too much now for me an' Decket to handle, though Decket's a good accountant."

"Well, I'm glad I'm out of it," said Captain Crowe. "I don't want the bother o' business. I don't need to slave."

"No; you shouldn't have too much to carry at your time o' life," rejoined his friend, in a tone that was anything but soothing; and at this moment Maria Lunn returned with her best lamp in full brilliancy. She had listened eagerly to their exchange of compliments, and thought it would be wise to change the subject.

"What's been goin' on down street today?" she asked. "I haven't had occasion to go out, and I don't have anybody to bring me the news, as I used to."

"Here's Cap'n Shaw makin' me out to be old enough to be his grandfather," insisted Captain Crowe, laughing gently, as if he had taken it as a joke. "Now, everybody knows I ain't but five years the oldest. Shaw, you mustn't be settin' up for a young dandy. I've had a good deal more sea service than you. I believe you never went out on a long voyage round the Cape or the like o' that; those long voyages count a man two years to one, if they're hard passages."

"No; I only made some few trips; the rest you might call coastin'," said Captain Shaw handsomely. The two men felt more at ease and reasonable

with this familiar subject of experience and discussion. "I come to the conclusion I'd better stop ashore. If I could ever have found me a smart, de-
pendable crew, I might have followed the sea longer than I did."

It was in the big captain's heart to say, "Poor master, poor crew;" but he
refrained. It had been well known that in spite of Shaw's ability as a money-
maker on shore, he was no seaman, and never had been. Mrs. Lunn was
sure to have heard his defects commented on, but she sat by the table, smiling, and gave no sign, though Captain Crowe looked at her eagerly for a
glance of understanding and contempt.

There was a moment of silence, and nobody seemed to know what to say
next. Mrs. Maria Lunn was not a great talker in company, although so delightful in confidence and consultation. She wished now, from the bottom of
her heart, that one of her admirers would go away; but at this instant there
was a loud tapping at a back door in the farther end of the house.

"I thought I heard somebody knocking a few minutes ago." Captain
Crowe rose like a buoy against the ceiling. "Here, now, I'm goin' to the door
for you, Mis' Lunn; there may be a tramp or somethin'."

"Oh, no," said the little woman, anxiously bustling past him, and lifting
the hand-lamp as she went. "I guess it's only somebody to speak about the
washing. Mrs. Dimmett's been sick"— The last words were nearly lost in
the distance, and in the draught a door closed after her, and the two captains were left alone. Some minutes went by before they suddenly heard the
sound of a familiar voice.

"I don't know but what I will, after all, step in an' set down for just a
minute," said the hearty voice of little Captain Witherspoon. "I'll just wash
my hands here at the sink, if you'll let me, same's I did the other day. I
shouldn't have bothered you so late about a mere fish, but they was such
prime mackerel, an' I thought like's not one of 'em would make you a
breakfast."

"You're always very considerate," answered Mrs. Lunn, in spite of what
she felt to be a real emergency. She was very fond of mackerel, and these
were the first of the season. "Walk right in, Cap'n Witherspoon, when you
get ready. You'll find some o' your friends. 'Tis 'The Cap'n,' gentlemen,"
she added, in a pleased tone, as she rejoined her earlier guests.

If Captain Witherspoon had also indulged a hope of finding his love
alone, he made no sign; it would be beneath so valiant and gallant a man to
show defeat. He shook hands with both his friends as if he had not seen
them for a fortnight, and then drew one of the Windsor chairs forward,
forcing the two companions into something like a social circle.

"What's the news?" he demanded. "Anything heard from the new minister yet, Crowe? I suppose, though, the ladies are likely to hear of those
matters first."

Mrs. Lunn was grateful to this promoter of friendly intercourse. "Yes, sir," she answered quickly; "I was told, just before tea, that he had written to Deacon Torby that he felt moved to accept the call."

Her eyes shone with pleasure at having this piece of news. She had been thinking a great deal about it just before the two captains came in, but their mutual dismay had been such an infliction that for once she had been in danger of forgetting her best resources. Now, with the interest of these parishioners in their new minister, the propriety, not to say the enjoyment, of the rest of the evening was secure. Captain Witherspoon went away earliest, as cheerfully as he had come; and Captain Shaw rose and followed him for the sake of having company along the street. Captain Crowe lingered a few moments, so obtrusively that he seemed to fill the whole sitting-room, while he talked about unimportant matters; and at last Mrs. Lunn knocked a large flat book off the end of the sofa for no other reason than to tell him that it was one of Captain Witherspoon's old log-books which she had taken great pleasure in reading. She did not explain that it was asked for because of other records; her late husband had also been in command—one voyage—of the ship Mary Susan.

Captain Crowe went grumbling away down the street. "I've seen his plaguy logs; and what she can find, I don't see. There ain't nothin' to a page but his figures, and what men were sick, and how the seas run, an' 'So ends the day.'" It was a terrible indication of rivalry that the captain felt at liberty to bring his confounded fish to any door he chose; and his very willingness to depart early and leave the field might prove him to possess a happy certainty, Captain Crowe was so jealous that he almost forgot to play his rôle of lover.

As for Mrs. Lunn herself, she blew out the best lamp at once, so that it would burn another night, and sat and pondered over her future. "'Twas real awkward to have 'em all call together; but I guess I passed it off pretty well," she consoled herself, casting an absent-minded glance at her little blurred mirror with the gilded wheat-sheaf at the top.

"Everybody's after her; I've got to look sharp," said Captain Asa Shaw to himself that night. I guess I'd better give her to understand what I'm worth."

"Both o' them old sea-dogs is steerin' for the same port as I be. I'll cut 'em out, if only for the name of it—see if I don't!" Captain Crowe muttered, as he smoked his evening pipe, puffing away with a great draught that made the tobacco glow and almost flare.

"I care a world more about poor Maria than anybody else does," said warm-hearted little Captain Witherspoon, making himself as tall as he could as he walked his bedroom deck to and fro.

III.

Down behind the old Witherspoon warehouse, built by the captain's father when the shipping interests of Longport were at their height of prosperity, there was a pleasant spot where one might sometimes sit in the cool of the afternoon. There were some decaying sticks of huge oak timber, stout and short, which served well for benches; the gray, rain-gnawed wall of the old warehouse, with its overhanging second story, was at the back; and in front was the wharf, still well graveled except where tenacious, wiry weeds and thin grass had sprouted, and been sunburned into sparse hay. There were some places, alas! where the planking had rotted away, and one could look down through and see the clear, green water underneath, and the black, sea-worn piles with their fringes of barnacles and seaweed. Captain Crowe gave a deep sigh as he sat heavily down on a stick of timber; then he heard a noise above, and looked up, to see at first only the rusty windlass under the high gable, with its end of frayed rope flying loose; then one of the wooden shutters was suddenly flung open, and swung to again, and fastened. Captain Crowe was sure now that he should gain a companion. Captain Witherspoon was in the habit of airing the empty warehouse once a week— Wednesdays, if pleasant; it was nearly all the active business he had left; and this was Thursday, but Wednesday had been rainy.

Presently the Captain appeared at the basement doorway, just behind where his friend was sitting. The door was seldom opened, but the owner of the property professed himself forgetful about letting in as much fresh air there as he did above, and announced that he should leave it open for half an hour. The two men moved a little way along the oak stick to be out of the cool draught which blew from the cellar-like place, empty save for the storage of some old fragments of vessels or warehouse gear. There was a musty odor of the innumerable drops of molasses which must have leaked into the hard earth there for half a century; there was still a fragrance of damp Liverpool salt, a reminder of even the dyestuffs and pepper and rich spices that had been stowed away. The two elderly men were carried back to the past by these familiar, ancient odors; they turned and sniffed once or twice with satisfaction, but neither spoke. Before them the great, empty harbor spread its lovely, shining levels in the low afternoon light. There were a few ephemeral pleasure-boats, but no merchantmen riding at anchor, no lines of masts along the wharves, with great wrappings of furled sails on the yards; there were no sounds of mallets on the ships' sides, or of the voices of men, busy with unlading, or moving the landed cargoes. The old warehouses were all shuttered and padlocked, as far as the two men could see.

"Looks lonesomer than ever, don't it?" said Captain Crowe, pensively. "I

vow it's a shame to see such a harbor as this, an' think o' all the back country, an' how things were goin' on here in our young days."

" 'Tis sad, sir, sad," growled brave little Captain Witherspoon. "They've
taken the wrong course for the country's good—some o' those folks in
Washington. When the worst of 'em have stuffed their own pockets as full
as they can get, p'r'aps they'll see what else can be done, and all catch hold
together and shore up the shipping int'rists. I see every night, when I go
after my paper, the whole sidewalk full o' louts that ought to be pushed off
to sea with a good smart master; they're going to the devil ashore, sir. Every
way you can look at it, shippin's a loss to us."

At this moment the shrill whistle of a locomotive sounded back of the
town, but the captains took no notice of it. Two idle boys suddenly came
scrambling up the broken landing-steps from the water, one of them clutching a distressed puppy. Then another, who had stopped to fasten the invisible boat underneath, joined them in haste, and all three fled round the corner. The elderly seamen had watched them severely.

"It used to cost but a ninepence to get a bar'l from Boston by sea," said
Captain Crowe, in a melancholy tone; "and now it costs twenty-five cents by
the railroad, sir."

In reply Captain Witherspoon shook his head gloomily.

"You an' I never expected to see Longport harbor look like this," resumed Captain Crowe, giving the barren waters a long gaze, and then leaning forward and pushing the pebbles about with his cane. "I don't know's I
ever saw things look so poor along these wharves as they do to-day. I've
seen six or seven large vessels at a time waitin' out in the stream there until
they could get up to the wharves. You could stand ashore an' hear their
masters rippin' an' swearin' aboard, an' fur's you could see from here, either
way, the masts and riggin' looked like the woods in winter-time. There
used to be somethin' doin' in this place when we was young men, Cap'n
Witherspoon."

"I feel it as much as anybody," acknowledged the captain. "Looks to me
very much as if there was a vessel comin' up, down there over Dimmett's
P'int; she may only be runnin' in closer'n usual on this light sou'easterly
breeze; yes, I s'pose that's all. What do you make her out to be, sir?"

The old shipmasters bent their keen, farsighted gaze seaward for a moment. "She ain't comin' in; she's only one o' them great schooners runnin'
west'ard. I'd as soon put to sea under a Monday's clothes-line, for my part,"
said Captain Crowe.

"Yes; give me a brig, sir, a good able brig," said Witherspoon eagerly. "I
don't care if she's a little chunky, neither. I'd make more money out of her
than out o' any o' these gre't new-fangled things. I'd as soon try to sail a
whole lumber-yard to good advantage. Gi' me an old-fashioned house an'

an old-style vessel; there was some plan an' reason to 'em. Now that new
house of Asa Shaw's he's put so much money in—looks as if a nor'west
wind took an' hove it together. Shaw's just the man to call for one o' them
schooners we just spoke of."

The mention of this rival's name caused deep feelings in their manly
breasts. The captains felt an instant resentment of Asa Shaw's wealth and
pretensions. Neither noticed that the subject was abruptly changed without apparent reason, when Captain Crowe asked if there was any truth
in the story that the new minister was going to take board with the
Widow Lunn.

"No, sir," exclaimed Captain Witherspoon, growing red in the face, and
speaking angrily; "I don't put any confidence in the story at all."

"It might be of mutual advantage," his companion urged a little maliciously. Captain Crowe had fancied that Mrs. Lunn had shown him special
favor that afternoon, and ventured to think himself secure.

"The new minister's a dozen years younger than she; must be all o' that,"
said the Captain, collecting himself. "I called him quite a young-lookin'
man when he preached for us as a candidate. Sing'lar he shouldn't be a
married man. Generally they be."

"You ain't the right one to make reflections," joked Captain Crowe,
mindful that Maria Lunn had gone so far that very day as to compliment
him upon owning the handsomest old place in town. "I used to think you
was a great beau among the ladies, Witherspoon."

"I never expected to die a single man," said his companion, with dignity.

"You're gettin' along in years," urged Captain Crowe. "You're gettin' to
where it's dangerous; a good-hearted elderly man's liable to be snapped up
by somebody he don't want. They say an old man ought to be married, but
he shouldn't get married. I don't know but it's so."

"I've put away my thoughts o' youth long since," said the little captain
nobly. "Though I ain't so old, sir, but what I've got some years before me
yet, unless I meet with accident; an' I'm so situated that I never yet had to
take anybody that I didn't want. But I do often feel that there's somethin' to
be said for the affections, an' I get to feelin' lonesome winter nights, thinkin'
that age is before me, an' if I should get hove on to a sick an' dyin' bed"—

The captain's hearty voice failed for once; then the pleasant face and
sprightly figure of the lady of his choice seemed to interpose, and to comfort
him. "Come, come!" he said, "ain't we gettin' into the doldrums, Crowe?
I'll just step in an' close up the warehouse; it must be time to make for
supper."

Captain Crowe walked slowly round by the warehouse lane into the
street, waiting at the door while his friend went through the old building,
carefully putting up the bars and locking the street door upon its emptiness

with a ponderous key; then the two captains walked away together, the tall one and the short one, clicking their canes on the flagstones. They turned up Barbadoes Street, where Mrs. Lunn lived, and bowed to her finely as they passed.

IV.

One Sunday morning in September the second bell was just beginning to toll, and Mrs. Lunn locked her front door, tried the great brass latch, put the heavy key into her best silk dress pocket, and stepped forth discreetly on her way to church. She had been away from Longport for several weeks, having been sent for to companion the last days of a cousin much older than herself; and her reappearance was now greeted with much friendliness. The siege of her heart had necessarily been in abeyance. She walked to her seat in the broad aisle with great dignity. It was a season of considerable interest in Longport, for the new minister had that week been installed, and that day he was to preach his first sermon. All the red East Indian scarfs and best raiment of every sort suitable for early autumn wear had been brought out of the camphor-chests, and there was an air of solemn festival.

Mrs. Lunn's gravity of expression was hardly borne out by her gayety of apparel, yet there was something cheerful about her look, in spite of her recent bereavement. The cousin who had just died had in times past visited Longport, so that Mrs. Lunn's friends were the more ready to express their regret. When one has passed the borders of middle life, such losses are sadly met; they break the long trusted bonds of old association, and remove a part of one's own life and belongings. Old friends grow dearer as they grow fewer; those who remember us as long as we remember ourselves become a part of ourselves at last, and leave us much the poorer when they are taken away. Everybody felt sorry for Mrs. Lunn, especially as it was known that this cousin had always been as generous as her income would allow; but she was chiefly dependent upon an annuity, and was thought to have but little to leave behind her.

Mrs. Lunn had reached home only the evening before, and, the day of her return having been uncertain, she was welcomed by no one, and had slipped in at her own door unnoticed in the dusk. There was a little stir in the congregation as she passed to her pew, but, being in affliction, she took no notice of friendly glances, and responded with great gravity only to her neighbor in the next pew, with whom she usually exchanged confidential whispers as late as the second sentence of the opening prayer.

The new minister was better known to her than to any other member of the parish; for he had been the pastor of the church to which her lately deceased cousin belonged, and Mrs. Lunn had seen him oftener and more intimately than ever in this last sad visit. He was a fine-looking man, no

longer young,—in fact, he looked quite as old as our heroine,—and though
at first the three captains alone may have regarded him with suspicion, by
the time church was over and the Rev. Mr. Farley had passed quickly by
some prominent parishioners who stood expectant at the doors of their
pews, in order to speak to Mrs. Lunn, and lingered a few moments holding
her affectionately by the hand—by this time gossip was fairly kindled.
Moreover, the minister had declined Deacon Torby's invitation to dinner,
and it was supposed, though wrongly, that he had accepted Mrs. Lunn's, as
they walked away together.

Now Mrs. Lunn was a great favorite in the social circles of Longport—
none greater; but there were other single ladies in the First Parish, and it
was something to be deeply considered whether she had the right, with so
little delay, to appropriate the only marriageable minister who had been settled over that church and society during a hundred and eighteen years.
There was a loud buzzing of talk that Sunday afternoon. It was impossible
to gainsay the fact that if there was a prospective engagement, Mrs. Lunn
had shown her usual discretion. The new minister had a proper income, but
no house and home; while she had a good house and home, but no income.
She was called hard names, which would have deeply wounded her, by
many of her intimate friends; but there were others who more generously
took her part, though they vigorously stated their belief that a young married pastor with a growing family had his advantages. The worst thing
seemed to be that the Rev. Mr. Farley was beginning his pastorate under
a cloud.

While all this tempest blew, and all eyes were turned her way, friends and
foes alike behaved as if not only themselves but the world were concerned
with Mrs. Maria Lunn's behavior, and as if the fate of empires hung upon
her choice of a consort. She was maligned by Captain Crowe's two sisters for
having extended encouragement to their brother, while the near relatives of
Captain Shaw told tales of her open efforts to secure his kind attention; but
in spite of all these things, and the antagonism that was in the very air, Mrs.
Lunn went serenely on her way. She even, after a few days' seclusion, ar-
rayed herself in her best, and set forth to make some calls with a pleasant,
unmindful manner which puzzled her neighbors a good deal. She had, or
professed to have, some excuse for visiting each house: of one friend she
asked instructions about her duties as newly elected officer of the sewing
society, the first meeting of which had been held in her absence; and another neighbor was kindly requested to give the latest news from an invalid
son at a distance. Mrs. Lunn did not make such a breach of good manners
as to go out making calls with no reason so soon after her cousin's death.
She appeared rather in her most friendly and neighborly character; and

furthermore gave much interesting information in regard to the new minister, telling many pleasant things about him and his relations to, and degree of success in, his late charge. There may or may not have been an air of proprietorship in her manner; she was frank and free of speech, at any rate; and so the flame of interest was fanned ever to a brighter blaze.

The reader can hardly be expected to sympathize with the great excitement in Longport society when it was known that the new minister had engaged board with Mrs. Lunn for an indefinite time. There was something very puzzling in this new development. If there was an understanding between them, then the minister and Mrs. Lunn were certainly somewhat indiscreet. Nobody could discredit the belief that they had a warm interest in each other; yet those persons who felt themselves most nearly concerned in the lady's behavior began to indulge themselves in seeing a ray of hope.

V.

Captain Asa Shaw had been absent for some time in New York on business, and Captain Crowe was confined to his handsome house with a lame ankle; but it happened that they both reappeared on the chief business street of Longport the very same day. One might have fancied that each wore an expression of anxiety; the truth was, they had made vows to themselves that another twenty-four hours should not pass over their heads before they made a bold push for the coveted prize. They were more afraid of the minister's rivalry than they knew; but not the least of each other's. There were angry lines down the middle of Captain Asa Shaw's forehead as he assured himself that he would soon put an end to the minister business, and Captain Crowe thumped his cane emphatically as he walked along the street. Captain John Witherspoon looked thin and eager, but a hopeful light shone in his eyes: his choice was not from his judgment, but from his heart.

It was strange that it should be so difficult—nay, impossible—for anybody to find an opportunity to speak with Mrs. Lunn upon this most private and sacred of personal affairs, and that day after day went by while the poor captains fretted and grew more and more impatient. They had it in mind to speak at once when the time came; neither Captain Crowe nor Captain Shaw felt that he could do himself or his feelings any justice in a letter.

On a rainy autumn afternoon, Mrs. Lunn sat down by her front window, and drew her wicker work-basket into her lap from the end of the narrow table before her. She was tired, and glad to rest. She had been busy all morning, putting in order the rooms that were to be set apart for the minister's sleeping-room and study. Her thoughts were evidently pleasant as she looked out into the street for a few minutes, and then crossed her plump hands over the work-basket. Presently, as a large, familiar green umbrella passed her window, she caught up a bit of sewing, and seemed to be busy with it, as some one opened her front door and came into the little square entry without knocking.

"May I take the liberty? I saw you settin' by the window this wet day," said Captain Shaw.

"Walk right in, sir; do!" Mrs. Lunn fluttered a little on her perch at the sight of him, and then settled herself quietly, as trig and demure as ever.

"I'm glad, ma'am, to find you alone. I have long had it in mind to speak with you on a matter of interest to us both." The captain felt more embarrassed than he had expected, but Mrs. Lunn remained tranquil, and glanced up at him inquiringly.

"It relates to the future," explained Captain Asa Shaw. "I make no doubt you have seen what my feelin's have been this good while. I can offer you a good home, and I shall want you to have your liberty."

"I enjoy a good home and my liberty now," said Mrs. Lunn stiffly, looking straight before her.

"I mean liberty to use my means, and to have plenty to do with, so as to make you feel comfortable," explained the captain, reddening. "Mis' Lunn, I'm a straightforward business man, and I intend business now. I don't know any of your flowery ways of sayin' things, but there ain't anybody in Longport I'd like better to see at the head of my house. You and I ain't young, but we"—

"Don't say a word, sir," protested Mrs. Lunn. "You can get you just as good housekeepers as I am. I don't feel to change my situation just at present, sir."

"Is that final?" said Captain Shaw, looking crestfallen. "Come now, Maria! I'm a good-hearted man, I'm worth over forty thousand dollars, and I'll make you a good husband, I promise. Here's the minister on your hands, I know. I did feel all ashore when I found you'd promised to take him in. I tried to get a chance to speak with you before you went off, but when I come home from New York 'twas the first news I heard. I don't deem it best for you; you can't make nothin' out o' one boarder, anyway. I tried it once myself."

"Excuse me, Mr. Shaw," said Mrs. Lunn coldly; "I know my own business best. You have had my answer, sir." She added in a more amiable tone, "Not but what I feel obliged to you for payin' me the compliment."

There was a sudden loud knocking at the side door, which startled our friends extremely. They looked at each other with apprehension; then Mrs. Lunn slowly rose and answered the summons.

The gentle voice of the giant was heard without. "Oh, Mis' Lunn," said Captain Crowe excitedly, "I saw some elegant mackerel brought ashore, blown up from the south'ard, I expect, though so late in the season; and I recalled that you once found some acceptable. I thought 'twould help you out."

"I'm obliged to you, Captain Crowe," said the mistress of the house; "and to think of your bringin' 'em yourself this drenchin' day! I take it very neighborly, sir." Her tone was entirely different from that in which she had conducted so decisive a conversation with the guest in the sitting-room. They heard the front door bang just as Captain Crowe entered with his fish.

"Was that the wind sprung up so quick?" he inquired, alert to any change of weather.

"I expect it was Captain Shaw, just leavin'," said Mrs. Lunn angrily. "He's always full o' business, ain't he? No wonder those children of his are without manners." There was no favor in her tone, and the spirits of Captain Crowe were for once equal to his height.

The daylight was fading fast. The mackerel were deposited in their proper place, and the donor was kindly bidden to come in and sit down. Mrs. Lunn's old-fashioned sitting-room was warm and pleasant, and the big captain felt that his moment had come; the very atmosphere was encouraging. He was sitting in the rocking-chair, and she had taken her place by the window. There was a pause; the captain remembered how he had felt once in the China Seas just before a typhoon struck the ship.

"Maria," he said huskily, his voice sounding as if it came from the next room,—"Maria, I s'pose you know what I'm thinkin' of?"

"I don't," said Mrs. Lunn, with cheerful firmness. "Cap'n Crowe, I know it ain't polite to talk about your goin' when you've just come in; but when you do go, I've got something I want to send over to your sister Eliza."

The captain gasped; there was something in her tone that he could not fathom. He began to speak, but his voice failed him altogether. There she sat, perfectly self-possessed, just as she looked every day.

"What are you payin' now for potatoes, sir?" continued Mrs. Lunn.

"Sixty cents a bushel for the last, ma'am," faltered the captain. "I wish you'd hear to me, Maria," he burst out. "I wish"—

"Now don't, cap'n," urged the pleasant little woman. "I've made other arrangements. At any rate," she added, with her voice growing more business-like than ever,—"at any rate, I deem it best to wait until the late potatoes come into market; they seem to keep better."

The typhoon had gone past, but the captain waited a moment, still apprehensive. Then he took his hat, and slowly and sadly departed without any words of farewell. In spite of his lame foot he walked some distance beyond his own house, in a fit of absent-mindedness that was born of deep regret. It was impossible to help respecting Mrs. Lunn's character and ability more than ever. "Oh! them ministers, them ministers!" he groaned, turning in at his high white gate between the tall posts with their funeral urns.

Mrs. Lunn heard the door close behind Captain Crowe; then she smoothed down her nice white apron abstractedly, and glanced out of the window to see if he were out of sight, but she could not catch a glimpse of the captain's broad, expressive back, to judge his feelings or the manner in which he was taking his rebuff. She felt unexpectedly sorry for him; it was lonely in his handsome, large house, where his two sisters made so poor a home for him and such a good one for themselves.

It was almost dark now, and the shut windows of the room made the afternoon seem more gloomy; the days were fast growing shorter. After her successful conduct of the affair with her two lovers, she felt a little lonely and uncertain. Although she had learned to dislike Captain Shaw, and had dismissed him with no small pleasure, with Captain Crowe it was different; he was a good, kind-hearted man, and she had made a great effort to save his feelings.

Just then her quick ears caught the sound of a footstep in the street. She listened intently for a moment, and then stood close to the window, looking out. The rain was falling steadily; it streaked the square panes in long lines, so that Mrs. Lunn's heart recognized the approach of a friend more easily than her eyes. But the expected umbrella tipped away on the wind as it passed, so that she could see the large ivory handle. She lifted the sash in an instant. "I wish you'd step in just one minute, sir, if it's perfectly convenient," she said appealingly, and then felt herself grow very red in the face as she crossed the room and opened the door.

"I'm 'most too wet to come into a lady's parlor," apologized Captain Witherspoon gallantly. "Command me, Mrs. Lunn, if there's any way I can serve you. I expect to go down street again this evening."

"Do you think you'd better, sir?" gently inquired Mrs. Lunn. There was something beautiful about the captain's rosy cheeks and his curly gray hair. His kind blue eyes beamed at her like a boy's.

"I have had some business fall to me, you see, Cap'n," she continued, blushing still more; "and I feel as if I'd better ask your advice. My late cousin, Mrs. Hicks, has left me all her property. The amount is very unexpected; I never looked for more than a small remembrance. There will have to be steps taken."

"Command me, madam," said the captain again, to whom it never for one moment occurred that Mrs. Lunn was better skilled in business matters than himself. He instantly assumed the place of protector, which she so unaffectedly offered. For a minute he stood like an admiral ready to do the honors of his ship; then he put out his honest hand.

"Maria," he faltered, and the walls about him seemed to flicker and grow unsteady,—"Maria, I dare say it's no time to say the word just now, but if you could feel toward me"—

He never finished the sentence; he never needed to finish it. Maria Lunn said no word in answer, but they each took a step forward. They may not have been young, but they knew all the better how to value happiness.

About half an hour afterward, the captain appeared again in the dark street, in all the rain, without his umbrella. As he paraded toward his lodgings, he chanced to meet the Reverend Mr. Farley, whom he saluted proudly. He had demurred a little at the minister's making a third in their household; but in the brief, delightful space of their engagement, Mrs. Lunn had laid before him her sensible plans, and persuaded Captain Witherspoon that the minister—dear, good man!—was one who always had his head in a book when he was in the house, and would never give a bit of trouble; and that they might as well have the price of his board and the pleasure of his company as anybody.

Mrs. Lunn sat down to her belated and solitary supper, and made an excellent meal. "'Twill be pleasant for me to have company again," she murmured. "I think 'tis better for a person." She had a way, as many lonely women have, of talking to herself, just for the sake of hearing the sound of a voice. "I guess Mr. Farley's situation is goin' to please him, too," she added; "I feel as if I'd done it all for the best." Mrs. Lunn rose, and crossed the room with a youthful step, and stood before the little looking-glass, holding her head this way and that, like a girl; then she turned, still blushing a little, and put away the tea-things. "'Tis about time now for the Cap'n to go down town after his newspaper," she whispered; and at that moment the Captain opened the door.

One day, the next spring, Captain Crowe, who had always honored the heroine of this tale for saving his self-respect, and allowing him to affirm with solemn asseverations that though she was a prize for any man, he never had really offered himself to Mrs. Lunn—Captain Crowe and Captain Witherspoon were sitting at the head of Long Wharf together in the sunshine.

"I've been a very fortunate man, sir," said the little captain boldly. "My own property has looked up a good deal since I was married, what with that piece of land I sold for the new hotel, and other things that have come to bear—this wharf property, for instance. I shall have to lay out considerable for new plank, but I'm able to do it."

"Yes, sir; things have started up in Longport a good deal this spring; but it never is goin' to be what it was once," answered Captain Crowe, who had grown as much older as his friend had grown younger since the autumn, though he always looked best out of doors. "Don't you think, Captain

Witherspoon," he said, changing his tone, "that you ought to consider the matter of re-shinglin' your house? You'll have to engage men now, anyway, to do your plankin'. I know of some extra cedar shingles that were landed yesterday from somewheres up river. Or was Mis' Witherspoon a little over-anxious last season?"

"I think, with proper attention, sir," said the Captain sedately, "that the present shingles may last us a number of years yet."

SARAH ORNE JEWETT
1849–1909

Growing up in the town of her birth, South Berwick, Maine, Sarah Orne Jewett was deeply impressed by the people of the area, particularly the fishermen and sailors. Her paternal grandfather had been a sea captain, and during retirement he ran a general store where the young girl could hear the talk of the captains who came to fraternize. She learned of a different side of life by accompanying her father, a medical doctor, on his rounds. Though she was graduated from Berwick Academy in 1865, she was more educated by these experiences than by school.

Under the pseudonyms "A. C. Eliot," "Alice Eliot," and "Sarah O. Sweet," she began publishing stories in 1868; in 1869, one of her tales, "Mr. Bruce," appeared in the *Atlantic Monthly*. With the encouragement of *Atlantic* editor William Dean Howells, Jewett wrote her first book, *Deephaven* (1877). Books of her short stories followed. *Play Days* (1878) was a collection for children. It was followed by *Old Friends and New* (1879), *Country By-Ways* (1881), *The Mate of the Daylight*, and *Friends Ashore* (1884), all of which helped establish her reputation as a realist who made creative use of the romantic tradition that many other writers of the day were discarding as useless.

A Country Doctor (1884), an imaginative novel rooted firmly in the adolescent experience of the authoress, was too complicated for her to handle without strain. *A White Heron and Other Stories* (1886) has as its title story one of the most intriguing of Jewett's tales. While the other books of stories that appeared throughout her career contain masterful examples of her talent, her acknowledged masterpiece is *The Country of the Pointed Firs* (1896), a novel more convincing in tone and characterization than any of her earlier work.

"All My Sad Captains," a tale of three retired sea captains in love with the same woman, was collected in *The Life of Nancy* (1895).

Being Ashore

BY JOHN MASEFIELD

IN THE NIGHTS, in the winter nights, in the nights of storm when the wind howls, it is then that I feel the sweet of it. Aha, I say, you howling cata-mount, I say, you may blow, wind, and crack your cheeks, for all I care. Then I listen to the noise of the elm trees and to the creak in the old floor-ings, and, aha, I say, you whining rantipoles, you may crack and you may creak, but here I shall lie till daylight.

There is a solid comfort in a roaring storm ashore here. But on a calm day, when it is raining, when it is muddy underfoot, when the world is the colour of a drowned rat, one calls to mind more boisterous days, the days of effort and adventure; and wasn't I a fool, I say, to come ashore to a life like this life. And I was surely daft, I keep saying, to think the sea as bad as I always thought it. And if I were in a ship now, I say, I wouldn't be doing what I'm trying to do. And, ah! I say, if I'd but stuck to the sea I'd have been a third in the Cunard, or perhaps a second in a P.S.N. coaster. I wouldn't be hunched at a desk, I say, but I'd be up on a bridge—up on a bridge with a helmsman, feeling her do her fifteen knots.

It is at such times that I remember the good days, the exciting days, the days of vehement and spirited living. One day stands out, above nearly all my days, as a day of joy.

We were at sea off the River Plate, running south like a stag. The wind had been slowly freshening for twenty-four hours, and for one whole day we had whitened the sea like a battleship. Our run for the day had been 271 knots, which we thought a wonderful run, though it has, of course, been exceeded by many ships. For this ship it was an exceptional run. The wind was on the quarter, her best point of sailing, and there was enough wind for a glutton. Our captain had the reputation of being a "cracker-on," and on this one occasion he drove her till she groaned. For that one wonderful day we staggered and swooped, and bounded in wild leaps, and burrowed down and shivered, and anon rose up shaking. The wind roared up aloft and boomed in the shrouds, and the sails bellied out as stiff as iron. We tore through the sea in great jumps—there is no other word for it. She seemed to leap clear from one green roaring ridge to come smashing down upon the next. (I have been in a fast steamer—a very fast turbine steamer—doing more than twenty knots, but she gave me no sense of great speed.) In this old sailing ship the joy of the hurry was such that we laughed and cried aloud. The noise of the wind booming, and the clack, clack, clack of the sheet-blocks, and the ridged seas roaring past us, and the groaning and whining of every block and plank, were like tunes for a dance. We seemed to be tearing through it at ninety miles an hour. Our wake whitened and broadened, and rushed away aft in a creamy fury. We were running here, and hurrying there, taking a small pull of this, and getting another inch of that, till we were weary. But as we hauled we sang and shouted. We were possessed of the spirits of the wind. We could have danced and killed each other. We were in an ecstasy. We were possessed. We half believed that the ship would leap from the waters and hurl herself into the heavens, like a winged god. Over her bows came the sprays in showers of sparkles. Her foresail was wet to the yard. Her scuppers were brooks. Her swing-ports spouted like cataracts. Recollect, too, that it was a day to make your heart glad. It was a clear day, a sunny day, a day of brightness and splendour. The sun was glorious in the sky. The sky was of a blue unspeakable. We were tearing along across a splendour of sea that made you sing. Far as one could see there was the water shining and shaking. Blue it was, and green it was, and of a dazzling brilliance in the sun. It rose up in hills and in ridges. It smashed into a foam and roared. It towered up again and toppled. It mounted and shook in a rhythm, in a tune, in a music. One could have flung one's body to it as a sacrifice. One longed to be in it, to be a part of it, to be beaten and banged by it. It was a wonder and a glory and a terror. It was a triumph, it was royal, to see that beauty.

And later, after a day of it, as we sat below, we felt our mad ship taking yet wilder leaps, bounding over yet more boisterous hollows, and shivering and exulting in every inch of her. She seemed filled with a fiery, unquiet life. She seemed inhuman, glorious, spiritual. One forgot that she was man's work. We forgot that we were men. She was alive, immortal, furious. We were her minions and servants. We were the star-dust whirled in the train of the comet. We banged our plates with the joy we had in her. We sang and shouted, and called her the glory of the seas.

There is an end to human glory. "Greatness a period hath, no sta-ti-on." The end to our glory came when, as we sat at dinner, the door swung back from its hooks and a mate in oilskins bade us come on deck "without stopping for our clothes." It was time. She was carrying no longer; she was dragging. To windward the sea was blotted in a squall. The line of the horizon was masked in a grey film. The glory of the sea had given place to greyness and grimness. Her beauty had become savage. The music of the wind had changed to a howl as of hounds.

And then we began to "take it off her," to snug her down, to check her in her stride. We went to the clewlines and clewed the royals up. Then it was, "Up there, you boys, and make the royals fast." My royal was the mizzen-royal, a rag of a sail among the clouds, a great grey rag, which was leaping and slatting a hundred and sixty feet above me. The wind beat me down against the shrouds, it banged me and beat me, and blew the tears from my eyes. It seemed to lift me up the futtocks into the top, and up the topmast rigging to the cross-trees. In the cross-trees I learned what wind was.

It came roaring past with a fervour and a fury which struck me breathless. I could only look aloft to the yard I was bound for and heave my panting body up the rigging. And there was the mizzen-royal. There was the sail I had come to furl. And a wonder of a sight it was. It was blowing and bellying in the wind, and leaping around "like a drunken colt," and flying over the yard, and thrashing and flogging. It was roaring like a bull with its slatting and thrashing. The royal mast was bending to the strain of it. To my eyes it was buckling like a piece of whalebone. I lay out on the yard, and the sail hit me in the face and knocked my cap away. It beat me and banged me, and blew from my hands. The wind pinned me flat against the yard, and seemed to be blowing all my clothes to shreds. I felt like a king, like an emperor. I shouted aloud with the joy of that "rastle" with the sail. Forward of me was the main mast, with another lad, fighting another royal; and beyond him was yet another, whose sail seemed tied in knots. Below me was the ship, a leaping mad thing, with little silly figures, all heads and shoulders, pulling silly strings along the deck. There was the sea, sheer under me, and it looked grey and grim, and streaked with the white of our smother.

Then, with a lashing swish, the rain-squall caught us. It beat down the sea. It blotted out the view. I could see nothing more but grey, driving rain, grey spouts of rain, grey clouds which burst rain, grey heavens which opened and poured rain. Cold rain. Icy-cold rain. Rain which drove the dye out of my shirt till I left blue tracks where I walked. For the next two hours I was clewing up, and furling, and snugging her down. By nightfall we were under our three lower topsails and a reefed forecourse. The next day we were hove-to under a weather cloth.

There are varieties of happiness; and, to most of us, that variety called excitement is the most attractive. On a grey day such as this, with the grass rotting in the mud, the image and memory of that variety are a joy to the heart. They are a joy for this, if for no other reason. They teach us that a little thing, a very little thing, a capful of wind even, is enough to make us exult in, and be proud of, our parts in the pageant of life.

On Growing Old

BY JOHN MASEFIELD

THE OTHER DAY I met an old sailor friend at a café. We dined together, talking of old times. He was just home, on long leave, from the Indian Marine, a service in which he is a lieutenant. At first we talked of our shipmates, and of the men we had known at sea or in foreign ports; but that kind of talk was too melancholy; we had to stop. Some had fallen from aloft, and some had fallen down the hold, and a derrick had killed one and a bursting boiler another. One had been burnt in his ship, another had been posted missing. One had been stabbed by a greaser; two or three had gone to the gold-fields; one was in gaol for fraud; and one or two had taken to "crooking their little fingers" in the saloons of the Far West. He and I, we reckoned, were all that remained alive of a group of fifteen who were photographed together only eleven years ago. Before we parted, my friend remarked that I had greatly changed since our last meeting. I had grown quite grey, he said, and I had a drawn, old look about the eyes, and no one (this is what grieved me) would ever think me young again. Then we shook hands and went our ways, wondering if we should have yet another meeting before we died.

I left him thinking of the sadness of life and of a man's folly in not sticking to his work. We had been friends, I thought, intimate friends, comrades, when we had been at sea together. We had shared our clothes, our money, our letters from home, our work, our ease. We had been a proverb and a by-word to a whole ship's company. We were going to stick to each other, we always said, and when we were old, we hoped, we would get a job on a lighthouse, and smoke our pipes and read the papers together, and perhaps write a book together, or invent a safety pawl or a new kind of logship. We had intended all these things. We had hoped never to separate. We had built our lighthouse in the air, and based it in the wash of breakers. Then life, in its strength and strangeness, had swept us apart; and we who had been comrades were now a little puzzled by each other. I was wondering how it was that he could see no beauty in poetry. He was thinking me a little touched by time, an ancient, one grown old prematurely, a fossil, a has-been.

Then I was startled to think that he was right; to think that I was, in sooth, a has-been; that I was grown grey and bent; and that I wore an overcoat. It was shocking to me. I had done with a part of my life, with my youth, with my comrades. I should have no more comrades till I died. I should have friends, and perhaps a wife, and acquaintances to ask to dinner, and people to take a hand at cards with; but of comrades I should have no more. They were things I had done with for ever. I should go a-roving no more. I should never furl a sail again with a lot of men in oilskins. I could hum to myself the chorus—

> To *my*
> Ay,
> And we'll *furl*
> Ay
> And pay Paddy Doyle for his boots,

but I should never hear it again, as I once heard it, on the great yellow yards, among "the crowd." That line of swaying figures on the foot-rope, and the faces under the sou'-wester brims, and the slatting canvas stiff with ice, and the roar and the howl of the wind, and the flogging of the gear. Well; I had done with all that; with that and much else. I was not among "the crowd" any more, nor could I get back to it. Those places on the map too, those haunting places, those places with the Spanish names, those magical places. Oh, you names, you beautiful names!

Then I thought that, after all, if my youth were gone, the fine flower of it, the beauty, was yet mine. That man, my friend, my old comrade, what had youth been to him? It had been a means to an end, a state of probation, the formula that made his present. Had it any value to him? Did it haunt him? Did it come flooding to his mind in the night watches? Did it say to him, "This was life, this was truth, this was the meaning of life"? Could his soul inhabit that past, like a king in a palace? What, of his life, had seemed significant to him? What, in the past, recurred to him? Did anything? I called to mind our first voyage together, with its long, long walks on the deck, under the stars, over the sharp shadows of the sails. I remembered the first whale we saw, and the intense silvery brightness of his spout against the blue water. It had been in a dog watch, and I had been washing on the booby-hatch, and we spoke a great sailing ship an hour later. She had come to the wind about half a mile away, a noble, great ship, under all sail. I remembered her name, the *Glaucus*, and the extreme stateliness with which she dipped, and then rose, and again dipped, in a slow, swaying rhythm. I remembered the first land we made after our long sailing. We had had the morning watch, and had seen the land at dawn, a faint blue on the horizon, topped with a bright peak or two that were ruddy with sunrise. The water alongside was no longer blue, but a dark green, which was not like the seas we had sailed. As it grew lighter the mist which had lain along the land was blown away. We saw the land we had come so far to see, the land we had struggled for, the land we had talked of. It lay in a line to leeward, a grey, irregular mass, with the sun shining on it. Over us was a sky of a deep, kindly blue, patrolled with soft, white clouds, little white Pacific clouds, delicately rounded, like the clouds of the Trade Winds. Under us was the green, tremulous, talking water, and there, towards us, came the birds of those parts, birds of the sea, flying low, dipping now and then for fish. Later, as we drew nearer, we saw the houses, the factory chimneys, the lighthouse, the gleam of a window. There were the ships in the bay, tier upon tier of them, their masts like a fence of sticks round a sand-dune. Over the quiet sea came a little tug, a little wooden tug, with her paint gone, with blisters on her smoke-stack. Slowly she came, clanging and groaning, making a knot an hour. Aboard her were the men we had come so far to see, the strangers, the men with Spanish names. In a few minutes we were to speak with them, we were to speak with strangers, the first we had met for four months. We should hear strange voices, we should see strange faces, they would have news for us. Eagerly we watched them, till the heads that had been dots upon her deck were become human. She drew up to us, clanging and groaning; she came within hail. We saw them, those strangers. A negro with a red cap; a little, pale man, smoking a cigar; a tall, brown fellow, his teeth green with coca; and a boy in a blue shirt teasing a monkey with a stick. Those were the strangers, the men we had come to see, the men we had struggled to through the months of sailing.

That was youth, the flower of youth, the glory of it, the adventure accomplished. It had been much to me; it is much still. It had been much to my friend; it was nothing to him now. I was getting old; yet the thing came back to me, I took a part in it. The thing comes back to me; the tug, the green water, the negro with the cap, the masts of the ships at anchor. It is eternal, it is my youth, I am young in it. It is my friend who is old; it is he who has lost his youth, it has gone from him, it is dead, he has lived his vision.

But when we get to our lighthouse he will have more of such tales to tell me than I to tell him. He has seen so much. He is still seeing so much. He will have a fuller memory to turn over, and arrange, and select from. And when our pipes are smoked out, and it is time for us to go to our hammocks, it is not great poetry we shall sing together. It will be the song we sang when we were comrades, when we sailed the green seas and saw the flying fish. It will be—

I dreamed a dream the other night,
    Lowlands, Lowlands, hurrah, my John;
I dreamed a dream the other night,
    My Lowlands a-ray,

or some other song that comes with its memory of work done, its suggestion of storm and of stress and of adventure accomplished.

JOHN MASEFIELD
1878–1967

Orphaned at the age of seven, John Masefield lived with an aunt and uncle in Ledbury, Herefordshire, until he entered the King's School. Finding life at the boarding school uncongenial, the youth often ran away, and his relatives despaired of his ever profiting by education.

At thirteen he went to sea on HMS *Conway*, a merchant training vessel. Masefield's love of the sea was immediately evident. He took to training well; he was initiated in the language of seamen and the lore of the sea; and he learned the art of storytelling on the *Conway*. By 1894 he was apprentice on a windjammer bound around Cape Horn to Chile. While on shore leave in Argentina, however, he signed on as the sixth officer of the White Star Line's *Adriatic*. Leaving the ship in New York, Masefield worked in a hotel saloon and then in a carpet factory. When he left New York in 1897, it was to return to England to become a writer.

Months of hardship followed, but Masefield began to meet literary artists who encouraged him, notably Yeats and Synge, and to publish. Between 1902 and 1910 he proved an indefatigable writer. *Salt Water Ballads* (1902) brought little recognition at the time but contained poems of such enduring value as "Sea-Fever" and "A Wanderer's Song." He also produced two collections of sea stories, *A Mainsail Haul* (1905) and *A Tarpaulin Muster* (1907); two novels; two naval histories, *Sea Life in Nelson's Time* (1905) and *On the Spanish Main* (1906); two plays; and *Ballads and Poems* (1910).

Poetry brought Masefield fame. *The Everlasting Mercy* (1911), *The Widow in the Bye Street* (1912), and *Dauber* (1913) revived the lagging narrative mode in poetry and gained widespread notice of his work. After an interlude of war service—he was a picket boat commander during the Dardanelles disaster, a historian of World War I, and a propagandist—Masefield settled down to write novels in the twenties. Two of his best, *The Bird of Dawning* (1933) and *Victorious Troy: or The Hurrying Angel* (1935), were written during this period.

In 1930, partly, it must be noted, because King George V was a sailor himself and loved Masefield's sea ballads, he became England's poet laureate. While he did not originally intend to write verse for royal or national events, by 1934 he was doing so. That official function and the advent of World War II, which demanded a great deal of Masefield's attention, largely spelled the end of his creative work. He spent many of his later years writing autobiographical works, including *New Chum* (1944), *So Long to Learn* (1952), and *Grace Before Plowing* (1966).

"Being Ashore" and "On Growing Old" appeared in *A Tarpaulin Muster*.

Mutiny

BY JOHN THOMASON

"There was no disorder on the *Kaiser*."—*Official reports on the German Naval Mutiny, November, 1918.*

WHEN I CAME ASHORE, they ordered me into an office to do research on a Chronicle of the Acts of the Second U.S. Division (Regular), A.E.F., there having been a brigade of Marines in that division. In the course of this duty, it became necessary to examine the records of the German divisions which disputed with us certain points in France, and since I am not good at German, I asked Headquarters for a person qualified to make translations.

Headquarters found such a person in the Post Bakery Detachment at Quantico, and shortly afterwards a squarely built Marine, extremely blond, in a new uniform, came up, clicked his heels, saluted and stated that Private First Class Franz reported for duty. His salute was entirely precise, but he held his hand more to the front than we do, and his palm more open than the German soldiers held theirs in the Rhineland.

I asked him where he had learned to salute that way. He said he had served three years in the Imperial Germany Navy, and unless he thought about it, every time, he forgot. I gave him the War Diary of the German Seventh Army in the original Gothic, and showed him a desk, and he dived forthwith into the events of May, 1918, on the Chemin des Dames.

Months afterwards, one November afternoon, with the rain drumming at the windows, we finished checking the painful adventures of the German 88th Division in the hard country this side of the Meuse River, and I asked him idly where he was, that week in 1918. Engineer-aspirant, he told me— which is a rating at the bottom of the ladder in the engineer branch of the German service—on S.M.S. *Kaiser.*

And I had from him this story, the story of *Oberheizer* Hinrik Glassen, S.M.S. *Kaiser*, who served four years in the High Sea Fleet, and did not want to die. It is also the story, I think, of many brave and simple men, in the time when their world fell around them.

I have set it down much as it was told me, and I have verified, from the official records, certain essential facts. It opens with the second week of November, 1918, on the battleship *Kaiser*, which was, with the Third Squadron of the High Sea Fleet, on station in the German Bight, guarding the sea-approaches to the Free Cities. It follows:

It was eleven-forty-five by the ship's clock on the bulkhead, the night of November seventh, and a stoker of the port watch ran through Starboard Compartment 10, smacking the hammocks with the wooden sole of his *Klinker* and chanting, *"Steht auf, steht auf, faule Leute,"* which are the German sailor's words for "Rise and shine!" The machinist's mate of the relief growled in the passage, sucking the dregs of his coffee from his mustache, and the starboard watch hit the deck.

Oberheizer—which is to say, fireman first class—Hinrik Glassen was the last man out of his blankets; he scratched and yawned, pulling on his trousers.

He was the senior stoker in the watch, and the biggest man aboard the *Kaiser*, and the details of compartment police were beneath him. Two youngsters ran to clew up his hammock and rush it to the nettings, while he hogged the coffee in the mess kettles as a matter of right. The mate called the roll, and the watch, still half asleep, trooped after him, seven decks down and through the blistering passage along the flanks of the boilers, to relieve Number 10 fireroom. The port watch was ready to go off, but Hinrik Glassen's opposite number, a beefy Holsteiner named Kaspar, stopped to pass a word.

"Coal's good," he said. "Hard clear through; no dust at all. But something's up. The mate was in here a minute ago, and said to let up on them two boilers—no use in cleaning fires. And what's more, I was on deck a while back—it was me that called you—and saw Norderney Light, two miles off to port! What do you make of that?"

Hinrik gave a grunt that implied total disbelief. *"Ja,"* he jeered. "And the old lightship skipper waved his hand at you—did you see that, too? Norderney Light!"

"Oh, well, good watch!" and the Holsteiner, declining to argue, shuffled out of the compartment, while Hinrik went about his job.

The fireroom was in action, through all its three compartments. Doors clanged back, searing the gloomy steel place with spurts of white-hot light. Slice bars clattered, and the bright, heavy scoops gritted and rang on the gratings. The water tenders passed along, checking their gauges, and the steady beat of the engines, felt rather than heard, dominated the whole.

It was not a time for reflection, and the *Oberheizer* put everything out of his mind but his fires, until the six of them were snoring comfortably along, and his gauges rode level. Then he wiped the perspiration from his eyes and leaned on his shovel to consider what Kaspar had told him.

Hinrik Glassen was a big East Frisian, with the brick-red, wind-bitten skin of those hardy islanders who snatch their living from the bleak North Sea. Meeting him ashore, you would never have taken him for a man of the black gang, who are a pale people, bleached to white and gray by the steaming hells where they keep their watches. He looked like the deck force, like a cox'n or a signalman, and the quantities of *Schnapps* and grog he took aboard did nothing to reduce his coloring.

In any company he was big, and in the close, fitfully lighted firerooms, he stood enormous. He was bull-necked and long of arm, with hands like hams, and when they saw his shoulders at the depot, back in 1914, after that last Kiel Week, they said, "There's a proper stoker for you!" and they flung him below with a scoop in his fist. He served in one fireroom after another through the four war years—the last three of them on *S.M.S. Kaiser*.

They would have rated him up long ago and transferred him to U-boats, as the best men were, or to the destroyers, as most of the incorrigibles were, had it not been for two things: he was drunk as often as he could get enough corn brandy, and he was too slow in the head to be trusted with any mechanism more complicated than a fire door and a shovel. But he was thoroughly without aspiration, and docile enough, and he stood a good watch, even when he was blind from a hangover. Now, his slaty-blue eyes were half closed under his straw-colored brows, and his broad, flat face was painfully corrugated with thought.

In the first place, old Kaspar was not a joker—Hinrik did not like jokers—and if those were the orders, he'd soon have a word from the mate about his own fires. But Norderney Light, now! His home was behind Borkum, which is one island west of Norderney, and he knew the Frisian Islands as he knew his hand. The ship had no business around there, just now.

He checked the days on his knuckles: the Third Squadron—*Kaiser, König, Kaiserin, Baden,* and *Bayern*—had left Schillig Roads on the fourth of November, one day ahead of schedule, for its routine two-weeks' hitch of guard patrol across the German Bight—Helgoland, and down towards the Hook of Holland, and back again, like policemen on a beat. This was the seventh—eleven days to go before they went back to port. Then Schillig Roads, and shore leave in turn.

That was how the war went. Kaspar was a blockhead. And yet, he thought, shifting uneasily on his feet, strange things were happening, and not all of them ashore. He hadn't given much attention to the war news for a year or so, because the French names all sounded the same, and the army never seemed to get anywhere. A rather helpless lot, the army. But there was the mutiny on the *Prinzregent Luitpold*. And the Russian prisoners in the dockyard at Wilhelmshaven refusing duty, and getting away with it.

Such things used to be handled with a strong hand, but now you heard of fellows being condemned to death, and then turned loose and restored to duty.

And the ship's *Wachtmeister*, the slick hound, always slinking through the compartments and listening in passages and hauling men aft for things you never heard of. Also, the civilians in the town were getting into an odd frame of mind.

Hinrik sucked the knuckles of his right hand, where the skin had not yet renewed itself, and recalled the shore-going *Schwein* who, a few days before, in his favorite Port Arthur groggery, had sung into his very nose, to the tune of *"Die Wacht am Rhein"*:

"Our Fatherland may safely rest,
The Fleet is sleeping in its nest—"

Or started to sing: when the civilian got that far, Hinrik had knocked him across two tables and a beer barrel, and had gone away before the fellow could recover and shout for police. But it showed you things were not right, in the fleet or out of it.

Of course he was sick of the war—everybody was, except maybe the officers. It had lasted too long, and the food was getting worse every day. But it never occurred to him that anything could be done about it. The navy was the navy, and you stood your watch. . . . Here the mate entered through the midships bulkhead, and Hinrik lunged guiltily at the nearest fire box, but the petty officer stopped him.

"No. Wait half an hour, and shut the dampers on your boiler. Don't feed it. At three-thirty, start throwing out your fire. Hard lines, eh?" The mate was gone before Hinrik could frame a question.

He trimmed his fires and stared into the flames for an answer to his bewilderment. Kaspar was right about the boilers. Norderney Light, now? Ashore, he lived with the girl Tietje; and her old man, a sour dock-worker, who never seemed entirely reassured by Hinrik's easy promise to marry Tietje as soon as the war was finished, had walked with them to the basin when they sailed the other day.

There was something he said, and with effort Hinrik recalled it: "*Ja*. You go to sea. But you will return sooner than you think. I tell you, things are happening in Germany!"

There was more, but Tietje had a tremulous rumor that they were going out to fight the English fleet, and she needed talking to, so Hinrik hadn't listened to the old croaker. . . . Tietje—there was a fine girl for you. He honestly intended to take Tietje home with him, when the war let him go. She'd make a good wife, even if she was a Baltic Province woman and no Frisian.

He felt a draft and turned to see the water-tight door swing open on a man from the starboard compartment. "So!" he said. "You laying down on the job, too?"

"Yes; only nine boilers running, now. Mine's nearly cold. Must be headed for port. What's up?"

"Don't know a thing. The mate was in here—" Hinrik repeated his orders and detailed, also, the prediction of Tietje's father.

The two put their thick heads together, and other stokers, released by the dying fires, joined them. All the crazy rumors of the last few weeks were brought out and picked to pieces. What could be the reason that the squadron was sent out a day early?

There was considerable speculation over a strange, hairy person who had been smuggled aboard just before the ship cleared, and who was being kept out of sight.

It was a short watch. When it ended, Hinrik passed up his bath, and went on deck. The ship was at anchor, and before he was through the hatch, he smelled the land. Running to the port side, he looked for the light, and it was Norderney, for a fact.

You couldn't raise the low coast in the thick November dawn, but he had known Norderney Light all his life—flash, one, two, three, four; flash—

The *Kaiser* lay well in, and not alone. Off astern, and a little to seaward, rode the tall hulks of the Third Squadron. Close aboard was the long shape of a battle cruiser. There were strings of light craft farther out, cruisers and destroyers. But they looked strange. They were in amazing disarray, not in orderly columns, by squadron and flotilla, as *S.M.* High Sea Fleet was wont to be.

And on the *Kaiser*, Hinrik, with sailor's instinct, sensed a strangeness. The old tight atmosphere, every man in his place and things humming steadily along, was missing. Port and starboard watches were on deck together, talking in small groups, standing aimlessly about. A little later, on the mess deck, Hinrik heard that the Naval Air Station on Borkum refused to answer the ship's calls.

He sat down in the compartment to consider, and went to sleep, and it was after morning colors when he came on deck again. The ship's routine had simply stopped. Most of the crew were out, and they could see that the decks of the other ships were black with men. The morning was calm, and a chill wind from the northeast blew just enough to hold the colors from the gaff.

Then some one cried out from the superstructure, "Look at the battle cruiser, there!"—and Hinrik joined the rush to the starboard side. Pushing aft for a clear place at the rail, he crossed the sacred white line which bounded off the quarterdeck, the officers' deck, from the rest of the ship.

Hinrik was horror-stricken. He looked quickly and anxiously about him and caught the eye of the sub-lieutenant on watch, coming around the turret. The last time he crossed that line, it meant fifteen days' bread and water, with the *Wachtmeister* doing him dirt by forgetting when his warm meal was due; and now he came despairingly to attention, accepting his fate. But an amazing thing happened: the young gentleman did not bawl for the guard. He grinned nervously at Hinrik and paced behind the turret.

Hinrik's muscles galvanized in a stumbling leap, which took him safely forward, and he shouldered his way into the mass on the rail. That was a near thing, that! But before he could turn it over in his mind, the battle cruiser took all his attention.

Over there, her people were clotted thick on the quarterdeck, climbing on the turrets and along the superstructure. A group swayed back and forth on her after signal bridge, and a confused babel of shouts and curses rolled down the wind to the *Kaiser*. There were screams, and pistol shots. Men swarmed up the ladders, and the mob on the signal bridge grew, but you could not see what went on in the midst of them. A figure broke loose and stood clear against the sky on the after turret, and a signalman, with a pair of binoculars from the bridge, called out that it was an officer—a two-striper, and that he was making a speech. Certainly you could see his arms wave, in frantic gestures. But they were after him. A man, two men, got on the turret, and he flung them off. A wave of men fell upon him and threw him to the deck below, where he was instantly surrounded.

He broke clear once and stood, with his clothes torn off, against the life lines, facing his attackers. Then he went down. He was trampled, kicked about, caught up above the heads of the men, and flung overboard.

A yelling broke out on the battle cruiser, and the Imperial Ensign came down from the gaff. In its place, to wild cheering, a red flag rose jerkily.

On the *Kaiser*, men turned and stared at each other. They looked for their officers, but not an officer was to be seen—not even the young lieutenant on the quarterdeck. The battle cruiser, meantime, got under way. From her wing bridge a man wigwagged rapidly, and the signaller with the binoculars called off the message to those around him: "Revolution ashore. Kaiser abdicated. Armistice declared with the English. Workmen's and Soldiers' Council in control. Wilhelmshaven—"

The sea boiled under the battle cruiser's stern; she came about and headed east for the Jade, under the red flag. Other ships were getting under way. But an event occurred upon the *Kaiser* that drove them out of mind.

First a few venturesome fellows, then more men, and finally the whole crew collected on the quarterdeck. The strange, hairy man discussed by Hinrik's watch appeared miraculously from the brig, mounted the cabin skylight, and began to make a speech. He was a Russian Bolshevik—the sound of his thick Baltic German was proof of that. He shrieked, he gesticulated, he shook his fists at the Ensign blowing out above, and he cried that it must come down. He dragged a greasy red cloth from his bosom: this, he said, was the glorious banner of the Revolution.

Voices were raised among the packed ship's company, some angry, and some approving, but most of them doubtful. There had always been discipline aboard the *Kaiser*, and the habit of it held the crew. Hinrik, standing with his legs wide apart in the press, tried to work it out: you step on the quarter-deck and the officer doesn't clap you into the brig; they throw a lieutenant into the water and drown him, and nothing happens; they raise the red flag and go to port. And now a flea-bitten Russky stands on a German deck and tells German sailors what they ought to do.

It was too much for Hinrik. He kneaded his shaven skull with his great fists, and saw Electrician's Mate First Class Karl Kappler barge out on deck, evidently in liquor. Well, if they were serving brandy to the crew, he would get his! And he plowed toward the hatch.

The crew, lashed by the Russky's tongue, gathered itself to an intention, and a rush of men forced Hinrik against the trunk of *Emil* turret. They ran towards the mainmast and began to mount the ladders to the after bridge. Then a great voice, over Hinrik's head, bellowed *"Achtung!"* Every man stopped mechanically, and they saw the captain on *Dora* turret, looking down at them.

His buttons shone gold in the gray sea light, and his stripes and insignia were bright and new on the fine blue cloth of his coat, and the Order for Merit glittered at his collar. He was taller than Hinrik Glassen, and almost as broad, and he stood straighter. His short, stiff beard was trimmed and brushed, and his narrow eyes were like chips of Baltic ice in his ruddy face. He stood with his hands easy at his sides, alone, and looked at the milling crew, and a full half of them brought heels together and fingers to the trouser-seams and shoulders back, to wait on what he had to say.

The German service was never an easy one, and the *Kaiser's* captain was a skipper of the old hard school. His punishments were sure and merciless, and his command had a name for tautness through the fleet. But the ship's company knew that their captain had himself gone to the galley and tasted the soup, on that amazing day a year ago when the stokers stood up and said the food wasn't right.

And when a handful of *Kaisers* had been involved in the disorders ashore, in early fall, and were brought before the squadron court with the men of other ships, their captain had fought for them, and delivered them aboard his own ship, to take his punishment. It was terrible, that punishment—but it was their own skipper, and no brass-bound court, that dealt with them. The electrician's mate, now beyond all decency, tried to raise a cheer and was suppressed, and the captain spoke:

"*Kinder*, I may never have another chance to talk to you. Together we have been through four terrible war years. We have seen the death of how many comrades, who gave their lives without a word of complaint! It has been hard on all of us. No one in His Majesty's Service has felt your suffering more keenly than I—"

The Russian screamed furiously, and somebody knocked him under the overhang of the turret. "Be silent, thou—" What the captain said was true, and they crowded closer to hear him.

"The old régime, under which you were born, and under which you have come to manhood and to glory among the nations—it is gone. Our Fatherland now faces trying days of reconstruction—maybe of civil strife. But"— his eyes swept their faces—"whatever the past régime failed in, it is not yours to condemn. Men come among you now, and tell you wild and foolish things. Men who have lived in safety while you were fighting, who never faced the enemy on land or stood out with us to keep our German seas.

"The Bolsheviki who have ruined Russia turn now to Germany. I will tell you of these Bolsheviki," and he told them in plain words what Bolshevism was and how it worked. He told them at length. "And remember this," he concluded. "Our old German land will never bear the fruit of the seeds of Bolshevism! Remember this, when you step ashore and meet the army of half-grown soldiers upon which Russia pins her hope to drag us down into that pit with her!"

Electrician's Mate Kappler sobbed loudly; the events of the day and the captain's words, superimposed on his lading of *Schnapps*, disintegrated him. A friend kicked him into the waterways, where he went to sleep. The captain's voice grew deeper:

"When we get into port, you will be freed from the last obligation of the oath you gave His Majesty . . . and may God bless you when you resume where you left off, four horrible years ago." He half wheeled and flung up his hand, pointing. "That flag"—the Ensign blew out in heavy folds— "throughout this war you have served it faithfully. Thousands on thousands have bled to death for it. In every sea around this earth have sunk to rest our German dead.

"You knew these men, how they were glad to serve and to die under that flag, for the things the flag means to us—for our homes and honor of the dear German land. They loved it. Will you tear it down now and trample it underfoot?"

The captain had no more words, and he stood with his eyes upon them, looking taller than any man in the world on the tall gray turret. His words burned in them, and they paid him the tribute of silence. They saw, in their minds, the places they called home, and they saw the men of the Dogger Bank and the Skagerrak, and the Cocos Keys and the Falklands, and of the lost submarines, who had gone out with them, high-hearted. And they saw, in shuddering vision, mobs beating down doors and trampling old men and womenfolk.

They watched the captain go forward over the turret and along the superstructure, and they went quietly to their stations. Presently the pipes shrilled and the anchor came up, and the ship stood eastward on Schillig Roads. The Russian disappeared. The rumor ran that a Workmen's and Sailors' Council was being formed aboard, and that its first order would provide for a double ration of grog to all hands. But orders were issued quietly and quietly carried out.

Most of the men off duty collected in sober knots through the compartments and discussed the thing that had come to pass. It was all very well to talk about revolution and social democracy, and lamp-posts for officers, but somebody had to give the orders, and they wondered, honestly, what was going to come next. They were a little scared, and content, at the moment, that the captain was in charge and not the Russian fellow.

As for Hinrik, he had a bottle of brandy from the medical stores—by the simple process of going forward and glaring at the little Bavarian in charge—and he squatted on his heels by his locker and drank, and growled, from time to time, that he'd like to be shown the man who could make a Bolshevik of him!

Next morning, in thick weather, they lay to off Schillighorn and flew the pilot flag, but no pilot came out, and the word was passed that the skipper was taking the old bucket in himself: critical seamen gathered on the bows and approved the skill which threaded the great ship through the shoals and the tide rips to the Wilhelmshaven Basin. There the *Kaiser* had to wait her turn, and the lock people were terribly slow about it.

It was afternoon before she came up, the last of the Third Squadron, and slid into the first lock. All the crew gathered on deck forward, and strained their eyes towards the town, but there was little to be seen, except that every mast in sight flew a red flag. They noted, too, how a clumsy riffraff took the lines ashore, and in the midst of caustic comment on their unhandiness, a non-commissioned officer of the army picked his way from the lock house and hailed.

He was a well-nourished man, in a new uniform, and he wore a long-barrelled Luger and a red armband. Every eye was on the captain, and the captain looked down from the bridge and boomed:

"What the devil do you want, young soldier?"

"By order of the Workmen's and Soldiers' Council of Wilhelmshaven!

No ship flying the so-called Imperial flag will be allowed through the locks! Haul it down, and hoist the red flag, and you will be allowed to proceed!" yelled the sergeant, straining his voice.

On the ship, nobody moved or spoke, but they looked at the quiet man on the bridge, and the captain ran his eye along their upturned faces. Hinrik Glassen, well forward, with liquor glowing pleasantly in him, quivered and clenched his fists. If the old skipper did such a thing, he, an *Oberheizer*, would certainly inform him on a German sailor's duty to his flag, and furthermore, he would have a word to offer about the propriety of an army sergeant giving orders to a battleship!

But the captain said nothing. He looked the sergeant up and down, turned without haste and walked away. The gesture was utterly contemptuous and final, and the ship's company ratified it with a delighted yell, and began at once to tell the sergeant things about his mother, his sisters and his remote ancestors. They saw the red surge into the man's face, and when they had run out of words, he screamed:

"You have one minute to raise the red flag! After one minute, I will fire on you!" He turned and trotted back to the lock house, and from sheds on each side of the gates two squads of soldiers ran with heavy machine guns, which they set up off the bows. The soldiers were awkward, and nondescript as to uniform, but the Maxims meant business.

Ashore, the riffraff threw down the lines and took cover. There was a moment's confusion on the *Kaiser*: the gun crews dived below to the secondary batteries, and others dashed to the stub masts, port and starboard, where the anti-aircraft searchlights and machine guns were mounted, and still others ran about the deck aimlessly.

At this stage of the tide, the deck was a little lower than the top of the locks, so that only the fifteen-centimetres abaft the bridge would bear, and the range was too close for it to be safe to fire them. At once the machine guns ashore swept the decks clean with gusts of fire, and Hinrik Glassen joined a frantic rush into the little armored room abaft the chart house. From its shelter, you could hear the bullets rattle on the steel plates outside, and there arose cries and curses from the men caught in the open.

A minute later, the guns on the stub masts were brought into action, and although they did not seem to be hitting anything, they had the effect of making the soldiers duck and fire wild. Some rating in the chart house shouted, and Hinrik ran with a dozen men aft, behind the break of the superstructure, to the place where the gangway was lashed up. Sodden and salt-crusted, it resisted their efforts until a decksman thought of his knife and cut it free, and some one cried that, as the ship swung, they could get ashore from the quarter-deck.

Waiting craftily, out of sight, until the port side lay in, and the gun on that bow was busy in a duel with the stub mast, they pushed the heavy planking out and swarmed over it, a disorderly mass of stokers, decksmen, and gunners, with never a firearm among them, brandishing spanners, wrenches and such things as a man might catch up, running. The machine gun saw them too late: they were at close quarters before the blunt muzzle could swing down and traverse to them. Just as they reached it, a burst tore through them, and men went down, kicking.

The sergeant was with this gun, and he stood up to them with his Luger, until somebody beat his head in. Hinrik himself whirled up the gunner and threw him into the lock. Every soldier there died, quickly and violently, and a deck rating turned the gun on its sister across the lock, which had been preoccupied with the ship. It was silenced, and the lock was quiet, except for the crying of the wounded.

The crew trooped ashore; they carried their own men back to the sick bay, and they threw the others, living and dead, into the water. Engineer petty officers flew at the lock machinery, and the deck force handled the lines.

Hinrik lifted one of the Maxims and brought it off, setting it up on the forward turret. He felt big and fine, swinging its muzzle this way and that, and fiddling with the sights.

So the *Kaiser* passed through, and went under her own steam to her berth. Most of the fleet was inside, and every ship had the red flag, but they all cheered the *Kaiser*, swinging by with her old Imperial at the gaff. The *Kaiser* cheered back.

When they were tied up, the port captain came aboard, and a little later the terms of the Armistice were published on the ship, which sobered the crew exceedingly. Enough men volunteered to stay aboard and send off the ammunition and carry out certain other measures. Those English *Schweine* shouldn't have everything.

Hinrik was not among the men who remained. He considered that the war was over, and he was going home. He made a roll, of his possessions and a little food from the petty officers' galley, shouldered it and went out through the dockyard.

He was going home, and the pale sentry with the red armband at the dockyard gate observed his size and elaborately looked the other way.

Hinrik took the tram to the Port Arthur district, where Tietje lived, in the best humor in the world. Tomorrow he would pack her up, and they would go out to Borkum and the wind-blown fishing village on the Frisian sands, where the *Mütterchen* waited, and his father would be glad of his weight on the trawl.

But *Ach!* there was Joachim, who died in the turret fire on the *Derfflinger* at the Skagerrak, and Karlchen, who put out on a submarine and never came back again—three that went, and one returning. Hinrik was over-come with grief, and pulled at his bottle to restore himself, and couldn't be roused to pay his fare; but the gloomy woman who collected the *Pfennige* grinned and left him.

Presently he was snuggled down in the grateful frowst of Tietje's room, with the girl on his knee and a steaming glass at his elbow. Outside, the easy ladies of Port Arthur entered upon a big evening, and eighty thousand sail-ors and soldiers and bitter workmen were getting drunk and ripening for mischief, but Hinrik was tranquil and content. . . .

I wish I could leave him so, with his glass and his girl, and the long war years behind him, happy, in complete incomprehension of world disaster. But if the war was finished with him, the revolution was not—and the story goes on:

After midnight some one knocked timidly at the door outside. "Let him knock," said Tietje, her head burrowed in his shoulder. "*Leibchen*, be still!" But Hinrik rolled to the door and the *Kaiser's Wachtmeister* slid into the tiny hall.

"For dear God's sake," he said, "hide me until daylight! They're killing us." Then he saw who it was, for he had tried the door at a venture, and his face went hopeless. The under-officer, always so dapper and precise, was rumpled and muddy, and the color of a tallow candle.

Hinrik was amused. Once he had been angry at this shivering rat! Ho! Ho! Hinrik couldn't, at the moment, recall just why he had been angry, and he wasn't angry any more. Peace had come.

Besides, how ridiculous was the *Herr Wachtmeister*, with his cravat under his ear, and the mud smear on his long nose! Hinrik laughed, and the *Wachtmeister* blinked at him. But Tietje, who had followed with the lamp, shook so that Hinrik took it from her and set it on a stool.

Outside, the narrow street was filled with the wordless growl of a mob. A man struck the door with a rifle butt, and there were voices: "You, there, within! Open! The officer went—"

Tietje sprang for the light, and Hinrik blocked her with his arm, slung her into the room, and locked the door. "You stay there," he said. He had not altogether decided about the *Wachtmeister*, but he was a free German and not to be hustled. "Just stand clear, thou," he said, "while I talk to these—"

He opened the door, and wolfish faces under caps and helmets, with a gleam of weapons among them, crowded the threshold. They did not cross it, for Hinrik, with the light behind him, bulked giant-size.

The *Wachtmeister* came out of the shadow. "It's no good, Glassen," he said, and to the door: "*Kameraden*, I am the man you want."

"Get back, you fool!" Hinrik shoved him violently. "Now, you gutted herrings! So, you—"

Half a dozen rifles crashed from the doorway, loud in the narrow hall. Hinrik recoiled a step. He sank to his knees, slumped forward on his face, and died. The *Wachtmeister* thrashed about and scraped the floor with his heels, and died also. The little lamp burned on, flickering in the draft.

Behind her locked door, Tietje screamed and beat with ineffectual fists, and a soldier laughed, drunkenly. The mob flowed on, and some white-faced boys dropped from the fringe of it and searched the pockets of the dead men.

There was derisive yelling, growing distant: *"Hoch! Hoch! Dreimal Hoch . . ."*

JOHN THOMASON
1893–1944

Born in Huntsville, Texas, John William Thomason, Jr., studied at assorted schools—Southwestern University, Sam Houston Normal Institute, the University of Texas, and the Art Students' League in New York—before becoming a reporter for the *Houston Chronicle* in 1916. When the United States entered World War I Thomason became a second lieutenant in the marine corps, fighting at Belleau Wood, Soissons, St. Mihiel, Blanc Mont, and the Meuse-Argonne. He won the Navy Cross and the Silver Star.

After the conflict he served tours at sea, in the West Indies, in Peking, and in Washington. Laurence Stallings, author of *What Price Glory*, took Thomason to *Scribner's Magazine* with a portfolio of his drawings in 1925 and obtained for him a commission for a set of drawings and stories. *Fix Bayonets!* (1926), Thomason's first book, resulted from that assignment. Encouraged by H. L. Mencken, Thomason contributed stories to *American Mercury*, *The New Yorker*, *The Saturday Evening Post*, and *Harpers*.

Additional volumes of stories written and illustrated by Thomason followed: *Red Pants* (1927), *Marines and Others* (1929), and *Salt Winds and Gobi Dust* (1934). One final collection of stories,—*and a Few Marines* (1943), contains the best of his writing and drawing from previous collections.

"Mutiny," first collected in *Salt Winds and Gobi Dust*, brings to life a report in Gothic script of a mutiny aboard SMS *Kaiser* in 1918.

Red

BY SOMERSET MAUGHAM

THE SKIPPER thrust his hand into one of his trouser pockets and with difficulty, for they were not at the sides but in front and he was a portly man, pulled out a large silver watch. He looked at it and then looked again at the declining sun. The Kanaka at the wheel gave him a glance, but did not speak. The skipper's eyes rested on the island they were approaching. A white line of foam marked the reef. He knew there was an opening large enough to get his ship through, and when they came a little nearer he counted on seeing it. They had nearly an hour of daylight still before them. In the lagoon the water was deep and they could anchor comfortably. The chief of the village which he could already see among the coconut trees was a friend of the mate's, and it would be pleasant to go ashore for the night. The mate came forward at that minute and the skipper turned to him.

"We'll take a bottle of booze along with us and get some girls in to dance," he said.

"I don't see the opening," said the mate.

He was a Kanaka, a handsome, swarthy fellow, with somewhat the look of a later Roman emperor, inclined to stoutness; but his face was fine and clean-cut.

"I'm dead sure there's one right here," said the captain, looking through his glasses. "I can't understand why I can't pick it up. Send one of the boys up the mast to have a look."

The mate called one of the crew and gave him the order. The captain watched the Kanaka climb and waited for him to speak. But the Kanaka shouted down that he could see nothing but the unbroken line of foam. The captain spoke Samoan like a native, and he cursed him freely.

"Shall he stay up there?" asked the mate.

"What the hell good does that do?" answered the captain. "The blame fool can't see worth a cent. You bet your sweet life I'd find the opening if I was up there."

He looked at the slender mast with anger. It was all very well for a native who had been used to climbing up coconut trees all his life. He was fat and heavy.

"Come down," he shouted. "You're no more use than a dead dog. We'll just have to go along the reef till we find the opening."

It was a seventy-ton schooner with paraffin auxiliary, and it ran, when there was no head wind, between four and five knots an hour. It was a bedraggled object; it had been painted white a very long time ago, but it was now dirty, dingy, and mottled. It smelt strongly of paraffin and of the copra which was its usual cargo. They were within a hundred feet of the reef now and the captain told the steersman to run along it till they came to the opening. But when they had gone a couple of miles he realised that they had missed it. He went about and slowly worked back again. The white foam of the reef continued without interruption and now the sun was setting. With a curse at the stupidity of the crew the skipper resigned himself to waiting till next morning.

"Put her about," he said. "I can't anchor here."

They went out to sea a little and presently it was quite dark. They anchored. When the sail was furled the ship began to roll a good deal. They said in Apia that one day she would roll right over; and the owner, a German-American who managed one of the largest stores, said that no money was big enough to induce him to go out in her. The cook, a Chinese in white trousers, very dirty and ragged, and a thin white tunic, came to say that supper was ready, and when the skipper went into the cabin he found the engineer already seated at table. The engineer was a long, lean man with a scraggy neck. He was dressed in blue overalls and a sleeveless jersey which showed his thin arms tattooed from elbow to wrist.

"Hell, having to spend the night outside," said the skipper.

The engineer did not answer, and they ate their supper in silence. The cabin was lit by a dim oil lamp. When they had eaten the canned apricots with which the meal finished the Chink brought them a cup of tea. The skipper lit a cigar and went on the upper deck. The island now was only a darker mass against the night. The stars were very bright. The only sound was the ceaseless breaking of the surf. The skipper sank into a deck-chair and smoked idly. Presently three or four members of the crew came up and sat down. One of them had a banjo and another a concertina. They began to play, and one of them sang. The native song sounded strange on these instruments. Then to the singing a couple began to dance. It was a barbaric dance, savage and primeval, rapid, with quick movements of the hands and feet and contortions of the body; it was sensual, sexual even, but sexual without passion. It was very animal, direct, weird without mystery, natural in short, and one might almost say childlike. At last they grew tired. They stretched themselves on the deck and slept, and all was silent. The skipper lifted himself heavily out of his chair and clambered down the companion.

He went into his cabin and got out of his clothes. He climbed into his bunk and lay there. He panted a little in the heat of the night.

But next morning, when the dawn crept over the tranquil sea, the opening in the reef which had eluded them the night before was seen a little to the east of where they lay. The schooner entered the lagoon. There was not a ripple on the surface of the water. Deep down among the coral rocks you saw little coloured fish swim. When he had anchored his ship the skipper ate his breakfast and went on deck. The sun shone from an unclouded sky, but in the early morning the air was grateful and cool. It was Sunday, and there was a feeling of quietness, a silence as though nature were at rest, which gave him a peculiar sense of comfort. He sat, looking at the wooded coast, and felt lazy and well at ease. Presently a slow smile moved his lips and he threw the stump of his cigar into the water.

"I guess I'll go ashore," he said. "Get the boat out."

He climbed stiffly down the ladder and was rowed to a little cove. The coconut trees came down to the water's edge, not in rows, but spaced out with an ordered formality. They were like a ballet of spinsters, elderly but flippant, standing in affected attitudes with the simpering graces of a bygone age. He sauntered idly through them, along a path that could be just seen winding its tortuous way, and it led him presently to a broad creek. There was a bridge across it, but a bridge constructed of single trunks of coconut trees, a dozen of them, placed end to end and supported where they met by a forked branch driven into the bed of the creek. You walked on a smooth, round surface, narrow and slippery, and there was no support for the hand. To cross such a bridge required sure feet and a stout heart. The skipper hesitated. But he saw on the other side, nestling among the trees, a white man's house; he made up his mind and, rather gingerly, began to walk. He watched his feet carefully, and where one trunk joined on to the next and there was a difference of level, he tottered a little. It was with a gasp of relief that he reached the last tree and finally set his feet on the firm ground of the other side. He had been so intent on the difficult crossing that he never noticed anyone was watching him, and it was with surprise that he heard himself spoken to.

"It takes a bit of nerve to cross these bridges when you're not used to them."

He looked up and saw a man standing in front of him. He had evidently come out of the house which he had seen.

"I saw you hesitate," the man continued, with a smile on his lips, "and I was watching to see you fall in."

"Not on your life," said the captain, who had now recovered his confidence.

"I've fallen in myself before now. I remember, one evening I came back from shooting, and I fell in, gun and all. Now I get a boy to carry my gun for me."

He was a man no longer young, with a small beard, now somewhat grey, and a thin face. He was dressed in a singlet, without arms, and a pair of duck trousers. He wore neither shoes nor socks. He spoke English with a slight accent.

"Are you Neilson?" asked the skipper.

"I am."

"I've heard about you. I thought you lived somewheres round here."

The skipper followed his host into the little bungalow and sat down heavily in the chair which the other motioned him to take. While Neilson went out to fetch whisky and glasses he took a look round the room. It filled him with amazement. He had never seen so many books. The shelves reached from floor to ceiling on all four walls, and they were closely packed. There was a grand piano littered with music, and a large table on which books and magazines lay in disorder. The room made him feel embarrassed. He remembered that Neilson was a queer fellow. No one knew very much about him, although he had been in the islands for so many years, but those who knew him agreed that he was queer. He was a Swede.

"You've got one big heap of books here," he said, when Neilson returned.

"They do no harm," answered Neilson with a smile.

"Have you read them all?" asked the skipper.

"Most of them."

"I'm a bit of a reader myself. I have the *Saturday Evening Post* sent me regler."

Neilson poured his visitor a good stiff glass of whisky and gave him a cigar. The skipper volunteered a little information.

"I got in last night, but I couldn't find the opening, so I had to anchor outside. I never been this run before, but my people had some stuff they wanted to bring over here. Gray, d'you know him?"

"Yes, he's got a store a little way along."

"Well, there was a lot of canned stuff that he wanted over, an' he's got some copra. They thought I might just as well come over as lie idle at Apia. I run between Apia and Pago-Pago mostly, but they've got smallpox there just now, and there's nothing stirring."

He took a drink of his whisky and lit a cigar. He was a taciturn man, but there was something in Neilson that made him nervous, and his nervousness made him talk. The Swede was looking at him with large dark eyes in which there was an expression of faint amusement.

"This is a tidy little place you've got here."

"I've done my best with it."

"You must do pretty well with your trees. They look fine. With copra at the price it is now. I had a bit of a plantation myself once, in Upolu it was, but I had to sell it."

He looked round the room again, where all those books gave him a feeling of something incomprehensible and hostile.

"I guess you must find it a bit lonesome here though," he said.

"I've got used to it. I've been here for twenty-five years."

Now the captain could think of nothing more to say, and he smoked in silence. Neilson had apparently no wish to break it. He looked at his guest with a meditative eye. He was a tall man, more than six feet high, and very stout. His face was red and blotchy, with a network of little purple veins on the cheeks, and his features were sunk into its fatness. His eyes were bloodshot. His neck was buried in rolls of fat. But for a fringe of long curly hair, nearly white, at the back of his head, he was quite bald; and that immense, shiny surface of forehead, which might have given him a false look of intelligence, on the contrary gave him one of peculiar imbecility. He wore a blue flannel shirt, open at the neck and showing his fat chest covered with a mat of reddish hair, and a very old pair of blue serge trousers. He sat in his chair in a heavy ungainly attitude, his great belly thrust forward and his fat legs uncrossed. All elasticity had gone from his limbs. Neilson wondered idly what sort of man he had been in his youth. It was almost impossible to imagine that this creature of vast bulk had ever been a boy who ran about. The skipper finished his whisky, and Neilson pushed the bottle towards him.

"Help yourself."

The skipper leaned forward and with his great hand seized it.

"And how come you in these parts anyways?" he said.

"Oh, I came out to the islands for my health. My lungs were bad and they said I hadn't a year to live. You see they were wrong."

"I meant, how come you to settle down right here?"

"I am a sentimentalist."

"Oh!"

Neilson knew that the skipper had not an idea what he meant, and he looked at him with an ironical twinkle in his dark eyes. Perhaps just because the skipper was so gross and dull a man the whim seized him to talk further.

"You were too busy keeping your balance to notice, when you crossed the bridge, but this spot is generally considered rather pretty."

"It's a cute little house you've got here."

"Ah, that wasn't here when I first came. There was a native hut, with its beehive roof and its pillars, overshadowed by a great tree with red flowers; and the croton bushes, their leaves yellow and red and golden, made a pied fence around it. And then all about were the coconut trees, as fanciful as

women, and as vain. They stood at the water's edge and spent all day looking at their reflections. I was a young man then—Good Heavens, it's a quarter of a century ago—and I wanted to enjoy all the loveliness of the world
in the short time allotted to me before I passed into the darkness. I thought
it was the most beautiful spot I had ever seen. The first time I saw it I had a
catch at my heart, and I was afraid I was going to cry. I wasn't more than
twenty-five, and though I put the best face I could on it, I didn't want to die.
And somehow it seemed to me that the very beauty of this place made it
easier for me to accept my fate. I felt when I came here that all my past life
had fallen away, Stockholm and its University, and then Bonn: it all seemed
the life of somebody else, as though now at last I had achieved the reality
which our doctors of philosophy—I am one myself, you know—had discussed so much. 'A year,' I cried to myself. 'I have a year. I will spend it here
and then I am content to die.'

"We are foolish and sentimental and melodramatic at twenty-five, but if
we weren't perhaps we should be less wise at fifty."

"Now drink, my friend. Don't let the nonsense I talk interfere with you."

He waved his thin hand towards the bottle, and the skipper finished
what remained in his glass.

"You ain't drinking nothin'," he said, reaching for the whisky.

"I am of a sober habit," smiled the Swede. "I intoxicate myself in ways
which I fancy are more subtle. But perhaps that is only vanity. Anyhow, the
effects are more lasting and the results less deleterious."

"They say there's a deal of cocaine taken in the States now," said the
captain.

Neilson chuckled.

"But I do not see a white man often," he continued, "and for once I don't
think a drop of whisky can do me any harm."

He poured himself out a little, added some soda, and took a sip.

"And presently I found out why the spot had such an unearthly loveliness. Here love had tarried for a moment like a migrant bird that happens
on a ship in mid-ocean and for a little while folds its tired wings. The fragrance of a beautiful passion hovered over it like the fragrance of hawthorn
in May in the meadows of my home. It seems to me that the places where
men have loved or suffered keep about them always some faint aroma of
something that has not wholly died. It is as though they had acquired a
spiritual significance which mysteriously affects those who pass. I wish I
could make myself clear." He smiled a little. "Though I cannot imagine that
if I did you would understand."

He paused.

"I think this place was beautiful because here had been loved beautifully." And now he shrugged his shoulders. "But perhaps it is only that my

aesthetic sense is gratified by the happy conjunction of young love and a suitable setting."

Even a man less thick-witted than the skipper might have been forgiven if we were bewildered by Neilson's words. For he seemed faintly to laugh at what he said. It was as though he spoke from emotion which his intellect found ridiculous. He had said himself that he was a sentimentalist, and when sentimentality is joined with scepticism there is often the devil to pay.

He was silent for an instant and looked at the captain with eyes in which there was a sudden perplexity.

"You know, I can't help thinking that I've seen you before somewhere or other," he said.

"I couldn't say as I remember you," returned the skipper.

"I have a curious feeling as though your face were familiar to me. It's been puzzling me for some time. But I can't situate my recollection in any place or at any time."

The skipper massively shrugged his heavy shoulders.

"It's thirty years since I first come to the islands. A man can't figure on remembering all the folk he meets in a while like that."

The Swede shook his head.

"You know how one sometimes has the feeling that a place one has never been to before is strangely familiar. That's how I seem to see you." He gave a whimsical smile. "Perhaps I knew you in some past existence. Perhaps, perhaps you were the master of a galley in ancient Rome and I was a slave at the oar. Thirty years have you been here?"

"Every bit of thirty years."

"I wonder if you knew a man called Red?"

"Red?"

"That is the only name I've ever known him by. I never knew him personally. I never even set eyes on him. And yet I seem to see him more clearly than many men, my brothers, for instance, with whom I passed my daily life for many years. He lives in my imagination with the distinctness of a Paolo Malatesta or a Romeo. But I daresay you have never read Dante or Shakespeare?"

"I can't say as I have," said the captain.

Neilson, smoking a cigar, leaned back in his chair and looked vacantly at the ring of smoke which floated in the still air. A smile played on his lips, but his eyes were grave. Then he looked at the captain. There was in his gross obesity something extraordinarily repellent. He had the plethoric self-satisfaction of the very fat. It was an outrage. It set Neilson's nerves on edge. But the contrast between the man before him and the man he had in mind was pleasant.

"It appears that Red was the most comely thing you ever saw. I've talked to quite a number of people who knew him in those days, white men, and they all agree that the first time you saw him his beauty just took your breath away. They called him Red on account of his flaming hair. It had a natural wave and he wore it long. It must have been of that wonderful colour that the pre-Raphaelites raved over. I don't think he was vain of it, he was much too ingenuous for that, but no one could have blamed him if he had been. He was tall, six feet and an inch or two—in the native house that used to stand here was the mark of his height cut with a knife on the central trunk that supported the roof—and he was made like a Greek god, broad in the shoulders and thin in the flanks; he was like Apollo, with just that soft roundness which Praxiteles gave him, and that suave, feminine grace which has in it something troubling and mysterious. His skin was dazzling white, milky, like satin; his skin was like a woman's."

"I had kind of a white skin myself when I was a kiddie," said the skipper, with a twinkle in his bloodshot eyes.

But Neilson paid no attention to him. He was telling his story now and interruption made him impatient.

"And his face was just as beautiful as his body. He had large blue eyes, very dark, so that some say they were black, and unlike most red-haired people he had dark eyebrows and long dark lashes. His features were perfectly regular and his mouth was like a scarlet wound. He was twenty."

On these words the Swede stopped with a certain sense of the dramatic. He took a sip of whisky.

"He was unique. There never was anyone more beautiful. There was no more reason for him than for a wonderful blossom to flower on a wild plant. He was a happy accident of nature.

"One day he landed at that cove into which you must have put this morning. He was an American sailor, and he had deserted from a man-of-war in Apia. He had induced some good-humoured native to give him a passage on a cutter that happened to be sailing from Apia to Safoto, and he had been put ashore here in a dugout. I do not know why he deserted. Perhaps life on a man-of-war with its restrictions irked him, perhaps he was in trouble, and perhaps it was the South Seas and these romantic islands that got into his bones. Every now and then they take a man strangely, and he finds himself like a fly in a spider's web. It may be that there was a softness of fibre in him, and these green hills with their soft airs, this blue sea, took the northern strength from him as Delilah took the Nazarite's. Anyhow, he wanted to hide himself, and he thought he would be safe in this secluded nook till his ship had sailed from Samoa.

"There was a native hut at the cove and as he stood there, wondering where exactly he should turn his steps, a young girl came out and invited him to enter. He knew scarcely two words of the native tongue and she as little English. But he understood well enough what her smiles meant, and her pretty gestures, and he followed her. He sat down on a mat and she gave him slices of pineapple to eat. I can speak of Red only from hearsay, but I saw the girl three years after he first met her, and she was scarcely nineteen then. You cannot imagine how exquisite she was. She had the passionate grace of the hibiscus and the rich colour. She was rather tall, slim, with the delicate features of her race, and large eyes like pools of still water under the palm trees; her hair, black and curling, fell down her back, and she wore a wreath of scented flowers. Her hands were lovely. They were so small, so exquisitely formed, they gave your heartstrings a wrench. And in those days she laughed easily. Her smile was so delightful that it made your knees shake. Her skin was like a field of ripe corn on a summer day. Good Heavens, how can I describe her? She was too beautiful to be real.

"And these two young things, she was sixteen and he was twenty, fell in love with one another at first sight. That is the real love, not the love that comes from sympathy, common interests, or intellectual community, but love pure and simple. That is the love that Adam felt for Eve when he awoke and found her in the garden gazing at him with dewy eyes. That is the love that draws the beasts to one another, and the Gods. That is the love that makes the world a miracle. That is the love which gives life its pregnant meaning. You have never heard of the wise, cynical French duke who said that with two lovers there is always one who loves and one who lets himself be loved; it is a bitter truth to which most of us have to resign ourselves; but now and then there are two who love and two who let themselves be loved. Then one might fancy that the sun stands still as it stood when Joshua prayed to the God of Israel.

"And even now after all these years, when I think of these two, so young, so fair, so simple, and of their love, I feel a pang. It tears my heart just as my heart is torn when on certain nights I watch the full moon shining on the lagoon from an unclouded sky. There is always pain in the contemplation of perfect beauty.

"They were children. She was good and sweet and kind. I know nothing of him, and I like to think that then at all events he was ingenuous and frank. I like to think that his soul was as comely as his body. But I daresay he had no more soul than the creatures of the woods and forests who made pipes from reeds and bathed in the mountain streams when the world was young, and you might catch sight of little fawns galloping through the glade on the back of a bearded centaur. A soul is a troublesome possession and when man developed it he lost the Garden of Eden.

"Well, when Red came to the island it had recently been visited by one of those epidemics which the white man has brought to the South Seas, and one third of the inhabitants had died. It seems that the girl had lost all her near kin and she lived now in the house of distant cousins. The household consisted of two ancient crones, bowed and wrinkled, two younger women, and a man and a boy. For a few days he stayed there. But perhaps he felt himself too near the shore, with the possibility that he might fall in with white men who would reveal his hiding-place; perhaps the lovers could not bear that the company of others should rob them for an instant of the delight of being together. One morning they set out, the pair of them, with the few things that belonged to the girl, and walked along a grassy path under the coconuts, till they came to the creek you see. They had to cross the bridge you crossed, and the girl laughed gleefully because he was afraid. She held his hand till they came to the end of the first tree, and then his courage failed him and he had to go back. He was obliged to take off all his clothes before he could risk it, and she carried them over for him on her head. They settled down in the empty hut that stood here. Whether she had any rights over it (land tenure is a complicated business in the islands), or whether the owner had died during the epidemic, I do not know, but anyhow no one questioned them, and they took possession. Their furniture consisted of a couple of grass-mats on which they slept, a fragment of looking-glass, and a bowl or two. In this pleasant land that is enough to start housekeeping on.

"They say that happy people have no history, and certainly a happy love has none. They did nothing all day long and yet the days seemed all too short. The girl had a native name, but Red called her Sally. He picked up the easy language very quickly, and he used to lie on the mat for hours while she chattered gaily to him. He was a silent fellow, and perhaps his mind was lethargic. He smoked incessantly the cigarettes which she made him out of the native tobacco and pandanus leaf, and he watched her while with deft fingers she made grass mats. Often natives would come in and tell long stories of the old days when the island was disturbed by tribal wars. Sometimes he would go fishing on the reef, and bring home a basket full of coloured fish. Sometimes at night he would go out with a lantern to catch lobster. There were plantains round the hut and Sally would roast them for their frugal meal. She knew how to make delicious messes from coconuts, and the breadfruit tree by the side of the creek gave them its fruit. On feast-days they killed a little pig and cooked it on hot stones. They bathed together in the creek; and in the evening they went down to the lagoon and paddled about in a dugout, with its great outrigger. The sea was deep blue, wine-coloured at sundown, like the sea of Homeric Greece; but in the lagoon the colour had an infinite variety, aquamarine and amethyst and emerald; and the setting sun turned it for a short moment to liquid gold. Then there was the colour of the coral, brown, white, pink, red, purple; and the shapes it took were marvellous. It was like a magic garden, and the hurrying fish were like butterflies. It strangely lacked reality. Among the coral were pools with a floor of white sand and here, where the water was dazzling clear, it was very good to bathe. Then, cool and happy, they wandered back in the gloaming over the soft grass road to the creek, walking hand in hand, and now the mynah birds filled the coconut trees with their clamour. And then the night, with that great sky shining with gold, that seemed to stretch more widely than the skies of Europe, and the soft airs that blew gently through the open hut, the long night again was all too short. She was sixteen and he was barely twenty. The dawn crept in among the wooden pillars of the hut and looked at those lovely children sleeping in one another's arms. The sun hid behind the great tattered leaves of the plantains so that it might not disturb them, and then, with playful malice, shot a golden ray, like the outstretched paw of a Persian cat, on their faces. They opened their sleepy eyes and they smiled to welcome another day. The weeks lengthened into months, and a year passed. They seemed to love one another as—I hesitate to say passionately, for passion has in it always a shade of sadness, a touch of bitterness or anguish, but as whole heartedly, as simply and naturally as on that first day on which, meeting, they had recognised that a god was in them.

"If you had asked them I have no doubt that they would have thought it impossible to suppose their love could ever cease. Do we not know that the essential element of love is a belief in its own eternity? And yet perhaps in Red there was already a very little seed, unknown to himself and unsuspected by the girl, which would in time have grown to weariness. For one day one of the natives from the cove told them that some way down the coast at the anchorage was a British whaling-ship.

"'Gee,' he said, 'I wonder if I could make a trade of some nuts and plantains for a pound or two of tobacco.'

"The pandanus cigarettes that Sally made him with untiring hands were strong and pleasant enough to smoke, but they left him unsatisfied; and he yearned on a sudden for real tobacco, hard, rank, and pungent. He had not smoked a pipe for many months. His mouth watered at the thought of it. One would have thought some premonition of harm would have made Sally seek to dissuade him, but love possessed her so completely that it never occurred to her any power on earth could take him from her. They went up into the hills together and gathered a great basket of wild oranges, green, but sweet and juicy; and they picked plantains from around the hut, and coconuts from their trees, and breadfruit and mangoes; and they carried them down to the cove. They loaded the unstable canoe with them, and Red and the native boy who had brought them the news of the ship paddled along outside the reef.

"It was the last time she ever saw him.

"Next day the boy came back alone. He was all in tears. This is the story he told. When after their long paddle they reached the ship and Red hailed it, a white man looked over the side and told them to come on board. They took the fruit they had brought with them and Red piled it up on the deck. The white man and he began to talk, and they seemed to come to some agreement. One of them went below and brought up tobacco. Red took some at once and lit a pipe. The boy imitated the zest with which he blew a great cloud of smoke from his mouth. Then they said something to him and he went into the cabin. Through the open door the boy, watching curiously, saw a bottle brought out and glasses. Red drank and smoked. They seemed to ask him something, for he shook his head and laughed. The man, the first man who had spoken to them, laughed too, and he filled Red's glass once more. They went on talking and drinking, and presently, growing tired of watching a sight that meant nothing to him, the boy curled himself up on the deck and slept. He was awakened by a kick; and, jumping to his feet, he saw that the ship was slowly sailing out of the lagoon. He caught sight of Red seated at the table, with his head resting heavily on his arms, fast asleep. He made a movement towards him, intending to wake him, but a rough hand seized his arm, and a man, with a scowl and words which he did not understand, pointed to the side. He shouted to Red, but in a moment he was seized and flung overboard. Helpless, he swam round to his canoe which was drifting a little way off, and pushed it on to the reef. He climbed in and, sobbing all the way, paddled back to shore.

"What had happened was obvious enough. The whaler, by desertion or sickness, was short of hands, and the captain when Red came aboard had asked him to sign on; on his refusal he had made him drunk and kidnapped him.

"Sally was beside herself with grief. For three days she screamed and cried. The natives did what they could to comfort her, but she would not be comforted. She would not eat. And then, exhausted, she sank into a sullen apathy. She spent long days at the cove, watching the lagoon, in the vain hope that Red somehow or other would manage to escape. She sat on the white sand, hour after hour, with the tears running down her cheeks, and at night dragged herself wearily back across the creek to the little hut where she had been happy. The people with whom she had lived before Red came to the island wished her to return to them, but she would not; she was convinced that Red would come back, and she wanted him to find her where he had left her. Four months later she was delivered of a still-born child, and the old woman who had come to help her through her confinement remained with her in the hut. All joy was taken from her life. If her anguish with time became less intolerable it was replaced by a settled melancholy. You would not have thought that among these people, whose emotions, though so violent, are very transient, a woman could be found capable of so enduring a passion. She never lost the profound conviction that sooner or later Red would come back. She watched for him, and every time someone crossed this slender little bridge of coconut trees she looked. It might at last be he."

Neilson stopped talking and gave a faint sigh.

"And what happened to her in the end?" asked the skipper.

Neilson smiled bitterly.

"Oh, three years afterwards she took up with another white man."

The skipper gave a fat, cynical chuckle.

"That's generally what happens to them," he said.

The Swede shot him a look of hatred. He did not know why that gross, obese man excited in him so violent a repulsion. But his thoughts wandered and he found his mind filled with memories of the past. He went back five and twenty years. It was when he first came to the island, weary of Apia, with its heavy drinking, its gambling and coarse sensuality, a sick man, trying to resign himself to the loss of the career which had fired his imagination with ambitious thoughts. He set behind him resolutely all his hopes of making a great name for himself and strove to content himself with the few poor months of careful life which was all that he could count on. He was boarding with a half-caste trader who had a store a couple of miles along the coast at the edge of a native village; and one day, wandering aimlessly along the grassy paths of the coconut groves, he had come upon the hut in which Sally lived. The beauty of the spot had filled him with a rapture so great that it was almost painful, and then he had seen Sally. She was the loveliest creature he had ever seen, and the sadness in those dark, magnificent eyes of hers affected him strangely. The Kanakas were a handsome race, and beauty was not rare among them, but it was the beauty of shapely animals. It was empty. But those tragic eyes were dark with mystery, and you felt in them the bitter complexity of the groping, human soul. The trader told him the story and it moved him.

"Do you think he'll ever come back?" asked Neilson.

"No fear. Why, it'll be a couple of years before the ship is paid off, and by then he'll have forgotten all about her. I bet he was pretty mad when he woke up and found he'd been shanghaied, and I shouldn't wonder but he wanted to fight somebody. But he'd got to grin and bear it, and I guess in a month he was thinking it the best thing that had ever happened to him that he got away from the island."

But Neilson could not get the story out of his head. Perhaps because he was sick and weakly, the radiant health of Red appealed to his imagination. Himself an ugly man, insignificant of appearance, he prized very highly comeliness in others. He had never been passionately in love, and certainly he had never been passionately loved. The mutual attraction of those two young things gave him a singular delight. It had the ineffable beauty of the Absolute. He went again to the little hut by the creek. He had a gift for languages and an energetic mind, accustomed to work, and he had already given much time to the study of the local tongue. Old habit was strong in him and he was gathering together material for a paper on the Samoan speech. The old crone who shared the hut with Sally invited him to come in and sit down. She gave him *kava* to drink and cigarettes to smoke. She was glad to have someone to chat with and while she talked he looked at Sally. She reminded him of the Psyche in the museum at Naples. Her features had the same clear purity of line, and though she had borne a child she had still a virginal aspect.

It was not till he had seen her two or three times that he induced her to speak. Then it was only to ask him if he had seen in Apia a man called Red. Two years had passed since his disappearance, but it was plain that she still thought of him incessantly.

It did not take Neilson long to discover that he was in love with her. It was only by an effort of will now that he prevented himself from going every day to the creek, and when he was not with Sally his thoughts were. At first, looking upon himself as a dying man, he asked only to look at her, and occasionally hear her speak, and his love gave him a wonderful happiness. He exulted in its purity. He wanted nothing from her but the opportunity to weave around her graceful person a web of beautiful fancies. But the open air, the equable temperature, the rest, the simple fare, began to have an unexpected effect on his health. His temperature did not soar at night to such alarming heights, he coughed less and began to put on weight; six months passed without his having a haemorrhage; and on a sudden he saw the possibility that he might live. He had studied his disease carefully, and the hope dawned upon him that with great care he might arrest its course. It exhilarated him to look forward once more to the future. He made plans. It was evident that any active life was out of the question, but he could live on the islands, and the small income he had, insufficient elsewhere, would be ample to keep him. He could grow coconuts; that would give him an occupation; and he would send for his books and a piano; but his quick mind saw that in all this he was merely trying to conceal from himself the desire which obsessed him.

He wanted Sally. He loved not only her beauty, but that dim soul which he divined behind her suffering eyes. He would intoxicate her with his passion. In the end he would make her forget. And in an ecstasy of surrender he fancied himself giving her too the happiness which he had thought never to know again, but had now so miraculously achieved.

He asked her to live with him. She refused. He had expected that and did not let it depress him, for he was sure that sooner or later she would yield. His love was irresistible. He told the old woman of his wishes, and found somewhat to his surprise that she and the neighbours, long aware of them, were strongly urging Sally to accept his offer. After all, every native was glad to keep house for a white man, and Neilson according to the standards of the island was a rich one. The trader with whom he boarded went to her and told her not to be a fool; such an opportunity would not come again, and after so long she could not still believe that Red would ever return. The girl's resistance only increased Neilson's desire, and what had been a very pure love now became an agonising passion. He was determined that nothing should stand in his way. He gave Sally no peace. At last, worn out by his persistence and the persuasions, by turns pleading and angry, of everyone around her, she consented. But the day after when, exultant, he went to see her he found that in the night she had burnt down the hut in which she and Red had lived together. The old crone ran towards him full of angry abuse of Sally, but he waved her aside; it did not matter; they would build a bungalow on the place where the hut had stood. A European house would really be more convenient if he wanted to bring out a piano and a vast number of books.

And so the little wooden house was built in which he had now lived for many years, and Sally became his wife. But after the first few weeks of rapture, during which he was satisfied with what she gave him he had known little happiness. She had yielded to him, through weariness, but she had only yielded what she set no store on. The soul which he had dimly glimpsed escaped him. He knew that she cared nothing for him. She still loved Red, and all the time she was waiting for his return. At a sign from him, Neilson knew that, notwithstanding his love, his tenderness, his sympathy, his generosity, she would leave him without a moment's hesitation. She would never give a thought to his distress. Anguish seized him and he battered at that impenetrable self of hers which sullenly resisted him. His love became bitter. He tried to melt her heart with kindness, but it remained as hard as before; he feigned indifference, but she did not notice it. Sometimes he lost his temper and abused her, and then she wept silently. Sometimes he thought she was nothing but a fraud, and that soul simply an invention of his own, and that he could not get into the sanctuary of her heart because there was no sanctuary there. His love became a prison from which he longed to escape, but he had not the strength merely to open the door—that was all it needed—and walk out into the open air. It was torture and at last he became numb and hopeless. In the end the fire burnt itself out and, when he saw her eyes rest for an instant on the slender bridge, it was no longer rage that filled his heart but impatience. For many years now they had lived together bound by the ties of habit and convenience, and it was with a smile that he looked back on his old passion. She was an old woman, for the women on the islands age quickly, and if he had no love for her any more he had tolerance. She left him alone. He was contented with his piano and his books.

His thoughts led him to a desire for words.

"When I look back now and reflect on that brief passionate love of Red and Sally, I think that perhaps they should thank the ruthless fate that separated them when their love seemed still to be at its height. They suffered, but they suffered in beauty. They were spared the real tragedy of love."

"I don't know exactly as I get you," said the skipper.

"The tragedy of love is not death or separation. How long do you think it would have been before one or other of them ceased to care? Oh, it is dreadfully bitter to look at a woman whom you have loved with all your heart and soul, so that you felt you could not bear to let her out of your sight, and realise that you would not mind if you never saw her again. The tragedy of love is indifference."

But while he was speaking a very extraordinary thing happened. Though he had been addressing the skipper he had not been talking to him, he had been putting his thoughts into words for himself, and with his eyes fixed on the man in front of him he had not seen him. But now an image presented itself to them, an image not of the man he saw, but of another man. It was as though he were looking into one of those distorting mirrors that make you extraordinarily squat or outrageously elongate, but here exactly the opposite took place, and in the obese, ugly old man he caught the shadowy glimpse of a stripling. He gave him now a quick, searching scrutiny. Why had a haphazard stroll brought him just to this place? A sudden tremor of his heart made him slightly breathless. An absurd suspicion seized him. What had occurred to him was impossible, and yet it might be a fact.

"What is your name?" he asked abruptly.

The skipper's face puckered and he gave a cunning chuckle. He looked then malicious and horribly vulgar.

"It's such a damned long time since I heard it that I almost forget it myself. But for thirty years now in the islands they've always called me Red."

His huge form shook as he gave a low, almost silent laugh. It was obscene. Neilson shuddered. Red was hugely amused, and from his bloodshot eyes tears ran down his cheeks.

Neilson gave a gasp, for at that moment a woman came in. She was a native, a woman of somewhat commanding presence, stout without being corpulent, dark, for the natives grow darker with age, with very grey hair. She wore a black Mother Hubbard, and its thinness showed her heavy breasts. The moment had come.

She made an observation to Neilson about some household matter and he answered. He wondered if his voice sounded as unnatural to her as it did to himself. She gave the man who was sitting in the chair by the window an indifferent glance, and went out of the room. The moment had come and gone.

Neilson for a moment could not speak. He was strangely shaken. Then he said:

"I'd be very glad if you'd stay and have a bit of dinner with me. Pot luck."

"I don't think I will," said Red. "I must go after this fellow Gray. I'll give him his stuff and then I'll get away. I want to be back in Apia tomorrow."

"I'll send a boy along with you to show you the way."

"That'll be fine."

Red heaved himself out of his chair, while the Swede called one of the boys who worked on the plantation. He told him where the skipper wanted to go, and the boy stepped along the bridge. Red prepared to follow him.

"Don't fall in," said Neilson.

"Not on your life."

Neilson watched him make his way across and when he had disappeared among the coconuts he looked still. Then he sank heavily in his chair. Was that the man who had prevented him from being happy? Was that the man whom Sally had loved all these years and for whom she had waited so desperately? It was grotesque. A sudden fury seized him so that he had an instinct to spring up and smash everything around him. He had been cheated. They had seen each other at last and had not known it. He began to laugh, mirthlessly, and his laughter grew till it became hysterical. The Gods had played him a cruel trick. And he was old now.

At last Sally came in to tell him dinner was ready. He sat down in front of her and tried to eat. He wondered what she would say if he told her now that the fat old man sitting in the chair was the lover whom she remembered still with the passionate abandonment of her youth. Years ago, when he hated her because she made him so unhappy, he would have been glad to tell her. He wanted to hurt her then as she hurt him, because his hatred was only love. But now he did not care. He shrugged his shoulders listlessly.

"What did that man want?" she asked presently.

He did not answer at once. She was old too, a fat old native woman. He wondered why he had ever loved her so madly. He had laid at her feet all the treasures of his soul, and she had cared nothing for them. Waste, what waste! And now, when he looked at her, he felt only contempt. His patience was at last exhausted. He answered her question.

"He's the captain of a schooner. He's come from Apia."

"Yes."

"He brought me news from home. My eldest brother is very ill and I must go back."

"Will you be gone long?"
He shrugged his shoulders.

SOMERSET MAUGHAM
1874–1965

William Somerset Maugham was born in the British Embassy in Paris. His father worked as a solicitor there, and his parents wanted him to enjoy the privilege of being born on British soil. Until the death of his parents—his mother died when he was only eight years old and his father two years later—Maugham lived in Paris. A tutor had to teach the orphan English before he could be sent back to England. After attending King's School in Canterbury and sitting in on philosophy and literature lectures at the University of Heidelberg for nine months, he entered St. Thomas's Hospital in London as a medical student.

Maugham's first novel, *Liza of Lambeth* (1897), reflected his familiarity with the slums of Lambeth, where he served several weeks as an obstetrics clerk. The book caused such a stir that the author decided to pursue a literary career instead of an assistantship at St. Thomas's.

He wrote constantly, but he did not enjoy the success his first book had portended. Then in 1907, the Royal Court Theatre put on a production of *Lady Frederick*, one of his comedies, and it was an immediate success. Within a year, four of his plays—*Lady Frederick*, *The Explorer*, *Jack Straw*, and *Mrs. Dot*—were running simultaneously in West End theaters. Overnight Maugham became affluent and widely known.

While he never confined himself to writing for the theater, Maugham did regularly write plays for the next twenty-six years. Then in 1933, after the production of *Sheppey*, he announced his retirement from the theater, saying that drama did not give him the freedom he needed in writing. One thing his popular plays and the films made from them did provide him, for more than a quarter of a century, was a handsome income.

Of Human Bondage (1915), an autobiographical novel, is still considered his most important fictional work, but *The Moon and Sixpence* (1919), a novelistic treatment of the life of the French artist Paul Gauguin, remains a favorite as well. Researching *The Moon and Sixpence*, Maugham traveled to Tahiti in 1916. He loved the place and returned to it in 1919. The South Seas stories in *The Trembling of a Leaf* (1921) were the result of his travels. *Cakes and Ale* (1930) and *The Razor's Edge* (1944) complete the list of his most enduring fiction.

During World War I Maugham twice served as an intelligence agent, first in a post in Geneva and then in St. Petersburg to help bolster the provisional government of Alexander Kerensky. He wrote of some of his experiences as an agent in *A Writer's Notebook* (1949).

From 1928, when he bought the Villa Maresque on Cap Ferrat, until his death in 1965, Maugham lived primarily in France. During World War II, however, when the Germans invaded France, he had to leave (Goebbels had personally denounced him). He traveled to the United States, wintering at Parker's Ferry, South Carolina, and passing the summers at Edgartown, Martha's Vineyard, until the cessation of hostilities.

"Red," a story that reflects Maugham's interest in life on the South Sea islands, appeared in *The Trembling of a Leaf* (1921).

The Rough Crossing

BY F. SCOTT FITZGERALD

I

ONCE ON THE LONG, covered piers, you have come into a ghostly country that is no longer Here and not yet There. Especially at night. There is a hazy yellow vault full of shouting, echoing voices. There is the rumble of trucks and the clump of trunks, the strident chatter of a crane and the first salt smell of the sea. You hurry through, even though there's time. The past, the continent, is behind you; the future is that glowing mouth in the side of the ship; this dim turbulent alley is too confusedly the present.

Up the gangplank, and the vision of the world adjusts itself, narrows. One is a citizen of a commonwealth smaller than Andorra. One is no longer so sure of anything. Curiously unmoved the men at the purser's desk, cell-like the cabin, disdainful the eyes of voyagers and their friends, solemn the officer who stands on the deserted promenade deck thinking something of his own as he stares at the crowd below. A last odd idea that one didn't really have to come, then the loud, mournful whistles, and the thing—certainly not the boat, but rather a human idea, a frame of mind—pushes forth into the big dark night.

Adrian Smith, one of the celebrities on board—not a very great celebrity, but important enough to be bathed in flash-light by a photographer who had been given his name, but wasn't sure what his subject "did"—Adrian Smith and his blonde wife, Eva, went up to the promenade deck, passed the melancholy ship's officer, and, finding a quiet aerie, put their elbows on the rail.

'We're going!' he cried presently, and they both laughed in ecstasy. 'We've escaped. They can't get us now.'

'Who?'

He waved his hand vaguely at the civic tiara.

'All those people out there. They'll come with their posses and their warrants and list of crimes we've committed, and ring the bell at our door on Park Avenue and ask for the Adrian Smiths, but what ho! the Adrian Smiths and their children and nurse are off for France.'

'You make me think we really have committed crimes.'

'They can't have you,' he said frowning. 'That's one thing they're after me about—they know I haven't got any right to a person like you, and they're furious. That's one reason I'm glad to get away.'

'Darling,' said Eva.

She was twenty-six—five years younger than he. She was something precious to everyone who knew her.

'I like this boat better than the *Majestic* or the *Aquitania*,' she remarked, unfaithful to the ships that had served their honeymoon.

'It's much smaller.'

'But it's very slick and it has all those little shops along the corridors. And I think the staterooms are bigger.'

'The people are very formal—did you notice?—as if they thought everyone else was a card sharp. And in about four days half of them will be calling the other half by their first names.'

Four of the people came by now—a quartet of young girls abreast, making a circuit of the deck. Their eight eyes swept momentarily toward Adrian and Eva, and then swept automatically back, save for one pair which lingered for an instant with a little start. They belonged to one of the girls in the middle, who was, indeed, the only passenger of the four. She was not more than eighteen—a dark little beauty with the fine crystal gloss over her that, in brunettes, takes the place of a blonde's bright glow.

'Now, who's that?' wondered Adrian. 'I've seen her before.'

'She's pretty,' said Eva.

'Yes.' He kept wondering, and Eva deferred momentarily to his distraction; then, smiling up at him, she drew him back into their privacy.

'Tell me more,' she said.

'About what?'

'About us—what a good time we'll have, and how we'll be much better and happier, and very close always.'

'How could we be any closer?' His arm pulled her to him.

'But I mean never even quarrel any more about silly things. You know, I made up my mind when you gave me my birthday present last week'—her fingers caressed the fine seed pearls at her throat—'that I'd try never to say a mean thing to you again.'

'You never have, my precious.'

Yet even as he strained her against his side he knew that the moment of utter isolation had passed almost before it had begun. His antennae were already out, feeling over this new world.

'Most of the people look rather awful,' he said—'little and swarthy and ugly. Americans didn't use to look like that.'

'They look dreary,' she agreed. 'Let's not get to know anybody, but just stay together.'

A gong was beating now, and stewards were shouting down the decks, 'Visitors ashore, please!' and voices rose to a strident chorus. For a while the gangplanks were thronged; then they were empty, and the jostling crowd behind the barrier waved and called unintelligible things, and kept up a grin of good will. As the stevedores began to work at the ropes a flat-faced, somewhat befuddled young man arrived in a great hurry and was assisted up the gangplank by a porter and a taxi driver. The ship having swallowed him as impassively as though he were a missionary for Beirut, a low, portentous vibration began. The pier with its faces commenced to slide by, and for a moment the boat was just a piece accidentally split off from it; then the faces became remote, voiceless, and the pier was one among many yellow blurs along the water front. Now the harbour flowed swiftly toward the sea.

On a northern parallel of latitude a hurricane was forming and moving south by southeast preceded by a strong west wind. On its course it was destined to swamp the *Peter I. Eudim* of Amsterdam, with a crew of sixty-six, to break a boom on the largest boat in the world, and to bring grief and want to the wives of several hundred seamen. This liner, leaving New York Sunday evening, would enter the zone of the storm Tuesday, and of the hurricane late Wednesday night.

II

Tuesday afternoon Adrian and Eva paid their first visit to the smoking room. This was not in accord with their intentions—they had 'never wanted to see a cocktail again' after leaving America—but they had forgotten the staccato loneliness of ships, and all activity centred about the bar. So they went in for just a minute.

It was full. There were those who had been there since luncheon, and those who would be there until dinner, not to mention a faithful few who had been there since nine this morning. It was a prosperous assembly, taking its recreation at bridge, solitaire, detective stories, alcohol, argument and love. Up to this point you could have matched it in the club or casino life of any country, but over it all played a repressed nervous energy, a barely disguised impatience that extended to old and young alike. The cruise had begun, and they had enjoyed the beginning, but the show was not varied enough to last six days, and already they wanted it to be over.

At a table near them Adrian saw the pretty girl who had stared at him on the deck the first night. Again he was fascinated by her loveliness; there was no mist upon the brilliant gloss that gleamed through the smoky confusion of the room. He and Eva had decided from the passenger list that she was probably 'Miss Elizabeth D'Amido and maid,' and he had heard her called Betsy as he walked past a deck-tennis game. Among the young people with her was the flat-nosed youth who had been 'poured on board,' the night of their departure; yesterday he had walked the deck morosely, but he was apparently reviving. Miss D'Amido whispered something to him, and he looked over at the Smiths with curious eyes. Adrian was new enough at being a celebrity to turn self-consciously away.

'There's a little roll. Do you feel it?' Eva demanded.

'Perhaps we'd better split a pint of champagne.'

While he gave the order a short colloquy was taking place at the other table; presently a young man rose and came over to them.

'Isn't this Mr Adrian Smith?'

'Yes.'

'We wondered if we couldn't put you down for the deck-tennis tournament. We're going to have a deck-tennis tournament.'

'Why—' Adrian hesitated.

'My name's Stacomb,' burst out the young man. 'We all know your—your plays or whatever it is, and all that—and we wondered if you wouldn't like to come over to our table.'

Somewhat overwhelmed, Adrian laughed: Mr Stacomb, glib, soft, slouching, waited; evidently under the impression that he had delivered himself of a graceful compliment.

Adrian, understanding that, too, replied: 'Thanks, but perhaps you'd better come over here.'

'We've got a bigger table.'

'But we're older and more—more settled.'

The young man laughed kindly, as if to say, 'That's all right.'

'Put me down,' said Adrian. 'How much do I owe you?'

'One buck. Call me Stac.'

'Why?' asked Adrian, startled.

'It's shorter.'

When he had gone they smiled broadly.

'Heavens,' Eva gasped, 'I believe they are coming over.'

They were. With a great draining of glasses, calling of waiters, shuffling of chairs, three boys and two girls moved to the Smiths' table. If there was any diffidence, it was confined to the hosts; for the new additions gathered around them eagerly, eyeing Adrian with respect—too much respect—as if to say: 'This was probably a mistake and won't be amusing, but maybe we'll get something out of it to help us in our after life, like at school.'

In a moment Miss D'Amido changed seats with one of the men and placed her radiant self at Adrian's side, looking at him with manifest admiration.

'I fell in love with you the minute I saw you,' she said audibly and without self-consciousness; 'so I'll take all the blame for butting in. I've seen your play four times.'

Adrian called a waiter to take their orders.

'You see,' continued Miss D'Amido, 'we're going into a storm, and you might be prostrated the rest of the trip, so I couldn't take any chances.'

He saw that there was no undertone or innuendo in what she said, nor the need of any. The words themselves were enough, and the deference with which she neglected the young men and bent her politeness on him was somehow very touching. A little glow went over him; he was having rather more than a pleasant time.

Eva was less entertained; but the flat-nosed young man, whose name was Butterworth, knew people that she did, and that seemed to make the affair less careless and casual. She did not like meeting new people unless they had 'something to contribute,' and she was often bored by the great streams of them, of all types and conditions and classes, that passed through Adrian's life. She herself 'had everything'—which is to say that she was well endowed with talents and with charm—and the mere novelty of people did not seem a sufficient reason for eternally offering everything up to them.

Half an hour later when she rose to go and see the children, she was content that the episode was over. It was colder on deck, with a damp that was almost rain, and there was a perceptible motion. Opening the door of her stateroom she was surprised to find the cabin steward sitting languidly on her bed, his head slumped upon the upright pillow. He looked at her listlessly as she came in, but made no move to get up.

'When you've finished your nap you can fetch me a new pillow-case,' she said briskly.

Still the man didn't move. She perceived then that his face was green.

'You can't be seasick in here,' she anounced firmly. 'You go and lie down in your own quarters.'

'It's me side,' he said faintly. He tried to rise, gave out a little rasping sound of pain and sank back again. Eva rang for the stewardess.

A steady pitch, toss, roll had begun in earnest and she felt no sympathy for the steward, but only wanted to get him out as quick as possible. It was outrageous for a member of the crew to be seasick. When the stewardess came in Eva tried to explain this, but now her own head was whirring, and throwing herself on the bed, she covered her eyes.

'It's his fault,' she groaned when the man was assisted from the room. 'I was all right and it made me sick to look at him. I wish he'd die.'

In a few minutes Adrian came in.

'Oh, but I'm sick!' she cried.

'Why, you poor baby.' He leaned over and took her in his arms. 'Why didn't you tell me?'

'I was all right upstairs, but there was a steward—Oh, I'm too sick to talk.'

'You'd better have dinner in bed.'

'Dinner! Oh, my heavens!'

He waited solicitously, but she wanted to hear his voice, to have it drown out the complaining sound of the beams.

'Where've you been?'

'Helping to sign up people for the tournament.'

'Will they have it if it's like this? Because if they do I'll just lose for you.'

He didn't answer; opening her eyes, she saw that he was frowning.

'I didn't know you were going in the doubles,' he said.

'Why, that's the only fun.'

'I told the D'Amido girl I'd play with her.'

'Oh.'

'I didn't think. You know I'd much rather play with you.'

'Why didn't you, then?' she asked coolly.

'It never occurred to me.'

She remembered that on their honeymoon they had been in the finals and won a prize. Years passed. But Adrian never frowned in this regretful way unless he felt a little guilty. He stumbled about, getting his dinner clothes out of the trunk, and she shut her eyes.

When a particular violent lurch startled her awake again he was dressed and tying his tie. He looked healthy and fresh, and his eyes were bright.

'Well, how about it?' he inquired. 'Can you make it, or no?'

'No.'

'Can I do anything for you before I go?'

'Where are you going?'

'Meeting those kids in the bar. Can I do anything for you?'

'No.'

'Darling, I hate to leave you like this.'

'Don't be silly. I just want to sleep.'

That solicitous frown—when she knew he was crazy to be out and away from the close cabin. She was glad when the door closed. The thing to do was to sleep, sleep.

Up—down—sideways. Hey there, not so far! Pull her round the corner there! Now roll her, right—left—Crea-eak! Wrench! Swoop!

Some hours later Eva was dimly conscious of Adrian bending over her. She wanted him to put his arms around her and draw her up out of this dizzy lethargy, but by the time she was fully awake the cabin was empty. He had looked in and gone. When she awoke next the cabin was dark and he was in bed.

The morning was fresh and cool, and the sea was just enough calmer to make Eva think she could get up. They breakfasted in the cabin and with Adrian's help she accomplished an unsatisfactory makeshift toilet and they went up on the boat deck. The tennis tournament had already begun and was furnishing action for a dozen amateur movie cameras, but the majority of passengers were represented by lifeless bundles in deck chairs beside untasted trays.

Adrian and Miss D'Amido played their first match. She was deft and graceful; blatantly well. There was even more warmth behind her ivory skin than there had been the day before. The strolling first officer stopped and talked to her; half a dozen men whom she couldn't have known three days ago called her Betsy. She was already the pretty girl of the voyage, the cynosure of starved ship's eyes.

But after a while Eva preferred to watch the gulls in the wireless masts and the slow slide of the roll-top sky. Most of the passengers looked silly with their movie cameras that they had all rushed to get and now didn't know what to use for, but the sailors painting the lifeboat stanchions were quiet and beaten and sympathetic, and probably wished, as she did, that the voyage was over.

Butterworth sat down on the deck beside her chair.

'They're operating on one of the stewards this morning. Must be terrible in this sea.'

'Operating? What for?' she asked listlessly.

'Appendicitis. They have to operate now because we're going into worse weather. That's why they're having the ship's party tonight.'

'Oh, the poor man!' she cried, realizing it must be her steward.

Adrian was showing off now by being very courteous and thoughtful in the game.

'Sorry. Did you hurt yourself? . . . No, it was my fault. . . . You better put on your coat right away, pardner, or you'll catch cold.'

The match was over and they had won. Flushed and hearty, he came up to Eva's chair.

'How do you feel?'

'Terrible.'

'Winners are buying a drink in the bar,' he said apologetically.

'I'm coming, too,' Eva said, but an immediate dizziness made her sink back in her chair.

'You'd better stay here. I'll send you up something.'

She felt that his public manner had hardened toward her slightly.

'You'll come back?'

'Oh, right away.'

She was alone on the boat deck, save for a solitary ship's officer who slanted obliquely as he paced the bridge. When the cocktail arrived she forced herself to drink it, and felt better. Trying to distract her mind with pleasant things, she reached back to the sanguine talks that she and Adrian had had before sailing: There was the little villa in Brittany, the children learning French—that was all she could think of now—the little villa in Brittany, the children learning French—so she repeated the words over and over to herself until they became as meaningless as the wide white sky. The why of their being here had suddenly eluded her; she felt unmotivated, accidental, and she wanted Adrian to come back quick, all responsive and tender, to reassure her. It was in the hope that there was some secret of graceful living, some real compensation for the lost, careless confidence of twenty-one, that they were going to spend a year in France.

The day passed darkly, with fewer people around and a wet sky falling. Suddenly it was five o'clock, and they were all in the bar again, and Mr Butterworth was telling her about his past. She took a good deal of champagne, but she was seasick dimly through it, as if the illness was her soul trying to struggle up through some thickening incrustation of abnormal life.

'You're my idea of a Greek goddess, physically,' Butterworth was saying.

It was pleasant to be Mr Butterworth's idea of a Greek goddess physically, but where was Adrian? He and Miss D'Amido had gone out on a forward deck to feel the spray. Eva heard herself promising to get out her colours and paint the Eiffel Tower on Butterworth's shirt front for the party to-night.

When Adrian and Betsy D'Amido, soaked with spray, opened the door with difficulty against the driving wind and came into the now-covered security of the promenade deck, they stopped and turned toward each other.

'Well?' she said. But he only stood with his back to the rail, looking at her, afraid to speak. She was silent, too, because she wanted him to be first; so for a moment nothing happened. Then she made a step toward him, and he took her in his arms and kissed her forehead.

'You're just sorry for me, that's all.' She began to cry a little. 'You're just being kind.'

'I feel terribly about it.' His voice was taut and trembling.

'Then kiss me.'

The deck was empty. He bent over her swiftly.

'No, really kiss me.'

He could not remember when anything had felt so young and fresh as her lips. The rain lay, like tears shed for him, upon the softly shining porcelain cheeks. She was all new and immaculate, and her eyes were wild.

'I love you,' she whispered. 'I can't help loving you, can I? When I first saw you—oh, not on the boat, but over a year ago—Grace Healy took me to a rehearsal and suddenly you jumped up in the second row and began telling them what to do. I wrote you a letter and tore it up.'

'We've got to go.'

She was weeping as they walked along the deck. Once more, impru-
dently, she held up her face to him at the door of her cabin. His blood was
beating through him in wild tumult as he walked on to the bar.

He was thankful that Eva scarcely seemed to notice him or to know that
he had been gone. After a moment he pretended an interest in what she was
doing.

'What's that?'

'She's painting the Eiffel Tower on my shirt front for tonight,' explained
Butterworth.

'There,' Eva laid away her brush and wiped her hands. 'How's that?'

'A *chef-d'œuvre.*'

Her eyes swept around the watching group, lingered casually upon
Adrian.

'You're wet. Go and change.'

'You come too.'

'I want another champagne cocktail.'

'You've had enough. It's time to dress for the party.'

Unwilling she closed her paints and preceded him.

'Stacomb's got a table for nine,' he remarked as they walked along the
corridor.

'The younger set,' she said with unnecessary bitterness. 'Oh, the younger
set. And you just having the time of your life—with a child.'

They had a long discussion in the cabin, unpleasant on her part and eva-
sive on his, which ended when the ship gave a sudden gigantic heave, and
Eva, the edge worn off her champagne, felt ill again. There was nothing to
do but to have a cocktail in the cabin, and after that they decided to go to
the party—she believed him now, or she didn't care.

Adrian was ready first—he never wore fancy dress.

'I'll go on up. Don't be long.'

'Wait for me, please; it's rocking so.'

He sat down on a bed, concealing his impatience.

'You don't mind waiting, do you? I don't want to parade up there all
alone.'

She was taking a tuck in an oriental costume rented from the barber.

'Ships make people feel crazy,' she said. 'I think they're awful.'

'Yes,' he muttered absently.

'When it gets very bad I pretend I'm in the top of a tree, rocking to and
fro. But finally I get pretending everything, and finally I have to pretend I'm
sane when I know I'm not.'

'If you get thinking that way you will go crazy.'

'Look, Adrian.' She held up the string of pearls before clasping them on.

'Aren't they lovely?'

In Adrian's impatience she seemed to move around the cabin like a figure in a slow-motion picture. After a moment he demanded:

'Are you going to be long? It's stifling in here.'

'You go on!' she fired up.

'I don't want—'

'Go on, please! You just make me nervous trying to hurry me.'

With a show of reluctance he left her. After a moment's hesitation he went down a flight to a deck below and knocked at a door.

'Betsy.'

'Just a minute.'

She came out in the corridor attired in a red pea-jacket and trousers borrowed from the elevator boy.

'Do elevator boys have fleas?' she demanded. 'I've got everything in the world on under this as a precaution.'

'I had to see you,' he said quickly.

'Careful,' she whispered. 'Mrs Worden, who's supposed to be chaperoning me, is across the way. She's sick.'

'I'm sick for you.'

They kissed suddenly, clung close together in the narrow corridor, swaying to and fro with the motion of the ship.

'Don't go away,' she murmured.

'I've got to. I've—'

Her youth seemed to flow into him, bearing him up into a delicate romantic ecstasy that transcended passion. He couldn't relinquish it; he had discovered something that he had thought was lost with his own youth forever. As he walked along the passage he knew that he had stopped thinking, no longer dared to think.

He met Eva going into the bar.

'Where've you been?' she asked with a strained smile.

'To see about the table.'

She was lovely; her cool distinction conquered the trite costume and filled him with a resurgence of approval and pride. They sat down at a table.

The gale was rising hour by hour and the mere traversing of a passage had become a rough matter. In every stateroom trunks were lashed to the washstands, and the *Vestris* disaster was being reviewed in detail by nervous ladies, tossing, ill and wretched, upon their beds. In the smoking-room a stout gentleman had been hurled backward and suffered a badly cut head; and now the lighter chairs and tables were stacked and roped against the wall.

The crowd who had donned fancy dress and were dining together had swollen to about sixteen. The only remaining qualification for membership was the ability to reach the smoking-room. They ranged from a Groton-Harvard lawyer to an ungrammatical broker they had nicknamed Gyp the Blood, but distinctions had disappeared; for the moment they were samurai, chosen from several hundred for their triumphant resistance to the storm.

The gala dinner, overhung sardonically with lanterns and streamers, was interrupted by great communal slides across the room, precipitate retirements and spilled wine, while the ship roared and complained that under the panoply of a palace it was a ship after all. Upstairs afterward a dozen couples tried to dance, shuffling and galloping here and there in a crazy fandango, thrust around fantastically by a will alien to their own. In view of the condition of tortured hundreds below, there grew to be something indecent about it like a revel in a house of mourning, and presently there was an egress of the ever-dwindling survivors toward the bar.

As the evening passed, Eva's feeling of unreality increased. Adrian had disappeared—presumably with Miss D'Amido—and her mind, distorted by illness and champagne, began to enlarge upon the fact; annoyance changed slowly to dark and brooding anger, grief to desperation. She had never tried to bind Adrian, never needed to—for they were serious people, with all sorts of mutual interests, and satisfied with each other—but this was a breach of the contract, this was cruel. How could he think that she didn't know?

It seemed several hours later that he leaned over her chair in the bar where she was giving some woman an impassioned lecture upon babies, and said:

'Eva, we'd better turn in.'

Her lip curled. 'So that you can leave me there and then come back to your eighteen-year—'

'Be quiet.'

'I won't come to bed.'

'Very well. Good night.'

More time passed and the people at the table changed. The stewards wanted to close up the room, and thinking of Adrian—her Adrian—off somewhere saying tender things to someone fresh and lovely, Eva began to cry.

'But he's gone to bed,' her last attendants assured her. 'We saw him go.'

She shook her head. She knew better. Adrian was lost. The long seven-year dream was broken. Probably she was punished for something she had done; as this thought occurred to her the shrieking timbers overhead began to mutter that she had guessed at last. This was for the selfishness to her mother, who hadn't wanted her to marry Adrian; for all the sins and omissions of her life. She stood up, saying she must go out and get some air.

The deck was dark and drenched with wind and rain. The ship pounded through valleys, fleeing from black mountains of water that roared toward it. Looking out at the night, Eva saw that there was no chance for them unless she could make atonement, propitiate the storm. It was Adrian's love that was demanded of her. Deliberately she unclasped her pearl necklace, lifted it to her lips—for she knew that with it went the freshest, fairest part of her life—and flung it out into the gale.

III

When Adrian awoke it was lunchtime, but he knew that some heavier sound than the bugle had called him up from his deep sleep. Then he realized that the trunk had broken loose from its lashings and was being thrown back and forth between a wardrobe and Eva's bed. With an exclamation he jumped up, but she was unharmed—still in costume and stretched out in deep sleep. When the steward had helped him secure the trunk, Eva opened a single eye.

'How are you?' he demanded, sitting on the side of her bed.

She closed the eye, opened it again.

'We're in a hurricane now,' he told her. 'The steward says it's the worst he's seen in twenty years.'

'My head,' she muttered. 'Hold my head.'

'How?'

'In front. My eyes are going out. I think I'm dying.'

'Nonsense. Do you want the doctor?'

She gave a funny little gasp that frightened him; he rang and sent the steward for the doctor.

The young doctor was pale and tired. There was a stubble of beard upon his face. He bowed curtly as he came in and, turning to Adrian, said with scant ceremony:

'What's the matter?'

'My wife doesn't feel well.'

'Well, what is it you want—a bromide?'

A little annoyed by his shortness, Adrian said: 'You'd better examine her and see what she needs.'

'She needs a bromide,' said the doctor. 'I've given orders that she is not to have any more to drink on this ship.'

'Why not?' demanded Adrian in astonishment.

'Don't you know what happened last night?'

'Why, no, I was asleep.'

'Mrs Smith wandered around the boat for an hour, not knowing what she was doing. A sailor was set to follow her, and then the medical stewardess tried to get her to bed, and your wife insulted her.'

'Oh, my heavens!' cried Eva faintly.

'The nurse and I had both been up all night with Steward Carton, who died this morning.' He picked up his case. 'I'll send down a bromide for Mrs Smith. Good-bye.'

For a few minutes there was silence in the cabin. Then Adrian put his arm around her quickly.

'Never mind,' he said. 'We'll straighten it out.'

'I remember now.' Her voice was an awed whisper. 'My pearls. I threw them overboard.'

'Threw them overboard!'

'Then I began looking for you.'

'But I was here in bed.'

'I didn't believe it; I thought you were with that girl.'

'She collapsed during dinner. I was taking a nap down here.'

Frowning, he rang the bell and asked the steward for luncheon and a bottle of beer.

'Sorry, but we can't serve any beer to your cabin, sir.'

When he went out Adrian exploded: 'This is an outrage. You were simply crazy from that storm and they can't be so high-handed. I'll see the captain.'

'Isn't that awful?' Eva murmured. 'The poor man died.'

She turned over and began to sob into her pillow. There was a knock at the door.

'Can I come in?'

The assiduous Mr Butterworth, surprisingly healthy and immaculate, came into the crazily tipping cabin.

'Well, how's the mystic?' he demanded of Eva. 'Do you remember praying to the elements in the bar last night?'

'I don't want to remember anything about last night.'

They told him about the stewardess, and with the telling the situation lightened; they all laughed together.

'I'm going to get you some beer to have with your luncheon,' Butterworth said. 'You ought to get up on deck.'

'Don't go,' Eva said. 'You look so cheerful and nice.'

'Just for ten minutes.'

When he had gone, Adrian rang for two baths.

'The thing is to put on our best clothes and walk proudly three times around the deck,' he said.

'Yes.' After a moment she added abstractedly: 'I like that young man. He was awfully nice to me last night when you'd disappeared.'

The bath steward appeared with the information that bathing was too dangerous today. They were in the midst of the wildest hurricane on the

North Atlantic in ten years; there were two broken arms this morning from attempts to take baths. An elderly lady had been thrown down a staircase and was not expected to live. Furthermore, they had received the SOS signal from several boats this morning.

'Will we go to help them?'

'They're all behind us, sir, so we have to leave them to the *Mauretania*. If we tried to turn in this sea the portholes would be smashed.'

This array of calamities minimized their own troubles. Having eaten a sort of luncheon and drunk the beer provided by Butterworth, they dressed and went on deck.

Despite the fact that it was only possible to progress step by step, holding on to rope or rail, more people were abroad than on the day before. Fear had driven them from their cabins, where the trunks bumped and the waves pounded the portholes and they awaited momentarily the call to the boats. Indeed, as Adrian and Eva stood on the transverse deck above the second class, there was a bugle call, followed by a gathering of stewards and stewardesses on the deck below. But the boat was sound; it had outlasted one of its cargo—Steward James Carton was being buried at sea.

It was very British and sad. There were the rows of stiff, disciplined men and women standing in the driving rain, and there was a shape covered by the flag of the Empire that lived by the sea. The chief purser read the service, a hymn was sung, the body slid off into the hurricane. With Eva's burst of wild weeping for this humble end, some last string snapped within her. Now she really didn't care. She responded eagerly when Butterworth suggested that he get some champagne to their cabin. Her mood worried Adrian; she wasn't used to so much drinking and he wondered what he ought to do. At his suggestion that they sleep instead, she merely laughed, and the bromide the doctor had sent stood untouched on the washstand. Pretending to listen to the insipidities of several Mr Stacombs, he watched her; to his surprise and discomfort she seemed on intimate and even sentimental terms with Butterworth and he wondered if this was a form of revenge for his attention to Betsy D'Amido.

The cabin was full of smoke, the voices went on incessantly, the suspension of activity, the waiting for the storm's end, was getting on his nerves. They had been at sea only four days; it was like a year.

The two Mr Stacombs left finally, but Butterworth remained. Eva was urging him to go for another bottle of champagne.

'We've had enough,' objected Adrian. 'We ought to go to bed.'

'I won't go to bed!' she burst out. 'You must be crazy! You play around all you want, and then, when I find somebody I—I like, you want to put me to bed.'

'You're hysterical.'

'On the contrary, I've never been so sane.'

'I think you'd better leave us, Butterworth,' Adrian said. 'Eva doesn't know what she's saying.'

'He won't go. I won't let him go.' She clasped Butterworth's hand passionately. 'He's the only person that's been half decent to me.'

'You'd better go, Butterworth,' repeated Adrian.

The young man looked at him uncertainly.

'It seems to me you're being unjust to your wife,' he ventured.

'My wife isn't herself.'

'That's no reason for bullying her.'

Adrian lost his temper. 'You get out of here!' he cried.

The two men looked at each other for a moment in silence. Then Butterworth turned to Eva, said, 'I'll be back later,' and left the cabin.

'Eva, you've got to pull yourself together,' said Adrian when the door closed.

She didn't answer, looked at him from sullen, half-closed eyes.

'I'll order dinner here for us both and then we'll try to get some sleep.'

'I want to go up and send a wireless.'

'Who to?'

'Some Paris lawyer. I want a divorce.'

In spite of his annoyance, he laughed. 'Don't be silly.'

'Then I want to see the children.'

'Well, go and see them. I'll order dinner.'

He waited for her in the cabin twenty minutes. Then impatiently he opened the door across the corridor; the nurse told him that Mrs Smith had not been there.

With a sudden prescience of disaster he ran upstairs, glanced in the bar, the salons, even knocked at Butterworth's door. Then a quick round of the decks, feeling his way through the black spray and rain. A sailor stopped him at a network of ropes.

'Orders are no one goes by, sir. A wave has gone over the wireless room.'

'Have you seen a lady?'

'There was a young lady here—' He stopped and glanced around. 'Hello, she's gone.'

'She went up the stairs!' Adrian said anxiously. 'Up to the wireless room!'

The sailor ran up to the boat deck; stumbling and slipping, Adrian followed. As he cleared the protected sides of the companionway, a tremendous body struck the boat a staggering blow and, as she keeled over to an angle of forty-five degrees, he was thrown in a helpless roll down the drenched deck, to bring up dizzy and bruised against a stanchion.

'Eva!' he called. His voice was soundless in the black storm. Against the faint light of the wireless-room window he saw the sailor making his way forward.

'Eva!'

The wind blew him like a sail up against a lifeboat. Then there was another shuddering crash, and high over his head, over the very boat, he saw a gigantic, glittering white wave, and in the split second that it balanced there he became conscious of Eva, standing beside a ventilator twenty feet away. Pushing out from the stanchion, he lunged desperately toward her, just as the wave broke with a smashing roar. For a moment the rushing water was five feet deep, sweeping with enormous force toward the side, and then a human body was washed against him, and frantically he clutched it and was swept with it back toward the rail. He felt his body bump against it, but desperately he held on to his burden; then, as the ship rocked slowly back, the two of them, still joined by his fierce grip, were rolled out exhausted on the wet planks. For a moment he knew no more.

IV

Two days later, as the boat train moved tranquilly south toward Paris, Adrian tried to persuade his children to look out the window at the Norman countryside.

'It's beautiful,' he assured them. 'All the little farms like toys. Why, in heaven's name, won't you look?'

'I like the boat better,' said Estelle.

Her parents exchanged an infanticidal glance.

'The boat is still rocking for me,' Eva said with a shiver. 'Is it for you?'

'No. Somehow, it all seems a long way off. Even the passengers looked unfamiliar going through the customs.'

'Most of them hadn't appeared above ground before.'

He hesitated. 'By the way, I cashed Butterworth's cheque for him.'

'You're a fool. You'll never see the money again.'

'He must have needed it pretty badly or he would not have come to me.'

A pale and wan girl, passing along the corridor, recognized them and put her head through the doorway.

'How do you feel?'

'Awful.'

'Me, too,' agreed Miss D'Amido. 'I'm vainly hoping my fiancé will recognize me at the Gare du Nord. Do you know two waves went over the wireless room?'

'So we heard,' Adrian answered dryly.

She passed gracefully along the corridor and out of their life.

'The real truth is that none of it happened,' said Adrian after a moment. 'It was a nightmare—an incredibly awful nightmare.'

'Then, where are my pearls?'

'Darling, there are better pearls in Paris. I'll take the responsibility for those pearls. My real belief is that you saved the boat.'

'Adrian, let's never get to know anyone else, but just stay together always—just we two.'

He tucked her arm under his and they sat close. 'Who do you suppose those Adrian Smiths on the boat were?' he demanded. 'It certainly wasn't me.'

'Nor me.'

'It was two other people,' he said, nodding to himself. 'There are so many Smiths in this world.'

F. SCOTT FITZGERALD
1896–1940

Born in St. Paul, Minnesota, Francis Scott Key Fitzgerald enjoyed the advantages of being raised in an upper-class home, specifically travel and an active social life. In 1917, after attending Princeton University, where he collaborated on shows sponsored by the Triangle Club with fellow student Edmund Wilson but did not complete his degree, Fitzgerald entered the army.

At the war's end he obtained a position as an advertising writer, and in the meantime he worked on stories, sketches, and a novel. By 1920 he had found a place in America's best magazines and had published *This Side of Paradise*, firmly establishing himself among the coterie of foremost writers. He consolidated his position as the leading recorder of the jazz age with the publication of *The Great Gatsby* (1925). His wife, Zelda, was institutionalized in the thirties after a breakdown, a fictionalized account of which is recorded in *Tender Is the Night* (1934).

Fitzgerald himself entered a long period of emotional and physical collapse, aggravated by Zelda's permanent confinement and his own alcoholism. The period of decline, during which he wrote for Hollywood movie studios and worked on *The Last Tycoon*, ended with his death in 1940.

"The Rough Crossing," distinguished both by the panache and the care that characterized Fitzgerald's work, is taken from *Flappers and Philosophers* (1921).

Lifeguard

BY JOHN UPDIKE

BEYOND DOUBT, I am a splendid fellow. In the autumn, winter, and spring, I execute the duties of a student of divinity; in the summer I disguise myself in my skin and become a lifeguard. My slightly narrow and gingerly hirsute but not necessarily unmanly chest becomes brown. My smooth back turns the color of caramel, which, in conjunction with the whipped cream of my white pith helmet, gives me, some of my teen-age satellites assure me, a delightfully edible appearance. My legs, which I myself can study, cocked as they are before me while I repose on my elevated wooden throne, are dyed a lustreless maple walnut that accentuates their articulate strength. Correspondingly, the hairs of my body are bleached blond, so that my legs have the pointed elegance of, within the flower, umber anthers dusted with pollen.

For nine months of the year, I pace my pale hands and burning eyes through immense pages of Biblical text barnacled with fudging commentary; through multivolumed apologetics couched in a falsely friendly Victorian voice and bound in subtly abrasive boards of finely ridged, prefaded red; through handbooks of liturgy and histories of dogma; through the bewildering duplicities of Tillich's divine politicking; through the suave table talk of Father D'Arcy, Etienne Gilson, Jacques Maritain, and other such moderns mistakenly put at their ease by the exquisite antique furniture and overstuffed larder of the hospitable St. Thomas; through the terrifying attempts of Kierkegaard, Berdyaev, and Barth to scourge God into being. I sway appalled on the ladder of minus signs by which theologians would surmount the void. I tiptoe like a burglar into the house of naturalism to steal the silver. An acrobat, I swing from wisp to wisp. Newman's iridescent cobwebs crush in my hands. Pascal's blackboard mathematics are erased by a passing shoulder. The cave drawings, astoundingly vital by candlelight, of those aboriginal magicians, Paul and Augustine, in daylight fade into mere anthropology. The diverting productions of literary flirts like Chesterton, Eliot, Auden, and Greene—whether they regard Christianity as a pastel forest designed for a fairyland romp or a deliciously miasmic pit from which chiaroscuro can be mined with mechanical buckets—in the end all infallibly strike, despite the comic variety of gongs and mallets, the note of the rich young man who on the coast of Judaea refused in dismay to sell all that he had.

Then, for the remaining quarter of the solar revolution, I rest my eyes on a sheet of brilliant sand printed with the runes of naked human bodies. That there is no discrepancy between my studies, that the texts of the flesh complement those of the mind, is the easy burden of my sermon.

On the back rest of my lifeguard's chair is painted a cross—true, a red cross, signifying bandages, splints, spirits of ammonia, and sunburn unguents. Nevertheless, it comforts me. Each morning, as I mount into my chair, my athletic and youthfully fuzzy toes expertly gripping the slats that make a ladder, it is as if I am climbing into an immense, rigid, loosely fitting vestment.

Again, in each of my roles I sit attentively perched on the edge of an immensity. That the sea, with its multiform and mysterious hosts, its savage and senseless rages, no longer comfortably serves as a divine metaphor indicates how severely humanism has corrupted the apples of our creed. We seek God now in flowers and good deeds, and the immensities of blue that surround the little scabs of land upon which we draw our lives to their unsatisfactory conclusions are suffused by science with vacuous horror. I myself can hardly bear the thought of stars, or begin to count the mortalities of coral. But from my chair the sea, slightly distended by my higher perspective, seems a misty old gentleman stretched at his ease in an immense armchair which has for arms the arms of this bay and for an antimacassar the freshly laundered sky. Sailboats float on his surface like idle and unrelated but benevolent thoughts. The soughing of the surf is the rhythmic lifting of his ripple-stitched vest as he breathes. Consider. We enter the sea with a shock; our skin and blood shout in protest. But, that instant, that leap, past, what do we find? Ecstasy and buoyance. Swimming offers a parable. We struggle and thrash, and drown; we succumb, even in despair, and float, and are saved.

With what timidity, with what a sense of trespass, do I set forward even this obliquely a thought so official! Forgive me. I am not yet ordained; I am too disordered to deal with the main text. My competence is marginal, and I will confine myself to the gloss of flesh with which this particular margin, this one beach, is annotated each day.

Here the cinema of life is run backwards. The old are the first to arrive. They are idle, and have lost the gift of sleep. Each of our bodies is a clock that loses time. Young as I am, I can hear in myself the protein acids ticking; I wake at odd hours and in the shuddering darkness and silence feel my death rushing toward me like an express train. The older we get, and the fewer the mornings left to us, the more deeply dawn stabs us awake. The old ladies wear wide straw hats and, in their hats' shadows, smiles as wide, which they bestow upon each other, upon salty shells they discover in the morning-smooth sand, and even upon me, downy-eyed from my night of dissipation. The gentlemen are often incongruous; withered white legs support brazen barrel chests, absurdly potent, bustling with white froth. How these old roosters preen on their "condition"! With what fatuous expertness they swim in the icy water—always, however, prudently parallel to the shore, at a depth no greater than their height.

Then come the middle-aged, burdened with children and aluminum chairs. The men are scarred with the marks of their vocation—the red forearms of the gasoline-station attendant, the pale X on the back of the overall-wearing mason or carpenter, the clammer's nicked ankles. The hair on their bodies has as many patterns as matted grass. The women are wrinkled but fertile, like the Iraqi rivers that cradled the seeds of our civilization. Their children are odious. From their gaunt faces leer all the vices, the greeds, the grating urgencies of the adult, unsoftened by maturity's reticence and fatigue. Except that here and there, a girl, the eldest daughter, wearing a knit suit striped horizontally with green, purple, and brown, walks slowly, carefully, puzzled by the dawn enveloping her thick smooth body, her waist not yet nipped but her throat elongated.

Finally come the young. The young matrons bring fat and fussing infants who gobble the sand like sugar, who toddle blissfully into the surf and bring me bolt upright on my throne. My whistle tweets. The mothers rouse. Many of these women are pregnant again, and sluggishly lie in their loose suits like cows tranced in a meadow. They gossip politics, and smoke incessantly, and lift their troubled eyes in wonder as a trio of flat-stomached nymphs parades past. These maidens take all our eyes. The vivacious redhead, freckled and white-footed, pushing against her boy and begging to be ducked; the solemn brunette, transporting the vase of herself with held breath; the dimpled blonde in the bib and diapers of her Bikini, the lambent fuzz of her midriff shimmering like a cat's belly. Lust stuns me like the sun.

You are offended that a divinity student lusts? What prigs the unchurched are. Are not our assaults on the supernatural lascivious, a kind of indecency? If only you knew what de Sadian degradations, what frightful psychological spelunking, our gentle transcendentalist professors set us to, as preparation for our work, which is to shine in the darkness.

I feel that my lust makes me glow; I grow cold in my chair, like a torch of ice, as I study beauty. I have studied much of it, wearing all styles of bathing suit and facial expression, and have come to this conclusion: a woman's beauty lies, not in any exaggeration of the specialized zones, nor in any general harmony that could be worked out by means of the *sectio aurea* or a similar aesthetic superstition; but in the arabesque of the spine. The curve by which the back modulates into the buttocks. It is here that grace sits and rides a woman's body.

I watch from my white throne and pity women, deplore the demented

judgment that drives them toward the braggart muscularity of the meso-
morph and the prosperous complacence of the endomorph when it is we
ectomorphs who pack in our scrawny sinews and exacerbated nerves the
most intense gift, the most generous shelter, of love. To desire a woman is to
desire to save her. Anyone who has endured intercourse that was neither
predatory nor hurried knows how through it we descend, with a partner,
into the grotesque and delicate shadows that until then have remained
locked in the most guarded recess of our soul: into this harbor we bring her.
A vague and twisted terrain becomes inhabited; each shadow, touched by
the exploration, blooms into a flower of act. As if we are an island upon
which a woman, tossed by her laboring vanity and blind self-seeking, is
blown, and there finds security, until, an instant before the anticlimax, Nature with a smile thumps down her trump, and the island sinks beneath
the sea.

There is great truth in those motion pictures which are slandered as true
neither to the Bible nor to life. They are—written though they are by demons and drunks—true to both. We are all Solomons lusting for a Sheba's
salvation. The God-filled man is filled with a wilderness that cries to be
populated. The stony chambers need jewels, furs, tints of cloth and flesh,
even though, as in Samson's case, the temple comes tumbling. Women are
an alien race of pagans set down among us. Every seduction is a conversion.

Who has loved and not experienced that sense of rescue? It is not true
that our biological impulses are tricked out with ribands of chivalry; rather,
our chivalric impulses go clanking in encumbering biological armor. Eu-
nuchs love. Children love. I would love.

My chief exercise, as I sit above the crowds, is to lift the whole mass into
immortality. It is not a light task; the throng is so huge, and its members so
individually unworthy. No *memento mori* is so clinching as a photograph of
a vanished crowd. Cheering Roosevelt, celebrating the Armistice, there it is,
wearing its ten thousand straw hats and stiff collars, a fearless and wooden-
faced bustle of life: it is gone. A crowd dies in the street like a derelict; it
leaves no heir, no trace, no name. My own persistence beyond the last rim of
time is easy to imagine; indeed, the effort of imagination lies the other
way—to conceive of my ceasing. But when I study the vast tangle of humanity that blackens the beach as far as the sand stretches, absurdities
crowd in on me. Is it as maiden, matron, or crone that the females will be
eternalized? What will they do without children to watch and gossip to exchange? What of the thousand deaths of memory and bodily change we
endure—can each be redeemed at a final Adjustments Counter? The sheer
numbers involved make the mind scream. The race is no longer a tiny clan
of simian aristocrats lording it over an ocean of grass; mankind is a plague
racing like fire across the exhausted continents. This immense clot gathered

on the beach, a fraction of a fraction—can we not say that this breeding swarm is its own immortality and end the suspense? The beehive in a sense survives; and is each of us not proved to be a hive, a galaxy of cells each of whom is doubtless praying, from its pew in our thumbnail or esophagus, for personal resurrection? Indeed, to the cells themselves cancer may seem a revival of faith. No, in relation to other people oblivion is sensible and sanitary.

This sea of others exasperates and fatigues me most on Sunday mornings. I don't know why people no longer go to church—whether they have lost the ability to sing or the willingness to listen. From eight-thirty onward they crowd in from the parking lot, ants each carrying its crumb of baggage, until by noon, when the remote churches are releasing their gallant and gaily dressed minority, the sea itself is jammed with hollow heads and thrashing arms like a great bobbing backwash of rubbish. A transistor radio somewhere in the sand releases in a thin, apologetic gust the closing peal of a transcribed service. And right here, here at the very height of torpor and confusion, I slump, my eyes slit, and the blurred forms of Protestantism's errant herd seem gathered by the water's edge in impassioned poses of devotion. I seem to be lying dreaming in the infinite rock of space before Creation, and the actual scene I see is a vision of impossibility: a Paradise. For had we existed before the gesture that split the firmament, could we have conceived of our most obvious possession, our most platitudinous blessing, the moment, the single ever-present moment that we perpetually bring to our lips brimful?

So: be joyful. Be Joyful is my commandment. It is the message I read in your jiggle. Stretch your skins like pegged hides curing in the miracle of the sun's moment. Exult in your legs' scissoring, your waist's swivel. Romp; eat the froth; be children. I am here above you; I have given my youth that you may do this. I wait. The tides of time have treacherous undercurrents. You are borne continually toward the horizon. I have prepared myself; my muscles are instilled with everything that must be done. Someday my alertness will bear fruit; from near the horizon there will arise, delicious, translucent, like a green bell above the water, the call for help, the call, a call, it saddens me to confess, that I have yet to hear.

JOHN UPDIKE
1932–

Updike was a fine student who became a widely touted author early in life. From the Shillington, Pennsylvania, public schools, he went to Harvard,

earning a B.A. *summa cum laude* in 1954. A year at the Ruskin School of
Drawing and Fine Arts at Oxford University preceded a two-year stint
(1955–57) on the staff of the *New Yorker*, which has printed many of his
poems and stories since.

From the publication of his first book, *The Carpentered Hen and Other
Tame Creatures* (1958), Updike has displayed remarkable versatility as a
writer. The first book was verse; the second, *The Poorhouse Fair* (1959), was
a novel with great promise, a promise partly fulfilled in *Rabbit Run* (1961), a
story Updike proclaims is propelled by "the great urgencies of sex and
death." Subsequent novels, including *The Centaur* (1962), *Of the Farm*
(1965), *Couples* (1968), *Rabbit Redux* (1971), *A Month of Sundays* (1975), and
Bech Is Back (1983), have enjoyed popularity and critical success.

His verse, contained in such volumes as *Telephone Poles* (1963), *Bath After
Sailing* (1968), *Midpoint and Other Poems* (1969), *Seventy Poems* (1972), *Six
Poems* (1973), and *The Dance of the Solids* (1964), utilizes clear, startling
imagery.

The short stories are his forte, however. From 1959 to 1973 he published
seven collections, among which are numbered *Pigeon Feathers and Other
Stories* (1962) and *The Music School* (1967). His stories use his characteris-
tically striking imagery and achieve a sense of importance absent from his
novels.

"The Lifeguard," one of Updike's most celebrated stories, was first published in *The New Yorker* and then collected in *Pigeon Feathers* (1962).

Sea Lore and Legend

PART OF THE LURE of the sea is expressed in the lore of the sea, that body of learning, wisdom, and superstition passed from one generation of seamen to the next without ever finding its way into a textbook. Sea lore does not give us knowledge of the scientific sort; it is too eclectic, too eccentric, often too "wrong" for that. But in the hands of a good storyteller, legends of ghost ships, treasure hunts, and unspeakable horrors do more than just put the listener—or reader—on the edge of his seat: they draw the reader in with an almost mythological force distilled from decades, even centuries, of experience on the sea.

"The Ambitious Jimmy Hicks," a John Masefield yarn hung on three half hitches, is as pure a tale of sea lore as there is. Mark Twain's "About All Kinds of Ships" might have been a prosaic period piece comparing the turn-of-the-century liner with its primitive predecessors, but the author transforms it into a rollicking tour of vessels throughout the ages, complete with a review of centuries of sea lore.

Legends are represented by two kinds of stories, the tall tale and the tale of supernatural occurrences. Lord Dunsany's "A Story of Land and Sea" is a tall tale. Chased by vessels from three nations, Captain Shard and his private band in the *Desperate Lurch* make good their escape and redefine the meaning of "ship of the desert" in the process. It is a story of exaggeration and high good humor.

The second type, the legends of terror and the supernatural, are more fully represented in this volume. John Masefield pictures the Devil and Davy Jones dicing for the souls of seamen in "Davy Jones's Gift," while in "The Roll Call of the Reef" Arthur Quiller-Couch tells the chilling story of a shipwreck and a ghostly muster. Frank Norris resurrects the dead in "The Ship That Saw a Ghost," but the story is more than the recounting of a terrifying event. What happens to the ship that encounters and is deterred by a two-hundred-year-old ghost ship?

A ship on an illegal search for oysters is detained by Malay authorities and hauled to a long anchorage, but the ship and her crew manage to wreak vengeance on their captors. Rudyard Kipling's "The Devil and the Deep Sea" is a story of cunning, action, and supernatural irony.

Odysseus had his mariners stuff their ears with wax and lash him to a mast so he could hear the enticing voices of the Sirens without being lured to his destruction on their dangerous rocks. E. M. Forster makes the legend live again in "The Story of the Siren," about a modern boy seduced by the voices of destruction; and in Anatole France's "The Ocean Christ" a wooden figure of the crucified Christ bereft of His cross rides the waves and miraculously brings God's blessing to a bereaved seaside people.

About All Kinds of Ships

BY MARK TWAIN

The Modern Steamer and the Obsolete Steamer

WE ARE VICTIMS of one common superstition—the superstition that we real-ize the changes that are daily taking place in the world because we read about them and know what they are. I should not have supposed that the modern ship could be a surprise to me, but it is. It seems to be as much of a surprise to me as it could have been if I had never read anything about it. I walk about this great vessel, the *Havel*, as she plows her way through the Atlantic, and every detail that comes under my eye brings up the miniature counterpart of it as it existed in the little ships I crossed the ocean in four-teen, seventeen, eighteen, and twenty years ago.

In the *Havel* one can be in several respects more comfortable than he can be in the best hotels on the continent of Europe. For instance, she has several bathrooms, and they are as convenient and as nicely equipped as the bath-rooms in a fine private house in America; whereas in the hotels of the conti-nent one bathroom is considered sufficient, and it is generally shabby and located in some out-of-the-way corner of the house; moreover, you need to give notice so long beforehand that you get over wanting a bath by the time you get it. In the hotels there are a good many different kinds of noises, and they spoil sleep; in my room in the ship I hear no sounds. In the hotels they usually shut off the electric light at midnight; in the ship one may burn it in one's room all night.

In the steamer *Batavia*, twenty years ago, one candle, set in the bulkhead between two staterooms, was there to light both rooms, but did not light either of them. It was extinguished at 11 at night, and so were all the saloon lamps except one or two, which were left burning to help the passenger see how to break his neck trying to get around in the dark. The passengers sat at table on long benches made of the hardest kind of wood; in the *Havel* one sits on a swivel chair with a cushioned back to it. In those old times the dinner bill of fare was always the same: a pint of some simple, homely soup or other, boiled codfish and potatoes, slab of boiled beef, stewed prunes for dessert—on Sundays "dog in a blanket," on Thursdays "plum duff." In the modern ship the *menu* is choice and elaborate, and is changed daily. In the old times dinner was a sad occasion; in our day a concealed orchestra enlivens it with charming music. In the old days the decks were always wet; in our day they are usually dry, for the promenade-deck is roofed over, and a sea seldom comes aboard. In a moderately disturbed sea, in the old days, a landsman could hardly keep his legs, but in such a sea in our day the decks are as level as a table. In the old days the inside of a ship was the plainest and barrenest thing, and the most dismal and uncomfortable that ingenuity could devise; the modern ship is a marvel of rich and costly decoration and sumptuous appointment, and is equipped with every comfort and convenience that money can buy. The old ships had no place of assembly but the dining-room, the new ones have several spacious and beautiful drawing-rooms. The old ships offered the passenger no chance to smoke except in the place that was called the "fiddle." It was a repulsive den made of rough boards (full of cracks) and its office was to protect the main hatch. It was grimy and dirty; there were no seats; the only light was a lamp of the rancid-oil-and-rag kind; the place was very cold, and never dry, for the seas broke in through the cracks every little while and drenched the cavern thoroughly. In the modern ship there are three or four large smoking-rooms, and they have card tables and cushioned sofas, and are heated by steam and lighted by electricity. There are few European hotels with such smoking-rooms.

The former ships were built of wood, and had two or three water-tight compartments in the hold with doors in them which were often left open, particularly when the ship was going to hit a rock. The modern leviathan is built of steel, and the water-tight bulkheads have no doors in them; they divide the ship into nine or ten water-tight compartments and endow her with as many lives as a cat. Their complete efficiency was established by the happy results following the memorable accident to the *City of Paris* a year or two ago.

One curious thing which is at once noticeable in the great modern ship is the absence of hubbub, clatter, rush of feet, roaring of orders. That is all gone by. The elaborate maneuvers necessary in working the vessel into her dock are conducted without sound; one sees nothing of the processes, hears no commands. A Sabbath stillness and solemnity reign, in place of the turmoil and racket of the earlier days. The modern ship has a spacious bridge fenced chin-high with sailcloth, and floored with wooden gratings; and this bridge, with its fenced fore-and-aft annexes, could accommodate a seated audience of a hundred and fifty men. There are three steering equipments, each competent if the others should break. From the bridge the ship is steered, and also handled. The handling is not done by shout or whistle, but by signalling with patent automatic gongs. There are three tell-tales, with plainly lettered dials—for steering, handling the engines, and for communicating orders to the invisible mates who are conducting the landing of the ship or casting off. The officer who is astern is out of sight and too far away to hear trumpet calls; but the gongs near him tell him to haul in, pay out, make fast, let go, and so on; he hears, but the passengers do not, and so the ship seems to land herself without human help.

This great bridge is thirty or forty feet above the water, but the sea climbs up there sometimes; so there is another bridge twelve or fifteen feet higher still, for use in these emergencies. The force of water is a strange thing. It slips between one's fingers like air, but upon occasion it acts like a solid body and will bend a thin iron rod. In the *Havel* it has splintered a heavy oaken rail into broom-straws instead of merely breaking it in two, as would have been the seemingly natural thing for it to do. At the time of the awful Johnstown disaster, according to the testimony of several witnesses, rocks were carried some distance on the surface of the stupendous torrent; and at St. Helena, many years ago, a vast sea wave carried a battery of cannon forty feet up a steep slope and deposited the guns there in a row. But the water has done a still stranger thing, and it is one which is credibly vouched for. A marlinspike is an implement about a foot long which tapers from its butt to the other extremity and ends in a sharp point. It is made of iron and is heavy. A wave came aboard a ship in a storm and raged aft, breast high, carrying a marlinspike point first with it, and with such lightning-like swiftness and force as to drive it three or four inches into a sailor's body and kill him.

In all ways the ocean greyhound of to-day is imposing and impressive to one who carries in his head no ship pictures of a recent date. In bulk she comes near to rivaling the Ark; yet this monstrous mass of steel is driven five hundred miles through the waves in twenty-four hours. I remember the brag run of a steamer which I traveled in once on the Pacific—it was two hundred and nine miles in twenty-four hours; a year or so later I was a passenger in the excursion tub *Quaker City*, and on one occasion in a level and glassy sea, it was claimed that she reeled off two hundred and eleven miles between noon and noon, but it was probably a campaign lie. That little steamer had seventy passengers, and a crew of forty men, and seemed a good deal of a beehive. But in this present ship we are living in a sort of solitude, these soft summer days, with sometimes a hundred passengers scattered about the spacious distances, and sometimes nobody in sight at all; yet, hidden somewhere in the vessel's bulk, there are (including crew) near eleven hundred people.

The stateliest lines in the literature of the sea are these:

"Britannia needs no bulwarks, no towers along the steep—
Her march is o'er the mountain waves, her home is on the deep!"

There it is. In those old times the little ships climbed over the waves and wallowed down into the trough on the other side; the giant ship of our day does not climb over the waves, but crushes her way through them. Her formidable weight and mass and impetus give her mastery over any but extraordinary storm waves.

The ingenuity of man! I mean in this passing generation. To-day I found in the chart-room a frame of removable wooden slats on the wall, and on the slats was painted uninforming information like this:

Trim-Tank,	Empty
Double-Bottom No. 1,	Full
Double-Bottom No. 2,	Full
Double-Bottom No. 3,	Full
Double-Bottom No. 4,	Full

While I was trying to think out what kind of a game this might be and how a stranger might best go to work to beat it, a sailor came in and pulled out the "Empty" end of the first slat and put it back with its reverse side to the front, marked "Full." He made some other change, I did not notice what. The slat-frame was soon explained. Its function was to indicate how the ballast in the ship was distributed. The striking thing was that the ballast was water. I did not know that a ship had ever been ballasted with water. I had merely read, some time or other, that such an experiment was to be tried. But that is the modern way; between the experimental trial of a new thing and its adoption, there is no wasted time, if the trial proves its value.

On the wall, near the slat-frame, there was an outline drawing of the ship, and this betrayed the fact that this vessel has twenty-two considerable lakes of water in her. These lakes are in her bottom; they are imprisoned between her real bottom and a false bottom. They are separated from each other, thwartships, by water-tight bulkheads, and separated down the middle by a bulkhead running from the bow four-fifths of the way to the stern. It is a chain of lakes four hundred feet long and from five to seven feet deep. Fourteen of the lakes contain fresh water brought from shore, and the aggregate weight of it is four hundred tons. The rest of the lakes contain salt water—six hundred and eighteen tons. Upwards of a thousand tons of water, altogether.

Think how handy this ballast is. The ship leaves port with the lakes all full. As she lightens forward through consumption of coal, she loses trim—her head rises, her stern sinks down. Then they spill one of the sternward lakes into the sea, and the trim is restored. This can be repeated right along as occasion may require. Also, a lake at one end of the ship can be moved to the other end by pipes and steam pumps. When the sailor changed the slat-frame to-day, he was posting a transference of that kind. The seas had been increasing, and the vessel's head needed more weighting, to keep it from rising on the waves instead of plowing through them; therefore, twenty-five tons of water had been transferred to the bow from a lake situated well towards the stern.

A water compartment is kept either full or empty. The body of water must be compact, so that it cannot slosh around. A shifting ballast would not do, of course.

The modern ship is full of beautiful ingenuities, but it seems to me that this one is the king. I would rather be the originator of that idea than of any of the others. Perhaps the trim of a ship was never perfectly ordered and preserved until now. A vessel out of trim will not steer, her speed is maimed, she strains and labors in the seas. Poor creature, for six thousand years she has had no comfort until these latest days. For six thousand years she swam through the best and cheapest ballast in the world, the only perfect ballast, but she couldn't tell her master and he had not the wit to find it out for himself. It is odd to reflect that there is nearly as much water inside of this ship as there is outside, and yet there is no danger.

Noah's Ark

The progress made in the great art of ship-building since Noah's time is quite noticeable. Also, the looseness of the navigation laws in the time of Noah is in quite striking contrast with the strictness of the navigation laws of our time. It would not be possible for Noah to do in our day what he was permitted to do in his own. Experience has taught us the necessity of being more particular, more conservative, more careful of human life. Noah would not be allowed to sail from Bremen in our day. The inspectors would come and examine the Ark, and make all sorts of objections. A person who knows Germany can imagine the scene and the conversation without difficulty and without missing a detail. The inspector would be in a beautiful military uniform; he would be respectful, dignified, kindly, the perfect gentleman, but steady as the north star to the last requirement of his duty. He would make Noah tell him where he was born, and how old he was, and what religious sect he belonged to, and the amount of his income, and the grade and position he claimed socially, and the name and style of his occupation, and how many wives and children he had, and how many servants, and the name, sex, and age of the whole of them; and if he hadn't a passport he would be courteously required to get one right away. Then he would take up the matter of the Ark:

"What is her length?"

"Six hundred feet."

"Depth?"

"Sixty-five."

"Beam?"

"Fifty or sixty."

"Built of—"

"Wood."

"What kind?"

"Shittim and gopher."

"Interior and exterior decorations?"

"Pitched within and without."

"Passengers?"

"Eight."

"Sex?"

"Half male, the others female."

"Ages?"

"From a hundred years up."

"Up to where?"

"Six hundred."

"Ah—going to Chicago; good idea, too. Surgeon's name?"

"We have no surgeon."

"Must provide a surgeon. Also an undertaker—particularly the undertaker. These people must not be left without the necessities of life at their age. Crew?"

"The same eight."

"The same eight?"

"The same eight."

"And half of them women?"

"Yes, sir."

"Have they ever served as seamen?"

"No, sir."

"Have the men?"

"No, sir."

"Have any of you ever been to sea?"

"No, sir."

"Where were you reared?"

"On a farm—all of us."

"This vessel requires a crew of eight hundred men, she not being a steamer. You must provide them. She must have four mates and nine cooks. Who is captain?"

"I am, sir."

"You must get a captain. Also a chambermaid. Also sick nurses for the old people. Who designed this vessel?"

"I did, sir."

"Is it your first attempt?"

"Yes, sir."

"I partly suspected it. Cargo?"

"Animals."

"Kinds?"

"All kinds."

"Wild, or tame?"

"Mainly wild."

"Foreign or domestic?"

"Mainly foreign."

"Principal wild ones?"

"Megatherium, elephant, rhinoceros, lion, tiger, wolf, snakes—all the wild things of all climes—two of each."

"Securely caged?"

"No, not caged."

"They must have iron cages. Who feeds and waters the menagerie?"

"We do."

"The old people?"

"Yes, sir."

"It is dangerous—for both. The animals must be cared for by a competent force. How many animals are there?"

"Big ones, seven thousand; big and little together, ninety-eight thousand."

"You must provide twelve hundred keepers. How is the vessel lighted?"

"By two windows."

"Where are they?"

"Up under the eaves."

"Two windows for a tunnel six hundred feet long and sixty-five feet deep? You must put in the electric light—a few arc lights and fifteen hundred incandescents. What do you do in case of leaks? How many pumps have you?"

"None, sir."

"You must provide pumps. How do you get water for the passengers and the animals?"

"We let down the buckets from the windows."

"It is inadequate. What is your motive power?"

"What is my which?"

"Motive power. What power do you use in driving the ship?"

"None."

"You must provide sails or steam. What is the nature of your steering apparatus?"

"We haven't any."

"Haven't you a rudder?"

"No, sir."

"How do you steer the vessel?"

"We don't."

"You must provide a rudder, and properly equip it. How many anchors have you?"

"None."

"You must provide six. One is not permitted to sail a vessel like this without that protection. How many life-boats have you?"

"None, sir."

"Provide twenty-five. How many life-preservers?"

"None."

"You will provide two thousand. How long are you expecting your voyage to last?"

"Eleven or twelve months."

"Eleven or twelve months. Pretty slow—but you will be in time for the Exposition. What is your ship sheathed with—copper?"

"Her hull is bare—not sheathed at all."

"Dear man, the wood-boring creatures of the sea would riddle her like a sieve and send her to the bottom in three months. She *cannot* be allowed to go away in this condition; she must be sheathed. Just a word more: Have you reflected that Chicago is an inland city and not reachable with a vessel like this?"

"Shecargo? What is Shecargo? I am not going to Shecargo."

"Indeed? Then may I ask what the animals are for?"

"Just to breed others from."

"Others? Is it possible that you haven't enough?"

"For the present needs of civilization, yes; but the rest are going to be drowned in a flood, and these are to renew the supply."

"A flood?"

"Yes, sir."

"Are you sure of that?"

"Perfectly sure. It is going to rain forty days and forty nights."

"Give yourself no concern about that, dear sir, it often does that here."

"Not this kind of rain. This is going to cover the mountain tops, and the earth will pass from sight."

"Privately—but of course not officially—I am sorry you revealed this, for it compels me to withdraw the option I gave you as to sails or steam. I must require you to use steam. Your ship cannot carry the hundredth part of an eleven-months water supply for the animals. You will have to have condensed water."

"But I tell you I am going to dip water from outside with buckets."

"It will not answer. Before the flood reaches the mountain tops the fresh waters will have joined the salt seas, and it will all be salt. You must put in steam and condense your water. I will now bid you good day, sir. Did I understand you to say that this was your very first attempt at ship building?"

"My very first, sir, I give you the honest truth. I built this Ark without having ever had the slightest training or experience or instruction in marine architecture."

"It is a remarkable work, sir, a most remarkable work. I consider that it contains more features that are new—absolutely new and unhackneyed— than are to be found in any other vessel that swims the seas."

"This compliment does me infinite honor, dear sir, infinite; and I shall cherish the memory of it while life shall last. Sir, I offer my duty and most grateful thanks. Adieu."

No, the German inspector would be limitlessly courteous to Noah, and would make him feel that he was among friends, but he wouldn't let him go to sea with that Ark.

Columbus's Craft

Between Noah's time and the time of Columbus naval architecture underwent some changes, and from being unspeakably bad was improved to a point which may be described as less unspeakably bad. I have read somewhere, some time or other, that one of Columbus's ships was a ninety-ton vessel. By comparing that ship with the ocean greyhounds of our time one is able to get down to a comprehension of how small that Spanish bark was, and how little fitted she would be to run opposition in the Atlantic passenger trade to-day. It would take seventy-four of her to match the tonnage of the *Havel* and carry the *Havel*'s trip. If I remember rightly, it took her ten weeks to make the passage. With our ideas this would now be considered an objectionable gait. She probably had a captain, a mate, and a crew consisting of four seamen and a boy. The crew of a modern greyhound numbers two hundred and fifty persons.

Columbus's ship being small and very old, we know that we may draw from these two facts several absolute certainties in the way of minor details which history has left unrecorded. For instance: being small, we know that she rolled and pitched and tumbled in any ordinary sea, and stood on her head or her tail, or lay down with her ear in the water, when storm seas ran high; also, that she was used to having billows plunge aboard and wash her decks from stem to stern; also, that the storm racks were on the table all the way over, and that nevertheless a man's soup was oftener landed in his lap than in his stomach; also, that the dining-saloon was about ten feet by seven, dark, airless, and suffocating with oil-stench; also, that there was only about one stateroom, the size of a grave, with a tier of two or three berths in it of the dimensions and comfortableness of coffins, and that when the light was out the darkness in there was so thick and real that you could bite into it and chew it like gum; also, that the only promenade was on the lofty poop-deck astern (for the ship was shaped like a high-quarter shoe)—a streak sixteen feet long by three feet wide, all the rest of the vessel being littered with ropes and flooded by the seas.

We know all these things to be true, from the mere fact that we know the vessel was small. As the vessel was old, certain other truths follow, as matters of course. For instance: she was full of rats; she was full of cockroaches; the heavy seas made her seams open and shut like your fingers, and she leaked like a basket; where leakage is, there also, of necessity, is bilgewater; and where bilgewater is, only the dead can enjoy life. This is on account of the smell. In the presence of bilgewater, Limburger cheese becomes odorless and ashamed.

From these absolutely sure data we can competently picture the daily life of the great discoverer. In the early morning he paid his devotions at the shrine of the Virgin. At eight bells he appeared on the poop-deck promenade. If the weather was chilly he came up clad from plumed helmet to spurred heel in magnificent plate armor inlaid with arabesques of gold, having previously warmed it at the galley fire. If the weather was warm he came up in the ordinary sailor toggery of the time—great slouch hat of blue velvet with a flowing brush of snowy ostrich plumes, fastened on with a flashing cluster of diamonds and emeralds; gold-embroidered doublet of green velvet with slashed sleeves exposing under-sleeves of crimson satin; deep collar and cuff ruffles of rich limp lace; trunk hose of pink velvet, with big knee-knots of brocaded yellow ribbon; pearl-tinted silk stockings, clocked and daintily embroidered; lemon-colored buskins of unborn kid, funnel-topped, and drooping low to expose the pretty stockings; deep gauntlets of finest white heretic skin, from the factory of the Holy Inquisition, formerly part of the person of a lady of rank; rapier with sheath crusted with jewels, and hanging from a broad baldric upholstered with rubies and sapphires.

He walked the promenade thoughtfully, he noted the aspects of the sky and the course of the wind; he kept an eye out for drifting vegetation and other signs of land; he jawed the man at the wheel for pastime; he got out an imitation egg and kept himself in practice on his old trick of making it stand on its end; now and then he hove a life-line below and fished up a sailor who was drowning on the quarter-deck; the rest of his watch he gaped and yawned and stretched, and said he wouldn't make the trip again to discover six Americas. For that was the kind of natural human person Columbus was when not posing for posterity.

At noon he took the sun and ascertained that the good ship had made three hundred yards in twenty-four hours, and this enabled him to win the pool. Anybody can win the pool when nobody but himself has the privilege of straightening out the ship's run and getting it right.

The Admiral has breakfasted alone, in state: bacon, beans, and gin; at noon he dines alone, in state: bacon, beans, and gin; at six he sups alone, in state: bacon, beans, and gin; at eleven P. M. he takes a night relish alone, in state: bacon, beans, and gin. At none of these orgies is there any music; the ship orchestra is modern. After his final meal he returned thanks for his many blessings, a little overrating their value, perhaps, and then he laid off his silken splendors or his gilded hardware, and turned in, in his little coffin-bunk, and blew out his flickering stencher and began to refresh his lungs with inverted sighs freighted with the rich odors of rancid oil and bilgewater. The sighs returned as snores, and then the rats and the cockroaches swarmed out in brigades and divisions and army corps and had a circus all over him. Such was the daily life of the great discoverer in his marine basket during several historic weeks; and the difference between his ship and his comforts and ours is visible almost at a glance.

When he returned, the King of Spain, marveling, said—as history records:

"This ship seems to be leaky. Did she leak badly?"

"You shall judge for yourself, sire. I pumped the Atlantic Ocean through her sixteen times on the passage."

This is General Horace Porter's account. Other authorities say fifteen.

It can be shown that the differences between that ship and the one I am writing these historical contributions in are in several respects remarkable. Take the matter of decoration, for instance. I have been looking around again, yesterday and to-day, and have noted several details which I conceive to have been absent from Columbus's ship, or at least slurred over and not elaborated and perfected. I observe stateroom doors three inches thick, of solid oak and polished. I note companion-way vestibules with walls, doors, and ceilings paneled in polished hardwoods, some light, some dark, all dainty and delicate joiner-work, and yet every joint compact and tight; with beautiful pictures inserted, composed of blue tiles—some of the pictures containing as many as sixty tiles—and the joinings of those tiles perfect. These are daring experiments. One would have said that the first time the ship went straining and laboring through a storm-tumbled sea those tiles would gape apart and drop out. That they have not done so is evidence that the joiner's art has advanced a good deal since the days when ships were so shackly that when a giant sea gave them a wrench the doors came unbolted. I find the walls of the dining-saloon upholstered with mellow pictures wrought in tapestry and the ceiling aglow with pictures done in oil. In other places of assembly I find great panels filled with embossed Spanish leather, the figures rich with gilding and bronze. Everywhere I find sumptuous

masses of color—color, color, color—color all about, color of every shade
and tint and variety; and, as a result, the ship is bright and cheery to the eye,
and this cheeriness invades one's spirit and contents it. To fully appreciate
the force and spiritual value of this radiant and opulent dream of color, one
must stand outside at night in the pitch dark and the rain, and look in
through a port, and observe it in the lavish splendor of the electric lights.
The old-time ships were dull, plain, graceless, gloomy, and horribly depressing. They compelled the blues; one could not escape the blues in them.
The modern idea is right: to surround the passenger with conveniences,
luxuries, and abundance of inspiriting color. As a result, the ship is the
pleasantest place one can be in, except, perhaps, one's home.

A Vanished Sentiment

One thing is gone, to return no more forever—the romance of the sea. Soft
sentimentality about the sea has retired from the activities of this life, and is
but a memory of the past, already remote and much faded. But within the
recollection of men still living, it was in the breast of every individual; and
the further any individual lived from salt water the more of it he kept in
stock. It was as pervasive, as universal, as the atmosphere itself. The mere
mention of the sea, the romantic sea, would make any company of people
sentimental and mawkish at once. The great majority of the songs that were
sung by the young people of the back settlements had the melancholy wanderer for subject and his mouthings about the sea for refrain. Picnic parties
paddling down a creek in a canoe when the twilight shadows were gathering always sang:

Homeward bound, homeward bound
From a foreign shore;

and this was also a favorite in the West with the passengers on sternwheel
steamboats. There was another:

My boat is by the shore
    And my bark is on the sea,
But before I go, Tom Moore,
    Here's a double health to thee.

And this one, also:

O pilot, 'tis a fearful night,
There's danger on the deep.

And this:

A life on the ocean wave
    And a home on the rolling deep,

Where the scattered waters rave
  And the winds their revels keep!

And this:

A wet sheet and a flowing sea,
  And a wind that follows fair.

And this:

My foot is on my gallant deck,
  Once more the rover is free!

And the "Larboard Watch"—the person referred to below is at the mast-head, or somewhere up there:

Oh, who can tell what joy he feels,
As o'er the foam his vessel reels,
And his tired eyelids slumb'ring fall,
He rouses at the welcome call
    Of "Larboard watch—ahoy!"

Yes, and there was forever and always some jackass-voiced person braying out:

Rocked in the cradle of the deep,
I lay me down in peace to sleep!

Other favorites had these suggestive titles: "The Storm at Sea;" "The Bird at Sea;" "The Sailor Boy's Dream;" "The Captive Pirate's Lament;" "We are far from Home on the Stormy Main"—and so on, and so on, the list is endless. Everybody on a farm lived chiefly amid the dangers of the deep in those days, in fancy.

But all that is gone now. Not a vestige of it is left. The iron-clad, with her unsentimental aspect and frigid attention to business, banished romance from the war marine, and the unsentimental steamer has banished it from the commercial marine. The dangers and uncertainties which made sea life romantic have disappeared and carried the poetic element along with them. In our day the passengers never sing sea-songs on board a ship, and the band never plays them. Pathetic songs about the wanderer in strange lands far from home, once so popular and contributing such fire and color to the imagination by reason of the rarity of that kind of wanderer, have lost their charm and fallen silent, because everybody is a wanderer in the far lands now, and the interest in that detail is dead. Nobody is worried about the wanderer; there are no perils of the sea for him, there are no uncertainties.

He is safer in the ship than he would probably be at home, for there he is always liable to have to attend some friend's funeral and stand over the grave in the sleet, bareheaded—and that means pneumonia for him, if he gets his deserts; and the uncertainties of his voyage are reduced to whether he will arrive on the other side in the appointed afternoon, or have to wait till morning.

The first ship I was ever in was a sailing vessel. She was twenty-eight days going from San Francisco to the Sandwich Islands. But the main reason for this particularly slow passage was, that she got becalmed and lay in one spot fourteen days in the center of the Pacific two thousand miles from land. I hear no sea-songs in this present vessel, but I heard the entire layout in that one. There were a dozen young people—they are pretty old now, I reckon—and they used to group themselves on the stern, in the starlight or the moonlight, every evening, and sing sea-songs till after midnight, in that hot, silent, motionless calm. They had no sense of humor, and they always sang "Homeward Bound," without reflecting that that was practically ridiculous, since they were standing still and not proceeding in any direction at all; and they often followed that song with " 'Are we almost there, are we almost there,' said the dying girl as she drew near home?"

It was a very pleasant company of young people, and I wonder where they are now. Gone, oh, none knows whither; and the bloom and grace and beauty of their youth, where is that? Among them was a liar; all tried to reform him, but none could do it. And so, gradually, he was left to himself; none of us would associate with him. Many a time since I have seen in fancy that forsaken figure, leaning forlorn against the taffrail, and have reflected that perhaps if we had tried harder, and been more patient, we might have won him from his fault and persuaded him to relinquish it. But it is hard to tell; with him the vice was extreme, and was probably incurable. I like to think—and, indeed, I do think—that I did the best that in me lay to lead him to higher and better ways.

There was a singular circumstance. The ship lay becalmed that entire fortnight in exactly the same spot. Then a handsome breeze came fanning over the sea, and we spread our white wings for flight. But the vessel did not budge. The sails bellied out, the gale strained at the ropes, but the vessel moved not a hair's breadth from her place. The captain was surprised. It was some hours before we found out what the cause of the detention was. It was barnacles. They collect very fast in that part of the Pacific. They had fastened themselves to the ship's bottom; then others had fastened themselves to the first bunch, others to these, and so on, down and down and down, and the last bunch had glued the column hard and fast to the bottom of the sea, which is five miles deep at that point. So the ship was simply become the handle of a walking cane five miles long—yes, and no more movable by wind and sail than a continent is. It was regarded by every one as remarkable.

Well, the next week—however, Sandy Hook is in sight.

MARK TWAIN
1835–1910

Samuel Langhorne Clemens was born in Florida, Missouri, attended school only briefly, and by age eighteen was doing itinerant newspaper work in various cities, including New York, Philadelphia, Washington, and Cincinnati. From 1856 to 1861 he was a riverboat pilot, the fine art of navigating on the Mississippi being taught to him by the legendary Horace Bixby. His pen name, Mark Twain, which means two fathoms deep, was a term used by leadsmen taking soundings on Mississippi steamers.

When the Civil War began he endured a brief enlistment in a volunteer unit, an experience later recounted in "The History of a Private Campaign that Failed," and made his way slowly but surely to California via Nevada, where he gave in to the craze for silver mining briefly.

Publication in the *Saturday Press* of a story, "The Notorious Jumping Frog of Calaveras County," brought him instant fame in 1865.

A trip to Europe and the Holy Land aboard the *Quaker City* was reported for the *Alta California*, and the reports were turned into a best-selling book about his experiences, *The Innocents Abroad* (1869).

He married Olivia Langdon in 1870 and planned to become editor of the Buffalo *Express*, but soon he moved to Hartford and was writing his first novel, *The Guilded Age* (1873), in collaboration with Charles Dudley Wagner. Other more important novels followed, notably *The Adventures of Tom Sawyer* (1876), *Adventures of Huckleberry Finn* (1885), and *A Connecticut Yankee at King Arthur's Court* (1889). Travel literature and lesser novels flowed from his pen, including *Life on the Mississippi* (1883), a nostalgic remembrance of steamboating days; *A Tramp Abroad* (1880); *Following the Equator* (1897); *The American Claimant* (1892); *The £1,000,000 Bank Note* (1893); *The Tragedy of Pudd'nhead Wilson* (1894); *Personal Recollections of Joan of Arc* (1896); *Tom Sawyer Abroad* (1894); and *Tom Sawyer, Detective* (1896).

Twain was not only a writer who was able to poke fun at American life; he was an entertainer as well, often taking to the lecture platform to delight audiences with his humor. He toured the country once with George Washington Cable, the two being billed as Twins of Genius.

The selection presented here comes from *The American Claimant and Other Stories and Sketches* (1892).

The Devil and the Deep Sea

BY RUDYARD KIPLING

All supplies very bad and dear, and there are no facilities for even the smallest repairs.—*Sailing Directions*.

HER NATIONALITY was British, but you will not find her house-flag in the list of our mercantile marine. She was a nine-hundred-ton, iron, schooner-rigged, screw cargo-boat, differing externally in no way from any other tramp of the sea. But it is with steamers as it is with men. There are those who will for a consideration sail extremely close to the wind; and, in the present state of a fallen world, such people and such steamers have their use. From the hour that the *Aglaia* first entered the Clyde—new, shiny, and innocent, with a quart of cheap champagne trickling down her cut-water—Fate and her owner, who was also her captain, decreed that she should deal with embarrassed crowned heads, fleeing Presidents, financiers of over-extended ability, women to whom change of air was imperative, and the lesser law-breaking Powers. Her career led her sometimes into the Admiralty Courts, where the sworn statements of her skipper filled his brethren with envy. The mariner cannot tell or act a lie in the face of the sea, or mislead a tempest; but, as lawyers have discovered, he makes up for chances withheld when he returns to shore, an affidavit in either hand.

The *Aglaia* figured with distinction in the great *Mackinaw* salvage-case. It was her first slip from virtue, and she learned how to change her name, but not her heart, and to run across the sea. As the *Guiding Light* she was very badly wanted in a South American port for the little matter of entering harbour at full speed, colliding with a coal-hulk and the State's only man-of-war, just as that man-of-war was going to coal. She put to sea without explanations, though three forts fired at her for half an hour. As the *Julia M'Gregor* she had been concerned in picking up from a raft certain gentlemen who should have stayed in Nouméa, but who preferred making themselves vastly unpleasant to authority in quite another quarter of the world; and as the *Shah-in-Shah* she had been overtaken on the high seas, indecently full of munitions of war, by the cruiser of an agitated Power at issue with its neighbour. That time she was very nearly sunk, and her riddled hull gave eminent lawyers of two countries great profit. After a season she reappeared as the *Martin Hunt*, painted a dull slate-colour, with pure saffron funnel, and boats of robin's-egg blue, engaging in the Odessa trade till she was invited (and the invitation could not well be disregarded) to keep away from Black Sea ports altogether.

She had ridden through many waves of depression. Freights might drop out of sight, Seamen's Unions throw spanners and nuts at certificated masters, or stevedores combine till cargo perished on the dock-head; but the boat of many names came and went, busy, alert, and inconspicuous always. Her skipper made no complaint of hard times, and port officers observed that her crew signed and signed again with the regularity of Atlantic liner boatswains. Her name she changed as occasion called; her well-paid crew never; and a large percentage of the profits of her voyages was spent with an open hand on her engine-room. She never troubled the underwriters, and very seldom stopped to talk with a signal-station, for her business was urgent and private.

But an end came to her tradings, and she perished in this manner. Deep peace brooded over Europe, Asia, Africa, America, Australasia, and Polynesia. The Powers dealt together more or less honestly; banks paid their depositors to the hour; diamonds of price came safely to the hands of their owners; Republics rested content with their Dictators; diplomats found no one whose presence in the least incommoded them; monarchs lived openly with their lawfully wedded wives. It was as though the whole earth had put on its best Sunday bib and tucker; and business was very bad for the *Martin Hunt*. The great, virtuous calm engulfed her, slate sides, yellow funnel, and all, but cast up in another hemisphere the steam whaler *Haliotis*, black and rusty, with a manure-coloured funnel, a litter of dingy white boats, and an enormous stove, or furnace, for boiling blubber on her forward well-deck. There could be no doubt that her trip was successful, for she lay at several ports not too well known, and the smoke of her trying-out insulted the beaches.

Anon she departed, at the speed of the average London four-wheeler, and entered a semi-inland sea, warm, still, and blue, which is, perhaps, the most strictly preserved water in the world. There she stayed for a certain time, and the great stars of those mild skies beheld her playing puss-in-the-corner among islands where whales are never found. All that while she smelt abominably, and the smell, though fishy, was not whalesome. One evening calamity descended upon her from the island of Pygang-Watai, and she fled, while her crew jeered at a fat black-and-brown gunboat puffing far behind. They knew to the last revolution the capacity of every boat, on those seas, that they were anxious to avoid. A British ship with a good conscience does not, as a rule, flee from the man-of-war of a foreign Power, and it is also considered a breach of etiquette to stop and search British ships at sea.

These things the skipper of the *Haliotis* did not pause to prove, but held on at an inspiriting eleven knots an hour till nightfall. One thing only he overlooked.

The Power that kept an expensive steam-patrol moving up and down those waters (they had dodged the two regular ships of the station with an ease that bred contempt) had newly brought up a third and a fourteen-knot boat with a clean bottom to help the work; and that was why the *Haliotis*, driving hard from the east to the west, found herself at daylight in such a position that she could not help seeing an arrangement of four flags, a mile and a half behind, which read: "Heave to, or take the consequences!"

She had her choice, and she took it. The end came when, presuming on her lighter draught, she tried to draw away northward over a friendly shoal. The shell that arrived by way of the Chief Engineer's cabin was some five inches in diameter, with a practice, not a bursting, charge. It had been intended to cross her bows, and that was why it knocked the framed portrait of the Chief Engineer's wife—and she was a very pretty girl—on to the floor, splintered his wash-hand stand, crossed the alleyway into the engine-room, and striking on a grating, dropped directly in front of the forward engine, where it burst, neatly fracturing both the bolts that held the connecting-rod to the forward crank.

What follows is worth consideration. The forward engine had no more work to do. Its released piston-rod, therefore, drove up fiercely, with nothing to check it, and started most of the nuts of the cylinder-cover. It came down again, the full weight of the steam behind it, and the foot of the disconnected connecting-rod, useless as the leg of a man with a sprained ankle, flung out to the right and struck the starboard, or right-hand, cast-iron supporting-column of the forward engine, cracking it clean through about six inches above the base, and wedging the upper portion outwards three inches towards the ship's side. There the connecting-rod jammed. Meantime, the after-engine, being as yet unembarrassed, went on with its work, and in so doing brought round at its next revolution the crank of the forward engine, which smote the already jammed connecting-rod, bending it and therewith the piston-rod cross-head—the big cross-piece that slides up and down so smoothly.

The cross-head jammed sideways in the guides, and, in addition to putting further pressure on the already broken starboard supporting-column, cracked the port, or left-hand, supporting-column in two or three places. There being nothing more that could be made to move, the engines brought up, all standing, with a hiccup that seemed to lift the *Haliotis* a foot out of the water; and the engine-room staff, opening every steam outlet that they could find in the confusion, arrived on deck somewhat scalded, but calm. There was a sound below of things happening—a rushing, clicking, purring, grunting, rattling noise that did not last for more than a minute. It was the machinery adjusting itself, on the spur of the moment, to a hundred altered conditions. Mr. Wardrop, one foot on the upper grating, inclined his ear sideways, and groaned. You cannot stop engines working at twelve knots an hour in three seconds without disorganising them. The *Haliotis* slid forward in a cloud of steam, shrieking like a wounded horse. There was nothing more to do. The five-inch shell with a reduced charge had settled the situation. And when you are full, all three holds, of strictly preserved pearls; when you have cleaned out the Tanna Bank, the Sea-Horse Bank, and four other banks from one end to the other of the Amanala Sea—when you have ripped out the very heart of a rich Government monopoly so that five years will not repair your wrongdoings—you must smile and take what is in store. But the skipper reflected, as a launch put out from the man-of-war, that he had been bombarded on the high seas, with the British flag—several of them—picturesquely disposed above him, and tried to find comfort from the thought.

"Where," said the stolid naval lieutenant hoisting himself aboard, "where are those dam' pearls?"

They were there beyond evasion. No affidavit could do away with the fearful smell of decayed oysters, the diving-dresses, and the shell-littered hatches. They were there to the value of seventy thousand pounds, more or less; and every pound poached.

The man-of-war was annoyed; for she had used up many tons of coal, she had strained her tubes, and, worse than all, her officers and crew had been hurried. Every one on the *Haliotis* was arrested and rearrested several times, as each officer came aboard; then they were told by what they esteemed to be the equivalent of a midshipman that they were to consider themselves prisoners, and finally were put under arrest.

"It's not the least good," said the skipper, suavely. "You'd much better send us a tow—"

"Be still—you are arrest!" was the reply.

"Where the devil do you expect we are going to escape to? We're helpless. You've got to tow us into somewhere, and explain why you fired on us. Mr. Wardrop, we're helpless, aren't we?"

"Ruined from end to end," said the man of machinery. "If she rolls, the forward cylinder will come down and go through her bottom. Both columns are clean cut through. There's nothing to hold anything up."

The council of war clanked off to see if Mr. Wardrop's words were true. He warned them that it was as much as a man's life was worth to enter the engine-room, and they contented themselves with a distant inspection through the thinning steam. The *Haliotis* lifted to the long, easy swell, and the starboard supporting-column ground a trifle, as a man grits his teeth under the knife. The forward cylinder was depending on that unknown force men call the pertinacity of materials, which now and then balances that other heartbreaking power, the perversity of inanimate things.

"You see!" said Mr. Wardrop, hurrying them away. "The engines aren't worth their price as old iron."

"We tow," was the answer. "Afterwards we shall confiscate."

The man-of-war was short-handed, and did not see the necessity for putting a prize-crew aboard the *Haliotis*. So she sent one sublieutenant, whom the skipper kept very drunk, for he did not wish to make the tow too easy, and, moreover, he had an inconspicuous little rope hanging from the stern of his ship.

Then they began to tow at an average speed of four knots an hour. The *Haliotis* was very hard to move, and the gunnery-lieutenant, who had fired the five-inch shell, had leisure to think upon consequences. Mr. Wardrop was the busy man. He borrowed all the crew to shore up the cylinders with spars and blocks from the bottom and sides of the ship. It was a day's risky work; but anything was better than drowning at the end of a tow-rope; and if the forward cylinder had fallen, it would have made its way to the sea-bed, and taken the *Haliotis* after.

"Where are we going to, and how long will they tow us?" he asked of the skipper.

"God knows! and this prize-lieutenant's drunk. What do you think you can do?"

"There's just the bare chance," Mr. Wardrop whispered, though no one was within hearing—"there's just the bare chance o' repairin' her, if a man knew how. They've twisted the very guts out of her, bringing her up with that jerk; but I'm saying that, with time and patience, there's just the chance o' making steam yet. *We* could do it."

The skipper's eye brightened. "Do you mean," he began, "that she is any good?"

"Oh, no," said Mr. Wardrop. "She'll need three thousand pounds in repairs, at the lowest, if she's to take the sea again, an' that apart from any injury to her structure. She's like a man fallen down five pair o' stairs. We can't tell for months what has happened; but we know she'll never be good again without a new inside. Ye should see the condenser-tubes an' the steam connections to the donkey, for two things only. I'm not afraid of them repairin' her. I'm afraid of them stealin' things."

"They've fired on us. They'll have to explain that."

"Our reputation's not good enough to ask for explanations. Let's take what we have and be thankful. Ye would not have consuls rememberin' the *Guidin' Light*, an' the *Shah-in-Shah*, an' the *Aglaia*, at this most alarmin' crisis. We've been no better than pirates these ten years. Under Providence we're no worse than thieves now. We've much to be thankful for—if we e'er get back to her."

"Make it your own way, then," said the skipper. "If there's the least chance—"

"I'll leave none," said Mr. Wardrop—"none that they'll dare to take. Keep her heavy on the tow, for we need time."

The skipper never interfered with the affairs of the engine-room, and Mr. Wardrop—an artist in his profession—turned to and composed a work terrible and forbidding. His background was the dark-grained sides of the engine-room; his material the metals of power and strength, helped out with spars, baulks, and ropes. The man-of-war towed sullenly and viciously. The *Haliotis* behind her hummed like a hive before swarming. With extra and totally unneeded spars her crew blocked up the space round the forward engine till it resembled a statue in its scaffolding, and the butts of the shores interfered with every view that a dispassionate eye might wish to take. And that the dispassionate mind might be swiftly shaken out of its calm, the well-sunk bolts of the shores were wrapped round untidily with loose ends of ropes, giving a studied effect of most dangerous insecurity. Next, Mr. Wardrop took up a collection from the after-engine, which, as you will remember, had not been affected in the general wreck. The cylinder escape-valve he abolished with a flogging-hammer. It is difficult in far-off ports to come by such valves, unless, like Mr. Wardrop, you keep duplicates in store. At the same time men took off the nuts of two of the great holding-down bolts that serve to keep the engines in place on their solid bed. An engine violently arrested in mid-career may easily jerk off the nut of a holding-down bolt, and this accident looked very natural.

Passing along the tunnel, he removed several shaft coupling-bolts and -nuts, scattering other and ancient pieces of iron underfoot. Cylinder-bolts he cut off to the number of six from the after-engine cylinder, so that it might match its neighbour, and stuffed the bilge- and feed-pumps with cotton-waste. Then he made up a neat bundle of the various odds and ends that he had gathered from the engines—little things like nuts and valve-spindles, all carefully tallowed—and retired with them under the floor of the engine-room, where he sighed, being fat, as he passed from manhole to manhole of the double bottom, and in a fairly dry submarine compartment hid them. Any engineer, particularly in an unfriendly port, has a right to keep his spare stores where he chooses; and the foot of one of the cylinder shores blocked all entrance into the regular store-room, even if that had not been already closed with steel wedges. In conclusion, he disconnected the after-engine, laid piston and connecting-rod, carefully tallowed, where it would be most inconvenient to the casual visitor, took out three of the eight collars of the thrust-block, hid them where only he could find them again, filled the boilers by hand, wedged the sliding doors of the coal-bunkers, and rested from his labours. The engine-room was a cemetery, and it did not need the contents of the ash-lift through the skylight to make it any worse.

He invited the skipper to look at the completed work.

"Saw ye ever such a forsaken wreck as that?" said he, proudly. "It almost frights *me* to go under those shores. Now, what d' you think they'll do to us?"

"Wait till we see," said the skipper. "It'll be bad enough when it comes."

He was not wrong. The pleasant days of towing ended all too soon, though the *Haliotis* trailed behind her a heavily weighted jib stayed out into the shape of a pocket; and Mr. Wardrop was no longer an artist of imagination, but one of seven-and-twenty prisoners in a prison full of insects. The man-of-war had towed them to the nearest port, not to the headquarters of the colony, and when Mr. Wardrop saw the dismal little harbour, with its ragged line of Chinese junks, its one crazy tug, and the boat-building shed that, under the charge of a philosophical Malay, represented a dockyard, he sighed and shook his head.

"I did well," he said. "This is the habitation o' wreckers an' thieves. We're at the uttermost ends of the earth. Think you they'll ever know in England?"

"Doesn't look like it," said the skipper.

They were marched ashore with what they stood up in, under a generous escort, and were judged according to the customs of the country, which, though excellent, are a little out of date. There were the pearls; there were the poachers; and there sat a small but hot Governor. He consulted for a while, and then things began to move with speed, for he did not wish to keep a hungry crew at large on the beach, and the man-of-war had gone up the coast. With a wave of his hand—a stroke of the pen was not necessary—he consigned them to the *blakgang-tana*, the back-country, and the hand of the Law removed them from his sight and the knowledge of men. They were marched into the palms, and the back-country swallowed them up—all the crew of the *Haliotis*.

Deep peace continued to brood over Europe, Asia, Africa, America, Australasia, and Polynesia.

It was the firing that did it. They should have kept their counsel; but when a few thousand foreigners are bursting with joy over the fact that a ship under the British flag has been fired at on the high seas, news travels quickly; and when it came out that the pearl-stealing crew had not been allowed access to their consul (there was no consul within a few hundred miles of that lonely port) even the friendliest of Powers has a right to ask questions. The great heart of the British public was beating furiously on account of the performance of a notorious race-horse, and had not a throb to waste on distant accidents; but somewhere deep in the hull of the ship of State there is machinery which more or less accurately takes charge of foreign affairs. That machinery began to revolve, and who so shocked and surprised as the Power that had captured the *Haliotis?* It explained that colonial governors and far-away men-of-war were difficult to control, and promised that it would most certainly make an example both of the Governor and the vessel. As for the crew reported to be pressed into military service in tropical climes, it would produce them as soon as possible, and it would apologise, if necessary. Now, no apologies were needed. When one nation apologises to another, millions of amateurs who have no earthly concern with the difficulty hurl themselves into the strife and embarrass the trained specialist. It was requested that the crew be found, if they were still alive—they had been eight months beyond knowledge—and it was promised that all would be forgotten.

The little Governor of the little port was pleased with himself. Seven-and-twenty white men made a very compact force to throw away on a war that had neither beginning nor end—a jungle-and-stockade fight that flickered and smouldered through the wet hot years in the hills a hundred miles away, and was the heritage of every wearied official. He had, he thought, deserved well of his country; and if only some one would buy the unhappy *Haliotis*, moored in the harbour below his verandah, his cup would be full. He looked at the neatly silvered lamps that he had taken from her cabins, and thought of much that might be turned to account. But his countrymen in that moist climate had no spirit. They would peep into the silent engine-room, and shake their heads. Even the men-of-war would not tow her further up the coast, where the Governor believed that she could be repaired. She was a bad bargain; but her cabin carpets were undeniably beautiful, and his wife approved of her mirrors.

Three hours later cables were bursting round him like shells, for, though he knew it not, he was being offered as a sacrifice by the nether to the upper millstone, and his superiors had no regard for his feelings. He had, said the cables, grossly exceeded his power, and failed to report on events. He would, therefore—at this he cast himself back in his hammock—produce the crew of the *Haliotis*. He would send for them, and, if that failed, he would put his dignity on a pony and fetch them himself. He had no conceivable right to make pearl-poachers serve in any war. He would be held responsible.

Next morning the cables wished to know whether he had found the crew of the *Haliotis*. They were to be found, freed and fed—he was to feed them—till such time as they could be sent to the nearest English port in a man-of-war. If you abuse a man long enough in great words flashed over the sea-beds, things happen. The Governor sent inland swiftly for his prisoners, who were also soldiers; and never was a militia regiment more anxious to reduce its strength. No power short of death could make these mad men wear the uniform of their service. They would not fight, except with their fellows, and it was for that reason the regiment had not gone to war, but stayed in a stockade, reasoning with the new troops. The autumn campaign had been a fiasco, but here were the Englishmen. All the regiment marched back to guard them, and the hairy enemy, armed with blow-pipes, rejoiced in the forest. Five of the crew had died, but there lined up on the Governor's verandah two-and-twenty men marked about the legs with the scars of leech-bites. A few of them wore fringes that had once been trousers; the others used loin-cloths of gay patterns; and they existed beautifully but simply in the Governor's verandah, and when he came out they sang at him. When you have lost seventy thousand pounds' worth of pearls, your pay, your ship, and all your clothes, and have lived in bondage for five months beyond the faintest pretences of civilisation, you know what true independence means, for you become the happiest of created things—natural man.

The Governor told the crew that they were evil, and they asked for food. When he saw how they ate, and when he remembered that none of the pearl patrol-boats were expected for two months, he sighed. But the crew of the *Haliotis* lay down in the verandah, and said that they were pensioners of the Governor's bounty. A grey-bearded man, fat and bald-headed, his one garment a green-and-yellow loin-cloth, saw the *Haliotis* in the harbor, and bellowed for joy. The men crowded to the verandah-rail, kicking aside the long cane chairs. They pointed, gesticulated, and argued freely, without shame. The militia regiment sat down in the Governor's garden. The Governor retired to his hammock—it was as easy to be killed lying as standing—and his women squeaked from the shuttered rooms.

"She sold?" said the grey-bearded man, pointing to the *Haliotis*. He was Mr. Wardrop.

"No good," said the Governor, shaking his head. "No one come buy."

"He's taken my lamps, though," said the skipper. He wore one leg of a pair of trousers, and his eye wandered along the verandah. The Governor quailed. There were cuddy camp-stools and the skipper's writing-table in plain sight.

"They've cleaned her out, o' course," said Mr. Wardrop. "They would. We'll go aboard and take an inventory. See!" He waved his hands over the harbour. "We—live—there—now. Sorry?"

The Governor smiled a smile of relief.

"He's glad of that," said one of the crew, reflectively. "I shouldn't wonder."

They flocked down to the harbour-front, the militia regiment clattering behind, and embarked themselves in what they found—it happened to be the Governor's boat. Then they disappeared over the bulwarks of the *Haliotis*, and the Governor prayed that they might find occupation inside.

Mr. Wardrop's first bound took him to the engine-room; and when the others were patting the well-remembered decks, they heard him giving God thanks that things were as he had left them. The wrecked engines stood over his head untouched; no inexpert hand had meddled with his shores; the steel wedges of the store-room were rusted home; and, best of all, the hundred and sixty tons of good Australian coal in the bunkers had not diminished.

"I don't understand it," said Mr. Wardrop. "Any Malay knows the use o' copper. They ought to have cut away the pipes. And with Chinese junks coming here, too. It's a special interposition o' Providence."

"You think so," said the skipper, from above. "There's only been one thief here, and he's cleaned her out of all *my* things, anyhow."

Here the skipper spoke less than the truth, for under the planking of his cabin, only to be reached by a chisel, lay a little money which never drew any interest—his sheet-anchor to windward. It was all in clean sovereigns that pass current the world over, and might have amounted to more than a hundred pounds.

"He's left me alone. Let's thank God," repeated Mr. Wardrop.

"He's taken everything else; look!"

The *Haliotis*, except as to her engine-room, had been systematically and scientifically gutted from one end to the other, and there was strong evidence that an unclean guard had camped in the skipper's cabin to regulate that plunder. She lacked glass, plate, crockery, cutlery, mattresses, cuddy carpets and chairs, all boats, and her copper ventilators. These things had been removed, with her sails and as much of the wire rigging as would not imperil the safety of the masts.

"He must have sold those," said the skipper. "The other things are in his house, I suppose."

Every fitting that could be pried or screwed out was gone. Port, starboard, and masthead lights; teak gratings; sliding sashes of the deck-house; the captain's chest of drawers, with charts and chart-table; photographs, brackets, and looking-glasses; cabin doors; rubber cuddy mats; hatch-irons; half the funnel-stays; cork fenders; carpenter's grindstone and tool-chest; holystones, swabs, squeegees; all cabin and pantry lamps; galley-fittings *en bloc*; flags and flag-locker; clocks, chronometers; the forward compass and the ship's bell and belfry, were among the missing.

There were great scarred marks on the deck-planking over which the cargo-derricks had been hauled. One must have fallen by the way, for the bulwark-rails were smashed and bent and the side-plates bruised.

"It's the Governor," said the skipper. "He's been selling her on the instalment plan."

"Let's go up with spanners and shovels, and kill 'em all," shouted the crew. "Let's drown him, and keep the woman!"

"Then we'll be shot by that black-and-tan regiment—*our* regiment. What's the trouble ashore? They've camped our regiment on the beach."

"We're cut off, that's all. Go and see what they want," said Mr. Wardrop. "You've the trousers."

In his simple way the Governor was a strategist. He did not desire that the crew of the *Haliotis* should come ashore again, either singly or in detachments, and he proposed to turn their steamer into a convict-hulk. They would wait—he explained this from the quay to the skipper in the barge—and they would continue to wait till the man-of-war came along, exactly where they were. If one of them set foot ashore, the entire regiment would open fire, and he would not scruple to use the two cannon of the town. Meantime food would be sent daily in a boat under an armed escort. The skipper, bare to the waist, and rowing, could only grind his teeth; and the Governor improved the occasion, and revenged himself for the bitter words in the cables, by saying what he thought of the morals and manners of the crew. The barge returned to the *Haliotis* in silence, and the skipper climbed aboard, white on the cheekbones and blue about the nostrils.

"I knew it," said Mr. Wardrop; "and they won't give us good food, either. We shall have bananas morning, noon, and night, an' a man can't work on fruit. *We* know that."

Then the skipper cursed Mr. Wardrop for importing frivolous side-issues into the conversation; and the crew cursed one another, and the *Haliotis*, the voyage, and all that they knew or could bring to mind. They sat down in silence on the empty decks, and their eyes burned in their heads. The green harbour water chuckled at them overside. They looked at the palm-fringed hills inland, at the white houses above the harbour road, at the single tier of native craft by the quay, at the stolid soldiery sitting round the two cannon, and, last of all, at the blue bar of the horizon. Mr. Wardrop was buried in thought, and scratched imaginary lines with his untrimmed finger-nails on the planking.

"I make no promise," he said, at last, "for I can't say what may or may not have happened to them. But here's the ship, and here's us."

There was a little scornful laughter at this, and Mr. Wardrop knitted his brows. He recalled that in the days when he wore trousers he had been Chief Engineer of the *Haliotis*.

"Harland, Mackesy, Noble, Hay, Naughton, Fink, O'Hara, Trumbull."

"Here, sir!" The instinct of obedience waked to answer the roll-call of the engine-room.

"Below!"

They rose and went.

"Captain, I'll trouble you for the rest of the men as I want them. We'll get my stores out, and clear away the stores we don't need, and then we'll patch her up. *My* men will remember that they're in the *Haliotis*,—under *me*."

He went into the engine-room, and the others stared. They were used to the accidents of the sea, but this was beyond their experience. None who had seen the engine-room believed that anything short of new engines from end to end could stir the *Haliotis* from her moorings.

The engine-room stores were unearthed, and Mr. Wardrop's face, red with the filth of the bilges and the exertion of travelling on his stomach, lit with joy. The spare gear of the *Haliotis* had been unusually complete, and two-and-twenty men, armed with screw-jacks, differential blocks, tackle, vices, and a forge or so, can look Kismet between the eyes without winking. The crew were ordered to replace the holding-down and shaft-bearing bolts, and return the collars of the thrust-block. When they had finished, Mr. Wardrop delivered a lecture on repairing compound engines without the aid of the shops, and the men sat about on the cold machinery. The cross-head jammed in the guides leered at them drunkenly, but offered no help. They ran their fingers hopelessly into the cracks of the starboard supporting-column, and picked at the ends of the ropes round the shores, while Mr. Wardrop's voice rose and fell echoing, till the quick tropic night closed down over the engine-room skylight.

Next morning the work of reconstruction began.

It has been explained that the foot of the connecting-rod was forced against the foot of the starboard supporting-column, which it had cracked through and driven outward towards the ship's skin. To all appearance the job was more than hopeless, for rod and column seemed to have been welded into one. But herein Providence smiled on them for one moment to hearten them through the weary weeks ahead. The second engineer—more reckless than resourceful—struck at random with a cold chisel into the cast-iron of the column, and a greasy, grey flake of metal flew from under the imprisoned foot of the connecting-rod, while the rod itself fell away slowly, and brought up with a thunderous clang somewhere in the dark of the crank-pit. The guides-plates above were still jammed fast in the guides, but the first blow had been struck. They spent the rest of the day grooming the donkey-engine, which stood immediately forward of the engine-room hatch. Its tarpaulin, of course, had been stolen, and eight warm months had not improved the working parts. Further, the last dying hiccup of the

Haliotis seemed—or it might have been the Malay from the boat-house—to have lifted the thing bodily on its bolts, and set it down inaccurately as regarded its steam connections.

"If we only had one single cargo-derrick!" Mr. Wardrop sighed. "We can take the cylinder-cover off by hand, if we sweat; but to get the rod out o' the piston's not possible unless we use steam. Well, there'll be steam the morn, if there's nothing else. She'll fizzle!"

Next morning men from the shore saw the *Haliotis* through a cloud, for it was as though the deck smoked. Her crew were chasing steam through the shaken and leaky pipes to its work in the forward donkey-engine; and where oakum failed to plug a crack, they stripped off their loincloths for lapping, and swore, half-boiled and mother-naked. The donkey-engine worked—at a price—the price of constant attention and furious stoking— worked long enough to allow a wire-rope (it was made up of a funnel and a foremast-stay) to be led into the engine-room and made fast on the cylinder-cover of the forward engine. That rose easily enough, and was hauled through the skylight and on to the deck, many hands assisting the doubtful steam. Then came the tug of war, for it was necessary to get to the piston and the jammed piston-rod. They removed two of the piston junk-ring studs, screwed in two strong iron eye-bolts by way of handles, doubled the wire-rope, and set half a dozen men to smite with an extemporised battering-ram at the end of the piston-rod, where it peered through the piston, while the donkey-engine hauled upwards on the piston itself. After four hours of this furious work, the piston-rod suddenly slipped, and the piston rose with a jerk, knocking one or two men over into the engine-room. But when Mr. Wardrop declared that the piston had not split, they cheered, and thought nothing of their wounds; and the donkey-engine was hastily stopped; its boiler was nothing to tamper with.

And day by day their supplies reached them by boat. The skipper humbled himself once more before the Governor, and as a concession had leave to get drinking-water from the Malay boat-builder on the quay. It was not good drinking-water, but the Malay was anxious to supply anything in his power, if he were paid for it.

Now when the jaws of the forward engine stood, as it were, stripped and empty, they began to wedge up the shores of the cylinder itself. That work alone filled the better part of three days—warm and sticky days, when the hands slipped and sweat ran into the eyes. When the last wedge was hammered home there was no longer an ounce of weight on the supporting-columns; and Mr. Wardrop rummaged the ship for boiler-plate three-quarters of an inch thick, where he could find it. There was not much available, but what there was was more than beaten gold to him. In one desperate forenoon the entire crew, naked and lean, hauled back, more or less into place, the starboard supporting-column, which, as you remember, was cracked clean through. Mr. Wardrop found them asleep where they had finished the work, and gave them a day's rest, smiling upon them as a father while he drew chalk-marks about the cracks. They woke to new and more trying labour; for over each one of those cracks a plate of three-quarter inch boiler-iron was to be worked hot, the rivet-holes being drilled by hand. All that time they were fed on fruits, chiefly bananas, with some sago.

Those were the days when men swooned over the ratchet-drill and the hand-forge, and where they fell they had leave to lie unless their bodies were in the way of their fellows' feet. And so, patch upon patch, and a patch over all, the starboard supporting-column was clouted; but when they thought all was secure, Mr. Wardrop decreed that the noble patchwork would never support working engines; at the best, it could only hold the guide-bars approximately true. The dead-weight of the cylinders must be borne by vertical struts; and, therefore, a gang would repair to the bows, and take out, with files, the big bow-anchor davits, each of which was some three inches in diameter. They threw hot coals at Wardrop, and threatened to kill him, those who did not weep (they were ready to weep on the least provocation); but he hit them with iron bars heated at the end, and they limped forward, and the davits came with them when they returned. They slept sixteen hours on the strength of it, and in three days two struts were in place, bolted from the foot of the starboard supporting-column to the under side of the cylinder. There remained now the port, or condenser-column, which, though not so badly cracked as its fellow, had also been strengthened in four places with boiler-plate patches, but needed struts. They took away the main stanchions of the bridge for that work, and, crazy with toil, did not see till all was in place that the rounded bars of iron must be flattened from top to bottom to allow the air-pump levers to clear them. It was Wardrop's oversight, and he wept bitterly before the men as he gave the order to unbolt the struts and flatten them with hammer and the flame. Now the broken engine was underpinned firmly, and they took away the wooden shores from under the cylinders, and gave them to the robbed bridge, thanking God for even half a day's work on gentle, kindly wood instead of the iron that had entered into their souls. Eight months in the back-country among the leeches, at a temperature of 84° moist, is very bad for the nerves.

They had kept the hardest work to the last, as boys save Latin prose, and, worn though they were, Mr. Wardrop did not dare to give them rest. The piston-rod and connecting-rod were to be straightened, and this was a job for a regular dockyard with every appliance. They fell to it, cheered by a little chalk showing of work done and time consumed which Mr. Wardrop wrote up on the engine-room bulkhead. Fifteen days had gone—fifteen days of killing labour—and there was hope before them.

It is curious that no man knows how the rods were straightened. The crew of the *Haliotis* remember that week very dimly, as a fever patient re-members the delirium of a long night. There were fires everywhere, they say; the whole ship was one consuming furnace, and the hammers were never still. Now, there could not have been more than one fire at the most, for Mr. Wardrop distinctly recalls that no straightening was done except under his own eye. They remember, too, that for many years voices gave orders which they obeyed with their bodies, but their minds were abroad on all the seas. It seems to them that they stood through days and nights slowly sliding a bar backwards and forwards through a white glow that was part of the ship. They remember an intolerable noise in their burning heads from the walls of the stoke-hole, and they remember being savagely beaten by men whose eyes seemed asleep. When their shift was over they would draw straight lines in the air, anxiously and repeatedly, and would question one another in their sleep, crying, "Is she straight?"

At last—they do not remember whether this was by day or by night—Mr. Wardrop began to dance clumsily, and wept the while; and they too danced and wept, and went to sleep twitching all over; and when they woke, men said that the rods were straightened, and no one did any work for two days, but lay on the decks and ate fruit. Mr. Wardrop would go below from time to time, and pat the two rods where they lay, and they heard him singing hymns.

Then his trouble of mind went from him, and at the end of the third day's idleness he made a drawing in chalk upon the deck, with letters of the alphabet at the angles. He pointed out that, though the piston-rod was more or less straight, the piston-rod cross-head—the thing that had been jammed sideways in the guides—had been badly strained, and had cracked the lower end of the piston-rod. He was going to forge and shrink a wrought-iron collar on the neck of the piston-rod where it joined the cross-head, and from the collar he would bolt a Y-shaped piece of iron whose lower arms should be bolted into the cross-head. If anything more were needed, they could use up the last of the boiler-plate.

So the forges were lit again, and men burned their bodies, but hardly felt the pain. The finished connection was not beautiful, but it seemed strong enough—at least, as strong as the rest of the machinery; and with that job their labours came to an end. All that remained was to connect up the en-gines, and to get food and water. The skipper and four men dealt with the Malay boat-builder—by night chiefly; it was no time to haggle over the price of sago and dried fish. The others stayed aboard and replaced piston, piston-rod, cylinder-cover, cross-head, and bolts, with the aid of the faithful donkey-engine. The cylinder-cover was hardly steam-proof, and the eye of science might have seen in the connecting-rod a flexure something like that of a Christmas-tree candle which has melted and been straightened by hand over a stove, but, as Mr. Wardrop said, "She didn't hit anything."

As soon as the last bolt was in place, men tumbled over one another in their anxiety to get to the hand starting-gear, the wheel and worm, by which some engines can be moved when there is no steam aboard. They nearly wrenched off the wheel, but it was evident to the blindest eye that the engines stirred. They did not revolve in their orbits with any enthusiasm, as good machines should; indeed, they groaned not a little; but they moved over and came to rest in a way which proved that they still recognised man's hand. Then Mr. Wardrop sent his slaves into the darker bowels of the engine-room and the stoke-hole, and followed them with a flare-lamp. The boilers were sound, but would take no harm from a little scaling and cleaning. Mr. Wardrop would not have any one over-zealous, for he feared what the next stroke of the tool might show. "The less we know about her now," said he, "the better for us all, I'm thinkin'. Ye'll understand me when I say that this is in no sense regular engineerin'."

As his raiment, when he spoke, was his grey beard and uncut hair, they believed him. They did not ask too much of what they met, but polished and tallowed and scraped it to a false brilliancy.

"A lick of paint would make me easier in my mind," said Mr. Wardrop, plaintively. "I know half the condenser-tubes are started; and the propeller-shaftin' 's God knows how far out of the true, and we'll need a new air-pump, an' the main-steam leaks like a sieve, and there's worse each way I look; but—paint's like clothes to a man, an' ours is near all gone."

The skipper unearthed some stale ropy paint of the loathsome green that they used for the galleys of sailing-ships, and Mr. Wardrop spread it abroad lavishly to give the engines self-respect.

His own was returning day by day, for he wore his loin-cloth continuously; but the crew, having worked under orders, did not feel as he did. The completed work satisfied Mr. Wardrop. He would at the last have made shift to run to Singapore, and gone home without vengeance taken to show his engines to his brethren in the craft; but the others and the captain forbade him. They had not yet recovered their self-respect.

"It would be safer to make what ye might call a trial trip, but beggars mustn't be choosers; an' if the engines will go over to the hand-gear, the probability—I'm only saying it's a probability—the chance is that they'll hold up when we put steam on her."

"How long will you take to get steam?" said the skipper.

"God knows! Four hours—a day—half a week. If I can raise sixty pound I'll not complain."

"Be sure of her first; we can't afford to go out half a mile, and break down."

"My soul and body, man, we're one continuous breakdown, fore an' aft! We might fetch Singapore, though."

"We'll break down at Pygang-Watai, where we can do good," was the answer, in a voice that did not allow argument. "She's *my* boat, and—I've had eight months to think in."

No man saw the *Haliotis* depart, though many heard her. She left at two in the morning, having cut her moorings, and it was none of her crew's pleasure that the engines should strike up a thundering half-seas-over chanty that echoed among the hills. Mr. Wardrop wiped away a tear as he listened to the new song.

"She's gibberin'—she's just gibberin'," he whimpered. "Yon's the voice of a maniac."

And if engines have any soul, as their masters believe, he was quite right. There were outcries and clamours, sobs and bursts of chattering laughter, silences where the trained ear yearned for the clear note, and torturing re-duplications where there should have been one deep voice. Down the screw-shaft ran murmurs and warnings, while a heart-diseased flutter without told that the propeller needed re-keying.

"How does she make it?" said the skipper.

"She moves, but—but she's breakin' my heart. The sooner we're at Pygang-Watai, the better. She's mad, and we're waking the town."

"Is she at all near safe?"

"What do *I* care how safe she is? She's mad. Hear that, now! To be sure, nothing's hittin' anything, and the bearin's are fairly cool, but—can ye not hear?"

"If she goes," said the skipper, "I don't care a curse. And she's *my* boat, too."

She went, trailing a fathom of weed behind her. From a slow two knots an hour she crawled up to a triumphant four. Anything beyond that made the struts quiver dangerously, and filled the engine-room with steam. Morning showed her out of sight of land, and there was a visible ripple under her bows; but she complained bitterly in her bowels, and, as though the noise had called it, there shot along across the purple sea a swift, dark proa, hawk-like and curious, which presently ranged alongside and wished to know if the *Haliotis* were helpless. Ships, even the steamers of the white men, had been known to break down in those waters, and the honest Malay and Javanese traders would sometimes aid them in their own peculiar way. But this ship was not full of lady passengers and well-dressed officers. Men, white, naked and savage, swarmed down her sides—some with red-hot iron bars, and others with large hammers—threw themselves upon those innocent inquiring strangers, and, before any man could say what had happened, were in full possession of the proa, while the lawful owners bobbed in the water overside. Half an hour later the proa's cargo of sago and trepang, as well as a doubtful-minded compass, was in the *Haliotis*. The two huge triangular mat sails, with their seventy-foot yards and booms, had followed the cargo, and were being fitted to the stripped masts of the steamer.

They rose, they swelled, they filled, and the empty steamer visibly laid over as the wind took them. They gave her nearly three knots an hour, and what better could men ask? But if she had been forlorn before, this new purchase made her horrible to see. Imagine a respectable charwoman in the tights of a ballet-dancer rolling drunk along the streets, and you will come to some faint notion of the appearance of that nine-hundred-ton, well-decked, once schooner-rigged cargo-boat as she staggered under her new help, shouting and raving across the deep. With steam and sail that marvellous voyage continued; and the bright-eyed crew looked over the rail, desolate, unkempt, unshorn, shamelessly clothed—beyond the decencies.

At the end of the third week she sighted the island of Pygang-Watai, whose harbour is the turning-point of a pearl sea-patrol. Here the gunboats stay for a week ere they retrace their line. There is no village at Pygang-Watai; only a stream of water, some palms, and a harbour safe to rest in till the first violence of the southeast monsoon has blown itself out. They opened up the low coral beach, with its mound of whitewashed coal ready for supply, the deserted huts for the sailors, and the flagless flagstaff.

Next day there was no *Haliotis*—only a little proa rocking in the warm rain at the mouth of the harbour, whose crew watched with hungry eyes the smoke of a gunboat on the horizon.

Months afterwards there were a few lines in an English newspaper to the effect that some gunboat of some foreign Power had broken her back at the mouth of some far-away harbour by running at full speed into a sunken wreck.

RUDYARD KIPLING
1865–1936

The son of a connoisseur of Indian art, Kipling lived in Bombay until he was six, learning English and Hindustani at the same time. Although he was put in the care of a relative in Swansea, England, he did not attend school until he was twelve. At the United Services College in North Devon he demonstrated an interest in writing. He edited the school magazine and had verses published in a local paper.

Rejecting university study, Kipling returned to India in 1882 to join the staff of the Lahore *Civil and Military Gazette and Pioneer*, not only reporting but contributing short stories and verses to the paper. While working in Lahore he published *Departmental Ditties* (1886), a collection of verse that had first appeared in the *Gazette*. *Plain Tales from the Hills* (1888), containing stories about the celebrated "soldiers three," was not issued until he had moved to Allahabad to write. Additional exploits of the three characters he created appeared in *Soldiers Three* (1888). Kipling was prolific, as the number of additional books of fiction issued in 1888 shows: *The Story of the Gadsbys*, *In Black and White*, *Under the Deodars*, *The Phantom 'Rickshaw*, and *Wee Willie Winkie*. Most of the stories had been previously published in *The Week's News*, but even so the output was staggering.

His paper sent him to London via Japan, San Francisco, and New York in 1889. *Letters of Marque* (1891) and *From Sea to Sea* (1899) were the result of his travels. In London Kipling published his best-known book, *Barrack-Room Ballads* (1892), and married Caroline Balestier, an American with property in Vermont. The couple moved there and Kipling wrote constantly, producing among other books *The Jungle Book* (1894), *The Seven Seas* (1896), and a tale of bravery at sea, *Captains Courageous* (1897).

Other nautical work followed. After returning to England in 1896 and settling at Torquay, Kipling cruised with the channel fleet. After this experience he wrote the brilliant *A Fleet in Being*. In 1916 *Sea Warfare*, a compilation of his newspaper pieces, appeared, and *Sea and Sussex* was published a decade later.

After returning from South Africa, where he had reported on the Boer War, Kipling settled first by the sea at Rottingdean and then in the Sussex village of Burwash. In 1901 *Kim*, an extremely successful novel depicting Indian custom, character, and social life, appeared. In 1907 he received the Nobel Prize for literature.

During World War I, Kipling became a propagandist, writing *The New Army in Training* (1915) and *France at War* (1915). He edited *The Irish Guards in the Great War* (1923).

"The Devil and the Deep Sea," said to be Kipling's most successful ship story, was written during his residence in America and collected in *The Day's Work* (1898).

Davy Jones's Gift

BY JOHN MASEFIELD

"Once upon a time," said the sailor, "the Devil and Davy Jones came to Cardiff, to the place called Tiger Bay. They put up at Tony Adams's, not far from Pier Head, at the corner of Sunday Lane. And all the time they stayed there they used to be going to the rum-shop, where they sat at a table, smoking their cigars, and dicing each other for different persons' souls. Now you must know that the Devil gets landsmen, and Davy Jones gets sailor-folk; and they get tired of having always the same, so then they dice each other for some of another sort.

"One time they were in a place in Mary Street, having some burnt brandy, and playing red and black for the people passing. And while they were looking out on the street and turning the cards, they saw all the people on the sidewalk breaking their necks to get into the gutter. And they saw all the shop-people running out and kowtowing, and all the carts pulling up, and all the police saluting. 'Here comes a big nob,' said Davy Jones. 'Yes,' said the Devil; 'it's the Bishop that's stopping with the Mayor.' 'Red or black?' said Davy Jones, picking up a card. 'I don't play for bishops,' said the Devil. 'I respect the cloth,' he said. 'Come on, man,' said Davy Jones. 'I'd give an admiral to have a bishop. Come on, now; make your game. Red or black?' 'Well, I say red,' said the Devil. 'It's the ace of clubs,' said Davy Jones; 'I win; and it's the first bishop ever I had in my life.' The Devil was mighty angry at that—at losing a bishop. 'I'll not play any more,' he said; 'I'm off home. Some people gets too good cards for me. There was some queer shuffling when that pack was cut, that's my belief.'

"'Ah, stay and be friends, man,' said Davy Jones. 'Look at what's coming down the street. I'll give you that for nothing.'

"Now, coming down the street there was a reefer—one of those apprentice fellows. And he was brass-bound fit to play music. He stood about six feet, and there were bright brass buttons down his jacket, and on his collar, and on his sleeves. His cap had a big gold badge, with a house-flag in seven different colours in the middle of it, and a gold chain cable of a chinstay twisted round it. He was wearing his cap on three hairs, and he was walking on both the sidewalks and all the road. His trousers were cut like windsails round the ankles. He had a fathom of red silk tie rolling out over his chest. He'd a cigarette in a twisted clay holder a foot and a half long. He was chewing tobacco over his shoulders as he walked. He'd a bottle of rum—hot in one hand, a bag of jam tarts in the other, and his pockets were full of love-letters from every port between Rio and Callao, round by the East.

"'You mean to say you'll give me that?' said the Devil. 'I will,' said Davy Jones, 'and a beauty he is. I never see a finer.' 'He is, indeed, a beauty,' said the Devil. 'I take back what I said about the cards. I'm sorry I spoke crusty. What's the matter with some more burnt brandy?' 'Burnt brandy be it,' said Davy Jones. So then they rang the bell, and ordered a new jug and clean glasses.

"Now the Devil was so proud of what Davy Jones had given him, he couldn't keep away from him. He used to hang about the East Bute Docks, under the red-brick clock-tower, looking at the barque the young man worked aboard. Bill Harker his name was. He was in a West Coast barque, the *Coronel*, loading fuel for Hilo. So at last, when the *Coronel* was sailing, the Devil shipped himself aboard her, as one of the crowd in the fo'c'sle, and away they went down the Channel. At first he was very happy, for Bill Harker was in the same watch, and the two would yarn together. And though he was wise when he shipped, Bill Harker taught him a lot. There was a lot of things Bill Harker knew about. But when they were off the River Plate, they got caught in a pampero, and it blew very hard, and a big green sea began to run. The *Coronel* was a wet ship, and for three days you could stand upon her poop, and look forward and see nothing but a smother of foam from the break of the poop to the jib-boom. The crew had to roost on the poop. The fo'c'sle was flooded out. So while they were like this the flying jib worked loose. 'The jib will be gone in half a tick,' said the mate. 'Out there, one of you, and make it fast, before it blows away.' But the boom was dipping under every minute, and the waist was four feet deep, and green water came aboard all along her length. So none of the crowd would go forward. Then Bill Harker shambled out, and away he went forward, with the green seas smashing over him, and he lay out along the jib-boom and made the sail fast, and jolly nearly drowned he was. 'That's a brave lad, that Bill Harker,' said the Devil. 'Ah, come off,' said the sailors. 'Them reefers, they haven't got souls to be saved.' It was that that set the Devil thinking.

"By and by they came up with the Horn; and if it had blown off the Plate, it now blew off the roof. Talk about wind and weather. They got them both for sure aboard the *Coronel*. And it blew all the sails off her, and she rolled all her masts out, and the seas made a breach of her bulwarks, and the ice knocked a hole in her bows. So watch and watch they pumped the old *Coronel*, and the leak gained steadily, and there they were hove to under a weather cloth, five and a half degrees to the south of anything. And while they were like this, just about giving up hope, the old man sent the watch below, and told them they could start prayers. So the Devil crept on to the top of the half-deck, to look through the scuttle, to see what the reefers were doing, and what kind of prayers Bill Harker was putting up. And he saw them all sitting round the table, under the lamp, with Bill Harker at the head. And each of them had a hand of cards, and a length of knotted rope-yarn, and they were playing able-whackets. Each man in turn put down a card, and swore a new blasphemy, and if his swear didn't come as he played the card, then all the others hit him with their teasers. But they never once had a chance to hit Bill Harker. 'I think they were right about his soul,' said the Devil. And he sighed, like he was sad.

"Shortly after that the *Coronel* went down, and all hands drowned in her, saving only Bill and the Devil. They came up out of the smothering green seas, and saw the stars blinking in the sky, and heard the wind howling like a pack of dogs. They managed to get aboard the *Coronel's* hen-house, which had come adrift, and floated. The fowls were all drowned inside, so they lived on drowned hens. As for drink, they had to do without, for there was none. When they got thirsty they splashed their faces with salt water; but they were so cold they didn't feel thirst very bad. They drifted three days and three nights, till their skins were all cracked and salt-caked. And all the Devil thought of was whether Bill Harker had a soul. And Bill kept telling the Devil what a thundering big feed they would have as soon as they fetched to port, and how good a rum-hot would be, with a lump of sugar and a bit of lemon peel.

"And at last the old hen-house came bump on to Terra del Fuego, and there were some natives cooking rabbits. So the Devil and Bill made a raid of the whole jing bang, and ate till they were tired. Then they had a drink out of a brook, and a warm by the fire, and a pleasant sleep, 'Now,' said the Devil, 'I will see if he's got a soul. I'll see if he give thanks.' So after an hour or two Bill took a turn up and down and came to the Devil. 'It's mighty dull on this forgotten continent,' he said. 'Have you got a ha'penny?' 'No,' said the Devil. 'What in joy d'ye want with a ha'penny?' 'I might have played you pitch and toss,' said Bill. 'It was better fun on the hen-coop than here.' 'I give you up,' said the Devil; 'you've no more soul than the inner part of an empty barrel.' And with that the Devil vanished in a flame of sulphur.

"Bill stretched himself, and put another shrub on the fire. He picked up a few round shells, and began a game of knucklebones."

Ambitious Jimmy Hicks

BY JOHN MASEFIELD

"WELL," said the captain of the foretop to me, "it's our cutter today, and you're the youngest hand, and you'll be bowman. Can you pull an oar?" "No," I answered. "Well, you'd better pull one today, my son, or mind your eye. You'll climb Zion's Hill tonight if you go catching any crabs." With that he went swaggering along the deck, chewing his quid of sweet-cake. I thought lugubriously of Zion's Hill, a very different place from the one in the Bible, and the longer I thought, the chillier came the sweat on my palms. "Away cutters," went the pipe a moment later. "Down to your boat, foretopmen." I skidded down the gangway into the bows of the cutter, and cast the turns from the painter, keeping the boat secured by a single turn. A strong tide was running, and the broken water was flying up in spray. Dirty water ran in trickles down my sleeves. The thwarts were wet. A lot of dirty water was slopping about in the well. "Bowman," said the captain of the foretop, "why haven't you cleaned your boat out?" "I didn't know I had to." "Well, next time you don't know we'll jolly well duck you in it. Let go forrard. Back a stroke, starboard. Down port, and shove her off." "Where are we going?" asked the stroke. "We're going to the etceteraed slip to get the etceteraed love-letters. Now look alive in the bows there. Get your oars out and give way. If I come forward with the tiller your heads'll ache for a week." I got out my oar, or rather I got out the oar which had been left to me. It was one of the midship oars, the longest and heaviest in the boat. With this I made a shift to pull till we neared the slip, when I had to lay my oar in, gather up the painter, and stand by to leap on to the jetty to make the boat fast as we came alongside. I have known some misery in my time, but the agony of that moment, wondering if I should fall headlong on the slippery green weed, in the sight of the old sailors smoking there, was as bitter as any I have suffered. The cutter's nose rubbed the dangling seaweed. I made a spring, slipped, steadied myself, cast the painter around the mooring-hook, and made the boat fast. "A round turn and two half hitches," I murmured, as I passed the turns, "and a third half hitch for luck." "Come off with your third half hitch," said one of the old sailors. "You and your three half hitches. You're like Jimmy Hicks, the come-day go-day. You want to do too much, you do. You'd go dry the keel with a towel, wouldn't you, rather than take a caulk? Come off with your third hitch."

Late that night I saw the old sailor in the lamproom, cleaning the heavy copper lamps. I asked if I might help him, for I wished to hear the story of Jimmy Hicks. He gave me half a dozen lamps to clean, with a mass of cotton waste and a few rags, most of them the relics of our soft cloth working caps. "Heave round, my son," he said, "and get an appetite for your supper." When I had cleaned two or three of my lamps I asked him to tell me about Jimmy Hicks.

"Ah," he said, "you want to be warned by him. You're too ambitious altogether. Look at you coming here to clean my lamps. And you after pulling in the cutter. I wouldn't care to be like Jimmy Hicks. No. I wouldn't that. It's only young fellies like you wants to be like Jimmy Hicks." "Who was Jimmy Hicks?" I asked; "and what was it he did?"

"Ah," said the old man, "did you ever hear tell of the Black Ball Line? Well, there's no ships like them ships now. You think them Cunarders at the buoy there; you think them fine. You should a seen the *Red Jacket*, or the *John James Green*, or the *Thermopylæ*. By dad, that *was* a sight. Spars—talk of spars. And skysail yards on all three masts, and a flying jib-boom the angels could have picked their teeth with. Sixty-six days they took, the Thames to Sydney Heads. It's never been done before nor since. Well, Jimmy Hicks he was a young, ambitious felly, the same as you. And he was in one of them ships. I was shipmates with him myself.

"Well, of all the red-headed ambitious fellies I think Jimmy Hicks was the worst. Yes, sir. I think he was the worst. The day they got to sea the bosun set him to scrub the fo'c'sle. So he gets some sand and holystone and a three-cornered scraper, and he scrubs that fo'c'sle fit for an admiral. He begun that job at three bells in the morning watch, and he was doing it at eight bells, and half his watch below he was doing it, and when they called him for dinner he was still doing it. Talk about white. White was black alongside them planks. So in the afternoon it came on to blow. Yes, sir, it breezed up. So they had to snug her down. So Jimmy Hicks he went up and made the skysails fast, and then he made the royals fast. And then he come down to see had he got a good furl on them. And then up he went again and put a new stow on the skysail. And then he went up again to tinker the main royal bunt. Them furls of his, by dad, they reminded me of Sefton Park. Yes, sir; they was that like Sunday clothes.

"He was always like that. He wasn't never happy unless he was putting whippings on ropes' ends, or pointing the topgallant and royal braces, or polishing the brass on the ladders till it was as bright as gold. Always doing something. Always doing more than his piece. The last to leave the deck and the first to come up when hands were called. If he was told to whip a rope, he pointed it and gave it a rub of slush and Flemish-coiled it. If he was told to broom down the top of a deckhouse he got it white with a holystone. He was like the poet—

Double, double, toil and trouble.—Shakespeare.

That was Jimmy Hicks. Yes, Sir, that was him. You want to be warned by him. You hear the terrible end he come to.

"Now they was coming home in that ship. And what do you suppose they had on board? Well, they had silks. My word they was silks. Light as muslin. Worth a pound a fathom. All yellow and blue and red. All the colours. And a gloss. It was like so much moonlight. Well. They had a lot of that. Then they had china tea, and it wasn't none of your skilly. No, sir. It was tea the King of Spain could have drunk in the golden palaces of Rome. There was flaviour. Worth eighteen shilling a pound that tea was. The same as the Queen drunk. It was like meat that tea was. You didn't want no meat if you had a cup of that. Worth two hundred thousand pound that ship's freight was. And a general in the army was a passenger. Besides a bishop.

"So as they were coming home they got caught in a cyclone, off of the Mauritius. Whoo! You should a heard the wind. O mommer, it just blew. And the cold green seas they kept coming aboard. Ker-woosh, they kept coming. And the ship she groaned and she strained, and she worked her planking open. So it was all hands to the pumps, general and bishop and all, and they kept pumping out tea, all ready made with salt water. That was all they had to live on for three days. Salt-water tea. Very wholesome it is, too, for them that like it. *And* for them that's inclined to consumption.

"By and by the pumps choked. 'The silks is in the well,' said the mate. 'To your prayers, boys. We're gone up.' 'Hold on with prayers,' said the old man. 'Get a tackle rigged and hoist the boat out. You can pray afterwards. Work is prayer,' he says, 'so long as I command.' 'Lively there,' says the mate. 'Up there one of you with a block. Out to the mainyard arm and rig a tackle! Lively now. Stamp and go. She's settling under us.' So Jimmy Hicks seizes a tackle and they hook it on to the longboat, and Jimmy nips into the rigging with one of the blocks in his hand. And they clear it away to him as he goes. And she was settling like a stone all the time. 'Look slippy there, you!' cries the mate, as Jimmy lays out on the yard. For the sea was crawling across the deck. It was time to be gone out of that.

"And Jimmy gets to the yard-arm, and he takes a round turn with his lashing, and he makes a half hitch, and he makes a second half hitch. 'Yard-arm, there!' hails the mate. 'May we hoist away?' 'Hold on,' says Jimmy, 'till I make her fast,' he says. And just as he makes his third half hitch and yells to them to sway away—Ker-woosh! there comes a great green sea. And down they all go—ship, and tea, and mate, and bishop, and general, and Jimmy, and the whole lash-up. All the whole lot of them. And all because he would wait to take the third half hitch. So you be warned by Jimmy Hicks, my son. And don't you be neither red-headed nor ambitious."

JOHN MASEFIELD*
1878–1967

The narratives "Davy Jones's Gift" and "Ambitious Jimmy Hicks" both appeared in Masefield's *A Tarpaulin Muster* (1907).

*For a look at the author's life and work, see page 55.

The Roll-Call of the Reef

BY ARTHUR QUILLER-COUCH

"Yes, sir," said my host the quarryman, reaching down the relics from their hook in the wall over the chimney-piece; "they've hung there all my time, and most of my father's. The women won't touch 'em; they're afraid of the story. So here they'll dangle, and gather dust and smoke, till another tenant comes and tosses 'em out o' doors for rubbish. Whew! 'tis coarse weather."

He went to the door, opened it, and stood studying the gale that beat upon his cottage-front, straight from the Manacle Reef. The rain drove past him into the kitchen aslant like threads of gold silk in the shine of the wreckwood fire. Meanwhile by the same firelight I examined the relics on my knee. The metal of each was tarnished out of knowledge. But the trumpet was evidently an old cavalry trumpet, and the threads of its parti-coloured sling, though frayed and dusty, still hung together. Around the side-drum, beneath its cracked brown varnish, I could hardly trace a royal coat-of-arms, and a legend running—*Per Mare per Terram*—the motto of the Marines. Its parchment, though coloured and scented with wood-smoke, was limp and mildewed; and I began to tighten up the straps—under which the drumsticks had been loosely thrust—with the idle purpose of trying if some music might be got out of the old drum yet.

But as I turned it on my knee, I found the drum attached to the trumpet-sling by a curious barrel-shaped padlock, and paused to examine this. The body of the lock was composed of half a dozen brass rings, set accurately edge to edge; and, rubbing the brass with my thumb, I saw that each of the six had a series of letters engraved around it.

I knew the trick of it, I thought. Here was one of those word-padlocks, once so common; only to be opened by getting the rings to spell a certain word, which the dealer confides to you.

My host shut and barred the door, and came back to the hearth.

"'Twas just such a wind—east by south—that brought in what you've got between your hands. Back in the year 'nine it was; my father has told me the tale a score o' times. You're twisting round the rings, I see. But you'll never guess the word. Parson Kendall, he made the word, and locked down a couple o' ghosts in their graves with it; and when his time came, he went to his own grave and took the word with him."

"Whose ghosts, Matthew?"

"You want the story, I see, sir. My father could tell it better than I can. He was a young man in the year 'nine, unmarried at the time, and living in this very cottage just as I be. That's how he came to get mixed up with the tale."

He took a chair, lit a short pipe, and unfolded the story in a low musing voice, with his eyes fixed on the dancing violet flames.

"Yes, he'd ha' been about thirty year old in January, of the year 'nine. The storm got up in the night o' the twenty-first o' that month. My father was dressed and out long before daylight; he never was one to 'bide in bed, let be that the gale by this time was pretty near lifting the thatch over his head. Besides which, he'd fenced a small 'taty-patch that winter, down by Lowland Point, and he wanted to see if it stood the night's work. He took the path across Gunner's Meadow—where they buried most of the bodies afterwards. The wind was right in his teeth at the time, and once on the way (he's told me this often) a great strip of ore-weed came flying through the darkness and fetched him a slap on the cheek like a cold hand. But he made shift pretty well till he got to Lowland, and then had to drop upon his hands and knees and crawl, digging his fingers every now and then into the shingle to hold on, for he declared to me that the stones, some of them as big as a man's head, kept rolling and driving past till it seemed the whole foreshore was moving westward under him. The fence was gone, of course; not a stick left to show where it stood; so that, when first he came to the place, he thought he must have missed his bearings. My father, sir, was a very religious man; and if he reckoned the end of the world was at hand—there in the great wind and night, among the moving stones—you may believe he was certain of it when he heard a gun fired, and, with the same, saw a flame shoot up out of the darkness to windward, making a sudden fierce light in all the place about. All he could find to think or say was, 'The Second Coming—The Second Coming! The Bridegroom cometh, and the wicked He will toss like a ball into a large country!' and being already upon his knees, he just bowed his head and 'bided, saying this over and over.

"But by'm-by, between two squalls, he made bold to lift his head and look, and then by the light—a bluish colour 'twas—he saw all the coast clear away to Manacle Point, and off the Manacles, in the thick of the weather, a sloop-of-war with top-gallants housed, driving stern foremost towards the reef. It was she, of course, that was burning the flare. My father could see the white streak and the ports of her quite plain as she rose to it, a little outside the breakers, and he guessed easy enough that her captain had just managed to wear ship, and was trying to force her nose to the sea with the help of her small bower anchor and the scrap or two of canvas that hadn't yet been blown out of her. But while he looked, she fell off, giving her broadside to it foot by foot, and drifting back on the breakers around

Carn dû and the Varses. The rocks lie so thick thereabouts, that 'twas a toss up which she struck first; at any rate, my father couldn't tell at the time, for just then the flare died down and went out.

"Well, sir, he turned then in the dark and started back for Coverack to cry the dismal tidings—though well knowing ship and crew to be past any hope; and as he turned, the wind lifted him and tossed him forward 'like a ball,' as he'd been saying, and homeward along the foreshore. As you know, 'tis ugly work, even by daylight, picking your way among the stones there, and my father was prettily knocked about at first in the dark. But by this 'twas nearer seven than six o'clock, and the day spreading. By the time he reached North Corner, a man could see to read print; hows'ever, he looked neither out to sea nor towards Coverack, but headed straight for the first cottage—the same that stands above North Corner to-day. A man named Billy Ede lived there then, and when my father burst into the kitchen bawling, 'Wreck! wreck!' he saw Billy Ede's wife, Ann, standing there in her clogs, with a shawl over her head, and her clothes wringing wet.

"'Save the chap!' says Billy Ede's wife, Ann. 'What d' 'ee mean by crying stale fish at that rate?'

"'But 'tis a wreck, I tell 'ee. I've a-zeed 'n!'

"'Why, so 'tis,' says she, 'and I've a-zeed 'n too; and so has everyone with an eye in his head.'

"And with that she pointed straight over my father's shoulder, and he turned; and there, close under Dolor Point, at the end of Coverack town, he saw *another* wreck washing, and the point black with people, like emmets, running to and fro in the morning light. While he stood staring at her, he heard a trumpet sounded on board, the notes coming in little jerks, like a bird rising against the wind; but faintly, of course, because of the distance and the gale blowing—though this had dropped a little.

"'She's a transport,' said Billy Ede's wife, Ann, 'and full of horse soldiers, fine long men. When she struck they must ha' pitched the hosses over first to lighten the ship, for a score of dead hosses had washed in afore I left, half an hour back. An' three or four soldiers, too—fine long corpses in white breeches and jackets of blue and gold. I held the lantern to one. Such a straight young man!'

"My father asked her about the trumpeting.

"'That's the queerest bit of all. She was burnin' a light when me an' my man joined the crowd down there. All her masts had gone; whether they carried away, or were cut away to ease her, I don't rightly know. Anyway, there she lay 'pon the rocks with her decks bare. Her keelson was broke under her and her bottom sagged and stove, and she had just settled down like a sitting hen—just the leastest list to starboard; but a man could stand there easy. They had rigged up ropes across her, from bulwark to bulwark, an' beside these the men were mustered, holding on like grim death whenever the sea made a clean breach over them, an' standing up like heroes as soon as it passed. The captain an' the officers were clinging to the rail of the quarter-deck, all in their golden uniforms, waiting for the end as if 'twas King George they expected. There was no way to help, for she lay right beyond cast of line, though our folk tried it fifty times. And beside them clung a trumpeter, a whacking big man, an' between the heavy seas he would lift his trumpet with one hand, and blow a call; and every time he blew, the men gave a cheer. There' (she says) '—hark 'ee now—there he goes agen! But you won't hear no cheering any more, for few are left to cheer, and their voices weak. Bitter cold the wind is, and I reckon it numbs their grip o' the ropes, for they were dropping off fast with every sea when my man sent me home to get his breakfast. *Another* wreck, you say? Well, there's no hope for the tender dears, if 'tis the Manacles. You'd better run down and help yonder; though 'tis little help that any man can give. Not one came in alive while I was there. The tide's flowing, an' she won't hold together another hour, they say.'

"Well, sure enough, the end was coming fast when my father got down to the point. Six men had been cast up alive, or just breathing—a seaman and five troopers. The seaman was the only one that had breath to speak; and while they were carrying him into the town, the word went round that the ship's name was the *Despatch*, transport, homeward bound from Corunna, with a detachment of the 7th Hussars, that had been fighting out there with Sir John Moore. The seas had rolled her farther over by this time, and given her decks a pretty sharp slope; but a dozen men still held on, seven by the ropes near the ship's waist, a couple near the break of the poop, and three on the quarter-deck. Of these three my father made out one to be the skipper; close by him clung an officer in full regimentals—his name, they heard after, was Captain Duncanfield; and last came the tall trumpeter; and if you'll believe me, the fellow was making shift there, at the very last, to blow *God Save the King*. What's more, he got to *Send us victorious* before an extra big sea came bursting across and washed them off the deck—every man but one of the pair beneath the poop—and *he* dropped his hold before the next wave; being stunned, I reckon. The others went out of sight at once, but the trumpeter—being, as I said, a powerful man as well as a tough swimmer—rose like a duck, rode out a couple of breakers, and came in on the crest of the third. The folks looked to see him broke like an egg at their feet; but when the smother cleared, there he was, lying face downward on a ledge below them; and one of the men that happened to have a rope round him—I forget the fellow's name, if I ever heard it—jumped down and grabbed him by the ankle as he began to slip back. Before the next big sea, the pair were hauled high enough to be out of harm, and another heave brought them up to grass. Quick work; but master trumpeter wasn't quite dead; nothing worse than a cracked head and three staved ribs. In twenty minutes or so they had him in bed, with the doctor to tend him.

"Now was the time—nothing being left alive upon the transport—for my father to tell of the sloop he'd seen driving upon the Manacles. And when he got a hearing, though the most were set upon salvage, and believed a wreck in the hand, so to say, to be worth half a dozen they couldn't see, a good few volunteered to start off with him and have a look. They crossed Lowland Point; no ship to be seen on the Manacles, nor anywhere upon the sea. One or two was for calling my father a liar. 'Wait till we come to Dean Point,' said he. Sure enough, on the far side of Dean Point, they found the sloop's mainmast washing about with half a dozen men lashed to it—men in red jackets—every mother's son drowned and staring; and a little farther on, just under the Dean, three or four bodies cast up on the shore, one of them a small drummer-boy, side-drum and all; and, near by, part of a ship's gig, with 'H.M.S. *Primrose*' cut on the stern-board. From this point on, the shore was littered thick with wreckage and dead bodies—the most of them Marines in uniform; and in Godrevy Cove, in particular, a heap of furniture from the captain's cabin, and amongst it a water-tight box, not much damaged, and full of papers; by which, when it came to be examined next day, the wreck was easily made out to be the *Primrose*, of eighteen guns, outward bound from Portsmouth, with a fleet of transports for the Spanish War— thirty sail, I've heard, but I've never heard what became of them. Being handled by merchant skippers, no doubt they rode out the gale and reached the Tagus safe and sound. Not but what the captain of the *Primrose* (Mein was his name) did quite right to try and club-haul his vessel when he found himself under the land: only he never ought to have got there if he took proper soundings. But it's easy talking.

"The *Primrose*, sir, was a handsome vessel—for her size, one of the handsomest in the King's service—and newly fitted out at Plymouth Dock. So the boys had brave pickings from her in the way of brasswork, ship's instruments, and the like, let alone some barrels of stores not much spoiled. They loaded themselves with as much as they could carry, and started for home, meaning to make a second journey before the preventive men got wind of their doings and came to spoil the fun. But as my father was passing back under the Dean, he happened to take a look over his shoulder at the bodies there. 'Hullo,' says he, and dropped his gear: 'I do believe there's a leg moving!' And, running fore, he stooped over the small drummer-boy that I told you about. The poor little chap was lying there, with his face a mass of bruises and his eyes closed: but he had shifted one leg an inch or two, and was still breathing. So my father pulled out a knife and cut him free from his drum—that was lashed on to him with a double turn of Manilla rope—and took him up and carried him along here, to this very room that we're sitting in. He lost a good deal by this, for when he went back to fetch his bundle the preventive men had got hold of it, and were thick as thieves along the foreshore; so that 'twas only by paying one or two to look the other way that he picked up anything worth carrying off: which you'll allow to be hard, seeing that he was the first man to give news of the wreck.

"Well, the inquiry was held, of course, and my father gave evidence; and for the rest they had to trust to the sloop's papers: for not a soul was saved besides the drummer-boy, and he was raving in a fever, brought on by the cold and the fright. And the seamen and the five troopers gave evidence about the loss of the *Despatch*. The tall trumpeter, too, whose ribs were healing, came forward and kissed the Book; but somehow his head been hurt in coming ashore, and he talked foolish-like, and 'twas easy seen he would never be a proper man again. The others were taken up to Plymouth, and so went their ways; but the trumpeter stayed on in Coverack; and King George, finding he was fit for nothing, sent him down a trifle of a pension after a while—enough to keep him in board and lodging, with a bit of tobacco over.

"Now the first time that this man—William Tallifer, he called himself—met with the drummer-boy, was about a fortnight after the little chap had bettered enough to be allowed a short walk out of doors, which he took, if you please, in full regimentals. There never was a soldier so proud of his dress. His own suit had shrunk a brave bit with the salt water; but into ordinary frock an' corduroys he declared he would not get—not if he had to go naked the rest of his life; so my father, being a good-natured man and handy with the needle, turned to and repaired damages with a piece or two of scarlet cloth cut from the jacket of one of the drowned Marines. Well, the poor little chap chanced to be standing, in this rig-out, down by the gate of Gunner's Meadow, where they had buried two score and over of his comrades. The morning was a fine one, early in March month; and along came the cracked trumpeter, likewise taking a stroll.

"'Hullo!' says he; 'good mornin'! And what might you be doin' here?'

"'I was a-wishin',' says the boy, 'I had a pair o' drum-sticks. Our lads were buried yonder without so much as a drum tapped or a musket fired; and that's not Christian burial for British soldiers.'

"'Phut!' says the trumpeter, and spat on the ground; 'a parcel of Marines!'

"The boy eyed him a second or so, and answered up: 'If I'd a tab of turf handy, I'd bung it at your mouth, you greasy cavalryman, and learn you to speak respectful of your betters. The Marines are the handiest body of men in the service.'

"The trumpeter looked down on him from the height of six foot two, and asked: 'Did they die well?'

"'They died very well. There was a lot of running to and fro at first, and some of the men began to cry, and a few to strip off their clothes. But when the ship fell off for the last time, Captain Mein turned and said something to Major Griffiths, the commanding officer on board, and the Major called out to me to beat to quarters. It might have been for a wedding, he sang it out so cheerful. We'd had word already that 'twas to be parade order, and the men fell in as trim and decent as if they were going to church. One or two even tried to shave at the last moment. The Major wore his medals. One of the seamen, seeing I had hard work to keep the drum steady—the sling being a bit loose for me and the wind what you remember—lashed it tight with a piece of rope; and that saved my life afterwards, a drum being as good as a cork until 'tis stove. I kept beating away until every man was on deck; and then the Major formed them up and told them to die like British soldiers, and the chaplain read a prayer or two—the boys standin' all the while like rocks, each man's courage keeping up the others'. The chaplain was in the middle of a prayer when she struck. In ten minutes she was gone. That was how they died, cavalryman.'

"'And that was very well done, drummer of the Marines. What's your name?'

"'John Christian.'

"'Mine is William George Tallifer, trumpeter, of the 7th Light Dragoons—the Queen's Own. I played *God Save the King* while our men were drowning. Captain Duncanfield told me to sound a call or two, to put them in heart; but that matter of *God Save the King* was a notion of my own. I won't say anything to hurt the feelings of a Marine, even if he's not much over five-foot tall; but the Queen's Own Hussars is a tearin' fine regiment. As between horse and foot, 'tis a question o' which gets the chance. All the way from Sahagun to Corunna 'twas we that took and gave the knocks—at Mayorga and Rueda, and Bennyventy.' (The reason, sir, I can speak the names so pat is that my father learnt 'em by heart afterwards from the trumpeter, who was always talking about Mayorga and Rueda and Bennyventy.) 'We made the rear-guard, under General Paget, and drove the French every time; and all the infantry did was to sit about in wine-shops till we whipped 'em out, an' steal an' straggle an' play the tom-fool in general. And when it came to a stand-up fight at Corunna, 'twas the horse, or the best part of it, that had to stay sea-sick aboard the transports, an' watch the infantry in the thick o' the caper. Very well they behaved, too; 'specially the 4th Regiment, an' the 42nd Highlanders an' the Dirty Half-Hundred. Oh, ay; they're decent regiments, all three. But the Queen's Own Hussars is a tearin' fine regiment. So you played on your drum when the ship was goin' down? Drummer John Christian, I'll have to get you a new pair o' drum-sticks for that.'

"Well, sir, it appears that the very next day the trumpeter marched into Helston, and got a carpenter there to turn him a pair of box-wood drum-sticks for the boy. And this was the beginning of one of the most curious friendships you ever heard tell of. Nothing delighted the pair more than to borrow a boat off my father and pull out to the rocks where the *Primrose* and the *Despatch* had struck and sunk; and on still days 'twas pretty to hear them out there off the Manacles, the drummer playing his tattoo—for they always took their music with them—and the trumpeter practising calls, and making his trumpet speak like an angel. But if the weather turned rough-ish, they'd be walking together and talking; leastwise, the youngster listened while the other discoursed about Sir John's campaign in Spain and Portugal, telling how each little skirmish befell; and of Sir John himself, and General Baird and General Paget, and Colonel Vivian, his own commanding officer, and what kind of men they were; and of the last bloody standup at Corruna, and so forth, as if neither could have enough.

"But all this had to come to an end in the late summer; for the boy, John Christian, being now well and strong again, must go up to Plymouth to report himself. 'Twas his own wish (for I believe King George had forgotten all about him), but his friend wouldn't hold him back. As for the trumpeter, my father had made an arrangement to take him on as a lodger as soon as the boy left; and on the morning fixed for the start, he was up at the door here by five o'clock, with his trumpet slung by his side, and all the rest of his kit in a small valise. A Monday morning it was, and after breakfast he had fixed to walk with the boy some way on the road towards Helston, where the coach started. My father left them at breakfast together, and went out to meat the pig, and do a few odd morning jobs of that sort. When he came back, the boy was still at table, and the trumpeter standing here by the chimney-place with the drum and trumpet in his hands, hitched together just as they be at this moment.

"'Look at this,' he says to my father, showing him the lock; 'I picked it up off a starving brass-worker in Lisbon, and it is not one of your common locks that one word of six letters will open at any time. There's *janius* in this lock; for you've only to make the rings spell any six-letter word you please, and snap down the lock upon that, and never a soul can open it—not the maker, even—until somebody comes along that knows the word you snapped it on. Now Johnny here's goin', and he leaves his drum behind him; for, though he can make pretty music on it, the parchment sags in wet weather, by reason of the sea-water getting at it; an' if he carries it to Plymouth, they'll only condemn it and give him another. And, as for me, I shan't have the heart to put lip to the trumpet any more when Johnny's gone. So we've chosen a word together, and locked 'em together upon that; and, by your leave, I'll hang 'em here together on the hook over your fire-place. Maybe Johnny'll come back; maybe not. Maybe, if he comes, I'll be dead an' gone, an' he'll take 'em apart an' try their music for old sake's sake. But if he never comes, nobody can separate 'em; for nobody beside knows the word. And if you marry and have sons, you can tell 'em that here are tied together the souls of Johnny Christian, drummer of the Marines, and William George Tallifer, once trumpeter of the Queen's Own Hussars. Amen.'

"With that he hung the two instruments 'pon the hook there; and the boy stood up and thanked my father and shook hands; and the pair went forth of the door, towards Helston.

"Somewhere on the road they took leave of one another; but nobody saw the parting, nor heard what was said between them. About three in the afternoon the trumpeter came walking back over the hill; and by the time my father came home from the fishing, the cottage was tidied up and the tea ready, and the whole place shining like a new pin. From that time for five years he lodged here with my father, looking after the house and tilling the garden; and all the while he was steadily failing, the hurt in his head spreading, in a manner, to his limbs. My father watched the feebleness growing on him, but said nothing. And from first to last neither spake a word about the drummer, John Christian; nor did any letter reach them, nor word of his doings.

"The rest of the tale you'm free to believe, sir, or not, as you please. It stands upon my father's words, and he always declared he was ready to kiss the Book upon it before judge and jury. He said, too, that he never had the wit to make up such a yarn; and he defied anyone to explain about the lock, in particular, by any other tale. But you shall judge for yourself.

"My father said that about three o'clock in the morning, April fourteenth of the year 'fourteen, he and William Tallifer were sitting here, just as you and I, sir, are sitting now. My father had put on his clothes a few minutes before, and was mending his spiller by the light of the horn lantern, mean-ing to set off before daylight to haul the trammel. The trumpeter hadn't been to bed at all. Towards the last he mostly spent his nights (and his days, too) dozing in the elbow-chair where you sit at this minute. He was dozing then (my father said), with his chin dropped forward on his chest, when a knock sounded upon the door, and the door opened, and in walked an up-right young man in scarlet regimentals.

"He had grown a brave bit, and his face was the colour of wood-ashes; but it was the drummer, John Christian. Only his uniform was different from the one he used to wear, and the figures '38' shone in brass upon his collar.

"The drummer walked past my father as if he never saw him, and stood by the elbow-chair and said:

"'Trumpeter, trumpeter, are you one with me?'

"And the trumpeter just lifted the lids of his eyes, and answered, 'How should I not be one with you, drummer Johnny—Johnny boy? The men are patient. 'Till you come, I count; while you march, I mark time; until the discharge comes.'

"'The discharge has come to-night,' said the drummer, 'and the word is Corunna no longer'; and stepping to the chimney-place, he unhooked the drum and trumpet, and began to twist the brass rings of the lock, spelling the word aloud, so—C-O-R-U-N-A. When he had fixed the last letter, the padlock opened in his hand.

"Did you know, trumpeter, that when I came to Plymouth they put me into a line regiment?'

"'The 38th is a good regiment,' answered the old Hussar, still in his dull voice. 'I went back with them from Sahagun to Corunna. At Corunna they stood in General Fraser's division, on the right. They behaved well.'

"'But I'd fain see the Marines again,' says the drummer, handing him the trumpet; 'and you—you shall call once more for the Queen's Own. Matthew,' he says, suddenly, turning on my father—and when he turned, my father saw for the first time that his scarlet jacket had a round hole by the breast-bone, and that the blood was welling there—'Matthew, we shall want your boat.'

"Then my father rose on his legs like a man in a dream, while they two slung on, the one his drum, and t'other his trumpet. He took the lantern, and went quaking before them down to the shore, and they breathed heavily behind him; and they stepped into his boat, and my father pushed off.

"'Row you first for Dolor Point,' says the drummer. So my father rowed them out past the white houses of Coverack to Dolor Point, and there, at a word, lay on his oars. And the trumpeter, William Tallifer, put his trumpet to his mouth and sounded the Revelly. The music of it was like rivers running.

"'They will follow,' said the dummer. 'Matthew, pull you now for the Manacles.'

"So my father pulled for the Manacles, and came to an easy close outside Carn dû. And the drummer took his sticks and beat a tattoo, there by the edge of the reef; and the music of it was like a rolling chariot.

"'That will do,' says he, breaking off; 'they will follow. Pull now for the shore under Gunner's Meadow.'

"Then my father pulled for the shore, and ran his boat in under Gunner's

Meadow. And they stepped out, all three, and walked up to the meadow. By the gate the drummer halted and began his tattoo again, looking out towards the darkness over the sea.

"And while the drum beat, and my father held his breath, there came up out of the sea and the darkness a troop of many men, horse and foot, and formed up among the graves; and others rose out of the graves and formed up—drowned Marines with bleached faces, and pale Hussars riding their horses, all lean and shadowy. There was no clatter of hoofs or accoutrements, my father said, but a soft sound all the while, like the beating of a bird's wing, and a black shadow lying like a pool about the feet of all. The drummer stood upon a little knoll just inside the gate, and beside him the tall trumpeter, with hand on hip, watching them gather; and behind them both my father, clinging to the gate. When no more came, the drummer stopped playing, and said, 'Call the roll.'

"Then the trumpeter stepped towards the end man of the rank and called, 'Troop-Sergeant-Major Thomas Irons!' and the man in a thin voice answered 'Here!'

"'Troop-Sergeant-Major Thomas Irons, how is it with you?'

"The man answered, 'How should it be with me? When I was young, I betrayed a girl; and when I was grown, I betrayed a friend; and for these things I must pay. But I died as a man ought. God save the King!'

"The trumpeter called to the next man, 'Trooper Henry Buckingham!' and the next man answered, 'Here!'

"'Trooper Henry Buckingham, how is it with you?'

"'How should it be with me? I was a drunkard, and I stole, and in Lugo, in a wine-shop, I knifed a man. But I died as a man should. God save the King!'

"So the trumpeter went down the line; and when he had finished, the drummer took it up, hailing the dead Marines in their order. Each man answered to his name, and each man ended with 'God save the King!' When all were hailed, the drummer stepped back to his mound, and called:

"'It is well. You are content, and we are content to join you. Wait yet a little while.'

"With this he turned and ordered my father to pick up the lantern, and lead the way back. As my father picked it up, he heard the ranks of dead men cheer and call, 'God save the King!' all together, and saw them waver and fade back into the dark, like a breath fading off a pane.

"But when they came back here to the kitchen, and my father set the lantern down, it seemed they'd both forgot about him. For the drummer turned in the lantern-light—and my father could see the blood still welling out of the hole in his breast—and took the trumpet-sling from around the other's neck, and locked drum and trumpet together again, choosing the letters on the lock very carefully. While he did this he said:

"'The word is no more Corunna, but Bayonne. As you left out an "n" in Corunna, so must I leave out an "n" in Bayonne.' And before snapping the padlock, he spelt out the word slowly—'B-A-Y-O-N-E.' After that, he used no more speech; but turned and hung the two instruments back on the hook; and then took the trumpeter by the arm; and the pair walked out into the darkness, glancing neither to right nor left.

"My father was on the point of following, when he heard a sort of sigh behind him; and there, sitting in the elbow-chair, was the very trumpeter he had just seen walk out by the door! If my father's heart jumped before, you may believe it jumped quicker now. But after a bit, he went up to the man asleep in the chair, and put a hand upon him. It was the trumpeter in flesh and blood that he touched; but though the flesh was warm, the trumpeter was dead.

"Well, sir, they buried him three days after; and at first my father was minded to say nothing about his dream (as he thought it). But the day after the funeral, he met Parson Kendall coming from Helston market: and the parson called out: 'Have 'ee heard the news the coach brought down this mornin'?' 'What news?' says my father. 'Why, that peace is agreed upon.' 'None too soon,' says my father. 'Not soon enough for our poor lads at Bayonne,' the parson answered. 'Bayonne!' cries my father, with a jump. 'Why, yes'; and the parson told him all about a great sally the French had made on the night of April 13th. 'Do you happen to know if the 38th Regiment was engaged?' my father asked. 'Come, now,' said Parson Kendall, 'I didn't know you was so well up in the campaign. But, as it happens, I *do* know that the 38th was engaged, for 'twas they that held a cottage and stopped the French advance.'

"Still my father held his tongue; and when, a week later, he walked into Helston and bought a *Mercury* off the Sherborne rider, and got the landlord of the 'Angel' to spell out the list of killed and wounded, sure enough, there among the killed was Drummer John Christian, of the 38th Foot.

"After this, there was nothing for a religious man but to make a clean breast. So my father went up to Parson Kendall and told the whole story. The parson listened, and put a question or two, and then asked:

"'Have you tried to open the lock since that night?'

"'I han't dared to touch it,' says my father.

"'Then come along and try.' When the parson came to the cottage here, he took the things off the hook and tried the lock. 'Did he say "*Bayonne*"? The word has seven letters.'

"'Not if you spell it with one "n" as *he* did,' says my father.

"The parson spelt it out—B-A-Y-O-N-E. 'Whew!' says he, for the lock had fallen open in his hand.

"He stood considering it a moment, and then he says, 'I tell you what. I shouldn't blab this all round the parish, if I was you. You won't get no credit for truth-telling, and a miracle's wasted on a set of fools. But if you like, I'll shut down the lock again upon a holy word that no one but me shall know, and neither drummer nor trumpeter, dead nor alive, shall frighten the secret out of me.'

"'I wish to gracious you would, parson,' said my father.

"The parson chose the holy word there and then, and shut the lock back upon it, and hung the drum and trumpet back in their place. He is gone long since, taking the word with him. And till the lock is broken by force, nobody will ever separate those twain."

ARTHUR QUILLER-COUCH
1863-1944

Arthur Thomas Quiller-Couch entered Trinity College, Oxford, in 1882. He wrote for the *Oxford Magazine* while there, doing parodies of English poets and first using the pseudonym Q, by which he became well known. In 1887 he published a romantic novel, *Dead Man's Rock*, and then left Oxford to take up journalism in London. *The Astonishing History of Troy Town* (1888) introduced the place that resurfaced in much of his fiction and would later be identified with the small Cornish seaport town, Fowey.

In 1890 Quiller-Couch became an assistant editor of *The Speaker*, a weekly, contributing a short story for each issue as well as occasional pieces. At the same time he was working long hours writing novels and doing freelance work for other periodicals until 1892.

A desire to live by the sea, his love of Fowey, and a Cornish wife prompted Quiller-Couch to abandon his journalism career in London in 1892 and head for the seaside town. He continued until 1899 to do some writing for *The Speaker*, and he did not stop free-lancing until 1912. Most of his fiction was written during these years, a period when he also indulged his passion for yachting.

Never confining himself solely to fiction, Quiller-Couch also became an anthologist, editing the world-renowned *Oxford Book of English Verse* (1900) and the *Oxford Book of Ballads* (1910).

Honors were heaped upon Quiller-Couch. In 1910 he was knighted, and two years later he was appointed King Edward VII Professor of English Literature at Cambridge and elected fellow of Jesus College.

For the rest of his life he spent the school term at Cambridge, returning to his home at the shore during vacations. His lectures, models of perfection, were collected in, among other volumes, *On the Art of Writing* (1916), *On the Art of Reading* (1920), *Charles Dickens and Other Victorians* (1925), and *The Poet as Citizen and Other Papers* (1934). A versatile writer, his serious poetry appeared in 1930 under the simple title *Poems*, and his light verse the same year in the volume *Green Bags*.

The Ship That Saw a Ghost

BY FRANK NORRIS

VERY MUCH of this story must remain untold, for the reason that if it were definitely known what business I had aboard the tramp steam-freighter *Glarus*, three hundred miles off the South American coast on a certain summer's day, some few years ago, I would very likely be obliged to answer a great many personal and direct questions put by fussy and impertinent experts in maritime law—who are paid to be inquisitive. Also, I would get "Ally Bazan," Strokher and Hardenberg into trouble.

Suppose on that certain summer's day, you had asked of Lloyds' agency where the *Glarus* was, and what was her destination and cargo. You would have been told that she was twenty days out from Callao, bound north to San Francisco in ballast; that she had been spoken by the bark *Medea* and the steamer *Benevento*; that she was reported to have blown out a cylinder head, but being manageable was proceeding on her way under sail.

That is what Lloyds would have answered.

If you know something of the ways of ships and what is expected of them, you will understand that the *Glarus*, to be some half a dozen hundred miles south of where Lloyds' would have her, and to be still going south, under full steam, was a scandal that would have made her brothers and sisters ostracize her finally and forever.

And that is curious, too. Humans may indulge in vagaries innumerable, and may go far afield in the way of lying; but a ship may not so much as quibble without suspicion. The least lapse of "regularity," the least difficulty in squaring performance with intuition, and behold she is on the black list, and her captain, owners, officers, agents and consignors, and even supercargoes, are asked to explain.

And the *Glarus* was already on the black list. From the beginning her stars had been malign. As the *Breda*, she had first lost her reputation, seduced into a filibustering escapade down the South American coast, where in the end a plain-clothes United States detective—that is to say, a revenue cutter—arrested her off Buenos Ayres and brought her home, a prodigal daughter, besmirched and disgraced.

After that she was in some dreadful blackbirding business in a far quarter of the South Pacific; and after that—her name changed finally to the

Glarus—poached seals for a syndicate of Dutchmen who lived in Tacoma, and who afterward built a club-house out of what she earned.

And after that we got her.

We got her, I say, through Ryder's South Pacific Exploitation Company. The "President" had picked out a lovely little deal for Hardenberg, Strok-her and Ally Bazan (the Three Black Crows), which he swore would make them "independent rich" the rest of their respective lives. It is a promising deal (B. 300 it is on Ryder's map), and if you want to know more about it you may write to ask Ryder what B. 300 is. If he chooses to tell you, that is his affair.

For B. 300—let us confess it—is, as Hardenberg puts it, as crooked as a dog's hind leg. It is as risky as barratry. If you pull it off you may—after paying Ryder his share—divide sixty-five, or possibly sixty-seven, thousand dollars between you and your associates. If you fail, and you are perilously like to fail, you will be sure to have a man or two of your companions shot, maybe yourself obliged to pistol certain people, and in the end fetch up at Tahiti, prisoner in a French patrol-boat.

Observe that B. 300 is spoken of as still open. It is so, for the reason that the Three Black Crows did not pull it off. It still stands marked up in red ink on the map that hangs over Ryder's desk in the San Francisco office; and any one can have a chance at it who will meet Cyrus Ryder's terms. Only he can't get the *Glarus* for the attempt.

For the trip to the island after B. 300 was the last occasion on which the *Glarus* will smell blue water or taste the trades. She will never clear again. She is lumber.

And yet the *Glarus* on this very blessed day of 1902 is riding to her buoys off Sausalito in San Francisco Bay, complete in every detail (bar a broken propeller shaft), not a rope missing, not a screw loose, not a plank started— a perfectly equipped steam-freighter.

But you may go along the "Front" in San Francisco from Fisherman's Wharf to the China steamships' docks and shake your dollars under the seamen's noses, and if you so much as whisper *Glarus* they will edge suddenly off and look at you with scared suspicion, and then, as like as not, walk away without another word. No pilot will take the *Glarus* out; no captain will navigate her; no stoker will feed her fires; no sailor will walk her decks. The *Glarus* is suspect. She has seen a ghost.

It happened on our voyage to the island after this same B. 300. We had stood well off from shore for day after day, and Hardenberg had shaped our course so far from the track of navigation that since the *Benevento* had hulled down and vanished over the horizon no stitch of canvas nor smudge of smoke had we seen. We had passed the equator long since, and would fetch a long circuit to the southard, and bear up against the island by a circuitous route. This to avoid being spoken. It was tremendously essential that the *Glarus* should not be spoken.

I suppose, no doubt, that it was the knowledge of our isolation that impressed me with the dreadful remoteness of our position. Certainly the sea in itself looks no different at a thousand than at a hundred miles from shore. But as day after day I came out on deck at noon, after ascertaining our position on the chart (a mere pin-point in a reach of empty paper), the sight of the ocean weighed down upon me with an infinitely great awesomeness— and I was no new hand to the high seas even then.

But at such times the *Glarus* seemed to me to be threading a loneliness beyond all worlds and beyond all conception desolate. Even in more populous waters, when no sail notches the line of the horizon, the propinquity of one's kind is nevertheless a thing understood, and to an unappreciated degree comforting. Here, however, I knew we were out, far out in the desert. Never a keel for years upon years before us had parted these waters; never a sail had bellied to these winds. Perfunctorily, day in and day out we turned our eyes through long habit toward the horizon. But we knew, before the look, that the searching would be bootless. Forever and forever, under the pitiless sun and cold blue sky stretched the indigo of the ocean floor. The ether between the planets can be no less empty, no less void.

I never, till that moment, could have so much as conceived the imagination of such loneliness, such utter stagnant abomination of desolation. In an open boat, bereft of comrades, I should have gone mad in thirty minutes.

I remember to have approximated the impression of such empty immensity only once before, in my younger days, when I lay on my back on a treeless, bushless mountainside and stared up into the sky for the better part of an hour.

You probably know the trick. If you do not, you must understand that if you look up at the blue long enough, the flatness of the thing begins little by little to expand, to give here and there; and the eye travels on and on and up and up, till at length (well for you that it lasts but the fraction of a second), you all at once see space. You generally stop there and cry out, and—your hands over your eyes—are only too glad to grovel close to the good old solid earth again. Just as I, so often on short voyage, was glad to wrench my eyes away from that horrid vacancy, to fasten them upon our sailless masts and stack, or to lay my grip upon the sooty smudged taffrail of the only thing that stood between me and the Outer Dark.

For we had come at last to that region of the Great Seas where no ship goes, the silent sea of Coleridge and the Ancient One, the unplumbed, untracked, uncharted Dreadfulness, primordial, hushed, and we were as much alone as a grain of star-dust whirling in the empty space beyond Uranus and the ken of the greater telescopes.

So the *Glarus* plodded and churned her way onward. Every day and all day the same pale-blue sky and the unwinking sun bent over that moving speck. Every day and all day the same black-blue water-world, untouched by any known wind, smooth as a slab of syenite, colourful as an opal, stretched out and around and beyond and before and behind us, forever, illimitable, empty. Every day the smoke of our fires veiled the streaked whiteness of our wake. Every day Hardenberg (our skipper) at noon pricked a pin-hole in the chart that hung in the wheel-house, and that showed we were so much farther into the wilderness. Every day the world of men, of civilization, of newspapers, policemen and street-railways receded, and we steamed on alone, lost and forgotten in that silent sea.

"Jolly lot o' room to turn raound in," observed Ally Bazan, the colonial, "withaout steppin' on y'r neighbour's toes."

"We're clean, clean out o' the track o' navigation," Hardenberg told him. "An' a blessed good thing for us, too. Nobody ever comes down into these waters. Ye couldn't pick no course here. Everything leads to nowhere."

"Might as well be in a bally balloon," said Strokher.

I shall not tell of the nature of the venture on which the *Glarus* was bound, further than to say it was not legitimate. It had to do with an ill thing done more than two centuries ago. There was money in the venture, but it was not to be gained by a violation of metes and bounds which are better left intact.

The island toward which we were heading is associated in the minds of men with a Horror. A ship had called there once, two hundred years in advance of the *Glarus*—a ship not much unlike the crank high-prowed caravel of Hudson, and her company had landed, and having accomplished the evil they had set out to do, made shift to sail away. And then, just after the palms of the island had sunk from sight below the water's edge, the unspeakable had happened. The Death that was not Death had arisen from out the sea and stood before the ship, and over it, and the blight of the thing lay along the decks like mould, and the ship sweated in the terror of that which is yet without a name.

Twenty men died in the first week, all but six in the second. These six, with the shadow of insanity upon them, made out to launch a boat, returned to the island and died there, after leaving a record of what had happened.

The six left the ship exactly as she was, sails all set, lanterns all lit—left her in the shadow of the Death that was not Death.

She stood there, becalmed, and watched them go. She was never heard of again.

Or was she—well, that's as may be.

But the main point of the whole affair, to my notion, has always been this. The ship was the last friend of those six poor wretches who made back for the island with their poor chests of plunder. She was their guardian, as it were, would have defended and befriended them to the last; and also we, the Three Black Crows and myself, had no right under heaven, nor before the law of men, to come prying and peeping into this business—into this affair of the dead and buried past. There was sacrilege in it. We were no better than body-snatchers.

When I heard the others complaining of the loneliness of our surroundings, I said nothing at first. I was no sailor man, and I was on board only by tolerance. But I looked again at the maddening sameness of the horizon— the same vacant, void horizon that we had seen now for sixteen days on end, and felt in my wits and in my nerves that same formless rebellion and protest such as comes when the same note is reiterated over and over again.

It may seem a little thing that the mere fact of meeting with no other ship should have ground down the edge of the spirit. But let the incredulous—bound upon such a hazard as ours—sail straight into nothingness for sixteen days on end, seeing nothing but the sun, hearing nothing but the thresh of his own screw, and then put the question.

And yet, of all things, we desired no company. Stealth was our one great aim. But I think there were moments—toward the last—when the Three Crows would have welcomed even a cruiser.

Besides, there was more cause for depression, after all, than mere isolation.

On the seventh day Hardenberg and I were forward by the cat-head, adjusting the grain with some half-formed intent of spearing the porpoises that of late had begun to appear under our bows, and Hardenberg had been computing the number of days we were yet to run.

"We are some five hundred odd miles off that island by now," he said, "and she's doing her thirteen knots handsome. All's well so far—but do you know, I'd just as soon raise that point o' land as soon as convenient."

"How so?" said I, bending on the line. "Expect some weather?"

"Mr. Dixon," said he, giving me curious glance, "the sea is a queer proposition, put it any ways. I've been a seafarin' man since I was big as a minute, and I know the sea, and what's more, the Feel o' the sea. Now, look out yonder. Nothin', hey? Nothin' but the same ol' skyline we've watched all the way out. The glass is as steady as a steeple, and this ol' hooker, I reckon, is as sound as the day she went off the ways. But just the same if I were to home now, a-foolin' about Gloucester way in my little dough-dish—d'ye know what? I'd put into port. I sure would. Because why? Because I got the Feel o' the Sea, Mr. Dixon. I got the Feel o' the Sea."

I had heard old skippers say something of this before, and I cited to Hardenberg the experience of a skipper captain I once knew who had turned turtle in a calm sea off Trincomalee. I asked him what this Feel of the

Sea was warning him against just now (for on the high sea any premonition is a premonition of evil, not of good). But he was not explicit.

"I don't know," he answered moodily, and as if in great perplexity, coiling the rope as he spoke. "I don't know. There's some blame thing or other close to us, I'll bet a hat. I don't know the name of it, but there's a big Bird in the air, just out of sight som'eres, and," he suddenly exclaimed, smacking his knee and leaning forward, "I—don't—like—it—one—dam'—bit."

The same thing came up in our talk in the cabin that night, after the dinner was taken off and we settled down to tobacco. Only, at this time, Hardenberg was on duty on the bridge. It was Ally Bazan who spoke instead.

"Seems to me," he hazarded, "as haow they's somethin' or other a-goin' to bump up pretty blyme soon. I shouldn't be surprised, naow, y'know, if we piled her up on some bally uncharted reef along o' to-night and went strite daown afore we'd had a bloomin' charnce to s'y 'So long, gen'lemen all.'"

He laughed as he spoke, but when, just at that moment, a pan clattered in the galley, he jumped suddenly with an oath, and looked hard about the cabin.

Then Strokher confessed to a sense of distress also. He'd been having it since day before yesterday, it seemed.

"And I put it to you the glass is lovely," he said, "so it's no blow. I guess," he continued, "we're all a bit seedy and ship-sore."

And whether or not this talk worked upon my own nerves, or whether in very truth the Feel of the Sea had found me also, I do not know; but I do know that after dinner that night, just before going to bed, a queer sense of apprehension came upon me, and that when I had come to my stateroom, after my turn upon deck, I became furiously angry with nobody in particular, because I could not at once find the matches. But here was a difference. The other man had been merely vaguely uncomfortable.

I could put a name to my uneasiness. I felt that we were being watched.

It was a strange ship's company we made after that. I speak only of the Crows and myself. We carried a scant crew of stokers, and there was also a chief engineer. But we saw so little of him that he did not count. The Crows and I gloomed on the quarterdeck from dawn to dark, silent, irritable, working upon each other's nerves till the creak of a block would make a man jump like cold steel laid to his flesh. We quarreled over absolute nothings, glowered at each other for half a word, and each one of us, at different times, was at some pains to declare that never in the course of his career had he been associated with such a disagreeable trio of brutes. Yet we were always together, and sought each other's company with painful insistence.

Only once were we all agreed, and that was when the cook, a Chinaman, spoiled a certain batch of biscuits. Unanimously we fell foul of the creature with so much vociferation as fishwives till he fled the cabin in actual fear of mishandling, leaving us suddenly seized with noisy hilarity—for the first time in a week. Hardenberg proposed a round of drinks from our single remaining case of beer. We stood up and formed an Elk's chain and then drained our glasses to each other's health with profound seriousness.

That same evening, I remember, we all sat on the quarterdeck till late and—oddly enough—related each one his life's history up to date; and then went down to the cabin for a game of euchre before turning in.

We had left Strokher on the bridge—it was his watch—and had forgotten all about him in the interest of the game, when—I suppose it was about one in the morning—I heard him whistle long and shrill. I laid down my cards and said:

"Hark!"

In the silence that followed we heard at first only the muffled lope of our engines, the cadenced snorting of the exhaust, and the ticking of Hardenberg's big watch in his waistcoat that he had hung by the arm-hole to the back of his chair. Then from the bridge, above our deck, prolonged, intoned—a wailing cry in the night—came Strokher's voice:

"Sail oh-h-h."

And the cards fell from our hands, and, like men turned to stone, we sat looking at each other across the soiled red cloth for what seemed an immeasurably long minute.

Then stumbling and swearing, in a hysteria of hurry, we gained the deck.

There was a moon, very low and reddish, but no wind. The sea beyond the taffrail was as smooth as lava, and so still that the swells from the cutwater of the *Glarus* did not break as they rolled away from the bows.

I remember that I stood staring and blinking at the empty ocean—where the moonlight lay like a painted stripe reaching to the horizon—stupid and frowning, till Hardenberg, who had gone on ahead, cried:

"Not here—on the bridge!"

We joined Strokher, and as I came up the others were asking:

"Where? Where?"

And there, before he had pointed, I saw—we all of us saw— And I heard Hardenberg's teeth come together like a spring trap, while Ally Bazan ducked as though to a blow, muttering:

"Gord 'a' mercy, what nyme do ye put to a ship like that?"

And after that no one spoke for a long minute, and we stood there, moveless black shadows, huddled together for the sake of the blessed elbow touch that means so incalculably much, looking off over our port quarter.

For the ship that we saw there—oh, she was not a half-mile distant—was unlike any ship known to present day construction.

She was short, and high-pooped, and her stern, which was turned a little toward us, we could see, was set with curious windows, not unlike a house. And on either side of this stern were two great iron cressets such as once were used to burn signal-fires in. She had three masts with mighty yards swung 'thwart ship, but bare of all sails save a few rotting streamers. Here and there about her a tangled mass of rigging drooped and sagged.

And there she lay, in the red eye of the setting moon, in that solitary ocean, shadowy, antique, forlorn, a thing the most abandoned, the most sinister I ever remember to have seen.

Then Strokher began to explain volubly and with many repetitions.

"A derelict, of course. I was asleep; yes, I was asleep. Gross neglect of duty. I say I was asleep—on watch. And we worked up to her. When I woke, why—you see, when I woke, there she was," he gave a weak little laugh, "and—and now, why, there she is, you see. I turned around and saw her sudden like—when I woke up, that is."

He laughed again, and as he laughed the engines far below our feet gave a sudden hiccough. Something crashed and struck the ship's sides till we lurched as we stood. There was a shriek of steam, a shout—and then silence.

The noise of the machinery ceased; the *Glarus* slid through the still water, moving only by her own decreasing momentum.

Hardenberg sang, "Stand by!" and called down the tube to the engine-room.

"What's up?"

I was standing close enough to him to hear the answer in a small, faint voice:

"Shaft gone, sir."

"Broke?"

"Yes, sir."

Hardenberg faced about.

"Come below. We must talk." I do not think any of us cast a glance at the Other Ship again. Certainly I kept my eyes away from her. But as we started down the companionway I laid my hand on Strokher's shoulder. The rest were ahead. I looked him straight between the eyes as I asked:

"Were you asleep? Is that why you saw her so suddenly?"

It is now five years since I asked the question. I am still waiting for Strokher's answer.

Well, our shaft was broken. That was flat. We went down into the engine-room and saw the jagged fracture that was the symbol of our broken hopes. And in the course of the next five minutes' conversation with the chief we found that, as we had not provided against such a contingency, there was to be no mending of it. We said nothing about the mishap coinciding with the appearance of the Other Ship. But I know we did not consider the break with any degree of surprise after a few moments.

We came up from the engine-room and sat down to the cabin table.

"Now what?" said Hardenberg, by way of beginning.

Nobody answered at first.

It was by now three in the morning. I recall it all perfectly. The ports opposite where I sat were open and I could see. The moon was all but full set. The dawn was coming up with a copper murkiness over the edge of the world. All the stars were yet out. The sea, for all the red moon and copper dawn, was gray, and there, less than half a mile away, still lay our consort. I could see her through the portholes with each slow careening of the *Glarus*.

"I vote for the island," cried Ally Bazan, "shaft or no shaft. We rigs a bit o' syle, y'know—" and thereat the discussion began.

For upward of two hours it raged, with loud words and shaken fore-fingers, and great noisy bangings of the table, and how it would have ended I do not know, but at last—it was then maybe five in the morning—the lookout passed word down to the cabin:

"Will you come on deck, gentlemen?" It was the mate who spoke, and the man was shaken—I could see that—to the very vitals of him. We started and stared at one another, and I watched little Ally Bazan go slowly white to the lips. And even then no word of the ship, except as it might be this from Hardenberg:

"What is it? Good God Almighty, I'm no coward, but this thing is getting one too many for me."

Then without further speech he went on deck.

The air was cool. The sun was not yet up. It was that strange, queer mid-period between dark and dawn, when the night is over and the day not yet come, just the gray that is neither light nor dark, the dim dead blink as of the refracted light from extinct worlds.

We stood at the rail. We did not speak; we stood watching. It was so still that the drip of steam from some loosened pipe far below was plainly audi-ble, and it sounded in that lifeless, silent grayness like—God knows what—a death tick.

"You see," said the mate, speaking just above a whisper, "there's no mis-take about it. She is moving—this way."

"Oh, a current, of course," Strokher tried to say cheerfully, "sets her to-ward us."

Would the morning never come?

Ally Bazan—his parents were Catholic—began to mutter to himself.

Then Hardenberg spoke aloud.

"I particularly don't want—that—out—there—to cross our bows. I don't want it to come to that. We must get some sails on her."

"And I put it to you as man to man," said Strokher, "where might be your wind."

He was right. The *Glarus* floated in absolute calm. On all that slab of ocean nothing moved but the Dead Ship.

She came on slowly; her bows, the high, clumsy bows pointed toward us, the water turning from her forefoot. She came on; she was near at hand. We saw her plainly—saw the rotted planks, the crumbling rigging, the rust-corroded metal-work, the broken rail, the gaping deck, and I could imagine that the clean water broke away from her sides in refluent wavelets as though in recoil from a thing unclean. She made no sound. No single thing stirred aboard the hulk of her—but she moved.

We were helpless. The *Glarus* could stir no boat in any direction; we were chained to the spot. Nobody had thought to put out our lights, and they still burned on through the dawn, strangely out of place in their red-and-green garishness, like maskers surprised by daylight.

And in the silence of that empty ocean, in that queer half-light between dawn and day, at six o'clock, silent as the settling of the dead to the bottomless bottom of the ocean, gray as fog, lonely, blind, soulless, voiceless, the Dead Ship crossed our bows.

I do not know how long after this the Ship disappeared, or what was the time of day when we at last pulled ourselves together. But we came to some sort of decision at last. This was to go on—under sail. We were too close to the island now to turn back for—for a broken shaft.

The afternoon was spent fitting on the sails to her, and when after nightfall the wind at length came up fresh and favourable, I believe we all felt heartened and a deal more hardy—until the last canvas went aloft, and Hardenberg took the wheel.

We had drifted a good deal since the morning, and the bows of the *Glarus* were pointed homeward, but as soon as the breeze blew strong enough to get steerageway Hardenberg put the wheel over and, as the booms swung across the deck, headed for the island again.

We had not gone on this course half an hour—no, not twenty minutes—before the wind shifted a whole quarter of the compass and took the *Glarus* square in the teeth, so that there was nothing for it but to tack. And then the strangest thing befell.

I will make allowance for the fact that there was no centre-board nor keel to speak of to the *Glarus*. I will admit that the sails upon a nine-hundred-ton freighter are not calculated to speed her, nor steady her. I will even admit the possibility of a current that set from the island toward us. All this may be true, yet the *Glarus* should have advanced. We should have made a wake.

And instead of this, our stolid, steady, trusty old boat was—what shall I say?

I will say that no man may thoroughly understand a ship—after all. I will say that new ships are cranky and unsteady; that old and seasoned ships have their little crochets, their little fussinesses that their skippers must learn and humour if they are to get anything out of them; that even the best ships may sulk at times, shirk their work, grow unstable, perverse, and refuse to answer helm and handling. And I will say that some ships that for years have sailed blue water as soberly and as docilely as a street-car horse has plodded the treadmill of the 'tween-tracks, have been known to balk, as stubbornly and as conclusively as any old Bay Billy that ever wore a bell. I know this has happened, because I have seen it. I saw, for instance, the *Glarus* do it.

Quite literally and truly we could do nothing with her. We will say, if you like, that that great jar and wrench when the shaft gave way shook her and crippled her. It is true, however, that whatever the cause may have been, we could not force her toward the island. Of course, we all said "current"; but why didn't the log-line trail?

For three days and three nights we tried it. And the *Glarus* heaved and plunged and shook herself just as you have seen a horse plunge and rear when his rider tries to force him at the steam-roller.

I tell you I could feel the fabric of her tremble and shudder from bow to stern-post, as though she were in a storm; I tell you she fell off from the wind, and broad-on drifted back from her course till the sensation of her shrinking was as plain as her own staring lights and a thing pitiful to see.

We roweled her, and we crowded sail upon her, and we coaxed and bullied and humoured her, till the Three Crows, their fortune only a plain sail two days ahead, raved and swore like insensate brutes, or shall we say like mahouts trying to drive their stricken elephant upon the tiger—and all to no purpose. "Damn the damned current and the damned luck and the damned shaft and all," Hardenberg would exclaim, as from the wheel he would catch the *Glarus* falling off. "Go on, you old hooker—you tub of junk! My God, you'd think she was scared!"

Perhaps the *Glarus* was scared, perhaps not; that point is debatable. But it was beyond doubt of debate that Hardenberg was scared.

A ship that will not obey is only one degree less terrible than a mutinous crew. And we were in a fair way to have both. The stokers, whom we had impressed into duty as A. B.'s, were of course superstitious; and they knew how the *Glarus* was acting, and it was only a question of time before they got out of hand.

That was the end. We held a final conference in the cabin and decided that there was no help for it—we must turn back.

And back we accordingly turned, and at once the wind followed us, and the "current" helped us, and the water churned under the forefoot of the *Glarus*, and the wake whitened under her stern, and the log-line ran out from the trail and strained back as the ship worked homeward.

We had never a mishap from the time we finally swung her about; and, considering the circumstances, the voyage back to San Francisco was propitious.

But an incident happened just after we had started back. We were perhaps some five miles on the homeward track. It was early evening and Strokher had the watch. At about seven o'clock he called me up on the bridge.

"See her?" he said.

And there, far behind us, in the shadow of the twilight, loomed the Other Ship again, desolate, lonely beyond words. We were leaving her rapidly astern. Strokher and I stood looking at her till she dwindled to a dot. Then Strokher said:

"She's on post again."

And when months afterward we limped into the Golden Gate and cast anchor off the "Front" our crew went ashore as soon as discharged, and in half a dozen hours the legend was in every sailors' boarding-house and in every seaman's dive, from Barbary Coast to Black Tom's.

It is still there, and that is why no pilot will take the *Glarus* out, no captain will navigate her, no stoker feed her fires, no sailor walk her decks. The *Glarus* is suspect. She will never smell blue water again, nor taste the trades. She has seen a Ghost.

FRANK NORRIS
1870–1902

Benjamin Franklin Norris, Jr., lived with his affluent parents in Chicago and later in Oakland and San Francisco. He was never an excellent student, and indulgent parents allowed him to pursue his interests, which changed often. He went to an exclusive college preparatory school, transferred to a school for business training, and then attended the San Francisco Art Association. Interest in painting led to study in Paris, Florence, and Rome, but this gave way to a fascination for medieval armor. By age nineteen Norris had published his first article, "Clothes of Steel," in the San Francisco *Chronicle*.

His elective studies did not prepare him for regular admission to college, but he was admitted to the University of California at Berkeley as a student with limited status. He stayed there for four years, leaving without a degree in 1894 to study creative writing at Harvard with Lewis Gater.

After a trip to South Africa Norris returned to California in 1896, where he became assistant to the editor of the San Francisco *Wave*. The paper, founded to publicize a Del Monte resort hotel, provided Norris an outlet for his early work. In 1898 *Moran of the Lady Letty* appeared in the *Wave* and then was published in book form.

In the same year Norris served briefly as a correspondent in the Spanish-American War, returning to the States to publish *McTeague* and *Blix* in 1899. As a reader for Doubleday, he doggedly pushed for publication of Dreiser's *Sister Carrie* in the face of opposition. He published *A Man's Woman* (1900) and completed *The Octopus* (1901), the first novel in his projected trilogy on wheat. In 1901 Norris went to Chicago to collect material for the second book, *The Pit* (1903). That novel was published after Norris died, at age thirty-two, of a perforated appendix and peritonitis. Other works also appeared after his death—*A Deal in Wheat and Other Stories of the New and Old West* (1903), *The Responsibilities of a Novelist* (1903), and *Vandover and the Brute* (1914).

"The Ship That Saw a Ghost" was printed posthumously in *A Deal in Wheat and Other Stories*.

A Story of Land and Sea

BY LORD DUNSANY

IT IS WRITTEN in the first Book of Wonder how Captain Shard of the bad ship *Desperate Lark*, having looted the sea-coast city Bombasharna, retired from active life; and resigning piracy to younger men, with the goodwill of the North and South Atlantic, settled down with a captured queen on his floating island.

Sometimes he sank a ship for the sake of old times, but he no longer hovered along the trade-routes; and timid merchants watched for other men.

It was not age that caused him to leave his romantic profession; nor unworthiness of its traditions, nor gunshot wound, nor drink; but grim necessity and *force majeure*. Five navies were after him. How he gave them the slip one day in the Mediterranean, how he fought with the Arabs, how a ship's broadside was heard in Lat. 23 N. Long. 4 E. for the first time and the last, with other things unknown to Admiralties, I shall proceed to tell.

He had had his fling, had Shard, captain of pirates, and all his merry men wore pearls in their ear-rings; and now the English fleet was after him under full sail along the coast of Spain with a good north wind behind them. They were not gaining much on Shard's rakish craft, the bad ship *Desperate Lark*, yet they were closer than was to his liking, and they interfered with business.

For a day and a night they had chased him, when off Cape St. Vincent at about 6 a.m. Shard took that step that decided his retirement from active life, he turned for the Mediterranean. Had he held on southwards down the African coast it is doubtful whether in face of the interference of England, Russia, France, Denmark and Spain, he could have made piracy pay; but in turning for the Mediterranean he took what we may call the penultimate step of his life which meant for him settling down. There were three great courses of action invented by Shard in his youth, upon which he pondered by day and brooded by night, consolations in all his dangers, secret even from his men, three means of escape as he hoped from any peril that might meet him on the sea. One of these was the floating island that the Book of Wonder tells of, another was so fantastic that we may doubt if even the brilliant audacity of Shard could ever have found it practicable, at least he never tried it so far as is known in that tavern by the sea in which I glean my news, and the third he determined on carrying out as he turned that morning for the Mediterranean. True, he might yet have practised piracy in spite of the step that he took, a little later when the seas grew quiet, but that penultimate step was like that small house in the country that the business man has his eye on; like some snug investment put away for old age, there are certain final courses in men's lives which after taking they never go back to business.

He turned then for the Mediterranean with the English fleet behind him, and his men wondered.

What madness was this—muttered Bill, the boatswain, in Old Frank's only ear—with the French fleet waiting in the Gulf of Lyons and the Spaniards all the way between Sardinia and Tunis: for they knew the Spaniards' ways. And they made a deputation and waited upon Captain Shard, all of them sober and wearing their costly clothes; and they said that the Mediterranean was a trap, and all he said was that the north wind should hold. And the crew said they were done.

So they entered the Mediterranean, and the English Fleet came up and closed the straits. And Shard went tacking along the Moroccan coast with a dozen frigates behind him. And the north wind grew in strength. And not till evening did he speak to his crew, and then he gathered them all together except the man at the helm, and politely asked them to come down to the hold. And there he showed them six immense steel axles and a dozen low iron wheels of enormous width which none had seen before; and he told his crew how all unknown to the world his keel had been specially fitted for these same axles and wheels, and how he meant soon to sail to the wide Atlantic again, though not by the way of the straits. And when they heard the name of the Atlantic all his merry men cheered, for they looked on the Atlantic as a wide safe sea.

And night came down and Captain Shard sent for his diver. With the sea getting up it was hard work for the diver, but by midnight things were done to Shard's satisfaction; and the diver said that of all the jobs he had done, . . . but finding no apt comparison, and being in need of a drink, silence fell on him and soon sleep, and his comrades carried him away to his hammock. All the next day the chase went on with the English well in sight, for Shard had lost time overnight with his wheels and axles, and the danger of meeting the Spaniards increased every hour; and evening came when every minute seemed dangerous, yet they still went tacking on towards the East where they knew the Spaniards must be.

And at last they sighted their topsails right ahead, and still Shard went on. It was a close thing, but night was coming on, and the Union Jack which he hoisted helped Shard with the Spaniards for the last few anxious minutes, though it seemed to anger the English, but as Shard said, "There's no pleasing everyone," and then the twilight shivered into darkness.

"Hard to starboard," said Captain Shard.

The north wind which had risen all day was now blowing a gale. I do not know what part of the coast Shard steered for, but Shard knew, for the coasts of the world were to him what Margate is to some of us.

At a place where the desert rolling up from mystery and from death, yea from the heart of Africa, emerges upon the sea, no less grand than she, no less terrible, even there they sighted the land quite close, almost in darkness. Shard ordered every man to the hinder part of the ship and all the ballast too; and soon the *Desperate Lark*, her prow a little high out of the water, doing her eighteen knots before the wind, struck a sandy beach and shuddered; she heeled over a little, then righted herself, and slowly headed into the interior of Africa.

The men would have given three cheers, but after the first Shard silenced them and, steering the ship himself, he made them a short speech while the broad wheels pounded slowly over the African sand, doing barely five knots in a gale. The perils of the sea, he said, had been greatly exaggerated. Ships had been sailing the sea for hundreds of years, and at sea you knew what to do, but on land this was different. They were on land now and they were not to forget it. At sea you might make as much noise as you pleased and no harm was done, but on land anything might happen. One of the perils of the land that he instanced was that of hanging. For every hundred men that they hung on land, he said, not more than twenty would be hung at sea. The men were to sleep at their guns. They would not go far that night; for the risk of being wrecked at night was another danger peculiar to the land, while at sea you might sail from set of sun till dawn: yet it was essential to get out of sight of the sea, for if anyone knew they were there they'd have cavalry after them. And he had sent back Smerdrak (a young lieutenant of pirates) to cover their tracks where they came up from the sea. And the merry men vigorously nodded their heads though they did not dare to cheer, and presently Smerdrak came running up and they threw him a rope by the stern. And when they had done fifteen knots they anchored, and Captain Shard gathered his men about him and, standing by the land-wheel in the bows, under the large and clear Algerian stars, he explained his system of steering. There was not much to be said for it; he had with considerable ingenuity detached and pivoted the portion of the keel that held the leading axle and could move it by chains which were controlled from the land-wheel, thus the front pair of wheels could be deflected at will, but only very slightly, and they afterwards found that in a hundred yards they could only turn their ship four yards from her course. But let not captains of comfortable battleships, or owners even of yachts, criticize too harshly a man who was not of their time and who knew not modern contrivances; it should be remembered also that Shard was no longer at sea. His steering may have been clumsy but he did what he could.

When the use and limitations of his land-wheel had been made clear to his men, Shard bade them all turn in except those on watch. Long before dawn he woke them and by the very first gleam of light they got their ship under way, so that when those two fleets that had made so sure of Shard closed in like a great crescent on the Algerian coast there was no sign to see of the *Desperate Lark* either on sea or land; and the flags of the Admiral's ship broke out into a hearty English oath.

The gale blew for three days and, Shard using more sail by daylight, they scudded over the sands at little less than ten knots, though on the report of rough water ahead (as the look-out man called rocks, low hills or uneven surface before he adapted himself to his new surroundings) the rate was much decreased. Those were long summer days and Shard, who was anxious while the wind held good to outpace the rumour of his own appearance, sailed for nineteen hours a day, lying to at ten in the evening and hoisting sail again at 3 a.m., when it first began to be light.

In those three days he did five hundred miles; then the wind dropped to a breeze, though it still blew from the north, and for a week they did no more than two knots an hour. The merry men began to murmur then. Luck had distinctly favoured Shard at first, for it sent him at ten knots through the only populous districts well ahead of crowds except those who chose to run, and the cavalry were away on a local raid. As for the runners they soon dropped off when Shard pointed his cannon though he did not dare to fire, up there near the coast; for much as he jeered at the intelligence of the English and Spanish Admirals in not suspecting his manoeuvre, the only one as he said that was possible in the circumstances, yet he knew that cannon had an obvious sound which would give his secret away to the weakest mind. Certainly luck had befriended him, and when it did so no longer he made out of the occasion all that could be made; for instance, while the wind held good he had never missed opportunities to revictual; if he passed by a village its pigs and poultry were his, and whenever he passed by water he filled his tanks to the brim, and now that he could only do two knots he sailed all night with a man and a lantern before him: thus in that week he did close on four hundred miles while another man would have anchored at night and have missed five or six hours out of the twenty-four. Yet his men murmured. Did he think the wind would last for ever, they said. And Shard only smoked. It was clear that he was thinking, and thinking hard. "But what is he thinking about?" said Bill to Bad Jack. And Bad Jack answered: "He may think as hard as he likes, but thinking won't get us out of the Sahara if this wind were to drop."

And towards the end of that week Shard went to his chart-room and laid a new course for his ship a little to the east and towards cultivation. And one day towards evening they sighted a village, and twilight came and the wind dropped altogether. Then the murmurs of the merry men grew to oaths and nearly to mutiny. "Where were they now?" they asked, and were they being treated like poor honest men?

Shard quieted them by asking what they wished to do themselves, and when no one had any better plan than going to the villagers and saying that they had been blown out of their course by a storm, Shard unfolded his scheme to them.

Long ago he had heard how they drove carts with oxen in Africa; oxen were very numerous in these parts wherever there was any cultivation, and for this reason when the wind had begun to drop he had laid his course for the village: that night the moment it was dark they were to drive off fifty yoke of oxen; by midnight they must all be yoked to the bows and then away they would go at a good round gallop.

So fine a plan as this astonished the men and they all apologized for their want of faith in Shard, shaking hands with him every one, and spitting on their hands before they did so in token of goodwill.

The raid that night succeeded admirably; but ingenious as Shard was on land, and a past-master at sea, yet it must be admitted that lack of experience in this class of seamanship led him to make a mistake, a slight one it is true, and one that a little practice would have prevented altogether: the oxen could not gallop. Shard swore at them, threatened them with his pistol, said they should have no food, and all to no avail: that night and as long as they pulled the bad ship *Desperate Lark* they did one knot an hour and no more. Shard's failures like everything that came his way were used as stones in the edifice of his future success, he went at once to his chart-room and worked out all his calculations anew.

The matter of the oxen's pace made pursuit impossible to avoid. Shard therefore countermanded his order to his lieutenant to cover the tracks in the sand, and the *Desperate Lark* plodded on into the Sahara on her new course trusting to her guns.

The village was not a large one, and the little crowd that was sighted astern next morning disappeared after the first shot from the cannon in the stern. At first Shard made the oxen wear rough iron bits, another of his mistakes, and strong bits too, "For if they run away," he had said, "we might as well be driving before a gale, and there's no saying where we'd find ourselves," but after a day or two he found that the bits were no good and, like the practical man he was, immediately corrected his mistake.

And now the crew sang merry songs all day, bringing out mandolins and clarionettes and cheering Captain Shard. All were jolly except the captain himself whose face was moody and perplexed; he alone expected to hear

188 SEA LORE AND LEGEND

more of those villagers; and the oxen were drinking up the water every day; he alone feared that there was no more to be had, and a very unpleasant fear that is when your ship is becalmed in a desert. For over a week they went on like this, doing ten knots a day, and the music and singing got on the captain's nerves, but he dared not tell his men what the trouble was. And then one day the oxen drank up the last of the water. And Lieutenant Smerdrak came and reported the fact.

"Give them rum," said Shard, and he cursed the oxen. "What is good enough for me," he said, "should be good enough for them," and he swore that they should have rum.

"Aye, aye, sir," said the young lieutenant of pirates.

Shard should not be judged by the orders he gave that day; for nearly a fortnight he had watched the doom that was coming slowly towards him, discipline cut him off from anyone that might have shared his fear and discussed it, and all the while he had had to navigate his ship, which even at sea is an arduous responsibility. These things had fretted the calm of that clear judgment that had once baffled five navies. Therefore he cursed the oxen and ordered them rum, and Smerdrak had said "Aye, aye, sir," and gone below.

Towards sunset Shard was standing on the poop, thinking of death; it would not come to him by thirst; mutiny first, he thought. The oxen were refusing rum for the last time, and the men were beginning to eye Captain Shard in a very ominous way, not muttering, but each man looking at him with a side-long look of the eye as though there were only one thought among them all that had no need of words. A score of geese like a long letter "V" were crossing the evening sky, they slanted their necks and all went twisting downwards somewhere about the horizon. Captain Shard rushed to his chart-room, and presently the men came in at the door with Old Frank in front looking awkward and twisting his cap in his hand.

"What is it?" said Shard as though nothing were wrong.

Then Old Frank said what he had come to say: "We want to know what you be going to do."

And the men nodded grimly.

"Get water for the oxen," said Captain Shard, "as the swine won't have rum, and they'll have to work for it, the lazy beasts. Up anchor!"

And at the word water a look came into their faces like when some wanderer suddenly thinks of home.

"Water!" they said.

"Why not?" said Captain Shard. And none of them ever knew that but for those geese, that slanted their necks and suddenly twisted downwards, they would have found no water that night nor ever after, and the Sahara would have taken them as she has taken so many and shall take so many more. All that night they followed their new course: at dawn they found an oasis and the oxen drank.

And here, on this green acre or so with its palm trees and its well, beleaguered by thousands of miles of desert and holding out through the ages, here they decided to stay: for those who have been without water for a while in one of Africa's deserts come to have for that simple fluid such a regard as you, O reader, might not easily credit. And here each man chose a site where he would build his hut, and settle down, and marry perhaps, and even forget the sea; when Captain Shard having filled his tanks and barrels peremptorily ordered them to weigh anchor. There was much dissatisfaction, even some grumbling, but when a man has twice saved his fellows from death by the sheer freshness of his mind they come to have a respect for his judgment that is not shaken by trifles. It must be remembered that in the affair of the dropping of the wind and again when they ran out of water these men were at their wits' end: so was Shard on the last occasion, but that they did not know. All this Shard knew, and he chose this occasion to strengthen the reputation that he had in the minds of the men of that bad ship by explaining to them his motives, which usually he kept secret. The oasis, he said, must be a port of call for all the travellers within hundreds of miles: how many men did you see gathered together in any part of the world where there was a drop of whiskey to be had! And water here was rarer than whiskey in decent countries and, such was the peculiarity of the Arabs, even more precious. Another thing he pointed out to them, the Arabs were a singularly inquisitive people and if they came upon a ship in the desert they would probably talk about it; and the world having a wickedly malicious tongue would never construe in its proper light their difference with the English and Spanish fleets, but would merely side with the strong against the weak.

And the men sighed, and sang the capstan song, and hoisted the anchor and yoked the oxen up, and away they went doing their steady knot, which nothing could increase. It may be thought strange that with all sail furled in dead calm and while the oxen rested they should have cast anchor at all. But custom is not easily overcome and long survives its use. Rather enquire how many such useless customs we ourselves preserve: the flaps, for instance, to pull up the tops of hunting boots though the tops no longer pull up, the bows on our evening shoes that neither tie nor untie. They said they felt safer that way, and there was an end of it.

Shard lay a course of south by west and they did ten knots that day, the next day they did seven or eight and Shard hove to. Here he intended to stop; they had huge supplies of fodder on board for the oxen, for his men he had a pig or so, plenty of poultry, several sacks of biscuits and ninety-eight oxen (for two were already eaten), and they were only twenty miles from water. Here he said they would stay till folks forgot their past, someone would invent something or some new thing would turn up to take folks' minds off them and the ships he had sunk: he forgot that there are men who are well paid to remember.

Half-way between him and the oasis he established a little depot where he buried his water-barrels. As soon as a barrel was empty he sent half a dozen men to roll it by turns to the depot. This they would do at night, keeping hid by day, and next night they would push on to the oasis, fill the barrel and roll it back. Thus only ten miles away he soon had a store of water, unknown to the thirstiest native of Africa, from which he could safely replenish his tanks at will. He allowed his men to sing and even within reason to light fires. Those were jolly nights while the rum held out; sometimes they saw gazelles watching them curiously, sometimes a lion went by over the sand, the sound of his roar added to their sense of the security of their ship; all round them level, immense lay the Sahara. "This is better than an English prison," said Captain Shard.

And still the dead calm lasted, not even the sand whispered at night to little winds; and when the rum gave out and it looked like trouble, Shard reminded them what little use it had been to them when it was all they had and the oxen wouldn't look at it.

And the days wore on with singing, and even dancing at times, and at nights round a cautious fire in a hollow of sand, with only one man on watch, they told tales of the sea. It was all a relief after arduous watches and sleeping by the guns, a rest to strained nerves and eyes; and all agreed, for all that they missed their rum, that the best place for a ship like theirs was the land.

This was in latitude 23 north, longitude 4 east, where, as I have said, a ship's broadside was heard for the first time and the last. It happened this way.

They had been there several weeks and had eaten perhaps ten or a dozen oxen and all that while there had been no breath of wind and they had seen no one: when one morning about two bells when the crew were at breakfast the look-out man reported cavalry on the port side. Shard, who had already surrounded his ship with sharpened stakes, ordered all his men on board; the young trumpeter, who prided himself on having picked up the ways of the land, sounded "Prepare to receive cavalry"; Shard sent a few men below with pikes to the lower port-holes, two more aloft with muskets, the rest to the guns; he changed the "grape" or "canister" with which the guns were loaded in case of a surprise, for shot, cleared the decks, drew in ladders, and before the cavalry came within range everything was ready for them. The oxen were always yoked in order that Shard could manoeuvre his ship at a moment's notice.

When first sighted the cavalry were trotting, but they were coming on now at a slow canter. Arabs in white robes on good horses. Shard estimated that there were two or three hundred of them. At six hundred yards Shard opened with one gun; he had had the distance measured, but had never practised for fear of being heard at the oasis: the shot went high. The next one fell short and ricochetted over the Arabs' heads. Shard had the range then, and by the time the ten remaining guns of his broadside were given the same elevation as that of his second gun the Arabs had come to the spot where the last shot pitched. The broadside hit the horses, mostly low, and ricochetted on amongst them; one cannon-ball striking a rock at the horses' feet shattered it and sent fragments flying amongst the Arabs with the peculiar scream of things set free by projectiles from their motionless harmless state, and the cannon-ball went on with them with a great howl; this shot alone killed three men.

"Very satisfactory," said Shard, rubbing his chin. "Load with grape," he added sharply.

The broadside did not stop the Arabs nor even reduce their speed, but they crowded in closer together as though for company in their time of danger, which they should not have done. They were four hundred yards off now, three hundred and fifty; and then the muskets began, for the two men in the crow's-nest had thirty loaded muskets besides a few pistols; the muskets all stood round them leaning against the rail; they picked them up and fired them one by one. Every shot told, but still the Arabs came on. They were galloping now. It took some time to load the guns in those days. Three hundred yards, two hundred and fifty, men dropping all the way, two hundred yards; Old Frank for all his one ear had terrible eyes; it was pistols now, they had fired all their muskets; a hundred and fifty; Shard had marked the fifties with little white stones. Old Frank and Bad Jack up aloft felt pretty uneasy when they saw the Arabs had come to that little white stone, they both missed their shots.

"All ready?" said Captain Shard.

"Aye, aye, sir," said Smerdrak.

"Right," said Captain Shard, raising a finger.

A hundred and fifty yards is a bad range at which to be caught by grape (or "case" as we call it now), the gunners can hardly miss and the charge has time to spread. Shard estimated afterwards that he got thirty Arabs by that broadside alone and as many horses.

There were close on two hundred of them still on their horses, yet the broadside of grape had unsettled them, they surged round the ship but seemed doubtful what to do. They carried swords and scimitars in their hands, though most had strange long muskets slung behind them; a few unslung them and began firing wildly. They could not reach Shard's merry men with their swords. Had it not been for that broadside that took them when it did they might have climbed up from their horsès and carried the bad ship by sheer force of numbers, but they would have had to have been very steady, and the broadside spoiled all that. Their best course was to have concentrated all their efforts in setting fire to the ship, but this they did not attempt. Part of them swarmed all round the ship brandishing their swords and lookingly vainly for an easy entrance; perhaps they expected a door, they were not seafaring people; but their leaders were evidently set on driving off the oxen, not dreaming that the *Desperate Lark* had other means of travelling. And this to some extent they succeeded in doing. Thirty they drove off, cutting the traces, twenty they killed on the spot with their scimitars though the bow gun caught them twice as they did their work, and ten more were unluckily killed by Shard's bow gun. Before they could fire a third time from the bows they all galloped away, firing back at the oxen with their muskets and killing three more, and what troubled Shard more than the loss of his oxen was the way that they manoeuvred, galloping off just when the bow gun was ready and riding off by the port bow where the broadside could not get them, which seemed to him to show more knowledge of guns than they could have learned on that bright morning. What, thought Shard to himself, if they should bring big guns against the *Desperate Lark*! And the mere thought of it made him rail at Fate. But the merry men all cheered when they rode away. Shard had only twenty-two oxen left, and then a score or so of the Arabs dismounted while the rest rode further on leading their horses. And the dismounted men lay down on the port bow behind some rocks two hundred yards away and began to shoot at the oxen. Shard had just enough of them left to manoeuvre his ship with an effort, and he turned his ship a few points to the starboard so as to get a broadside at the rocks. But grape was of no use here, as the only way he could get an Arab was by hitting one of the rocks with shot behind which an Arab was lying, and the rocks were not easy to hit except by chance, and as often as he manoeuvred his ship the Arabs changed their ground. This went on all day while the mounted Arabs hovered out of range watching what Shard would do; and all the while the oxen were growing fewer, so good a mark were they, until only ten were left and the ship could manoeuvre no longer. But then they all rode off.

The merry men were delighted, they calculated that one way and another they had unhorsed a hundred Arabs, and on board there had been no more than one man wounded: Bad Jack had been hit in the wrist; probably by a bullet meant for the men at the guns, for the Arabs were firing high. They had captured a horse and had found quaint weapons on the bodies of the dead Arabs and an interesting kind of tobacco. It was evening now and they talked over the fight, made jokes about their luckier shots, smoked their new tobacco and sang: altogether it was the jolliest evening they'd had. But Shard alone on the quarter-deck paced to and fro pondering, brooding and wondering. He had chopped off Bad Jack's wounded hand and given him a hook out of store, for captain does doctor upon these occasions, and Shard, who was ready for most things, kept half a dozen or so of neat new limbs, and of course a chopper. Bad Jack had gone below swearing a little and said he'd lie down for a bit, the men were smoking and singing on the sand, and Shard was there alone. The thought that troubled Shard was: What would the Arabs do? They did not look like men to go away for nothing. And at back of all his thoughts was one that reiterated guns, guns, guns. He argued with himself that they could not drag them all that way on the sand, that the *Desperate Lark* was not worth it, that they had given it up. Yet he knew in his heart that that was what they would do. He knew there were fortified towns in Africa, and as for its being worth it, he knew that there was no pleasant thing left now to those defeated men except revenge, and if the *Desperate Lark* had come over the sand, why not guns? He knew that the ship could never hold out against guns and cavalry, a week perhaps, two weeks, even three: what difference did it make how long it was? And the men sang:

> Away we go,
> Oho, Oho, Oho,
> A drop of rum for you and me,
> And the world's as round as the letter O,
> And round it runs the sea.

A melancholy settled down on Shard.

About sunset Lieutenant Smerdrak came up for orders. Shard ordered a trench to be dug along the port side of the ship. The men wanted to sing and grumbled at having to dig, especially as Shard never mentioned his fear of guns, but he fingered his pistols and in the end Shard had his way. No one on board could shoot like Captain Shard. That is often the way with captains of pirate ships, it is a difficult position to hold. Discipline is essential to those that have the right to fly the skull-and-cross-bones, and Shard was the man to enforce it. It was starlight by the time the trench was dug to the captain's satisfaction, and the men that it was to protect when the worst came to the worst swore all the time as they dug. And when it was finished they clamoured to make a feast on some of the killed oxen, and this Shard let them do. And they lit a huge fire for the first time, burning abundant scrub, they thinking that the Arabs daren't return, Shard knowing that concealment was now useless. All that night they feasted and sang, and Shard sat up in his chart-room making his plans.

When morning came they rigged up the cutter, as they called the captured horse, and told off her crew. As there were only two men that could ride at all these became the crew of the cutter. Spanish Dick and Bill the Boatswain were the two.

Shard's orders were that turn and turn about they should take command of the cutter and cruise about five miles off to the north-east all the day, but at night they were to come in. And they fitted the horse up with a flagstaff in front of the saddle so that they could signal from her, and carried an anchor behind for fear she should run away.

And as soon as Spanish Dick had ridden off Shard sent some men to roll all the barrels back from the depot, where they were buried in the sand, with orders to watch the cutter all the time, and, if she signalled, to return as fast as they could.

They buried the Arabs that day, removing their water-bottles and any provisions they had, and that night they got all the water-barrels in, and for days nothing happened. One event of extraordinary importance did indeed occur: the wind got up one day, but it was due south, and as the oasis lay to the north of them, and beyond that they might pick up the camel track, Shard decided to stay where he was. If it had looked to him like lasting Shard might have hoisted sail, but it dropped at evening as he knew it would, and in any case it was not the wind he wanted. And more days went by, two weeks without a breeze. The dead oxen would not keep and they had had to kill three more; there were only seven left now.

Never before had the men been so long without rum. And Captain Shard had doubled the watch, besides making two more men sleep at the guns. They had tired of their simple games, and most of their songs; and their tales that were never true were no longer new. And then one day the monotony of the desert came down upon them.

There is a fascination in the Sahara: a day there is delightful, a week is pleasant, a fortnight is a matter of opinion, but it was running into months. The men were perfectly polite, but the boatswain wanted to know when Shard thought of moving on. It was an unreasonable question to ask of the captain of any ship in a dead calm in a desert, but Shard said he would set a course and let him know in a day or two. And a day or two went by over the monotony of the Sahara, who for monotony is unequalled by all the parts of the earth. Great marshes cannot equal it, nor plains of grass nor the sea; the Sahara alone lies unaltered by the seasons, she has no altering surface, no flowers to fade or grow, year in year out she is changeless for hundreds and hundreds of miles. And the boatswain came again and took off his cap and asked Captain Shard to be so kind as to tell them about his new course. Shard said he meant to stay until they had eaten three more of the oxen as they could only take three of them in the hold, there were only six left now. But what if there was no wind? the boatswain said. And at that moment the faintest breeze from the north ruffled the boatswain's forelock as he stood with his cap in his hand.

"Don't talk about the wind to *me*," said Captain Shard: and Bill was a little frightened for Shard's mother had been a gipsy.

But it was only a breeze astray, a trick of the Sahara. And another week went by and they ate two more oxen.

They obeyed Captain Shard ostentatiously now, but they wore ominous looks. Bill came again and Shard answered him in Romany.

Things were like this one hot Sahara morning when the cutter signalled. The look-out man told Shard and Shard read the message. "Cavalry astern" it read, and then a little later she signalled "With guns."

"Ah," said Captain Shard.

One ray of hope Shard had; the flags on the cutter fluttered. For the first time for five weeks a light breeze blew from the north, very light, you hardly felt it. Spanish Dick rode in and anchored his horse to starboard and the cavalry came on slowly from the port.

Not till the afternoon did they come in sight, and all the while that little breeze was blowing.

"One knot," said Shard at noon. "Two knots," he said at six bells, and still it grew and the Arabs trotted nearer. By five o'clock the merry men of the bad ship *Desperate Lark* could make out twelve long old-fashioned guns on low-wheeled carts dragged by horses, and what looked like lighter guns carried on camels. The wind was blowing a little stronger now.

"Shall we hoist sail, sir?" said Bill.

"Not yet," said Shard.

By six o'clock the Arabs were just outside the range of cannon and there they halted. Then followed an anxious hour or so, but the Arabs came no nearer. They evidently meant to wait till dark to bring their guns up. Probably they intended to dig a gun epaulement from which they could safely pound away at the ship.

"We could do three knots," said Shard half to himself, he was walking up and down his quarter-deck with very fast short paces. And then the sun set and they heard the Arabs praying, and Shard's merry men cursed at the top of their voices to show that they were as good men as they.

The Arabs had come no nearer, waiting for night. They did not know how Shard was longing for it too, he was gritting his teeth and sighing for it, he even would have prayed, but that he feared that it might remind Heaven of him and his merry men.

Night came and the stars. "Hoist sail," said Shard. The men sprang to their places, they had had enough of that silent lonely spot. They took the oxen on board and let the great sails down; and like a lover coming from over sea, long dreamed of, long expected, like a lost friend seen again after many years, the north wind came into the pirates' sails. And before Shard could stop it a ringing English cheer went away to the wondering Arabs.

They started off at three knots, and soon they might have done four, but Shard would not risk it at night. All night the wind held good, and doing three knots from ten to four they were far out of sight of the Arabs when daylight came. And then Shard hoisted more sail and they did four knots, and by eight bells they were doing four and a half. The spirits of those volatile men rose high, and discipline became perfect. So long as there was wind in the sails and water in the tanks Captain Shard felt safe at least from mutiny. Great men can only be overthrown while their fortunes are at their lowest. Having failed to depose Shard when his plans were open to criticism and he himself scarce knew what to do next, it was hardly likely they could do it now; and whatever we think of his past and his way of living we cannot deny that Shard was among the great men of the world.

Of defeat by the Arabs he did not feel so sure. It was useless to try to cover his tracks even if he had had time, the Arab cavalry could have picked them up anywhere. And he was afraid of their camels with those light guns on board, he had heard they could do seven knots and keep it up most of the day, and if as much as one shot struck the mainmast . . . and Shard taking his mind off useless fears worked out on his chart when the Arabs were likely to overtake them. He told his men that the wind would hold good for a week, and, gipsy or no, he certainly knew as much about the wind as is good for a sailor to know.

Alone in his chart-room he worked it out like this: mark two hours to the good for surprise and finding the tracks and delay in starting, say three hours if the guns were mounted in their epaulements, then the Arabs should start at seven. Supposing the camels go twelve hours a day at seven knots they would do eighty-four knots a day, while Shard doing three knots from ten to four, and four knots the rest of the time, was doing ninety and actually gaining. But when it came to it he wouldn't risk more than two knots at night while the enemy were out of sight, for he rightly regarded anything more than that as dangerous when sailing on land at night, so he too did eighty-four knots a day. It was a pretty race. I have not troubled to see if Shard added up his figures wrongly or if he underrated the pace of camels, but whatever it was the Arabs gained slightly, for on the fourth day Spanish Jack, five knots astern on what they called the cutter, sighted the camels a very long way off and signalled the fact to Shard. They had left their cavalry behind as Shard supposed they would. The wind held good, they had still two oxen left, and could always eat their "cutter," and they had a fair, though not ample, supply of water; but the appearance of the Arabs was a blow to Shard, for it showed him that there was no getting away from them, and of all things he dreaded guns. He made light of it to the men:

said they would sink the lot before they had been in action half an hour: yet he feared that once the guns came up it was only a question of time before his rigging was cut or his steering gear disabled.

One point the *Desperate Lark* scored over the Arabs and a very good one too, darkness fell just before they could have sighted her, and now Shard used the lantern ahead as he dared not do on the first night when the Arabs were close, and with the help of it managed to do three knots. The Arabs encamped in the evening and the *Desperate Lark* gained twenty knots. But the next evening they appeared again, and this time they saw the sails of the *Desperate Lark*.

On the sixth day they were close. On the seventh they were closer. And then, a line of verdure across their bows, Shard saw the Niger River.

Whether he knew that for a thousand miles it rolled its course through forest, whether he even knew that it was there at all; what his plans were, or whether he lived from day to day like a man whose days are numbered, he never told his men. Nor can I get an indication on this point from the talk that I hear from sailors in their cups in a certain tavern I know of. His face was expressionless, his mouth shut, and he held his ship to her course. That evening they were up to the edge of the tree-trunks and the Arabs camped and waited ten knots astern, and the wind had sunk a little.

There Shard anchored a little before sunset and landed at once. At first he explored the forest a little on foot. Then he sent for Spanish Dick. They had slung the cutter on board some days ago when they found she could not keep up. Shard could not ride, but he sent for Spanish Dick and told him he must take him as a passenger. So Spanish Dick slung him in front of the saddle "before the mast," as Shard called it, for they still carried a mast on the front of the saddle, and away they galloped together. "Rough weather," said Shard, but he surveyed the forest as he went, and the long and short of it was he found a place where the forest was less than half a mile thick and the *Desperate Lark* might get through: but twenty trees must be cut. Shard marked the trees himself, sent Spanish Dick right back to watch the Arabs and turned the whole of his crew on to those twenty trees. It was a frightful risk, the *Desperate Lark* was empty, with an enemy no more than ten knots astern, but it was a moment for bold measures and Shard took the chance of being left without his ship in the heart of Africa in the hope of being repaid by escaping altogether.

The men worked all night on those twenty trees, those that had no axes bored with bradawls and blasted, and then relieved those that had.

Shard was indefatigable, he went from tree to tree, showing exactly what way every one was to fall, and what was to be done with them when they were down. Some had to be cut down because their branches would get in

the way of the masts, others because their trunks would be in the way of the
wheels; in the case of the last the stumps had to be made smooth and low
with saws and perhaps a bit of the trunk sawn off and rolled away. This was
the hardest work they had. And they were all large trees; on the other hand,
had they been small, there would have been many more of them and they
could not have sailed in and out, sometimes for hundreds of yards, without cutting any at all: and all this Shard calculated on doing if only there
was time.

The light before dawn came and it looked as if they would never do it at
all. And then dawn came and it was all done but one tree, the hard part of
the work had all been done in the night and a sort of final rush cleared
everything up except that one huge tree. And then the cutter signalled the
Arabs were moving. At dawn they had prayed, and now they had struck
their camp. Shard at once ordered all his men to the ship except ten whom
he left at the tree; they had some way to go and the Arabs had been moving
some ten minutes before they got there. Shard took in the cutter, which
wasted five minutes, hoisted sail short-handed and that took five minutes
more, and slowly got under way.

The wind was dropping still, and by the time the *Desperate Lark* had
come to the edge of that part of the forest through which Shard had laid his
course the Arabs were no more than five knots away. He had sailed east half
a mile, which he ought to have done overnight so as to be ready, but he
could not spare time or thought or men away from those twenty trees. Then
Shard turned into the forest and the Arabs were dead astern. They hurried
when they saw the *Desperate Lark* enter the forest.

"Doing ten knots," said Shard as he watched them from the deck. The
Desperate Lark was doing no more than a knot and a half, for the wind was
weak under the lee of the trees. Yet all went well for a while. The big tree
had just come down some way ahead, and the ten men were sawing bits off
the trunk.

And then Shard saw a branch that he had not marked on the chart, it
would just catch the top of the mainmast. He anchored at once and sent a
man aloft who sawed it half-way through and did the rest with a pistol, and
now the Arabs were only three knots astern. For a quarter of a mile Shard
steered them through the forest till they came to the ten men and that bad
big tree; another foot had yet to come off one corner of the stump, for the
wheels had to pass over it. Shard turned all hands on to the stump, and it
was then that the Arabs came within shot. But they had to unpack their
gun. And before they had it mounted Shard was away. If they had charged
things might have been different. When they saw the *Desperate Lark* under
way again the Arabs came on to within three hundred yards and there they
mounted two guns. Shard watched them along his stern gun but would

not fire. They were six hundred yards away before the Arabs could fire, and then they fired too soon and both guns missed. And Shard and his merry men saw clear water only ten fathoms ahead. Then Shard loaded his stern gun with canister instead of shot and at the same moment the Arabs charged on their camels; they came galloping down through the forest waving long lances. Shard left the steering to Smerdrak and stood by the stern gun; the Arabs were within fifty yards and still Shard did not fire; he had most of his men in the stern with muskets beside him. Those lances carried on camels were altogether different from swords in the hands of horsemen, they could reach the men on deck. The men could see the horrible barbs on the lance-heads, they were almost at their faces when Shard fired; and at the same moment the *Desperate Lark* with her dry and sun-cracked keel in air on the high bank of the Niger fell forward like a diver. The gun went off through the tree-tops, a wave came over the bows and swept the stern, the *Desperate Lark* wriggled and righted herself, she was back in her element.

The merry men looked at the wet decks and at their dripping clothes. "Water," they said almost wonderingly.

The Arabs followed a little way through the forest, but when they saw that they had to face a broadside instead of one stern gun and perceived that a ship afloat is less vulnerable to cavalry even than when on shore, they abandoned ideas of revenge, and comforted themselves with a text out of their sacred book which tells how in other days and other places our enemies shall suffer even as we desire.

For a thousand miles with the flow of the Niger and the help of occasional winds, the *Desperate Lark* moved seawards. At first he sweeps east a little and then southwards, till you come to Akassa and the open sea.

I will not tell you how they caught fish and ducks, raided a village here and there and at last came to Akassa, for I have said much already of Captain Shard. Imagine them drawing nearer and nearer the sea, bad men all, and yet with a feeling for something where we feel for our king, our country or our home, a feeling for something that burned in them not less ardently than our feelings in us, and that something the sea. Imagine them nearing it till sea birds appeared and they fancied they felt sea breezes and all sang songs again that they had not sung for weeks. Imagine them heaving at last on the salt Atlantic again.

I have said much already of Captain Shard and I fear lest I shall weary you, O my reader, if I tell you any more of so bad a man. I, too, at the top of a tower all alone am weary.

And yet it is right that such a tale should be told. A journey almost due south from near Algiers to Akassa in a ship that we should call no more than a yacht. Let it be a stimulus to younger men.

Guarantee to the Reader

Since writing down for your benefit, O my reader, all this long tale that I heard in the tavern by the sea, I have travelled in Algeria and Tunisia as well as in the Desert. Much that I saw in those countries seems to throw doubt on the tale that the sailor told me. To begin with, the Desert does not come within hundreds of miles of the coast, and there are more mountains to cross than you would suppose, the Atlas mountains in particular. It is just possible Shard might have got through by El Cantara, following the camel road which is many centuries old; or he may have gone by Algiers and Bou Saada and through the mountain pass El Finita Dem, though that is a bad enough way for camels to go (let alone bullocks with a ship), for which reason the Arabs call it Finita Dem—the Path of Blood.

I should not have ventured to give this story the publicity of print had the sailor been sober when he told it, for fear that he should have deceived you, O my reader; but this was never the case with him, as I took good care to ensure: *in vino veritas* is a sound old proverb, and I never had cause to doubt his word unless that proverb lies.

If it should prove that he has deceived me, let it pass; but if he has been the means of deceiving you, there are little things about him that I know, the common gossip of that ancient tavern whose leaded bottle-glass windows watch the sea, which I will tell at once to every judge of my acquaintance, and it will be a pretty race to see which of them will hang him.

Meanwhile, O my reader, believe the story, resting assured that if you are taken in the thing shall be a matter for the hangman.

LORD DUNSANY
1878–1957

Edward John Moreton Drax Plunkett, the eighteenth baron of Dunsany, was born in London and passed his boyhood at Danstall Priory in Kent, although after 1889 some holidays were spent in Ireland at his father's ancestral home, Dunsany Castle, County Meath.

In the auspicious year of 1899 he joined the Coldstream Guards and then succeeded to the title of Lord Dunsany. During most of the Boer War he served as a second lieutenant, putting the knowledge he gained of Africa to use in later writing.

At the family home in Ireland Dunsany began to write, publishing *The Gods of Pegana*, a book of stories, in 1905. In 1909 his first play, *The Glittering Gate*, was produced in Dublin at the Abbey Theatre. *The Gods of the*

Mountain played in a London theater in 1911, and after 1916 his plays, first staged in Britain, became extremely popular in the United States.

He wrote novels, the early ones including *The Chronicles of Rodriguez* (1922) and *The Blessing of Pan* (1927). *The Curse of the Wise Woman* (1933), *Rory and Bran* (1936), and others using Irish themes came somewhat later. Dunsany also composed verse, his best work in that genre being the narrative poem *Journey* (1943) about his adventures, including his evacuation from Turkey while under German aerial fire.

Though he worked in many genres, Dunsany was at his best writing stories of exaggeration like the one printed here. "A Story of Land and Sea" was collected in *The Last Book of Wonder* (1916).

The Story of the Siren

BY E. M. FORSTER

FEW THINGS have been more beautiful than my notebook on the Deist Controversy as it fell downward through the waters of the Mediterranean. It dived, like a piece of black slate, but opened soon, disclosing leaves of pale green, which quivered into blue. Now it had vanished, now it was a piece of magical india-rubber stretching out to infinity, now it was a book again, but bigger than the book of all knowledge. It grew more fantastic as it reached the bottom, where a puff of sand welcomed it and obscured it from view. But it reappeared, quite sane though a little tremulous, lying decently open on its back, while unseen fingers fidgeted among its leaves.

"It is such pity," said my aunt, "that you will not finish your work in the hotel. Then you would be free to enjoy yourself and this would never have happened."

"Nothing of it but will change into something rich and strange," warbled the chaplain, while his sister said, "Why, it's gone in the water!" As for the boatmen, one of them laughed, while the other, without a word of warning, stood up and began to take his clothes off.

"Holy Moses," cried the Colonel. "Is the fellow mad?"

"Yes, thank him, dear," said my aunt: "that is to say, tell him he is very kind, but perhaps another time."

"All the same I do want my book back," I complained. "It's for my Fellowship Dissertation. There won't be much left of it by another time."

"I have an idea," said some woman or other through her parasol. "Let us leave this child of nature to dive for the book while we go on to the other grotto. We can land him either on this rock or on the ledge inside, and he will be ready when we return."

The idea seemed good; and I improved it by saying I would be left behind too, to lighten the boat. So the two of us were deposited outside the little grotto on a great sunlit rock that guarded the harmonies within. Let us call them blue, though they suggest rather the spirit of what is clean—cleanliness passed from the domestic to the sublime, the cleanliness of all the sea gathered together and radiating light. The Blue Grotto at Capri contains only more blue water, not bluer water. That colour and that spirit are the heritage of every cave in the Mediterranean into which the sun can shine and the sea flow.

As soon as the boat left I realized how imprudent I had been to trust myself on a sloping rock with an unknown Sicilian. With a jerk he became alive, seizing my arm and saying, "Go to the end of the grotto, and I will show you something beautiful."

He made me jump off the rock on to the ledge over a dazzling crack of sea; he drew me away from the light till I was standing on the tiny beach of sand which emerged like powdered turquoise at the farther end. There he left me with his clothes, and returned swiftly to the summit of the entrance rock. For a moment he stood naked in the brilliant sun, looking down at the spot where the book lay. Then he crossed himself, raised his hands above his head, and dived.

If the book was wonderful, the man is past all description. His effect was that of a silver statue, alive beneath the sea, through whom life throbbed in blue and green. Something infinitely happy, infinitely wise—but it was impossible that it should emerge from the depths sunburned and dripping, holding the notebook on the Deist Controversy between its teeth.

A gratuity is generally expected by those who bathe. Whatever I offered, he was sure to want more, and I was disinclined for an argument in a place so beautiful and also so solitary. It was a relief that he should say in conversational tones, "In a place like this one might see the Siren."

I was delighted with him for thus falling into the key of his surroundings. We had been left together in a magic world, apart from all the commonplaces that are called reality, a world of blue whose floor was the sea and whose walls and roof of rock trembled with the sea's reflections. Here only the fantastic would be tolerable, and it was in that spirit I echoed his words, "One might easily see the Siren."

He watched me curiously while he dressed. I was parting the sticky leaves of the notebook as I sat on the sand.

"Ah," he said at last. "You may have read the little book that was printed last year. Who would have thought that our Siren would have given the foreigners pleasure!"

(I read it afterwards. Its account is, not unnaturally, incomplete, in spite of there being a woodcut of the young person, and the words of her song.)

"She comes out of this blue water, doesn't she," I suggested, "and sits on the rock at the entrance, combing her hair."

I wanted to draw him out, for I was interested in his sudden gravity, and there was a suggestion of irony in his last remark that puzzled me.

"Have you ever seen her?" he asked.

"Often and often."

"I, never."

"But you have heard her sing?"

He put on his coat and said impatiently, "How can she sing under the water? Who could? She sometimes tries, but nothing comes from her but great bubbles."

"She should climb on to the rock."

"How can she?" he cried again, quite angry. "The priests have blessed the air, so she cannot breathe it, and blessed the rocks, so that she cannot sit on them. But the sea no man can bless, because it is too big, and always changing. So she lives in the sea."

I was silent.

At this his face took a gentler expression. He looked at me as though something was on his mind, and going out to the entrance rock gazed at the external blue. Then returning into our twilight he said, "As a rule only good people see the Siren."

I made no comment. There was a pause, and he continued. "That is a very strange thing, and the priests do not know how to account for it; for she of course is wicked. Not only those who fast and go to Mass are in danger, but even those who are merely good in daily life. No one in the village had seen her for two generations. I am not surprised. We all cross ourselves before we enter the water, but it is unnecessary. Giuseppe, we thought, was safer than most. We loved him, and many of us he loved: but that is a different thing from being good."

I asked who Giuseppe was.

"That day—I was seventeen and my brother was twenty and a great deal stronger than I was, and it was the year when the visitors, who have brought such prosperity and so many alterations into the village, first began to come. One English lady in particular, of very high birth, came, and has written a book about the place, and it was through her that the Improvement Syndicate was formed, which is about to connect the hotels with the station by a funicular railway."

"Don't tell me about that lady in here," I observed.

"That day we took her and her friends to see the grottoes. As we rowed close under the cliffs I put out my hand, as one does, and caught a little crab, and having pulled off its claws offered it as a curiosity. The ladies groaned, but a gentleman was pleased, and held out money. Being inexperienced, I refused it, saying that his pleasure was sufficient reward! Giuseppe, who was rowing behind, was very angry with me and reached out with his hand and hit me on the side of the mouth, so that a tooth cut my lip, and I bled. I tried to hit him back, but he always was too quick for me, and as I stretched round he kicked me under the armpit, so that for a moment I could not even row. There was a great noise among the ladies, and I heard afterward that they were planning to take me away from my brother and train me as a waiter. That, at all events, never came to pass.

"When we reached the grotto—not here, but a larger one—the gentleman was very anxious that one of us should dive for money, and the ladies consented, as they sometimes do. Giuseppe, who had discovered how much pleasure it gives foreigners to see us in the water, refused to dive for anything but silver, and the gentleman threw in a two-lira piece.

"Just before my brother sprang off he caught sight of me holding my bruise, and crying, for I could not help it. He laughed and said, 'This time, at all events, I shall not see the Siren!' and went into the water without crossing himself. But he saw her."

He broke off and accepted a cigarette. I watched the golden entrance rock and the quivering walls and the magic water through which great bubbles constantly rose.

At last he dropped his hot ash into the ripples and turned his head away, and said, "He came up without the coin. We pulled him into the boat, and he was so large that he seemed to fill it, and so wet that we could not dress him. I have never seen a man so wet. I and the gentleman rowed back, and we covered Giuseppe with sacking and propped him up in the stern."

"He was drowned, then?" I murmured, supposing that to be the point.

"He was not," he cried angrily. "He saw the Siren. I told you."

I was silenced again.

"We put him to bed, though he was not ill. The doctor came, and took money, and the priest came and spattered him with holy water. But it was no good. He was too big—like a piece of the sea. He kissed the thumb-bones of San Biagio and they never dried till evening."

"What did he look like?" I ventured.

"Like any one who has seen the Siren. If you have seen her 'often and often' how is it you do not know? Unhappy, unhappy because he knew everything. Every living thing made him unhappy because he knew it would die. And all he cared to do was sleep."

I bent over my note-book.

"He did no work, he forgot to eat, he forgot whether he had his clothes on. All the work fell on me, and my sister had to go out to service. We tried to make him into a beggar, but he was too robust to inspire pity, and as for an idiot, he had not the right look in his eyes. He would stand in the street looking at people, and the more he looked at them the more unhappy he became. When a child was born he would cover his face with his hands. If any one was married—he was terrible then, and would frighten them as they came out of church. Who would have believed he would marry himself! I caused that, I. I was reading out of the paper how a girl at Ragusa had 'gone mad through bathing in the sea.' Giuseppe got up, and in a week he and that girl came in.

"He never told me anything, but it seems that he went straight to her house, broke into her room, and carried her off. She was the daughter of a rich mineowner, so you may imagine our peril. Her father came down, with a clever lawyer, but they could do no more than I. They argued and they threatened, but at last they had to go back and we lost nothing—that is to say, no money. We took Giuseppe and Maria to the church and had them married. Ugh! that wedding! The priest made no jokes afterward, and coming out the children threw stones. . . . I think I would have died to make her happy; but as always happens, one could do nothing."

"Were they unhappy together then?"

"They loved each other, but love is not happiness. We can all get love. Love is nothing. I had two people to work for now, for she was like him in everything—one never knew which of them was speaking. I had to sell our own boat and work under the bad old man you have today. Worst of all, people began to hate us. The children first—everything begins with them—and then the women and last of all the men. For the cause of every misfortune was— You will not betray me?"

I promised good faith, and immediately he burst into the frantic blasphemy of one who has escaped from supervision, cursing the priests, who had ruined his life, he said. "Thus are we tricked!" was his cry, and he stood up and kicked at the azure ripples with his feet, till he had obscured them with a cloud of sand.

I too was moved. The story of Giuseppe, for all its absurdity and superstition, came nearer to reality than anything I had known before. I don't know why, but it filled me with desire to help others—the greatest of all our desires, I suppose, and the most fruitless. The desire soon passed.

"She was about to have a child. That was the end of everything. People said to me, 'When will your charming nephew be born? What a cheerful, attractive child he will be, with such a father and mother!' I kept my face steady and replied, 'I think he may be. Out of sadness shall come gladness'—it is one of our proverbs. And my answer frightened them very much, and they told the priests, who were frightened too. Then the whisper started that the child would be Antichrist. You need not be afraid: he was never born.

"An old witch began to prophesy, and no one stopped her. Giuseppe and the girl, she said, had silent devils, who could do little harm. But the child would always be speaking and laughing and perverting, and last of all he would go into the sea and fetch up the Siren into the air and all the world would see her and hear her sing. As soon as she sang, the Seven Vials would be opened and the Pope would die and Mongibello flame, and the veil of Santa Agata would be burned. Then the boy and the Siren would marry, and together they would rule the world, for ever and ever.

"The whole village was in tumult, and the hotel-keepers became alarmed, for the tourist season was just beginning. They met together and decided that Giuseppe and the girl must be sent inland until the child was born, and they subscribed the money. The night before they were to start there was a full moon and wind from the east, and all along the coast the sea shot up over the cliffs in silver clouds. It is a wonderful sight, and Maria said she must see it once more.

"'Do not go,' I said. 'I saw the priest go by, and some one with him. And the hotel-keepers do not like you to be seen, and if we displease them also we shall starve.'

"'I want to go,' she replied. 'The sea is stormy, and I may never feel it again.'

"'No, he is right,' said Giuseppe. 'Do not go—or let one of us go with you.'

"'I want to go alone,' she said; and she went alone.

"I tied up their luggage in a piece of cloth, and then I was so unhappy at thinking I should lose them that I went and sat down by my brother and put my arm around his neck, and he put his arm round me, which he had not done for more than a year, and we remained thus I don't remember how long.

"Suddenly the door flew open and moonlight and wind came in together, and a child's voice said laughing, 'They have pushed her over the cliffs into the sea.'

"I stepped to the drawer where I keep my knives.

"'Sit down again,' said Giuseppe—Giuseppe of all people! 'If she is dead, why should others die too?'

"'I guess who it is,' I cried, 'and I will kill him.'

"I was almost out of the door, and he tripped me up and, kneeling upon me, took hold of both my hands and sprained my wrists; first my right one, then my left. No one but Giuseppe would have thought of such a thing. It hurt more than you would suppose, and I fainted. When I woke up, he was gone, and I never saw him again."

But Giuseppe disgusted me.

"I told you he was wicked," he said. "No one would have expected him to see the Siren."

"How do you know he did see her?"

"Because he did not see her 'often and often,' but once."

"Why do you love him if he is wicked?"

He laughed for the first time. That was his only reply.

"Is that the end?" I asked.

"I never killed her murderer, for by the time my wrists were well he was in America; and one cannot kill a priest. As for Giuseppe, he went all over the world too, looking for some one else who had seen the Siren—either a man, or, better still, a woman, for then the child might still have been born. At last he came to Liverpool—is the district probable?—and there he began to cough, and spat blood until he died.

"I do not suppose there is any one living now who has seen her. There has seldom been more than one in a generation, and never in my life will there be both a man and a woman from whom that child can be born, who will fetch up the Siren from the sea, and destroy silence, and save the world!"

"Save the world?" I cried. "Did the prophecy end like that?"

He leaned back against the rock, breathing deep. Through all the blue-green reflections I saw him colour. I heard him say: "Silence and loneliness cannot last for ever. It may be a hundred or a thousand years, but the sea lasts longer, and she shall come out of it and sing." I would have asked him more, but at that moment the whole cave darkened, and there rode in through its narrow entrance the returning boat.

E. M. FORSTER
1879–1970

Before Edward Morgan Forster was two years old his father died. He and his mother left London for Herefordshire. After attending Tonbridge School as a day boy, he matriculated at King's College, Cambridge, where he was elected to the Cambridge Conversazione Society (the Apostles).

Following graduation in 1901, he traveled for a year in Italy and Austria with his mother. In 1903 he began to publish essays and short stories in the *Independent Review* and other magazines.

Between 1903 and 1910 Forster wrote four novels: *Where Angels Fear to Tread* (1905) and *A Room with a View* (1908) have Italian settings; *The Longest Journey* (1907), a Tonbridge and Cambridge setting; and *Howard's End* (1910), a Herefordshire setting. *Howard's End* signaled Forster's arrival as a major author, but it also brought to an end the steady productivity in long fiction that had characterized his early career.

Forster, after meeting Syed Ross Masood, became his Latin tutor and closest friend. Largely because of this friendship the writer visited India in 1912–13 and began work on *A Passage to India*, his masterpiece. The work, finished only after a second visit to India in 1921–22, was published to unanimous acclaim in 1924. The following year he received both the Femina Vie Heureuse and James Tait Black prizes for the book. No other novels appeared in Forster's lifetime, though *Maurice* (1971) and the unfinished *Arctic Summer* (1980) were published posthumously.

After 1924 he produced largely nonfiction prose, most notably *Abinger Harvest* (1936), *Two Cheers for Democracy* (1951), and *The Hill of Devi* (1953). Along with Eric Crozier, Forster adapted Herman Melville's sea tale, *Billy Budd*, as a libretto for Benjamin Britten's opera.

Between 1924 and 1945 Forster and his mother lived in Abinger Hammer, Surrey. Upon her death in 1945, Forster took up permanent residence in King's College, Cambridge, where he had been elected an honorary fellow.

"The Story of the Siren," though it dates from 1904 or earlier, was not published until 1920, when it appeared in a hand-printed Hogarth Press edition published by Leonard and Virginia Woolf.

The Ocean Christ

BY ANATOLE FRANCE

THAT YEAR many of the fishers of Saint-Valéry had been drowned at sea. Their bodies were found on the beach cast up by the waves with the wreckage of their boats; and for nine days, up the steep road leading to the church were to be seen coffins borne by hand and followed by widows, who were weeping beneath their great black-hooded cloaks, like women in the Bible.

Thus were the skipper Jean Lenoël and his son Désiré laid in the great nave, beneath the vaulted roof from which they had once hung a ship in full rigging as an offering to Our Lady. They were righteous men and God-fearing. Monsieur Guillaume Truphème, priest of Saint-Valéry, having pronounced the Absolution, said in a tearful voice:

"Never were laid in consecrated ground there to await the judgment of God better men and better Christians than Jean Lenoël and his son Désiré."

And while barques and their skippers perished near the coast, in the high seas great vessels foundered. Not a day passed that the ocean did not bring in some flotsam of wreck. Now one morning some children who were steering a boat saw a figure lying on the sea. It was a figure of Jesus Christ, life-size, carved in wood, painted in natural colouring, and looking as if it were very old. The Good Lord was floating upon the sea with arms outstretched. The children towed the figure ashore and brought it up into Saint-Valéry. The head was encircled with the crown of thorns. The feet and hands were pierced. But the nails were missing as well as the cross. The arms were still outstretched ready for sacrifice and blessing, just as He appeared to Joseph of Arimathea and the holy women when they were burying him.

The children gave it to Monsieur le Curé Truphème, who said to them:

"This image of the Saviour is of ancient workmanship. He who made it must have died long ago. Although to-day in the shops of Amiens and Paris excellent statues are sold for a hundred francs and more, we must admit that the earlier sculptors were not without merit. But what delights me most is the thought that if Jesus Christ be thus come with open arms to Saint-Valéry, it is in order to bless the parish, which has been so cruelly tried, and in order to announce that he has compassion on the poor folk who go a-fishing at the risk of their lives. He is the God who walked upon the sea and blessed the nets of Cephas."

And Monsieur le Curé Truphème, having had the Christ placed in the church on the cloth of the high altar, went off to order from the carpenter Lemerre a beautiful cross in heart of oak.

When it was made, the Saviour was nailed to it with brand new nails, and it was erected in the nave above the churchwarden's pew.

Then it was noticed that His eyes were filled with mercy and seemed to glisten with tears of heavenly pity.

One of the churchwardens, who was present at the putting up of the crucifix, fancied he saw tears streaming down the divine face. The next morning when Monsieur le Curé with a choir-boy entered the church to say his mass, he was astonished to find the cross above the churchwarden's pew empty and the Christ lying upon the altar.

As soon as he had celebrated the divine sacrifice he had the carpenter called and asked him why he had taken the Christ down from his cross. But the carpenter replied that he had not touched it. Then, after having questioned the beadle and the sidesmen, Monsieur Truphème made certain that no one had entered the church since the crucifix had been placed over the churchwarden's pew.

Thereupon he felt that these things were miraculous, and he meditated upon them discreetly. The following Sunday in his exhortation he spoke of them to his parishioners, and he called upon them to contribute by their gifts to the erection of a new cross more beautiful than the first and more worthy to bear the Redeemer of the world.

The poor fishers of Saint-Valéry gave as much money as they could and the widows brought their wedding-rings. Wherefore Monsier Truphème was able to go at once to Abbeville and to order a cross of ebony highly polished and surmounted by a scroll with the inscription I.N.R.I. in letters of gold. Two months later it was erected in the place of the former and the Christ was nailed to it between the lance and the sponge.

But Jesus left this cross as He had left the other; and as soon as night fell He went and stretched Himself upon the altar.

Monsieur le Curé, when he found Him there in the morning, fell on his knees and prayed for a long while. The fame of this miracle spread throughout the neighbourhood, and the ladies of Amiens made a collection for the Christ of Saint-Valéry. Monsieur Truphème received money and jewels from Paris, and the wife of the Minister of Marine, Madame Hyde de Neuville, sent him a heart of diamonds. Of all these treasures, in the space of two years, a goldsmith of La Rue St. Sulpice, fashioned a cross of gold and precious stones which was set up with great pomp in the church of Saint-Valéry on the second Sunday after Easter in the year 18—. But He who had not refused the cross of sorrow, fled from this cross of gold and again stretched Himself upon the white linen of the altar.

For fear of offending Him He was left there this time; and He had lain upon the altar for more than two years, when Pierre, son of Pierre Caillou, came to tell Monsieur le Curé Truphème that he had found the true cross of Our Lord on the beach.

Pierre was an innocent; and, because he had not sense enough to earn a livelihood, people gave him bread out of charity; he was liked because he never did any harm. But he wandered in his talk and no one listened to him.

Nevertheless Monsieur Truphème, who had never ceased meditating on the Ocean Christ, was struck by what the poor imbecile had just said. With the beadle and two sidesmen he went to the spot, where the child said he had seen a cross, and there he found two planks studded with nails, which had long been washed by the sea and which did indeed form a cross.

They were the remains of some old shipwreck. On one of these boards could still be read two letters painted in black, a J and an L; and there was no doubt that this was a fragment of Jean Lenoël's barque, he who with his son Désiré had been lost at sea five years before.

At the sight of this, the beadle and the sidesmen began to laugh at the innocent who had taken the broken planks of a boat for the cross of Jesus Christ. But Monsieur le Curé Truphème checked their merriment. He had meditated much and prayed long since the Ocean Christ had arrived among the fisherfolk, and the mystery of infinite charity began to dawn upon him. He knelt down upon the sand, repeated the prayer for the faithful departed, and then told the beadle and the sidesmen to carry the flotsam on their shoulders and to place it in the church. When this had been done he raised the Christ from the altar, placed it on the planks of the boat and himself nailed it to them, with the nails that the ocean had corroded.

By the priest's command, the very next day this cross took the place of the cross of gold and precious stones over the churchwarden's pew. The Ocean Christ has never left it. He has chosen to remain nailed to the planks on which men died invoking His name and that of His Mother. There, with parted lips, august and afflicted He seems to say:

"My cross is made of all men's woes, for I am in truth the God of the poor and the heavy-laden."

ANATOLE FRANCE
1844–1924

The son of a bookseller, Jacques Anatole François Thibault was born in Paris. After graduation from the College Stanislaus in 1864, he began writing under the pseudonym Anatole France. Two poems published in *La Gazette rimée* in 1867 helped bring about political suppression of the magazine. His first book, *Alfred de Vigny* (1868), which paid tribute to the poet, is inadequate as a biography, incomplete as a discussion of Vigny's writing, and vague in its critical judgments. Subsequently France pursued his own career as a poet, writing two books of poems, *Les Poèmes dorés* (1873) and *Les Noces corinthiennes* (1876). While the latter has the reputation as the dramatic masterpiece of the Parnassian poets, France's poetic attitudes are better understood in the work he did for the French poetry anthology *Le Parnasse contemporain*. He had two poems accepted for the second edition of the book; and by the time contributions for the third edition were being received, he was on the editorial board. He rejected Mallarmé's *L'Après-midi d'un faune* and work by Paul Verlaine. If his judgments were not always wise, he at least had the influence to make them stick.

Turning his attention to fiction, France wrote a prize-winning novel, *Le Crime de Sylvestre Bonnard* by 1881. Other impressive fiction followed: *Thaïs* (1890), *La Rôtisserie de la reine Pédauque* (1893), *Le Lys rouge* (1894), and *Le Jardin d'epicure* (1894). *L'Etui de nacre* (1892) contained his most famous short story, "The Procurator of Judea." France's election to the French Academy in 1896 came in recognition of the stature of his fiction.

For some years he was a journalist, serving as literary critic of *Le Temps* between 1886 and 1891 and contributing at various times to *L'Echo de Paris*, *Le Figaro*, and *l'Humanite*.

His later work included *La Vie de Jeanne d'Arc* (1908), a biography that presented a highly unorthodox view of the Maid of Orleans, and *L'Île des pingouins* (1908), a brilliant parody of French history which made the skeptic's anticlerical bias plain. The Roman Catholic Church put all his works on the papal index in 1922.

Throughout his life France wrote quasi-fictional books about his childhood, including *Le Livre de mon ami* (1885), *Pierre Nozière* (1889), *Le Petit Pierre* (1919), and *La Vie en fleur* (1922).

France was named Nobel Laureate in 1921. The extraordinary breadth of his achievement—he mastered the genres of poetry, fiction, satire, and the essay—is matched by but a few literary artists.

Adventures at Sea

Is it possible to mention sea adventure without conjuring up visions of swashbuckling pirates and billowing sails? *Treasure Island* and an endless parade of movies made in the forties and fifties have imprinted the image indelibly on our minds, but the writers represented here, including Robert Louis Stevenson himself, give us an alternative version of adventure on the high seas. There is piracy, but not piracy carried out under the ensign of the skull and crossbones. There are sailing ships, but there are also twentieth-century mechanical marvels that travel the sea.

Writers realize, of course, that in the sea they have a strong and easily controlled setting for an adventure story. With the sea they have a platform to write about man's battles with nature; about his conflicts with fellow human beings; and about the ships that are the products of his ingenuity and on which his life depends. The ship itself can be a whole universe in which one or two people battle in isolation; it can be an Eden invaded by evil forces; or it can be a model of the perfect world.

A spy, the threat of death, and dramatic isolation are the ingredients that combine to make Wilkie Collins's "Blow Up with the Brig!" a masterful suspense story. In Guy de Maupassant's tale adventure sets the stage for a moral dilemma so wrenching that the reader faces it as if it were his own. "At Sea" is the story of the master of a fishing boat caught between his duty to make a profit and his obligation to save life and limb.

"The Merry Men," the title of Robert Louis Stevenson's macabre story of superstition, shipwreck, mental aberration and murder, has an appropriately ironic ring. Unlike the other stories in this section, Stevenson's takes place on land, on the storm-swept island of Eilean Aros; but the sea, as always, manages to work its pervasive power on the landscape and the characters.

Rounding Cape Horn to get from the east coast of the Americas to the west was one of the most hazardous and nerve-wracking chores for the captain of a sailing ship. Waiting for winds that would give the sails a proper angle might take weeks or months. And what might a captain have to endure if he took advantage of those winds when they came? Sleepless nights, the ire of his crew, murder? In "Make Westing" Jack London tells just how far shipmaster Dan Cullen is willing to go to get around the Cape.

William Faulkner is best known for his novels about Southern life, but in "Turn About" he channels his talent in a different direction to tell an exciting tale of American aviators and English boatmen in World War I. C. S. Forester's "Night Stalk" is a story of the equally daring men engaged in submarine attack and submarine hunting.

"HMS *Marlborough* Will Enter Harbour" is Nicholas Monsarrat's magnificent story of endurance. Can a ship, torpedoed and barely able to limp along, with more than half her complement of officers and men killed, make it to a friendly port? The fight the characters throw themselves into is one of nerves and perseverance.

"Blow Up with the Brig!"

BY WILKIE COLLINS

I HAVE GOT an alarming confession to make. I am haunted by a Ghost.

If you were to guess for a hundred years, you would never guess what my ghost is. I shall make you laugh to begin with—and afterward I shall make your flesh creep. My Ghost is the ghost of a Bedroom Candlestick.

Yes, a bedroom candlestick and candle, or a flat candlestick and candle— put it which way you like—that is what haunts me. I wish it was something pleasanter and more out of the common way; a beautiful lady, or a mine of gold and silver, or a cellar of wine and a coach and horses, and such like. But, being what it is, I must take it for what it is, and make the best of it; and I shall thank you kindly if you will help me out by doing the same.

I am not a scholar myself, but I make bold to believe that the haunting of any man with any thing under the sun begins with the frightening of him. At any rate, the haunting of me with a bedroom candlestick and candle began with the frightening of me with a bedroom candlestick and candle— the frightening of me half out of my life; and, for the time being, the frightening of me altogether out of my wits. That is not a very pleasant thing to confess before stating the particulars; but perhaps you will be the readier to believe that I am not a downright coward, because you find me bold enough to make a clean breast of it already, to my own great disadvantage so far.

Here are the particulars, as well as I can put them:

I was apprenticed to the sea when I was about as tall as my own walking-stick; and I made good enough use of my time to be fit for a mate's berth at the age of twenty-five years.

It was in the year eighteen hundred and eighteen, or nineteen, I am not quite certain which, that I reached the before-mentioned age of twenty-five. You will please to excuse my memory not being very good for dates, names, numbers, places, and such like. No fear, though, about the particulars I have undertaken to tell you of; I have got them all shipshape in my recollection; I can see them, at this moment, as clear as noonday in my own mind. But there is a mist over what went before, and, for the matter of that, a mist likewise over much that came after—and it's not very likely to lift at my time of life, is it?

Well, in eighteen hundred and eighteen, or nineteen, when there was peace in our part of the world—and not before it was wanted, you will say—there was fighting, of a certain scampering, scrambling kind, going on in that old battle-field which we seafaring men know by the name of the Spanish Main.

The possessions that belonged to the Spaniards in South America had broken into open mutiny and declared for themselves years before. There was plenty of bloodshed between the new Government and the old; but the new had got the best of it, for the most part, under one General Bolivar—a famous man in his time, though he seems to have dropped out of people's memories now. Englishmen and Irishmen with a turn for fighting, and nothing particular to do at home, joined the general as volunteers; and some of our merchants here found it a good venture to send supplies across the ocean to the popular side. There was risk enough, of course, in doing this; but where one speculation of the kind succeeded, it made up for two, at the least, that failed. And that's the true principle of trade, wherever I have met with it, all the world over.

Among the Englishmen who were concerned in this Spanish-American business, I, your humble servant, happened, in a small way, to be one.

I was then mate of a brig belonging to a certain firm in the City, which drove a sort of general trade, mostly in queer out-of-the-way places, as far from home as possible; and which freighted the brig, in the year I am speaking of, with a cargo of gunpowder for General Bolivar and his volunteers. Nobody knew anything about our instructions, when we sailed, except the captain; and he didn't half seem to like them. I can't rightly say how many barrels of powder we had on board, or how much each barrel held—I only know we had no other cargo. The name of the brig was the *Good Intent*—a queer name enough, you will tell me, for a vessel laden with gunpowder, and sent to help a revolution. And as far as this particular voyage was concerned, so it was. I mean that for a joke, and I hope you will encourage me by laughing at it.

The *Good Intent* was the craziest tub of a vessel I ever went to sea in, and the worst found in all respects. She was two hundred and thirty, or two hundred and eighty tons burden, I forget which; and she had a crew of eight, all told—nothing like as many as we ought by rights to have had to work the brig. However, we were well and honestly paid our wages; and we had to set that against the chance of foundering at sea, and, on this occasion, likewise the chance of being blown up into the bargain.

In consideration of the nature of our cargo, we were harassed with new regulations, which we didn't at all like, relative to smoking our pipes and lighting our lanterns; and, as usual in such cases, the captain, who made the regulations, preached what he didn't practise. Not a man of us was allowed to have a bit of lighted candle in his hand when he went below—except the skipper; and he used his light, when he turned in, or when he looked over his charts on the cabin table, just as usual.

This light was a common kitchen candle or "dip," and it stood in an old battered flat candlestick, with all the japan worn and melted off, and all the tin showing through. It would have been more seaman-like and suitable in every respect if he had had a lamp or a lantern; but he stuck to his old candlestick; and that same old candlestick has ever afterward stuck to *me*. That's another joke, if you please, and a better one than the first, in my opinion.

Well (I said "well" before, but it's a word that helps a man on like), we sailed in the brig, and shaped our course, first, for the Virgin Islands, in the West Indies; and, after sighting them, we made for the Leeward Islands next, and then stood on due south, till the lookout at the masthead hailed the deck and said he saw land. That land was the coast of South America. We had had a wonderful voyage so far. We had lost none of our spars or sails, and not a man of us had been harassed to death at the pumps. It wasn't often the *Good Intent* made such a voyage as that, I can tell you.

I was sent aloft to make sure about the land, and I did make sure of it.

When I reported the same to the skipper, he went below and had a look at his letter of instructions and the chart. When he came on deck again, he altered our course a trifle to the eastward—I forget the point on the compass, but that don't matter. What I do remember is, that it was dark before we closed in with the land. We kept the lead going, and hove the brig to in from four to five fathoms water, or it might be six—I can't say for certain. I kept a sharp eye to the drift of the vessel, none of us knowing how the currents ran on that coast. We all wondered why the skipper didn't anchor; but he said No, he must first show a light at the foretopmast-head, and wait for an answering light on shore. We did wait, and nothing of the sort appeared. It was starlight and calm. What little wind there was came in puffs off the land. I suppose we waited, drifting a little to the westward, as I made it out, best part of an hour before anything happened—and then, instead of seeing the light on shore, we saw a boat coming toward us, rowed by two men only.

We hailed them, and they answered "Friends!" and hailed us by our name. They came on board. One of them was an Irishman, and the other was a coffee-coloured native pilot, who jabbered a little English.

The Irishman handed a note to our skipper, who showed it to me. It informed us that the part of the coast we were off was not oversafe for discharging our cargo, seeing that spies of the enemy (that is to say, of the old Government) had been taken and shot in the neighbourhood the day before. We might trust the brig to the native pilot; and he had his instructions to take us to another part of the coast. The note was signed by the proper parties; so we let the Irishman go back alone in the boat, and allowed the pilot to exercise his lawful authority over the brig. He kept us stretching off from the land till noon the next day—his instructions, seemingly, ordering him to keep up well out of sight of the shore. We only altered our course in the afternoon, so as to close in with the land again a little before midnight.

This same pilot was about as ill-looking a vagabond as ever I saw; a skinny, cowardly, quarrelsome mongrel, who swore at the men in the vilest broken English, till they were every one of them ready to pitch him overboard. The skipper kept them quiet, and I kept them quiet; for the pilot being given us by our instructions, we were bound to make the best of him. Near nightfall, however, with the best will in the world to avoid it, I was unlucky enough to quarrel with him.

He wanted to go below with his pipe, and I stopped him, of course, because it was contrary to orders. Upon that he tried to hustle by me, and I put him away with my hand. I never meant to push him down; but somehow I did. He picked himself up as quick as lightning, and pulled out his knife. I snatched it out of his hand, slapped his murderous face for him, and threw his weapon overboard. He gave me one ugly look, and walked aft. I didn't think much of the look then, but I remembered it a little too well afterward.

We were close in with the land again, just as the wind failed us, between eleven and twelve that night, and dropped our anchor by the pilot's directions.

It was pitch-dark, and a dead, airless calm. The skipper was on deck, with two of our best men for watch. The rest were below, except the pilot, who coiled himself up, more like a snake than a man, on the forecastle. It was not my watch till four in the morning. But I didn't like the look of the night, or the pilot, or the state of things generally, and I shook myself down on deck to get my nap there, and be ready for anything at a moment's notice. The last I remember was the skipper whispering to me that he didn't like the look of things either, and that he would go below and consult his instructions again. That is the last I remember, before the slow, heavy, regular roll of the old brig on the ground-swell rocked me off to sleep.

I was awoke by a scuffle on the forecastle and a gag in my mouth. There was a man on my breast and a man on my legs, and I was bound hand and foot in half a minute.

The brig was in the hands of the Spaniards. They were swarming all over her. I heard six heavy splashes in the water, one after another. I saw the captain stabbed to the heart as he came running up the companion, and I heard a seventh splash in the water. Except myself, every soul of us on board had been murdered and thrown into the sea. Why I was left I couldn't think, till I saw the pilot stoop over me with a lantern, and look, to make sure of who I was. There was a devilish grin on his face, and he nodded his head at me, as much as to say, *You* were the man who hustled me down and slapped my face, and I mean to play the game of cat and mouse with you in return for it!

I could neither move nor speak, but I could see the Spaniards take off the main hatch and rig the purchases for getting up the cargo. A quarter of an hour afterward I heard the sweeps of a schooner, or other small vessel, in the water. The strange craft was laid alongside of us, and the Spaniards set to work to discharge our cargo into her. They all worked hard except the pilot; and he came from time to time, with his lantern, to have another look at me, and to grin and nod, always in the same devilish way. I am old enough now not to be ashamed of confessing the truth, and I don't mind acknowledging that the pilot frightened me.

The fright, and the bonds, and the gag, and the not being able to stir hand or foot, had pretty nigh worn me out by the time the Spaniards gave over work. This was just as the dawn broke. They had shifted a good part of our cargo on board their vessel, but nothing like all of it, and they were sharp enough to be off with what they had got before daylight.

I need hardly say that I had made up my mind by this time to the worst I could think of. The pilot, it was clear enough, was one of the spies of the enemy, who had wormed himself into the confidence of our consignees without being suspected. He, or more likely his employers, had got knowledge enough of us to suspect what our cargo was; we had been anchored for the night in the safest berth for them to surprise us in; and we had paid the penalty of having a small crew, and consequently an insufficient watch. All this was clear enough—but what did the pilot mean to do with *me?*

On the word of a man, it makes my flesh creep now, only to tell you what he did with me.

After all the rest of them were out of the brig, except the pilot and two Spanish seamen, these last took me up, bound and gagged as I was, lowered me into the hold of the vessel, and laid me along on the floor, lashing me to it with ropes' ends, so that I could just turn from one side to the other, but could not roll myself fairly over, so as to change my place. They then left me. Both of them were the worse for liquor; but the devil of a pilot was sober—mind that!—as sober as I am at the present moment.

I lay in the dark for a little while, with my heart thumping as if it was going to jump out of me. I lay about five minutes or so when the pilot came down into the hold alone.

He had the captain's cursed flat candlestick and a carpenter's awl in one hand, and a long thin twist of cotton yarn, well oiled, in the other. He put the candlestick, with a new "dip" candle lighted in it, down on the floor about two feet from my face, and close against the side of the vessel. The light was feeble enough; but it was sufficient to show a dozen barrels of gunpowder or more left all round me in the hold of the brig. I began to suspect what he was after the moment I noticed the barrels. The horrors laid hold of me from head to foot, and the sweat poured off my face like water.

I saw him go next to one of the barrels of powder standing against the side of the vessel in a line with the candle, and about three feet, or rather better, away from it. He bored a hole in the side of the barrel with his awl, and the horrid powder came trickling out, as black as hell, and dripped into the hollow of his hand, which he held to catch it. When he had got a good handful, he stopped up the hole by jamming one end of his oiled twist of cotton-yarn fast into it, and he then rubbed the powder into the whole length of the yarn till he had blackened every hair-breadth of it.

The next thing he did—as true as I sit here, as true as the heaven above us all—the next thing he did was to carry the free end of his long, lean, black, frightful slow-match to the lighted candle alongside my face. He tied it (the bloody-minded villain!) in several folds round the tallow dip, about a third of the distance down, measuring from the flame of the wick to the lip of the candlestick. He did that; he looked to see that my lashings were all safe; and then he put his face close to mine, and whispered in my ear, "Blow up with the brig!"

He was on deck again the moment after, and he and the two others shoved the hatch on over me. At the farthest end from where I lay they had not fitted it down quite true, and I saw a blink of daylight glimmering in when I looked in that direction. I heard the sweeps of the schooner fall into the water—splash! splash! fainter and fainter, as they swept the vessel out in the dead calm, to be ready for the wind in the offing. Fainter and fainter, splash, splash! for a quarter of an hour or more.

While those receding sounds were in my ears, my eyes were fixed on the candle.

It had been freshly lighted. If left to itself, it would burn for between six and seven hours. The slow-match was twisted round it about a third of the way down, and therefore the flame would be about two hours reaching it. There I lay, gagged, bound, lashed to the floor; seeing my own life burning down with the candle by my side—there I lay, alone on the sea, doomed to be blown to atoms, and to see that doom drawing on, nearer and nearer with every fresh second of time, through nigh on two hours to come; powerless to help myself, and speechless to call for help to others. The wonder to me is that I didn't cheat the flame, the slow-match, and the powder, and die of the horror of my situation before my first half-hour was out in the hold of the brig.

I can't exactly say how long I kept the command of my senses after I had ceased to hear the splash of the schooner's sweeps in the water. I can trace back everything I did and everything I thought up to a certain point; but, once past that, I get all abroad, and lose myself in my memory now, much as I lost myself in my own feelings at the time.

The moment the hatch was covered over me, I began, as every other man would have begun in my place, with a frantic effort to free my hands. In the mad panic I was in, I cut my flesh with the lashings as if they had been knife blades, but I never stirred them. There was less chance still of freeing my legs, or of tearing myself from the fastenings that held me to the floor. I gave in when I was all but suffocated for want of breath. The gag, you will be pleased to remember, was a terrible enemy to me; I could only breathe freely through my nose—and that is but a poor vent when a man is straining his strength as far as ever it will go.

I gave in and lay quiet, and got my breath again, my eyes glaring and straining at the candle all the time.

While I was staring at it, the notion struck me of trying to blow out the flame by pumping a long breath at it suddenly through my nostrils. It was too high above me, and too far away from me, to be reached in that fashion. I tried, and tried, and tried; and then I gave in again, and lay quiet again, always with my eyes glaring at the candle, and the candle glaring at *me*. The splash of the schooner's sweeps was very faint by this time. I could only just hear them in the morning stillness. Splash! splash!—fainter and fainter—splash! splash!

Without exactly feeling my mind going, I began to feel it getting queer as early as this. The snuff of the candle was growing taller and taller, and the length of tallow between the flame and the slow-match, which was the length of my life, was getting shorter and shorter. I calculated that I had rather less than an hour and a half to live.

An hour and a half! Was there a chance in that time of a boat pulling off to the brig from shore? Whether the land near which the vessel was anchored was in possession of our side, or in possession of the enemy's side, I made out that they must, sooner or later, send to hail the brig merely because she was a stranger in those parts. The question for *me* was, how soon? The sun had not risen yet, as I could tell by looking through the chink in the hatch. There was no coast village near us, as we all knew, before the brig was seized, by seeing no lights on shore. There was no wind, as I could tell by listening, to bring any strange vessel near. If I had had six hours to live, there might have been a chance for me, reckoning from sunrise to noon. But with an hour and a half, which had dwindled to an hour and a quarter by this time—or, in other words, with the earliness of the morning, the uninhabited coast, and the dead calm all against me—there was not the ghost of a chance. As I felt that, I had another struggle—the last—with my bonds, and only cut myself the deeper for my pains.

I gave in once more, and lay quiet, and listened for the splash of the sweeps.

Gone! Not a sound could I hear but the blowing of a fish now and then on the surface of the sea, and the creak of the brig's crazy old spars, as she rolled gently from side to side with the little swell there was on the quiet water.

An hour and a quarter. The wick grew terribly as the quarter slipped away, and the charred top of it began to thicken and spread out mushroom-shape. It would fall off soon. Would it fall off red-hot, and would the swing of the brig cant it over the side of the candle and let it down on the slow-match? If it would, I had about ten minutes to live instead of an hour.

This discovery set my mind for a minute on a new tack altogether. I began to ponder with myself what sort of a death blowing up might be. Painful! Well, it would be, surely, too sudden for that. Perhaps just one crash inside me, or outside me, or both; and nothing more! Perhaps not even a crash; that and death and the scattering of this living body of mine into millions of fiery sparks, might all happen in the same instant! I couldn't make it out; I couldn't settle how it would be. The minute of calmness in my mind left it before I had half done thinking; and I got all abroad again.

When I came back to my thoughts, or when they came back to me (I can't say which), the wick was awfully tall, the flame was burning with a smoke above it, the charred top was broad and red, and heavily spreading out to its fall.

My despair and horror at seeing it took me in a new way, which was good and right, at any rate, for my poor soul. I tried to pray—in my own heart, you will understand, for the gag put all lip-praying out of my power. I tried, but the candle seemed to burn it up in me. I struggled hard to force my eyes from the slow, murdering flame, and to look up through the chink in the hatch at the blessed daylight. I tried once, tried twice; and gave it up. I next tried only to shut my eyes, and keep them shut—once—twice—and the second time I did it. "God bless old mother, and sister Lizzie; God keep them both, and forgive *me*." That was all I had time to say, in my own heart, before my eyes opened again, in spite of me, and the flame of the candle flew into them, flew all over me, and burned up the rest of my thoughts in an instant.

I couldn't hear the fish blowing now; I couldn't hear the creak of the spars; I couldn't think; I couldn't feel the sweat of my own death agony on my face—I could only look at the heavy, charred top of the wick. It swelled, tottered, bent over to one side, dropped—red-hot at the moment of its fall—black and harmless, even before the swing of the brig had canted it over into the bottom of the candlestick.

I caught myself laughing.

Yes! laughing at the safe fall of the bit of wick. But for the gag, I should have screamed with laughter. As it was, I shook with it inside me—shook till the blood was in my head, and I was all but suffocated for want of breath. I had just sense enough left to feel that my own horrid laughter at that awful moment was a sign of my brain going at last. I had just sense enough left to make another struggle before my mind broke loose like a frightened horse, and ran away with me.

One comforting look at the blink of daylight through the hatch was what I tried for once more. The fight to force my eyes from the candle and to get that one look at the daylight was the hardest I had had yet; and I lost the fight. The flame had hold of my eyes as fast as the lashings had hold of my hands. I couldn't look away from it. I couldn't even shut my eyes, when I tried that next, for the second time. There was the wick growing tall once more. There was the space of unburned candle between the light and the slow-match shortened to an inch or less.

How much life did that inch leave me? Three-quarters of an hour? Half an hour? Fifty minutes? Twenty minutes? Steady! an inch of tallow candle would burn longer than twenty minutes. An inch of tallow! the notion of a man's body and soul being kept together by an inch of tallow! Wonderful! Why, the greatest king that sits on a throne can't keep a man's body and soul together; and here's an inch of tallow that can do what the king can't! There's something to tell mother when I get home which will surprise her more than all the rest of my voyages put together. I laughed inwardly again at the thought of that, and shook and swelled and suffocated myself, till the light of the candle leaped in through my eyes, and licked up the laughter, and burned it out of me, and made me all empty and cold and quiet once more.

Mother and Lizzie. I don't know when they came back; but they did come back—not, as it seemed to me, into my mind this time, but right down bodily before me, in the hold of the brig.

Yes: sure enough, there was Lizzie, just as lighthearted as usual, laughing at me. Laughing? Well, why not? Who is to blame Lizzie for thinking I'm lying on my back, drunk in the cellar, with the beer barrels all round me? Steady! she's crying now—spinning round and round in a fiery mist, wringing her hands, screeching out for help—fainter and fainter, like the splash of the schooner's sweeps. Gone—burned up in the fiery mist! Mist? fire? no; neither one nor the other. It's mother makes the light—mother knitting, with ten flaming points at the ends of her fingers and thumbs, and slow-matches hanging in bunches all round her face instead of her own grey hair. Mother in her old armchair, and the pilot's long skinny hands hanging over the back of the chair, dripping with gunpowder. No! no gunpowder, no chair, no mother—nothing but the pilot's face, shining red-hot, like a sun, in the fiery mist; turning upside down in the fiery mist; running backward and forward along the slow-match, in the fiery mist; spinning millions of miles in a minute, in the fiery mist—spinning itself smaller and smaller into one tiny point, and that point darting on a sudden straight into my head—and then, all fire and all mist—no hearing, no seeing, no thinking, no feeling—the brig, the sea, my own self, the whole world, all gone together!

After what I've just told you, I know nothing and remember nothing, till I woke up (as it seemed to me) in a comfortable bed, with two rough-and-ready men like myself sitting on each side of my pillow, and a gentleman standing watching me at the foot of the bed. It was about seven in the morning. My sleep (or what seemed like my sleep to me) had lasted better than eight months—I was among my own countrymen in the island of Trinidad—the men at each side of my pillow were my keepers, turn and turn about—and the gentleman standing at the foot of the bed was the doctor. What I said and did in those eight months I never have known, and never shall. I woke out of it as if it had been one long sleep—that's all I know.

It was another two months or more before the doctor thought it safe to answer the questions I asked him.

An American vessel, becalmed in the offing, had made out the brig as the sun rose; and the captain, seeing her anchored where no vessel had any reason to be, had manned one of his boats and sent his mate to look into the matter and report of what he saw.

What he saw, when he and his men found the brig deserted and boarded her, was a gleam of candlelight through the chink in the hatchway. The flame was within about a thread's breadth of the slow-match when he lowered himself into the hold; and if he had not had the sense and coolness to cut the match in two with his knife before he touched the candle, he and his men might have been blown up along with the brig as well as me. The match caught, and turned into sputtering red fire, in the very act of putting the candle out. . . .

What became of the Spanish schooner and the pilot I have never heard from that day to this.

As for the brig, the Yankees took her, as they took me, to Trinidad, and claimed their salvage, and got it, I hope, for their own sakes. I was landed just in the same state as when they rescued me from the brig—that is to say, clean out of my senses. But please to remember, it was a long time ago; and, take my word for it, I was discharged cured, as I have told you. Bless your hearts, I'm all right now, as you may see. I'm a little shaken by telling the story, as is only natural—a little shaken, my good friends, that's all.

WILKIE COLLINS
1824–89

William Wilkie Collins was the elder son of the well-known painter William Collins. Apprenticed to the principal partner in a large firm of tea merchants, young Wilkie seemed destined for a career in business; nevertheless, after five years in the apprenticeship Collins obtained a release. He then became a student of law at Lincoln's Inn. But neither business nor law interested him.

In 1843, while still an apprentice, Collins published "The Last Stage-coachman." In 1847 his father died, and the next year Collins published *The Memories of the Life of William Collins, Esq., R.A.* The pace of his production quickened in 1850. That year *Antonina, or the Fall of Rome*, Collins's first novel, was published, and his play, *A Court Duel*, opened at Miss Kelly's Theatre.

Charles Dickens and Collins met in 1851, became friends, and by 1856 were collaborators. The alliance lasted until 1867. (One of their collaborative efforts, "The Wreck of the *Golden Mary*," appears on page 375.)

A prolific writer, Collins had published more than thirty books by 1889. Two are still widely read and respected by common readers and literary critics alike—*The Woman In White* (1860) and *The Moonstone* (1868). These are the books that gave Collins the epithet "father of the English detective novel."

"Blow Up with the Brig!" is not detective fiction, but it has the suspense that characterizes mystery writing at its spine-tingling best. The story, under the rather strange title "The Ghost in the Cupboard Room," was first published in the Christmas 1859 issue of *All the Year Round*, a magazine of which Collins was an editor.

At Sea

BY GUY DE MAUPASSANT

THE FOLLOWING LINES recently appeared in the press:

"BOULOGNE-SUR-MER, January 22.
"From our correspondent.
"A frightful disaster has occurred which throws into consternation our maritime population, so grievously afflicted for the last two years. The fishing boat, commanded by Captain Javel, entering into port, was carried to the west, and broken upon the rocks of the breakwater near the pier. In spite of the efforts of the life-boat, and of life-lines shot out to them, four men and a cabin boy perished. The bad weather continues. Further wrecks are feared."

Who is this Captain Javel? Is he the brother of the one-armed Javel? If this poor man tossed by the waves, and dead perhaps, under the *débris* of his boat cut in pieces, is the one I think he is, he witnessed, eighteen years ago, another drama, terrible and simple as are all the formidable dramas of the sea.

Javel senior was then master of a smack. The smack is the fishing boat *par excellence*. Solid, fearing no kind of weather, with round body, rolled incessantly by the waves, like a cork, always lashed by the harsh, salty winds of the Channel, it travels the sea indefatigably, with sail filled, carrying in its wake a net which reaches the bottom of the ocean, detaching all the sleeping creatures from the rocks, the flat fishes glued to the sand, the heavy crabs with their hooked claws, and the lobster with his pointed mustaches.

When the breeze is fresh and the waves choppy, the boat puts about to fish. A rope is fastened to the end of a great wooden shank tipped with iron, which is let down by means of two cables slipping over two spools at the extreme end of the craft. And the boat, driving under wind and current, drags after her this apparatus, which ravages and devastates the bottom of the sea.

Javel had on board his younger brother, four men, and a cabin boy. He had set out from Boulogne in fair weather to cast the nets. Then, suddenly, the wind arose and a squall drove the boat before the wind. It reached the coast of England; but a tremendous sea was beating against the cliffs and the shore so that it was impossible to enter port. The little boat put to sea again and returned to the coast of France. The storm continued to make the piers unapproachable, enveloping with foam, noise and danger every place of refuge.

The fishing boat set out again, running along the tops of the billows, tossed about, shaken up, streaming, buffeted by mountains of water, but game in spite of all, accustomed to heavy weather, which sometimes kept it wandering for five or six days between the two countries, unable to land in the one or the other.

Finally, the hurricane ceased, when they came out into open sea, and although the sea was still high, the Old Man ordered them to cast the net. Then the great fishing tackle was thrown overboard, and two men at one side and two at the other began to unwind from windlasses the cable which held it. Suddenly it touched the bottom, but a high wave tipped the boat forward. Javel junior, who was in the prow directing the casting of the net, tottered and found his arm caught between the cable, slackened an instant by the motion, and the wood on which it was turning. He made a desperate effort with his other hand to lift the cable, but the net was dragging again and the taut cable would not yield.

Rigid with pain, he called. Every one ran to him. His brother left the helm. They threw their full force upon the rope, forcing it away from the arm it was grinding. It was in vain. "We must cut it," said a sailor, and he drew from his pocket a large knife which could, in two blows, save young Javel's arm. But to cut was to lose the net, and the net meant money, much money—fifteen hundred francs; it belonged to the elder Javel, who was keen on his property.

In anguish he cried out: "No, don't cut; I'll luff the ship." And he ran to the wheel, putting the helm about. The boat scarcely obeyed, paralyzed by the net, which counteracted its power, and driven besides by the force of the leeway and the wind.

Young Javel fell to his knees with set teeth and haggard eyes. He said nothing. His brother returned, still anxious about the sailor's knife.

"Wait! wait!" he said, "don't cut; we must cast anchor."

The anchor was thrown overboard, all the chain paid out, and they then tried to take a turn around the capstan with the cables in order to loosen them from the weight of the net. The cables finally relaxed, and they released the arm, which hung inert under a sleeve of bloody woolen cloth.

Young Javel seemed to have lost his mind. They removed his jersey, and then saw something horrible; a mass of bruised flesh, from which the blood was gushing, as if it were forced by a pump. The man himself looked at his arm and murmured: "Done for."

Then, as the hæmorrhage made a pool on the deck of the boat, the sailors cried: "He'll lose all his blood. We must bind the artery!"

They then took some twine, thick, black, tarred twine, and, twisting it around the limb above the wound, bound it with all their strength. Little by little the jets of blood stopped, and finally ceased altogether.

Young Javel arose, his arm hanging by his side. He took it by the other hand, raised it, turned it, shook it. Everything was broken; the bones were crushed completely; only the muscles held it to his body. He looked at it thoughtfully, with sad eyes. Then he seated himself on a folded sail, and his comrades came around him, advising him to soak it continually to prevent gangrene.

They put a bucket near him and every moment he would dip into it with a glass and bathe the horrible wound by letting a thin stream of clear water fall upon it.

"You would be better down below," said his brother. He went down, but after an hour he came up again, feeling better not to be alone. And then, he preferred the open air. He sat down again upon the sail and continued bathing his arm.

The fishing was good. The huge fish with white bodies were lying beside him, shaken by the spasms of death. He looked at them without ceasing to sprinkle the mangled flesh.

When they started to return to Boulogne, another gale of wind began to blow. The little boat resumed its mad course, bounding, and tumbling, shaking the poor wounded man.

Night came on. The weather was heavy until daybreak. At sunrise, they could see England again, but as the sea was a little less rough, they turned toward France, beating against the wind.

Toward evening, young Javel called his comrades and showed them black traces and the hideous signs of decay around that part of his arm which was no longer joined to his body.

The sailors looked at it, giving advice: "That must be gangrene," said one.

"It must have salt water on it," said another.

Then they brought salt water and poured it on the wound. The wounded man became livid, grinding his teeth, and twisting with pain; but he uttered no cry.

When the burning grew less, he said to his brother: "Give me your knife." The brother gave it to him.

"Hold this arm up for me, and pull it."

His brother did as he was asked.

Then he began to cut. He cut gently, with caution, severing the last tendons with the blade as sharp as a razor. Soon he had only a stump. He heaved a deep sigh and said: "That had to be done. Otherwise, it would be all up."

He seemed relieved and breathed energetically. He continued to pour water on the part of his arm remaining to him.

The night was still bad and they could not land. When the day appeared, young Javel took his severed arm and examined it carefully. Putrefaction had begun. His comrades came also and examined it, passing it from hand to hand, touching it, turning it over, and smelling it.

His brother said: "It's about time to throw that into the sea."

Young Javel was angry; he replied: "No, oh! no! I will not. It is mine, isn't it? Since it is my arm—" He took it and held it between his legs.

"It won't grow any less putrid," said the elder.

Then an idea came to the wounded man. In order to keep the fish when they remained a long time at sea, they had with them barrels of salt. "Couldn't I put it in there in the brine?" he asked.

"That's so," declared the others.

Then they emptied one of the barrels, already full of fish from the last few days, and, at the bottom, they deposited the arm. Then they turned salt upon it and replaced the fishes, one by one.

One of the sailors made a little joke: "Take care we don't happen to sell it at the fish market."

And everybody laughed except the Javel brothers.

The wind still blew. They beat about in sight of Boulogne until the next day at ten o'clock. The wounded man still poured water on his arm. From time to time he would get up and walk from one end of the boat to the other. His brother, who was at the wheel, shook his head and followed him with his eye.

Finally, they came into port.

The doctor examined the wound and declared it was doing well. He dressed it properly and ordered rest. But Javel could not go to bed without having his arm again, and went quickly back to the dock to find the barrel, which he had marked with a cross.

They emptied it in front of him, and he found his arm well preserved in the salt, wrinkled and in good condition. He wrapped it in a napkin brought for this purpose, and took it home.

His wife and children examined carefully this fragment of their father, touching the fingers, taking up the grains of salt that had lodged under the nails. Then they sent for the carpenter, who measured it for a little coffin.

The next day the complete crew of the fishing smack followed the funeral of the severed arm. The two brothers, side by side, conducted the ceremony. The parish beadle held the coffin under his arm.

Javel junior gave up going to sea. He obtained a small position in port, and, later, whenever he spoke of the accident, he would say to his auditor, in a low tone: "If my brother had been willing to cut the net, I should still have my arm, for certain. But he was thinking of his valuable property."

GUY DE MAUPASSANT
1850–93

Spending much of his youth at Étretat on the French sea coast, Henri René Albert Guy de Maupassant early learned how those people dependent on the sea for their livelihood fared. He also learned early of his mother's literary ambitions for him, ambitions spawned because in him she saw the image of his brother, Alfred le Poittevin, Flaubert's literary tutor-confessor, who died prematurely. Maupassant was like a son to Flaubert, and the master's influence on the young man was pervasive. Nevertheless, Maupassant did not produce his impressive work early; his talent came to a head in a ten-year span near the end of his life.

In 1869 he became a law student in Paris, parlaying his training and connections into a position in the Ministry of the Marine in 1872. While at the ministry Maupassant began to publish in obscure journals. Later he formed a friendship with the group of French writers who published their stories under the title *Les Soirées de Médan*.

With Flaubert's help he published *Boule de Suif* (1880), a book that freed him from the necessity of working for a ministry and which made it obvious that fiction was his forte. Unfortunately he did not recognize that his talent for the short story did not adapt well to the novel. Because of his admiration for Flaubert and his erroneous assumption that glory and money awaited the novelist, Maupassant tried to master the longer form. He wrote five novels with varying degrees of success. One of them, *Pierre et Jean* (1888), was both a popular and critical success, but the effort to produce a longer more complicated work finally led to the ill-fated *Fort comme la mort* (1899). Maupassant's real contributions to literature are his short stories.

The influence of the sea is everywhere in Maupassant's essays, novels, and short stories. "At Sea" exemplifies that influence and shows Maupassant's understanding of complex moral and ethical questions. The story appeared under the title "Selfishness" in *The Complete Short Stories of Guy de Maupassant* (1955).

The Merry Men

BY ROBERT LOUIS STEVENSON

I

Eilean Aros

IT WAS a beautiful morning in the late July when I set forth on foot for the last time for Aros. A boat had put me ashore the night before at Grisapol; I had such breakfast as the little inn afforded, and, leaving all my baggage till I had an occasion to come round for it by sea, struck right across the promontory with a cheerful heart.

I was far from being a native of these parts, springing, as I did, from an unmixed Lowland stock. But an uncle of mine, Gordon Darnaway, after a poor, rough youth, and some years at sea, had married a young wife in the islands; Mary Maclean she was called, the last of her family; and when she died in giving birth to a daughter, Aros, the sea-girt farm, had remained in his possession. It brought him in nothing but the means of life, as I was well aware; but he was a man whom ill-fortune had pursued; he feared, cumbered as he was with the young child, to make a fresh adventure upon life; and remained in Aros, biting his nails at destiny. Years passed over his head in that isolation, and brought neither help nor contentment. Meantime our family was dying out in the Lowlands; there is little luck for any of that race; and perhaps my father was the luckiest of all, for not only was he one of the last to die, but he left a son to his name and a little money to support it. I was a student of Edinburgh University, living well enough at my own charges, but without kith or kin; when some news of me found its way to Uncle Gordon on the Ross of Grisapol; and he, as he was a man who held blood thicker than water, wrote to me the day he heard of my existence, and taught me to count Aros as my home. Thus it was that I came to spend my vacations in that part of the country, so far from all society and comfort, between the codfish and the moorcocks; and thus it was that now, when I had done with my classes, I was returning thither with so light a heart that July day.

The Ross, as we call it, is a promontory neither wide nor high, but as rough as God made it to this day; the deep sea on either hand of it, full of rugged isles and reefs most perilous to seamen—all overlooked from the eastward by some very high cliffs and the great peak of Ben Kyaw. *The*

Mountain of the Mist, they say the words signify in the Gaelic tongue; and it is well named. For that hill-top, which is more than three thousand feet in height, catches all the clouds that come blowing from the seaward; and, indeed, I used often to think that it must make them for itself; since when all heaven was clear to the sea-level, there would ever be a streamer on Ben Kyaw. It brought water, too, and was mossy to the top in consequence. I have seen us sitting in broad sunshine on the Ross, and the rain falling black like crape upon the mountain. But the wetness of it made it often appear more beautiful to my eyes; for when the sun struck upon the hill-sides, there were many wet rocks and watercourses that shone like jewels even as far as Aros, fifteen miles away.

The road that I followed was a cattle-track. It twisted so as nearly to double the length of my journey; it went over rough boulders so that a man had to leap from one to another, and through soft bottoms where the moss came nearly to the knee. There was no cultivation anywhere, and not one house in the ten miles from Grisapol to Aros. Houses of course there were—three at least; but they lay so far on the one side or the other that no stranger could have found them from the track. A large part of the Ross is covered with big granite rocks, some of them larger than a two-roomed house, one beside another, with fern and deep heather in between them where the vipers breed. Any way the wind was, it was always sea-air, as salt as on a ship; the gulls were as free as moorfowl over all the Ross; and whenever the way rose a little, your eye would kindle with the brightness of the sea. From the very midst of the land, on a day of wind and a high spring, I have heard the Roost roaring like a battle where it runs by Aros, and the great and fearful voices of the breakers that we call the Merry Men.

Aros itself—Aros Jay, I have heard the natives call it, and they say it means *the House of God*—Aros itself was not properly a piece of the Ross, nor was it quite an islet. It formed the south-west corner of the land, fitted close to it, and was in one place only separated from the coast by a little gut of the sea, not forty feet across the narrowest. When the tide was full, this was clear and still, like a pool on a land river; only there was a difference in the weeds and fishes and the water itself was green instead of brown; but when the tide went out, in the bottom of the ebb, there was a day or two in every month when you could pass dryshod from Aros to the mainland. There was some good pasture, where my uncle fed the sheep he lived on; perhaps the feed was better because the ground rose higher on the islet than the main level of the Ross, but this I am not skilled enough to settle. The house was a good one for that country, two stories high. It looked westward over a bay, with a pier hard by for a boat, and from the door you could watch the vapours blowing on Ben Kyaw.

On all this part of the coast, and especially near Aros, these great granite rocks that I have spoken of go down together in troops into the sea, like cattle on a summer's day. There they stand, for all the world like their neighbours ashore; only the salt water sobbing between them instead of the quiet earth, and clots of sea-pink blooming on their sides instead of heather; and the great sea-conger to wreathe about the base of them instead of the poisonous viper of the land. On calm days you can go wandering between them in a boat for hours, echoes following you about the labyrinth; but when the sea is up, Heaven help the man that hears that caldron boiling.

Off the south-west end of Aros these blocks are very many, and much greater in size. Indeed, they must grow monstrously bigger out to sea, for there must be ten sea-miles of open water sown with them as thick as a country place with houses, some standing thirty feet above the tides, some covered, but all perilous to ships; so that on a clear, westerly blowing day, I have counted, from the top of Aros, the great rollers breaking white and heavy over as many as six-and-forty buried reefs. But it is nearer inshore that the danger is worst; for the tide, here running like a mill-race, makes a long belt of broken water—a *Roost* we call it—at the tail of the land. I have often been out there in a dead calm at the slack of the tide; and a strange place it is, with the sea swirling and combing up and boiling like the caldrons of a linn, and now and again a little dancing mutter of sound as though the Roost were talking to itself. But when the tide begins to run again, and above all in heavy weather, there is no man could take a boat within half a mile of it, nor a ship afloat that could either steer or live in such a place. You can hear the roaring of it six miles away. At the seaward end there comes the strongest of the bubble; and it's here that these big breakers dance together—the dance of death, it may be called—that have got the name, in these parts, of the Merry Men. I have heard it said that they run fifty feet high; but that must be the green water only, for the spray runs twice as high as that. Whether they got the name from their movements, which are swift and antic, or from the shouting they make about the turn of the tide, so that all Aros shakes with it, is more than I can tell.

The truth is, that in a south-westerly wind that part of our archipelago is no better than a trap. If a ship got through the reefs, and weathered the Merry Men, it would be to come ashore on the south coast of Aros, in Sandag Bay, where so many dismal things befell our family, as I propose to tell. The thought of all these dangers, in the place I knew so long, makes me particularly welcome the works now going forward to set lights upon the headlands and buoys along the channels of our iron-bound, inhospitable islands.

The country people had many a story about Aros, as I used to hear from my uncle's man, Rorie, an old servant of the Macleans, who had transferred his services without afterthought on the occasion of the marriage. There was some tale of an unlucky creature, a sea-kelpie, that dwelt and did business in some fearful manner of his own among the boiling breakers of the Roost. A mermaid had once met a piper on Sandag beach, and there sang to him a long, bright midsummer's night, so that in the morning he was found stricken crazy, and from thenceforward, till the day he died, said only one form of words; what they were in the original Gaelic I cannot tell, but they were thus translated: "Ah, the sweet singing out of the sea." Seals that haunted that coast have been known to speak to man in his own tongue, presaging great disasters. It was here that a certain saint first landed on his voyage out of Ireland to convert the Hebrideans. And, indeed, I think he had some claim to be called saint; for, with the boats of that past age, to make so rough a passage, and land on such a ticklish coast, was surely not far short of the miraculous. It was to him, or to some of his monkish underlings who had a cell there, that the islet owes its holy and beautiful name, the House of God.

Among these old wives' stories there was one which I was inclined to hear with more credulity. As I was told, in that tempest which scattered the ships of the Invincible Armada over all the north and west of Scotland, one great vessel came ashore on Aros, and before the eyes of some solitary people on a hill-top, went down in a moment with all hands, her colours flying even as she sank. There was some likelihood in this tale; for another of that fleet lay sunk on the north side, twenty miles from Grisapol. It was told, I thought, with more detail and gravity than its companion stories, and there was one particularity which went far to convince me of its truth: the name, that is, of the ship was still remembered, and sounded in my ears, Spanishly. The *Espirito Santo* they called it, a great ship of many decks of guns, laden with treasure and grandees of Spain, and fierce soldadoes, that now lay fathom deep to all eternity, done with her wars and voyages, in Sandag Bay, upon the west of Aros. No more salvos of ordnance for that tall ship, the "Holy Spirit," no more fair winds or happy ventures; only to rot there deep in the sea-tangle and hear the shoutings of the Merry Men as the tide ran high about the island. It was a strange thought to me first and last, and only grew stranger as I learned the more of the way in which she had set sail with so proud a company, and King Philip, the wealthy king, that sent her on that voyage.

And now I must tell you, as I walked from Grisapol that day, the *Espirito Santo* was very much in my reflections. I had been favourably remarked by our then Principal in Edinburgh College, the famous writer Dr. Robertson, and by him had been set to work on some papers of an ancient date to rearrange and sift of what was worthless; and in one of these, to my great wonder, I found a note of this very ship, the *Espirito Santo*, with her captain's name, and how she carried a great part of the Spaniard's treasure, and had been lost upon the Ross of Grisapol; but in what particular spot, the wild tribes of that place and period would give no information to the King's inquiries. Putting one thing with another, and taking our island tradition together with this note of old King Jamie's perquisitions after wealth, it had come strongly on my mind that the spot for which he sought in vain could be no other than the small bay of Sandag on my uncle's land; and being a fellow of a mechanical turn, I had ever since been plotting how to weigh that good ship up again with all her ingots, ounces, and doubloons, and bring back our house of Darnaway to its long-forgotten dignity and wealth.

This was a design of which I soon had reason to repent. My mind was sharply turned on different reflections; and since I became the witness of a strange judgment of God's, the thought of dead men's treasures has been intolerable to my conscience. But even at that time I must acquit myself of sordid greed; for if I desired riches, it was not for their own sake, but for the sake of a person who was dear to my heart—my uncle's daughter, Mary Ellen. She had been educated well, and had been a time to school upon the mainland; which, poor girl, she would have been happier without. For Aros was no place for her with old Rorie the servant, and her father, who was one of the unhappiest men in Scotland, plainly bred up in a country place among Cameronians, long a skipper sailing out of the Clyde about the islands, and now, with infinite discontent, managing his sheep and a little 'long-shore fishing for the necessary bread. If it was sometimes weariful to me, who was there but a month or two, you may fancy what it was to her who dwelt in that same desert all the year round, with the sheep and flying seagulls, and the Merry Men singing and dancing in the Roost!

II
What the Wreck Had Brought to Aros

It was half-flood when I got the length of Aros; and there was nothing for it but to stand on the far shore and whistle for Rorie with the boat. I had no need to repeat the signal. At the first sound, Mary was at the door flying a handkerchief by way of answer, and the old long-legged serving-man was shambling down the gravel to the pier. For all his hurry, it took him a long while to pull across the bay; and I observed him several times to pause, go into the stern, and look over curiously into the wake. As he came nearer, he seemed to me aged and haggard, and I thought he avoided my eye. The coble had been repaired, with two new thwarts and several patches of some rare and beautiful foreign wood, the name of it unknown to me.

"Why, Rorie," said I, as we began the return voyage, "this is fine wood. How came you by that?"

"It will be hard to cheesel," Rorie opined reluctantly; and just then, dropping the oars, he made another of those dives into the stern which I had remarked as he came across to fetch me, and, leaning his hand on my shoulder, stared with an awful look into the waters of the bay.

"What is wrong?" I asked, a good deal startled.

"It will be a great feesh," said the old man, returning to his oars; and nothing more could I get out of him, but strange glances and an ominous nodding of the head. In spite of myself, I was infected with a measure of uneasiness; I turned also, and studied the wake. The water was still and transparent, but, out here in the middle of the bay, exceeding deep. For some time I could see naught; but at last it did seem to me as if something dark—a great fish, or perhaps only a shadow—followed studiously in the track of the moving coble. And then I remembered one of Rorie's superstitions: how in a ferry in Morven, in some great exterminating feud among the clans, a fish, the like of it unknown in all our waters, followed for some years the passage of the ferry-boat, until no man dared to make the crossing.

"He will be waiting for the right man," said Rorie.

Mary met me on the beach, and led me up the brae and into the house of Aros. Outside and inside there were many changes. The garden was fenced with the same wood that I had noted in the boat; there were chairs in the kitchen covered with strange brocade; curtains of brocade hung from the window; a clock stood silent on the dresser; a lamp of brass was swinging from the roof; the table was set for dinner with the finest of linen and silver; and all these new riches were displayed in the plain old kitchen that I knew so well, with the high-backed settle, and the stools, and the closet-bed for Rorie; with the wide chimney the sun shone into, and the clear-smouldering peats; with the pipes on the mantelshelf and the three-cornered spittoons, filled with sea-shells instead of sand, on the floor; with the bare stone walls and the bare wooden floor, and the three patchwork rugs that were of yore its sole adornment—poor man's patchwork, the like of it unknown in cities, woven with homespun, and Sunday black, and sea-cloth polished on the bench of rowing. The room, like the house, had been a sort of wonder in that country-side, it was so neat and habitable; and to see it now, shamed by these incongruous additions, filled me with indignation and a kind of anger. In view of the errand I had come upon to Aros, the feeling was baseless and unjust; but it burned high, at the first moment, in my heart.

"Mary, girl," said I, "this is the place I had learned to call my home, and I do not know it."

"It is my home by nature, not by the learning," she replied; "the place I was born and the place I'm like to die in; and I neither like these changes, nor the way they came, nor that which came with them. I would have liked better, under God's pleasure, they had gone down into the sea, and the Merry Men were dancing on them now."

Mary was always serious; it was perhaps the only trait that she shared with her father; but the tone with which she uttered these words was even graver than of custom.

"Ay," said I, "I feared it came by wreck, and that's by death; yet when my father died, I took his goods without remorse."

"Your father died a clean-strae death, as the folk say," said Mary.

"True," I returned; "and a wreck is like a judgment. What was she called?"

"They ca'd her the *Christ-Anna*," said a voice behind me; and, turning round, I saw my uncle standing in the doorway.

He was a sour, small, bilious man, with a long face and very dark eyes; fifty-six years old, sound and active in body, and with an air somewhat between that of a shepherd and that of a man following the sea. He never laughed, that I heard; read long at the Bible; prayed much, like the Cameronians he had been brought up among; and indeed, in many ways, used to remind me of one of the hill-preachers in the killing times before the Revolution. But he never got much comfort, nor even, as I used to think, much guidance, by his piety. He had his black fits, when he was afraid of hell; but he had led a rough life, to which he would look back with envy, and was still a rough, cold, gloomy man.

As he came in at the door out of the sunlight, with his bonnet on his head and a pipe hanging in his button-hole, he seemed, like Rorie, to have grown older and paler, the lines were deeplier ploughed upon his face, and the whites of his eyes were yellow, like old stained ivory, or the bones of the dead.

"Ay," he repeated, dwelling upon the first part of the word, "the *Christ-Anna*. It's an awfu' name."

I made him my salutations, and complimented him upon his look of health; for I feared he had perhaps been ill.

"I'm in the body," he replied, ungraciously enough; "aye in the body and the sins of the body, like yoursel'. Denner," he said abruptly to Mary, and then ran on to me: "They're grand braws, thir that we hae gotten, are they no'? Yon's a bonny knock, but it'll no gang; and the napery's by ordnar. Bonny, bairnly braws; it's for the like o' them folk sells the peace of God that passeth understanding; it's for the like o' them, an' maybe no' even sae muckle worth, folk daunton God to His face and burn in muckle hell; and it's for that reason the Scripture ca's them, as I read the passage, the accursed thing. Mary, ye girzie," he interrupted himself to cry out with some asperity, "what for hae ye no' put out the twa candlesticks?"

"Why should we need them at high noon?" she asked.

But my uncle was not to be turned from his idea. "We'll bruik them

while we may," he said; and so two massive candlesticks of wrought silver were added to the table equipage, already so unsuited to that rough seaside farm.

"She cam' ashore Februar' 10, about ten at nicht," he went on to me.
"There was nae wind, and a sair run o' sea; and she was in the sook o' the
Roost, as I jaloose. We had seen her a' day, Rorie and me, beating to the
wind. She wasna a handy craft, I'm thinking, that *Christ-Anna*; for she
would neither steer nor stey wi' them. A sair day they had of it; their hands
was never aff the sheets, and it perishin' cauld—ower cauld to snaw; and
aye they would get a bit nip o' wind, and awa' again, to pit the emp'y hope
into them. Eh, man! but they had a sair day for the last o't! He would have
had a prood, prood heart that won ashore upon the back o' that."

"And were all lost?" I cried. "God help them!"

"Wheesht!" he said sternly. "Nane shall pray for the deid on my hearth-
stane."

I disclaimed a Popish sense for my ejaculation; and he seemed to accept
my disclaimer with unusual facility, and ran on once more upon what had
evidently become a favourite subject.

"We fand her in Sandag Bay, Rorie an' me, and a' thae braws in the inside
of her. There's a kittle bit, ye see, about Sandag; whiles the sook rins strong
for the Merry Men; an' whiles again, when the tide's makin' hard an' ye can
hear the Roost blawin' at the far-end of Aros, there comes a back-spang of
current straucht into Sandag Bay. Weel, there's the thing that got the grip on
the *Christ-Anna*. She but to have come in ram-stam an' stern forrit; for the
bows of her are aften under, and the back-side of her is clear at hie-water o'
neaps. But, man! the dunt that she cam doon wi' when she struck! Lord save
us a'! but it's an unco life to be a sailor—a cault, wanchancy life. Mony's the
gliff I got mysel' in the great deep; and why the Lord should hae made yon
unco water is mair than ever I could win to understand. He made the vales
and the pastures, the bonny green yaird, the halesome, canty land—

"'And now they shout and sing to Thee,
For Thou hast made them glad,'

as the Psalms say in the metrical version. No, that I would preen my faith to
that clink neither; but it's bonny, and easier to mind. 'Who go to sea in
ships,' they hae't again—

"'and in
Great waters trading be,
Within the deep these men God's works
And His great wonders see.'

Weel, it's easy sayin' sae. Mabe Dauvit wasna very weel acquaint wi' the sea. But troth, if it wasna prentit in the Bible, I wad whiles be temp'it to think it wasna the Lord, but the muckle black deil that made the sea. There's naething good comes oot o't but the fish; an' the spentacle o' God riding on the tempest to be shüre, whilk would be what Dauvit was likely ettling at. But, man, they were sair wonders that God showed to the *Christ-Anna*— wonders, do I ca' them? Judgments, rather: judgments in the mirk nicht among the draygons o' the deep. And their souls—to think o' that—their souls, man, maybe no prepared! The sea—a muckle yett to hell!"

I observed, as my uncle spoke, that his voice was unnaturally moved and his manner unwontedly demonstrative. He leaned forward at these last words, for example, and touched me on the knee with his spread fingers, looking up into my face with a certain pallor, and I could see that his eyes shone with a deep-seated fire, and that the lines about his mouth were drawn and tremulous.

Even the entrance of Rorie, and the beginning of our meal, did not detach him from his train of thought beyond a moment. He condescended, indeed, to ask me some questions as to my success at College, but I thought it was with half his mind; and even in his extempore grace, which was, as usual, long and wandering, I could find the trace of his preoccupation, praying, as he did, that God would "remember in mercy fower puir, feckless, fiddling, sinful creatures here by their lee-lane beside the great and dowie waters."

Soon there came an interchange of speeches between him and Rorie.

"Was it there?" asked my uncle.

"Ou, ay!" said Rorie.

I observed that they both spoke in a manner of aside, and with some show of embarrassment, and that Mary herself appeared to colour, and looked down on her plate. Partly to show my knowledge, and so relieve the party from an awkward strain, partly because I was curious, I pursued the subject.

"You mean the fish?" I asked.

"Whatten fish?" cried my uncle. "Fish, quo' he! Fish! Your een are fu' o' fatness, man; your heid dozened wi' carnal leir. Fish! it's a bogle!"

He spoke with great vehemence, as though angry; and perhaps I was not very willing to be put down so shortly, for young men are disputatious. At least I remember I retorted hotly, crying out upon childish superstitions.

"And ye come frae the College!" sneered Uncle Gordon. "Gude kens what they learn folk there; it's no muckle service, onyway. Do ye think, man, that there's naething in a' yon saut wilderness o' a world oot wast there, wi' the sea-grasses growin', an' the sea-beasts fechtin', an' the sun glintin' down into it, day by day? Na; the sea's like the land, but fearsomer. If there's folk ashore, there's folk in the sea—deid they may be, but they're folk whatever; and as for deils, there's nane that's like the sea-deils. There's no sae muckle harm in the land-deils, when a's said and done. Lang syne, when I was a callant in the south country, I mind there was an auld, bald bogle in the Peewie Moss. I got a glisk o' him mysel', sittin' on his hunkers in a hag, as grey's a tombstane. An', troth, he was a fearsome-like taed. But he steered naebody. Nae doobt, if ane that was a reprobate, ane the Lord hated, had gane by there wi' his sin still upon his stamach, nae doobt the creature would hae lowped upo' the likes o' him. But there's deils in the deep sea would yoke on a communicant! Eh, sirs, if ye had gane doon wi' the puir lads in the *Christ-Anna*, ye would ken by now the mercy o' the seas. If ye had sailed it for as lang as me, ye would hate the thocht of it as I do. If ye had but used the een God gave ye, ye would hae learned the wickedness o' that fause, saut, cauld, bullering creature, and of a' that's in it by the Lord's permission: labsters an' partans, an' sic-like, howking in the deid; muckle, gutsy, blawing whales; an' fish—the hale clan o' them—cauld-wamed, blind-ee'd uncanny ferlies. Oh, sirs," he cried, "the horror—the horror o' the sea!"

We were all somewhat staggered by this outburst; and the speaker himself, after that last hoarse apostrophe, appeared to sink gloomily into his own thoughts. But Rorie, who was greedy of superstitious lore, recalled him to the subject by a question.

"You will not ever have seen a teevil of the sea?" he asked.

"No' clearly," replied the other, "I misdoobt if a mere man could see ane clearly and conteenue in the body. I hae sailed wi' a lad—they ca'd him Sandy Gabart; he saw ane, shüre eneuch, an' shüre eneuch it was the end of him. We were seeven days oot frae the Clyde—a sair wark we had had—gaun north wi' seeds an' braws an' things for the Macleod. We had got in ower near under the Cutchull'ns, an' had just gane about by Soa, an' were off on a lang tack, we thocht would maybe hauld as far's Copnahow. I mind the nicht weel; a mune smoored wi' mist; a fine gaun breeze upon the water, but no' steedy; an'—what nane o' us likit to hear—anither wund gurlin' owerheid, amang thae fearsome, auld stane craigs o' the Cutchull'ns. Weel, Sandy was forrit wi' the jib sheet; we couldna see him for the mains'l, that had just begude to draw, when a' at ance he gied a skirl. I luffed for my life, for I thocht we were ower near Soa; but na, it wasna that, it was puir Sandy Gabart's deid skreigh, or near-hand, for he was deid in half an hour. A't he could tell was that a sea-deil, or sea-bogle, or sea-spenster, or sic-like, had clum up by the bowsprit, an' gi'en him ae cauld, uncanny look. An', or the life was oot o' Sandy's body, we kent weel what the thing betokened,

and why the wund gurled in the taps o' the Cutchull'ns; for doon it cam'—
a wund do I ca' it! it was the wund o' the Lord's anger—an' a' that nicht we
foucht like men dementit, and the neist that we kenned we were ashore in
Loch Uskevagh, an' the cocks were crawing in Benbecula."

"It will have been a merman," Rorie said.

"A merman!" screamed my uncle, with immeasurable scorn. "Auld
wives' clavers! There's nae sic things as mermen."

"But what was the creature like?" I asked.

"What like was it? Gude forbid that we suld ken what like it was! It had
a kind of a heid upon it—man could say nae mair."

Then Rorie, smarting under the affront, told several tales of mermen,
mermaids and sea-horses that had come ashore upon the islands and attacked the crews of boats upon the sea; and my uncle, in spite of his incredulity, listened with uneasy interest.

"Aweel, aweel," he said, "it may be sae; I may be wrang; but I find nae
word o' mermen in the Scriptures."

"And you will find nae word of Aros Roost, maybe," objected Rorie, and
his argument appeared to carry weight.

When dinner was over, my uncle carried me forth with him to a bank
behind the house. It was a very hot and quiet afternoon; scarce a ripple
anywhere upon the sea, nor any voice but the familiar voice of sheep and
gulls; and perhaps in consequence of this repose in nature, my kinsman
showed himself more rational and tranquil than before. He spoke evenly
and almost cheerfully of my career, with every now and then a reference to
the lost ship or the treasure it had brought to Aros. For my part, I listened to
him in a sort of trance, gazing with all my heart in that remembered scene,
and drinking gladly the sea-air and the smoke of peats that had been lit
by Mary.

Perhaps an hour had passed when my uncle, who had all the while been
covertly gazing on the surface of the little bay, rose to his feet and bade me
follow his example. Now I should say that the great run of tide at the south-
west end of Aros exercises a perturbing influence round all the coast. In
Sandag Bay, to the south, a strong current runs at certain periods of the
flood and ebb respectively; but in this northern bay—Aros Bay as it is
called—where the house stands and on which my uncle was now gazing,
the only sign of disturbance is towards the end of the ebb, and even then it is
too slight to be remarkable. When there is any swell, nothing can be seen at
all; but when it is calm, as it often is, there appear certain strange, un-
decipherable marks—sea-runes, as we may name them—on the glassy surface of the bay. The like is common in a thousand places on the coast; and
many a boy must have amused himself as I did, seeking to read in them

some reference to himself or those he loved. It was to these marks that my uncle now directed my attention, struggling, as he did so, with an evident reluctance.

"Do ye see yon scart upo' the water?" he inquired; "yon ane wast the grey stane? Ay? Weel, it'll no' be like a letter, wull it?"

"Certainly it is," I replied. "I have often remarked it. It is like a C."

He heaved a sigh as if heavily disappointed with my answer, and then added below his breath: "Ay, for the *Christ-Anna*."

"I used to suppose, sir, it was for myself," said I; "for my name is Charles."

"And so ye saw't afore?" he ran on, not heeding my remark. "Weel, weel, but that's unco strange. Maybe, it's been there waitin', as a man wad say, through a' the weary ages. Man, but that's awfu'." And then, breaking off: "Ye'll no' see anither, will ye?" he asked.

"Yes," said I. "I see another very plainly, near the Ross side, where the road comes down—an M."

"An M," he repeated very low; and then, again after another pause: "An' what wad ye make o' that?" he inquired.

"I had always thought it to mean Mary, sir," I answered, growing some-what red, convinced as I was in my own mind that I was on the threshold of a decisive explanation.

But we were each following his own train of thought to the exclusion of the other's. My uncle once more paid no attention to my words: only hung his head and held his peace; and I might have been led to fancy that he had not heard me, if his next speech had not contained a kind of echo from my own.

"I would say naething o' thae clavers to Mary," he observed, and began to walk forward.

There is a belt of turf along the side of Aros Bay where walking is easy; and it was along this that I silently followed my silent kinsman. I was per-haps a little disappointed at having lost so good an opportunity to declare my love; but I was at the same time far more deeply exercised at the change that had befallen my uncle. He was never an ordinary, never, in the strict sense, an amiable man; but there was nothing in even the worst that I had known of him before, to prepare me for so strange a transformation. It was impossible to close the eyes against one fact; that he had, as the saying goes, something on his mind; and as I mentally ran over the different words which might be represented by the letter M—misery, mercy, marriage, money and the like—I was arrested with a sort of start by the word murder. I was still considering the ugly sound and fatal meaning of the word, when the direction of our walk brought us to a point from which a view was to be had to either side, back towards Aros Bay and homestead, and forward on the ocean, dotted to the north with isles, and lying to the southward blue and open to the sky. There my guide came to a halt, and stood staring for a while on that expanse. Then he turned to me and laid a hand on my arm.

"Ye think there's naething there?" he said, pointing with his pipe; and then cried out aloud, with a kind of exultation: "I'll tell ye, man! The deid are down there—thick like rattons!"

He turned at once, and, without another word, we retraced our steps to the house of Aros.

I was eager to be alone with Mary; yet it was not till after supper, and then but for a short while, that I could have a word with her. I lost no time beating about the bush, but spoke out plainly what was on my mind.

"Mary," I said, "I have not come to Aros without a hope. If that should prove well founded, we may all leave and go somewhere else, secure of daily bread and comfort; secure, perhaps, of something far beyond that, which it would seem extravagant in me to promise. But there's a hope that lies nearer to my heart than money." And at that I paused. "You can guess fine what that is, Mary," I said. She looked away from me in silence, and that was small encouragement, but I was not to be put off. "All my days I have thought the world of you," I continued; "the time goes on and I think always the more of you; I could not think to be happy or hearty in my life without you: you are the apple of my eye." Still she looked away, and said never a word; but I thought I saw that her hands shook. "Mary," I cried in fear, "do ye no' like me?"

"Oh, Charlie man," she said, "is this a time to speak of it? Let me be a while; let me be the way I am; it'll not be you that loses by the waiting!"

I made out by her voice that she was nearly weeping, and this put me out of any thought but to compose her. "Mary Ellen," I said, "say no more; I did not come to trouble you: your way shall be mine, and your time too; and you have told me all I wanted. Only just this one thing more: what ails you?"

She owned it was her father, but would enter into no particulars, only shook her head, and said he was not well and not like himself, and it was a great pity. She knew nothing of the wreck. "I havena been near it," said she. "What for would I go near it, Charlie lad? The poor souls are gone to their account long syne; and I would just have wished they had ta'en their gear with them—poor souls!"

This was scarcely any great encouragement for me to tell her of the *Espirito Santo*; yet I did so, and at the very first word she cried out in surprise. "There was a man at Grisapol," she said, "in the month of May—a little, yellow, black-avised body, they tell me, with gold rings upon his fingers, and a beard; and he was speiring high and low for that same ship."

It was towards the end of April that I had been given these papers to sort out by Dr. Robertson: and it came suddenly back upon my mind that they were thus prepared for a Spanish historian, or a man calling himself such, who had come with high recommendations to the Principal, on a mission of inquiry as to the dispersion of the great Armada. Putting one thing with another, I fancied that the visitor "with the gold rings upon his fingers" might be the same with Dr. Robertson's historian from Madrid. If that were so, he would be more likely after treasure for himself than information for a learned society. I made up my mind, I should lose no time over my undertaking; and if the ship lay sunk in Sandag Bay, as perhaps both he and I supposed, it should not be for the advantage of this ringed adventurer, but for Mary and myself, and for the good old, honest, kindly family of the Darnaways.

III
Land and Sea in Sandag Bay

I was early afoot next morning; and as soon as I had a bite to eat, set forth upon a tour of exploration. Something in my heart distinctly told me that I should find the ship of the Armada; and although I did not give way entirely to such hopeful thoughts, I was still very light in spirits and walked upon air. Aros is a very rough islet, its surface strewn with great rocks and shaggy with fern and heather; and my way lay almost north and south across the highest knoll; and though the whole distance was inside of two miles, it took more time and exertion than four upon a level road. Upon the summit, I paused. Although not very high—not three hundred feet, as I think—it yet out-tops all the neighbouring lowlands of the Ross, and commands a great view of sea and islands. The sun, which had been up some time, was already hot upon my neck; the air was listless and thundery, although purely clear; away over the north-west, where the isles lie thickliest congregated, some half a dozen small and ragged clouds hung together in a covey; and the head of Ben Kyaw wore, not merely a few streamers, but a solid hood of vapour. There was a threat in the weather. The sea, it is true, was smooth like glass: even the Roost was but a seam on that wide mirror, and the Merry Men no more than caps of foam; but to my eye and ear, so long familiar with these places, the sea also seemed to lie uneasily; a sound of it, like a long sigh, mounted to me where I stood; and, quiet as it was, the Roost itself appeared to be revolving mischief. For I ought to say that all we dwellers in these parts attributed, if not prescience, at least a quality of warning, to that strange and dangerous creature of the tides.

I hurried on, then, with the greater speed, and had soon descended the slope of Aros to the part that we call Sandag Bay. It is a pretty large piece of water compared with the size of the isle; well sheltered from all but the prevailing wind; sandy and shoal and bounded by low sand-hills to the west, but to the eastward lying several fathoms deep along a ledge of rocks.

It is upon that side that, at a certain time each flood, the current mentioned by my uncle sets so strong into the bay; a little later, when the Roost begins to work higher, an undertow runs still more strongly in the reverse direction; and it is the action of this last, as I suppose, that has scoured that part so deep. Nothing is to be seen out of Sandag Bay but one small segment of the horizon and, in heavy weather, the breakers flying high over a deep sea-reef.

From half-way down the hill, I had perceived the wreck of February last, a brig of considerable tonnage, lying, with her back broken, high and dry on the east corner of the sands; and I was making directly towards it, and already almost on the margin of the turf, when my eyes were suddenly arrested by a spot, cleared of fern and heather, and marked by one of those long, low, and almost human-looking mounds that we see so commonly in graveyards. I stopped like a man shot. Nothing had been said to me of any dead man or interment on the island; Rorie, Mary and my uncle had all equally held their peace; of her at least, I was certain that she must be ignorant; and yet here, before my eyes, was proof indubitable of the fact. Here was a grave; and I had to ask myself, with a chill, what manner of man lay there in his last sleep, awaiting the signal of the Lord in that solitary, sea-beat resting-place? My mind supplied no answer but what I feared to entertain. Shipwrecked, at least, he must have been; perhaps, like the old Armada mariners, from some far and rich land oversea; or perhaps one of my own race, perishing within eyesight of the smoke of home. I stood a while uncovered by his side, and I could have desired that it had lain in our religion to put up some prayer for that unhappy stranger, or, in the old classic way, outwardly to honour his misfortune. I knew, although his bones lay there, a part of Aros, till the trumpet sounded, his imperishable soul was forth and far away, among the raptures of the everlasting Sabbath or the pangs of hell; and yet my mind misgave me even with a fear, that perhaps he was near me where I stood, guarding his sepulchre and lingering on the scene of his unhappy fate.

Certainly it was with a spirit somewhat overshadowed that I turned away from the grave to the hardly less melancholy spectacle of the wreck. Her stem was above the first arc of the flood; she was broken in two a little abaft the foremast—though indeed she had none, both masts having broken short in her disaster; and as the pitch of the beach was very sharp and sudden, and the bows lay many feet below the stern, the fracture gaped widely open, and you could see right through her poor hull upon the farther side. Her name was much defaced, and I could not make out clearly whether she was called *Christiania*, after the Norwegian city, or *Christiana*, after the good woman, Christian's wife, in that old book *The Pilgrim's Progress*. By her build she was a foreign ship, but I was not certain of her nationality. She had been painted green, but the colour was faded and weathered, and the paint peeling off in strips. The wreck of the mainmast lay alongside, half-buried in sand. She was a forlorn sight, indeed, and I could not look without emotion at the bits of rope that still hung about her, so often handled of yore by shouting seamen; or the little scuttle where they had passed up and down to their affairs; or that poor noseless angel of a figure-head that had dipped into so many running billows.

I do not know whether it came most from the ship or from the grave, but I fell into some melancholy scruples, as I stood there, leaning with one hand against the battered timbers. The homelessness of men, and even of inanimate vessels, cast away upon strange shores, came strongly in upon my mind. To make a profit of such pitiful misadventures seemed an unmanly and a sordid act; and I began to think of my then quest as of something sacrilegious in its nature. But when I remembered Mary, I took heart again. My uncle would never consent to an imprudent marriage, nor would she, as I was persuaded, wed without his full approval. It behoved me, then, to be up and doing for my wife; and I thought with a laugh how long it was since that great sea-castle, the *Espirito Santo*, had left her bones in Sandag Bay, and how weak it would be to consider rights so long extinguished and misfortunes so long forgotten in the process of time.

I had my theory of where to seek for her remains. The set of the current and the soundings both pointed to the east side of the bay under the ledge of rocks. If she had been lost in Sandag Bay, and if, after these centuries, any portion of her held together, it was there that I should find it. The water deepens, as I have said, with great rapidity, and even close alongside the rocks several fathoms may be found. As I walked upon the edge I could see far and wide over the sandy bottom of the bay; the sun shone clear and green and steady in the deeps; the bay seemed rather like a great transparent crystal, as one sees them in a lapidary's shop; there was naught to show that it was water but an internal trembling, a hovering within of sun-glints and netted shadows, and now and then a faint lap and a dying bubble round the edge. The shadows of the rocks lay out for some distance at their feet, so that my own shadow, moving, pausing, and stooping on the top of that, reached sometimes half across the bay. It was above all in this belt of shadows that I hunted for the *Espirito Santo*; since it was there the undertow ran strongest, whether in or out. Cool as the whole water seemed this broiling day, it looked, in that part, yet cooler, and had a mysterious invitation for the eyes. Peer as I pleased, however, I could see nothing but a few fishes or a bush of sea-tangle, and here and there a lump of rock that had fallen from above and now lay separate on the sandy floor. Twice did I pass from one end to the other of the rocks, and in the whole distance I could see nothing of the wreck, nor any place but one where it was possible for it to be. This was a large terrace in five fathoms of water, raised off the surface of the sand to a considerable height, and looking from above like a mere outgrowth of the rocks on which I walked. It was one mass of great sea-tangles like a grove, which prevented me judging of its nature, but in shape and size it bore some likeness to a vessel's hull. At least it was my best chance. If the *Espirito Santo* lay not there under the tangles, it lay nowhere at all in Sandag Bay; and I prepared to put the question to the proof, once and for all, and either go back to Aros a rich man or cured for ever of my dreams of wealth.

I stripped to the skin, and stood on the extreme margin with my hands clasped, irresolute. The bay at that time was utterly quiet; there was no sound but from a school of porpoises somewhere out of sight behind the point; yet a certain fear withheld me on the threshold of my venture. Sad sea-feelings, scraps of my uncle's superstitions, thoughts of the dead, of the grave, of the old broken ships, drifted through my mind. But the strong sun upon my shoulders warmed me to the heart, and I stooped forward and plunged into the sea.

It was all that I could do to catch a trail of the sea-tangle that grew so thickly on the terrace; but once so far anchored I secured myself by grasping a whole armful of these thick and slimy stalks, and, planting my feet against the edge, I looked around me. On all sides the clear sand stretched forth unbroken; it came to the foot of the rocks, scoured into the likeness of an alley in a garden by the action of the tides; and before me, for as far as I could see, nothing was visible but the same many-folded sand upon the sun-bright bottom of the bay. Yet the terrace to which I was then holding was as thick with strong sea-growths as a tuft of heather, and the cliff from which it bulged hung draped below the water-line with brown lianas. In this complexity of forms, all swaying together in the current, things were hard to be distinguished; and I was still uncertain whether my feet were pressed upon the natural rock or upon the timbers of the Armada treasure-ship, when the whole tuft of tangle came away in my hand, and in an instant I was on the surface, and the shores of the bay and the bright water swam before my eyes in a glory of crimson.

I clambered back upon the rocks, and threw the plant of tangle at my feet. Something at the same moment rang sharply, like a falling coin. I stooped, and there, sure enough, crusted with the red rust, there lay an iron shoe-buckle. The sight of this poor human relic thrilled me to the heart, but not with hope nor fear, only with a desolate melancholy. I held it in my hand and the thought of its owner appeared before me like the presence of an actual man. His weather-beaten face, his sailor's hands, his sea-voice hoarse with singing at the capstan, the very foot that had once worn that buckle and trod so much along the swerving decks—the whole human fact of him, as a creature like myself with hair and blood and seeing eyes, haunted me in that sunny, solitary place, not like a spectre, but like some friend whom I had basely injured. Was the great treasure-ship indeed below there, with her guns and chain and treasure, as she had sailed from Spain; her decks a garden for the sea-weed, her cabin a breeding-place for fish, soundless but for the dredging water, motionless but for the waving of the tangle upon her battlements—that old, populous sea-riding castle, now a reef in Sandag Bay? Or, as I thought it likelier, was this a waif from the disaster of the foreign brig—was this shoe-buckle bought but the other day and worn by a man of my own period in the world's history, hearing the same news from day to day, thinking the same thoughts, praying, perhaps, in the same temple with myself? However it was, I was assailed with dreary thoughts; my uncle's words, "the dead are down there," echoed in my ears; and though I determined to dive once more, it was with a strong repugnance that I stepped forward to the margin of the rocks.

A great change passed at that moment over the appearance of the bay. It was no more that clear, visible interior, like a house roofed with glass, where the green, submarine sunshine slept so stilly. A breeze, I suppose, had flawed the surface, and a sort of trouble and blackness filled its bosom, where flashes of light and clouds of shadow tossed confusedly together. Even the terrace below obscurely rocked and quivered. It seemed a graver thing to venture on this place of ambushes; and when I leaped into the sea the second time it was with a quaking in my soul.

I secured myself as at first, and groped among the waving tangle. All that met my touch was cold and soft and gluey. The thicket was alive with crabs and lobsters, trundling to and fro lop-sidedly, and I had to harden my heart against the horror of their carrion neighbourhood. On all sides I could feel the grain and the clefts of hard, living stone; no planks, no iron, not a sign of any wreck; the *Espirito Santo* was not there. I remember I had almost a sense of relief in my disappointment, and I was about ready to leave go, when something happened that sent me to the surface with my heart in my mouth. I had already stayed somewhat late over my explorations; the current was freshening with the change of the tide, and Sandag Bay was no longer a safe place for a single swimmer. Well, just at the last moment there came a sudden flush of current, dredging through the tangles like a wave. I lost one hold, was flung sprawling on my side, and, instinctively grasping for a fresh support, my fingers closed on something hard and cold. I think I knew at that moment what it was. At least I instantly left hold of the tangle, leaped for the surface, and clambered out next moment on the friendly rocks with the bone of a man's leg in my grasp.

Mankind is a material creature, slow to think and dull to perceive connections. The grave, the wreck of the brig and the rusty shoe-buckle were surely plain advertisements. A child might have read their dismal story, and yet it was not until I touched that actual piece of mankind that the full horror of the charnel ocean burst upon my spirit. I laid the bone beside the buckle, picked up my clothes, and ran as I was along the rocks towards the human shore. I could not be far enough from the spot; no fortune was vast enough to tempt me back again. The bones of the drowned dead should henceforth roll undisturbed by me, whether on tangle or minted gold. But as soon as I trod the good earth again and had covered my nakedness against the sun, I knelt down over against the ruins of the brig, and out of the fullness of my heart prayed long and passionately for all poor souls upon the sea. A generous prayer is never presented in vain; the petition may be refused, but the petitioner is always, I believe, rewarded by some gracious visitation. The horror, at least, was lifted from my mind; I could look with calm of spirit on that great bright creature, God's ocean; and as I set off homeward up the rough sides of Aros, nothing remained of any concern beyond a deep determination to meddle no more with the spoils of wrecked vessels or the treasures of the dead.

I was already some way up the hill before I paused to breathe and look behind me. The sight that met my eyes was doubly strange.

For, first, the storm that I had foreseen was now advancing with almost tropical rapidity. The whole surface of the sea had been dulled from its conspicuous brightness to an ugly hue of corrugated lead; already in the distance the white waves, the "skipper's daughters," had begun to flee before a breeze that was still insensible on Aros; and already along the curve of Sandag Bay there was a splashing run of sea that I could hear from where I stood. The change upon the sky was even more remarkable. There had begun to arise out of the south-west a huge and solid continent of scowling cloud; here and there, through rents in its contexture, the sun still poured a sheaf of spreading rays; and here and there, from all its edges, vast inky streamers lay forth along the yet unclouded sky. The menace was express and imminent. Even as I gazed, the sun was blotted out. At any moment the tempest might fall upon Aros in its might.

The suddenness of this change of weather so fixed my eyes on heaven that it was some seconds before they alighted on the bay, mapped out below my feet, and robbed a moment later of the sun. The knoll which I had just surmounted overflanked a little amphitheatre of lower hillocks sloping towards the sea, and beyond that the yellow arc of beach and the whole extent of Sandag Bay. It was a scene on which I had often looked down, but where I had never before beheld a human figure. I had but just turned my back upon it and left it empty, and my wonder may be fancied when I saw a boat and several men in that deserted spot. The boat was lying by the rocks. A pair of fellows, bare-headed, with the sleeves rolled up and one with a boathook, kept her with difficulty to her moorings, for the current was growing brisker every moment. A little way off upon the ledge two men in black clothes, whom I judged to be superior in rank, laid their heads together over some task which at first I did not understand, but a second after I had made it out—they were taking bearings with the compass; and just then I saw one of them unroll a sheet of paper and lay his finger down, as though identifying features in a map. Meanwhile a third was walking to and fro, poking among the rocks and peering over the edge into the water. While I was still watching them with the stupefaction of surprise, my mind hardly yet able to work on what my eyes reported, this third person suddenly stooped and summoned his companions with a cry so loud that it reached my ears upon the hill. The others ran to him, even dropping the compass in their hurry, and I could see the bone and the shoe-buckle going from hand to hand, causing the most unusual gesticulations of surprise and interest. Just then I could hear the seamen crying from the boat, and saw them point westward to that cloud continent which was ever the more rapidly unfurling its blackness over heaven. The others seemed to consult; but the danger was too pressing to be braved, and they bundled into the boat carrying my relics with them, and set forth out of the bay with all speed of oars.

I made no more ado about the matter, but turned and ran for the house. Whoever these men were, it was fit my uncle should be instantly informed. It was not then altogether too late in the day for a descendent of the Jacobites; and maybe Prince Charlie, whom I knew my uncle to detest, was one of the three superiors whom I had seen upon the rock.

Yet as I ran, leaping from rock to rock, and turned the matter loosely in my mind, this theory grew ever the longer the less welcome to my reason. The compass, the map, the interest awakened by the buckle, and the conduct of that one among the strangers who had looked so often below him in the water, all seemed to point to a different explanation of their presence on that outlying, obscure islet of the western sea. The Madrid historian, the search instituted by Dr. Robertson, the bearded stranger with the rings, my own fruitless search that very morning in the deep water of Sandag Bay, ran together, piece by piece, in my memory, and I made sure that these strangers must be Spaniards in quest of ancient treasure and the lost ship of the Armada. But the people living in outlying islands, such as Aros, are answerable for their own security; there is none near by to protect or even to help them; and the presence in such a spot of a crew of foreign adventurers— poor, greedy, and most likely lawless—filled me with apprehensions for my uncle's money, and even for the safety of his daughter.

I was still wondering how we were to get rid of them when I came, all breathless, to the top of Aros. The whole world was shadowed over; only in the extreme east, on a hill of the mainland, one last gleam of sunshine lingered like a jewel. Rain had begun to fall, not heavily, but in great drops;

the sea was rising with each moment, and already a band of white encircled Aros and the nearer coasts of Grisapol. The boat was still pulling seaward, but I now became aware of what had been hidden from me lower down—a large, heavily sparred, handsome schooner, lying-to at the south end of Aros. Since I had not seen her in the morning when I had looked around so closely at the signs of the weather, and upon these lone waters where a sail was rarely visible, it was clear she must have lain last night behind the uninhabited Eilean Gour; and this proved conclusively that she was manned by strangers to our coast, for that anchorage, though good enough to look at, is little better than a trap for ships. With such ignorant sailors upon so wild a coast, the coming gale was not unlikely to bring death upon its wings.

IV
The Gale

I found my uncle at the gable-end, watching the signs of the weather, with a pipe in his fingers.

"Uncle," said I, "there were men ashore at Sandag Bay—"

I had no time to go further; indeed, I not only forgot my words, but even my weariness, so strange was the effect on Uncle Gordon. He dropped his pipe and fell back against the end of the house with his jaw fallen, his eyes staring, and his long face as white as paper. We must have looked at one another silently for a quarter of a minute, before he made answer in this extraordinary fashion: "Had he a hair kep on?"

I knew as well as if I had been there that the man who now lay buried at Sandag had worn a hairy cap, and that he had come ashore alive. For the first and only time, I lost toleration for the man who was my benefactor and the father of the woman I hoped to call my wife.

"These were living men," said I, "perhaps Jacobites, perhaps the French, perhaps pirates, perhaps adventurers come here to seek the Spanish treasure-ship; but, whatever they may be, dangerous at least to your daughter and my cousin. As for your own guilty terrors, man, the dead sleeps well where you have laid him. I stood this morning by his grave; he will not wake before the trump of doom."

My kinsman looked upon me, blinking, while I spoke; then he fixed his eyes for a little on the ground, and pulled his fingers foolishly; but it was plain that he was past the power of speech.

"Come," said I. "You must think for others. You must come up the hill with me, and see this ship."

He obeyed without a word or a look, following slowly after my impatient strides. The spring seemed to have gone out of his body, and he scrambled heavily up and down the rocks, instead of leaping, as he was wont, from one to another. Nor could I, for all my cries, induce him to make better haste.

Only once he replied to me complainingly, and like one in bodily pain: "Ay, ay, man, I'm coming." Long before we had reached the top, I had no other thought for him but pity. If the crime had been monstrous, the punishment was in proportion.

At last we emerged above the skyline of the hill, and could see around us. All was black and stormy to the eye; the last gleam of sun had vanished; a wind had sprung up, not yet high, but gusty and unsteady to the point; the rain, on the other hand, had ceased. Short as was the interval, the sea already ran vastly higher than when I had stood there last; already it had begun to break over some of the outward reefs, and already it moaned aloud in the sea-caves of Aros. I looked, at first in vain, for the schooner.

"There she is," I said at last. But her new position, and the course she was now lying, puzzled me. "They cannot mean to beat to sea," I cried.

"That's what they mean," said my uncle, with something like joy; and just then the schooner went about and stood upon another tack, which put the question beyond the reach of doubt. These strangers, seeing a gale on hand, had thought first of sea-room. With the wind that threatened, in these reef-sown waters and contending against so violent a stream of tide, their course was certain death.

"Good God!" said I, "they are all lost."

"Ay," returned my uncle, "a'—a' lost. They hadna a chance but to rin for Kyle Dona. The gate they're gaun the noo, they couldna win through an the muckle deil were there to pilot them. Eh, man," he continued, touching me on the sleeve, "it's a braw nicht for a shipwreck! Twa in ae twalmonth! Eh, but the Merry Men'll dance bonny!"

I looked at him, and it was then that I began to fancy him no longer in his right mind. He was peering up to me, as if for sympathy, a timid joy in his eyes. All that had passed between us was already forgotten in the prospect of this fresh disaster.

"If it were not too late," I cried, with indignation, "I would take the coble and go out to warn them."

"Na, na," he protested, "ye maunna interfere; ye maunna meddle wi' the like o' that. It's His"—doffing his bonnet—"His wull. And, eh man! but it's a braw nicht for 't!"

Something like fear began to creep into my soul; and, reminding him that I had not yet dined, I proposed we should return to the house. But no; nothing would tear him from his place of outlook.

"I maun see the hail thing, man Charlie," he explained; and then as the schooner went about a second time, "Eh, but they han'le her bonny!" he cried. "The *Christ-Anna* was naething to this."

Already the men on board the schooner must have begun to realize some part, but not yet the twentieth, of the dangers that environed their doomed ship. At every lull of the capricious wind they must have seen how fast the current swept them back. Each tack was made shorter, as they saw how little it prevailed. Every moment the rising swell began to boom and foam upon another sunken reef; and ever and again a breaker would fall in sounding ruin under the very bows of her, and the brown reef and streaming tangle appear in the hollow of the wave. I tell you, they had to stand to their tackle; there was no idle man aboard that ship, God knows. It was upon the progress of a scene so horrible to any humane-hearted man that my misguided uncle now pored and gloated like a connoisseur. As I turned to go down the hill, he was lying on his belly on the summit, with his hands stretched forth and clutching in the heather. He seemed rejuvenated, mind and body.

When I got back to the house already dismally affected, I was still more sadly downcast at the sight of Mary. She had her sleeves rolled up over her strong arms, and was quietly making bread. I got a bannock from the dresser and sat down to eat it in silence.

"Are ye wearied, lad?" she asked after a while.

"I am not so much wearied, Mary," I replied, getting on my feet, "as I am weary of delay, and perhaps of Aros too. You know me well enough to judge me fairly, say what I like. Well, Mary, you may be sure of this: you had better be anywhere but here."

"I'll be sure of one thing," she returned: "I'll be where my duty is."

"You forget you have a duty to yourself," I said.

"Ay, man," she replied, pounding at the dough; "will you have found that in the Bible, now?"

"Mary," I said solemnly, "you must not laugh at me just now. God knows I am in no heart for laughing. If we could get your father with us, it would be best; but with him or without him, I want you far away from here, my girl; for your own sake, and for mine, ay, and for your father's too, I want you far—far away from here. I came with other thoughts; I came here as a man comes home; now it is all changed, and I have no desire nor hope but to flee—for that's the word—flee, like a bird out of the fowler's snare, from this accursed island."

She had stopped her work by this time.

"And do you think, now," said she, "do ye think, now, I have neither eyes nor ears? Do ye think I havena broken my heart to have these braws (as he calls them, God forgive him!) thrown into the sea? Do ye think I have lived with him, day in, day out, and not seen what you saw in an hour or two? No," she said, "I know there's wrong in it; what wrong, I neither know nor want to know. There was never an ill thing made better by meddling, that I could hear of. But, my lad, you must never ask me to leave my father. While the breath is in his body, I'll be with him. And he's not long for here, either:

that I can tell you, Charlie—he's not long for here. The mark is on his brow; and better so—maybe better so."

I was a while silent, not knowing what to say; and when I roused my head at last to speak, she got before me.

"Charlie," she said, "what's right for me, needna be right for you. There's sin upon this house and trouble; you are a stranger; take your things upon your back and go your ways to better places and to better folk, and if you were ever minded to come back, though it were twenty years syne, you would find me aye waiting."

"Mary Ellen," I said, "I asked you to be my wife, and you said as good as yes. That's done for good. Wherever you are, I am; as I shall answer to my God."

As I said the words, the winds suddenly burst out raving, and then seemed to stand still and shudder round the house of Aros. It was the first squall, or prologue, of the coming tempest, and as we started and looked about us, we found that a gloom, like the approach of evening, had settled round the house.

"God pity all poor folks at sea!" she said. "We'll see no more of my father till the morrow's morning."

And then she told me, as we sat by the fire and hearkened to the rising gusts, of how this change had fallen upon my uncle. All last winter he had been dark and fitful in his mind. Whenever the Roost ran high, or, as Mary said, whenever the Merry Men were dancing, he would lie out for hours together on the Head, if it were at night, or on the top of Aros by day, watching the tumult of the sea, and sweeping the horizon for a sail. After February the tenth, when the wealth-bringing wreck was cast ashore at Sandag, he had been at first unnaturally gay, and his excitement had never fallen in degree, but only changed in kind from dark to darker. He neglected his work, and kept Rorie idle. They two would speak together by the hour at the gable-end, in guarded tones and with an air of secrecy and almost of guilt; and if she questioned either, as at first she sometimes did, her inquiries were put aside with confusion. Since Rorie had first remarked the fish that hung about the ferry, his master had never set foot but once upon the mainland of the Ross. That once—it was in the height of the springs—he had passed dry-shod while the tide was out; but, having lingered over-long on the far side, found himself cut off from Aros by the returning waters. It was with a shriek of agony that he had leaped across the gut, and he had reached home thereafter in a fever-fit of fear. A fear of the sea, a constant haunting thought of the sea, appeared in his talk and devotions, and even in his looks when he was silent.

Rorie alone came in to supper; but a little later my uncle appeared, took a bottle under his arm, put some bread in his pocket, and set forth again to his outlook, followed this time by Rorie. I heard that the schooner was losing ground, but the crew were still fighting every inch with hopeless ingenuity and courage; and the news filled my mind with blackness.

A little after sundown the full fury of the gale broke forth, such a gale as I have never seen in summer, nor, seeing how swiftly it had come, even in winter. Mary and I sat in silence, the house quaking overhead, the tempest howling without, the fire between us sputtering with raindrops. Our thoughts were far away with the poor fellows on the schooner, or my not less unhappy uncle, houseless on the promontory; and yet ever and again we were startled back to ourselves, when the wind would rise and strike the gable like a solid body, or suddenly fall and draw away, so that the fire leaped into flame and our hearts bounded in our sides. Now the storm in its might would seize and shake the four corners of the roof, roaring like Leviathan in anger. Anon, in a lull, cold eddies of tempest moved shudderingly in the room, lifting the hair upon our heads and passing between us as we sat. And again the wind would break forth in a chorus of melancholy sounds, hooting low in the chimney, wailing with flute-like softness round the house.

It was perhaps eight o'clock when Rorie came in and pulled me mysteriously to the door. My uncle, it appeared, had frightened even his constant comrade; and Rorie, uneasy at his extravagance, prayed me to come out and share the watch. I hastened to do as I was asked; the more readily as, what with fear and horror, and the electrical tension of the night, I was myself restless and disposed for action. I told Mary to be under no alarm, for I should be a safeguard on her father; and wrapping myself warmly in a plaid, I followed Rorie into the open air.

The night, though we were so little past midsummer, was as dark as January. Intervals of a groping twilight alternated with spells of utter blackness; and it was impossible to trace the reason of these changes in the flying horror of the sky. The wind blew the breath out of a man's nostrils; all heaven seemed to thunder overhead like one huge sail; and when there fell a momentary lull on Aros, we could hear the gusts dismally sweeping in the distance. Over all the lowlands of the Ross, the wind must have blown as fierce as on the open sea; and God only knows the uproar that was raging around the head of Ben Kyaw. Sheets of mingled spray and rain were driven in our faces. All round the isle of Aros the surf, with an incessant, hammering thunder, beat upon the reefs and beaches. Now louder in one place, now lower in another, like the combinations of orchestral music, the constant mass of sound was hardly varied for a moment. And loud above all this hurly-burly I could hear the changeful voices of the Roost and the intermittent roaring of the Merry Men. At that hour, there flashed into my mind the reason of the name that they were called. For the noise of them seemed almost mirthful, as it out-topped the other noises of the night; or if not mirthful, yet instinct with a portentous joviality. Nay, and it seemed even human. As when savage men have drunk away their reason, and, discarding speech, bawl together in their madness by the hour; so, to my ears, these deadly breakers shouted by Aros in the night.

Arm in arm, and staggering against the wind, Rorie and I won every yard of ground with conscious effort. We slipped on the wet sod, we fell together sprawling on the rocks. Bruised, drenched, beaten, and breathless, it must have taken us near half an hour to get from the house down to the Head that overlooks the Roost. There, it seemed, was my uncle's favourite observatory. Right in the face of it, where the cliff is highest and most sheer, a hump of earth, like a parapet, makes a place of shelter from the common winds, where a man may sit in quiet and see the tide and the mad billows contending at his feet. As he might look down from the window of a house upon some street disturbance, so, from this post, he looks down upon the tumbling of the Merry Men. On such a night, of course, he peers upon a world of blackness, where the waters wheel and boil, where the waves joust together with the noise of an explosion, and the foam towers and vanishes in the twinkling of an eye. Never before had I seen the Merry Men thus violent. The fury, height, and transiency of their spoutings was a thing to be seen and not recounted. High over our heads on the cliff rose their white columns in the darkness; and the same instant, like phantoms, they were gone. Sometimes three at a time would thus aspire and vanish; sometimes a gust took them, and the spray would fall about us, heavy as a wave. And yet the spectacle was rather maddening in its levity than impressive by its force. Thought was beaten down by the confounding uproar; a gleeful vacancy possessed the brains of men, a state akin to madness; and I found myself at times following the dance of the Merry Men as it were a tune upon a jigging instrument.

I first caught sight of my uncle when we were still some yards away in one of the flying glimpses of twilight that chequered the pitch darkness of the night. He was standing up behind the parapet, his head thrown back and the bottle to his mouth. As he put it down, he saw and recognized us with a toss of one hand fleeringly above his head.

"Has he been drinking?" shouted I to Rorie.

"He will aye be drunk when the wind blaws," returned Rorie, in the same high key, and it was all that I could do to hear him.

"Then—was he so—in February?" I inquired.

Rorie's "Ay" was a cause of joy to me. The murder, then, had not sprung in cold blood from calculation; it was an act of madness, no more to be condemned than to be pardoned. My uncle was a dangerous madman, if you will, but he was not cruel and base as I had feared. Yet what a scene for a carouse, what an incredible vice was this that the poor man had chosen! I have always thought drunkenness a wild and almost fearful pleasure, rather demoniacal than human; but drunkenness, out here in the roaring blackness, on the edge of a cliff above that hell of waters, the man's head spinning like the Roost, his foot tottering on the edge of death, his ear watching for the signs of shipwreck, surely that, if it were credible in any one, was morally impossible in a man like my uncle, whose mind was set upon a damnatory creed and haunted by the darkest superstitions. Yet so it was; and as we reached the bight of shelter and could breathe again, I saw the man's eye shining in the night with an unholy glimmer.

"Eh, Charlie man, it's grand!" he cried. "See to them!" he continued, dragging me to the edge of the abyss from whence arose that deafening clamour and those clouds of spray; "see to them dancin', man! Is that no' wicked?"

He pronounced the word with gusto, and I thought it suited the scene.

"They're yowlin' for thon schooner," he went on, his thin, insane voice clearly audible in the shelter of the bank, "an' she's comin' aye nearer, aye nearer, aye nearer an' nearer an' nearer; an' they ken't, the folk kens it, they ken weel it's by wi' them. Charlie, lad, they're a' drunk in yon schooner, a' dozened wi' drink. They were a' drunk in the *Christ-Anna*, at the hinder end. There's nane could droon at sea wantin' the brandy. Hoot awa, what do you ken?" with a sudden blast of anger. "I tell ye, it canna be; they daurna droon withoot it. Ha'e," holding out the bottle, "tak' a sowp."

I was about to refuse, but Rorie touched me as if in warning; and indeed I had already thought better of the movement. I took the bottle, therefore, and not only drank freely myself, but contrived to spill even more as I was doing so. It was pure spirit, and almost strangled me to swallow. My kinsman did not observe the loss, but, once more throwing back his head, drained the remainder to the dregs. Then, with a loud laugh, he cast the bottle forth among the Merry Men, who seemed to leap up, shouting, to receive it.

"Ha'e, bairns!" he cried, "there's your han'sel. Ye'll get bonnier nor that, or morning."

Suddenly, out in the black night before us, and not two hundred yards away, we heard, at a moment when the wind was silent, the clear note of a human voice. Instantly the wind swept howling down upon the Head, and the Roost bellowed, and churned, and danced with a new fury. But we had heard the sound, and we knew, with agony, that this was the doomed ship now close on ruin, and that what we had heard was the voice of her master issuing his last command. Crouching together on the edge, we waited, straining every sense, for the inevitable end. It was long, however, and to us it seemed like ages, ere the schooner suddenly appeared for one brief instant, relieved against a tower of glimmering foam. I still see her reefed mainsail flapping loose, as the boom fell heavily across the deck; I still see the black outline of the hull, and still think I can distinguish the figure of a man stretched upon the tiller. Yet the whole sight we had of her passed swifter than lightning; the very wave that disclosed her fell burying her for ever; the mingled cry of many voices at the point of death rose and was quenched in the roaring of the Merry Men. And with that the tragedy was at an end. The strong ship, with all her gear, and the lamp perhaps still burning in the cabin, the lives of so many men, precious surely to others, dear, at least, as heaven to themselves, had all, in that one moment, gone down into the surging waters. They were gone like a dream. And the wind still ran and shouted, and the senseless waters in the Roost still leaped and tumbled as before.

How long we lay there together, we three, speechless and motionless, is more than I can tell, but it must have been for long. At length, one by one, and almost mechanically, we crawled back into the shelter of the bank. As I lay against the parapet, wholly wretched and not entirely master of my mind, I could hear my kinsman maundering to himself in an altered and melancholy mood. Now he would repeat to himself with maudlin iteration, "Sic a fecht as they had—sic a sair fecht as they had, puir lads, puir lads!" and anon he would bewail that "a' the gear was as gude's tint," because the ship had gone down among the Merry Men instead of stranding on the shore; and throughout the name—the *Christ-Anna*—would come and go in his divagations, pronounced with shuddering awe. The storm all this time was rapidly abating. In half an hour the wind had fallen to a breeze, and the change was accompanied or caused by a heavy, cold, and plumping rain. I must then have fallen asleep, and when I came to myself, drenched, stiff, and unrefreshed, day had already broken, grey, wet, discomfortable day; the wind blew in faint and shifting capfuls, the tide was out, the Roost was at its lowest, and only the strong beating surf round all the coasts of Aros remained to witness of the furies of the night.

V
A Man Out of the Sea

Rorie set out for the house in search of warmth and breakfast; but my uncle was bent upon examining the shores of Aros, and I felt it a part of duty to accompany him throughout. He was now docile and quiet, but tremulous and weak in mind and body; and it was with the eagerness of a child that he pursued his exploration. He climbed far down upon the rocks; on the beaches, he pursued the retreating breakers. The merest broken plank or rag of cordage was a treasure in his eyes, to be secured at the peril of his life. To see him, with weak and stumbling footsteps, expose himself to the pursuit of the surf, or the snares and pitfalls of the weedy rock, kept me in a perpetual terror. My arm was ready to support him, my hand clutched him by the skirt, I helped him to draw his pitiful discoveries beyond the reach of the returning wave; a nurse accompanying a child of seven would have had no different experience.

Yet, weakened as he was by the reaction from his madness of the night before, the passions that smouldered in his nature were those of a strong man. His terror of the sea, although conquered for the moment, was still undiminished; had the sea been a lake of living flames, he could not have shrunk more panically from its touch; and once, when his foot slipped and he plunged to the midleg into a pool of water, the shriek that came up out of his soul was like the cry of death. He sat still for a while, panting like a dog, after that; but his desire for the spoils of shipwreck triumphed once more over his fears; once more he tottered among the curded foam; once more he crawled upon the rocks among the bursting bubbles; once more his whole heart seemed to be set on driftwood, fit, if it was fit for anything, to throw upon the fire. Pleased as he was with what he found, he still incessantly grumbled at his ill-fortune.

"Aros," he said, "is no' a place for wrecks ava'—no' ava'. A' the years I've dwalt here, this ane maks the second; and the best o' the gear clean tint!"

"Uncle," said I, for we were now on a stretch of open sand, where there was nothing to divert his mind, "I saw you last night as I never thought to see you—you were drunk."

"Na, na," he said, "no' as bad as that. I had been drinking, though. And to tell ye the God's truth, it's a thing I canna mend. There's nae soberer man than me in my ordnar; but when I hear the wind blaw in my lug, it's my belief that I gang gyte."

"You are a religious man," I replied, "and this is sin."

"Ou," he returned, "if it wasna sin, I dinna ken that I would care for't. Ye see, man, it's defiance. There's a sair spang o' the auld sin o' the warld in yon sea; it's an unchristian business at the best o't; an' whiles when it gets up, an' the wind skreighs—the wind an' her are a kind of sib, I'm thinking—an' thae Merry Men, the daft callants, blawin' and lauchin', and puir souls in the deid thraws warstlin' the leelang nicht wi' their bit ships—weel, it comes ower me like a glamour. I'm a deil, I ken't. But I think naething o' the puir sailor lads; I'm wi' the sea, I'm just like ane o' her ain Merry Men."

I thought I should touch him in a joint of his harness. I turned me towards the sea; the surf was running gaily, wave after wave, with their manes blowing behind them, riding one after another up the beach, towering, curving, falling one upon another on the trampled sand. Without, the salt air, the scared gulls, the widespread army of the sea-chargers, neighing to each other, as they gathered together to the assault of Aros; and close before us, that line on the flat sands that, with all their number and their fury, they might never pass.

"Thus far shalt thou go," said I, "and no farther." And then I quoted, as solemnly as I was able, a verse that I had often before fitted to the chorus of the breakers:

"But yet the Lord that is on high
  Is more of might by far,
Than noise of many waters is,
  Or great sea-billows are."

"Ay," said my kinsman, "at the hinder end, the Lord will triumph; I dinna misdoobt that. But here on earth, even silly men-folk daur Him to His face. It is no' wise; I am no' sayin' that it's wise; but it's the pride of the eye, and it's the lust o' life, an' it's the wale o' pleesures."

I said no more, for we had now begun to cross a neck of land that lay between us and Sandag; and I withheld my last appeal to the man's better reason till we should stand upon the spot associated with his crime. Nor did he pursue the subject; but he walked beside me with a firmer step. The call that I had made upon his mind acted like a stimulant, and I could see that he had forgotten his search for worthless jetsam, in a profound, gloomy, and yet stirring train of thought. In three or four minutes we had topped the brae and begun to go down upon Sandag. The wreck had been roughly handled by the sea; the stem had been spun round and dragged a little lower down; and perhaps the stern had been forced a little higher, for the two parts now lay entirely separate on the beach. When we came to the grave I stopped, uncovered my head in the thick rain, and, looking my kinsman in the face, addressed him.

"A man," said I, "was in God's providence suffered to escape from mortal dangers; he was poor, he was naked, he was wet, he was weary, he was a stranger; he had every claim upon the bowels of your compassion; it may be that he was the salt of the earth, holy, helpful, and kind; it may be he was a man laden with iniquities to whom death was the beginning of torment. I ask you in the sight of Heaven: Gordon Darnaway, where is the man for whom Christ died?"

He started visibly at the last words; but there came no answer, and his face expressed no feeling but a vague alarm.

"You were my father's brother," I continued: "you have taught me to count your house as if it were my father's house; and we are both sinful men walking before the Lord among the sins and dangers of this life. It is by our evil that God leads us into good; we sin, I dare not say by His temptation, but I must say with His consent; and to any but the brutish man his sins are the beginning of wisdom. God has warned you by this crime; He warns you still by the bloody grave between our feet; and if there shall follow no repentance, no improvement, no return to Him, what can we look for but the following of some memorable judgment?"

Even as I spoke the words, the eyes of my uncle wandered from my face. A change fell upon his looks that cannot be described; his features seemed to dwindle in size, the colour faded from his cheeks, one hand rose waveringly and pointed over my shoulder into the distance, and the oft-repeated name fell once more from his lips: "The *Christ-Anna*!"

I turned; and if I was not appalled to the same degree, as I return thanks to Heaven that I had not the cause, I was still startled by the sight that met my eyes. The form of a man stood upright on the cabin-hutch of the wrecked ship; his back was towards us; he appeared to be scanning the offing with shaded eyes, and his figure was relieved to its full height, which was plainly very great, against the sea and sky. I have said a thousand times that I am not superstitious; but at that moment, with my mind running upon death and sin, the unexplained appearance of a stranger on that sea-girt, solitary island filled me with a surprise that bordered close on terror. It seemed scarce possible that any human soul should have come ashore alive in such a sea as had raged last night along the coasts of Aros; and the only vessel within miles had gone down before our eyes among the Merry Men. I was assailed with doubts that made suspense unbearable, and, to put the matter to the touch at once, stepped forward and hailed the figure like a ship.

He turned about, and I thought he started to behold us. At this my courage instantly revived, and I called and signed to him to draw near, and he, on his part, dropped immediately to the sands and began slowly to approach, with many stops and hesitations. At each repeated mark of the man's uneasiness I grew the more confident myself; and I advanced another step, encouraging him as I did so with my head and hand. It was plain the castaway had heard indifferent accounts of our island hospitality; and indeed, about this time, the people farther north had a sorry reputation.

"Why," I said, "the man is black!"

And just at that moment, in a voice that I could scarce have recognized, my kinsman began swearing and praying in a mingled stream. I looked at him; he had fallen on his knees, his face was agonized; at each step of the castaway's the pitch of his voice rose, the volubility of his utterance and the fervour of his language redoubled. I call it prayer, for it was addressed to God; but surely no such ranting incongruities were ever before addressed to the Creator by a creature: surely if prayer can be a sin, this mad harangue was sinful. I ran to my kinsman, I seized him by the shoulders, I dragged him to his feet.

"Silence, man," said I, "respect your God in words, if not in action. Here, on the very scene of your transgressions, He sends you an occasion of atonement. Forward and embrace it; welcome like a father yon creature who comes trembling to your mercy."

With that, I tried to force him towards the black; but he felled me to the ground, burst from my grasp, leaving the shoulder of his jacket, and fled up the hill-side towards the top of Aros like a deer. I staggered to my feet again, bruised and somewhat stunned; the negro had paused in surprise, perhaps in terror, some half-way between me and the wreck; my uncle was already far away, bounding from rock to rock; and I thus found myself torn for a time between two duties. But I judged, and I pray Heaven that I judged rightly, in favour of the poor wretch upon the sands; his misfortune was at least not plainly of his own creation; it was one, besides, that I could certainly relieve; and I had begun by that time to regard my uncle as an incurable and dismal lunatic. I advanced accordingly towards the black, who now awaited my approach with folded arms, like one prepared for either destiny. As I came nearer, he reached forth his hand with a great gesture, such as I had seen from the pulpit, and spoke to me in something of a pulpit voice, but not a word was comprehensible. I tried him first in English, then in Gaelic, both in vain; so that it was clear we must rely upon the tongue of looks and gestures. Thereupon I signed to him to follow me, which he did readily and with a grave obeisance like a fallen king; all the while there had come no shade of alteration in his face, neither of anxiety while he was still waiting, nor of relief now that he was reassured; if he were a slave, as I supposed, I could not but judge he must have fallen from some high place in his own country, and fallen as he was, I could not but admire his bearing. As we passed the grave, I paused and raised my hands and eyes to heaven in token of respect and sorrow for the dead; and he, as if in answer, bowed low and spread his hands abroad; it was a strange motion, but done like a thing of common custom; and I supposed it was ceremonial in the land from which he came. At the same time he pointed to my uncle, whom he could just see perched upon a knoll, and touched his head to indicate that he was mad.

We took the long way round the shore, for I feared to excite my uncle if we struck across the island; and as we walked, I had time enough to mature the little dramatic exhibition by which I hoped to satisfy my doubts. Accordingly, pausing on a rock, I proceeded to imitate before the negro the action of the man whom I had seen the day before taking bearings with the compass at Sandag. He understood me at once, and, taking the imitation out of my hands, showed me where the boat was, pointed out seaward as if to indicate the position of the schooner, and then down along the edge of the rock with the words "Espirito Santo," strangely pronounced, but clear enough for recognition. I had thus been right in my conjecture; the pretended historical inquiry had been but a cloak for treasure-hunting; the man who had played Dr. Robertson was the same as the foreigner who visited Grisapol in spring, and now, with many others, lay dead under the Roost of Aros; there had their greed brought them, there should their bones be tossed for evermore. In the meantime the black continued his imitation of the scene, now looking up skyward as though watching the approach of the storm; now, in the character of a seaman, waving the rest to come aboard; now as an officer running along the rock and entering the boat; and anon bending over imaginary oars with the air of a hurried boatman; but all with the same solemnity of manner, so that I was never even moved to smile. Lastly, he indicated to me, by a pantomime not to be described in words, how he himself had gone up to examine the stranded wreck, and, to his grief and indignation, had been deserted by his comrades; and thereupon folded his arms once more, and stooped his head, like one accepting fate.

The mystery of his presence being thus solved for me, I explained to him by means of a sketch the fate of the vessel and of all aboard her. He showed no surprise nor sorrow, and, with a sudden lifting of his open hand, seemed to dismiss his former friends or masters (whichever they had been) into God's pleasure. Respect came upon me and grew stronger, the more I observed him; I saw he had a powerful mind and a sober and severe character, such as I loved to commune with; and before we reached the house of Aros I had almost forgotten, and wholly forgiven him, his uncanny colour.

To Mary I told all that had passed without suppression, though I own my heart failed me; but I did wrong to doubt her sense of justice.

"You did the right," she said. "God's will be done." And she set out meat for us at once.

As soon as I was satisfied, I bade Rorie keep an eye upon the castaway, who was still eating, and set forth again myself to find my uncle. I had not gone far before I saw him sitting in the same place, upon the very topmost knoll, and seemingly in the same attitude as when I had last observed him. From that point, as I have said, the most of Aros and the neighbouring Ross would be spread below him like a map; and it was plain that he kept a bright lookout in all directions, for my head had scarcely risen above the summit of the first ascent before he had leaped to his feet and turned as if to face me. I hailed him at once, as well as I was able, in the same tones and words as I had often used before, when I had come to summon him to dinner. He made not so much as a movement in reply. I passed on a little farther, and again tried parley, with the same result. But when I began a second time to advance, his insane fears blazed up again, and still in dead silence, but with incredible speed, he began to flee from before me along the rocky summit of the hill. An hour before, he had been dead weary, and I had been comparatively active. But now his strength was recruited by the fervour of insanity, and it would have been vain for me to dream of pursuit. Nay, the very attempt, I thought, might have inflamed his terrors, and thus increased the miseries of our position. And I had nothing left but to turn homeward and make my sad report to Mary.

She heard it, as she had heard the first, with a concerned composure, and, bidding me lie down and take that rest of which I stood so much in need, set forth herself in quest of her misguided father. At that age it would have been a strange thing that put me from either meat or sleep; I slept long and deep; and it was already long past noon before I awoke and came downstairs into the kitchen. Mary, Rorie, and the black castaway were seated about the fire in silence; and I could see that Mary had been weeping. There was cause enough, as I soon learned, for tears. First she, and then Rorie, had been forth to seek my uncle; each in turn had found him perched upon the hill-top, and from each in turn he had silently and swiftly fled. Rorie had tried to chase him, but in vain; madness lent a new vigour to his bounds; he sprang from rock to rock over the widest gullies; he scoured like the wind along the hill-tops; he doubled and twisted like a hare before the dogs; and Rorie at length gave in; and the last that he saw, my uncle was seated as before upon the crest of Aros. Even during the hottest excitement of the chase, even when the fleet-footed servant had come, for a moment, very near to capture him, the poor lunatic had uttered not a sound. He fled, and he was silent, like a beast; and this silence had terrified his pursuer.

There was something heart-breaking in the situation. How to capture the madman, how to feed him in the meanwhile, and what to do with him when he was captured, were the three difficulties that we had to solve.

"The black," said I, "is the cause of this attack. It may even be his presence in the house that keeps my uncle on the hill. We have done the fair thing; he has been fed and warmed under this roof; now I propose that Rorie put him across the bay in the coble, and take him through the Ross as far as Grisapol."

In this proposal Mary heartily concurred; and bidding the black follow us, we all three descended to the pier. Certainly, Heaven's will was declared against Gordon Darnaway; a thing had happened, never paralleled before in Aros; during the storm the coble had broken loose, and, striking on the rough splinters of the pier, now lay in four feet of water with one side stove in. Three days of work at least would be required to make her float. But I was not to be beaten. I led the whole party round to where the gut was narrowest, swam to the other side, and called to the black to follow me. He signed, with the same clearness and quiet as before, that he knew not the art; and there was truth apparent in his signals, it would have occurred to none of us to doubt his truth; and that hope being over, we must all go back even as we came to the house of Aros, the negro walking in our midst without embarrassment.

All we could do that day was to make one more attempt to communicate with the unhappy madman. Again he was visible on his perch; again he fled in silence. But food and a great cloak were at least left for his comfort; the rain, besides, had cleared away, and the night promised to be even warm. We might compose ourselves, we thought, until the morrow; rest was the chief requisite, that we might be strengthened for unusual exertions; and as none cared to talk, we separated at an early hour.

I lay long awake, planning a campaign for the morrow. I was to place the black on the side of Sandag, whence he should head my uncle towards the house; Rorie in the west, I on the east, were to complete the cordon, as best we might. It seemed to me, the more I recalled the configuration of the island, that it should be possible, though hard, to force him down upon the low ground along Aros Bay; and once there, even with the strength of his madness, ultimate escape was hardly to be feared. It was on his terror of the black that I relied; for I made sure, however he might run, it would not be in the direction of the man whom he supposed to have returned from the dead, and thus one point of the compass at least would be secure.

When at length I fell asleep, it was to be awakened shortly after by a dream of wrecks, black men, and submarine adventure; and I found myself so shaken and fevered that I arose, descended the stair, and stepped out before the house. Within, Rorie and the black were asleep together in the kitchen; outside was a wonderful clear night of stars, with here and there a cloud still hanging, last stragglers of the tempest. It was near the top of the flood, and the Merry Men were roaring in the windless quiet of the night. Never, not even in the height of the tempest, had I heard their song with greater awe. Now, when the winds were gathered home, when the deep was dandling itself back into its summer slumber, and when the stars rained their gentle light over land and sea, the voice of these tide-breakers was still raised for havoc. They seemed, indeed, to be a part of the world's evil and the tragic side of life. Nor were their meaningless vociferations the only sounds that broke the silence of the night. For I could hear, now shrill and thrilling and now almost drowned, the note of a human voice that accompanied the uproar of the Roost. I knew it for my kinsman's; and a great fear fell upon me of God's judgments, and the evil in the world. I went back again into the darkness of the house as into a place of shelter, and lay long upon my bed, pondering these mysteries.

It was late when I again woke, and I leaped into my clothes and hurried to the kitchen. No one was there; Rorie and the black had both stealthily departed long before; and my heart stood still at the discovery. I could rely on Rorie's heart, but I placed no trust in his discretion. If he had thus set out without a word, he was plainly bent upon some service to my uncle. But what service could he hope to render even alone, far less in the company of the man in whom my uncle found his fears incarnated? Even if I were not already too late to prevent some deadly mischief, it was plain I must delay no longer. With the thought I was out of the house; and often as I have run on the rough sides of Aros, I never ran as I did that fatal morning. I do not believe I put twelve minutes to the whole ascent.

My uncle was gone from his perch. The basket had indeed been torn open and the meat scattered on the turf; but, as we found afterwards, no mouthful had been tasted; and there was not another trace of human existence in that wide field of view. Day had already filled the clear heavens; the sun already lighted in a rosy bloom upon the crest of Ben Kyaw; but all below me the rude knolls of Aros and the shield of the sea lay steeped in the clear darkling twilight of the dawn.

"Rorie!" I cried; and again "Rorie!" My voice died in the silence, but there came no answer back. If there were indeed an enterprise afoot to catch my uncle, it was plainly not in fleetness of foot, but in dexterity of stalking, that the hunters placed their trust. I ran on farther, keeping the higher spurs, and looking right and left, nor did I pause again till I was on the mount above Sandag. I could see the wreck, the uncovered belt of sand, the waves idly beating the long ledge of rocks, and on either hand the tumbled knolls, boulders, and gullies of the island. But still no human thing.

At a stride the sunshine fell on Aros, and the shadows and colours leaped into being. Not half a moment later, below me to the west, sheep began to scatter as in a panic. There came a cry. I saw my uncle running. I saw the black jump up in hot pursuit; and before I had time to understand, Rorie also had appeared, calling directions in Gaelic as to a dog herding sheep.

I took to my heels to interfere, and perhaps I had done better to have waited where I was, for I was the means of cutting off the madman's last escape. There was nothing before him from that moment but the grave, the wreck, and the sea in Sandag Bay. And yet Heaven knows that what I did was for the best.

My Uncle Gordon saw in what direction, horrible to him, the chase was driving him. He doubled, darting to the right and left; but high as the fever ran in his veins, the black was still the swifter. Turn where he would, he was still forestalled, still driven toward the scene of his crime. Suddenly he began to shriek aloud, so that the coast re-echoed; and now both I and Rorie were calling on the black to stop. But all was vain, for it was written otherwise. The pursuer still ran, the chase still sped before him screaming; they avoided the grave and skimmed close past the timbers of the wreck; in a breath they had cleared the sand; and still my kinsman did not pause, but dashed straight into the surf; and the black, now almost within reach, still followed swiftly behind him. Rorie and I both stopped, for the thing was now beyond the hands of men, and these were the decrees of God that came to pass before our eyes. There was never a sharper ending. On that steep beach they were beyond their depth at a bound; neither could swim; the black rose once for a moment with a throttling cry; but the current had them, racing seaward; and if ever they came up again, which God alone can tell, it would be ten minutes after, at the far end of Aros Roost, where the sea-birds hover fishing.

ROBERT LOUIS STEVENSON
1850–94

Beset by ill health from his youth, Stevenson's early education was irregular. When he entered Edinburgh University at seventeen he was expected to study engineering, the family profession, but he eventually obtained his father's consent to study law instead.

In 1873 Stevenson suffered a severe respiratory illness. In 1875 he was admitted to the Scottish bar, though he never practiced law. What he did do was travel. Two of his journeys inspired him to write *An Inland Voyage* (1878) and *Travels With a Donkey in the Cévennes* (1879).

He fell in love with Fanny Vandegrift Osbourne, a married American woman, and followed her to California in 1879, recording the events of his difficult journey in *Across the Plains* (1892) and *The Amateur Emigrant* (1895). After Mrs. Osbourne's divorce in 1880, she and Stevenson married and honeymooned near an abandoned silver mine. The record of that honeymoon appeared in Stevenson's *The Silverado Squatters* (1883).

After traveling to Scotland for a reconciliation with Stevenson's parents, the couple and Lloyd Osbourne, Fanny's son, moved to Davos, Switzerland, for a time. Davos had been recommended by doctors as a good place for Stevenson, by this time suffering from tuberculosis.

Beginning in 1881 Stevenson's novel *The Sea Cook* was serialized in *Young Folks* magazine. In slightly altered form it was published as *Treasure Island* (1883). In Davos Stevenson also worked on *Prince Otto* (1885). Back in Scotland in the spring and summer of 1882, he had lung hemorrhages, but they did not prevent him from writing two of his best short stories, "Thrawn Jane" and "The Merry Men."

During a sojourn in Hyeres, France, from 1882 to 1884, Stevenson began *The Black Arrow* (1888) and *A Child's Garden of Verses* (1885). In Bournemouth, England, he wrote *Kidnapped* (1886) and *The Strange Case of Dr. Jekyll and Mr. Hyde* (1886).

In search of a healthy climate, Stevenson returned to America in 1887 to find himself a famous man. He settled briefly in the Adirondacks, where he started *The Master of Ballantrae* (1889) and contributed to *Scribner's Magazine*.

In 1888 Stevenson settled in Samoa with his family. His Pacific travels provided material for *A Footnote to History* (1892) and *In the South Seas* (1896). His fiction from the period includes the sequel to *Kidnapped*, *Catriona* (1893), known as *David Balfour* in the United States; the magnificent story "The Beach of Falesa" (1892); and *The Ebb Tide* (1894), an unfinished masterpiece. *St. Ives*, also left uncompleted, was finished by Arthur Quiller-Couch.

"The Merry Men" is the title story of a collection published in 1886.

Make Westing

BY JACK LONDON

Whatever you do, make westing! make westing!
  —Sailing directions for Cape Horn.

FOR SEVEN WEEKS the *Mary Rogers* had been between 50° south in the Atlantic and 50° south in the Pacific, which meant that for seven weeks she had been struggling to round Cape Horn. For seven weeks she had been either in dirt, or close to dirt, save once, and then, following upon six days of excessive dirt, which she had ridden out under the shelter of the redoubtable Tierra Del Fuego coast, she had almost gone ashore during a heavy swell in the dead calm that had suddenly fallen. For seven weeks she had wrestled with the Cape Horn graybeards, and in return been buffeted and smashed by them. She was a wooden ship, and her ceaseless straining had opened her seams, so that twice a day the watch took its turn at the pumps.

The *Mary Rogers* was strained, the crew was strained, and big Dan Cullen, master, was likewise strained. Perhaps he was strained most of all, for upon him rested the responsibility of that titanic struggle. He slept most of the time in his clothes, though he rarely slept. He haunted the deck at night, a great, burly, robust ghost, black with the sunburn of thirty years of sea and hairy as an orangutan. He, in turn, was haunted by one thought of action, a sailing direction for the Horn: *Whatever you do, make westing! make westing!* It was an obsession. He thought of nothing else, except, at times, to blaspheme God for sending such bitter weather.

Make westing! He hugged the Horn, and a dozen times lay hove to with the iron Cape bearing east-by-north, or north-north-east, a score of miles away. And each time the eternal west wind smote him back and he made easting. He fought gale after gale, south to 64°, inside the antarctic drift-ice, and pledged his immortal soul to the Powers of Darkness for a bit of westing, for a slant to take him around. And he made easting. In despair, he had tried to make the passage through the Straits of Le Maire. Halfway through, the wind hauled to the north'ard of northwest, the glass dropped to 28.88, and he turned and ran before a gale of cyclonic fury, missing, by a hair's-breadth, piling up the *Mary Rogers* on the black-toothed rocks. Twice he had made west to the Diego Ramirez Rocks, one of the times saved between two snow-squalls by sighting the gravestones of ships a quarter of a mile dead ahead.

Blow! Captain Dan Cullen instanced all his thirty years at sea to prove that never had it blown so before. The *Mary Rogers* was hove to at the time he gave the evidence, and, to clinch it, inside half an hour the *Mary Rogers* was hove down to the hatches. Her new maintopsail and brand new spencer were blown away like tissue paper; and five sails, furled and fast under double gaskets, were blown loose and stripped from the yards. And before morning the *Mary Rogers* was hove down twice again, and holes were knocked in her bulwarks to ease her decks from the weight of ocean that pressed her down.

On an average of once a week Captain Dan Cullen caught glimpses of the sun. Once, for ten minutes, the sun shone at midday, and ten minutes afterward a new gale was piping up, both watches were shortening sail, and all was buried in the obscurity of a driving snow-squall. For a fortnight, once, Captain Dan Cullen was without a meridian or a chronometer sight. Rarely did he know his position within half a degree, except when in sight of land; for sun and stars remained hidden behind the sky, and it was so gloomy that even at the best the horizons were poor for accurate observations. A gray gloom shrouded the world. The clouds were gray; the great driving seas were leaden gray; the smoking crests were a gray churning; even the occasional albatrosses were gray, while the snow-flurries were not white, but gray, under the sombre pall of the heavens.

Life on board the *Mary Rogers* was gray,—gray and gloomy. The faces of the sailors were blue-gray; they were afflicted with sea-cuts and sea-boils, and suffered exquisitely. They were shadows of men. For seven weeks, in the forecastle or on deck, they had not known what it was to be dry. They had forgotten what it was to sleep out a watch, and all watches it was, "All hands on deck!" They caught snatches of agonized sleep, and they slept in their oilskins ready for the everlasting call. So weak and worn were they that it took both watches to do the work of one. That was why both watches were on deck so much of the time. And no shadow of a man could shirk duty. Nothing less than a broken leg could enable a man to knock off work; and there were two such, who had been mauled and pulped by the seas that broke aboard.

One other man who was the shadow of a man was George Dorety. He was the only passenger on board, a friend of the firm, and he had elected to make the voyage for his health. But seven weeks of Cape Horn had not bettered his health. He gasped and panted in his bunk through the long, heaving nights; and when on deck he was so bundled up for warmth that he resembled a peripatetic old-clothes shop. At midday, eating at the cabin table in a gloom so deep that the swinging sea-lamps burned always, he

looked as blue-gray as the sickest, saddest man for'ard. Nor did gazing
across the table at Captain Dan Cullen have any cheering effect upon him.
Captain Cullen chewed and scowled and kept silent. The scowls were for
God, and with every chew he reiterated the sole thought of his existence,
which was *make westing*. He was a big, hairy brute, and the sight of him
was not stimulating to the others' appetite. He looked upon George Dorety
as a Jonah, and told him so, once each meal, savagely transferring the scowl
from God to the passenger and back again.

Nor did the mate prove a first aid to a languid appetite. Joshua Higgins
by name, a seaman by profession and pull, but a potwalloper by capacity, he
was a loose-jointed, sniffling creature, heartless and selfish and cowardly,
without a soul, in fear of his life of Dan Cullen, and a bully over the sailors,
who knew that behind the mate was Captain Cullen, the lawgiver and com-
peller, the driver and the destroyer, the incarnation of a dozen bucko mates.
In that wild weather at the southern end of the earth, Joshua Higgins ceased
washing. His grimy face usually robbed George Dorety of what little appetite he managed to accumulate. Ordinarily this lavatorial dereliction would
have caught Captain Cullen's eye and vocabulary, but in the present his
mind was filled with making westing, to the exclusion of all other things
not contributory thereto. Whether the mate's face was clean or dirty had no
bearing upon westing. Later on, when 50° south in the Pacific had been
reached, Joshua Higgins would wash his face very abruptly. In the meantime, at the cabin table, where gray twilight alternated with lamplight while
the lamps were being filled, George Dorety sat between the two men, one a
tiger and the other a hyena, and wondered why God had made them. The
second mate, Matthew Turner, was a true sailor and a man, but George
Dorety did not have the solace of his company, for he ate by himself, solitary, when they had finished.

On Saturday morning, July 24, George Dorety awoke to a feeling of life
and headlong movement. On deck he found the *Mary Rogers* running off
before a howling southeaster. Nothing was set but the lower topsails and the
foresail. It was all she could stand, yet she was making fourteen knots,
as Mr. Turner shouted in Dorety's ear when he came on deck. And it was
all westing. She was going around the Horn at last . . . if the wind held.
Mr. Turner looked happy. The end of the struggle was in sight. But Captain Cullen did not look happy. He scowled at Dorety in passing. Captain
Cullen did not want God to know that he was pleased with that wind. He
had a conception of a malicious God, and believed in his secret soul that if
God knew it was a desirable wind, God would promptly efface it and send a
snorter from the west. So he walked softly before God, smothering his joy
down under scowls and muttered curses, and, so, fooling God, for God was
the only thing in the universe of which Dan Cullen was afraid.

All Saturday and Saturday night the *Mary Rogers* raced her westing. Persistently she logged her fourteen knots, so that by Sunday morning she had covered three hundred and fifty miles. If the wind held, she would make around. If it failed, and the snorter came from anywhere between southwest and north, back the *Mary Rogers* would be hurled and be no better off than she had been seven weeks before. And on Sunday morning the wind *was* failing. The big sea was going down and running smooth. Both watches were on deck setting sail after sail as fast as the ship could stand it. And now Captain Cullen went around brazenly before God, smoking a big cigar, smiling jubilantly, as if the failing wind delighted him, while down underneath he was raging against God for taking the life out of the blessed wind. *Make westing!* So he would, if God would only leave him alone. Secretly, he pledged himself anew to the Powers of Darkness, if they would let him make westing. He pledged himself so easily because he did not believe in the Powers of Darkness. He really believed only in God, though he did not know it. And in his inverted theology God was really the Prince of Darkness. Captain Cullen was a devilworshipper, but he called the devil by another name, that was all.

At midday, after calling eight bells, Captain Cullen ordered the royals on. The men went aloft faster than they had gone in weeks. Not alone were they nimble because of the westing, but a benignant sun was shining down and limbering their stiff bodies. George Dorety stood aft, near Captain Cullen, less bundled in clothes than usual, soaking in the grateful warmth as he watched the scene. Swiftly and abruptly the incident occurred. There was a cry from the foreroyal-yard of "Man overboard!" Somebody threw a life buoy over the side, and at the same instant the second mate's voice came aft, ringing and peremptory:—

"Hard down your helm!"

The man at the wheel never moved a spoke. He knew better, for Captain Dan Cullen was standing alongside of him. He wanted to move a spoke, to move all the spokes, to grind the wheel down, hard down, for his comrade drowning in the sea. He glanced at Captain Dan Cullen, and Captain Dan Cullen gave no sign.

"Down! Hard down!" the second mate roared, as he sprang aft.

But he ceased springing and commanding, and stood still, when he saw Dan Cullen by the wheel. And big Dan Cullen puffed at his cigar and said nothing. Astern, and going astern fast, could be seen the sailor. He had caught the life buoy and was clinging to it. Nobody spoke. Nobody moved. The men aloft clung to the royal yards and watched with terror-stricken faces. And the *Mary Rogers* raced on, making her westing. A long, silent minute passed.

"Who was it?" Captain Cullen demanded.

"Mops, sir," eagerly answered the sailor at the wheel.

Mops topped a wave astern and disappeared temporarily in the trough. It was a large wave, but it was no graybeard. A small boat could live easily in such a sea, and in such a sea the *Mary Rogers* could easily come to. But she could not come to and make westing at the same time.

For the first time in all his years, George Dorety was seeing a real drama of life and death—a sordid little drama in which the scales balanced an unknown sailor named Mops against a few miles of longitude. At first he had watched the man astern, but now he watched big Dan Cullen, hairy and black, vested with power of life and death, smoking a cigar.

Captain Dan Cullen smoked another long, silent minute. Then he removed the cigar from his mouth. He glanced aloft at the spars of the *Mary Rogers*, and overside at the sea.

"Sheet home the royals!" he cried.

Fifteen minutes later they sat at table, in the cabin, with food served before them. On one side of George Dorety sat Dan Cullen, the tiger, on the other side, Joshua Higgins, the hyena. Nobody spoke. On deck the men were sheeting home the skysails. George Dorety could hear their cries, while a persistent vision haunted him of a man called Mops, alive and well, clinging to a life buoy miles astern in that lonely ocean. He glanced at Captain Cullen, and experienced a feeling of nausea, for the man was eating his food with relish, almost bolting it.

"Captain Cullen," Dorety said, "you are in command of this ship, and it is not proper for me to comment now upon what you do. But I wish to say one thing. There is a hereafter, and yours will be a hot one."

Captain Cullen did not even scowl. In his voice was regret as he said:—

"It was blowing a living gale. It was impossible to save the man."

"He fell from the royal-yard," Dorety cried hotly. "You were setting the royals at the time. Fifteen minutes afterward you were setting the skysails."

"It was a living gale, wasn't it, Mr. Higgins?" Captain Cullen said, turning to the mate.

"If you'd brought her to, it'd have taken the sticks out of her," was the mate's answer. "You did the proper thing, Captain Cullen. The man hadn't a ghost of a show."

George Dorety made no answer, and to the meal's end no one spoke. After that, Dorety had his meals served in his stateroom. Captain Cullen scowled at him no longer, though no speech was exchanged between them, while the *Mary Rogers* sped north toward warmer latitudes. At the end of the week, Dan Cullen cornered Dorety on deck.

"What are you going to do when we get to 'Frisco?" he demanded bluntly.

"I am going to swear out a warrant for your arrest," Dorety answered quietly. "I am going to charge you with murder, and I am going to see you hanged for it."

"You're almighty sure of yourself," Captain Cullen sneered, turning on his heel.

A second week passed, and one morning found George Dorety standing in the coach-house companionway at the for'ard end of the long poop, taking his first gaze around the deck. The *Mary Rogers* was reaching full-and-by, in a stiff breeze. Every sail was set and drawing, including the staysails. Captain Cullen strolled for'ard along the poop. He strolled carelessly, glancing at the passenger out of the corner of his eye. Dorety was looking the other way, standing with head and shoulders outside the companionway, and only the back of his head was to be seen. Captain Cullen, with swift eye, embraced the mainstaysail-block and the head and estimated the distance. He glanced about him. Nobody was looking. Aft, Joshua Higgins, pacing up and down, had just turned his back and was going the other way. Captain Cullen bent over suddenly and cast the staysail-sheet off from its pin. The heavy block hurtled through the air, smashing Dorety's head like an egg-shell and hurtling on and back and forth as the staysail whipped and slatted in the wind. Joshua Higgins turned around to see what had carried away, and met the full blast of the vilest portion of Captain Cullen's profanity.

"I made the sheet fast myself," whimpered the mate in the first lull, "with an extra turn to make sure. I remember it distinctly."

"Made fast?" the Captain snarled back, for the benefit of the watch as it struggled to capture the flying sail before it tore to ribbons. "You couldn't make your grandmother fast, you useless hell's scullion. If you made that sheet fast with an extra turn, why in hell didn't it stay fast? That's what I want to know. Why in hell didn't it stay fast?"

The mate whined inarticulately.

"Oh, shut up!" was the final word of Captain Cullen.

Half an hour later he was as surprised as any when the body of George Dorety was found inside the companionway on the floor. In the afternoon, alone in his room, he doctored up the log.

"Ordinary seaman, Karl Brun," he wrote, "lost overboard from foreroyal-yard in a gale of wind. Was running at the time, and for the safety of the ship did not dare come up to the wind. Nor could a boat have lived in the sea that was running."

On another page, he wrote:—

"Had often warned Mr. Dorety about the danger he ran because of his carelessness on deck. I told him, once, that some day he would get his head knocked off by a block. A carelessly fastened mainstaysail sheet was the cause of the accident, which was deeply to be regretted because Mr. Dorety was a favorite with all of us."

Captain Dan Cullen read over his literary effort with admiration, blotted the page, and closed the log. He lighted a cigar and stared before him. He felt the *Mary Rogers* lift, and heel, and surge along, and knew that she was making nine knots. A smile of satisfaction slowly dawned on his black and hairy face. Well, anyway, he had made his westing and fooled God.

JACK LONDON
1876–1916

The only child of Flora Wellman, who named William Henry Chaney, an itinerant astrologer, as the father, Jack London was accepted by and named after the man his mother married in 1876. After the completion of grammar school, the boy, who had already been working before school each day to augment the family income, went to work full time in a cannery. Then, with a loan of three hundred dollars, London purchased the sloop *Razzle-Dazzle* and became an oyster pirate at age fifteen.

In 1893 he took a seven-month voyage on the *Sophia Sutherland*, a sailing schooner, and the following year he tramped across the country. He was arrested for vagrancy near Niagara Falls and thrown into jail for thirty days without a trial. Returning to Oakland, California, he entered school at Oakland High. There he wrote for the student magazine and began to prepare for college by reading voraciously.

After a semester at the University of California, where he became impatient with the slow pace of classes, London joined the Klondike stampede to search for gold. He returned empty-handed from Alaska but with memories that would provide him with material for a career as a writer, which he was now determined to pursue. In 1899 London sold one of his Northland stories, "To the Man on Trail," to the *Overland Monthly*. "An Odyssey of the North" appeared in the *Atlantic Monthly* the following year.

In 1902 London published a novel, *A Daughter of the Snows*; but it was *The Call of the Wild* (1903) that brought him worldwide adulation, a reputation bolstered by publication of *The Sea-Wolf* (1904) and *White Fang* (1906). Lecture tours carried him to the East Coast in 1905 and 1906 and included engagements at Harvard, Yale, and Carnegie Hall.

Always enamored of the sea, London had recorded a fictionalized picture of himself as an oyster pirate for juveniles in *The Cruise of the Dazzler* (1902). Likewise, *Tales of the Fish Patrol* (1905) recalled youthful adventures on the water. Not content to be confined to land, London prepared to set sail again, this time in a new boat, the *Snark*. By 1907 he was on his way to Hawaii, the Marquesas, and Tahiti, a trip that continued until mid-1909 and took him on the South Seas to Ecuador, through Panama, and finally to New Orleans. The voyages encouraged a steady stream of writing: *The Cruise of the Snark* (1911), a book of travel sketches; *The South Sea Tales* (1911); and *The House of Pride and Other Tales of Hawaii* (1912). Always in quest of new adventure, London sailed around Cape Horn in 1912.

Several events called for London to turn reporter. In 1904 he filed stories with the Hearst organization about the Russo-Japanese War; in 1906 he reported the San Francisco earthquake for *Colliers*; and in 1914 he wrote on the Mexican Revolution for the same magazine. The last assignment was cut short by illness. Troubled by alcoholism and financial difficulties, London died of uremic poisoning in 1916, at the age of forty.

"Make Westing" was included in *When God Laughs* (1911), a collection of short stories.

Turn About

BY WILLIAM FAULKNER

God bless all men in little boats. In punts and wherries and ketches; in scows and dhows and dugouts; in junks, sampans and catamarans; in cutters and skiffs and sloops; in prams and shells and dinghies; in dories, canoes and whale-boats; and even, God, in motorboats. Amen.

I

THE AMERICAN—the older one—wore no pink Bedfords. His breeches were of plain whipcord, like the tunic. And the tunic had no long London-cut skirts, so that below the Sam Browne the tail of it stuck straight out like the tunic of a military policeman beneath his holster belt. And he wore simple puttees and the easy shoes of a man of middle age, instead of Savile Row boots, and the shoes and the puttees did not match in shade, and the ordnance belt did not match either of them, and the pilot's wings on his breast were just wings. But the ribbon beneath them was a good ribbon, and the insigne on his shoulders were the twin bars of a captain. He was not tall. His face was thin, a little aquiline; the eyes intelligent and a little tired. He was past twenty-five; looking at him, one thought, not Phi Beta Kappa exactly, but Skull and Bones perhaps, or possibly a Rhodes scholarship.

One of the men who faced him probably could not see him at all. He was being held on his feet by an American military policeman. He was quite drunk, and in contrast with the heavy-jawed policeman who held him erect on his long, slim, boneless legs, he looked like a masquerading girl. He was possibly eighteen, tall, with a pink-and-white face and blue eyes, and a mouth like a girl's mouth. He wore a pea-coat, buttoned awry and stained with recent mud, and upon his blond head, at that unmistakable and rakish swagger which no other people can ever approach or imitate, the cap of a Royal Naval Officer.

"What's this, corporal?" the American captain said. "What's the trouble? He's an Englishman. You'd better let their M.P.'s take care of him."

"I know he is," the policeman said. He spoke heavily, breathing heavily, in the voice of a man under physical strain; for all his girlish delicacy of limb, the English boy was heavier—or more helpless—than he looked. "Stand up!" the policeman said. "They're officers!"

The English boy made an effort then. He pulled himself together, focusing his eyes. He swayed, throwing his arms about the policeman's neck, and with the other hand he saluted, his hand flicking, fingers curled a little, to his right ear, already swaying again and catching himself again. "Cheer-o, sir," he said. "Name's not Beatty, I hope."

"No," the captain said.

"Ah," the English boy said. "Hoped not. My mistake. No offense, what?"

"No offense," the captain said quietly. But he was looking at the policeman. The second American spoke. He was a lieutenant, also a pilot. But he was not twenty-five and he wore the pink breeches, the London boots, and his tunic might have been a British tunic save for the collar.

"It's one of those navy eggs," he said. "They pick them out of the gutters here all night long. You don't come to town often enough."

"Oh," the captain said. "I've heard about them. I remember now." He also remarked now that, though the street was a busy one—it was just outside a popular café—and there were many passers, soldier, civilian, women, yet none of them so much as paused, as though it were a familiar sight. He was looking at the policeman. "Can't you take him to his ship?"

"I thought of that before the captain did," the policeman said. "He says he can't go aboard his ship after dark because he puts the ship away at sundown."

"Puts it away?"

"Stand up, sailor!" the policeman said savagely, jerking at his lax burden. "Maybe the captain can make sense out of it. Damned if I can. He says they keep the boat under the wharf. Run it under the wharf at night, and that they can't get it out again until the tide goes out tomorrow."

"Under the wharf? A boat? What is this?" He was now speaking to the lieutenant. "Do they operate some kind of aquatic motorcycles?"

"Something like that," the lieutenant said. "You've seen them—the boats. Launches, camouflaged and all. Dashing up and down the harbor. You've seen them. They do that all day and sleep in the gutters here all night."

"Oh," the captain said. "I thought those boats were ship commanders' launches. You mean to tell me they use officers just to—"

"I don't know," the lieutenant said. "Maybe they use them to fetch hot water from one ship to another. Or buns. Or maybe to go back and forth fast when they forget napkins or something."

"Nonsense," the captain said. He looked at the English boy again.

"That's what they do," the lieutenant said. "Town's lousy with them all night long. Gutters full, and their M.P.'s carting them away in batches, like nursemaids in a park. Maybe the French give them the launches to get them out of the gutters during the day."

"Oh," the captain said, "I see." But it was clear that he didn't see, wasn't listening, didn't believe what he did hear. He looked the English boy. "Well, you can't leave him here in that shape," he said.

Again the English boy tried to pull himself together. "Quite all right, 'sure you," he said glassily, his voice pleasant, cheerful almost, quite courteous. "Used to it. Confounded rough *pavé*, though. Should force French do something about it. Visiting lads jolly well deserve decent field to play on, what?"

"And he was jolly well using all of it too," the policeman said savagely. "He must think he's a one-man team, maybe."

At that moment a fifth man came up. He was a British military policeman. "Nah then," he said, "What's this? What's this?" Then he saw the Americans' shoulder bars. He saluted. At the sound of his voice the English boy turned, swaying, peering.

"Oh, hullo, Albert," he said.

"Nah then, Mr. Hope," the British policeman said. He said to the American policeman, over his shoulder: "What is it this time?"

"Likely nothing," the American said. "The way you guys run a war. But I'm a stranger here. Here. Take him."

"What is this, corporal?" the captain said. "What was he doing?"

"He won't call it nothing," the American policeman said, jerking his head at the British policeman. "He'll just call it a thrush or a robin or something. I turn into this street about three blocks back a while ago, and I find it blocked with a line of trucks going up from the docks, and the drivers all hollering ahead what the hell the trouble is. So I come on, and I find it is about three blocks of them, blocking the cross streets too; and I come on to the head of it where the trouble is, and I find about a dozen of the drivers out in front, holding a caucus or something in the middle of the street, and I come up and I say, 'What's going on here?' and they leave me through and I find this egg here laying—"

"Yer talking about one of His Majesty's officers, my man," the British policeman said.

"Watch yourself, corporal," the captain said. "And you found this officer—"

"He had done gone to bed in the middle of the street, with an empty basket for a pillow. Laying there with his hands under his head and his knees crossed, arguing with them about whether he ought to get up and move or not. He said that the trucks could turn back and go around by another street, but that he couldn't use any other street, because this street was his."

"His street?"

The English boy had listened, interested, pleasant. "Billet, you see," he said. "Must have order, even in war emergency. Billet by lot. This street

mine; no poaching, eh? Next street Jamie Wutherspoon's. But trucks can go
by that street because Jamie not using it yet. Not in bed yet. Insomnia. Knew
so. Told them. Trucks go that way. See now?"

"Was that it, corporal?" the captain said.

"He told you. He wouldn't get up. He just laid there, arguing with them.
He was telling one of them to go somewhere and bring back a copy of their
articles of war—"

"King's Regulations; yes," the captain said.

"—and see if the book said whether he had the right of way, or the
trucks. And then I got him up, and then the captain come along. And that's
all. And with the captain's permission I'll now hand him over to His Majesty's wet nur—"

"That'll do, corporal," the captain said. "You can go. I'll see to this." The
policeman saluted and went on. The British policeman was now supporting
the English boy. "Can't you take him home?" the captain said. "Where are
their quarters?"

"I don't rightly know, sir, if they have quarters or not. We—I usually see
them about the pubs until daylight. They don't seem to use quarters."

"You mean, they really aren't off of ships?"

"Well, sir, they might be ships, in a manner of speaking. But a man
would have to be a bit sleepier than him to sleep in one of them."

"I see," the captain said. He looked at the policeman. "What kind of
boats are they?"

This time the policeman's voice was immediate, final and completely in-
flectionless. It was like a closed door. "I don't rightly know, sir."

"Oh," the captain said. "Quite. Well, he's in no shape to stay about pubs
until daylight this time."

"Perhaps I can find him a bit of a pub with a back table, where he can
sleep," the policeman said. But the captain was not listening. He was looking across the street, where the lights of another café fell across the pave-
ment. The English boy yawned terrifically, like a child does, his mouth pink
and frankly gaped as a child's.

The captain turned to the policeman:

"Would you mind stepping across there and asking for Captain Bogard's
driver? I'll take care of Mr. Hope."

The policeman departed. The captain now supported the English boy,
his hand beneath the other's arm. Again the boy yawned like a weary child.
"Steady," the captain said. "The car will be here in a minute."

"Right," the English boy said through the yawn.

II

Once in the car he went to sleep immediately with the peaceful suddenness of babies, sitting between the two Americans. But though the aerodrome was only thirty minutes away, he was awake when they arrived, apparently quite fresh, and asking for whisky. When they entered the mess he appeared quite sober, only blinking a little in the lighted room, in his raked cap and his awry-buttoned pea-jacket and a soiled silk muffler, embroidered with a club insignia which Bogard recognized to have come from a famous preparatory school, twisted about his throat.

"Ah," he said, his voice fresh, clear now, not blurred, quite cheerful, quite loud, so that the others in the room turned and looked at him. "Jolly. Whisky, what?" He went straight as a bird dog to the bar in the corner, the lieutenant following. Bogard had turned and gone on to the other end of the room, where five men sat about a card table.

"What's he admiral of?" one said.

"Of the whole Scotch navy, when I found him," Bogard said.

Another looked up. "Oh, I thought I'd seen him in town." He looked at the guest. "Maybe it's because he was on his feet that I didn't recognize him when he came in. You usually see them lying down in the gutter."

"Oh," the first said. He, too, looked around. "Is he one of those guys?"

"Sure. You've seen them. Sitting on the curb, you know, with a couple of limey M.P.'s hauling at their arms."

"Yes. I've seen them," the other said. They all looked at the English boy. He stood at the bar, talking, his voice loud, cheerful. "They all look like him too," the speaker said. "About seventeen or eighteen. They run those little boats that are always dashing in and out."

"Is that what they do?" a third said. "You mean, there's a male marine auxiliary to the Waacs? Good Lord, I sure made a mistake when I enlisted. But this war never was advertised right."

"I don't know," Bogard said. "I guess they do more than just ride around."

But they were not listening to him. They were looking at the guest. "They run by clock," the first said. "You can see the condition of one of them after sunset and almost tell what time it is. But what I don't see is, how a man that's in that shape at one o'clock every morning can even see a battleship the next day."

"Maybe when they have a message to send out to a ship," another said, "they just make duplicates and line the launches up and point them toward the ship and give each one a duplicate of the message and let them go. And the ones that miss the ship just cruise around the harbor until they hit a dock somewhere."

"It must be more than that," Bogard said.

He was about to say something else, but at that moment the guest turned from the bar and approached, carrying a glass. He walked steadily enough, but his color was high and his eyes were bright, and he was talking, loud, cheerful, as he came up.

"I say. Won't you chaps join——." He ceased. He seemed to remark something; he was looking at their breasts. "Oh, I say. You fly. All of you. Oh, good gad! Find it jolly, eh?"

"Yes," somebody said. "Jolly."

"But dangerous, what?"

"A little faster than tennis," another said. The guest looked at him, bright, affable, intent.

Another said quickly, "Bogard says you command a vessel."

"Hardly a vessel. Thanks, though. And not command. Ronnie does that. Ranks me a bit. Age."

"Ronnie?"

"Yes. Nice. Good egg. Old, though. Stickler."

"Stickler?"

"Frightful. You'd not believe it. Whenever we sight smoke and I have the glass, he sheers away. Keeps the ship hull down all the while. No beaver then. Had me two down a fortnight yesterday."

The Americans glanced at one another. "No beaver?"

"We play it. With basket masts, you see. See a basket mast. Beaver! One up. The *Ergenstrasse* doesn't count any more, though."

The men about the table looked at one another. Bogard spoke. "I see. When you or Ronnie see a ship with basket masts, you get a beaver on the other. I see. What is the *Ergenstrasse*?"

"She's German. Interned. Tramp steamer. Foremast rigged so it looks something like a basket mast. Booms, cables, I dare say. I didn't think it looked very much like a basket mast, myself. But Ronnie said yes. Called it one day. Then one day they shifted her across the basin and I called her on Ronnie. So we decided to not count her any more. See now, eh?"

"Oh," the one who had made the tennis remark said, "I see. You and Ronnie run about in the launch, playing beaver. H'm'm. That's nice. Did you ever pl——"

"Jerry," Bogard said. The guest had not moved. He looked down at the speaker, still smiling, his eyes quite wide.

The speaker still looked at the guest. "Has yours and Ronnie's boat got a yellow stern?"

"A yellow stern?" the English boy said. He had quit smiling, but his face was still pleasant.

"I thought that maybe when the boats had two captains, they might paint the stern yellow or something."

"Oh," the guest said. "Burt and Reeves aren't officers."

"Burt and Reeves," the other said, in a musing tone. "So they go, too. Do they play beaver too?"

"Jerry," Bogard said. The other looked at him. Bogard jerked his head a little. "Come over here." The other rose. They went aside. "Lay off of him," Bogard said. "I mean it, now. He's just a kid. When you were that age, how much sense did you have? Just about enough to get to chapel on time."

"My country hadn't been at war going on four years, though," Jerry said. "Here we are, spending our money and getting shot at by the clock, and it's not even our fight, and these limeys that would have been goose-stepping twelve months now if it hadn't been—"

"Shut it," Bogard said. "You sound like a Liberty Loan."

"—taking it like it was a fair or something. 'Jolly.'" His voice was now falsetto, lilting. "'But dangerous, what?'"

"Sh-h-h-h," Bogard said.

"I'd like to catch him and his Ronnie out in the harbor, just once. Any harbor. London's. I wouldn't want anything but a Jenny, either. Jenny? Hell, I'd take a bicycle and a pair of water wings! I'll show him some war."

"Well, you lay off him now. He'll be gone soon."

"What are you going to do with him?"

"I'm going to take him along this morning. Let him have Harper's place out front. He says he can handle a Lewis. Says they have one on the boat. Something he was telling me—about how he once shot out a channel-marker light at seven hundred yards."

"Well, that's your business. Maybe he can beat you."

"Beat me?"

"Playing beaver. And then you can take on Ronnie."

"I'll show him some war, anyway," Bogard said. He looked at the guest. "His people have been in it three years now, and he seems to take it like a sophomore in town for the big game." He looked at Jerry again. "But you lay off him now."

As they approached the table, the guest's voice was loud and cheerful: ". . . if he got the glasses first, he would go in close and look, but when I got them first, he'd sheer off where I couldn't see anything but the smoke. Frightful stickler. Frightful. But *Ergenstrasse* not counting any more. And if you make a mistake and call her, you lose two beaver from your score. If Ronnie were only to forget and call her we'd be even."

III

At two o'clock the English boy was still talking, his voice bright, innocent and cheerful. He was telling them how Switzerland had been spoiled by 1914, and instead of the vacation which his father had promised him for his sixteenth birthday, when that birthday came he and his tutor had had to do with Wales. But that he and the tutor had got pretty high and that he dared to say—with all due respect to any present who might have had the advantage of Switzerland, of course—that one could see probably as far from Wales as from Switzerland. "Perspire as much and breathe as hard, anyway," he added. And about him the Americans sat, a little hardbitten, a little sober, somewhat older, listening to him with a kind of cold astonishment. They had been getting up for some time now and going out and returning in flying clothes, carrying helmets and goggles. An orderly entered with a tray of coffee cups, and the guest realized that for some time now he had been hearing engines in the darkness outside.

At last Bogard rose. "Come along," he said. "We'll get your togs." When they emerged from the mess, the sound of the engines was quite loud—an idling thunder. In alignment along the invisible tarmac was a vague rank of short banks of flickering blue-green fire suspended apparently in mid-air. They crossed the aerodrome to Bogard's quarters, where the lieutenant, McGinnis, sat on a cot fastening his flying boots. Bogard reached down a Sidcott suit and threw it across the cot. "Put this on," he said.

"Will I need all this?" the guest said. "Shall we be gone that long?"

"Probably," Bogard said. "Better use it. Cold upstairs."

The guest picked up the suit. "I say," he said. "I say. Ronnie and I have a do ourselves, tomor—today. Do you think Ronnie won't mind if I am a bit late? Might not wait for me."

"We'll be back before teatime," McGinnis said. He seemed quite busy with his boot. "Promise you." The English boy looked at him.

"What time should you be back?" Bogard said.

"Oh, well," the English boy said, "I dare say it will be all right. They let Ronnie say when to go, anyway. He'll wait for me if I should be a bit late."

"He'll wait," Bogard said. "Get your suit on."

"Right," the other said. They helped him into the suit. "Never been up before," he said, chattily, pleasantly. "Dare say you can see farther than from mountains, eh?"

"See more, anyway," McGinnis said. "You'll like it."

"Oh, rather. If Ronnie only waits for me. Lark. But dangerous, isn't it?"

"Go on," McGinnis said. "You're kidding me."

"Shut your trap, Mac," Bogard said. "Come along. Want some more coffee?" He looked at the guest, but McGinnis answered:

"No. Got something better than coffee. Coffee makes such a confounded stain on the wings."

"On the wings?" the English boy said. "Why coffee on the wings?"

"Stow it, I said, Mac," Bogard said. "Come along."

They recrossed the aerodrome, approaching the muttering banks of flame. When they drew near, the guest began to discern the shape, the outlines, of the Handley-Page. It looked like a Pullman coach run upslanted aground into the skeleton of the first floor of an incomplete skyscraper. The guest looked at it quietly.

"It's larger than a cruiser," he said in his bright, interested voice. "I say, you know. This doesn't fly in one lump. You can't pull my leg. Seen them before. It comes in two parts: Captain Bogard and me in one; Mac and 'nother chap in other. What?"

"No," McGinnis said. Bogard had vanished. "It all goes up in one lump. Big lark, eh? Buzzard, what?"

"Buzzard?" the guest murmured. "Oh, I say. A cruiser. Flying. I say, now."

"And listen," McGinnis said. His hand came forth; something cold fumbled against the hand of the English boy—a bottle. "When you feel yourself getting sick, see? Take a pull at it."

"Oh, shall I get sick?"

"Sure. We all do. Part of flying. This will stop it. But if it doesn't. See?"

"What? Quite. What?"

"Not overside. Don't spew it overside."

"Not overside?"

"It'll blow back in Bogy's and my face. Can't see. Bingo. Finished. See?"

"Oh, quite. What shall I do with it?" Their voices were quiet, brief, grave as conspirators.

"Just duck your head and let her go."

"Oh, quite."

Bogard returned. "Show him how to get into the front pit, will you?" he said. McGinnis led the way through the trap. Forward, rising to the slant of the fuselage, the passage narrowed; a man would need to crawl.

"Crawl in there and keep going," McGinnis said.

"It looks like a dog kennel," the guest said.

"Doesn't it, though?" McGinnis agreed cheerfully. "Cut along with you." Stooping, he could hear the other scuttling forward. "You'll find a Lewis gun up there, like as not," he said into the tunnel.

The voice of the guest came back: "Found it."

"The gunnery sergeant will be along in a minute and show you if it is loaded."

"It's loaded," the guest said; almost on the heels of his words the gun fired, a brief staccato burst. There were shouts, the loudest from the ground beneath the nose of the aeroplane. "It's quite all right," the English boy's voice said. "I pointed it west before I let it off. Nothing back there but Marine office and your brigade headquarters. Ronnie and I always do this before we go anywhere. Sorry if I was too soon. Oh, by the way," he added, "my name's Claude. Don't think I mentioned it."

On the ground, Bogard and two other officers stood. They had come up running. "Fired it west," one said. "How in hell does he know which way is west?"

"He's a sailor," the other said. "You forgot that."

"He seems to be a machine gunner too," Bogard said.

"Let's hope he doesn't forget that," the first said.

IV

Nevertheless, Bogard kept an eye on the silhouetted head rising from the round gunpit in the nose ten feet ahead of him. "He did work that gun, though," he said to McGinnis beside him. "He even put the drum on himself, didn't he?"

"Yes," McGinnis said. "If he just doesn't forget and think that that gun is him and his tutor looking around from a Welsh alp."

"Maybe I should not have brought him," Bogard said. McGinnis didn't answer. Bogard jockeyed the wheel a little. Ahead, in the gunner's pit, the guest's head moved this way and that continuously, looking. "We'll get there and unload and haul air for home," Bogard said. "Maybe in the dark— Confound it, it would be a shame for his country to be in this mess for four years and him not even to see a gun pointed in his direction."

"He'll see one tonight if he don't keep his head in," McGinnis said.

But the boy did not do that. Not even when they had reached the objective and McGinnis had crawled down to the bomb toggles. And even when the searchlights found them and Bogard signaled to the other machines and dived, the two engines snarling full speed into and through the bursting shells, he could see the boy's face in the searchlight's glare, leaned far overside, coming sharply out as a spotlighted face on a stage, with an expression upon it of childlike interest and delight. "But he's firing that Lewis," Bogard thought. "Straight too"; nosing the machine farther down, watching the pinpoints swing into the sights, his right hand lifted, waiting to drop into McGinnis' sight. He dropped his hand; above the noise of the engines he seemed to hear the click and whistle of the released bombs as the machine freed of the weight, shot zooming in a long upward bounce that carried it for an instant out of the light. Then he was pretty busy for a time, coming into and through the shells again, shooting athwart another beam that caught and held long enough for him to see the English boy leaning far over the side, looking back and down past the right wing, the undercarriage. "Maybe he's read about it somewhere," Bogard thought, turning, looking back to pick up the rest of the flight.

Then it was all over, the darkness cool and empty and peaceful and almost quiet, with only the steady sound of the engines. McGinnis climbed
back into the office, and standing up in his seat, he fired the colored pistol
this time and stood for a moment longer, looking backward toward where
the searchlights still probed and sabered. He sat down again.

"O.K.," he said. "I counted all four of them. Let's haul air." Then he
looked forward. "What's become of the King's Own? You didn't hang him
onto a bomb release, did you?" Bogard looked. The forward pit was empty.
It was in dim silhouette again now, against the stars, but there was nothing
there now save the gun. "No," McGinnis said; there he is. See? Leaning
overside. Dammit, I told him not to spew it! There he comes back!" The
guest's head came into view again. But again it sank out of sight.

"He's coming back," Bogard said. "Stop him. Tell him we're going to
have every squadron in the Hun Channel group on top of us in thirty
minutes."

McGinnis swung himself down and stooped at the entrance to the passage. "Get back!" he shouted. The other was almost out; they squatted so,
face to face like two dogs, shouting at another above the noise of the still-
unthrottled engines on either side of the fabric walls. The English boy's
voice was thin and high.

"Bomb!" he shrieked.

"Yes," McGinnis shouted. "They were bombs! We gave them hell! Get
back I tell you! Have every Hun in France on us in ten minutes! Get back to
your gun!"

Again the boy's voice came, high, faint above the noise: "Bomb! All
right?"

"Yes! Yes! All right. Back to your gun, damn you!"

McGinnis climbed back into the office. "He went back. Want me to take
her awhile?"

"All right," Bogard said. He passed McGinnis the wheel. "Ease her back
some. I'd just as soon it was daylight when they come down on us."

"Right," McGinnis said. He moved the wheel suddenly. "What's the
matter with that right wing?" he said. "Watch it. . . . See? I'm flying on the
right aileron and a little rudder. Feel it."

Bogard took the wheel a moment. "I didn't notice that. Wire somewhere,
I guess. I didn't think any of those shells were that close. Watch her, though."

"Right," McGinnis said. "And so you are going with him on his boat
tomorrow—today."

"Yes, I promised him. Confound it, you can't hurt a kid, you know."

"Why don't you take Collier along, with his mandolin? Then you could
said around and sing."

"I promised him," Bogard said. "Get that wing up a little."

"Right," McGinnis said.

Thirty minutes later it was beginning to be dawn; the sky was gray. Presently McGinnis said: "Well, here they come. Look at them! They look like mosquitoes in September. I hope he don't get worked up now and think he's playing beaver. If he does he'll just be one down to Ronnie, provided the devil has a beard. . . . Want the wheel?"

V

At eight o'clock the beach, the Channel, was beneath them. Throttled back, the machine drifted down as Bogard ruddered it gently into the Channel wind. His face was strained, a little tired.

McGinnis looked tired, too, and he needed a shave.

"What do you guess he is looking at now?" he said. For again the English boy was leaning over the right side of the cockpit, looking backward and downward past the right wing.

"I don't know," Bogard said. "Maybe bullet holes." He blasted the port engine. "Must have the riggers——"

"He could see some closer than that," McGinnis said. "I'll swear I saw tracer going into his back at one time. Or maybe it's the ocean he's looking at. But he must have seen that when he came over from England." Then Bogard leveled off; the nose rose sharply, the sand, the curling tide edge fled along-side. Yet still the English boy hung far overside, looking backward and downward at something beneath the right wing, his face rapt, with utter and childlike interest. Until the machine was completely stopped he continued to do so. Then he ducked down, and in the abrupt silence of the engines they could hear him crawling in the passage. He emerged just as the two pilots climbed stiffly down from the office, his face bright, eager; his voice high, excited.

"Oh, I say! Oh, good gad! What a chap! What a judge of distance! If Ronnie could only have seen! Oh, good gad! Or maybe they aren't like ours—don't load themselves as soon as the air strikes them."

The Americans looked at him. "What don't what?" McGinnis said.

"The bomb. It was magnificent; I say, I shan't forget it. Oh, I say, you know! It was splendid!"

After a while McGinnis said, "The bomb?" in a fainting voice. Then the two pilots glared at each other; they said in unison: "That right wing!" Then as one they clawed down through the trap and, with the guest at their heels, they ran around the machine and looked beneath the right wing. The bomb, suspended by its tail, hung straight down like a plumb bob beside the right wheel, its tip just touching the sand. And parallel with the wheel track was the long delicate line in the sand where its ultimate tip had dragged. Behind them the English boy's voice was high, clear, childlike:

"Frightened, myself. Tried to tell you. But realized you knew your business better than I. Skill. Marvelous. Oh, I say, I shan't forget it."

VI

A marine with a bayoneted rifle passed Bogard onto the wharf and directed him to the boat. The wharf was empty, and he didn't even see the boat until he approached the edge of the wharf and looked directly down into it and upon the backs of two stooping men in greasy dungarees, who rose and glanced briefly at him and stooped again.

It was about thirty feet long and about three feet wide. It was painted with gray-green camouflage. It was quarter-decked forward, with two blunt, raked exhaust stacks. "Good Lord," Bogard thought, "if all that deck is engine—" Just aft the deck was the control seat; he saw a big wheel, an instrument panel. Rising to a height of about a foot above the freeboard, and running from the stern forward to where the deck began, and continuing on across the after edge of the deck and thence back down the other gunwale to the stern, was a solid screen, also camouflaged, which inclosed the boat save for the width of the stern, which was open. Facing the steerman's seat like an eye was a hole in the screen about eight inches in diameter. And looking down into the long, narrow, still, vicious shape, he saw a machine gun swiveled at the stern, and he looked at the low screen—including which the whole vessel did not sit much more than a yard above water level—with its single empty forward-staring eye, and he thought quietly: "It's steel. It's made of steel." And his face was quite sober, quite thoughtful, and he drew his trench coat about him and buttoned it, as though he were getting cold.

He heard steps behind him and turned. But it was only an orderly from the aerodrome, accompanied by the marine with the rifle. The orderly was carrying a largish bundle wrapped in paper.

"From Lieutenant McGinnis to the captain," the orderly said.

Bogard took the bundle. The orderly and the marine retreated. He opened the bundle. It contained some objects and a scrawled note. The objects were a new yellow silk sofa cushion and a Japanese parasol, obviously borrowed, and a comb and a roll of toilet paper. The note said:

> Couldn't find a camera anywhere and Collier wouldn't let me have his mandolin. But maybe Ronnie can play on the comb.
>
> Mac.

Bogard looked at the objects. But his face was still quite thoughtful, quite grave. He rewrapped the things and carried the bundle on up the wharf a way and dropped it quietly into the water.

As he returned toward the invisible boat he saw two men approaching. He recognized the boy at once—tall, slender, already talking, voluble, his head bent a little toward his shorter companion, who plodded along beside him, hands in pockets, smoking a pipe. The boy still wore the pea-coat beneath a flapping oilskin, but in place of the rakish and casual cap he now wore an infantryman's soiled Balaclava helmet, with, floating behind him as though upon the sound of his voice, a curtainlike piece of cloth almost as long as a burnous.

"Hullo, there!" he cried, still a hundred yards away.

But it was the second man that Bogard was watching, thinking to himself that he had never in his life seen a more curious figure. There was something stolid about the very shape of his hunched shoulders, his slightly down-looking face. He was a head shorter than the other. His face was ruddy, too, but its mold was a profound gravity that was almost dour. It was the face of a man of twenty who has been for a year trying, even while asleep, to look twenty-one. He wore a high-necked sweater and dungaree slacks; above this a leather jacket; and above this a soiled naval officer's warmer that reached almost to his heels and which had one shoulder strap missing and not one remaining button at all. On his head was a plaid fore-and-aft deer stalker's cap, tied on by a narrow scarf brought across and down, hiding his ears, and then wrapped once about his throat and knotted with a hangman's noose beneath his left ear. It was unbelievably soiled, and with his hands elbow-deep in his pockets and his hunched shoulders and his bent head, he looked like someone's grandmother hung, say, for witch. Clamped upside down between his teeth was a short brier pipe.

"Here he is!" the boy cried. "This is Ronnie. Captain Bogard."

"How are you?" Bogard said. He extended his hand. The other said no word, but his hand came forth, limp. It was quite cold, but it was hard, calloused. But he said no word; he just glanced briefly at Bogard and then away. But in that instant Bogard caught something in the look, something strange—a flicker; a kind of covert and curious respect, something like a boy of fifteen looking at a circus trapezist.

But he said no word. He ducked on; Bogard watched him drop from sight over the wharf edge as though he had jumped feet first into the sea. He remarked now that the engines in the invisible boat were running.

"We might get aboard too," the boy said. He started toward the boat, then he stopped. He touched Bogard's arm. "Yonder!" he hissed. "See?" His voice was thin with excitement.

"What?" Bogard also whispered; automatically he looked backward and upward, after old habit. The other was gripping his arm and pointing across the harbor.

"There! Over there. The *Ergenstrasse*. They have shifted her again." Across the harbor lay an ancient, rusting, sway-backed hulk. It was small and nondescript, and, remembering, Bogard saw the foremast was a strange mess of cables and booms, resembling—allowing for a great deal of license or looseness of imagery—a basket mast. Beside him the boy was almost chortling. "Do you think that Ronnie noticed?" he hissed. "Do you?"

"I don't know," Bogard said.

"Oh, good gad! If he should glance up and call her before he notices, we'll be even. Oh, good gad! But come along." He went on; he was still chortling. "Careful," he said. "Frightful ladder."

He descended first, the two men in the boat rising and saluting. Ronnie had disappeared, save for his backside, which now filled a small hatch leading forward beneath the deck. Bogard descended gingerly.

"Good Lord," he said. "Do you have to climb up and down this every day?"

"Frightful, isn't it?" the other said, in his happy voice. "But you know yourself. Try to run a war with makeshifts, then wonder why it takes so long." The narrow hull slid and surged, even with Bogard's added weight. "Sits right on top, you see," the boy said. "Would float on a lawn, in a heavy dew. Goes right over them like a bit of paper."

"It does?" Bogard said.

"Oh, absolutely. That's why, you see." Bogard didn't see, but he was too busy letting himself gingerly down to a sitting posture. There were no thwarts; no seats save a long, thick, cylindrical ridge which ran along the bottom of the boat from the driver's seat to the stern. Ronnie had backed into sight. He now sat behind the wheel, bent over the instrument panel. But when he glanced back over his shoulder he did not speak. His face was merely interrogatory. Across his face there was now a long smudge of grease. The boy's face was empty, too, now.

"Right," he said. He looked forward, where one of the seamen had gone. "Ready forward?" he said.

"Aye, sir," the seaman said.

The other seaman was at the stern line. "Ready aft?"

"Aye, sir."

"Cast off." The boat sheered away, purring, a boiling of water under the stern. The boy looked down at Bogard. "Silly business. Do it shipshape, though. Can't tell when silly fourstriper—" His face changed again, immediate, solicitous. "I say. Will you be warm? I never thought to fetch—"

"I'll be all right," Bogard said. But the other was already taking off his oilskin. "No, no," Bogard said. "I won't take it."

"You'll tell me if you get cold?"

"Yes. Sure." He was looking down at the cylinder on which he sat. It was a half cylinder—that is, like the hot-water tank to some Gargantuan stove, sliced down the middle and bolted, open side down, to the floor plates. It was twenty feet long and more than two feet thick. Its top rose as high as the gunwales and between it and the hull on either side was just room enough for a man to place his feet to walk.

"That's Muriel," the boy said.

"Muriel?"

"Yes. The one before that was Agatha. After my aunt. The first one Ronnie and I had was Alice in Wonderland. Ronnie and I were the White Rabbit. Jolly, eh?"

"Oh, you and Ronnie have had three, have you?"

"Oh, yes," the boy said. He leaned down. "He didn't notice," he whispered. His face was again bright, gleeful. "When we come back," he said. "You watch."

"Oh," Bogard said. "The *Ergenstrasse*." He looked astern, and then he thought: "Good Lord! We must be going—traveling." He looked out now, broadside, and saw the harbor line fleeing past, and he thought to himself that the boat was well-nigh moving at the speed at which the Handley-Page flew, left the ground. They were beginning to bound now, even in the sheltered water, from one wave crest to the next with a distinct shock. His hand still rested on the cylinder on which he sat. He looked down at it again, following it from where it seemed to emerge beneath Ronnie's seat, to where it beveled into the stern. "It's the air in here, I suppose."

"The what?" the boy said.

"The air. Stored up in here. That makes the boat ride high."

"Oh, yes. I dare say. Very likely. I hadn't thought about it." He came forward, his burnous whipping in the wind, and sat down beside Bogard. Their heads were below the top of the screen.

Astern the harbor fled, diminishing, sinking into the sea. The boat had begun to lift now, swooping forward and down, shocking almost stationary for a moment, then lifting and swooping again; a gout of spray came aboard over the bows like a flung shovelful of shot. "I wish you'd take this coat," the boy said.

Bogard didn't answer. He looked around at the bright face. "We're outside, aren't we?" he said quietly.

"Yes. . . . Do take it, won't you?"

"Thanks, no. I'll be all right. We won't be long, anyway, I guess."

"No. We'll turn soon. It won't be so bad then."

"Yes. I'll be all right when we turn." Then they did turn. The motion became easier. That is, the boat didn't bang head-on, shuddering, into the swells. They came up beneath now, and the boat fled with increased speed, with a long, sickening, yawning motion, first to one side and then the other.

But it fled on, and Bogard looked astern with that same soberness with which he had first looked down into the boat. "We're going east now," he said.

"With just a spot of north," the boy said. "Makes her ride a bit better, what?"

"Yes," Bogard said. Astern there was nothing now save empty sea and the delicate needlelike cant of the machine gun against the boiling and slewing wake, and the two seamen crouching quietly in the stern. "Yes. It's easier." Then he said: "How far do we go?"

The boy leaned closer. He moved closer. His voice was happy, confidential, proud, though lowered a little: "It's Ronnie's show. He thought of it. Not that I wouldn't have, in time. Gratitude and all that. But he's the older, you see. Thinks fast. Courtesy, *noblesse oblige*—all that. Thought of it soon as I told him this morning. I said, 'Oh, I say. I've been there. I've seen it'; and he said, 'Not flying?'; and I said, 'Strewth'; and he said 'How far? No lying now'; and I said, 'Oh, far. Tremendous. Gone all night'; and he said, 'Flying all night. That must have been to Berlin'; and I said, 'I don't know. I dare say'; and he thought. I could see him thinking. Because he is the older, you see. More experience in courtesy, right thing. And he said, 'Berlin. No fun to that chap, dashing out and back with us.' And he thought and I waited, and I said, 'But we can't take him to Berlin. Too far. Don't know the way, either'; and he said—fast, like a shot—said, 'But there's Kiel'; and I knew—"

"What?" Bogard said. Without moving, his whole body sprang. "Kiel? In this?"

"Absolutely. Ronnie thought of it. Smart, even if he is a stickler. Said at once 'Zeebrugge no show at all for that chap. Must do best we can for him. Berlin,' Ronnie said. 'My gad! Berlin.'"

"Listen," Bogard said. He had turned now, facing the other, his face quite grave. "What is this boat for?"

"For?"

"What does it do?" Then, knowing beforehand the answer to his own question, he said, putting his hand on the cylinder: "What is this in here? A torpedo, isn't it?"

"I thought you knew," the boy said.

"No," Bogard said. "I didn't know." His voice seemed to reach him from a distance, dry, cricketlike: "How do you fire it?"

"Fire it?"

"How do you get it out of the boat? When that hatch was open a while ago I could see the engines. They were right in front of the end of this tube."

"Oh," the boy said. "You pull a gadget there and the torpedo drops out astern. As soon as the screw touches the water it begins to turn, and then the torpedo is ready, loaded. Then all you have to do is turn the boat quickly and the torpedo goes on."

"You mean—" Bogard said. After a moment his voice obeyed him again. "You mean you aim the torpedo with the boat and release it and it starts moving, and you turn the boat out of the way and the torpedo passes through the same water that the boat just vacated?"

"Knew you'd catch on," the boy said. "Told Ronnie so. Airman. Tamer than yours, though. But can't be helped. Best we can do, just on water. But knew you'd catch on."

"Listen," Bogard said. His voice sounded to him quite calm. The boat fled on, yawing over the swells. He sat quite motionless. It seemed to him that he could hear himself talking to himself: "Go on. Ask him. Ask him what? Ask him how close to the ship do you have to be before you fire. . . . Listen," he said, in that calm voice. "Now, you tell Ronnie, you see. You just tell him—just say—" He could feel his voice ratting off on him again, so he stopped it. He sat quite motionless, waiting for it to come back; the boy leaning now, looking at his face. Again the boy's voice was solicitous:

"I say. You're not feeling well. These confounded shallow boats."

"It's not that," Bogard said. "I just— Do your orders say Kiel?"

"Oh, no. They let Ronnie say. Just so we bring the boat back. This is for you. Gratitude. Ronnie's idea. Tame, after flying. But if you'd rather, eh?"

"Yes, some place closer. You see, I—"

"Quite. I see. No vacations in wartime. I'll tell Ronnie." He went forward. Bogard did not move. The boat fled in long, slewing swoops. Bogard looked quietly astern, at the scudding sea, the sky.

"My God!" he thought. "Can you beat it? Can you beat it?"

The boy came back; Bogard turned to him a face the color of dirty paper. "All right now," the boy said. "Not Kiel. Nearer place, hunting probably just as good. Ronnie says he knows you will understand." He was tugging at his pocket. He brought out a bottle. "Here. Haven't forgot last night. Do the same for you. Good for the stomach, eh?"

Bogard drank, gulping—a big one. He extended the bottle, but the boy refused. "Never touch it on duty," he said. "Not like you chaps. Tame here."

The boat fled on. The sun was already down the west. But Bogard had lost all count of time, of distance. Ahead he could see white seas through the round eye opposite Ronnie's face, and Ronnie's hand on the wheel and the granite-like jut of his profiled jaw and the dead upside-down pipe. The boat fled on.

Then the boy leaned and touched his shoulder. He half rose. The boy was pointing. The sun was reddish; against it, outside them and about two miles away, a vessel—a trawler, it looked like—at anchor swung a tall mast.

"Lightship!" the boy shouted. "Theirs." Ahead Bogard could see a low, flat mole—the entrance to a harbor. "Channel!" the boy shouted. He swept his arm in both directions. "Mines!" His voice swept back on the wind. "Place filthy with them. All sides. Beneath us too, Lark, eh?"

VII

Against the mole a fair surf was beating. Running before the seas now, the boat seemed to leap from one roller to the next; in the intervals while the screw was in the air the engine seemed to be trying to tear itself out by the roots. But it did not slow; when it passed the end of the mole the boat seemed to be standing almost erect on its rudder, like a sailfish. The mole was a mile away. From the end of it little faint lights began to flicker like fireflies. The boy leaned. "Down," he said. "Machine guns. Might stop a stray."

"What do I do?" Bogard shouted. "What can I do?"

"Stout fellow! Give them hell, what? Knew you'd like it!"

Crouching, Bogard looked up at the boy, his face wild. "I can handle the machine gun!"

"No need," the boy shouted back. "Give them first innings. Sporting. Visitors, eh?" He was looking forward. "There she is. See?" They were in the harbor now, the basin opening before them. Anchored in the channel was a big freighter. Painted midships of the hull was a huge Argentine flag. "Must get back to stations!" the boy shouted down to him. Then at that moment Ronnie spoke for the first time. The boat was hurtling along now in smoother water. Its speed did not slacken and Ronnie did not turn his head when he spoke. He just swung his jutting jaw and the clamped cold pipe a little, and said from the side of his mouth a single word:

"Beaver."

The boy, stooped over what he had called his gadget, jerked up, his expression astonished and outraged. Bogard also looked forward and saw Ronnie's arm pointing to starboard. It was a light cruiser at anchor a mile away. She had basket masts, and as he looked a gun flashed from her after turret. "Oh, damn!" the boy cried. "Oh, you putt! Oh, confound you, Ronnie! Now I'm three down!" But he had already stooped again over his gadget, his face bright and empty and alert again; not sober; just calm, waiting. Again Bogard looked forward and felt the boat pivot on its rudder and head directly for the freighter at terrific speed. Ronnie now with one hand on the wheel and the other lifted and extended at the height of his head.

But it seemed to Bogard that the hand would never drop. He crouched, not sitting, watching with a kind of quiet horror the painted flag increase like a moving picture of a locomotive taken from between the rails. Again the gun crashed from the cruiser behind them, and the freighter fired point-blank at them from its poop. Bogard heard neither shot.

"Man, man!" he shouted. "For God's sake!"

Ronnie's hand dropped. Again the boat spun on its rudder. Bogard saw the bow rise, pivoting; he expected the hull to slam broadside on into the ship. But it didn't. It shot off on a long tangent. He was waiting for it to make a wide sweep, heading seaward, putting the freighter astern, and he thought of the cruiser again. "Get a broadside, this time, once we clear the freighter," he thought. Then he remembered the freighter, the torpedo, and looked back toward the freighter to watch the torpedo strike, and saw to his horror that the boat was now bearing down on the freighter again, in a skidding turn. Like a man in a dream, he watched himself rush down upon the ship and shoot past under her counter, still skidding, close enough to see the faces on her decks. "They missed and they are going to run down the torpedo and catch it and shoot it again," he thought idiotically.

So the boy had to touch his shoulder before he knew he was behind him. The boy's voice was quite calm: "Under Ronnie's seat there. A bit of a crank handle. If you'll just hand it to me——"

He found the crank. He passed it back; he was thinking dreamily: "Mac would say they had a telephone on board." But he didn't look at once to see what the boy was doing with it, for in that still and peaceful horror he was watching Ronnie, the cold pipe rigid in his jaw, hurling the boat at top speed round and round the freighter, so near that he could see the rivets in the plates. Then he looked aft, his face wild, importunate, and he saw what the boy was doing with the crank. He had fitted it into what was obviously a small windlass low on one flank of the tube near the head. He glanced up and saw Bogard's face. "Didn't go that time!" he shouted cheerfully.

"Go?" Bogard shouted. "It didn't— The torpedo—"

The boy and one of the seamen were quite busy, stooping over the windlass and the tube. "No. Clumsy. Always happening. Should think clever chaps like engineers— Happens, though. Draw her in and try her again."

"But the nose, the cap!" Bogard shouted. It's still in the tube, isn't it? It's all right, isn't it?"

"Absolutely. But it's working now. Loaded. Screw's started turning. Get it back and drop it clear. If we should stop or slow up it would overtake us. Drive back into the tube. Bingo! What?"

Bogard was on his feet now, turned, braced to the terrific merry-go-round of the boat. High above them the freighter seemed to be spinning on her heel like a trick picture in the movies. "Let me have that winch!" he cried.

"Steady!" the boy said. "Mustn't draw her back too fast. Jam her into the head of the tube ourselves. Same bingo! Best let us. Every cobbler to his last, what?"

"Oh, quite," Bogard said. "Oh, absolutely." It was like someone else using his mouth. He leaned, braced, his hands on the cold tube, beside the others. He was hot inside, but his outside was cold. He could feel all his flesh jerking with cold as he watched the blunt, grained hand of the seaman turning the windlass in short, easy, inch-long arcs, while at the head of the tube the boy bent, tapping the cylinder with a spanner, lightly, his head turned with listening delicate and deliberate as a watchmaker. The boat rushed on in those furious, slewing turns. Bogard saw a long, drooping thread loop down from somebody's mouth, between his hands, and he found that the thread came from his own mouth.

He didn't hear the boy speak, nor notice when he stood up. He just felt the boat straighten out, flinging him to his knees beside the tube. The seaman had gone back to the stern and the boy stooped again over his gadget. Bogard knelt now, quite sick. He did not feel the boat when it swung again, nor hear the gun from the cruiser which had not dared to fire and the freighter which had not been able to fire, firing again. He did not feel anything at all when he saw the huge, painted flag directly ahead, and increasing with locomotive speed, and Ronnie's lifted hand drop. But this time he knew that the torpedo was gone; in pivoting and spinning this time the whole boat seemed to leave the water; he saw the bow of the boat shoot skyward like the nose of a pursuit ship going into a wingover. Then his outraged stomach denied him. He saw neither the geyser nor heard the detonation as he sprawled over the tube. He felt only a hand grasp him by the slack of his coat, and the voice of one of the seamen: "Steady all, sir. I've got you."

VIII

A voice roused him, a hand. He was half sitting in the narrow starboard runway, half lying across the tube. He had been there for quite a while; quite a while ago he had felt someone spread a garment over him. But he had not raised his head. "I'm all right," he said, "You keep it."

"Don't need it," the boy said. "Going home now."

"I'm sorry I—" Bogard said.

"Quite. Confounded shallow boats. Turn any stomach until you get used to them. Ronnie and I both, at first. Each time. You wouldn't believe it. Believe human stomach hold so much. Here." It was the bottle. "Good drink. Take enormous one. Good for stomach."

Bogard drank. Soon he did feel better, warmer. When the hand touched him later, he found that he had been asleep.

It was the boy again. The pea-coat was too small for him; shrunken, perhaps. Below the cuffs his long, slender, girl's wrists were blue with cold. Then Bogard realized what the garment was that had been laid over him. But before Bogard could speak, the boy leaned down, whispering; his face was gleeful: "He didn't notice!"

"What?"

"*Ergenstrasse!* He didn't notice that they had shifted her. Gad, I'd be just one down, then." He watched Bogard's face with bright, eager eyes. "Beaver, you know. I say. Feeling better, eh?"

"Yes," Bogard said. "I am."

"He didn't notice at all. Oh, gad! Oh, Jove!"

Bogard rose and sat on the tube. The entrance to the harbor was just ahead; the boat had slowed a little. It was just dusk. He said quietly: "Does this often happen?" The boy looked at him. Bogard touched the tube. "This. Failing to go out."

"Oh, yes. When they put the windlass on them. That was later. Made first boat; whole thing blew up one day. So put on windlass."

"But it happens sometimes, even now? I mean, sometimes they blow up, even with the windlass?"

"Well, can't say, of course. Boats go out. Not come back. Possible. Not ever know, of course. Not heard of one captured yet, though. Possible. Not to us, though. Not yet."

"Yes," Bogard said. "Yes." They entered the harbor, the boat moving still fast, but throttled now and smooth, across the dusk-filled basin. Again the boy leaned down, his voice gleeful.

"Not a word, now!" he hissed. "Steady all!" He stood up; he raised his voice: "I say, Ronnie." Ronnie did not turn his head, but Bogard could tell that he was listening. "That Argentine ship was amusing, eh? In there. How do you suppose it got past us here? Might have stopped here as well. French would buy the wheat." He paused, diabolical—Machiavelli with the face of a strayed angel. "I say. How long has it been since we had a strange ship in here? Been months, eh?" Again he leaned, hissing. "Watch, now!" But Bogard could not see Ronnie's head move at all. "He's looking, though!" the boy whispered, breathed. And Ronnie was looking, though his head had not moved at all. Then there came into view, in silhouette against the dusk-filled sky, the vague, basket-like shape of the interned vessel's foremast. At once Ronnie's arm rose, pointing; again he spoke without turning his head, out of the side of his mouth, past the cold, clamped pipe, a single word:

"Beaver."

The boy moved like a released spring, like a heeled dog freed. "Oh, damn you!" he cried. "Oh, you putt! It's the *Ergenstrasse!* Oh, confound you! I'm just one down now!" He had stepped one stride completely over

Bogard, and he now leaned down over Ronnie. "What?" The boat was slowing in toward the wharf, the engine idle. "Aren't I, Ronnie? Just one down now?"

The boat drifted in; the seamen had again crawled forward onto the deck. Ronnie spoke for the third and last time. "Right," he said.

IX

"I want," Bogard said, "a case of Scotch. The best we've got. And fix it up good. It's to go to town. And I want a responsible man to deliver it." The responsible man came. "This is for a child," Bogard said, indicating the package. "You'll find him in the Street of the Twelve Hours, somewhere near the Café Twelve Hours. He'll be in the gutter. You'll know him. A child about six feet long. Any English M.P. will show him to you. If he is asleep, don't wake him. Just sit there and wait until he wakes up. Then give him this. Tell him it is from Captain Bogard."

X

About a month later a copy of the English Gazette which had strayed onto an American aerodrome carried the following item in the casualty lists:

> MISSING; Torpedo Boat XOOI. Midshipmen R. Boyce Smith and L. C. W. Hope, R. N. R., Boatswain's Mate Burt and Able Seaman Reeves, Channel Fleet, Light Torpedo Division. Failed to return from coast patrol duty.

Shortly after that the American Air Service headquarters also issued a bulletin:

> For extraordinary valor over and beyond the routine of duty, Captain H. S. Bogard, with his crew, composed of Second Lieutenant Darrel McGinnis and Aviation Gunners Watts and Harper, on a daylight raid and without scout protection, destroyed with bombs an ammunition depot several miles behind the enemy's lines. From here, beset by enemy aircraft in superior numbers, these men proceeded with what bombs remained to the enemy's corps headquarters at Blank and partially demolished this château, and then returned safely without loss of a man.

And regarding which exploit, it might have been added, had it failed and had Captain Bogard come out of it alive, he would have been immediately and thoroughly court-martialed.

Carrying his remaining two bombs, he had dived the Handley-Page at the château where the generals sat at lunch, until McGinnis, at the toggles below him, began to shout at him, before he ever signaled. He didn't signal until he could discern separately the slate tiles of the roof. Then his hand dropped and he zoomed, and he held the aeroplane so, in its wild snarl, his lips parted, his breath hissing, thinking: "God! God! If they were all there— all the generals, the admirals, the presidents, and the kings—theirs, ours— all of them."

WILLIAM FAULKNER
1897–1962

Born in New Albany, Mississippi, Faulkner was raised in nearby Oxford. He left high school to join the Royal Canadian Flying Corps as a pilot, but World War I ended before he completed his training.

He returned to Oxford where, except for a tour of Europe and brief residencies in New Orleans, New York, and Hollywood, he spent the rest of his life in seclusion. A few close friends believed in the power of his writing early on. Sherwood Anderson helped him get his first novel, *Soldier's Pay* (1926), into print.

His most famous work recounts the history of the residents of his fictitious Yoknapatawpha county, a microcosm of the South as a whole. The following novels are only a sampling of his prolific output: *Sartoris* (1929), *The Sound and the Fury* (1929), *As I Lay Dying* (1930), *Sanctuary* (1931), *Light in August* (1932), *Absalom, Absalom!* (1936), *The Hamlet* (1940), *Go Down Moses* (1942), and *The Town* (1957).

In 1949 Faulkner received the Nobel Prize for literature and the National Book Award for his *Collected Stories* (1959). He also won the Pulitzer Prize for two novels, *A Fable* (1954) and *The Reivers* (1962).

While most of his fiction takes place on land, Faulkner wrote several sea stories, among them "Once Aboard the Lugger" and the selection included here, both from *Dr. Martino and Other Stories* (1934).

Night Stalk

BY C. S. FORESTER

"There aren't any whales in the Mediterranean," said Nickleby, the flotilla gunnery officer, in tones of deep satisfaction.

"There are big tunny fish, though, that go in shoals," said Rowles, the navigating officer.

"What about cold currents?" asked Captain Crowe. This discussion dealt with the sort of technical point to solve for which he had been specially surrounded by his highly trained staff officers, but he knew enough of the subject to take part in the argument.

"Nothing here worth mentioning, sir," said Rowles. "Of course, there may be a casual freak."

"Wrecks?" asked Holby.

"Plenty of those," admitted Rowles.

The flotilla was creeping through the night, guided by the most minute physical influences imaginable—too minute really for the human imagination to grasp, thought Crowe; the merest echoes of something already beyond human senses. They were trailing a submarine. Somewhere inside H.M.S. *Apache* a skilled rating was sending out sound waves into the sea with an apparatus that had never been thought of before Crowe became captain. It was all very difficult, for these sound waves were not the sort that one could hear; they were too high-pitched for that. Crowe could remember being shown a dog whistle once which blew a note too high for the human ear, but which yet could be heard by a dog. The sounds being sent out through the water were the same kind of noiseless sounds—what an absurd expression!—but even higher in pitch.

The principle was that when these radiating waves struck a solid body in the water, a minute proportion of them bounced back and could be picked up in the ship by an apparatus even more novel than the one which sent them out.

The fantastic sensitiveness of the whole affair could lead sometimes to curious results—the shoals of pilchards off the Cornish coast had been depth-charged more than once, and the dividing wall between a cold current and a warm current could reflect enough of the waves as well as refracting the rest to produce a positive indication in the receiver, so that the ship might find itself launching an attack upon nothing at all, like a blindfolded fighter assaulting a whiff of cigaret smoke.

It was like some deadly game of blindman's buff, or like two men stalking each other with revolvers in a completely dark room, for the submarine was by no means helpless; as she crept about underwater her own instruments could tell her, roughly, the bearing of her enemy, and when she was pressed too hard she could endeavor to relieve herself of her enemy's attentions by a salvo of torpedoes loosed off in the general direction of the pursuing ship.

The little chartroom was hot with the heat of the Mediterranean summer night and the stuffiness which comes with the inevitable interference with ventilation caused by the complete darkening of the ship. Rowles was bent over a large sheet of squared paper on which, with the aid of protractor and dividers, he was plotting the moves of the deadly game.

"*Cheyenne* signals, 'Three-four-O,'" came the voice of the chief yeoman of signals down the voice pipe from the bridge.

"Three-forty degrees!" exclaimed Rowles eagerly. "That gives us a fix."

Cheyenne was in the second division of destroyers out to port and she was giving the bearing of the unseen submarine as deduced from her instruments. Crowe could picture the transmission of the signal, the tiny flashes of the signaling lamp, screened and hooded, so that only the *Apache*, and no possible enemy, could pick them up. Rowles drew another line on his squared paper and made a cabalistic sign at the end of it. "Mmm," he said, "don't think it can be a cold current. And it seems to have moved, so it's not a wreck. Too many propellers going for the hydrophones to help us out."

Twenty years ago the hydrophone had been the only instrument which could be used for tracking a submarine; it actually listened to the beat of the submarine's propeller, and all the efforts of all the scientists had not yet succeeded in improving it to the point where it could pick up and follow the sound of a submarine's propeller through the noise of those of a whole flotilla.

The message tube buzzed, and Holby snatched the little brass cylinder from it, took out the message and tossed it across to Rowles, who read it eagerly. He ruled another line on his squared paper; the diagram he was drawing there was beginning to take some kind of shape, for the lines all had a general trend, and the little ringed numbers made a series which, though wavering, still had definition.

"I'd like to alter course, sir, if you please," said Rowles, and Crowe nodded.

Rowles spoke first into one voice tube and then into another. It was only an alteration of five degrees, but, with the flotilla fanned out on a wide front in pitch-darkness and with signals restricted to the barest minimum, it was not such a simple matter to wheel the line round as might at first be supposed. A moment later Rowles asked for an increase in speed, and the officers sitting in the silent little cabin were conscious for a brief space of a change in the tempo of the throbbing of the propellers; at the end of that time they were accustomed to the new rhythm and the throbbing passed unnoticed again. Then came fresh information, messages from the sonic apparatus below and from other destroyers in the flotilla.

"He's altered course," said Rowles.

The captain of the hunted submarine was receiving indications as well, and was turning his boat in a desperate effort to get out of the path of his enemies. But submerged as he was he could only creep along at six knots, while the destroyers were charging down on him at twenty-five. If only they could maintain contact with him, his end was certain. Rowles wheeled the flotilla farther round to intercept him.

Another voice tube in the little chartroom squeaked a warning, and Holby answered it.

"Torpedoes fired," he announced. The hydrophone apparatus had picked up the heavy underwater concussion. The Italian was trying to rid himself of pursuit by launching his torpedoes into the midst of his pursuers. Firing underwater and aiming only on the strength of the data supplied him by his sound apparatus, he could not hope for very accurate aim; the deployed destroyers made a wide target, but one with a good many gaps in it.

"One hundred and sixty seconds, I should say," said Holby, and all eyes turned involuntarily on the stopwatch ticking away on the chartroom table. With torpedoes and destroyers approaching one another at eighty knots, each little jump of the hand brought potential death forty yards nearer. Crowe took his attention from the watch and turned it upon Rowles' diagram. The destroyers were headed straight for the submarine, meeting the torpedoes head-on, therefore. That was the best way to receive a torpedo attack—a destroyer is ten times as long as she is wide, and, consequently, the chances of a blind shot missing were ten times as great. There was nothing to be done except wait.

The messages were still coming in, even during that two and a half minutes.

"Gone to ground," said Rowles, "on the bottom. It's his best chance, I suppose."

Lying absolutely silent and still on the bottom, the submarine would give no indication of its position to the hydrophone listeners and precious little to the sonic apparatus. And the Italian captain had taken his action while there was still plenty of time, while the English still were not absolutely sure of his position, and while there was a chance that the arrival of his torpedoes might distract his enemies, throw them off their course and upset their calculations. If he pinned much hope on this, however, he did not know the grim little group that was sitting round the chartroom table plotting his doom. The stopwatch hand was creeping inexorably round. Suddenly the *Apache* stopped as if she had run into a brick wall, throwing them all across the chartroom, and then she reared and then she plunged, standing almost up on her stern and then crashing down again, with the lights flickering spasmodically, while the memory of a tremendous crash of sound echoed in their ears. Crowe had been flung against the bulkhead and the breath driven from his body; it was pure instinct that carried him out onto the bridge; as his eyes were accustoming themselves to the darkness he could feel the *Apache* heeling and turning sharply. A black ghost of a ship whisked past their stern, missing them by a hairbreadth—that was *Navaho*, that had been following them. The officers and ratings on the bridge, flung down by the explosion, were only now picking themselves up.

"Hard-a-starboard there!" roared Hammett.

"She won't answer, sir!" came the helmsman's reply. "Wheel's right over!"

The *Apache* was turning sharply in defiance of her helm.

"Bow's a bit twisted, I should say," said Crowe, peering forward into the darkness, alongside Hammett; he could feel now that the bows were canted sharply downward as well, but in the utter darkness he could form no estimate at all of the amount of damage. The only thing that was certain was that the *Apache* was not on fire; a destroyer full of oil fuel, hit by a torpedo, can sometimes in a few seconds be changed into a blazing volcano.

"Midships!" said Hammet to the quartermaster, and then busied himself with the engine-room telegraph before explaining to Crowe, "I thought I'd let her complete the turn, sir."

"Go astern with the starboard engine as she comes round," said Crowe, and was promptly annoyed with himself for interfering with Hammett when the latter was doing perfectly well.

There were voices to be heard forward now as the stunned members of the crew picked themselves up and the emergency party reached the seat of the damage. The *Apache* was completing her turn, having lost a good deal of her way.

"Hard-a-starboard!" said Hammett again to the helmsman, and the ship trembled with the vibration of the starboard propeller going astern.

From forward there came a tremendous crackling as rivets sheared; the bows of the ship rose perceptibly, she lost her list and drifted straight on her original course as Hammett stopped the engines.

"We've broken something off," said Crowe, and a moment later the reports began to come in from for'ard, confirming his suggestion. The torpedo seemed to have hit almost squarely on the bows of the ship and had blown the first ten feet of the ship round at right angles to the rest. It was that which had forced the ship into the turn and which had now broken off. Number 1 bulkhead was holding, however, and the water which was pouring in was no more than the pumps could deal with adequately.

"Get that bulkhead shored up, Mr. Garland," said Hammett.

"Aye aye, sir," said a voice from the darkness.

"Go ahead with all the speed that the bulkhead will stand," said Crowe, before he went back into the chartroom.

His staff was still at the table planning the attack on the submarine; Rowles was a little white, and conscious of a stabbing pain every time he breathed, but it was not till sometime later that Crowe knew that his navigating officer had broken a couple of ribs when the explosion flung him against the table.

"We'll stay afloat for some time yet," announced Crowe, "and we'll make three or four knots, I hope."

"Splendid, sir," said Rowles, addressing himself to his squared paper. "I didn't want the little beggar to get away."

It is even harder to pick up the trail of a hostile submarine than it is to dispose of her, once she is detected; nothing must be allowed to interfere with the hunt when it is in full cry. While the emergency party faced sudden death shoring up the bulkhead, another signal winked from the battered flagship to the rest of the flotilla, gathering in for the kill. Out on the bridge again, Crowe looked forward through the darkness. He could not see them, but he knew that his other destroyers were arranging themselves in a neat pattern while the poor old *Apache* was panting up after them.

A fresh signal flashed from the *Apache's* masthead, and it was answered by a sound like a roll of thunder as the depth charges exploded. Only that signal was necessary; Crowe knew that his well-drilled flotilla was weaving round in the darkness as though taking part in an elaborate dance, and every few seconds a fresh roll of thunder announced the completion of a new figure as they systematically depth-charged every possible spot where a submarine might be lying. The sonic apparatus had given them the submarine's position within half a mile; a depth charge bursting within a hundred yards would do grave damage, and it was the business of the flotilla to see that at least one charge burst within a hundred yards. The *Apache* crept slowly over the sea toward the distant thunder; soon she was pitching and tossing perceptibly as the tremendous ripples of the explosions met her. They continued long after the explosions had ceased.

"We ought to be coming up to them now, sir," said Hammett, gazing into the darkness.

"What's that?" exclaimed Crowe, pointing suddenly.

It was a ghostly white triangle sticking out above the surface of the sea, thirty feet of it or so.

The words were hardly out of Crowe's mouth when one of the forward guns went off with a crash and a blinding flash. That triangle was the bows of a submarine protruding above the surface as she hung nearly vertically between wind and water, helpless and shattered; but a gun's crew, tense and eager for a target, will fire at the first sight of an enemy, and a submarine, once seen, must always be destroyed beyond all chance of escape and repair. The firing ceased, leaving everyone temporarily helpless in the darkness, but, blink their dazzled eyes as they might, Crowe and Hammett could see nothing of that pale triangle.

"She's gone," said Hammett.

Crowe sniffed the night air, trying to sort out the various smells which reached his nostrils. "That's her oil I can smell, isn't it?" he said.

Hammett sniffed as well. "Must be," he agreed, "there was no smell of our own oil before this happened."

The pungent, bitter smell was unmistakable; as they leaned over the rail at the end of the bridge it rose more penetratingly to their nostrils; they could picture the enormous pool of oil which was spreading round them, invisible in the night. And, as they leaned and looked, a vast bubble burst close alongside of the *Apache* as some fresh bulkhead gave way in the rent hull of the submarine sinking down to the bottom, and the enclosed air came bursting upward. They heard the sound and, faint in the darkness, they saw a white fragment whirl on the sea's surface.

"There's a bit of wreckage," said Crowe to Hammett. "Better get it for identification."

Wreckage indeed it was, for it was the dead body of a man. They carried it into the captain's day cabin as the nearest lighted place and laid it on the deck. Water ran from the soiled coveralls which it wore, forming a little pool, which washed backward and forward with the motion of the ship. The stars of gold on the shoulder straps indicated lieutenant commander's rank; the distorted face was young for a man of that seniority. The arms were clasped across his breast, and there was what looked like a red stain beneath them. Blood? Crowe stooped closer and then took hold of the cold hands and tried to pry the rigid arms upward; they were clasping to the lieutenant commander's breast a flat red book, and it was only with difficulty that they worked it loose, so fierce was the grip the corpse was maintaining upon it.

"Send for Mortimer!" snapped Crowe. "He speaks Italian!"

Most of the Italian that Lord Edward had spoken had been pretty little sentences asking, "When can we meet again?" and things like that. But he had a good academic knowledge of the language and it took no more than a glance for him to see the importance of what he was looking at.

"It's his orders, sir," he said, turning the wet pages with care and peering at the smudged handwriting and the typewritten orders that were clipped to the wet sheets.

"What does all this mean?" demanded Crowe. "Here's a latitude and longitude—I can see that for myself. Translate the Italian."

"He's three days out from Taranto, sir," said Mortimer, "and—by George, sir, this looks like a rendezvous! It is, by jingo! And here's the recognition signal."

As Mortimer translated the typewritten material Crowe looked back at the dead man lying in the puddle on the deck. He thought of the hunted submarine struggling desperately to throw off pursuit, and the final refuge taken at the bottom of the sea, of the rain of depth charges that had brought her up again, shattered and helpless; there would be the rush to destroy the secret documents, and before that could be effected came the shells from the *Apache*, blowing the shattered hull above and giving the captain his death-blow, even while the invading water whirled him to the surface.

"It's authentic all right," commented Nickleby, peering over Mortimer's shoulder.

"Yes," said Crowe; "let's hear it over again. . . . Go on, Mortimer."

The sunken submarine had an appointment with another, in two days' time, so that the one newly come from port could exchange information with the one returning—there was a day, a time and a position. Above all, there was the underwater recognition signal, the sequence of dots and dashes which, sent out in sound waves through the water, would be picked up by the other vessel as a signal for them both to rise to the surface at dawn to effect the exchange.

"I think somebody ought to keep that appointment," said Crowe, looking quizzically at his assistants.

"There's a bit of difference in pitch between the sound of our underwater signal and theirs," demurred Holby.

"Not enough to matter," said Crowe. "If they get the signal they're expecting, the right signal, at the right time and place, they won't stop to think about a trifling difference in pitch. Put yourself in their place, man."

The staff nodded. There was something fascinating and magnetic about their captain's determination to do the enemy all possible harm. But it was their duty to look at all sides of a question.

"What about surface propeller noises?" said Rowles, but Crowe shook his head.

"There won't be any," he explained. "We'll send one ship—there's no sense in taking the whole flotilla—and she'll get there early, in the dark, so she can drift. Who's got the steadiest nerves?"

"Marion?" suggested Nickleby, and as Crowe looked round at the others they nodded an agreement.

"Right!" said Crowe. "Get the orders out for him now."

That was how H.M.S. *Cheyenne*, Lieutenant Commander Edward Marion, D.S.C., came to detach herself from the Twentieth Flotilla at the end of that day to undertake an independent operation while the rest of the flotilla shepherded the wounded *Apache* back to port. It explains how an Italian submarine happened to rise to the surface close alongside her to find herself, much to her astonishment, swept by a torrent of fire from the waiting guns. The official British communiqué, issued sometime later, describing the capture, whole, of an Italian submarine, puzzled most of the people who read it. And yet the explanation is not a very complex one.

C. S. FORESTER
1899–1966

Born in Cairo, Egypt, as Cecil Lewis Troughton Smith, Forester was educated in England. He began to study medicine in 1918 at Guy's Hospital in London, but he dropped out of medical school and broke with his family three years later.

When he began life as a professional writer he adopted the pen name C. S. Forester. *Payment Deferred* (1924), his first important work, was adapted by him for stage and screen. Time spent on his boat, the *Annie Marble*, named after a character in *Payment Deferred*, provided material for two books published in quick succession, *The Voyage of the* Annie Marble (1929) and *The* Annie Marble *in Germany* (1930).

In 1932 Forester moved to California. In ensuing years his most widely read work was written. *The African Queen* appeared in 1935, *The General* in 1936. His most popular creation was the character of Horatio Hornblower in *The Happy Return* (1939), known under the title *Beat to Quarters* in America. Hornblower caught Forester's and the public's imagination, and after the publication of two more Hornblower novels—*Flying Colours* and *Ship of the Line* in 1938—the Book Society of England and the Book-of-the-Month Club (under the title *Captain Horatio Hornblower*) chose the trilogy for their subscribers. Forester won the James Tait Black Memorial Prize for literature in 1938 with *Ship of the Line*.

Though he made an effort to create an American Hornblower, Captain Josiah Peabody, in *The Captain From Connecticut* (1941), it was the British character who dominated much of Forester's writing until his death. *Com-*

modore Hornblower (1945) first saw publication in serial form in the *Saturday Evening Post*, where it created a stir because it depicted an adulterous relationship. Many other Hornblower novels followed.

"Night Stalk" was collected in *Gold from Crete: Ten Stories by C. S. Forester* (1970).

"HMS Marlborough *Will Enter Harbour*"

BY NICHOLAS MONSARRAT

I

THE SLOOP *Marlborough*, 1,200 tons, complement 8 officers and 130 men, was torpedoed at dusk on the last day of 1942 while on independent passage from Iceland to the Clyde. She was on her way home for refit, and for the leave that went with it, after a fourteen-month stretch of North Atlantic convoy escort with no break, except for routine boiler-cleaning. Three weeks' leave to each watch—that had been the buzz going round the ship's company when they left Reykjavik after taking in the last convoy; but many of them never found out how much truth there was in that buzz, for the torpedo struck at the worst moment, with two-thirds of the ship's company having tea below decks, and when it exploded under the forward mess-deck at least sixty of them were killed outright.

HMS *Marlborough* was an old ship, seventeen years old, and she took the outrage as an old lady of breeding should. At the noise and jar of the explosion a delicate shudder went all through her: then as her speed fell off there was stillness, while she seemed to be making an effort to ignore the whole thing: and then, brought face to face with the fury of this mortal attack, gradually and disdainfully she conceded the victory.

The deck plating of the fo'c'sle buckled and sagged, pulled downwards by the weight of the anchors and cables: all this deck, indeed, crumpled as far as the four-inch gun-mounting, which toppled forwards until the gun-muzzles were pointing foolishly to the sea; a big lurch tore loose many of the ammunition lockers and sent them cascading over the side. Until the way of her sixteen knots fell off, there were crunching noises as successive bulkheads took the weight of water, butted at it for a moment, and then gave in: and thus, after a space, she lay—motionless, cruelly hit, two hundred miles south-west of the Faeroes and five hundred miles from home.

So far it had been an affair of metal: now swiftly it became an affair of men. From forward came muffled shouting—screaming, some of it—borne on the wind down the whole length of the ship, to advertise the shambles buried below. The dazed gun's crew from 'A' gun, which had been directly over the explosion, climbed down from their sagging platform and drew off aft. There was a noise of trampling running feet from all over the ship:

along alleyways, up ladders leading from the untouched spaces aft: confused voices, tossed to and fro by the wind, called as men tried to find out how bad the damage was, what the orders were, whether their friends had been caught or not.

On the upper deck, near the boats and at the foot of the bridgeladders, the clatter and slur of feet and voices reached its climax. In the few moments before a firm hand was taken, with every light in the ship out and only the shock of the explosion as a guide to what had happened, there was confusion, noisy and urgent: the paramount need to move quickly clashed with indecision and doubt as to where that move could best be made. The dusk, the rising sea, the bitterly cold wind, which carried an acrid smell in sharp eddying puffs, were all part of this discordant aftermath: the iron trampling of those racing feet all over the ship bound it together, coordinating fear into a vast uneasy whole, a spur for panic if panic ever showed itself.

It never did show itself. The first disciplined reaction, one of many such small reassurances, to reach the bridge was the quartermaster's voice, admirably matter-of-fact, coming up the wheel-house voicepipe: 'Gyro compass gone dead, sir!' The midshipman, who shared the watch with the First Lieutenant and was at that moment licking a lip split open on the edge of the glass dodger, looked round uncertainly, found he was the only officer on the bridge, and answered: 'Very good. Steer by magnetic,' before he realized the futility of this automatic order. Then he jerked his head sideways, level with another voice-pipe, the one leading to the Captain's cabin, and called: 'Captain, sir!'

There was no answer. Probably the Captain was on his way up already. God, suppose he'd been killed, though. . . . The midshipman called again: 'Captain, sir!' and a voice behind him said: 'All right, Mid. I heard it.'

He turned round, to find the comforting bulk of the Captain's dufflecoat outlined against the dusk. It was not light enough to see the expression on his face, nor was there anything in his voice to give a clue to it. It did not occur to the midshipman to speculate about this, in any case: for him, this was simply the Captain, the man he had been waiting for, the man on whom every burden could now be squarely placed.

'Torpedo, sir.'

'Yes.'

The Captain, moving with purpose but without hurry, stepped up on to the central compass platform, glanced once round him—and sat down. There was something special in that act of sitting down, there in the middle of the noise and movement reaching the bridge from all over the ship, and everyone near him caught it. The Captain, on the bridge, sitting in the Captain's chair. Of course: that was what they had been waiting for. . . . It was the beginning, the tiny tough centre, of control and order. Soon it would spread outwards.

'Which side was it from?'

'Port, sir. Just under "A" gun.'

'Tell the engine-room what's happened. . . . Where is the First Lieutenant?'

'He must have gone down, sir. I suppose he's with the damage control party.'

Up the voice-pipe came the quartermaster's voice again: 'She won't come round, sir. The wheel's hard a-starboard.'

'Never mind.' The Captain turned his head slightly. 'Pilot!'

A figure, bent over the chart table behind him, straightened up. 'Sir?'

'Work out our position, and we'll send a signal.'

'Just getting it out now.'

The Captain bent forward to the voice-pipe again. 'Bos'n's Mate!'

'Sir?'

'Find the First Lieutenant. He'll be forrard somewhere. Tell him to report the damage as soon as he can.'

'Aye, aye, sir.'

That, at least, was a small space cleared. . . . Under him the ship felt sluggish and helpless; on the upper deck the voices clamoured, from below the cries still welled up. He looked round him, trying in the increasing darkness to find out who was on the bridge. Not everyone he expected to see, not all the men who should have collected at such a moment, were there. The signalman and the bridge messenger. Two look-outs. Bridger, his servant, standing just behind him. Pilot and the Mid. Someone else he could not make out.

He called: 'Coxswain?'

There was a pause, and then a voice said: 'He was below, sir.'

'Who's that?'

'Adams, sir.'

Adams was the Chief Bos'n's Mate, and the second senior rating on board. After a moment the Captain said:

'If he doesn't get out, you take over, Adams. . . . You'd better organize three or four of your quartermasters, for piping round the ship. I'll want you to stay by me. If there's anything to be piped you can pass it on.'

"Aye, aye, sir.'

There was too much noise on the upper deck, for a start. But perhaps it would be better if he spoke to them over the loud-hailer. Once more the Captain turned his head.

'Yeoman!'

Another pause, and then the same definitive phrase, this time from the signalman of the watch: 'He was below, sir.'

A wicked lurch, and another tearing noise from below, covered the silence after the words were spoken. But the Captain seemed to take them in his stride.

'See if the hailer's working,' he said to the signalman.

'I've got the position, sir,' said Haines, the navigating officer. 'Will you draft a signal?'

'Get on to the W/T office and see if they can send it, first.'

'The hailer's all right, sir,' said the signalman. 'Batteries still working.'

'Very good. Train the speaker aft.'

He clicked on the microphone, and from force of habit blew through it sharply. A healthy roar told him that the thing was in order. He cleared his throat.

'Attention, please! This is the Captain speaking.' His voice, magnified without distortion, overcame the wind and the shouting, which died away to nothing. 'I want to tell you what's happened. We've been torpedoed on the port side, under "A" gun. The First Lieutenant is finding out about the damage now. I want you all to keep quiet, and move about as little as possible, until I know what the position is. . . . "X" gun's crew will stand fast, the rest of the watch-on-deck clear away the boats and rafts ready for lowering. Do *not* start lowering, or do anything else, until I give the order over this hailer, or until you hear the pipe. That is all.'

The speaker clicked off, leaving silence on the bridge and all over the upper deck. Only the voices hidden below still called. He became aware that Haines was standing by his elbow, preparing to speak.

'What is it, Pilot?'

'It's the W/T office, sir. They can't transmit.'

'Who's down there?'

'The leading tel., sir. The PO tel. was below.' (That damned phrase again. If those two messes, the Chiefs' and the Petty Officers', were both written off, it was going to play hell wth organizing the next move, whatever it was.) 'But he knows what he's doing, sir,' Haines went on. 'The dynamo's been thrown off the board, but the set's had a hell of a knock anyway.'

'Go down yourself and make sure.' Haines, as well as being navigating officer, was an electrical expert, and this was in fact his department.

'Aye, aye, sir.'

'Midshipman!'

'Sir?'

'Pass the word to the Gunnery Officer—'

'I'm here, sir.' Guns' tall figure loomed up behind him. 'I've been looking at "A" gun.'

'Well?'

'It's finished, I'm afraid, sir.'

Guns knew his job, and the Captain did not ask him to elaborate. Instead he said:

'I think we'll try a little offensive action while we're waiting, in case those ———— come up to take a look at us.' He considered. 'Close up on "X" gun, go into local control, fire a spread of star-shell through this arc'—he indicated the port bow and beam—'and let fly if you see anything. I'll leave the details to you.'

'Aye, aye, sir.'

Guns clumped off down the ladder on his way aft. It was one of his idiosyncrasies to wear street-cleaner's thigh-boots with thick wooden soles, and his movements up and down the ship were easily traceable, earning indeed a good deal of fluent abuse from people who were trying to get to sleep below. As the heavy footfalls receded aft, the Captain stood up and leant over the port side of the bridge, staring down at the tumbling water. There was nothing to be seen of the main area of the damage, which was hidden by the outward flare of the bows; but the ship had less freedom of movement now—she was deeper, more solidly settled in the water. They must have taken tons of it in the ripped-up spaces forward: the fo'c'sle covering them looked like a slowly crumbling ruin. It was about time the First Lieutenant came through with his report. If they had to—

'What's that?' he asked suddenly.

A thin voice was calling 'Bridge, Bridge,' from one of the voicepipes. He bent down to the row nearest to him, but from none of them did the voice issue clearly. Behind him the midshipman was conducting the same search on his side. The voice went on calling 'Bridge, Bridge, Bridge,' in a patient monotone. It was the Captain's servant, Bridger, who finally traced it—a voice-pipe low down on the deck, its antispray cover still clipped on.

The man bent down to it and snapped back the cover. 'Bridge here.'

A single murmured sentence answered him. Bridger looked up to the Captain. 'It's the Engineer Officer, sir, speaking from the galley flat.'

The Captain bent down. A waft of bitter fume-laden air met his nostrils. 'Yes, Chief?'

'I'm afraid Number One got caught by that last bulkhead, sir.'

'What happened? I heard it go a little while back.'

'We thought it would hold, sir.' The level voice, coming from the heart of the ruined fo'c'sle, had an apologetic note, as if the speaker, even in that shambles, had had the cool honesty to convict himself of an error of judgment. 'It did look like holding for a bit, too. Number One was with the damage control party, between the seamen's messdeck and the bathrooms. They'd shut the watertight door behind them, and were just going to shore up, when the forrard bulkhead went.' Chief paused. 'You know what it's like, sir. We can't get at them without opening up.'

'Can't do that now, Chief.'

'No, sir.'

'Can you hear anything?'

'Not now.'

'How many were there with the First Lieutenant?'

'Fourteen, sir. Mostly stokers.' There was another pause. 'I took charge down here, sir. We're shoring up the next one.'

'What do you think of it?'

'Not too good. It's badly strained already, and leaking down one seam.' There was, now, a slightly sharpened note in the voice traveling up from below. 'There's a hell of a mess down here, sir. And if this one goes, that'll mean the whole lot.'

'Yes, I know.' The Captain thought quickly, while overhead and to port the sea was suddenly lit up by a cold yellow glare—the first spread of star-shell, four slowly dropping lights shadowing their spinning parachutes against the cloud overhead. Very pretty. . . . The news from below could hardly have been worse: it added up to fully a third of the ship flooded, all the forward mess-decks cut off, fourteen men drowned at one stroke, and God knows how many more caught by the original explosion. 'Look here, Chief, I don't want any more men lost like that. You must use your own judgment about getting out in a hurry. See how the shoring up goes, and let me know as soon as you can if you think it'll hold.'

'All right, sir.'

'We're firing star-shell at the moment, to see if there's anything on the surface. "X" gun may be firing independently, any time from now on.'

'All right, sir.'

'Take care of yourself, Chief.'

He could almost hear the other man smiling at what was, from the Captain, an unexpected remark. 'I'll do that, sir.'

The voice-pipe went dead. Walking back to his chair, the Captain allowed himself a moment of profound depression and regret. The First Lieutenant gone. A good kid, doing his first big job in the Navy and tremendously keen to do it properly. With a young wife, too—the three of them had had dinner at the Adelphi in Liverpool, not two weeks ago. There was a bad letter to be written there, later on. And the loss might make a deal of difference to the next few hours.

The star-shell soared and dropped again. Sitting in his chair, waiting for Chief's report, listening to the green seas slapping and thumping against the side as *Marlborough* sagged downwind in the wave troughs with a new, ugly motion, he was under no illusions as to what the next few hours might bring, and the chances of that 'bad letter' ever being written by himself. But that was not what he was now concentrating on: that was not in the mapped-out programme. . . . This was the moment for which the Navy had long been preparing him: for years his training and experience had had this precise occasion in view; that was why he was a commander, and the Captain of *Marlborough* when she was hit. Taking charge, gauging chances, foreseeing the next eventuality and if necessary forestalling it—none of it could take him by surprise, any more than could the chapter headings of a favourite book. When the moment had arrived he had recognized it instantly, and the sequence of his behaviour had lain before him like a familiar pattern, of which he now had to take the tenth or twentieth tracing. He had not been torpedoed before, but no matter: tucked away in his mind and brain there had always been a picture of a torpedoed ship, and of himself as, necessarily, the key figure in this picture. Now that the curtain was drawn, and the image became the reality, he simply had to play his assigned part with as much intelligence, skill, and endurance as he could muster. The loss of the First Lieutenant and over half the ship's company already was a bitter stroke, both personally and professionally: it would return in full force later; but for the moment it was only a debit item which had to be fitted into the evolving picture.

'Signalman!'

'Sir.'

'Get the Gunnery Officer on the quarter-deck telephone.'

A pause. More star-shell, reflected on a waste of cold tumbling water, dropped slowly till they were drowned in darkness again. There wasn't really much point in going on with the illumination now: the U-boat probably thought they had other ships in company ready to counterattack, and had sheered off. She had, indeed, cause to be satisfied, without pursuing the advantage further. . . .

'Gunnery Officer on the telephone, sir.'

The Captain took the proffered receiver. 'Guns?'

'Yes, sir?'

'I'm afraid Number One has been killed. I want you to take over.'

'Oh—all right, sir.'

Hearing the shocked surprise in his voice, the Captain remembered that the two of them had been very good friends. But that, again, was something to be considered later: only the bald announcement was part of the present pattern. He continued:

'I think you had better stay aft, as if we were still at full action stations.

Chief is in charge of damage control forrard. Stop star-shell now—I take it you've seen nothing.'

'Nothing, sir.'

'Right. You'd better have all the depth-charges set to safe—in fact have the primers withdrawn and dropped over the side. And I want someone to have a look at our draught-marks aft.'

'I've just had them checked, sir. There's nothing to go on, I'm afraid: they're right clear of the water.'

'Are the screws out of the water too?'

"Can't see in this light, sir. The top blades, probably.'

'Right. Get going on those depth-charges.'

The Captain handed back the receiver, at the same time saying to the signalman: 'Get your confidential books in the weighted bags, ready for ditching. And tell the W/T office to do the same.'

'Aye, aye, sir.'

'Bridger.'

'Yes, sir.'

'Go down and get the black hold-all, and come back here.'

'Aye, aye, sir.' Bridger's tough, unemotional expression did not alter, but his shoulders stiffened instinctively. He knew what the order meant. The black hold-all was, in his own phrase, the scram-bag: it held a bottle of brandy, morphine ampoules, a first-aid kit, some warm clothes, and a few personal papers. It had been tucked away in a corner of the skipper's cabin for nearly three years. It was as good as a ticket over the side. They'd start swimming any moment now.

The report from aft about the draught-marks had certainly quickened the tempo a little: his orders to Bridger and to the signalman were an endorsement of this. But quick tempo or slow, there was still the same number of things to be fitted into the available time, the same number of lines in the pattern to be traced. Now, in the darkness, as he turned to the next task, very little noise or movement reached the bridge from anywhere in the ship: only a sound of hammering from deep below (the damage control party busy on their shoring job), a voice calling 'Take a turn, there', as the whaler was swung out, the endless thump and surge of the waves driving down wind—only these were counter-distractions in the core of heart and brain which the bridge had now become. Indeed, the Captain was much less conscious of these than of the heavy breathing of Adams, the Chief Bos'n's Mate, who stood by his elbow as close and attentive as a spaniel at the butts. Adams had heard the order to Bridger, and had guessed what it meant: it had aroused, not his curiosity—matters were past such a faint reaction as curiosity now—but the same tough determination as the Captain himself

had felt. They were both men of the same stamp: seamen first, human beings afterwards; the kind of men whom *Marlborough*, in her extremity,
most needed and most deserved.

'Mid!'

'Yes, sir?'

'Go along to the sick bay, and—'

One of the voice-pipe bells rang sharply. The midshipman listened for a
moment, and then said: 'That's the doctor now, sir.'

The Captain bent down. 'Yes, doc?'

'I wanted to report about casualties, sir.'

'What's the position?'

'I've got nine down here, sir. Burns, mostly. One stoker with a broken
arm. I got a stretcher-party organized, and brought them down aft.'

'I was hoping there'd be more.'

'Afraid not, sir.'

'Do you need any hands to help you?'

'No, I'm all right, sir. I've got one sick-berth attendant—Jamieson was
caught forrard, I'm afraid—and the leading steward is giving a hand.'

'Very well. But you'll have to start moving them, I'm afraid. Get them on
the upper deck, on the lee side. Ask Guns to lend you some hands from "X"
gun.'

There was a pause. Then the doctor's voice came through again, more
hesitantly. 'They shouldn't really be moved, sir, unless—'

'That's what I meant. You understand?'

'Yes, sir.'

'Send the walking cases up to the boat-deck, and see to the others yourself. Divide them up between the two boats. I'll leave the details to you.'

'Very well, sir.'

Thank God for a good doctor, anyway—as bored, cynical, and impatient
as most naval doctors were for three-quarters of their time, with nothing to
do but treat warts and censor the mail: and then, on an occasion like this,
summoning all the resource and skill that had been kept idle, and throwing
them instantly into the breach. The doctor was going to be an asset during
the next few hours. So, indeed, was every officer and man left to the ship.

He would have liked to muster the remaining hands, to see how many
the explosion had caught and how many he had left to work with; but that
would disrupt things too much, at a time when there must be no halting in
the desperate race to save the ship or, at least, as many of the remaining lives
as possible. But as he sat back in his chair, waiting for what he was now
almost sure must happen, the Captain reviewed his officers one by one,
swiftly tabulating their work at this moment, speculating whether they
could be better employed. Number One was gone, of course. Guns in charge

aft, Haines in the wireless office (time he was back, incidentally). Chief working the damage control party—that was technically his responsibility anyway, and there was a first-class Chief ERA in charge of the engine-room. The Mid here on the bridge. The doctor with his hands full in the sick bay. Merrett—the Captain frowned suddenly. Where the devil was Merrett? He'd forgotten all about him—and indeed it was easy to overlook the shy, newly-joined sub who had startled the wardroom on his first night by re-marking: 'My father went to prison as a conscientious objector during the last war, so he's rather ashamed of me in this one,' but had then relapsed into the negative, colourless attitude which seemed natural to him. Where had he got to now?

The Captain repeated the query aloud to the midshipman.

'I haven't seen him at all, sir,' the latter answered. 'He was in the ward-room when I came on watch. Shall I call them up?'

'Yes, do.'

After a moment at one of the voice-pipes the midshipman came through with the answer: 'He was there a moment ago, sir. They think he's on the upper deck somewhere.'

'Send one of the bos'n's mates to—' The Captain paused. No, that might not be a good move. 'See if you can find him, Mid, and ask him to come up here.'

When the midshipman had left the bridge the Captain frowned again. Why in God's name had Merrett been in the wardroom a moment ago? What was he doing there at a time like this? Any sort of alarm or cri-sis meant that officers went to their action stations automatically: Merrett should have gone first to 'A' gun, where he was in charge, and then, as that was out of action, up to the bridge for orders. Now all that was known of him was that he had been in the wardroom, right aft. The Captain hoped there was a good explanation, not the attack of nerves or the breakdown of self-control he had been guessing at when he sent the midshipman to find Merrett. He could understand such a thing happening—the boy was barely twenty, and this was his first ship—but they just could not afford it now.

His guess had been right: so much became obvious as soon as Merrett was standing in front of him. Even in the darkness, with the exact expres-sion on his face blurred and shadowed, he seemed to manifest an almost exalted state of terror. The movements of foot and hand, the twitching shoulders, the slight, uncontrolled chattering of the teeth, the shine of sweat on the forehead—all were here, a distillation of fear which would, in full daylight, have been horrible to look at. So that was it. . . . For a moment the Captain hesitated, trying to balance their present crucial danger, and his own controlled reaction to it, against the almost unknown feelings of a boy, a landsman-turned-sailor, confronted with the same ordeal; but then the overriding necessity of everyone on board doing his utmost, swept away any readiness to make allowances for failure in this respect. The details, the pros and cons, the fine-drawn questions could wait; nothing but one hundred per cent effectiveness would suffice now, and that was what he must reestablish.

'Where have you been?' he asked curtly.

Merrett swallowed, looked across the shattered fo'c'sle to the wild sea, and drew no comfort or reassurance from it. He said, in a dry strained voice: 'I'm sorry, sir. I didn't know what to do, exactly.'

'Then you should come and ask me. Do you expect me to come and tell you?' It was rough: it was, in Merrett's present state, brutally so: but it was clearly dictated by the situation they were in. 'Where were you when we were hit?'

'I'd just gone up to "A" gun, sir.'

'Must have shaken you up a bit.' So much allowance, and no more, did the Captain make for what he could only guess at now—youth, uncertainty, self-distrust, perhaps an inherited horror of violence. 'But I don't want to have to send for individual officers at a time like this. You understand?'

'Yes, sir.' It was a whisper, almost a sigh. He'd been drinking whisky, too, the Captain thought. Well, that didn't matter as long as it had the right result; and this, and the tonic effect of giving him a definite job to do, could be put to the test now.

'Very well. . . . There's something I want you to do,' he went on, changing his tone in such a way as to indicate clearly that a fresh start could now be made. 'Go down to the boat-deck and see how they're getting on with the boats. They're to be swung out ready for lowering, and all the rafts cleared away as well. You'd better check up on the boats' crews, too: remember we've only got this one watch of seamen to play with, so far as we know. You'll want a coxswain, a stoker, and a bowman told off for the motor-boat, and a coxswain and a bowman for the whaler. Got that?'

'Yes, sir.'

It seemed that he had: already he was making some attempt to take a grip on his body, and his voice was more under control. Watching him turn and make for the bridge-ladder, the Captain felt ready to bet that he would make a good job of it. The few minutes had not been wasted.

But they had been no more than an odd, irrelevant delay in the main flow of the current; and now, in quick succession, as if to re-establish the ordained pace of disaster, three more stages came and were passed. Bridger appeared with the black hold-all, and with something else which he handed to the Captain almost furtively. 'Better have this, sir,' he said, as the Captain's hand closed over it. It was his safety-light, which he had forgotten to clip on to his life-jacket—one of the small watertight bulb-and-battery sets which were meant to be plugged in and switched on when in the water. The Captain took it with a grunt and fastened it on, his eyes turned instinctively to the black expanse of water washing and swirling round them. Yes, better have the light ready. . . .

Then Haines came up the ladder from below, starting to speak almost before he was on the bridge:

'I'm afraid they were right about the W/T set, sir,' he began. 'It's finished. And the main switchboard has blown, too. Even if we got the dynamo back on the board—'

'All right, Pilot,' said the Captain suddenly. And then, to the figure he had discerned at the top of the ladder, the third messenger of evil, he said: 'Yes, Chief?'

The engineer officer did not speak until he was standing close by the Captain, but there was no hesitation about his opening words. 'I don't think it's any good, sir.' He spoke with a clipped intensity, which did not disguise an exhaustion of spirit. 'That bulkhead—it might go any minute, and she'll probably break in two when it happens. That means a lot more men caught, sir.'

'You've shored up completely?'

'Yes, sir. But the space is too big, and the bulkhead was warped too much before we got the shores to it. It's working badly already. I can't see it holding more than another hour, if that.'

'It's the last one worth shoring,' said the Captain, almost to himself.

'Yes, sir.' Chief hesitated. 'I've still seven or eight hands down in the engine-room, I'd like to get them out in good time. Is that all right, sir?'

Chief was looking at him. They were all looking at him—Haines, the midshipman, the signalman, Adams, the look-outs, the hard-breathing Bridger—all waiting for the one plain order, which they now knew must come. Until that moment he had been refusing to look squarely at this order as it drew nearer and nearer; he could not believe that his loved ship must be given up, and even now, as he hesitated, and the men round him wondered, the idea still had no sort of reality about it. For this man on whom they all relied, this man to whom they attributed no feelings or qualities apart from the skill and forethought of seamanship, was not quite the stock figure, the thirty-eight-year-old RN commander, that they took him to be.

True, he fitted the normal mould well enough. He had always done so, from Dartmouth onwards, and the progress from midshipman to commander had followed its appointed course—twenty years of naval routine in which a mistake, a stepping-out-of-line, would have denied him his present rank. He never had stepped out of line; he had been, and still was, normal about everything except this ship; but for her he had a special feeling, a romantic conception, which would have astounded the men waiting round him. It was not the Navy, or his high sense of duty, or the fact that he commanded her, which had given him this feeling: it was love.

The old *Marlborough*. . . . The Captain was not married, and if he had been it might not have made any difference: he was profoundly and exclusively in love with this ship, and the passion, fed especially on the dangers and ordeals of the past three war years, left no room for a rival. It had started in 1926, when she was brand new and he had commissioned her: it had been his first job as First Lieutenant, and his proudest so far. She had been the very latest in ships then—a new sloop, Clyde-built, twin turbines, two four-inch guns (the twin mountings came later), and a host of gadgets and items of novel equipment which were sharp on the palate. . . . There had been other ships, of course, in the sixteen years between; his first command had been a river gunboat, his second a destroyer: but he had never forgotten *Marlborough*. He had kept an eye on her all the time, checking her movements as she transferred from the Home Fleet to the Mediterranean, thence to the China Station, then home again: looking up her officers in the Navy List and wondering if they were taking proper care of her: making a special trip up to Rosyth on one of his leaves, to have another look at her; and when, at the outbreak of war, he had been given command of her, it had been like coming home again, to someone dearly loved who was not yet past the honeymoon stage.

She was not, in point of fact, much of a command for a commander, even as the senior ship of an escort group, and he could have done better if he had wished. But he did not wish. Old-fashioned she might be, battered with much hard driving, none too comfortable, at least three knots slower than the job really demanded; but she could still show her teeth and she still ran as sweet as a sewing machine, and the last three years had been the happiest of his career. He was intensely jealous of her efficiency when contrasted with more up-to-date ships, and he went to endless trouble over this, intriguing for the fitting of new equipment 'for experimental purposes', demanding the replacement of officers or key-ratings if any weak point in the team began to show itself. In three years of North Atlantic convoy work he had spared neither himself nor his ship's company any of the intense strain which the job imposed; but *Marlborough* he had nursed continuously, so that the prodigious record of hours steamed and miles covered had cost the minimum of wear.

He knew her from end to end, not only with the efficient 'technical' eye of the man who had watched the last five months of her building, but with an added, intimate regard for every part of her, a loving admiration, an eye tenderly blind to her shortcomings.

Now she was going. No wonder he could not phrase that final order, no wonder he stared back almost angrily at the Chief, delaying what he knew must happen, waiting for the miracle to forestall it.

Up to the bridge came a new, curious noise. It came from deep within the fo'c'sle, a blend of thud and iron clang which coincided with the ship's rolling. Something very solid must have broken adrift down there, either through the shock or the unusual level of their trim, and was now washing to and fro out of control. Chief, his face puckered, tried to place it; it might have been any one of a dozen bits of heavy equipment in the forward store. The big portable pump, most likely. There must be the hell of a mess down there. Men and gear smashing up together—it hardly bore thinking of. And the noise was unnerving; it sounded like the toll of a bell, half sunk, tied to a wreck and washing with the tide. A damned sight too appropriate.

The Captain said suddenly: 'I'll come down and look at that bulkhead, Chief. Haines, take over here.' He turned to Adams. 'You come with me. Bring one of the quartermasters, too.'

There might be some piping to do in a hurry.

The journey down, deck by deck, had the same element of compulsion in it as, in a nightmare, distinguishes the random lunatic journey which can only lead to some inescapable horror at its end. The boat-deck was crowded: two loaded stretchers lay near the whaler, the figures on them not more than vague impressions of pain in the gloom: Merrett was directing the un-lashing of a raft near by: on the lee side of the funnel a dozen hands, staring out at the water, were singing 'Home on the Range', in low-pitched chorus. The small party—Captain, Chief, Adams, the quartermaster—made their way aft, past the figures grouped round 'X' gun, and down another ladder. At the iron-deck level, a few feet from the water, all was deserted. 'I sent the damage control party up, as soon as we'd finished, sir,' the Chief said, as he stepped through the canvas screen into the alleyway leading forward. 'There was nothing else for them to do.'

Under cover now, the four of them moved along the rocking passage: Chief's torch picking out the way, flicking from side to side of the hollow tunnel against which the water was already lapping. Under their stumbling scraping feet the slope led fatally downwards. The clanging toll seemed to advance to meet them. They passed the entrance to the engine-room: just within, feet straddled on the grating, stood a young stoker, the link with the outside world in case the bridge voice-pipe failed. To him, as they passed, the Chief said: 'No orders yet. I'll be coming back in a minute,' and the stoker drew back into the shadows to pass the message on. Then they came to a closed watertight door, and this they eased slowly open, a clip at a time, so that any pressure of water within would show immediately. But it was still dry . . . the door swung back, and they stepped inside the last water-tight space that lay between floating and sinking.

It was dimly lit, by two battery lanterns clipped to overhead brackets: the light struck down on a tangle of joists and beams, heel-pieces, wedges, cross-battens—the work of the damage control party. The deck was wet underfoot, and as *Marlborough* rolled, some inches of dirty water slopped from side to side, carrying with it a scummy flotsam of caps, boots, and ditty-boxes. The Captain switched on his torch, ducked under a transverse beam, and stepped up close to the bulkhead. It was, as the Chief had said, in bad shape; bulging towards him, strained and leaking all down one seam, responding to the ship's movements with a long-drawn-out, harsh creaking. For a single moment, as he watched it, he seemed to be looking through into the space beyond, where Number One and his fourteen damage control hands had been caught. The forbidden picture—forbidden in the strict scheme of his captaincy—gave place to another one, conjured up in its turn by the clanging which now sounded desperately loud and clear: the three flooded messdecks underneath his feet, the sealed-off shambles of the explosion area. Then his mind swung back, guiltily, to the only part of it that mattered now, the shored-up section he was standing in, and he nodded to himself as he glanced round it once more. It confirmed what he had been expecting but had only now faced fairly and squarely: Chief had done a good job, but it just wasn't good enough.

He turned quickly. 'All right, Chief. Bring your engine-room party out on to the upper deck. Adams! Pipe "Hands to stations for—"'

The words 'Abandon ship' were cut off by a violent explosion above their heads.

For a moment the noise was so puzzling that he could not assign it to anything: it was just an interruption, almost supernatural, which had stopped him finishing that hated sentence. Then another piece of the pattern clicked into place, and he said: 'That was a shell, by God!' and made swiftly for the doorway.

Outside, he called back over his shoulder: 'Chief—see to the door again!' and then started to run. His footsteps rang in the confined space: he heard Adams following close behind him down the passageway, the noise echoing and clattering all round him, urging him on. Reaching the open air at last was like escaping from a nightmare into a sweating wakefulness which must somehow be instantly co-ordinated and controlled. As he went up the ladder to the boat-deck there was a brilliant flash and another explosion up on the bridge, followed by the sharp reek of the shell-burst. Damned good shooting from somewhere . . . something shot past his head and spun into a ventilator with a loud clang. He began to run again, brushing close by a figure making for 'X' gun shouting, 'Close up again! Load star-shell!' Guns, at least, had his part of it under control.

He passed the space between the two boats. It was here, he saw, that the first shell had struck: the motor-boat was damaged, one of the stretchers was overturned, and there were three separate groups of men bending over figures stretched out on deck. He wanted to stop and find out how bad the damage was, and, especially, how many men had been killed or hurt, but he could not: the bridge called him, and had prior claim.

It was while he was climbing quickly up the ladder that he realized that the moon had now risen, low in the sky, and that *Marlborough* must be cleanly silhouetted against the horizon. If no one on the upper deck had seen the flash of the submarine's firing, the moon ought to give them a line on her position. Guns would probably work that out for himself. But it would be better to make sure.

Now he was at the top of the ladder, his eyes grown accustomed to the gloom, his nostrils assailed by the acrid stink of the explosion. The shell he had seen land when he first came out on deck had caught the bridge fair and square, going through one wing and exploding against the chart-house. Only two men were still on their feet—the signalman and one of the look-outs: the other look-out was lying, headless, against his machine-gun mounting. Adams, at his shoulder, drew in his breath sharply at the sight, but the Captain's eyes had already moved farther on, to where three other figures—who must be Haines, the midshipman, and the messenger—had fallen in a curiously theatrical grouping round the compass platform. The light there was too dim to show any details: the dark shambles could only be guessed at. But one of the figures was still moving. It was the midshipman, clinging to a voice-pipe and trying to hoist himself upright.

He said quickly: "Lie still, Mid,' and then: 'Signalman, give me the hailer,' and lastly, to Adams: 'Do what you can for them.' He caught sight of the young, shocked face of the other look-out staring at him, and he called out sharply: 'Don't look in-board. Watch your proper arc. Use your glasses.' Then he switched on the microphone, and spoke into it:

'X gun, X gun—illuminate away from the moon—illuminate away from the moon.' He paused, then continued: 'Doctor or sick-berth attendant report to the bridge now—doctor or sick-berth attendant.'

Pity had inclined him to put the last order first: the instinct of command had told him otherwise. But almost before he stopped speaking, the sharp crack of 'X' gun came from aft, and the star-shell soared. Guns had had the same idea as himself.

Adams, who was kneeling down and working away at a rough tourniquet, said over his shoulder:

'Shall I carry on with that pipe, sir?'

'No. Wait.'

The U-boat coming to the surface had altered everything. The ship was now only a platform for 'X' gun, and not to be abandoned while 'X' gun still had work to do.

As the star-shell burst and hung, lighting up the grey moving sea, the Captain raised his glasses and swept the arc of water that lay on their beam.

Almost immediately he saw the U-boat, stopped on the surface, broadside on to them and not more than a mile away. Before he had time to speak over the hailer, or give any warning, there was a noise from aft as Guns shouted a fresh order; and then things happened very quickly.

'X' gun roared. A spout of water, luminous under the star-shell, leapt upwards, just beyond the U-boat and dead in line—a superb sighting shot, considering the suddenness of this new crisis. There was a pause, while the Captain's mind raced over the two possibilities now open—that the U-boat, guessing she had only a badly crippled ship to deal with, would fight it out on the surface, or that she would submerge to periscope depth and fire another torpedo. Then came the next shot, to settle all his doubts.

It came from both ships, and it was almost farcically conclusive. The flash of both guns was instantaneous. The U-boat's shell exploded aft, right on 'X' gun, ripping the whole platform to pieces; but from the U-Boat herself a brilliant orange flash spurted suddenly, to be succeeded by the crump of an explosion. Then she disappeared completely.

'X' gun, mortally wounded itself, had made its last shot a mortal one for the enemy.

Silence now over all the ship, save for a faint moaning from aft. The Captain reached for the hailer, and then paused. No point in saying anything at this moment: they would be looking after 'X' gun's crew, what was left of them, and there was no more enemy to deal with. He listened for a moment to Adams's heavy breathing as he bent over the midshipman, and then turned as a figure showed itself at the top of the bridge-ladder.

'Captain, sir.'

'What is it?'

'SBA, sir. The doctor's gone aft to the gun.'

'All right. Bear a hand here. Who's that behind you?'

'It's me, sir,' said Bridger's voice from the top of the ladder. 'I was helping the SBA.'

'Were you up here when the second shell landed?'

'No, sir—just missed it.' Bridger sounded competent and unsurprised, as if he had arranged the thing that way. 'I went down to give them a hand when the first one hit the boat-deck, sir.'

'How much damage down there?'

'Killed three of the lads, sir.' The sick-berth attendant's voice breaking in was strained and rather uneven. 'Mr. Merrett's gone, too. He was just by the motor-boat.'

Another officer lost. Guns had probably been killed, too. That meant— the Captain checked suddenly, running over the list in his mind. Number One, caught by that bulkhead. Haines and the midshipman finished up here; Merrett gone, dying typically in a quiet corner, escaping his notice. Guns almost certainly killed at 'X' gun. That meant that there were no executive officers left at all: only Chief and the doctor. If they didn't abandon ship—if somehow they got her going again—it would be an almost impossible job, single-handed. . . . He put the thought on one side for the moment, and said to the sick-berth attendant:

'Take over from Petty Officer Adams. Have a look at the others first, and then get the midshipman aft to the wardroom.'

He waited again, as the man got to work. The heavy clanging from below, which had stopped momentarily when the gun was fired, now started once more. Presently the doctor came up to the bridge, to report what he had been expecting to hear—that Guns, and the whole crew of seven, had been killed by the last shot from the U-boat. Even though he had been prepared for it, it was impossible to hear the news with indifference. But for some reason it confirmed a thought which had been growing in his mind, ever since the U-boat had been sunk. They were on their own now, and the only danger was from the sea. His loved *Marlborough* had survived so much, had produced such a brilliant last-minute counter-stroke, that he could not leave her now. Reason told him to carry on with the order he had given down below, but reason seemed to have had no part in the last few minutes: something else, some product of heart and instinct, seemed to have taken control of them all. That last shot of 'X' gun had been a miracle. Suppose there were more miracles on the way?

Adams, straightening up as the sick-berth attendant took over, once again tried, respectfully, to recall the critical moment to him:

'Carry on with that pipe, sir?'

'No.' The Captain, divining the uncertainty in the man's mind, smiled in the darkness. 'No, Adams, I hadn't forgotten. But we'll wait till daylight.'

2

There were fourteen hours till daylight: fourteen hours to review that decision, to ascribe it correctly either to emotion or to a reasonable assessment of chance, and to foresee the outcome. What struck the Captain most strongly about it was the unprofessional aspect of what he had done. Down there in the shored-up fo'c'sle, he had made a precise, technical examination of the damage and the repairs to it, and come to a clear decision: if the U-boat's shell had not hit them, and interrupted the order, they would now be sitting in the boats, lying off in the darkness and waiting for *Marlborough* to go down. But something had intervened: not simply the absolute necessity of fighting the U-boat as long as possible, not even second thoughts on their chances of keeping the ship afloat, but something stronger still. It was so long since the Captain had changed his mind about any personal or professional decision that he hardly knew how to analyse it. But certainly the change of mind was there.

He could find excuses for it now, though not very adequate ones. Daylight would give them more chance to survey the damage properly. (But he had done that already.) With the motor-boat wrecked by the first shell-burst, there were not enough boats for the crew to take to. (But some of them would always have to use rafts anyway, and if *Marlborough* sank they would have no choice in the matter.) They had a number of badly-wounded men on board who must be sheltered for as long as possible, if they were not to die of neglect or exposure. (But they certainly stood more chance of surviving an orderly abandonment of the ship, rather than a last-minute emergency retreat.) No, none of these ideas had really any part in it. It boiled down to nothing more precise than a surge of feeling which had attacked him as soon as the U-boat was sunk: a foolish emotional idea, product both of the past years and of this last tremendous stroke, that after *Marlborough* had done so much for them they could not leave her to die. It wasn't an explanation which would look well in the Report of Proceedings; but it was as near the truth as he could phrase it.

The answer would come with daylight, anyway; till then he must wait. If the bulkhead held, and the weather moderated, and Chief was able to get things going again (that main switchboard would have to be rewired, for a start), then they might be able to do something: creep southwards, perhaps, till they were athwart the main convoy route and could get help. It was the longest chance he had ever taken: sitting there in his chair up on the bridge, brooding in the darkness, he tried to visualize its successive stages. Funnier things had happened at sea. . . . But the final picture, the one that remained with him all that night, was of a ship—his ship—drawing thirty-two feet forward and nothing aft, drifting helplessly downwind with little prospect of surviving till daylight.

No one ashore knew anything about them, and no one would start worrying for at least three days.

Within the ship, ignoring and somehow isolating itself against this preposterous weight of odds, there was much to do; and with no officers to call on except the doctor, who was busy with casualties, and the Chief, whom he left to make a start in the engine-room, the Captain set to work to organize it himself. He kept Bridger by him, to relay orders, and a signalman, in case something unexpected happened (there was a faint chance of an aircraft on passage being in their area, and within signalling distance): Adams was installed as a virtual First Lieutenant; and from this nucleus the control and routine of the ship was set in motion again.

The bulkhead he could do nothing about: Chief set to work on the main switchboard, the first step towards raising steam again, and the leading telegraphist was working on the wireless transmitter; the boats and rafts were left in instant readiness, and the more severe casualties taken back under cover again. (A hard decision, this; but to keep them on the upper deck in this bitter weather was a degree nearer killing them than running the risk of trapping them below.) Among the casualties was the midshipman, still alive after a cruel lacerated wound in the chest and now in the sick bay waiting for a blood transfusion. The bodies of the other three who had been killed on the bridge—Haines, the look-out, and the bridge messenger— had been taken aft to the quarter-deck, to join the rest, from 'X' gun's crew and the party on the boat-deck, awaiting burial.

Then, after a spell of cleaning up, which included the chaos of loose gear and ammunition round 'A' gun, which had been directly over the explosion, the Captain told Adams to muster what was left of the ship's company and report the numbers. He was still in his chair on the bridge, sipping a mug of cocoa, which Bridger had cooked up in the wardroom pantry, when Adams came up with his report, and he listened to the details with an attention which he tried to rid of all personal feeling. These crude figures, which Adams, bending over the chart-table light, was reading out, were men, some of them well known and liked, some of them shipmates of two and three years' standing, all of them sailors; but from now on they must only be numbers, only losses on a chart of activity and endurance. The dead were not to be sailors any more: just 'missing potential', 'negative assets'—some damned phrase like that.

Adams said: 'I've written it all down, sir, as well as I could.' He had, in his voice, the same matter-of-fact impersonal tone as the Captain would have used: the words 'as well as I could' might have referred to some trifling clerical inconvenience instead of the difficulty of sorting out the living, the dead, and the dying in the pitch darkness. 'There's the ones we know about, first. There's three officers and twelve ratings killed—that's the Gunnery Officer, Lieutenant Haines, and Mr. Merrett, and the gun's crew and the ones on the boat-deck and the two up here. The surgeon-lieutenant has one officer and sixteen men in the sick bay. We'll have to count most of them out, I'm afraid, sir. Nine of them were out of the fo'c'sle. Then there's'—he paused—'one officer and seventy-four men missing.' He stopped again, expecting the Captain to say something, but as no word came from the dark figure in the chair he went on: 'Then what we've got left, sir. There's yourself, and the surgeon-lieutenant, and the engineer—that's three officers, and twenty-eight men out of the Red Watch, the one that was on duty.'

'Twenty-eight. Is that all?'

'That's all, sir. They lost seven seamen at 'X' gun, three by the boats, and two here. Then there's seven of them down in the sick bay. That's forty-seven altogether.'

'How are the twenty-eight made up? How many seamen have we?'

Adams straightened up and turned round from the table. This part of it he evidently knew by heart. 'There's myself, sir, and Leading Seaman Tapper, and seven ABs: the quartermaster and the bos'n's mate, that were in the wheelhouse: and Bridger. That's twelve. Then there's the hands who were on watch in the W/T office; the leading tel. and two others, and two coders. That makes seventeen altogether. The signalman up here, eighteen. The SBA, nineteen. The leading steward, twenty.'

'Any other stewards?'

'No, sir.'

It didn't matter, thought the Captain: no officers, either.

'The rest were all engine-room branch, sir,' Adams went on. 'Eight of them altogether.'

'How are they made up?'

'It's pretty good, sir, as far as experience goes. The Chief ERA and one of the younger ones, and a stoker petty officer and five stokers. If it was just one watch they'd be all right. But of course there's no reliefs for them, and they'll have to be split into two watches if it comes to steaming.' Adams paused, on the verge of a question, but the Captain, seeing it coming, interrupted him. He didn't yet feel ready to discuss their chances of getting under way again.

'Just give me those figures again, Adams,' he said, 'as I say the headings. Let's have the fit men first.'

Adams bent down to the light once more. 'Yourself and two officers and twenty-eight men, sir.'

'Killed and wounded?'

Adams added quickly: 'Four officers and twenty-eight.'

'And missing, the First Lieutenant and seventy-four.' He had no need to be reminded of that item: that 'seventy-four' would stay with him always. Not counting the accident to Number One's damage control party, there must have been sixty men killed or cut off by the first explosion. All of them still there, deep down underneath his feet. Twenty-eight left out of a hundred and thirty. Whatever he was able to do with the *Marlborough* now, the weight of those figures could never be lightened.

'Will I make some more cocoa, sir?' said Bridger suddenly. He had been waiting in silence all this time, standing behind the Captain's chair. The numbers and details which Adams had produced, even though they concerned Bridger's own messmates, were real to him only so far as they affected the Captain: this moment, he judged instinctively, was the worst so far, and he tried to dissipate it in the only way open to him.

The Captain's figure, which had been hunched deep in the chair, straightened suddenly. He shook himself. The cold air was stiffening his legs, and he stood up. 'No thanks, Bridger,' he answered. 'I'm going to turn in, in a minute. Bring up my sleeping-bag and a pillow, and I'll sleep in the asdic hut.'

'Aye, aye, sir.' Bridger clumped off at a solid workmanlike pace, his heavy sea-boots ringing their way down the ladder. The Captain turned to Adams again. 'We'd better work out a routine for the time between now and daylight,' he said briskly. 'We can leave the engine-room out of it for the moment: they're busy enough. You'd better arrange the seamen in two watches: the telegraphists and coders can work in with them, except for the leading tel.—he can stay on the set. Send half the hands off watch now: they can sleep in the wardroom alleyway or on the upper deck, whichever they prefer. The rest can carry on with cleaning up.'

'The doctor may want some help down there, sir.'

'Yes—see about that too. . . . Keep two look-outs on the upper deck for the rest of tonight: tell them they're listening for aircraft as well. We'll show an Aldis lamp if we hear anything, and chance it being hostile. You'd better put the signalman up here, with those instructions; and pick out the most intelligent coder, and have him work watch-and-watch with the signalman. That's about all, I think. See that I'm called if anything happens.'

'Do you want a hand to watch that bulkhead, sir?'

'No. The engine-room will cover that: they're nearest. About meals. . . .' The Captain scratched his chin. 'We'll just have to do our best with the wardroom pantry. There were some dry provisions in the after-store, weren't there?'

'Corned beef and biscuits, sir, and some tinned milk, I think. And there's plenty of tea. We'll not go short.'

'Right. . . . That'll do for tonight, then. I'll see what things are like in the morning: there'll be plenty of squaring up to do. You'll have to get those bodies sewn up, too. If we do get under way again,' the Captain tried, and failed, to say this in a normal voice, 'you'll have to work out a scheme of guns' crews and look-outs and quartermasters.'

'Better take the wheel myself, sir.'

The Captain smiled. 'It won't exactly be fleet manoeuvres, Adams.'

The expected question came at last. 'How much chance have we got, sir?'

'Hard to say.' He answered it as unemotionally as he could. 'You saw the state that bulkhead was in. It might go any time, or it might hold indefinitely. But even very slow headway would make a big difference to the strain on it, unless the bows stay rigid where they are, and take most of the weight. Almost everything depends on the weather.'

As he said this, the arrangements he had been making with Adams receded into the background, and he became aware of the ship again, and of her sluggish motion under his feet. She was quieter now, certainly: no shock or grinding from below, no advertisement of distress. But he could feel, as if it were going on inside his own body, the strain on the whole ship, the anguish of that slow cumbersome roll downwind. Earlier she had seemed to be dying: this now was the rallying process, infinitely painful both to endure and to watch. Long after Adams had left the bridge, the Captain still stood there, suffering all that the ship suffered, aware that the only effective anaesthetic was death.

It was an idea which at any other time he would have dismissed as fanciful and ridiculous, unseamanlike as a poet talking of his soul. Now it was natural, deeply felt and deeply resented. His professional responsibility for *Marlborough* was transformed: he felt for her nothing save anger and pity.

Just before he turned in, Chief came up from below to report progress. He stood at the top of the ladder, a tired but not dispirited figure, and his voice had the old downright confidence on which the Captain had come to rely. He had been in *Marlborough* for nearly three years; as an engineering lieutenant he, too, could probably have got a better job, but he had never shown any signs of wanting one.

'We've made a good start on the switchboard, sir,' he began. 'We ought to get the fans going some time tomorrow.' There was nothing in his tone to suggest the danger, which he must have felt all the time, of working deep down below decks at a time like this. 'The boiler-room's in a bit of a mess—there's a lot of water about—but we'll clear that up as soon as we can get pressure on the pumps.'

'What about the bulkhead, Chief?'

'It's about the same, sir. I've been in once myself, and I've a hand listening all the time outside the next watertight door. There's nothing to report there.' He turned, and looked behind him down the length of the ship, and then up at the sky. 'She seems a lot easier, sir.'

'Yes, the wind's doing down.' The phrase was like a blessing.

'By God, we'll do it yet!' Chief, preparing to go down again, slurred his feet along the deck and found it sticky. 'Bit of a mess here,' he commented.

'Blood,' said the Captain shortly. 'They haven't cleaned up yet.'

'We're going to be pretty shorthanded,' said Chief, following a natural train of thought. 'But that's tomorrow's worry. Good night, sir.'

'Good night, Chief. Get some sleep if you can.'

But later he himself found sleep almost impossible to achieve, weary as he was after nearly nine hours on the bridge. He lay in his sleeping-bag on the hard floor of the asdic hut, feeling underneath him the trials and tremors of the ship's painful labouring. It was very cold. Poor *Marlborough*, he thought, losing between waking and sleeping the full control of his thoughts. Poor old *Marlborough*. We shouldn't do this to you. None of us should: not us, or the Germans, or those poor chaps washing about in the fo'c'sle. No ship deserved an ordeal as evil as this. Only human beings, immeasurably base, deserved such punishment.

Bridger woke him at first light, with a mug of tea and an insinuating 'Seven o'clock, sir!' so normal as to make him smile. But the smile was not much more than a momentary flicker. Under him he felt the ship very slowly rolling to and fro, without will and without protest: she seemed more a part of the sea itself than a separate burden on it. The weather must have moderated a lot, but *Marlborough* might be deeper in the water as well.

Cold and stiff, he lay for a few minutes before getting up, collecting his thoughts and remembering what was waiting for him outside the asdic hut. It would be bitterly cold, possibly wet as well: the ship would seem deformed and ugly, the damage meeting his eyes at every turn: the blood on the bridge would be dried black. All over the upper deck there would be men, grey-faced and shivering, waking to face the day: not cheerful and noisy as they usually were, but dully astonished that the ship was still afloat and that they had survived so far; unwilling, even, to meet each other's eye, in the embarrassment of fear and disbelief of the future. And there were those other men down in the fo'c'sle, who would not wake. There were the burials to see to. There was the bulkhead.

He got up.

The bulkhead first, with the Chief and Adams. The rating outside the watertight door said: 'Haven't heard anything, sir,' in a noncommittal way, as if he did not really believe that they were not all wasting their time. He was a young stoker: sixteen men in his mess had been caught forward: no hope of any sort had yet been communicated to him. Noting this, the Captain thought: I'll have to talk to them, some time this morning. . . . Inside, things were as before: there was a little more water, and the atmosphere was now thick and sour: but nothing had shifted, and with the decrease in the ship's rolling the bulkhead itself was rigid, without sound or movement.

'I think it's even improved a bit, sir,' said the Chief. He ran his hand down the central seam, which before had been leaking: his fingers now came away dry. 'This seems to have worked itself watertight again. If we could alter the trim a bit, so that even part of this space is above the waterline, we might be able to save it.'

'That's going to be today's job,' said the Captain, 'moving everything we can aft, so as to bring her head up a bit. I'll go into details when we get outside.'

On his way back he visited the boiler- and engine-rooms. The boiler-room was deserted, and already cooling fast: here again the forward bulkhead was a tangle of shores and joists, braced against the anglepieces that joined the frames.

'What about this one?' he asked.

'Doesn't seem to be any strain on it, sir,' Chief answered. 'I think the space next to it—that's the drying-room and the small bos'n's store—must still be watertight.'

The Captain nodded without saying anything. He was beginning to feel immensely and unreasonably cheerful, but to communicate that feeling to anyone else seemed frivolous in the extreme. There was so little to go on: it might all be a product of what he felt about the ship herself, and unfit to be shared with anyone.

The engine-room was very much alive. Two men—the Chief ERA and a young telegraphist—were working on the main switchboard: the telegraphist, lying flat on his back behind it, was pulling through a length of thick insulated cable and connecting it up. Two more hands were busy on one of the main steam valves. There was an air of purpose here, of men who knew clearly what the next job was to be, and how to set about it.

The Chief ERA, an old pensioner with a smooth bald head in odd contrast with the craggy wrinkles on his face, smiled when he saw the Captain. They came from the same Kentish village, and the Chief ERA's appointment to *Marlborough* had been the biggest wangle the Captain had ever undertaken. But it had been justified a score of times in the last two years, and obviously it was in process of being justified again now.

'Well, Chief?'

'Going on all right, sir. It won't be much to look at, but I reckon it'll serve.'

'That's all we want.' The Captain turned to the engineer officer. 'Any other troubles down here?'

'I'm a bit worried about the port engine, sir. That torpedo was a big shock. It may have knocked the shaft out.'

'It doesn't matter if we only have one screw. We couldn't go more than a few knots anyway, with that bulkhead.'

'That's what I thought, sir.'

The Chief ERA, presuming on their peace-time friendship in a way which the Captain had anticipated, and did not mind, said:

'Do you think we'll be able to steam, sir?'

Everyone in the engine-room stopped work to listen to the answer. The Captain hesitated a moment, and then said:

'If the weather stays like it is now, and we can correct the trim a bit, I think we ought to make a start.'

'How far to go, sir?'

'About five hundred miles.' That was as much as he wanted to talk about and he nodded and turned to go. With his foot on the ladder he said: 'I expect we'll be able to count every one of them.'

The laughter as he began to climb was a tonic for himself as well. It hadn't been a very good joke, but it was the first one for a long time.

The sick bay next. The doctor was asleep in an arm-chair when he came in, his young sensitive face turned away from the light, his hands splayed out on the arms of the chair as if each individual finger were resting after an exhaustive effort. The sick-berth attendant was bending over one of the lower cots, where a bandaged figure lay with closed, deeply-circled eyes. There were eight men altogether: after the night's turmoil the room was surprisingly tidy, save for a pile of bloodstained swabs and dressings which had overflowed from the waste-basket. The tidiness and the sharp aseptic smell were reassuring.

He put his hand out, and touched the sleeping figure.

'Good morning, Doctor.'

Soundlessly the doctor woke, opened his eyes, and sat up. Even this movement seemed part of some controlled competent routine.

'Hallo, sir!'

'Busy night?'

'Very, sir. All right, though.'

'Just what you were waiting for?' The Captain smiled.

The doctor looked at the Captain, and smiled back, and said: 'I haven't felt so well for years.'

It must be odd to feel like that, about what must surely have been the goriest night of his life. But it was natural, if you were proud and confident of your professional skill, and for three years you felt you had been utterly wasted. This young man, who had barely been qualified when war broke out, must now feel, with justice, that the initials after his name had at last come to life.

The Captain looked round the sick bay. 'Where are the rest of them? Adams said you had sixteen.'

'Four died.' It was extraordinary how the simplicity of phrase and tone still conveyed an assurance that the lives had been fought for, and only surrendered in the last extremity. 'I've spread the rest over the officers' cabins, where they'll be more comfortable. There's one in yours, sir.'

'That's all right. . . . How's the midshipman?'

'Bad. In fact going, I'm afraid, sir. That chest wound was too deep, and he lost too much blood. Do you want to take a look at him? He's in his own cabin.'

'Is he conscious?'

The doctor shook his head. 'No. I've had to dope him pretty thoroughly. That's the trouble: if I go on doping him he'll die of it, and if I let him wake up there's enough shock and pain to kill him almost immediately. That's why it's no good.' Again the simple tone seemed able to imply an infinity of skill and care, which had proved unavailing.

'I won't bother, then.' The phrase sounded callous, but he did not bother to qualify it: he was suddenly impatient to leave this antiseptic corner, and get to work on the ship. She, at least, was still among the living: no dope, no ordered death-bed for her. He had skill and care of his own sort. . . .

As he came out on the quarter-deck he checked his step, for there, arranged in neat rows, which somehow seemed a caricature of the whole idea of burial, were the sewn-up bodies which he must later commit to the deep. Nineteen of them: three officers and sixteen men. There had not been enough ensigns to cover them all, he noted: here and there three of them shared one flag, crowding under it in a pathetic, last-minute symbolism. . . . Adams, who had been waiting for him, straightened up as he emerged. He had only been bending down to adjust one of the formal canvas packages; but the Captain had a sudden ghoulish fancy that Adams had been giving it the traditional 'last stitch'—the needle and thread through the nose, by which the sailmaker used to satisfy himself that the body he was sewing up was beyond doubt that of a dead man. The Captain looked away, and up at the sky. It was full light now: a grey cold day, the veiled sun shedding the thinnest watery gleam, the waste of water round them reduced to a long flat swell. The passing of the storm, or some lull in its centre, had brought a windless day for their respite.

Chief, who had waited behind in the engine-room, now joined them, and together the three men crossed the upper deck towards the fo'c'sle. The Captain led the party, picking his way past the bloody ruin of 'X' gun, and the men who were at work cleaning up. He was conscious of them looking at him: conscious of a suppressed, heightened tension among them all: conscious, for example, that Leading Seaman Tapper, not an outstanding personality, had this morning assumed a new, almost heroic bearing. As the only leading seaman left alive, he was already rising to the challenge. . . . With the coming of daylight all these men had won back what the stoker, working and waiting below decks, still lacked: hope in the future, confidence in themselves and the ship. 'The ship is your best lifebelt'—a phrase in his Standing Orders for damage control returned to him. By God, that was still true; and all the men up here trusted and believed it.

Presently they were standing on the fo'c'sle by 'A' gun. From here the deck, buckled and distorted, led steeply downwards, till the bullring in the bows was not more than three or four feet from the water: even allowing for this downward curve of the deck, *Marlborough* must be drawing about twenty-eight feet instead of her normal sixteen. Obviously, the first essential was to correct this if possible: not only to ease the pressure forward when they started moving, but also to bring the screws fully under water again.

The Captain stepped forward carefully till he was standing directly over the explosion area: there he leant over the rail, staring down into the water a few feet away. From somewhere below an oily scum oozed out, trailing aft and away like some disgusting suppuration; but of the wound itself nothing could be seen. Unprofessionally, he was glad of that: it was sufficiently distressing to note the broad outlines of *Marlborough*'s plight on this cold grey morning, without being confronted with the gross details. He realized suddenly that this must now be treated as a technical problem, and nothing more, and after a quick look-round the rest of the fo'c'sle he turned back to the Chief and Adams.

'I've got three ideas,' he said briskly. 'You may have some more. . . . For a start, we'll get rid of as much as possible of this'—he tapped one of the lowered barrels of 'A' gun, askew on its drooping platform. 'It wouldn't be safe to fire them anyway, so we can ditch the barrels—and even the mounting itself if we can lift it clear.'

'The derrick can deal with the barrels, sir,' said Adams. 'I don't know about the rest.'

'We'll see. . . . Then there are the anchors. We can either let them run out altogether, with their cables, or else let the anchors go by themselves, and manhandle the cable aft as a counterweight. What do you think, Chief?'

'The second idea is the best one, sir. But without steam on the windlass we can't get the cable out of the locker.'

'We'll have to do that by hand.' The Captain turned to Adams again. 'We've still got one of those weapons, haven't we?—the ratchet-and-pawl lever?'

'Yes, sir. It's a long job, though.'

'I know.' They had once had to weigh anchor by this archaic method, a long time ago, bringing in the cable link by link, half a link to each stroke of the lever, which needed four men to operate it. It had been an agonizingly slow process, taking nearly six hours and everyone's temper. Now they would have to do it to each cable in turn. . . . 'But it's worth it, to get some of the weight aft. Then there's the windlass itself. If we pull it to pieces and use a sheer-legs to lift the heavy parts, we might get rid of a lot of weight that way.'

The Engineer Officer nodded, rather abstractedly. It would be his job later to account for all this, item by item, in triplicate at least, and the whole thing was a horrid distortion of the principles of storekeeping. But he put the thought on one side, and produced an idea which must have been professionally more acceptable.

'I was wondering about the fore-peak, sir,' he began. 'You know we've kept it flooded for the last two trips, to balance the weight of those extra depth-charges aft. We can't pump it out now, because the suction-line is broken. But if we took this cover-plate off'—he pointed to the small plate screwed to the deck, right up in the bows—'and made sure the compartment was still isolated, we could pump it out by hand. That would give us some buoyancy just where we need it.'

The Captain nodded quickly. 'Good idea, Chief. You'll have to go carefully, though, in case the bulkhead's gone and it's all part of the explosion area. By the way, what's the fuel situation going to be, with all this part isolated?'

'Oh, we'll have plenty, sir, especially if we're only steaming on one boiler. We've still got the two big tanks aft.'

'Right. . . .' He looked out at the sea again, and then at his watch. It was nearly nine. 'I'll read the burial service in half an hour, Adams, if you'll have everything ready by then. Then you can make a start on the weight-lifting programme—the gun first, and then the anchors. Can you spare any stokers, Chief?'

'Maybe two, sir.'

'The fresh air will be a nice change for them. . . .'

His spirits were rising.

But there was nothing artificial, no formal assumption of mourning, in what he felt half an hour later, as he opened his prayer book, gave 'Off caps' in a low, almost gentle voice, and prepared to read the service. All that remained of his ship's company stood in a rough square on the quarter-deck: at their feet the nineteen bodies, in their canvas shrouds, seemed like some sinister carpet from which they could not take their eyes. There were altogether too many of them: barely did the living outnumber the dead, and if the men caught in the fo'c'sle were reckoned, the living were only curious survivals of a vanished time. . . . That pause in the service, when he said 'We do now commit their bodies to the deep', and then waited, as the burial party got to work and the nineteen bodies made their successive splashes, their long dive—that pause seemed to be lasting for ever.

The men in their stained sea-boots and duffle-coats stood silent, their hair ruffled, watching the bodies go: flanking him, the doctor and the Chief completed the square of witnesses. The rough canvases scraped the deck as they were dragged across; the bodies splashed and vanished; the ship rolled, and all their feet shifted automatically to meet it; a seaman coughed; the silence under the cold sky was oppressive and somehow futile. He himself, with an appalling clarity of feeling, was conscious of cruel loss. These had been his own men: to see them 'discharged dead' in this perfunctory whole-sale fashion only deepened the sense of personal bereavement which was in his face and his voice as he took up the reading again.

When it was done he put the book away and faced his ship's company: in their expression, too, was something of the wastage and sadness of the moment. It was not what he wished to dwell on, but he could not dismiss it without a word: that would have been as cruelly artificial as using the dead men to whip up hatred, or additional energy for the task ahead. It was no time for anything save sincerity.

'I shall never need reminding of this moment,' he began, 'and I know that is true for all of you too. We have lost good men, good shipmates, and there are many more whom we cannot even reach to give them proper burial. We can't forget them, any more than we can forget the three officers and sixteen men we've just seen over the side. But,' he raised his voice a little, 'one of the hardest things of war is that there is never any spare time to think about these things, or to mourn men like these as they deserve. That has to come later: there's always something to do; and in this case it's going to be the toughest job any of us has ever undertaken. I may as well tell you that I nearly gave the order to abandon ship last night: for the moment the weather has saved us, and we must do our utmost to profit by it. I'm not going to hold out too much hope: but if the weather holds, and the bulk-head, which is taking most of the strain, doesn't collapse, and if I can correct the trim, we stand a good chance of getting in—or at least of going far enough south to meet other ships.' He smiled. 'You can see there are a lot of "ifs" about this job. But it would be a hundred times worth trying, even if our lives didn't depend on it. I myself am going to do my utmost to get this ship in, and I'm counting on every man to back me up. Remember there are only thirty-one of us altogether, and that means a double and triple effort from each one of you. . . . We'll stand easy now, and then get to work. And keep this idea in the back of your minds: if we do get *Marlborough* in, it will be the finest thing any of us have ever done.'

He wanted to say more: affected as he had been by the burials, he wanted to dwell on this aspect of sacrifice, and on *Marlborough* as a measure of its validity and as something dear to them all. But he was afraid of sounding theatrical: better perhaps to leave it like this, a challenge to their endurance and seamanship, and look to the outcome.

When he returned to the bridge he took out the deck-log and began to make an entry concerning the death and burial of his men. It was while he was adding the nineteen names and ratings that he noticed it was the morning of New Year's Day.

3

All that day they lay there, the ship's only motion a sluggish rolling. But within her the movement and the noises were cheerful. The ditching of 'A' gun barrels and the greater part of the mounting was easy: the breaking and moving of the anchor cables a long-drawn-out effort which lasted till well after dark. But the cables, hauled in sections along the upper deck and stowed right aft among the depth-charges, made an appreciable difference to their trim: so did the jettisoned windlass, which disappeared overboard bit by bit, as in some mysterious conjuring trick. (It was too heavy and unwieldy to move aft.) But the pumping out of the fore-peak (the triangular section which makes up the bows) was the most successful of all. It acted as a buoyancy chamber where it could exert the most leverage, and it brought the bows up cheerfully. Altogether, by the time the programme was fulfilled, the draught forrard had improved to twenty-four feet, and the screws aft were deep enough to get a firm grip of the water. Of course, she would steer like a mongrel waving its tail; but that wouldn't matter. There was no one watching.

One curious accident attended the lightening process. As *Marlborough's* draught forrard began to alter decisively, two bodies, released by some chance movement of the hull, floated out from the hole in the port side. They drifted away before they could be recovered: they were both badly burned, and both sprawling in relaxed, ungainly attitudes as though glad to be quit of their burden. The Captain, looking down from the bridge, watched them with absorbed attention, obsessed by the fancy that they were a first instalment of the sacrifice which must be paid before the ship got under way. He heard a rating on the fo'c'sle say: 'The second one was Fletcher— poor bastard,' and he felt angry at the curt epitaph, as if its informality might somehow weaken the magic. He could not remember having had thoughts like that since he was a small boy. Perhaps it was the beginning of feeling really tired.

For him it had been a long day, and now at dusk, with the prospect of another night of drifting, he felt impatient to put thing to the test. He had been all over the ship again: he had seen the midshipman and two ratings who were also dying: he had looked at the radio set (from which the leading tel. had at last stood back and said: 'It's no good, sir—there's too much smashed'): he had made a third examination of the bulkhead, where they had been able to insert another shore and a felt-and-tallow patch, to take up the slack as the pressure on it relaxed. He had directed the work on the cables, Adams being busy on 'A' gun. Now he had nothing to do but wait for Chief's report from the engine-room: the hardest part of all. He had the sky to watch, and the barometer, low but steady; and that was all. The main ordeal still lay ahead.

It was nine o'clock that evening before the engineer officer came up with his report: the Captain was sitting in the deserted wardroom aft, eating the corned beef hash which was now their staple diet and remembering other parties which this room had witnessed, when there were eight of them, with Number One's wife and Guns' fiancée and one of the Mid's colourful young women to cheer them. Now the dead men and the mourning women outnumbered the living: no charm, no laughter could enliven any of the absent. . . . Impatiently he ground a half-smoked cigarette into his plate, cursing these ridiculous thoughts and fancies, unlike any he could remember, which were beginning to crowd in on him. There was no time to spare for such irrelevances: he had one supreme task to concentrate on, and anything else was a drain on energy and attention alike.

Chief came in, shedding a pair of oily gauntlets, looking down apologetically at his stained white overalls.

'Well, Chief?'

'Pretty good, sir.' He crossed to the pantry hatch and hammered on it, demanding his supper. Then he sat down in his usual place at the foot of the table, and leant back. 'The switchboard's done, and they're working on the dynamo now: it had a bad shake-up, but I think we'll manage.' He was obviously very tired, eyelids drooping in a grey lined face. The Captain suddenly realized how much depended on this man's skill. 'I'll be flashing up when I've finished supper.'

'How long before we can steam?'

'Can't say to the nearest hour, sir. It'll be some time tomorrow, unless we run into more snags. There's the boiler-room to pump out, and a lot of cleaning up besides. It'll only be one screw, I'm afraid. The other's nearly locked: the shaft must be badly bent.'

'It doesn't matter.'

Bridger came in with the Chief's supper, and for a little while there was silence as he ate. Then, between bites, he asked:

'How's the midshipman, sir?'

'Pretty nearly gone. God knows what keeps him alive. His chest's in an awful mess.'

Chief looked round the room, and said: 'It's funny to see this place empty.'

There was silence again till he had finished eating. They shared the same thoughts, but it was less discomforting to leave them unspoken. Bridger, coming in with the Chief's coffee, broke the silence by asking the Captain:

'Will you be sleeping down here, sir?'

'No, in the asdic hut again.'

'Will you see Petty Officer Adams, sir?'

'Yes. Tell him to come in.'

There was a whispering in the pantry, and Adams came in, cap in hand. 'Same routine tonight, sir?' he asked.

'Yes, Adams. Two look-outs, and the signalman on the bridge. I'll be in the asdic hut.'

'Aye, aye, sir.'

'Things seem to be going all right. We should get going some time tomorrow.'

Adams's severe face cracked into a grin. 'Can I tell the hands, sir?'

'Yes, do.' The Captain stood up, and began to put on his duffle-coat. 'How about some sleep for you, Chief?'

The Chief nodded. "As soon as I've finished up, sir. There'll be a bit of time to spare then.' Relaxing, with coffee-cup in hand, he looked around the wardroom. 'New Year's Day. I wish we had the radio. It feels so cut off.'

'With luck you'll have your bedtime music tomorrow.' He went out, stepping over the dozen sleeping men who crowded the alleyway, and made his way forward to the bridge again. With luck tomorrow might bring everything they were waiting for.

The sea was still calm, the glass unwaveringly steady.

He awoke suddenly at five o'clock, startled and uneasy. For a moment he puzzled over what had disturbed him: then he realized gratefully what it was. The lights had come on, and the little heater screwed to the bulkhead was glowing. It meant that the dynamos were now running properly, and the switchboard, which the Chief had been reserving for the engine-room circuit, was able to deal with the full load. With a surge of thankfulness almost light-headed, he got up and went over to the side-table. On it lay a chart and pair of dividers, ready for a job which, impelled by yet another of those queer fancies, he had sworn not to tackle until this moment had arrived. The course for home. . . . He took out his pencil and prepared to calculate.

The only mark on the chart was Pilot's neat cross (too damned appropriate) marking their estimated position when the torpedo struck them, with the time and date—1630/31/12. From this he started to measure off. Distance to the Clyde—520 miles. Distance to the nearest of the Faeroes—210 miles, and nothing much when you got there. Distance to the nearest point of Britain—the Butt of Lewis, 270 miles. And just around the corner, another 30 miles or so—Stornoway. . . . That was the place to make for, he knew. It had no big repairing facilities, but it would be shelter enough, and they would be able to send tugs to bring them the rest of the way home. Stornaway—300 miles. Say three knots. A hundred hours. Four days. Good enough.

Now for the course. The magnetic course, it must be: the master gyro-compass had been wrecked, and they would have to depend on the magnetic compasses, trusting that the explosion and the shifting of ballast had not put them out. South-east would do it. South-east for four days. Butt of Lewis was a good mark for them (he checked it on the chart): a flashing light, visible fourteen miles. That would bring them in all right. And what a landfall. . . .

When finally he laid down his pencil he was still in the same state of exultation as had possessed him when he saw the lights come on. The desire to sleep had vanished: impelled to some sort of activity, he left the shelter of the asdic hut and began to pace up and down outside. By God, once they got going there would be no stopping them. . . . What did four days matter?— they could keep going for four weeks if it meant *Marlborough* making harbour at the end. There was no depression now, no morbid brooding about sacrifices or the cost in men. It was *Marlborough* against the sea and the enemy, and tomorrow would see her cheating them both. He looked up at the sky, clear and frosty: a night for action, for steering small, for laughing and killing at the same time. The first night of 1943. And tomorrow they would sail into the new year like a prizefighter going in for the finish. Nothing was going to stop them now.

Midday found them still drifting, still powerless. A succession of minor breakdowns involving in turn the fans and the steering-engine held up everything during the morning: at noon a defect in one of the oil pumps led to more delay. The suspended activity, the anti-climax after that first rush of feeling, was a severe test of patience: it was with difficulty that the Captain, walking the upper deck, managed to exhibit a normal confidence. Part of the morning was taken up with the burying of two more men who had died during the night, but for the remainder he had little to occupy him; and as the afternoon advanced and the light declined, a dull stupor, matching his own indolence, seemed to envelop the ship. Stricken with the curse of immobility, she accepted the dusk as if it were all that her languor deserved.

Then, as swiftly as that first torpedo strike, the good news came. Chief, presenting himself in the wardroom with a cheerful grin, announced that his repairs were complete: he used the classic formula 'Ready to proceed, sir!' and he seemed to shed ten years in saying it. The Captain got up slowly, smiling in answer.

'Thank you, Chief. . . . A remarkable effort.'

'We're all touching wood, sir.' But he was almost boyish in his good humour.

'I want to start very gently. Twenty or thirty revs, not more. Will you put a reliable hand on the bulkhead?'

'I'll go myself, sir. The Chief ERA can take charge in the engine-room.'

'All right.' The Captain raised his voice. 'Pantry!'

The leading steward appeared.

'Ask Petty Officer Adams to come up to the bridge.'

'Aye, aye, sir.'

'I'll just ring "Slow ahead" when I'm ready, Chief. We can do the rest by voice-pipe. If you hear anything at all from the bulkhead, stop engines straightaway, of your own accord.'

Within a minute or so he was on the bridge, the signalman by his side, Adams in the wheelhouse below. Leaning across the faintly-lit compass he called down the voice-pipe:

'How's her head down there?'

'South, eighty west, sir.'

The two compasses were in agreement. 'Right. . . . Our course is south-east, Adams. Bring her round very slowly when we begin to move.'

'Aye, aye, sir.' Adams's voice, like the signalman's hard breathing at his elbow, reflected the tension that was binding them all.

The Captain took a deep breath. 'Slow ahead starboard.'

'Slow ahead starboard, sir.'

The telegraph rang. There was a pause, then a slight tremor, then the beginning of a smooth pulsation. Very slowly *Marlborough* began to move. A thin ripple of bow-wave stood out in the luminous twilight: then another. In the compass bowl the floating disk stirred, edging away to the right. The ship started her turn, a slow, barely perceptible turn, 125 degrees to port in a wide half-circle nearly a mile across.

Presently he called down the voice-pipe: 'Steering all right?'

'Yes, sir. Five degrees of port wheel on.'

The engine-room bell rang, and he bent to the voice-pipe, his throat constricted. 'What is it?'

From the background of noise below an anonymous voice said: 'Message from the engineer, sir. "Nothing to report".'

'Thank you.'

A long pause, with nothing but smooth sliding movement. Then from Adams, suddenly: 'Course—south-east, sir.'

'Very good.'

They were started. Forty-eight hours after the torpedoing: two days and two nights adrift. Course south-east.

The wind, now growing cold on his cheek, was like a caress.

That first night, those first fourteen hours of darkness on the bridge, had the intensity and the disquiet of personal dedication. It was as if he were taking hold of *Marlborough*—a sick, uncertain, but brave accomplice—and nursing her through the beginnings of a desperate convalescence. He rarely stirred from his chair, because he could see all he wanted from there—the sagging fo'c'sle, the still rigid bows—and he could hear and feel all the subtleties of her movement forward: but occasionally he stepped to the wing of the bridge and glanced aft, where their pale wake glittered and spread. Of all that his eyes could rest on, that was the most heartening. . . . Then back to his chair, and the stealthy advance of the bows, and the perpetual humming undercurrent that came from the engine-room voice-pipe, as comforting as the steady beat of an aircraft engine in mid-ocean. He was not in the least tired: sustained by love and hope, he felt ready to lend to *Marlborough* all his reserves of endurance.

At midnight the Chief came up to join him. His report was good: the engine had settled down, the bulkhead seemed unaffected by their forward movement. They discussed the idea of increasing speed, and decided against it: the log showed a steady three knots, sufficient for his plans.

'There's no point in taking bigger chances,' said the Captain finally. 'She's settled down so well that it would be stupid to fool about with the revs. I think we'll leave things as they are.'

'Suits me, sir. It'll be a lot easier, seeing how shorthanded we are down there.'

'You're working watch-and-watch, I suppose?'

'Got to, sir, with only two ERAs. I'd stand a watch myself, but there's all the auxiliary machinery to look after.' He yawned and stretched. 'How about you, sir? Shall I give you a spell?'

'No, I'm all right, thanks, Chief. You turn in now, and get some sleep.' The Captain smiled. 'I always seem to be saying that to you. I hope you're doing it.'

Chief smiled back. 'Trust me, sir. Good night.'

Presently, up the voice-pipe, came Adams's voice: 'All right to hand over, sir?'

'Who's taking the wheel?'

'Leading Seaman Tapper, sir.'

'All right, Adams. What does the steering feel like now?'

'A bit lumpy, sir. It takes a lot to bring her round if she starts swinging off. But it's nothing out of the way, really.'

'I don't want anyone except you or Tapper to take the wheel until daylight.'

'Aye, aye, sir.'

It meant a long trick at the wheel for both these two; but inexpert steering might put too great a strain on the hull, and he wanted its endurance to be fully demonstrated before running any risks.

A moment later he heard the confirmatory 'Course south-east—starboard engine slow ahead—Leading Seaman Tapper on the wheel', as Adams was relieved. Then the bridge settled down to its overall watchful tranquillity again.

Indeed, his only other visitor, save for Bridger with a two-hourly relay of cocoa, was the doctor, who came up to tell him that the midshipman was dead. It was news which he had been waiting for, news with no element of surprise in it; but coming at a time of tension and weariness, towards the dawn, when he was cold and stiff and his eyes felt rimmed with tiredness, it was profoundly depressing. The midshipman, as captain's secretary, had spent a great deal of time with him: he was a cheerful, still irresponsible young man who had the makings of a first-class sailor. Now, at daylight, they would be burying him—and that only after alternate periods of agony and stupor, which had robbed death of every dignity. This, the latest and the most touching of the sacrifices that had been demanded of them, destroyed for the moment all the night's achievement.

Dawn restored it: a grey sunless dawn, only a lightening of the dull arch above them: but the new and blessed day for all that. As the gloom round them retreated and he was able to see, first the full outline of *Marlborough's* hull, then the shades of colour in the water, and then the horizon all round them, the triumph of the moment grew and warmed within him, dissolving all other feeling. By God, he thought, we can keep going for ever like this. . . . They were forty miles to the good already: there were only 260 more— three more nights, three more heartening dawns such as this: and *Marlborough*, creeping ahead over the smooth paling sea, was as strong as ever. If they could hold on to that (he touched the wood of his chair) then they were home.

At eight o'clock, the change of the watch, he called Leading Seaman Tapper to the bridge, and told him to turn over the wheel to the regular quartermaster and to take over as officer of the watch. It was irregular (he smiled as he realized how irregular), but he had to get some rest and there was no one else available to take his place: Chief was owed many hours of sleep, the doctor had been up all night with the midshipman, Adams had been on the wheel since four o'clock. It simply could not be helped.

He lay down at the back of the bridge, drew the hood of his duffle-coat over his face, and closed his eyes against the frosty light. It was such bliss to relax at last, to sink away from care, that he found himself grinning foolishly. Fourteen hours on the bridge: and God knows how many the night before. . . . He would have to watch that. Might get the doc. to fix him up. Leading Seaman Tapper—*Acting* Leading Seaman Tapper. . . . No, it couldn't be helped. In any case there was nothing to guard, nothing to watch for, nothing for them to fight with. Now, they had simply to endure.

4

It was at midday that the wind began to freshen, from the south.

The noise, slight as it was, woke the Captain. It began as no more than an occasional wave-slap against the bows, and a gentle lifting to the increased swell; but into his deep drugged sleep it stabbed like a sliver of ice. He lay still for a moment, getting the feel of the ship again, guessing at what had happened: by the way *Marlborough* was moving, the wind was slightly off the bow, and already blowing crisply. Then he stood up, shook off his blankets, and walked to the front of the bridge.

It was as he had thought: a fresh breeze, curling the wave-top, was now meeting them, about twenty degrees off the starboard bow. Of the two, that was the better side, as it kept the torpedoed area under shelter: but the angle was still bad, it could still impart to their progress a twisting movement which might become a severe strain. While he was considering it, Adams came up to relieve Tapper, and they all three stood in silence for a moment, watching the waves as they slapped and broke against *Marlborough's* lowered bows.

'You'd better go back on the wheel, Adams,' said the Captain presently. 'If this gets any worse we'll have to turn directly into it, and slow down.'

It did get worse, in the next hour he spent in his chair, and when the first wave, breaking right over the bows, splashed the fo'c'sle itself, he rang the bell to the engine-room. Chief himself answered.

'I'll have to take the revs off, Chief, I'm afraid,' he said. 'It's getting too lively altogether. What are they now?'

'Thirty-five, sir.'

'Make that twenty. Have you got a hand on the bulkhead?'

'No, sir. I'll put one on.'

'Right.' He turned to the wheel-house voice-pipe. 'Steer south, twenty-five east, Adams. And tell me if she's losing steerage-way. I want to keep the wind dead ahead.'

'Aye, aye, sir.'

The alteration, and the decrease in speed, served them well for an hour: then it suddenly seemed to lose its effect, and their movements became thoroughly strained and awkward. He decreased speed again, to fifteen revolutions—bare steerage-way—but still the awkwardness and the distress persisted: it became a steady thumping as each wave hit them, a recurrent lift-and-crunch which might have been specially designed to threaten their weakest point. It was now blowing steadily and strongly from the south: he listened to the wind rising with a murderous attention. At about half-past three it backed suddenly to the south-east, and he followed it: it meant they were heading for home again—the sole good point in a situation rapidly deteriorating. He looked at the seas running swiftly past them, and felt the ones breaking at the bows, and he knew that all their advantage was ebbing away from them. This was how it had been when he had been ready to abandon ship, three nights ago; it was this that was going to destroy them.

Quick steps rang on the bridge ladder, and he turned. It was the Chief: in the failing light his face looked grey and defeated.

'That bulkhead can't take this, sir,' he began immediately. 'I've been in to have a look, and it's started working again—there's the same leak down that seam. We'll have to stop.'

The Captain shook his head. 'That's no good, Chief. If we stop in this sea, we'll just bang ourselves to bits.' A big wave hit them as he spoke, breaking down on the bows, driving them under. *Marlborough* came up from it very slowly indeed. 'We've got to keep head to wind, at all costs.'

'Can we go any slower, sir?'

'No. She'll barely steer as it is.'

Another wave took them fair and square on the fo'c'sle, sweeping along the upper deck as *Marlborough* sagged into the trough. The wind tugged at them. It was as if the death-bed scene were starting all over again.

The Chief looked swiftly at the Captain. 'Could we go astern into it?'

'Probably pull the bows off, Chief.'

'Better than this, sir. This is just murder.'

'Yes. . . . All right. . . . She may not come round.' He leant over to the voice-pipe. 'Stop starboard.'

'Stop starboard, sir.' The telegraph clanged.

'Adams, I'm going astern, and up into the wind stern first. Put the wheel over hard a-starboard.'

'Hard a-starboard, sir.'

'Slow astern starboard.'

The bell clanged again. 'Starboard engine slow astern, wheel hard a-starboard, sir.'

'Very good.'

They waited. Those few minutes before *Marlborough* gathered sternway were horrible. She seemed to be standing in the jaws of the wind and sea, mutely undergoing a wild torture. She came down upon one wave with so solid a crash that it seemed impossible that the whole bows should not be wrenched off: a second, with a cruelty and malice almost deliberate, hit them a treacherous slewing blow on the port side. Slowly *Marlborough* backed away, shaking and staggering as if from a mortal thrust. The compass faltered, and started very slowly to turn: then as the wind caught the bows she began to swing sharply. He called out: 'Watch it, Adams! Meet her! Bring her head on to northwest,' and his hands as he gripped the pedestal were as white as the compass-card. The last few moments, before *Marlborough* was safely balanced with her stern into the teeth of the wind, were like the sweating end of a nightmare.

Behind him the Chief sighed deeply. 'Thank God for that. What revs do you want, sir?'

'We'll try twenty.'

It was by now almost dark. *Marlborough* settled down to her awkward progress: both Adams and then Tapper wrestled steadily to keep her stern to the wind, while the waves mounted and steepened and broke solidly upon the quarter-deck. That whole night, which the Captain spent on the bridge, had had a desperate quality of unrelieved distress. All the time the wind blew with great force from the southeast, all the time the seas ran against them as if powered by a living hate, and the vicious spray lashed the funnel and the bridge structure. At first light it began to snow: the driving clouds settled and lay thick all over them, crusting the upper deck in total icy whiteness. *Marlborough* might have been sailing backwards off a Christmas cake . . . but still, with unending, hopeless persistence, she butted her way southwards.

Five days later—one hundred and twenty-one hours—she was still doing it. The snow was gone, and the gale had eased to a stiff southerly breeze; but the sea was still running too high for them to risk turning their bows into it, and so they maintained, stern first, their ludicrous progress. The whole afterpart of the ship had been drenched with water ever since they turned; the wardroom had been made uninhabitable by a leaking skylight, the alleyway in which the men slept was six inches awash with a frothy residue of spray. It was hardly to be wondered at, thought the Captain as he slopped through it on his way back to the bridge: poor old *Marlborough* hadn't been designed for this sort of thing.

He was very tired. He had hardly had two consecutive hours of sleep in the last five days: the strain had settled in his face like a tight and ugly mask. The doctor had done his best to relieve him, by taking an occasional spell on the bridge when the remaining four serious patients could be left; but even this seemed of no avail—his weariness, and the hours of concentration on *Marlborough*'s foolish movements, pursued him like a hypnosis, twitching his eyelids when he sought sleep, making his scalp prickle and the brain inside flutter. Hope of rest was destroyed by a twanging tension such as sometimes made him want to scream aloud. When he sat down in his chair on that fifth night of stern-way—the ninth since they were torpedoed—and hunched his stiff shoulders against the cold, he was conscious of nothing save an appalling lassitude. Even to stare and search ahead, in quest of those shorelights that never showed themselves, was effort enough to make him feel sick in doing it.

He had no idea where they were. They had seen nothing—no lights at night, no aircraft, not a single smudge of smoke anywhere on the horizon. The sextant had been smashed by the shellfire, and there was no sun anyway to take sights by. Even at two knots, even at one and a half, they should have raised Butt of Lewis light by now, if their course was correct. That was the hellish, the insane part of it. Probably it wasn't correct: probably the torpedoing and the weightshifting had put everything out, and the magnetic compasses were completely haywire. Probably they were heading straight out into the Atlantic instead of pointing for home. And Hell! he thought, this bloody cock-eyed way of steaming . . . you couldn't tell where the ship was going to. They might be anywhere. They might be going around in circles, digging their own grave.

Bridger, the admirable unassailable Bridger, appeared at his elbow. The cup of cocoa which seemed to be part of his right arm was once more tendered. While he drank it, Bridger stood in silence, looking out at the sea. Then he said:

'Easing off a bit, sir.'

'Just a little, yes.'

There was another pause: then Bridger added: 'It's a lot drier aft, sir.'

'Good.' It was impossible not to respond to this effort at raising his spirits, or to be unaffected by it; and he said suddenly: 'What do the hands think about all this?' It was the sort of question he had never before asked any rating except the Coxswain.

Bridger considered. It was entirely novel to him, too; what the lower deck thought of things, and what they said about them to their officers, were two differing aspects of truth. At length:

'They're a bit sick of the corned beef, sir.'

The Captain laughed, for the first time for many days. 'Is that all?'

'Just about, sir. But we're having a sweepstake on when we get in.'

For some reason the Captain felt like crying at that one. He said, after a moment:

'Has your number come up yet?'

'No, sir. Six more days to run.'

There was much more that the Captain wanted to ask: did they really think *Marlborough* would get in: were they still confident in his judgment, after all these days and nights of blundering along: did they trust him absolutely?—questions he would never even have thought of, save in a lightheaded hunger for reassurance. But suddenly Bridger said:

'They hope you're getting enough sleep, sir!'

Then he sucked in his breath, as though discovered in some appalling breach of discipline, took the cup from the top of the compass, and quickly left the bridge. Alone once more, the Captain smiled tautly at the most moving thing that had ever been said to him, and settled back in his chair to take up the watch again. He *wasn't* getting enough sleep, but the fact that the ship's company realized this, and wished him well over it, was as sustaining and comforting as a strong arm round his shoulders.

On the morning of the tenth day since they were torpedoed, he had a conference with the Chief on the bridge. They had seen little of each other during the preceding time: five days of having the reversing gear in continuous action had proved an unaccustomed strain, and the Chief had been kept busy below, nursing the one remaining engine through its ordeal. Now, at nine o'clock, he had come up with some fresh news.

'Have you noticed the fo'c'sle, sir?'

'No, Chief, I hadn't.' After yet another night on the bridge he felt no more and no less tired than usual: he seemed to be living in some nether hell of weariness which nothing could deepen. 'What's happened to it?'

'The bows have started to bend upwards again.' He pointed. 'You can just about see it from here, sir. There's a kink in the deck, like folding a bit of paper.'

'You mean the whole thing's being pulled off.'

'Something like that, sir. It's a slow process, but if it gets any worse we'll lose the buoyancy of the fore-peak, and that may bring the screws out of the water again.'

'What's the answer, technically?'

'Either slow down to nothing, or turn round and push them on again.'

The Captain gestured irritably. 'My God, it's like fooling around with a bundle of scrap-iron! "Push the bows on again"—it sounds like some blasted lid off a tin!'

'Yes, sir.' While Chief waited for the foolish spasm to spend itself, he wondered idly what the Captain *really* thought *Marlborough* should be like, after what she had gone through. 'Bundle of scrap-iron' wasn't far wide of the mark: she could float, she could lollop along backwards, and that was about all. 'Well, that's the choice, sir,' he said presently. 'I don't think we can carry on like this much longer.'

The Captain got hold of himself again: at this late hour, he wasn't going to start dramatizing the situation. It was all this damned tiredness. . . . 'We could just about turn round now,' he said slowly, looking at the sea with its long rolling swell and occasional breaking wavetops. 'It was a lot worse than this before we turned last time.'

'About how far have we got to go, sir?'

'I don't know, Chief.' He did not make the mistake of admitting his ig-norance in a totally normal voice, but he managed to imply that there was nothing to be gained either by a full discussion of it, or by surrendering to its hopeless implication. 'If we were on our proper course we should have raised Butt of Lewis a long time ago. Probably the compasses are faulty. I'm just going to keep on like this till we hit something.'

Stopping, and turning the bows into the wind again, was an even slower process than it had been five days earlier: at times it seemed that *Marlborough*, lying lumpishly off the wind and butting those fragile bows against the run of the waves, *would not* come up to her course. The Captain dared not increase speed, in order to give the rudder more leverage; and so for a full half-hour they tumbled athwart the wave-troughs, gaining a point on the compass-card, sagging back again, wavering on and off the wind like a creaking weathercock that no one trusts any longer. Down in the wheel-house, Leading Seaman Tapper leant against the wheel which he had put hard a-starboard, and waited, his eyes on the compass-card. If she wouldn't, she wouldn't: no good worrying, no good fiddling about. . . . All over the ship, during the past few days, that sort of thing had been growing: things either went right, or they didn't, and that was all there was to it. Between a deep weariness and a deeper fatalism, the whole crew accepted the situa-tion, and were carried sluggishly along with it.

At the end of half an hour, a lull allowed *Marlborough* to come round on her course. She settled down again slowly, as if she did not really believe in it, but knew she had no choice. South-east, it was, and one and a half knots. It *must* bring them home. It had to.

It did not bring them home: it did not seem to bring them anywhere. The steamed all that day, and all the next, and all the next, and all the next: four more days and nights, to add to the fantastic total of that south-easterly passage. But *was* it a south-easterly passage?—for if so, they should by now have been right through Scotland, and out the other side: eleven days steam-ing, it added up to, and thirteen days since they had been torpedoed. It just didn't make sense.

The weather did not help. It did not deteriorate, it did not improve: the stiff breeze held all the time, the sloppy uneven sea came running at them for hour after hour and day after day. The ship took it all with a tough determination which could not disguise a steady progressive breaking down. The bulkhead wavered and creaked, the water ran down the splitting seam, slopped about on the deck, increased in weight till it began to drag the bows down to a fatal level. The noise mounted gradually to an appalling racket: clanging, groaning, knocking, protesting—the whole hull in pain, ill-treated as an old galled horse sweating against the collar, fit only for the knacker's yard but hardly strong enough to drag itself there. Gallant, ramshackle, on her last legs, *Marlborough* bumped and rolled southwards, at a pace which was itself a wretched trial of patience.

Above all, there was now a smell—a sweetish, sickish smell seeping up the ventilators from the fo'c'sle. It penetrated to every part of the ship, it hung in the wind, it followed them till there seemed to be nothing around them in the sea or the sky but the gross stink of the dead, those seventy-odd corpses which they carried with them as their obscene ballast. It could not be escaped anywhere in the ship. Every man on board lived with it, tried to shut it out with sleep, woke with it sweet and beastly in his nostrils. It became the unmentionable horror that attended them wherever they went.

They all hated it, but there was so much more to hate. The tiredness of overstrained men working four hours on and four hours off, for day after day and night after night, lay all over the ship, a tangible weight of weariness that affected every yard of their progress. The ship's company, whether watching on the upper deck or tending the boilers and the engine-room, moved in a tired dream barely distinguishable from sleep. A grotesque fatigue assailed them all: they stayed on watch till their eyes ran raw and their bodies seemed ready to crumple: they ate like men who could scarcely move their jaws against some dry and tasteless substance: they fell asleep where they dropped, wedged against ventilators, curled up like bundles of rags in odd corners of the deck. All of them were filthy, bearded, grimed with spray and smoke: there was no water to wash with, no change of clothes, nothing to hearten them but tea and hard biscuit and corned beef, for every meal of every day of the voyage. All over the ship one met them, or stumbled over them: wild-eyed, dirty, slightly mad. And all around them, and above and below, hung that smell of death, a thick enveloping curtain, the price of sea-power translated into a squalid and disgusting currency.

And the Captain . . . he summed up, in his person, all that tiredness, all that stress and dirt, all that wild fatigue. He had had the least sleep of anyone on board, throughout the thirteen days: at the end of it he still held the whole thing in his grip, but it was a grip that had another quality besides strength—it had something cracked and desperate about it. His was the worry, his the responsibility, his the appalling doubt as to whether they were really going anywhere at all: he held on because there was no choice, because they could not give up, above all because this was *Marlborough*, his own ship, and he would not surrender her to God or man or the sea. Like a lover, light-headed and despairing, he hoped and strove and would not be foresworn.

The bridge was now his prison. . . . Wedged in his chair, chin on hand, a small thing was beginning to obsess him. On one of the instruments in front of him there was a splash of dried blood, overlooked when they cleaned up after the shell-burst. It had an odd shape, like a boot, like Italy: but the silly thing was that when he looked to one side that shape seemed to change, spinning round and round like a windmill, expanding and contracting as if the blood still lived and still moved to a pulse. He tried to catch it moving, but when he stared at it directly it became Italy again, a dirty brownish smear that no one wanted. He roared out suddenly: 'Signalman!' and then: 'For the Lord's sake clean that off—it's filthy!' and when the man, staring, set to work on the job, he watched him as if his sanity depended on it. Then he looked ahead again, scanning the horizon, the damned crystal-clear horizon. No change there: no shadow, no smudge of smoke, nothing. Where were they going to? Was there anything ahead but deep water? Was he leading *Marlborough*, and the wretched remnant of her ship's company, on a fantastic chase into the blue? And God Almighty! That smell from forrard. . . . It was like a curse, clamped down hard on their necks. Perhaps they were all going to perish of it in the end: perhaps the whole ship and her dead and dying crew, welded together in a solid mass of corruption, would one night dip soundlessly beneath the sea and touch bottom a thousand fathoms below.

At 4 a.m. on the morning of January 14, Petty Officer Adams came up on the bridge, to see the Captain before taking over the wheel. He had a pair of binoculars slung beneath the hood of his duffle-coat, and from force of habit he raised them and swept slowly round the horizon, a barely distinguishable line of shadow on that black moonless night. He did this twice: then, on the verge of lowering his glasses, he checked suddenly and stared for a long minute ahead, blinking at the rawness, the watery eyestrain, which even this slight effort induced. Then he said, in a compressed, almost croaking voice: 'There's a light dead ahead, sir.'

The words fell into the silence of the bridge like a rock in a pool. They all whipped up their glasses and stared in turn—the Captain, the signalman, Bridger, with his cocoa-cup forgotten: all of them intent, tremendously alert, checking their breathing as if afraid of losing an instant's concentration. Then Adams said again:

'There it is, sir—only the loom of it, but you can see it sweeping across.'

And the Captain, answering him, said very softly: 'Yes.'

It *was* a light—the faintest lifting of the gloom in the sky, like a spectral fan opening and closing, like a whisper—but it *was* a light. For a moment, the Captain was childishly annoyed that he had not seen it first: and then a terrific and overpowering relief seemed to rise in his throat, choking him, pricking his eyes, flooding all over his body in a shaking spasm. The soreness which he had felt around his heart all through the last few days rose to an agonizing twinge and then fell away, leaving him weak, almost gasping. He found the light again, and then dropped his binoculars and leant against his chair. The wish to cry, at the end of the fourteen days' tension, was almost insupportable.

Round him the others reacted in their own way, contributing to a moment of release so extraordinary that no extravagance of movement or word could have been out of place. The cup which Bridger had placed on a ledge fell and shattered. The signalman was whistling an imitation of a bosn's pipe, a triumphant skirl of sound. Adams, unknowing, muttered: 'Jesus Christ, Jesus Christ, Jesus Christ,' over and over again, in a voice from which everything save a sober humility had disappeared. They were men in a moment of triumph and of weakness, as vulnerable as young children, as unstable, as near to ecstasy or to weeping in the same single breath. They were men in entrancement.

It *was* a light—and soon there were others: three altogether, winking and beckoning them towards the vast promise of the horizon. The Captain took a grip of himself, the tightest grip yet, and went into the charthouse to work them out; while all over the ship men, awakened by some extraordinary urgency which ran everywhere like a licking flame, leant over the rails, and stared and whispered and laughed at what they saw. Lights ahead—land—home—they'd made it after all. Some of them stared up at the bridge, seeing nothing but feeling that they were looking at the heart of the ship, the thing that had brought them home, the man who more than anyone had worked the miracle. And then they would go back to the lights again, and count the flashes, and start singing or cursing in ragged chorus. There was no one anywhere in the ship who did not share in this moment: the hands on the upper deck shouted the news down to the engine-room, the signalman on the bridge gave a breathless running commentary to the wheelhouse. The release from ordeal moved them all to the same wild exultation.

Only the Captain, faced by the array of charts on the table, no longer shared the full measure of their relief. For he was now concentrating on something else, something he could not make out at all. They were lights all right—but what lights? The one that Adams had first seen was not Butt of Lewis: the other two did not seem to fit any part of the chart, either Lewis or the mainland round Cape Wrath, or the scattered islands centred on Scapa Flow and the Orkneys. He checked them again, he laid off the bearings on a piece of tracing-paper and then moved it here and there on the chart, hesitatingly, like a child with its first jigsaw puzzle. He even moved it up to Iceland, but the answer would not come—and it was an answer they *must* have before very long: they were running into something, closing an unknown coastline which might have any number of hazards—outlying rocks, dangerous overfalls, minefields barring any approach except by a single swept channel. Sucking his pencil, frowning at the harsh lamplight, he strove to find the answer: even at this last moment, delay might rob them of their triumph. But the answer would not come.

Presently he opened the charthouse door and came out again, ready to take fresh bearings and to make doubly certain of what the lights showed. Both the doctor and the Chief were now on the bridge, talking in low voices through which ran a strong note of satisfaction and assurance. The Chief turned as he heard the step, and then jerked his head at the lights.

'Finest sight I've seen in my life, sir.'

The Captain smiled. 'Same here, Chief.'

'Is that Butt of Lewis, sir?' asked the doctor.

'No.' He raised his glasses, checked the number of flashes, and bent to the compass to take a fresh bearing. 'No, Doc, I haven't worked out what it is yet.'

'It's something solid, anyway.'

'Enough for me,' said the Chief. 'All I want is the good old putty, anywhere between Cape Wrath and the Longships.'

To himself the Captain thought: I wish I could guarantee that.

'Another light, sir!' exclaimed the signalman suddenly. 'Port bow— about four-oh.'

The Captain raised his glasses once more.

'There it is, sir,' said the signalman again, before the Captain had found it. 'It's a red one this time.'

'Red?'

'Yes, sir. I got it clearly then.'

Red . . . that rang a bell, by God! There was a red light at the end of Rathlin Island, off the north coast of Ireland: it was the only one he could remember, in fact. But Rathlin Island. He walked quickly into the charthouse, and moved the tracing-paper southwards. The jigsaw suddenly resolved itself. It *was* Rathlin: the light they had first seen was Inistrahull, the others were Inishowen and something else he could not check—probably an aircraft beacon. Rathlin Island—that meant that they had come all down the coast of Scotland, over two hundred miles farther than he had thought: it meant that they must have been steering at least fifteen degrees off their proper course. Those bloody compasses! But what did it matter now? Rathlin Island. They could put in at Londonderry and get patched up, and then go home. Northern Ireland instead of Butt of Lewis—that would look good in the Report. But what the hell *did* it matter? They had made their landfall.

He walked back to his chair, sat down, and said, in as level a voice as he had ever used:

'That's the north coast of Ireland. We'll be going to Derry.'

It was a peerless morning: the clean grey sky, flecked with pearly grey clouds, turned suddenly to gold as the sun climbed over the eastern horizon. There was now land ahead: a dark bluish coastline, with noble hills beyond. The Captain's stiff stubbly face warmed slowly to the sunshine: the ache across his shoulders and around his heart seemed to melt away, taking with it his desperate fatigue. Not much longer—and then sleep, and sleep, and sleep. . . . Bridger handed him the morning cup of cocoa, his face one enormous grin. But all he said was: 'Cocoa, sir.'

'Thanks. . . . We made it, Bridger.'

'Yes, sir.'

'Who won that sweepstake?'

'The Buffer, sir—I mean Petty Officer Adams.'

The Captain laughed aloud. 'Bad luck!' For the ship's company that must be the one flaw in an otherwise perfect morning. There were a lot of the hands on the upper deck now, smiling and pointing. He felt bound to them as closely as one man can be to another. Later, he wanted to find some words that would give them an idea of that. And something about *Marlborough*, too, the ship he loved, the ship they had all striven for.

'Trawlers ahead, sir,' said the signalman, breaking in on his thoughts. 'Three of them. I think they're sweeping.'

Back to civilization: to lights, harbours, dawn mine-sweepers, patrolling aircraft, a guarded fairway.

'Call them up, signalman.'

But one of the trawlers was already flashing to them. The signalman acknowledged the message, and said: 'From the trawler, sir: "Can I help you?"'

'Make: "Thank you. Are you going into Londonderry?"'

A pause, while the lamps flickered. Then: 'Reply "Yes", sir!'

'Right. Make: "Will you pass a message to the Port War Signal Station for me, please?"'

Another pause. 'Reply, "Certainly", sir.'

The Captain drew a long breath, conscious deep within him of an enormous satisfaction. 'Write this down, and then send it to them. "To Flag Officer in Charge, Londonderry, v. *Marlborough*. HMS *Marlborough* will enter harbour at 1300 today. Ship is severely damaged above and below waterline. Request pilot, tugs, dockyard assistance and burial arrangements for one officer and seventy-four ratings." Got that?'

'Yes, sir.'
'Right. Send it off. . . . Bridger!'
'Sir?'
'Ask the surgeon-lieutenant to relieve me for an hour. I'm going to shave. And wash. And change. And then eat.'

NICHOLAS MONSARRAT
1910–79

Nicholas John Turney Monsarrat's love of the sea has its roots in his boyhood. He first learned to sail in a borrowed boat during the family's summers at Trearddur Bay, Wales; he quickly became an accomplished sailor and in later years was elected secretary of the Trearddur Bay Yachting Club.

He attended Trinity College, Cambridge, receiving his honors degree in law in 1931. He had spent only a short time in a solicitor's office before he decided that, as sailing was his choice of avocations, so writing was his choice of vocations.

From the beginning he was prolific. In the first year of his new profession Monsarrat wrote a novel and two articles on sailing. Major productions followed at the rate of one a year—a novel in 1935, a play in 1936, and another novel in 1937.

In 1940 Monsarrat joined the Royal Navy and served for five years. As a lieutenant commander he was in charge of a vessel on convoy escort duty in the Atlantic. Three novels immediately resulted from his experiences at sea—*H.M. Corvette* (1942), *East Coast Corvette* (1943), and *Corvette Command* (1944). The book about the war that gained widest recognition and on which much of his reputation still depends was not published until 1951; *The Cruel Sea* commanded attention on both sides of the Atlantic, sold 130,000 copies in its first month in Britain, won the Heinemann Award for literature in 1952, and was the first of Monsarrat's books to be made into a movie.

The Story of Esther Costello (1953) did not fare quite so well, but it was turned into a money-making movie. Subsequent novels—*The Tribe That Lost Its Head* (1956), *Richer Than All His Tribe* (1968), and *The White Rajah* (1961)—used the knowledge of African customs and problems that Monsarrat gained as a British public information officer in South Africa between 1946 and 1953.

Monsarrat wrote an autobiography, which was published in two separate volumes in 1966 and 1970 and finally issued together under the title *Breaking In, Breaking Out* (1971). It suffers from a lack of candor, yet it accurately pictures Monsarrat as a man out of his time, a man with romantic notions about honor and decency in a world that no longer appreciates those concepts.

At his death he had written one book of a projected series which was to be known as *The Master Mariner*; this novel, *Running Proud* (1978), quickly became a best-seller in Britain.

"HMS *Marlborough* Will Enter Harbour" is taken from *Depends on What You Mean by Love* (1947).

Storm and Shipwreck

MAN HAS LEARNED over the centuries how to make the ship into a habitable, even pleasant place as well as a reliable transport, but he has been less successful making it an impregnable fortress against nature's fiercest assaults. The *Titanic*, advertised as unsinkable, went to the bottom of the North Atlantic on her maiden voyage in the most tragic shipwreck of the century. Boasts that the power of the sea can be nullified, that man can insulate himself completely from it, inevitably prove frivolous, and mark those who believe them as foolish and ill-fated men.

"The Wreck of the *Golden Mary*," a work authored jointly by Charles Dickens and Wilkie Collins, pictures an inhospitable environment in which men and women battle for survival following a shipwreck. This sort of struggle characterizes many of the great sea stories in English. Less common but just as powerful are tales about shipwrecks themselves. Some of these stories, including Edgar Allan Poe's "MS. Found in a Bottle," are among the most complex and enigmatic in the language. On the surface the story tells of a diary flung overboard by a man whose ship is sinking. It is also a psychological thriller about a narrator tortured by a ghost ship and convinced of his terrible fate from the outset.

H. M. Tomlinson's "The Derelict" ushers in yet another ghost ship, this one sailing on its own, protecting its territory, its fate, and most of all, its treasure.

In Ernest Hemingway's "After the Storm" a man with only the power of his arm attempts to salvage a wrecked vessel. The cost of his enterprise is a loss of energy and personal esteem.

MS. Found in a Bottle

BY EDGAR ALLAN POE

Qui n'a plus qu'un moment à vivre
N'a plus rien à dissimuler.—Quinault—Atys.

OF MY COUNTRY and of my family I have little to say. Ill usage and length of
years have driven me from the one, and estranged me from the other. He-
reditary wealth afforded me an education of no common order, and a contemplative turn of mind enabled me to methodize the stores which early
study very diligently garnered up.—Beyond all things, the study of the German moralists gave me great delight; not from any ill-advised admiration of
their eloquent madness, but from the ease with which my habits of rigid
thought enabled me to detect their falsities. I have often been reproached
with the aridity of my genius; a deficiency of imagination has been imputed
to me as a crime; and the Pyrrhonism of my opinions has at all times rendered me notorious. Indeed, a strong relish for physical philosophy has, I
fear, tinctured my mind with a very common error of this age—I mean the
habit of referring occurrences, even the least susceptible of such reference, to
the principles of that science. Upon the whole, no person could be less liable
than myself to be led away from the severe precincts of truth by the *ignes
fatui* of superstition. I have thought proper to premise thus much, lest the
incredible tale I have to tell should be considered rather the raving of a
crude imagination, than the positive experience of a mind to which the reveries of fancy have been a dead letter and a nullity.

After many years spent in foreign travel, I sailed in the year 18—, from
the port of Batavia, in the rich and populous island of Java, on a voyage to
the Archipelago of the Sunda islands. I went as passenger—having no other
inducement than a kind of nervous restlessness which haunted me as a
fiend.

Our vessel was a beautiful ship of about four hundred tons, copper-
fastened, and built at Bombay of Malabar teak. She was freighted with
cotton-wool and oil, from the Lachadive islands. We had also on board coir,
jaggeree, ghee, cocoa-nuts, and a few cases of opium. The stowage was
clumsily done, and the vessel consequently crank.

We got under way with a mere breath of wind, and for many days stood along the eastern coast of Java, without any other incident to beguile the monotony of our course than the occasional meeting with some of the small grabs of the Archipelago to which we were bound.

One evening, leaning over the taffrail, I observed a very singular, isolated cloud, to the N.W. It was remarkable, as well for its color, as from its being the first we had seen since our departure from Batavia. I watched it attentively until sunset, when it spread all at once to the eastward and westward, girting in the horizon with a narrow strip of vapor, and looking like a long line of low beach. My notice was soon afterwards attracted by the dusky-red appearance of the moon, and the peculiar character of the sea. The latter was undergoing a rapid change, and the water seemed more than usually transparent. Although I could distinctly see the bottom, yet, heaving the lead, I found the ship in fifteen fathoms. The air now became intolerably hot, and was loaded with spiral exhalations similar to those arising from heated iron. As night came on, every breath of wind died away, and a more entire calm it is impossible to conceive. The flame of a candle burned upon the poop without the least perceptible motion, and a long hair, held between the finger and thumb, hung without the possibility of detecting a vibration. However, as the captain said he could perceive no indication of danger, and as we were drifting in bodily to shore, he ordered the sails to be furled, and the anchor let go. No watch was set, and the crew, consisting principally of Malays, stretched themselves deliberately upon deck. I went below—not without a full presentiment of evil. Indeed, every appearance warranted me in apprehending a Simoom. I told the captain my fears; but he paid no attention to what I said, and left me without deigning to give a reply. My uneasiness, however, prevented me from sleeping, and about midnight I went upon deck.—As I placed my foot upon the upper step of the companion-ladder, I was startled by a loud, humming noise, like that occasioned by the rapid revolution of a mill-wheel, and before I could ascertain its meaning, I found the ship quivering to its centre. In the next instant, a wilderness of foam hurled us upon our beam-ends, and, rushing over us fore and aft, swept the entire decks from stem to stern.

The extreme fury of the blast proved, in a great measure, the salvation of the ship. Although completely water-logged, yet, as her masts had gone by the board, she rose, after a minute, heavily from the sea, and, staggering awhile beneath the immense pressure of the tempest, finally righted.

By what miracle I escaped destruction, it is impossible to say. Stunned by the shock of the water, I found myself, upon recovery, jammed in between the stern-post and rudder. With great difficulty I gained my feet, and looking dizzily around, was, at first, struck with the idea of our being among breakers; so terrific, beyond the wildest imagination, was the whirlpool of

mountainous and foaming ocean within which we were engulfed. After a
while, I heard the voice of an old Swede, who had shipped with us at the
moment of our leaving port. I hallooed to him with all my strength, and
presently he came reeling aft. We soon discovered that we were the sole survivors of the accident. All on deck, with the exception of ourselves, had
been swept overboard;—the captain and mates must have perished as they
slept, for the cabins were deluged with water. Without assistance, we could
expect to do little for the security of the ship, and our exertions were at first
paralyzed by the momentary expectation of going down. Our cable had, of
course, parted like pack-thread, at the first breath of the hurricane, or we
should have been instantaneously overwhelmed. We scudded with frightful
velocity before the sea, and the water made clear breaches over us. The
frame-work of our stern was shattered excessively, and, in almost every respect, we had received considerable injury; but to our extreme joy we found
the pumps unchoked, and that we had made no great shifting of our ballast.
The main fury of the blast had already blown over, and we apprehended
little danger from the violence of the wind; but we looked forward to its
total cessation with dismay; well believing, that, in our shattered condition,
we should inevitably perish in the tremendous swell which would ensue.
But this very just apprehension seemed by no means likely to be soon verified. For five entire days and nights—during which our only subsistence
was a small quantity of jaggeree, procured with great difficulty from the
forecastle—the hulk flew at a rate defying computation, before rapidly succeeding flaws of wind, which, without equalling the first violence of the
Simoom, were still more terrific than any tempest I had before encountered.
Our course for the first four days was, with trifling variations, S.E. and by
S.; and we must have run down the coast of New Holland.—On the fifth
day the cold became extreme, although the wind had hauled round a point
more to the northward.—The sun arose with a sickly yellow lustre, and
clambered a very few degrees above the horizon—emitting no decisive
light.—There were no clouds apparent, yet the wind was upon the increase,
and blew with a fitful and unsteady fury. About noon, as nearly as we could
guess, our attention was again arrested by the appearance of the sun. It gave
out no light, properly so called, but a dull and sullen glow without reflection, as if all its rays were polarized. Just before sinking within the turgid
sea, its central fires suddenly went out, as if hurriedly extinguished by some
unaccountable power. It was a dim, silver-like rim, alone, as it rushed down
the unfathomable ocean.

We waited in vain for the arrival of the sixth day—that day to me has not
arrived—to the Swede, never did arrive. Thenceforward we were en-
shrouded in pitchy darkness, so that we could not have seen an object at

twenty paces from the ship. Eternal night continued to envelop us, all unrelieved by the phosphoric sea-brilliancy to which we had been accustomed in the tropics. We observed too, that, although the tempest continued to rage with unabated violence, there was no longer to be discovered the usual appearance of surf, or foam, which had hitherto attended us. All around were horror, and thick gloom, and a black sweltering desert of ebony.—Superstitous terror crept by degrees into the spirit of the old Swede, and my own soul was wrapped up in silent wonder. We neglected all care of the ship, as worse than useless, and securing ourselves, as well as possible, to the stump of the mizen-mast, looked out bitterly into the world of ocean. We had no means of calculating time, nor could we form any guess of our situation. We were, however, well aware of having made farther to the southward than any previous navigators, and felt great amazement at not meeting with the usual impediments of ice. In the meantime every moment threatened to be our last—every mountainous billow hurried to overwhelm us. The swell surpassed anything I had imagined possible, and that we were not instantly buried is a miracle. My companion spoke of the lightness of our cargo, and reminded me of the excellent qualities of our ship; but I could not help feeling the utter hopelessness of hope itself, and prepared myself gloomily for that death which I thought nothing could defer beyond an hour, as, with every knot of way the ship made, the swelling of the black stupendous seas became more dismally appalling. At times we gasped for breath at an elevation beyond the albatross—at times became dizzy with the velocity of our descent into some watery hell, where the air grew stagnant, and no sound disturbed the slumbers of the kraken.

We were at the bottom of one of these abysses, when a quick scream from my companion broke fearfully upon the night. "See! see!" cried he, shrieking in my ears, "Almighty God! see! see!" As he spoke, I became aware of a dull, sullen glare of red light which streamed down the sides of the vast chasm where we lay, and threw a fitful brilliancy upon our deck. Casting my eyes upwards, I beheld a spectacle which froze the current of my blood. At a terrific height directly above us, and upon the very verge of the precipitous descent, hovered a gigantic ship of, perhaps, four thousand tons. Although upreared upon the summit of a wave more than a hundred times her own altitude, her apparent size still exceeded that of any ship of the line or East Indiaman in existence. Her huge hull was of a deep dingy black, unrelieved by any of the customary carvings of a ship. A single row of brass cannon protruded from her open ports, and dashed from their polished surfaces the fires of innumerable battle-lanterns, which swung to and fro about her rigging. But what mainly inspired us with horror and astonishment, was that she bore up under a press of sail in the very teeth of that supernatural sea, and of that ungovernable hurricane. When we first discovered her, her bows were alone to be seen, as she rose slowly from the dim and horrible gulf beyond her. For a moment of intense terror she paused upon the giddy pinnacle, as if in contemplation of her own sublimity, then trembled and tottered, and—came down.

At this instant, I know not what sudden self-possession came over my spirit. Staggering as far aft as I could, I awaited fearlessly the ruin that was to overwhelm. Our own vessel was at length ceasing from her struggles, and sinking with her head to the sea. The shock of the descending mass struck her, consequently, in that portion of her frame which was already under water, and the inevitable result was to hurl me, with irresistible violence, upon the rigging of the stranger.

As I fell, the ship hove in stays, and went about; and to the confusion ensuing I attributed my escape from the notice of the crew. With little difficulty I made my way unperceived to the main hatchway, which was partially open, and soon found an opportunity of secreting myself in the hold. Why I did so I can hardly tell. An indefinite sense of awe, which at first sight of the navigators of the ship had taken hold of my mind, was perhaps the principle of my concealment. I was unwilling to trust myself with a race of people who had offered, to the cursory glance I had taken, so many points of vague novelty, doubt, and apprehension. I therefore thought proper to contrive a hiding-place in the hold. This I did by removing a small portion of the shifting-boards, in such a manner as to afford me a convenient retreat between the huge timbers of the ship.

I had scarcely completed my work, when a footstep in the hold forced me to make use of it. A man passed by my place of concealment with a feeble and unsteady gait. I could not see his face, but had an opportunity of observing his general appearance. There was about it an evidence of great age and infirmity. His knees tottered beneath a load of years, and his entire frame quivered under the burthen. He muttered to himself, in a low broken tone, some words of a language which I could not understand, and groped in a corner among a pile of singular-looking instruments, and decayed charts of navigation. His manner was a wild mixture of the peevishness of second childhood, and the solemn dignity of a God. He at length went on deck, and I saw him no more.

A feeling, for which I have no name, has taken possession of my soul—a sensation which will admit of no analysis, to which the lessons of by-gone times are inadequate, and for which I fear futurity itself will offer me no key. To a mind constituted like my own, the latter consideration is an evil. I shall never—I know that I shall never—be satisfied with regard to the nature of my conceptions. Yet it is not wonderful that these conceptions are indefinite, since they have their origin in sources so utterly novel. A new sense—a new entity is added to my soul.

It is long since I first trod the deck of this terrible ship, and the rays of my destiny are, I think, gathering to a focus. Incomprehensible men! Wrapped up in meditations of a kind which I cannot divine, they pass me by unnoticed. Concealment is utter folly on my part, for the people *will not* see. It was but just now that I passed directly before the eyes of the mate—it was no long while ago that I ventured into the captain's own private cabin, and took thence the materials with which I write, and have written. I shall from time to time continue this journal. It is true that I may not find an opportunity of transmitting it to the world, but I will not fail to make the endeavour. At the last moment I will enclose the MS. in a bottle, and cast it within the sea.

An incident has occurred which has given me new room for meditation. Are such things the operation of ungoverned Chance? I had ventured upon deck and thrown myself down, without attracting any notice, among a pile of ratlin-stuff and old sails, in the bottom of the yawl. While musing upon the singularity of my fate, I unwittingly daubed with a tar-brush the edges of a neatly-folded studding-sail which lay near me on a barrel. The studding-sail is now bent upon the ship, and the thoughtless touches of the brush are spread out into the word DISCOVERY.

I have made many observations lately upon the structure of the vessel. Although well armed, she is not, I think, a ship of war. Her rigging, build, and general equipment, all negative a supposition of this kind. What she *is not*, I can easily perceive—what she *is* I fear it is impossible to say. I know not how it is, but in scrutinizing her strange model and singular cast of spars, her huge size and overgrown suits of canvass, her severely simple bow and antiquated stern, there will occasionally flash across my mind a sensation of familiar things, and there is always mixed up with such indistinct shadows of recollection, an unaccountable memory of old foreign chronicles and ages long ago.

I have been looking at the timbers of the ship. She is built of a material to which I am a stranger. There is a peculiar character about the wood which strikes me as rendering it unfit for the purpose to which it has been applied. I mean its extreme *porousness*, considered independently of the worm-eaten condition which is a consequence of navigation in these seas, and apart from the rottenness attendant upon age. It will appear perhaps an observation somewhat overcurious, but this wood would have every characteristic of Spanish oak, if Spanish oak were distended by any unnatural means.

In reading the above sentence a curious apothegm of an old weather-beaten Dutch navigator comes full upon my recollection. "It is as sure," he was wont to say, when any doubt was entertained of his veracity, "as sure as there is a sea where the ship itself will grow in bulk like the living body of the seaman."

About an hour ago, I made bold to thrust myself among a group of the crew. They paid me no manner of attention, and, although I stood in the very midst of them all, seemed utterly unconscious of my presence. Like the one I had at first seen in the hold, they all bore about them the marks of a hoary old age. Their knees trembled with infirmity; their shoulders were bent double with decrepitude; their shrivelled skins rattled in the wind; their voices were low, tremulous and broken; their eyes glistened with the rheum of years; and their gray hairs streamed terribly in the tempest. Around them, on every part of the deck, lay scattered mathematical instruments of the most quaint and obsolete construction.

I mentioned some time ago the bending of a studding-sail. From that period the ship, being thrown dead off the wind, has continued her terrific course due south, with every rag of canvass packed upon her, from her trucks to her lower studding-sail booms, and rolling every moment her top-gallant yard-arms into the most appalling hell of water which it can enter into the mind of man to imagine. I have just left the deck, where I find it impossible to maintain a footing, although the crew seem to experience little inconvenience. It appears to me a miracle of miracles that our enormous bulk is not swallowed up at once and forever. We are surely doomed to hover continually upon the brink of Eternity, without taking a final plunge into the abyss. From billows a thousand times more stupendous than any I have ever seen, we glide away with the facility of the arrowy sea-gull; and the colossal waters rear their heads above us like demons of the deep, but like demons confined to simple threats and forbidden to destroy. I am led to attribute these frequent escapes to the only natural cause which can account for such effect.—I must suppose the ship to be within the influence of some strong current, or impetuous under-tow.

I have seen the captain face to face, and in his own cabin—but, as I expected, he paid me no attention. Although in his appearance there is, to a casual observer, nothing which might bespeak him more or less than man —still a feeling of irrepressible reverence and awe mingled with the sensation of wonder with which I regarded him. In stature he is nearly my own height; that is, about five feet eight inches. He is of a well-knit and compact frame of body, neither robust nor remarkably otherwise. But it is the singularity of the expression which reigns upon the face—it is the intense, the wonderful, the thrilling evidence of old age, so utter, so extreme, which excites within my spirit a sense—a sentiment ineffable. His forehead, although little wrinkled, seems to bear upon it the stamp of a myriad of years.—His gray hairs are records of the past, and his grayer eyes are Sybils of the future. The cabin floor was thickly strewn with strange, iron-clasped folios, and mouldering instruments of science, and obsolete long-forgotten charts. His head was bowed down upon his hands, and he pored, with a fiery unquiet eye, over a paper which I took to be a commission, and which, at all events, bore the signature of a monarch. He muttered to himself, as did the first seaman whom I saw in the hold, some low peevish syllables of a foreign tongue, and although the speaker was close at my elbow, his voice seemed to reach my ears from the distance of a mile.

The ship and all in it are imbued with the spirit of Eld. The crew glide to and fro like the ghosts of buried centuries; their eyes have an eager and uneasy meaning; and when their fingers fall athwart my path in the wild glare of the battle-lanterns, I feel as I have never felt before, although I have been all my life a dealer in antiquities, and have imbibed the shadows of fallen columns at Balbec, and Tadmor, and Persepolis, until my very soul has become a ruin.

When I look around me I feel ashamed of my former apprehensions. If I trembled at the blast which has hitherto attended us, shall I not stand aghast at a warring of wind and ocean, to convey any idea of which the words tornado and simoom are trivial and ineffective? All in the immediate vicinity of the ship is the blackness of eternal night, and a chaos of foamless water; but, about a league on either side of us, may be seen, indistinctly and at intervals, stupendous ramparts of ice, towering away into the desolate sky, and looking like the walls of the universe.

As I imagined, the ship proves to be in a current; if that appellation can properly be given to a tide which, howling and shrieking by the white ice, thunders on to the southward with a velocity like the headlong dashing of a cataract.

To conceive the horror of my sensations is, I presume, utterly impossible; yet a curiosity to penetrate the mysteries of these awful regions, predominates even over my despair, and will reconcile me to the most hideous aspect of death. It is evident that we are hurrying onwards to some exciting knowledge—some never-to-be-imparted secret, whose attainment is destruction. Perhaps this current leads us to the southern pole itself. It must be confessed that a supposition apparently so wild has every probability in its favor.

The crew pace the deck with unquiet and tremulous step; but there is upon their countenances an expression more of the eagerness of hope than of the apathy of despair.

In the meantime the wind is still in our poop, and, as we carry a crowd of canvass, the ship is at times lifted bodily from out the sea—Oh, horror upon horror! the ice opens suddenly to the right, and to the left, and we are whirling dizzily, in immense concentric circles, round and round the borders of a gigantic amphitheatre, the summit of whose walls is lost in the darkness and the distance. But little time will be left me to ponder upon my destiny—the circles rapidly grow small—we are plunging madly within the grasp of the whirlpool—and amid a roaring, and bellowing, and thundering of ocean and of tempest, the ship is quivering, oh God! and—going down.

EDGAR ALLAN POE
1809–49

Born to itinerant actors, Edgar Allan Poe was deserted by his father before the age of three and orphaned when his mother died on tour in Richmond, Virginia. Poe became the ward of the wealthy merchant John Allan, though he was never adopted.

During his childhood he lived for a time in Scotland and England with the Allans and attended school at Stoke Newington. A year at the University of Virginia (1826) revealed both his academic promise and his penchant for gambling.

After running away to Boston, Poe published *Tamerlane and Other Poems* (1827), his first book of verse. A stint in the army, acceptance to West Point, and dismissal from the academy all followed. Meanwhile he published *Al Aaraaf, Tamerlane, and Minor Poems* (1829) and, after his dismissal from West Point, *Poems* (1831), which he dedicated to the cadets.

The first of Poe's short stories saw publication in 1832 in the Philadelphia *Saturday Courier*. When he won a contest sponsored by the Baltimore *Saturday Visiter* in 1833, he met people who launched his career as a writer and editor. John Pendleton Kennedy, one of the judges of the *Visiter* contest, not only sent Poe's stories to his own publisher but secured the poverty-stricken young man an editorial post with the *Southern Literary Messenger*.

Poe's career took him from Richmond to Philadelphia and then to New York as editor for various magazines, including the *Messenger, Burton's Gentleman's Magazine*, and *Graham's Magazine*.

Tales of the Grostesque and Arabesque, his one major work of fiction, appeared in 1840; his principal volume of verse, *The Raven and Other Poems*, was published in 1845. Both books cut new literary paths. Poe formalized the short story, pioneered the genre of detective fiction, and introduced a new kind of tale told from the point of view of a demented narrator. He created intensity with his emphasis on beauty and horror, death and dream. His poems, which exploited a new symbolic mode, were especially influential with French poets.

"MS. Found in a Bottle" won the *Saturday Visiter* contest and launched Poe's career as a writer of fiction.

The Wreck of the Golden Mary

BY CHARLES DICKENS

(with Wilkie Collins)

The Wreck

I WAS APPRENTICED to the Sea when I was twelve years old, and I have encountered a great deal of rough weather, both literal and metaphorical. It has always been my opinion since I first possessed such a thing as an opinion, that the man who knows only one subject is next tiresome to the man who knows no subject. Therefore, in the course of my life I have taught myself whatever I could, and although I am not an educated man, I am able, I am thankful to say, to have an intelligent interest in most things.

A person might suppose, from reading the above, that I am in the habit of holding forth about number one. That is not the case. Just as if I was to come into a room among strangers, and must either be introduced or introduce myself, so I have taken the liberty of passing these few remarks, simply and plainly that it may be known who and what I am. I will add no more of the sort than that my name is William George Ravender, that I was born at Penrith half a year after my own father was drowned, and that I am on the second day of this present blessed Christmas week of one thousand eight hundred and fifty-six, fifty-six years of age.

When the rumour first went flying up and down that there was gold in California—which, as most people know, was before it was discovered in the British colony of Australia—I was in the West Indies, trading among the Islands. Being in command and likewise part-owner of a smart schooner, I had my work cut out for me, and I was doing it. Consequently, gold in California was no business of mine.

But, by the time when I came home to England again, the thing was as clear as your hand held up before you at noonday. There was Californian gold in the museums and in the goldsmiths' shops, and the very first time I went upon 'Change, I met a friend of mine (a seafaring man like myself), with a Californian nugget hanging to his watch-chain. I handled it. It was as like a peeled walnut with bits unevenly broken off here and there, and then electrotyped all over, as ever I saw anything in my life.

I am a single man (she was too good for this world and for me, and she died six weeks before our marriage-day), so when I am ashore, I live in my house at Poplar. My house at Poplar is taken care of and kept ship-shape by an old lady who was my mother's maid before I was born. She is as handsome and as upright as any old lady in the world. She is as fond of me as if she had ever had an only son, and I was he. Well do I know wherever I sail that she never lays down her head at night without having said, "Merciful Lord! bless and preserve William George Ravender, and send him safe home, through Christ our Saviour!" I have thought of it in many a dangerous moment, when it has done me no harm, I am sure.

In my house at Poplar, along with this old lady, I lived quiet for best part of a year: having had a long spell of it among the Islands, and having (which was very uncommon in me) taken the fever rather badly. At last, being strong and hearty, and having read every book I could lay hold of, right out, I was walking down Leadenhall Street in the City of London, thinking of turning-to again, when I met what I call Smithick and Watersby of Liverpool. I chanced to lift up my eyes from looking in at a ship's chronometer in a window, and I saw him bearing down upon me, head on.

It is, personally, neither Smithick, nor Watersby, that I here mention, nor was I ever acquainted with any man of either of those names, nor do I think that there has been any one of either of those names in that Liverpool House for years back. But, it is in reality the House itself that I refer to; and a wiser merchant or a truer gentleman never stepped.

"My dear Captain Ravender," says he. "Of all the men on earth, I wanted to see you most. I was on my way to you."

"Well!" says I. "That looks as if you *were* to see me, don't it?" With that I put my arm in his, and we walked on towards the Royal Exchange, and when we got there, walked up and down at the back of it where the Clock-Tower is. We walked an hour and more, for he had much to say to me. He had a scheme for chartering a new ship of their own to take out cargo to the diggers and emigrants in California, and to buy and bring back gold. Into the particulars of that scheme I will not enter, and I have no right to enter. All I say of it is, that it was a very original one, a very fine one, a very sound one, and a very lucrative one beyond doubt.

He imparted it to me as freely as if I had been a part of himself. After doing so, he made me the handsomest sharing offer that ever was made to me, boy or man—or I believe to any other captain in the Merchant Navy—and he took this round turn to finish with:

"Ravender, you are well aware that the lawlessness of that coast and country at present, is as special as the circumstances in which it is placed. Crews of vessels outward-bound, desert as soon as they make the land; crews of vessels homewardbound, ship at enormous wages, with the express intention of murdering the captain and seizing the gold freight; no man can trust another, and the devil seems let loose. Now," says he, "you know my opinion of you, and you know I am only expressing it, and with no singularity, when I tell you that you are almost the only man on whose integrity, discretion, and energy—" &c. &c. For, I don't want to repeat what he said, though I was and am sensible of it.

Notwithstanding my being, as I have mentioned, quite ready for a voyage, still I had some doubts of this voyage. Of course I knew, without being told, that there were peculiar difficulties and dangers in it, a long way over and above those which attend all voyages. It must not be supposed that I was afraid to face them; but, in my opinion a man has no manly motive or sustainment in his own breast for facing dangers, unless he has well considered what they are, and is able quietly to say to himself, "None of these perils can now take me by surprise; I shall know what to do for the best in any of them; all the rest lies in the higher and greater hands to which I humbly commit myself." On this principle I have so attentively considered (regarding it as my duty) all the hazards I have ever been able to think of, in the ordinary way of storm, shipwreck, and fire at sea, that I hope I should be prepared to do, in any of those cases, whatever could be done, to save the lives intrusted to my charge.

As I was thoughtful, my good friend proposed that he should leave me to walk there as long as I liked, and that I should dine with him by-and-by at his club in Pall Mall. I accepted the invitation and I walked up and down there, quarter-deck fashion, a matter of a couple of hours; now and then looking up at the weathercock as I might have looked up aloft; and now and then taking a look into Cornhill, as I might have taken a look over the side.

All dinner-time, and all after dinner-time, we talked it over again. I gave him my views of his plan, and he very much approved of the same. I told him I had nearly decided, but not quite. "Well, well," says he, "come down to Liverpool to-morrow with me, and see the Golden Mary." I liked the name (her name was Mary, and she was golden, if golden stands for good), so I began to feel that it was almost done when I said I would go to Liverpool. On the next morning but one we were on board the Golden Mary. I might have known, from his asking me to come down and see her, what she was. I declare her to have been the completest and most exquisite Beauty that ever I set my eyes upon.

We had inspected every timber in her, and had come back to the gangway to go ashore from the dock-basin, when I put out my hand to my friend. "Touch upon it," says I, "and touch heartily. I take command of this ship, and I am hers and yours, if I can get John Steadiman for my chief mate."

John Steadiman had sailed with me four voyages. The first voyage John was third mate out to China, and came home second. The other three voyages he was my first officer. At this time of chartering the Golden Mary, he was aged thirty-two. A brisk, bright, blue-eyed fellow, a very neat figure and rather under the middle size, never out of the way and never in it, a face that pleased everybody and that all children took to, a habit of going about singing as cheerily as a blackbird, and a perfect sailor.

We were in one of those Liverpool hackney-coaches in less than a minute, and we cruised about in her upwards of three hours, looking for John. John had come home from Van Diemen's Land barely a month before, and I had heard of him as taking a frisk in Liverpool. We asked after him, among many other places, at the two boarding-houses he was fondest of, and we found he had had a week's spell at each of them; but, he had gone here and gone there, and had set off "to lay out on the main-to'-gallant-yard of the highest Welsh mountain" (so he had told the people of the house), and where he might be then, or when he might come back, nobody could tell us. But it was surprising, to be sure, to see how every face brightened the moment there was mention made of the name of Mr. Steadiman.

We were taken aback at meeting with no better luck, and we had wore ship and put her head for my friends, when as we were jogging through the streets, I clap my eyes on John himself coming out of a toyshop! He was carrying a little boy, and conducting two uncommon pretty women to their coach, and he told me afterwards that he had never in his life seen one of the three before, but that he was so taken with them on looking in at the toyshop while they were buying the child a cranky Noah's Ark, very much down by the head, that he had gone in and asked the ladies' permission to treat him to a tolerably correct Cutter there was in the window, in order that such a handsome boy might not grow up with a lubberly idea of naval architecture.

We stood off and on until the ladies' coachman began to give way, and then we hailed John. On his coming aboard of us, I told him, very gravely, what I had said to my friend. It struck him, as he said himself, amidships. He was quite shaken by it. "Captain Ravender," were John Steadiman's words, "such an opinion from you is true commendation, and I'll sail round the world with you for twenty years if you hoist the signal, and stand by you for ever!" And now indeed I felt that it was done, and that the Golden Mary was afloat.

Grass never grew yet under the feet of Smithick and Watersby. The riggers were out of that ship in a fortnight's time, and we had begun taking in cargo. John was always aboard, seeing everything stowed with his own eyes; and whenever I went aboard myself early or late, whether he was below in the hold, or on deck at the hatchway, or overhauling his cabin, nailing up pictures in it of the Blush Roses of England, the Blue Bells of Scotland, and the female Shamrock of Ireland: of a certainty I heard John singing like a blackbird.

We had room for twenty passengers. Our sailing advertisement was no sooner out, than we might have taken these twenty times over. In entering our men, I and John (both together) picked them, and we entered none but good hands—as good as were to be found in that port. And so, in a good ship of the best build, well owned, well arranged, well officered, well manned, well found in all respects, we parted with our pilot at a quarter past four o'clock in the afternoon of the seventh of March, one thousand eight hundred and fifty-one, and stood with a fair wind out to sea.

It may be easily believed that up to that time I had had no leisure to be intimate with my passengers. The most of them were then in their berths sea-sick; however, in going among them, telling them what was good for them, persuading them not to be there, but to come up on deck and feel the breeze, and in rousing them with a joke, or a comfortable word, I made acquaintance with them, perhaps, in a more friendly and confidential way from the first, than I might have done at the cabin table.

Of my passengers, I need only particularise, just at present, a bright-eyed blooming young wife who was going out to join her husband in California, taking with her their only child, a little girl of three years old, whom he had never seen; a sedate young woman in black, some five years older (about thirty as I should say), who was going out to join a brother; and an old gentleman, a good deal like a hawk if his eyes had been better and not so red, who was always talking, morning, noon, and night, about the gold discovery. But, whether he was making the voyage, thinking his old arms could dig for gold, or whether his speculation was to buy it, or to barter for it, or to cheat for it, or to snatch it anyhow from other people, was his secret. He kept his secret.

These three and the child were the soonest well. The child was a most engaging child, to be sure, and very fond of me: though I am bound to admit that John Steadiman and I were borne on her pretty little books in reverse order, and that he was captain there, and I was mate. It was beautiful to watch her with John, and it was beautiful to watch John with her. Few would have thought it possible, to see John playing at bo-peep round the mast, that he was the man who had caught up an iron bar and struck a Malay and a Maltese dead, as they were gliding with their knives down the cabin stair aboard the barque Old England, when the captain lay ill in his cot, off Saugar Point. But he was; and give him his back against a bulwark, he would have done the same by half-a-dozen of them. The name of the young mother was Mrs. Atherfield, the name of the young lady in black was Miss Coleshaw, and the name of the old gentleman was Mr. Rarx.

As the child had a quantity of shining fair hair, clustering in curls all about her face, and as her name was Lucy, Steadiman gave her the name of the Golden Lucy. So, we had the Golden Lucy and the Golden Mary; and

John kept up the idea to that extent as he and the child went playing about the decks, that I believe she used to think the ship was alive somehow—a sister or companion, going to the same place as herself. She liked to be by the wheel, and in fine weather, I have often stood by the man whose trick it was at the wheel, only to hear her, sitting near my feet, talking to the ship. Never had a child such a doll before, I suppose; but she made a doll of the Golden Mary, and used to dress her up by tying ribbons and little bits of finery to the belaying-pins; and nobody ever moved them, unless it was to save them from being blown away.

Of course I took charge of the two young women, and I called them "my dear," and they never minded, knowing that whatever I said was said in a fatherly and protecting spirit. I gave them their places on each side of me at dinner; Mrs. Atherfield on my right and Miss Coleshaw on my left; and I directed the unmarried lady to serve out the breakfast, and the married lady to serve out the tea. Likewise I said to my black steward in their presence, "Tom Snow, these two ladies are equally the mistresses of this house, and do you obey their orders equally;" at which Tom laughed, and they all laughed.

Old Mr. Rarx was not a pleasant man to look at, nor yet to talk to, or to be with, for no one could help seeing that he was a sordid and selfish character, and that he had warped further and further out of the straight with time. Not but what he was on his best behaviour with us, as everybody was; for we had no bickering among us, for'ard or aft. I only mean to say, he was not the man one would have chosen for a messmate. If choice there had been, one might even have gone a few points out of one's course, to say, "No! Not him!" But, there was one curious inconsistency in Mr. Rarx. That was, that he took an astonishing interest in the child. He looked, and I may add, he was, one of the last of men to care at all for a child, or to care much for any human creature. Still, he went so far as to be habitually uneasy, if the child was long on deck, out of his sight. He was always afraid of her falling overboard, or falling down a hatchway, or of a block or what not coming down upon her from the rigging in the working of the ship, or of her getting some hurt or other. He used to look at her and touch her, as if she was something precious to him. He was always solicitous about her not injuring her health, and constantly entreated her mother to be careful of it. This was so much the more curious, because the child did not like him, but used to shrink away from him, and would not even put out her hand to him without coaxing from others. I believe that every soul on board frequently noticed this, and not one of us understood it. However, it was such a plain fact, that John Steadiman said more than once when old Mr. Rarx was not within earshot, that if the Golden Mary felt a tenderness for the dear old gentleman she carried in her lap, she must be bitterly jealous of the Golden Lucy.

Before I go any further with this narrative, I will state that our ship was a barque of three hundred tons, carrying a crew of eighteen men, a second mate in addition to John, a carpenter, an armourer or smith, and two apprentices (one a Scotch boy, poor little fellow). We had three boats; the Long-boat, capable of carrying twenty-five men; the Cutter, capable of carrying fifteen; and the Surf-boat, capable of carrying ten. I put down the capacity of these boats according to the numbers they were really meant to hold.

We had tastes of bad weather and head-winds, of course; but, on the whole we had as fine a run as any reasonable man could expect, for sixty days. I then began to enter two remarks in the ship's Log and in my Journal; first, that there was an unusual and amazing quantity of ice; second, that the nights were most wonderfully dark, in spite of the ice.

For five days and a half, it seemed quite useless and hopeless to alter the ship's course so as to stand out of the way of this ice. I made what southing I could; but, all that time, we were beset by it. Mrs. Atherfield after standing by me on deck once, looking for some time in an awed manner at the great bergs that surrounded us, said in a whisper, "O! Captain Ravender, it looks as if the whole solid earth had changed into ice, and broken up!" I said to her, laughing, "I don't wonder that it does, to your inexperienced eyes, my dear." But I had never seen a twentieth part of the quantity, and, in reality, I was pretty much of her opinion.

However, at two P.M. on the afternoon of the sixth day, that is to say, when we were sixty-six days out, John Steadiman who had gone aloft, sang out from the top, that the sea was clear ahead. Before four P.M. a strong breeze springing up right astern, we were in open water at sunset. The breeze then freshening into half a gale of wind, and the Golden Mary being a very fast sailer, we went before the wind merrily, all night.

I had thought it impossible that it could be darker than it had been, until the sun, moon, and stars should fall out of the Heavens, and Time should be destroyed; but, it had been next to light, in comparison with what it was now. The darkness was so profound, that looking into it was painful and oppressive—like looking, without a ray of light, into a dense black bandage put as close before the eyes as it could be, without touching them. I doubled the look-out, and John and I stood in the bow side-by-side, never leaving it all night. Yet I should no more have known that he was near me when he was silent, without putting out my arm and touching him, than I should if he had turned in and been fast asleep below. We were not so much looking out, all of us, as listening to the utmost, both with our eyes and ears.

Next day, I found that the mercury in the barometer, which had risen steadily since we cleared the ice, remained steady. I had had very good observations, with now and then the interruption of a day or so, since our departure. I got the sun at noon, and found that we were in Lat. 58° S., Long. 60° W., off New South Shetland; in the neighbourhood of Cape Horn. We were sixty-seven days out, that day. The ship's reckoning was accurately worked and made up. The ship did her duty admirably, all on board were well, and all hands were as smart, efficient, and contented, as it was possible to be.

When the night came on again as dark as before, it was the eighth night I had been on deck. Nor had I taken more than a very little sleep in the daytime, my station being always near the helm, and often at it, while we were among the ice. Few but those who have tried it can imagine the difficulty and pain of only keeping the eyes open—physically open—under such circumstances, in such darkness. They get struck by the darkness, and blinded by the darkness. They make patterns in it, and they flash in it, as if they had gone out of your head to look at you. On the turn of midnight, John Steadiman, who was alert and fresh (for I had always made him turn in by day), said to me, "Captain Ravender, I entreat of you to go below. I am sure you can hardly stand, and your voice is getting weak, Sir. Go below, and take a little rest. I'll call you if a block chafes." I said to John in answer, "Well, well, John! Let us wait till the turn of one o'clock, before we talk about that." I had just had one of the ship's lanterns held up, that I might see how the night went by my watch, and it was then twenty minutes after twelve.

At five minutes before one, John sang out to the boy to bring the lantern again, and when I told him once more what the time was, entreated and prayed of me to go below. "Captain Ravender," says he, "all's well; we can't afford to have you laid up for a single hour; and I respectfully and earnestly beg of you to go below." The end of it was, that I agreed to do so, on the understanding that if I failed to come up of my own accord within three hours, I was to be punctually called. Having settled that, I left John in charge. But I called him to me once afterwards, to ask him a question. I had been to look at the barometer, and had seen the mercury still perfectly steady, and had come up the companion again to take a last look about me—if I can use such a word in reference to such darkness—when I thought that the waves, as the Golden Mary parted them and shook them off, had a hollow sound in them; something that I fancied was a rather unusual reverberation. I was standing by the quarter-deck rail on the starboard side, when I called John aft to me, and bade him listen. He did so with the greatest attention. Turning to me he then said, "Rely upon it, Captain Ravender, you have been without rest too long, and the novelty is only in the state of your sense of hearing." I thought so too by that time, and I think so now, though I can never kow for absolute certain in this world, whether it was or not.

When I left John Steadiman in charge, the ship was still going at a great rate through the water. The wind still blew right astern. Though she was making great way, she was under shortened sail, and had no more than she could easily carry. All was snug, and nothing complained. There was a pretty sea running, but not a very high sea neither, nor at all a confused one.

I turned in, as we seamen say, all standing. The meaning of that is, I did not pull my clothes off—no, not even so much as my coat: though I did my shoes, for my feet were badly swelled with the deck. There was a little swing-lamp alight in my cabin. I thought, as I looked at it before shutting my eyes, that I was so tired of darkness, and troubled by darkness, that I could have gone to sleep best in the midst of a million of flaming gas-lights. That was the last thought I had before I went off, except the prevailing thought that I should not be able to get to sleep at all.

I dreamed that I was back at Penrith again, and was trying to get round the church, which had altered its shape very much since I last saw it, and was cloven all down the middle of the steeple in a most singular manner. Why I wanted to get round the church I don't know; but I was as anxious to do it as if my life depended upon it. Indeed, I believe it did in the dream. For all that, I could not get round the church. I was still trying, when I came against it with a violent shock, and was flung out of my cot against the ship's side. Shrieks and a terrific outcry struck me far harder than the bruising timbers, and amidst sounds of grinding and crashing, and a heavy rushing and breaking of water—sounds I understood too well—I made my way on deck. It was not an easy thing to do, for the ship heeled over frightfully, and was beating in a furious manner.

I could not see the men as I went forward, but I could hear that they were hauling in sail, in disorder. I had my trumpet in my hand, and, after directing and encouraging them in this till it was done, I hailed first John Steadiman, and then my second mate, Mr. William Rames. Both answered clearly and steadily. Now, I had practised them and all my crew, as I have ever made it a custom to practise all who sail with me, to take certain stations and wait my orders, in case of any unexpected crisis. When my voice was heard hailing, and their voices were heard answering, I was aware, through all the noises of the ship and sea, and all the crying of the passengers below, that there was a pause. "Are you ready, Rames?"—"Ay, ay, Sir!"—"Then light up, for God's sake!" In a moment he and another were burning blue-lights, and the ship and all on board seemed to be enclosed in a mist of light, under a great black dome.

The light shone up so high that I could see the huge Iceberg upon which we had struck, cloven at the top and down the middle, exactly like Penrith Church in my dream. At the same moment I could see the watch last relieved, crowding up and down on deck; I could see Mrs. Atherfield and Miss Coleshaw thrown about on the top of the companion as they struggled to bring the child up from below; I could see that the masts were going with the shock and the beating of the ship; I could see the frightful breach stove in on the starboard side, half the length of the vessel, and the sheathing and timbers spirting up; I could see that the Cutter was disabled, in a wreck of broken fragments; and I could see every eye turned upon me. It is my belief that if there had been ten thousand eyes there, I should have seen them all, with their different looks. And all this in a moment. But you must consider what a moment.

I saw the men, as they looked at me, fall towards their appointed stations, like good men and true. If she had not righted, they could have done very little there or anywhere but die—not that it is little for a man to die at his post—I mean they could have done nothing to save the passengers and themselves. Happily, however, the violence of the shock with which we had so determinedly borne down direct on that fatal Iceberg, as if it had been our destination instead of our destruction, had so smashed and pounded the ship that she got off in this same instant and righted. I did not want the carpenter to tell me she was filling and going down; I could see and hear that. I gave Rames the word to lower the Long-boat and the Surf-boat, and I myself told off the men for each duty. Not one hung back, or came before the other. I now whispered to John Steadiman, "John, I stand at the gangway here, to see every soul on board safe over the side. You shall have the next post of honour, and shall be the last but one to leave the ship. Bring up the passengers, and range them behind me; and put what provision and water you can get at, in the boats. Cast your eye for'ard, John, and you'll see you have not a moment to lose."

My noble fellows got the boats over the side as orderly as I ever saw boats lowered with any sea running, and, when they were launched, two or three of the nearest men in them as they held on, rising and falling with the swell, called out, looking up at me, "Captain Ravender, if anything goes wrong with us, and you are saved, remember we stood by you!"—"We'll all stand by one another ashore, yet, please God, my lads!" says I. "Hold on bravely, and be tender with the women."

The women were an example to us. They trembled very much, but they were quiet and perfectly collected. "Kiss me, Captain Ravender," says Mrs. Atherfield, "and God in heaven bless you, you good man!" "My dear," says I, "those words are better for me than a lifeboat." I held her child in my arms till she was in the boat, and then kissed the child and handed her safe down. I now said to the people in her, "You have got your freight, my lads, all but me, and I am not coming yet awhile. Pull away from the ship, and keep off!"

That was the Long-boat. Old Mr. Rarx was one of her complement, and he was the only passenger who had greatly misbehaved since the ship struck. Others had been a little wild, which was not to be wondered at, and not very blamable; but, he had made a lamentation and uproar which it was dangerous for the people to hear, as there is always contagion in weakness and selfishness. His incessant cry had been that he must not be separated from the child, that he couldn't see the child, and that he and the child must go together. He had even tried to wrest the child out of my arms, that he might keep her in his. "Mr. Rarx," said I to him when it came to that, "I have a loaded pistol in my pocket; and if you don't stand out of the gang-way, and keep perfectly quiet, I shall shoot you through the heart, if you have got one." Says he, "You won't do murder, Captain Ravender!" "No, Sir," says I, "I won't murder forty-four people to humour you, but I'll shoot you to save them." After that he was quiet, and stood shivering a little way off, until I named him to go over the side.

The Long-boat being cast off, the Surf-boat was soon filled. There only remained aboard the Golden Mary, John Mullion, the man who had kept on burning the blue-lights (and who had lighted every new one at every old one before it went out, as quietly as if he had been at an illumination); John Steadiman; and myself. I hurried those two into the Surf-boat, called to them to keep off, and waited with a grateful and relieved heart for the Long-boat to come and take me in, if she could. I looked at my watch, and it showed me, by the blue-light, ten minutes past two. They lost no time. As soon as she was near enough, I swung myself into her, and called to the men, "With a will, lads! She's reeling!" We were not an inch too far out of the inner vortex of her going down, when, by the blue-light which John Mullion still burnt in the bow of the Surf-boat, we saw her lurch, and plunge to the bottom head-foremost. The child cried, weeping wildly, "O the dear Golden Mary! O look at her! Save her! Save the poor Golden Mary!" And then the light burnt out, and the black dome seemed to come down upon us.

I suppose if we had all stood a-top of a mountain, and seen the whole remainder of the world sink away from under us, we could hardly have felt more shocked and solitary than we did when we knew we were alone on the wide ocean, and that the beautiful ship in which most of us had been securely asleep within half an hour was gone for ever. There was an awful silence in our boat, and such a kind of palsy on the rowers and the man at the rudder, that I felt they were scarcely keeping her before the sea. I spoke out then, and said, "Let every one here thank the Lord for our preserva-tion!" All the voices answered (even the child's), "We thank the Lord!" I

STORM AND SHIPWRECK

then said the Lord's Prayer, and all hands said it after me with a solemn murmuring. Then I gave the word "Cheerily, O men, Cheerily!" and I felt that they were handling the boat again as a boat ought to be handled.

The Surf-boat now burnt another blue-light to show us where they were, and we made for her, and laid ourselves as nearly alongside of her as we dared. I had always kept my boats with a coil or two of good stout stuff in each of them, so both boats had a rope at hand. We made a shift, with much labour and trouble, to get near enough to one another to divide the blue-lights (they were no use after that night, for the sea-water soon got at them), and to get a tow-rope out between us. All night long we kept together, sometimes obliged to cast off the rope, and sometimes getting it out again, and all of us wearying for the morning—which appeared so long in coming that old Mr. Rarx screamed out, in spite of his fears of me, "The world is drawing to an end, and the sun will never rise any more!"

When the day broke, I found that we were all huddled together in a miserable manner. We were deep in the water; being, as I found on mustering, thirty-one in number, or at least six too many. In the Surf-boat they were fourteen in number, being at least four too many. The first thing I did, was to get myself passed to the rudder—which I took from that time—and to get Mrs. Atherfield, her child, and Miss Coleshaw, passed on to sit next me. As to old Mr. Rarx, I put him in the bow, as far from us as I could. And I put some of the best men near us in order that if I should drop there might be a skilful hand ready to take the helm.

The sea moderating as the sun came up, though the sky was cloudy and wild, we spoke the other boat, to know what stores they had, and to over-haul what we had. I had a compass in my pocket, a small telescope, a double-barrelled pistol, a knife, and a fire-box and matches. Most of my men had knives, and some had a little tobacco: some, a pipe as well. We had a mug among us, and an iron spoon. As to provisions, there were in my boat two bags of biscuit, one piece of raw beef, one piece of raw pork, a bag of coffee, roasted but not ground (thrown in, I imagine, by mistake, for something else), two small casks of water, and about half-a-gallon of rum in a keg. The Surf-boat, having rather more rum than we, and fewer to drink it, gave us, as I estimated, another quart into our keg. In return, we gave them three double handfuls of coffee, tied up in a piece of a handkerchief; they reported that they had aboard besides, a bag of biscuit, a piece of beef, a small cask of water, a small box of lemons, and a Dutch cheese. It took a long time to make these exchanges, and they were not made without risk to both parties; the sea running quite high enough to make our ap-proaching near to one another very hazardous. In the bundle with the cof-fee, I conveyed to John Steadiman (who had a ship's compass with him), a paper written in pencil, and torn from my pocket-book, containing the course I meant to steer, in the hope of making land, or being picked up by some vessel—I say in the hope, though I had little hope of either deliverance. I then sang out to him, so as all might hear, that if we two boats could live or die together, we would; but, that if we should be parted by the weather, and join company no more, they should have our prayers and blessings, and we asked for theirs. We then gave them three cheers, which they returned, and I saw the men's heads droop in both boats as they fell to their oars again.

These arrangements had occupied the general attention advantageously for all, though (as I expressed in the last sentence) they ended in a sorrowful feeling. I now said a few words to my fellow-voyagers on the subject of the small stock of food on which our lives depended if they were preserved from the great deep, and on the rigid necessity of our eking it out in the most frugal manner. One and all replied that whatever allowance I thought best to lay down should be strictly kept to. We made a pair of scales out of a thin strap of iron-plating and some twine, and I got together for weights such of the heaviest buttons among us as I calculated made up some fraction over two ounces. This was the allowance of solid food served out once a-day to each, from that time to the end; with the addition of a coffee-berry, or sometimes half a one, when the weather was very fair, for breakfast. We had nothing else whatever, but half a pint of water each per day, and sometimes, when we were coldest and weakest, a teaspoonful of rum each, served out as a dram. I know how learnedly it can be shown that rum is poison, but I also know that in this case, as in all similar cases I have ever read of—which are numerous—no words can express the comfort and support derived from it. Nor have I the least doubt that it saved the lives of far more than half our number. Having mentioned half a pint of water as our daily allowance, I ought to observe that sometimes we had less, and sometimes we had more; for much rain fell, and we caught it in a canvas stretched for the purpose.

Thus, at that tempestuous time of the year, and in that tempestuous part of the world, we shipwrecked people rose and fell with the waves. It is not my intention to relate (if I can avoid it) such circumstances appertaining to our doleful condition as have been better told in many other narratives of the kind than I can be expected to tell them. I will only note, in so many passing words, that day after day and night after night we received the sea upon our backs to prevent it from swamping the boat; that one party was always kept baling, and that every hat and cap among us soon got worn out, though patched up fifty times, as the only vessels we had for that service; that another party lay down in the bottom of the boat, while a third rowed; and that we were soon all in boils and blisters and rags.

The other boat was a source of such anxious interest to all of us that I used to wonder whether, if we were saved, the time could ever come when the survivors in this boat of ours could be at all indifferent to the fortunes of the survivors in that. We got out a tow-rope whenever the weather permitted, but that did not often happen, and how we two parties kept within the same horizon, as we did, He, who mercifully permitted it to be so for our consolation, only knows. I never shall forget the looks with which, when the morning light came, we used to gaze about us over the stormy waters, for the other boat. We once parted company for seventy-two hours, and we believed them to have gone down, as they did us. The joy on both sides when we came within view of one another again, had something in a manner Divine in it; each was so forgetful of individual suffering, in tears of delight and sympathy for the people in the other boat.

I have been wanting to get round to the individual or personal part of my subject, as I call it, and the foregoing incident puts me in the right way. The patience and good disposition aboard of us, was wonderful. I was not surprised by it in the women; for all men born of women know what great qualities they will show when men will fail; but, I own I was a little surprised by it in some of the men. Among one-and-thirty people assembled at the best of times, there will usually, I should say, be two or three uncertain tempers. I knew that I had more than one rough temper with me among my own people, for I had chosen those for the Long-boat that I might have them under my eye. But, they softened under their misery, and were as considerate of the ladies, and as compassionate of the child, as the best among us, or among men—they could not have been more so. I heard scarcely any complaining. The party lying down would moan a good deal in their sleep, and I would often notice a man—not always the same man, it is to be understood, but nearly all of them at one time or other—sitting moaning at his oar, or in his place, as he looked mistily over the sea. When it happened to be long before I could catch his eye, he would go on moaning all the time in the dismallest manner; but, when our looks met, he would brighten and leave off. I almost always got the impression that he did not know what sound he had been making, but that he thought he had been humming a tune.

Our sufferings from cold and wet were far greater than our sufferings from hunger. We managed to keep the child warm; but, I doubt if any one else among us ever was warm for five minutes together; and the shivering, and the chattering of teeth, were sad to hear. The child cried a little at first for her lost playfellow, the Golden Mary; but hardly ever whimpered afterwards; and when the state of the weather made it possible, she used now and then to be held up in the arms of some of us, to look over the sea for John Steadiman's boat. I see the golden hair and the innocent face now, between me and the driving clouds, like an angel going to fly away.

It had happened on the second day, towards night, that Mrs. Atherfield, in getting Little Lucy to sleep, sang her a song. She had a soft, melodious voice, and, when she had finished it, our people up and begged for another. She sang them another, and after it had fallen dark ended with the Evening Hymn. From that time, whenever anything could be heard above the sea and wind, and while she had any voice left, nothing would serve the people but that she should sing at sunset. She always did, and always ended with the Evening Hymn. We mostly took up the last line, and shed tears when it was done, but not miserably. We had a prayer night and morning, also, when the weather allowed of it.

Twelve nights and eleven days we had been driving in the boat, when old Mr. Rarx began to be delirious, and to cry out to me to throw the gold overboard or it would sink us, and we should all be lost. For days past the child had been declining, and that was the great cause of his wildness. He had been over and over again shrieking out to me to give her all the remaining meat, to give her all the remaining rum, to save her at any cost, or we should all be ruined. At this time, she lay in her mother's arms at my feet. One of her little hands was almost always creeping about her mother's neck or chin. I had watched the wasting of the little hand, and I knew it was nearly over.

The old man's cries were so discordant with the mother's love and submission, that I called out to him in an angry voice, unless he held his peace on the instant, I would order him to be knocked on the head and thrown overboard. He was mute then, until the child died, very peacefully, an hour afterwards: which was known to all in the boat by the mother's breaking out into lamentations for the first time since the wreck—for, she had great fortitude and constancy, though she was a little gentle woman. Old Mr. Rarx then became quite ungovernable, tearing what rags he had on him, raging in imprecations, and calling to me that if I had thrown the gold overboard (always the gold with him!) I might have saved the child. "And now," says he, in a terrible voice, "we shall founder, and all go to the Devil, for our sins will sink us, when we have no innocent child to bear us up!" We so discovered with amazement, that this old wretch had only cared for the life of the pretty little creature dear to all of us, because of the influence he superstitiously hoped she might have in preserving him! Altogether it was too much for the smith or armourer, who was sitting next the old man, to bear. He took him by the throat and rolled him under the thwarts, where he lay still enough for hours afterwards.

All that thirteenth night, Miss Coleshaw, lying across my knees as I kept the helm, comforted and supported the poor mother. Her child, covered with a pea-jacket of mine, lay in her lap. It troubled me all night to think that there was no Prayer-Book among us, and that I could remember but very few of the exact words of the burial service. When I stood up at broad day, all knew what was going to be done, and I noticed that my poor fellows made the motion of uncovering their heads, though their heads had been stark bare to the sky and sea for many a weary hour. There was a long heavy swell on, but otherwise it was a fair morning, and there were broad fields of sunlight on the waves in the east. I said no more than this: "I am the Resurrection and the Life, saith the Lord. He raised the daughter of Jairus the ruler, and said she was not dead but slept. He raised the widow's son. He arose Himself, and was seen of many. He loved little children, saying, Suffer them to come unto Me, and rebuke them not, for of such is the kingdom of heaven. In His name, my friends, and committed to His merciful goodness!" With those words I laid my rough face softly on the placid little forehed, and buried the Golden Lucy in the grave of the Golden Mary.

Having had it on my mind to relate the end of this dear little child, I have omitted something from its exact place, which I will supply here. It will come quite as well here as anywhere else.

Foreseeing that if the boat lived through the stormy weather, the time must come, and soon come, when we should have absolutely no morsel to eat, I had one momentous point often in my thoughts. Although I had, years before that, fully satisfied myself that the instances in which human beings in the last distress have fed upon each other, are exceedingly few, and have very seldom indeed (if ever) occurred when the people in distress, however dreadful their extremity, have been accustomed to moderate forbearance and restraint; I say, though I had long before quite satisfied my mind on this topic, I felt doubtful whether there might not have been in former cases some harm and danger from keeping it out of sight and pretending not to think of it. I felt doubtful whether some minds, growing weak with fasting and exposure and having such a terrific idea to dwell upon in secret, might not magnify it until it got to have an awful attraction about it. This was not a new thought of mine, for it had grown out of my reading. However, it came over me stronger than it had ever done before— as it had reason for doing—in the boat, and on the fourth day I decided that I would bring out into the light that unformed fear which must have been more or less darkly in every brain among us. Therefore, as a means of beguiling the time and inspiring hope, I gave them the best summary in my power of Bligh's voyage of more than three thousand miles, in an open boat, after the Mutiny of the Bounty, and of the wonderful preservation of that boat's crew. They listened throughout with great interest, and I concluded by telling them, that, in my opinion, the happiest circumstance in the whole narrative was, that Bligh, who was no delicate man either, had solemnly placed it on record therein that he was sure and certain that under no conceivable circumstances whatever would that emaciated party, who had gone through all the pains of famine, have preyed on one another. I cannot describe the visible relief which this spread through the boat, and how the tears stood in every eye. From that time I was as well convinced as Bligh himself that there was no danger, and that this phantom, at any rate, did not haunt us.

Now, it was a part of Bligh's experience that when the people in his boat were most cast down, nothing did them so much good as hearing a story told by one of their number. When I mentioned that, I saw that it struck the general attention as much as it did my own, for I had not thought of it until I came to it in my summary. This was on the day after Mrs. Atherfield first sang to us. I proposed that, whenever the weather would permit, we should have a story two hours after dinner (I always issued the allowance I have mentioned at one o'clock, and called it by that name), as well as our song at sunset. The proposal was received with a cheerful satisfaction that warmed my heart within me; and I do not say too much when I say that those two periods in the four-and-twenty hours were expected with positive pleasure, and were really enjoyed by all hands. Spectres as we soon were in our bodily wasting, our imaginations did not perish like the gross flesh upon our bones. Music and Adventure, two of the great gifts of Providence to mankind, could charm us long after that was lost.

The wind was almost always against us after the second day; and for many days together we could not nearly hold our own. We had all varieties of bad weather. We had rain, hail, snow, wind, mist, thunder and lightning. Still the boats lived through the heavy seas, and still we perishing people rose and fell with the great waves.

Sixteen nights and fifteen days, twenty nights and nineteen days, twenty-four nights and twenty-three days. So the time went on. Disheartening as I knew that our progress, or want of progress, must be, I never deceived them as to my calculations of it. In the first place, I felt that we were all too near eternity for deceit; in the second place, I knew that if I failed, or died, the man who followed me must have a knowledge of the true state of things to begin upon. When I told them at noon, what I reckoned we had made or lost, they generally received what I said in a tranquil and resigned manner, and always gratefully towards me. It was not unusual at any time of the day for some one to burst out weeping loudly without any new cause; and, when the burst was over, to calm down a little better than before. I had seen exactly the same thing in a house of mourning.

During the whole of this time, old Mr. Rarx had had his fits of calling out to me to throw the gold (always the gold!) overboard, and of heaping violent reproaches upon me for not having saved the child; but now, the food being all gone, and I having nothing left to serve out but a bit of coffee-berry now and then, he began to be too weak to do this, and consequently fell silent. Mrs. Atherfield and Miss Coleshaw generally lay, each with an arm across one of my knees, and her head upon it. They never complained at all. Up to the time of her child's death, Mrs. Atherfield had bound up her own beautiful hair every day; and I took particular notice that this was always before she sang her song at night, when every one looked at her. But she never did it after the loss of her darling; and it would have been now all tangled with dirt and wet, but that Miss Coleshaw was careful of it long after she was herself, and would sometimes smooth it down with her weak thin hands.

We were past mustering a story now; but one day, at about this period, I reverted to the superstition of old Mr. Rarx, concerning the Golden Lucy, and told them that nothing vanished from the eye of God, though much might pass away from the eyes of men. "We were all of us," says I, "children once; and our baby feet have strolled in green woods ashore; and our baby hands have gathered flowers in gardens, where the birds were singing. The children that we were, are not lost to the great knowledge of our Creator. Those innocent creatures will appear with us before Him, and plead for us. What we were in the best time of our generous youth will arise and go with us too. The purest part of our lives will not desert us at the pass to which all of us here present are gliding. What we were then, will be as much in existence before Him, as what we are now." They were no less comforted by this consideration, than I was myself; and Miss Coleshaw, drawing my ear nearer to her lips, said, "Captain Ravender, I was on my way to marry a disgraced and broken man, whom I dearly loved when he was honourable and good. Your words seem to have come out of my own poor heart." She pressed my hand upon it, smiling.

Twenty-seven nights and twenty-six days. We were in no want of rain-water, but we had nothing else. And yet, even now, I never turned my eyes upon a waking face but it tried to brighten before mine. O, what a thing it is, in a time of danger and in the presence of death, the shining of a face upon a face! I have heard it broached that orders should be given in great new ships by electric telegraph. I admire machinery as much as any man, and am as thankful to it as any man can be for what it does for us. But it will never be a substitute for the face of a man, with his soul in it, encouraging another man to be brave and true. Never try it for that. It will break down like a straw.

I now began to remark certain changes in myself which I did not like. They caused me much disquiet. I often saw the Golden Lucy in the air above the boat. I often saw her I have spoken of before, sitting beside me. I saw the Golden Mary go down, as she really had gone down, twenty times in a day. And yet the sea was mostly, to my thinking, not sea neither, but moving country and extraordinary mountainous regions, the like of which have never been beheld. I felt it time to leave my last words regarding John Steadiman, in case any lips should last out to repeat them to any living ears. I said that John had told me (as he had on deck) that he had sung out

"Breakers ahead!" the instant they were audible, and had tried to wear ship, but she struck before it could be done. (His cry, I dare say, had made my dream.) I said that the circumstances were altogether without warning, and out of any course that could have been guarded against; that the same loss would have happened if I had been in charge; and that John was not to blame, but from first to last had done his duty nobly, like the man he was. I tried to write it down in my pocket-book, but could make no words, though I knew what the words were that I wanted to make. When it had come to that, her hands—though she was dead so long—laid me down gently in the bottom of the boat, and she and the Golden Lucy swung me to sleep.

All that follows, was written by John Steadiman, Chief Mate:

On the twenty-sixth day after the foundering of the Golden Mary at sea, I, John Steadiman, was sitting in my place in the stern-sheets of the Surf-boat, with just sense enough left in me to steer—that is to say, with my eyes strained, wide-awake, over the bows of the boat, and my brains fast asleep and dreaming—when I was roused upon a sudden by our second mate, Mr. William Rames.

"Let me take a spell in your place," says he. "And look you out for the Long-boat astern. The last time she rose on the crest of a wave, I thought I made out a signal flying aboard her."

We shifted our places, clumsily and slowly enough, for we were both of us weak and dazed with wet, cold, and hunger. I waited some time, watching the heavy rollers astern, before the Long-boat rose a-top of one of them at the same time with us. At last, she was heaved up for a moment well in view, and there, sure enough, was the signal flying aboard of her—a strip of rag of some sort, rigged to an oar, and hoisted in her bows.

"What does it mean?" says Rames to me in a quavering, trembling sort of voice. "Do they signal a sail in sight?"

"Hush, for God's sake!" says I, clapping my hand over his mouth. "Don't let the people hear you. They'll all go mad together if we mislead them about that signal. Wait a bit, till I have another look at it."

I held on by him, for he had set me all of a tremble with his notion of a sail in sight, and watched for the Long-boat again. Up she rose on the top of another roller. I made out the signal clearly, that second time, and saw that it was rigged half-mast high.

"Rames," says I, "it's a signal of distress. Pass the word forward to keep her before the sea, and no more. We must get the Long-boat within hailing distance of us, as soon as possible."

I dropped down into my old place at the tiller without another word—

for the thought went through me like a knife that something had happened to Captain Ravender. I should consider myself unworthy to write another line of this statement, if I had not made up my mind to speak the truth, the whole truth, and nothing but the truth—and I must, therefore, confess plainly that now, for the first time, my heart sank within me. This weakness on my part was produced in some degree, as I take it, by the exhausting effects of previous anxiety and grief.

Our provisions—if I may give that name to what we had left—were reduced to the rind of one lemon and about a couple of handsfull of coffee-berries. Besides these great distresses, caused by the death, the danger, and the suffering among my crew and passengers, I had had a little distress of my own to shake me still more, in the death of the child whom I had got to be very fond of on the voyage out—so fond that I was secretly a little jealous of her being taken in the Long-boat instead of mine when the ship foundered. It used to be a great comfort to me, and I think to those with me also, after we had seen the last of the Golden Mary, to see the Golden Lucy, held up by the men in the Long-boat, when the weather allowed it, as the best and brightest sight they had to show. She looked, at the distance we saw her from, almost like a little white bird in the air. To miss her for the first time, when the weather lulled a little again, and we all looked out for our white bird and looked in vain, was a sore disappointment. To see the men's heads bowed down and the captain's hand pointing into the sea when we hailed the Long-boat, a few day's after, gave me as heavy a shock and as sharp a pang of heartache to bear as ever I remember suffering in all my life. I only mention these things to show that if I did give way a little at first, under the dread that our captain was lost to us, it was not without having been a good deal shaken beforehand by more trials of one sort or another than often fall to one man's share.

I had got over the choking in my throat with the help of a drop of water, and had steadied my mind again so as to be prepared against the worst, when I heard the hail (Lord help the poor fellows, how weak it sounded!)—

"Surf-boat ahoy!"

I looked up, and there were our companions in misfortune tossing abreast of us; not so near that we could make out the features of any of them, but near enough, with some exertion for people in our condition, to make their voices heard in the intervals when the wind was weakest.

I answered the hail, and waited a bit, and heard nothing, and then sung out the captain's name. The voice that replied did not sound like his; the words that reached us were:

"Chief-mate wanted on board!"

Every man of my crew knew what that meant as well as I did. As second officer in command, there could be but one reason for wanting me on board the Long-boat. A groan went all round us, and my men looked darkly in each other's faces, and whispered under their breaths:

"The captain is dead!"

I commanded them to be silent, and not to make too sure of bad news, at such a pass as things had now come to with us. Then, hailing the Long-boat, I signified that I was ready to go on board when the weather would let me—stopped a bit to draw a good long breath—and then called out as loud as I could the dreadful question:

"Is the captain dead?"

The black figures of three or four men in the after-part of the Long-boat all stooped down together as my voice reached them. They were lost to view for about a minute; then appeared again—one man among them was held up on his feet by the rest, and he hailed back the blessed words (a very faint hope went a very long way with people in our desperate situation): "Not yet!"

The relief felt by me, and by all with me, when we knew that our captain, though unfitted for duty, was not lost to us, it is not in words—at least, not in such words as a man like me can command—to express. I did my best to cheer the men by telling them what a good sign it was that we were not as badly off yet as we had feared; and then communicated what instructions I had to give, to William Rames, who was to be left in command in my place when I took charge of the Long-boat. After that, there was nothing to be done, but to wait for the chance of the wind dropping at sunset, and the sea going down afterwards, so as to enable our weak crews to lay the two boats alongside each other, without undue risk—or, to put it plainer, without saddling ourselves with the necessity for any extraordinary exertion of strength or skill. Both the one and the other had now been starved out of us for days and days together.

At sunset the wind suddenly dropped, but the sea, which had been running high for so long a time past, took hours after that before it showed any signs of getting to rest. The moon was shining, the sky was wonderfully clear, and it could not have been, according to my calculations, far off midnight, when the long, slow, regular swell of the calming ocean fairly set in, and I took the responsibility of lessening the distance between the Long-boat and ourselves.

It was, I dare say, a delusion of mine; but I thought I had never seen the moon shine so white and ghastly anywhere, either at sea or on land, as she shone that night while we were approaching our companions in misery. When there was not much more than a boat's length between us, and the white light streamed cold and clear over all our faces, both crews rested on their oars with one great shudder, and stared over the gunwale of either boat, panic-stricken at the first sight of each other.

"Any lives lost among you?" I asked, in the midst of that frightful silence. The men in the Long-boat huddled together like sheep at the sound of my voice.

"None yet, but the child, thanks be to God!" answered one among them.

And at the sound of his voice, all my men shrank together like the men in the Long-boat. I was afraid to let the horror produced by our first meeting at close quarters after the dreadful changes that wet, cold, and famine had produced, last one moment longer than could be helped; so, without giving time for any more questions and answers, I commanded the men to lay the two boats close alongside of each other. When I rose up and committed the tiller to the hands of Rames, all my poor fellows raised their white faces imploringly to mine. "Don't leave us, Sir," they said, "don't leave us." "I leave you," says I, "under the command and the guidance of Mr. William Rames, as good a sailor as I am, and as trusty and kind a man as ever stepped. Do your duty by him, as you have done it by me; and remember to the last, that while there is life there is hope. God bless and help you all!" With those words I collected what strength I had left, and caught at two arms that were held out to me, and so got from the stern-sheets of one boat into the stern-sheets of the other.

"Mind where you step, Sir," whispered one of the men who had helped me into the Long-boat. I looked down as he spoke. Three figures were huddled up below me, with the moonshine falling on them in ragged streaks through the gaps between the men standing or sitting above them. The first face I made out was the face of Miss Coleshaw; her eyes were wide open and fixed on me. She seemed still to keep her senses, and, by the alternate parting and closing of her lips, to be trying to speak, but I could not hear that she uttered a single word. On her shoulder rested the head of Mrs. Atherfield. The mother of our poor little Golden Lucy must, I think, have been dreaming of the child she had lost; for there was a faint smile just ruffling the white stillness of her face, when I first saw it turned upward, with peaceful closed eyes towards the heavens. From her, I looked down a little, and there, with his head on her lap, and with one of her hands resting tenderly on his cheek—there lay the Captain, to whose help and guidance, up to this miserable time, we had never looked in vain,—there, worn out at last in our service, and for our sakes, lay the best and bravest man of all our company. I stole my hand in gently through his clothes and laid it on his heart, and felt a little feeble warmth over it, though my cold dulled touch could not detect even the faintest beating. The two men in the stern-sheets with me, noticing what I was doing—knowing I loved him like a brother —and seeing, I suppose, more distress in my face than I myself was conscious of its showing, lost command over themselves altogether, and burst into a piteous moaning, sobbing lamentation over him. One of the two drew aside a jacket from his feet, and showed me that they were bare, except where a wet, ragged strip of stocking still clung to one of them. When the ship struck the Iceberg, he had run on deck leaving his shoes in his cabin. All through the voyage in the boat his feet had been unprotected; and not a soul had discovered it until he dropped! As long as he could keep his eyes open, the very look of them had cheered the men, and comforted and up-held the women. Not one living creature in the boat, with any sense about him, but had felt the good influence of that brave man in one way or an-other. Not one but had heard him, over and over again, give the credit to others which was due only to himself; praising this man for patience, and thanking that man for help, when the patience and the help had really and truly, as to the best part of both, come only from him. All this, and much more, I heard pouring confusedly from the men's lips while they crouched down, sobbing and crying over their commander, and wrapping the jacket as warmly and tenderly as they could over his cold feet. It went to my heart to check them; but I knew that if this lamenting spirit spread any further, all chance of keeping alight any last sparks of hope and resolution among the boat's company would be lost for ever. Accordingly I sent them to their places, spoke a few encouraging words to the men forward, promis-ing to serve out, when the morning came, as much as I dared, of any eatable thing left in the lockers; called to Rames, in my old boat, to keep as near us as he safely could; drew the garments and coverings of the two poor suffer-ing women more closely about them; and, with a secret prayer to be directed for the best in bearing the awful responsibility now laid on my shoulders, took my Captain's vacant place at the helm of the Long-boat.

This, as well as I can tell it, is the full and true account of how I came to be placed in charge of the lost passengers and crew of the Golden Mary, on the morning of the twenty-seventh day after the ship struck the Iceberg, and foundered at sea.

CHARLES DICKENS
1812–70
WILKIE COLLINS*
1824–89

Charles John Huffam Dickens was the son of a clerk in the navy pay-office at Portsmouth. In 1824 financial difficulty sent his father to debtor's prison and twelve-year-old Dickens to work for a few months in a shoe-blacking

* See Collins's biography, page 227.

warehouse. He was a student for a short time (1824–27), a solicitor's clerk (1827–28), a free-lance reporter (1829–31), and a shorthand reporter of Parliamentary proceedings beginning in late 1831 or early 1832. His first story, "A Dinner at Poplar Walk," was published in the *Monthly Magazine* in December 1833.

By 1836 his first major work was written. In that year the collection *Sketches by Boz* was published, and between April 1836 and November 1837 *The Posthumous Papers of the Pickwick Club* appeared in monthly parts. Always attracted to theater, Dickens wrote two plays which were staged in 1836—*The Strange Gentlemen* and *The Village Coquettes*.

Before Dickens began collaborating with Wilkie Collins in 1856, *Nicholas Nickleby, The Old Curiosity Shop, Barnaby Rudge, Martin Chuzzlewit, A Christmas Carol, David Copperfield,* and *Hard Times* had been published. The two men worked together on both stories and plays until 1867.

Little Dorrit (1855–57), *A Tale of Two Cities* (1859), *Great Expectations* (1860), and *Our Mutual Friend* (1864–65) were the most prominent of Dickens's solo productions during the years of collaboration. After 1867 Dickens was beset by ill health. He began *The Mystery of Edwin Drood* but died before completing it.

"The Wreck of the *Golden Mary*" was the title piece of the first volume (1856) Dickens and Collins produced in collaboration.

The Wreck of the Visigoth

BY RUDYARD KIPLING

"Eternal Father, strong to save,
Whose arm hath bound the restless wave,
Who bidst the mighty ocean keep
Its own appointed limits deep."

THE LADY PASSENGERS were trying the wheezy old harmonium in front of the cuddy, because it was Sunday night. In the patch of darkness near the wheel-grating sat the Captain, and the end of his cheroot burned like a head-lamp. There was neither breath nor motion upon the waters through which the screw was thudding. They spread, dull silver, under the haze of the moonlight till they joined the low coast of Malacca away to the eastward. The voices of the singers at the harmonium were held down by the awnings, and came to us with force.

"Oh, hear us when we cry to Thee,
For those in peril on the sea!"

It was as though the little congregation were afraid of the vastness of the sea. But a laugh followed, and some one said, "Shall we take it through again a little quicker?" Then the Captain told the story of just such a night, lowering his voice for fear of disturbing the music and the minds of the passengers.

"She was the *Visigoth*,—five hundred tons, or it may have been six,—in the coasting trade; one of the best steamers and best found on the Kutch-Kasauli line. She wasn't six years old when the thing happened: on just such a night as this, with an oily-smooth sea, under brilliant starlight, about a hundred miles from land. To this day no one knows really what the matter was. She was so small that she could not have struck even a log in the water without every soul on board feeling the jar; and even if she had struck something, it wouldn't have made her go down as she did. I was fourth officer then; we had about seven saloon passengers, including the Captain's wife and another woman, and perhaps five hundred deck-passengers going up the coast to a shrine, on just such a night as this, when she was ripping through the level sea at a level nine knots an hour. The man on the bridge, whoever it was, saw that she was sinking at the head. Sinking by the head as she went along. That was the only warning we got. She began to sink as she went along. Of course the Captain was told, and he sent me to wake up the saloon passengers and tell them to come on deck. 'Sounds a curious sort of message that to deliver on a dead-still night. The people tumbled up in their dressing-gowns and *pyjamas*, and wouldn't believe me. We were just sinking as fast as we could, and I had to tell 'em that. Then the deck-passengers got wind of it, and all Hell woke up along the decks.

"The rule in these little affairs is to get your saloon passengers off first, then to fill the boats with the balance, and afterwards—God help the extras, that's all. I was getting the starboard stern boat—the mail-boat—away. It hung as it might be over yonder, and as I came along from the cuddy, the deck-passengers hung round me, shoving their money-belts into my hand, taking off their nose-rings and ear-rings, and thrusting 'em upon me to buy just one chance for life. If I hadn't been so desperately busy, I should have thought it horrible. I put biscuits and water into the boat, and got the two ladies in. One of 'em was the Captain's wife. She had to be put in by main force. You've no notion how women can struggle. The other woman was the wife of an officer going to meet her husband; and there were a couple of passengers beside the lascars. The Captain said he was going to stay with the ship. You see the rule in these affairs, I believe, is that the Captain has to bow gracefully from the bridge and go down. I haven't had a ship under my charge wrecked yet. When that comes, I'll have to do like the others. After the boats were away, and I saw that there was nothing to be got by waiting, I jumped overboard exactly as I might have vaulted over into a flat green field, and struck out for the mail-boat. Another officer did the same thing, but he went for a boat full of natives, and they whacked him on the chest with oars, so he had some difficulty in climbing in.

"It was as well that I reached the mail-boat. There was a compass in it, but the idiots had managed to fill the boat half full of water somehow or another, and none of the crew seemed to know what was required of them. Then the *Visigoth* went down and took every one with her—ships generally do that; the corpses don't cumber the sea for some time.

"What did I do? I kept all the boats together, and headed into the track of the coasting steamers. The aggravating thing was the thought that we were close to land as far as a big steamer was concerned, and in the middle of eternity as far as regarded a little boat. The sea looks hugeous big from a boat at night."

"Oh, Christ, whose voice the waters heard
And hushed their ravings at Thy word,
Who walkedst on the foaming deep

And calm amidst its rage did keep,—
Oh, hear us when we cry to Thee,
For those in peril on the sea!"

sang the passengers cheerily.

"That harmonium is disgracefully out of tune," said the Captain. "The sea air affects their insides. Well, as I was saying, we settled down in the boat. The Captain's wife was unconscious; she lay in the bottom of the boat and moaned. I was glad she wasn't threshing about the boat: but what I did think was wrong, was the way the two men passengers behaved. They were useless with funk—out-and-out fear. They lay in the boat and did nothing. Fetched a groan now and again to show they were alive; but that was all. But the other woman was a jewel. Damn it, it was worth being shipwrecked to have that woman in the boat; she was awfully handsome, and as brave as she was lovely. She helped me bail out the boat, and she worked like a man.

"So we kicked about the sea from midnight till seven the next evening, and then we saw a steamer. 'I'll—I'll give you anything I'm wearing to hoist as a signal of distress,' said the woman; but I had no need to ask her, for the steamer picked us up and took us back to Bombay. I forgot to tell you that, when the day broke, I couldn't recognise the Captain's wife—widow, I mean. She had changed in the night as if fire had gone over her. I met her a long time afterwards, and even then she hadn't forgiven me for putting her into the boat and obeying the Captain's orders. But the husband of the other woman—he's in the Army—wrote me no end of a letter of thanks. I don't suppose he considered that the way his wife behaved was enough to make any decent man do all he could. The other fellows, who lay in the bottom of the boat and groaned, I've never met. 'Don't want to. 'Shouldn't be civil to 'em if I did. And that's how the *Visigoth* went down, for no assignable reason, with eighty bags of mail, five hundred souls, and not a single packet insured, on just such a night as this."

"Oh, Trinity of love and power,
Our brethren shield in that dread hour,
From rock and tempest, fire and foe,
Protect them wheresoe'er they go.
Thus evermore shall rise to Thee
Glad hymns of praise by land and sea."

"'Strikes me they'll go on singing that hymn all night. 'Imperfect sort of doctrine in the last lines, don't you think? They might have run in an extra verse specifying sudden collapse—like the *Visigoth*'s. I'm going on to the bridge, now. Good night," said the Captain.

And I was left alone with the steady thud, thud, of the screw and the gentle creaking of the boats at the davits.

That made me shudder.

RUDYARD KIPLING*
1865–1939

"The Wreck of the Visigoth" first appeared in the American edition of *Soldiers Three*.

*See Kipling's biography, page 147.

The Derelict

BY H. M. TOMLINSON

IN A TRAMP STEAMER, which was overloaded, and in midwinter, I had crossed to America for the first time. What we experienced of the western ocean during that passage gave me so much respect for it that the prospect of the return journey, three thousand miles of those seas between me and home, was already a dismal foreboding.

The shipping posters of New York, showing stately liners too lofty even to notice the Atlantic, were arguments good enough for steerage passengers, who do, I know, reckon a steamer's worth by the number of its funnels; but the pictures did nothing to lessen my regard for that dark outer world I knew. And having no experience of ships installed with racquet courts, Parisian cafes, swimming baths, and pergolas, I was naturally puzzled by the inconsequential behavior of the first-class passengers at the hotel. They were leaving by the liner which was to take me, and, I gathered, were going to cross a bridge to England in the morning. Of course, this might have been merely the innocent profanity of the simple-minded.

Embarking at the quay next day, I could not see that our ship had either a beginning or an end. There was a blank wall which ran out of sight to the right and left. How far it went, and what it enclosed, were beyond me. Hundreds of us in a slow procession mounted stairs to the upper floor of a warehouse, and from thence a bridge led us to a door in the wall half-way in its height. No funnels could be seen. Looking straight up from the embarkation gangway, along what seemed the parapet of the wall was a row of far-off indistinguishable faces peering straight down at us. There was no evidence that this building we were entering, of which the high black wall was a part, was not an important and permanent feature of the city. It was in keeping with the magnitude of New York's skyscrapers, which this planet's occasionally non-irritant skin permits to stand there to afford man an apparent reason to be gratified with his own capacity and daring.

But with the knowledge that this wall must be afloat there came no sense of security when, going through that little opening in its altitude, I found myself in a spacious decorated interior which hinted nothing of a ship, for I was puzzled as to direction. My last ship could be surveyed in two glances; she looked, and was, a comprehensible ship, no more than a manageable handful for an able master. In that ship you could see at once where you were and what to do. But in this liner you could not see where you were, and would never know which way to take unless you had a good memory. No understanding came to me in that hall of a measured and shapely body, designed with a cunning informed by ages of sea-lore to move buoyantly and surely among the raging seas, to balance delicately, a quick and sensitive being, to every precarious slope, to recover a lost poise easily and with the grace natural to a quick creature controlled by an alert mind.

There was no shape at all to this structure. I could see no line the run of which gave me warrant that it was comprised in the rondure of a ship. The lines were all of straight corridors, which, for all I knew, might have ended blindly on open space, as streets which traverse a city and are bare in vacancy beyond the dwellings. It was possible we were encompassed by walls, but only one wall was visible. There we idled, all strangers, in a large hall roofed by a dome of colored glass. Quite properly, palms stood beneath. There were offices and doors everywhere. On a broad staircase a multitude of us wandered aimlessly up and down. Each side of the stairway were electric lifts, intermittent and brilliant apparitions. I began to understand why the saloon passengers thought nothing of the voyage. They were encountering nothing unfamiliar. They had but come to another hotel for a few days.

I attempted to find my cabin, but failed. A uniformed guide took care of me. But my cabin, curtained, upholstered, and warm, with mirrors and plated ware, sunk somewhere deeply among carpeted and silent streets down each of which the perspective of glow-lamps looked interminable, left me still questioning. The long walk had given me a fear that I was remote from important affairs which might be happening beyond. My address was 323. The street door—I was down a side turning, though—bore that number. A visitor could make no mistake, supposing he could find the street and my side turning. That was it. There was a very great deal in this place for everybody to remember, and most of us were strangers. No doubt, however, we were afloat, if the lifebelts in the rack meant anything. Yet the cabin, insulated from all noise, was not soothing, but disturbing. I had been used to a ship in which you could guess all that was happening even when in your bunk; a sensitive and communicative ship.

A steward appeared at my door, a stranger out of nowhere, and asked whether I had seen a bag not mine in the cabin. He might have been created merely to put that question, for I never saw him again on the voyage. This liner was a large province having irregular and shifting bounds, permitting incontinent entrance and disappearance. All this should have inspired me with an idea of our vastness and importance, but it did not. I felt I was one of a multitude included in a nebulous mass too vague to hold together unless we were constantly wary.

In the saloon there was the solid furniture of rare woods, the ornate decorations, and the light and shadows making vague its limits and giving it an
appearance of immensity, to keep the mind from the thought of our real
circumstances. At dinner we had valentine music, dreamy stuff to accord
with the shaded lamps which displayed the tables in a lower rosy light. It
helped to extend the mysterious and romantic shadows. The pale, disem-
bodied masks of the waiters swam in the dusk above the tinted light. I had
for a companion a vivacious American lady from the Middle West, and she
looked round that prospect we had of an expensive café, and said, "Well, but
I am disappointed. Why, I've been looking forward to seeing the ocean, you
know. And it isn't here."

"Smooth passage," remarked a man on the other side. "No sea at all
worth mentioning." Actually, I know there was a heavy beam sea running
before a half-gale. I could guess the officer in charge somewhere on the exposed roof might have another mind about it; but it made no difference to
us in our circle of rosy intimate light bound by those vague shadows which
were alive with ready servitude.

"And I've been reading *Captains Courageous* with this voyage in view.
Isn't this the month when the forties roar? I want to hear them roar, just
once, you know, and as gently as any sucking dove." We all laughed. "We
can't even tell we're in a ship."

She began to discuss Kipling's book. "There's some fine seas in that. Have
you read it? But I'd like to know where that ocean is he pretends to have
seen. I do believe the realists are no more reliable than the romanticists.
Here we are a thousand miles out, and none of us has seen the sea yet. Tell
me, does not a realist have to magnify his awful billows just to get them into
his reader's view?"

I murmured something feeble and sociable. I saw then why sailors never
talk directly of the sea. I, for instance, could not find my key at that moment—it was in another pocket somewhere—so I had no iron to touch.
Talking largely of the sea is something like the knowing talk of young men
about women; and what is a simple sailor man that he should open his
mouth on mysteries?

Only on the liner's boat-deck, where you could watch her four funnels
against the sky, could you see to what extent the liner was rolling. The arc
seemed to be considerable then, but slowly described. But the roll made
little difference to the promenaders below. Sometimes they walked a short
distance on the edges of their boots, leaning over as they did so, and swerving from the straight, as though they had turned giddy. The shadows
formed by the weak sunlight moved slowly out of ambush across the white
deck, but often moved indecisively, as though uncertain of a need to go; and
then slowly went into hiding again. The sea whirling and leaping past was

far below our wall side. It was like peering dizzily over a precipice when watching those green and white cataracts.

The passengers, wrapped and comfortable on the lee deck, chatted as blithely as at a garden-party, while the band played medleys of national airs to suit our varied complexions. The stewards came round with loaded trays. A diminutive and wrinkled dame in costly furs frowned through her golden spectacles at her book, while her maid sat attentively by. An American actress was the center of an eager group of grinning young men; she was unseen, but her voice was distinct. The two Vanderbilts took their brisk constitutional among us as though the liner had but two real passengers though many invisible nobodies. The children, who had not ceased laughing and playing since we left New York, waited for the slope of the deck to reach its greatest, and then ran down toward the bulwarks precipitously. The children, happy and innocent, completed for us the feeling of comfortable indifference and security which we found when we saw there was more ship than ocean. The liner's deck canted slowly to leeward, went over more and more, beyond what it had done yet, and a pretty little girl with dark curls riotous from under her red tam-o'shanter, ran down, and brought up against us violently with both hands, laughing heartily. We laughed too. Looking seaward, I saw receding the broad green hill, snow-capped, which had lifted us and let us down. The sea was getting up.

Near sunset, when the billows were mounting express along our run, sometimes to leap and snatch at our upper structure, and were rocking us with some ease, there was a commotion forward. Books and shawls went anywhere as the passengers ran. Something strange was to be seen upon the waters.

It looked like a big log out there ahead, over the starboard bow. It was not easy to make out. The light was failing. We overhauled it rapidly, and it began to shape as a ship's boat. "Oh, it's gone," exclaimed some one then. But the forlorn object lifted high again, and sank once more. Whenever it was glimpsed it was set in a patch of foam.

That flotsam, whatever it was, was of man. As we watched it intently, and before it was quite plain, we knew intuitively that hope was not there, that we were watching something past its doom. It drew abeam, and we saw what it was, a derelict sailing ship, mastless and awash. The alien wilderness was around us now, and we saw a sky that was overcast and driven, and seas that were uplifted, which had grown incredibly huge, swift, and perilous, and they had colder and more somber hues.

The derelict was a schooner, a lifeless and soddened hulk, so heavy and uncontesting that its foundering seemed at hand. The waters poured back and forth at her waist, as though holding her body captive for the assaults of the active seas which came over her broken bulwarks, and plunged ruthlessly about. There was something ironic in the indifference of her defenseless body to these unending attacks. It mocked this white and raging postmortem brutality, and gave her a dignity that was cold and superior to all the eternal powers could now do. She pitched helplessly head first into a hollow, and a door flew open under the break of her poop; it surprised and shocked us, for the dead might have signed to us then. She went astern of us fast, and a great comber ran at her, as if it had but just spied her, and thought she was escaping. There was a high white flash, and a concussion we heard. She had gone. But she appeared again far away, on a summit in desolation, black against the sunset. The stump of her bowsprit, the accusatory finger of the dead, pointed at the sky.

I turned, and there beside me was the lady who had wanted to find the sea. She was gazing at the place where the wreck was last seen, her eyes fixed, her mouth a little open in awe and horror.

H. M. TOMLINSON
1873–1958

Growing up in London's East End by the docks, Henry Major Tomlinson early loved ships, the sea, and the curious things that came to London from foreign ports. By his twelfth birthday he was a junior clerk for a shipping company, where he became acquainted with bills of lading and cargo manifests and dreamed of strange lands.

He continued the scribbling he had been doing since childhood and finally sent some of it out. His first acceptance came from the London *Morning Leader*, which gave him a staff position in 1904.

A voyage up the Amazon in 1912 provided material for his first book, *The Sea and the Jungle* (1912). From 1914 to 1917 he was a war correspondent in Belgium and France. He edited the *Nation and Athenaeum* until 1923 and then traveled to the East Indies for *Harpers Magazine* for nine months. With this experience behind him he wrote *Tidemarks* (1924).

Not until the publication of *Gallions Reach* (1927), which won the Femina Vie Heureuse Prize, was Tomlinson able to devote all his time to writing what he liked. His work during the thirties included fiction which he claimed was autobiographical: *All Our Yesterdays* (1930), *The Snows of Helicon* (1933), *All Hands* (1937), and *The Day Before* (1939). Tomlinson also produced nonfiction works in the first half of the decade: *Out of Soundings* (1931); *Norman Douglas* (1931); *South to Cadiz* (1934); *Below London Bridge*

(1934), a book illustrated by his son; and *Mars His Idiot* (1935). Other books, including *The Wind Is Rising* (1941) and *The Turn of the Tide* (1947), followed in the forties.

Tomlinson included "The Derelict" in the collection *Sea Stories of All Nations* (1930).

After the Storm

BY ERNEST HEMINGWAY

IT WASN'T ABOUT ANYTHING, something about making punch, and then we started fighting and I slipped and he had me down kneeling on my chest and choking me with both hands like he was trying to kill me and all the time I was trying to get the knife out of my pocket to cut him loose. Everybody was too drunk to pull him off me. He was choking me and hammering my head on the floor and I got the knife out and opened it up; and I cut the muscle right across his arm and he let go of me. He couldn't have held on if he wanted to. Then he rolled and hung onto that arm and started to cry and I said:

"What the hell you want to choke me for?"

I'd have killed him. I couldn't swallow for a week. He hurt my throat bad.

Well, I went out of there and there were plenty of them with him and some came out after me and I made a turn and was down by the docks and I met a fellow and he said somebody killed a man up the street. I said "Who killed him?" and he said "I don't know who killed him but he's dead all right," and it was dark and there was water standing in the street and no lights and windows broke and boats all up in the town and trees blown down and everything all blown and I got a skiff and went out and found my boat where I had her inside of Mango Key and she was all right only she was full of water. So I bailed her out and pumped her out and there was a moon but plenty of clouds and still plenty rough and I took it down along; and when it was daylight I was off Eastern Harbor.

Brother, that was some storm. I was the first boat out and you never saw water like that was. It was just as white as a lye barrel and coming from Eastern Harbor to Sou'west Key you couldn't recognize the shore. There was a big channel blown right out through the middle of the beach. Trees and all blown out and a channel cut through and all the water white as chalk and everything on it; branches and whole trees and dead birds, and all floating. Inside the keys were all the pelicans in the world and all kinds of birds flying. They must have gone inside there when they knew it was coming.

I lay at Sou'west Key a day and nobody came after me. I was the first boat out and I seen a spar floating and I knew there must be a wreck and I

started out to look for her. I found her. She was a three-masted schooner
and I could just see the stumps of her spars out of water. She was in too
deep water and I didn't get anything off of her. So I went on looking for
something else. I had the start on all of them and I knew I ought to get
whatever there was. I went on down over the sand-bars from where I left
that three-masted schooner and I didn't find anything and I went on a long
way. I was way out toward the quicksands and I didn't find anything so I
went on. Then when I was in sight of the Rebecca Light I saw all kinds of
birds making over something and I headed over for them to see what it was
and there was a cloud of birds all right.

I could see something looked like a spar up out of the water and when I
got over close the birds all went up in the air and stayed all around me. The
water was clear out there and there was a spar of some kind sticking out just
above the water and when I come up close to it I saw it was all dark under
water like a long shadow and I came right over it and there under water
was a liner; just lying there all under water as big as the whole world. I
drifted over her in the boat. She lay on her side and the stern was deep
down. The port holes were all shut tight and I could see the glass shine in
the water and the whole of her; the biggest boat I ever saw in my life laying
there and I went along the whole length of her and then I went over and
anchored and I had the skiff on the deck forward and I shoved it down into
the water and sculled over with the birds all around me.

I had a water glass like we use sponging and my hand shook so I could
hardly hold it. All the port holes were shut that you could see going along
over her but way down below near the bottom something must have been
open because there were pieces of things floating out all the time. You
couldn't tell what they were. Just pieces. That's what the birds were after.
You never saw so many birds. They were all around me; crazy yelling.

I could see everything sharp and clear. I could see her rounded over and
she looked a mile long under the water. She was lying on a clear white bank
of sand and the spar was a sort of foremast or some sort of tackle that
slanted out of water the way she was laying on her side. Her bow wasn't
very far under. I could stand on the letters of her name on her bow and my
head was just out of water. But the nearest port hole was twelve feet down.
I could just reach it with the grains pole and I tried to break it with that but
I couldn't. The glass was too stout. So I sculled back to the boat and got a
wrench and lashed it to the end of the grains pole and I couldn't break it.
There I was looking down through the glass at that liner with everything in
her and I was the first one to her and I couldn't get into her. She must have
had five million dollars worth in her.

It made me shaky to think how much she must have in her. Inside the
port hole that was closest I could see something but I couldn't make it out
through the water glass. I couldn't do any good with the grains pole and I

took off my clothes and stood and took a couple of deep breaths and dove over off the stern with the wrench in my hand and swam down. I could hold on for a second to the edge of the port hole and I could see in and there was a woman inside with her hair floating all out. I could see her floating plain and I hit the glass twice with the wrench hard and I heard the noise clink in my ears but it wouldn't break and I had to come up.

I hung onto the dinghy and got my breath and then I climbed in and took a couple of breaths and dove again. I swam down and took hold of the edge of the port hole with my fingers and held it and hit the glass as hard as I could with the wrench. I could see the woman floated in the water through the glass. Her hair was tied once close to her head and it floated all out in the water. I could see the rings on one of her hands. She was right up close to the port hole and I hit the glass twice and I didn't even crack it. When I came up I thought I wouldn't make it to the top before I'd have to breathe.

I went down once more and I cracked the glass, only cracked it, and when I came up my nose was bleeding and I stood on the bow of the liner with my bare feet on the letters of her name and my head just out and rested there and then I swam over to the skiff and pulled up into it and sat there waiting for my head to stop aching and looking down in the water glass, but I bled so I had to wash out the water glass. Then I lay back in the skiff and held my hand under my nose to stop it and I lay there with my head back looking up and there was a million birds above and all around.

When I quit bleeding I took another look through the glass and then I sculled over to the boat to try and find something heavier than the wrench but I couldn't find a thing; not even a sponge hook. I went back and the water was clearer all the time and you could see everything that floated out over that white bank of sand. I looked for sharks but there weren't any. You could have seen a shark a long way away. The water was so clear and the sand white. There was a grapple for an anchor on the skiff and I cut it off and went overboard and down with it. It carried me right down and past the port hole and I grabbed and couldn't hold anything and went on down and down, sliding along the curved side of her. I had to let go of the grapple. I heard it bump once and it seemed like a year before I came up through to the top of the water. The skiff was floated away with the tide and I swam over to her with my nose bleeding in the water while I swam and I was plenty glad there weren't sharks; but I was tired.

My head felt cracked open and I lay in the skiff and rested and then I sculled back. It was getting along in the afternoon. I went down once more with the wrench and it didn't do any good. That wrench was too light. It wasn't any good diving unless you had a big hammer or something heavy enough to do good. Then I lashed the wrench to the grains pole again and I watched through the water glass and pounded on the glass and hammered until the wrench came off and I saw it in the glass, clear and sharp, go sliding down along her and then off and down to the quicksand and go in. Then I couldn't do a thing. The wrench was gone and I'd lost the grapple so I sculled back to the boat. I was too tired to get the skiff aboard and the sun was pretty low. The birds were all pulling out and leaving her and I headed for Sou'west Key towing the skiff and the birds going on ahead of me and behind me. I was plenty tired.

That night it came on to blow and it blew for a week. You couldn't get out to her. They come out from town and told me the fellow I'd had to cut was all right except for his arm and I went back to town and they put me under five hundred dollar bond. It came out all right because some of them, friends of mine, swore he was after me with an ax, but by the time we got back out to her the Greeks had blown her open and cleaned her out. They got the safe out with dynamite. Nobody ever knows how much they got. She carried gold and they got it all. They stripped her clean. I found her and I never got a nickel out of her.

It was a hell of thing all right. They say she was just outside of Havana harbor when the hurricane hit and she couldn't get in or the owners wouldn't let the captain chance coming in; they say he wanted to try; so she had to go with it and in the dark they were running with it trying to go through the gulf between Rebecca and Tortugas when she struck on the quicksands. Maybe her rudder was carried away. Maybe they weren't even steering. But anyway they couldn't have known they were quicksands and when she struck the captain must have ordered them to open up the ballast tanks so she'd lay solid. But it was quicksand she'd hit and when they opened the tank she went in stern first and then over on her beam ends. There were four hundred and fifty passengers and the crew on board of her and they must all have been aboard of her when I found her. They must have opened the tanks as soon as she struck and the minute she settled on it the quicksands took her down. Then her boilers must have burst and that must have been what made those pieces that came out. It was funny there weren't any sharks though. There wasn't a fish. I could have seen them on that clear white sand.

Plenty of fish now though; jewfish, the biggest kind. The biggest part of her's under the sand now but they live inside of her; the biggest kind of jewfish. Some weigh three to four hundred pounds. Sometime we'll go out and get some. You can see the Rebecca light from where she is. They've got a buoy on her now. She's right at the end of the quicksand right at the edge of the gulf. She only missed going through by about a hundred yards. In the dark in the storm they just missed it; raining the way it was they couldn't have seen the Rebecca. Then they're not used to that sort of thing. The captain of a liner isn't used to scudding that way. They have a course and they tell me they set some sort of a compass and it steers itself. They probably didn't know where they were when they ran with that blow but they come close to making it. Maybe they'd lost the rudder though. Anyway there wasn't another thing for them to hit till they'd get to Mexico once they were in that gulf. Must have been something though when they struck in that rain and wind and he told them to open her tanks. Nobody could have been on deck in that blow and rain. Everybody must have been below. They couldn't have lived on deck. There must have been some scenes inside all right because you know she settled fast. I saw that wrench go into the sand. The captain couldn't have known it was quicksand when she struck unless he knew these waters. He just knew it wasn't rock. He must have seen it all up in the bridge. He must have known what it was about when she settled. I wonder how fast she made it. I wonder if the mate was there with him. Do you think they stayed inside the bridge or do you think they took it outside? They never found any bodies. Not a one. Nobody floating. They float a long way with life belts too. They must have took it inside. Well, the Greeks got it all. Everything. They must have come fast all right. They picked her clean. First there was the birds, then me, then the Greeks, and even the birds got more out of her than I did.

ERNEST HEMINGWAY
1898–1961

As a youth Ernest Miller Hemingway hunted and fished in Michigan's north woods, learning to value himself and others by the prowess these endeavors and sports like football and boxing demanded. Following graduation from high school, he worked for the Kansas City *Star* as a reporter, but the war in Europe lured him. He saw it as a test, much like hunting and fishing, by which personal worth might be measured. After volunteer service in an American ambulance unit in France, he transferred to a more active role, fighting on the Italian front with a volunteer infantry, the Italian Arditi. Receiving serious wounds in the process of proving himself, he won several decorations for valor.

Returning to newspaper work, he covered the Greco-Turkish War in 1920 and later became a Paris correspondent. There, among expatriate intellectuals, he served his literary apprenticeship. His first major book, *In Our Time* (1924), was a collection of short stories that took as their themes the prowess and endurance Hemingway's sports activities and warring had made into yardsticks of human worth.

The Sun Also Rises (1926), his first novel, depicted the life of the lost generation of expatriates, largely American, in Europe following World War I. Other major works followed: *A Farewell to Arms* (1929), *Death in the Afternoon* (1932), *Green Hills of Africa* (1935), and the best of all his novels, *For Whom the Bell Tolls* (1940). The indomitable spirit that Hemingway extolled in *For Whom the Bell Tolls* also reigns in *The Old Man and the Sea* (1952), for which he was awarded a Pulitzer Prize in 1953. He received the Nobel Prize for literature in 1954.

His early heroic figures were modeled in part on the author's own life, in part on the heroic ideals he tried to emulate. Later Hemingway heroes did not show the brashness or the vigor of Jake Barnes, Frederic Henry, or Robert Jordan; and at least one of them—Richard Cantwell, in *Across the River and Into the Trees* (1952)—prefigured Hemingway's end. Both the character and the writer struggled to overcome physical and mental illness unsuccessfully. Both eventually resorted to suicide. Hemingway's end came in 1961.

"After the Storm," a tale about a loser, is not typical of the large body of Hemingway's work. First published in *Cosmopolitan* in May 1932, the story reappeared in *Winner Take Nothing* (1933).

Great Stories of the Sea

HERE ARE FOUR STORIES that have gained in popularity over the years. They are about seafarers, but they are not for seafarers alone; dealing with crucial decisions that real men and women make, these stories include among their most devoted fans landlocked people who fear any body of water larger than a bathtub. They portray the sea as not only a physical object but also a symbolic one that can give man insights into the nature of life and death.

Herman Melville's chilling story "Benito Cereno" opens with the picture of a confident captain who wants to aid a derelict ship. Soon his confidence turns to pity; his pity, apprehension; and his apprehension, sheer terror. "The Open Boat" also calls up fear—the desperate fear of people facing death. Stephen Crane's characters, adrift in an open boat after their ship has sunk, battle the winds, the sun, and the waves for their lives. Some, not always the physically weak, succumb. In the battle for survival, what counts if brute strength does not? Who are the fittest to survive?

Joseph Conrad is represented here by two stories. In "Youth" a man remembers a reckless time spent aboard the leaky coal freighter *Judea* as she struggled toward Bangkok. Rather than give up on the ship, judged too dangerous for passage by a succession of crews, the narrator stays with her, relying on sinews not yet tired and a will not yet conquered to see him and his vessel through. The trip is one in which youth is lost and adulthood discovered.

"The Secret Sharer" is the haunting tale of a double who shares the captain's cabin. Is he a stowaway? Is he merely a projection of the captain's mind? Why is he protected so carefully, kept so secret? The questions multiply as Conrad gives full rein to his imagination.

Benito Cereno

BY HERMAN MELVILLE

IN THE YEAR 1799, Captain Amasa Delano, of Duxbury, in Massachusetts, commanding a large sealer and general trader, lay at anchor with a valuable cargo, in the harbor of St. Maria—a small, desert, uninhabited island toward the southern extremity of the long coast of Chili. There he had touched for water.

On the second day, not long after dawn, while lying in his berth, his mate came below, informing him that a strange sail was coming into the bay. Ships were then not so plenty in those waters as now. He rose, dressed, and went on deck.

The morning was one peculiar to that coast. Everything was mute and calm; everything gray. The sea, though undulated into long roods of swells, seemed fixed, and was sleeked at the surface like waved lead that has cooled and set in the smelter's mould. The sky seemed a gray surtout. Flights of troubled gray fowl, kith and kin with flights of troubled gray vapors among which they were mixed, skimmed low and fitfully over the waters, as swallows over meadows before storms. Shadows present, foreshadowing deeper shadows to come.

To Captain Delano's surprise, the stranger, viewed through the glass, showed no colors; though to do so upon entering a haven, however uninhabited in its shores, where but a single other ship might be lying, was the custom among peaceful seamen of all nations. Considering the lawlessness and loneliness of the spot, and the sort of stories, at that day, associated with those seas, Captain Delano's surprise might have deepened into some uneasiness had he not been a person of a singularly undistrustful good nature, not liable, except on extraordinary and repeated incentives, and hardly then, to indulge in personal alarms, any way involving the imputation of malign evil in man. Whether, in view of what humanity is capable, such a trait implies, along with a benevolent heart, more than ordinary quickness and accuracy of intellectual perception, may be left to the wise to determine.

But whatever misgivings might have obtruded on first seeing the stranger, would almost, in any seaman's mind, have been dissipated by observing that, the ship, in navigating into the harbor, was drawing too near the land; a sunken reef making out off her bow. This seemed to prove her a stranger, indeed, not only to the sealer, but the island; consequently, she could be no wonted freebooter on that ocean. With no small interest, Captain Delano continued to watch her—a proceeding not much facilitated by the vapors partly mantling the hull, through which the far matin light from her cabin streamed equivocally enough; much like the sun—by this time hemisphered on the rim of the horizon, and, apparently, in company with the strange ship entering the harbor—which, wimpled by the same low, creeping clouds, showed not unlike a Lima *intriguante's* one sinister eye peering across the Plaza from the Indian loop-hole of her dusk *saya-y-manta*.

It might have been but a deception of the vapors, but, the longer the stranger was watched the more singular appeared her manœuvres. Ere long it seemed hard to decide whether she meant to come in or no—what she wanted, or what she was about. The wind, which had breezed up a little during the night, was now extremely light and baffling, which the more increased the apparent uncertainty of her movements.

Surmising, at last, that it might be a ship in distress, Captain Delano ordered his whale-boat to be dropped, and, much to the wary opposition of his mate, prepared to board her, and, at the least, pilot her in. On the night previous, a fishing-party of the seamen had gone a long distance to some detached rocks out of sight from the sealer, and, an hour or two before daybreak, had returned, having met with no small success. Presuming that the stranger might have been long off soundings, the good captain put several baskets of the fish, for presents, into his boat, and so pulled away. From her continuing too near the sunken reef, deeming her in danger, calling to his men, he made all haste to apprise those on board of their situation. But, some time ere the boat came up, the wind, light though it was, having shifted, had headed the vessel off, as well as partly broken the vapors from about her.

Upon gaining a less remote view, the ship, when made signally visible on the verge of the leaden-hued swells, with the shreds of fog here and there raggedly furring her, appeared like a white-washed monastery after a thunder-storm, seen perched upon some dun cliff among the Pyrenees. But it was no purely fanciful resemblance which now, for a moment, almost led Captain Delano to think that nothing less than a shipload of monks was before him. Peering over the bulwarks were what really seemed, in the hazy distance, throngs of dark cowls; while, fitfully revealed through the open port-holes, other dark moving figures were dimly described, as of Black Friars pacing the cloisters.

Upon a still nigher approach, this appearance was modified, and the true character of the vessel was plain—a Spanish merchantman of the first class, carrying negro slaves, amongst other valuable freight, from one colonial port to another. A very large, and, in its time, a very fine vessel, such as in

those days were at intervals encountered along that main; sometimes super-
seded Acapulco treasure-ships, or retired frigates of the Spanish king's navy,
which, like superannuated Italian palaces, still, under a decline of masters,
preserved signs of former state.

As the whale-boat drew more and more nigh, the cause of the peculiar
pipe-clayed aspect of the stranger was seen in the slovenly neglect pervading
her. The spars, ropes, and great part of the bulwarks, looked woolly, from
long unacquaintance with the scraper, tar, and the brush. Her keel seemed
laid, her ribs put together, and she launched, from Ezekiel's Valley of Dry
Bones.

In the present business in which she was engaged, the ship's general
model and rig appeared to have undergone no material change from their
original warlike and Froissart pattern. However, no guns were seen.

The tops were large, and were railed about with what had once been
octagonal net-work, all now in sad disrepair. These tops hung overhead like
three ruinous aviaries, in one of which was seen perched, on a ratlin, a white
noddy, a strange fowl, so called from its lethargic, somnambulistic character,
being frequently caught by hand at sea. Battered and mouldy, the castel-
lated forecastle seemed some ancient turret, long ago taken by assault, and
then left to decay. Toward the stern, two high-raised quarter galleries—the
balustrades here and there covered with dry, tindery sea-moss—opening out
from the unoccupied state-cabin, whose dead-lights, for all the mild weather,
were hermetically closed and calked—these tenantless balconies hung over
the sea as if it were the grand Venetian canal. But the principal relic of faded
grandeur was the ample oval of the shield-like stern-piece, intricately carved
with the arms of Castile and Leon, medallioned about by groups of mythological or symbolical devices; uppermost and central of which was a dark
satyr in a mask, holding his foot on the prostrate neck of a writhing figure,
likewise masked.

Whether the ship had a figure-head, or only a plain beak, was not quite
certain, owing to canvas wrapped about that part, either to protect it while
undergoing a re-furbishing, or else decently to hide its decay. Rudely painted
or chalked, as in a sailor freak, along the forward side of a sort of pedestal
below the canvas, was the sentence, *"Seguid vuestro jefe,"* (follow your
leader); while upon the tarnished headboards, near by, appeared, in stately
capitals, once gilt, the ship's name, "SAN DOMINICK," each letter streakingly
corroded with tricklings of copper-spike rust; while, like mourning weeds,
dark festoons of sea-grass slimily swept to and fro over the name, with every
hearse-like roll of the hull.

As, at last, the boat was hooked from the bow along toward the gangway
amidship, its keel, while yet some inches separated from the hull, harshly
grated as on a sunken coral reef. It proved a huge bunch of conglobated

barnacles adhering below the water to the side like a wen—a token of baffling airs and long calms passed somewhere in those seas.

Climbing the side, the visitor was at once surrounded by a clamorous throng of whites and blacks, but the latter outnumbering the former more than could have been expected, negro transportation-ship as the stranger in port was. But, in one language, and as with one voice, all poured out a common tale of suffering; in which the negresses, of whom there were not a few, exceeded the others in their dolorous vehemence. The scurvy, together with the fever, had swept off a great part of their number, more especially the Spaniards. Off Cape Horn they had narrowly escaped shipwreck; then, for days together, they had lain tranced without wind; their provisions were low; their water next to none; their lips that moment were baked.

While Captain Delano was thus made the mark of all eager tongues, his one eager glance took in all faces, with every other object about him.

Always upon first boarding a large and populous ship at sea, especially a foreign one, with a nondescript crew such as Lascars or Manilla men, the impression varies in a peculiar way from that produced by first entering a strange house with strange inmates in a strange land. Both house and ship—the one by its walls and blinds, the other by its high bulwarks like ramparts—hoard from view their interiors till the last moment: but in the case of the ship there is this addition; that the living spectacle it contains, upon its sudden and complete disclosure, has, in contrast with the blank ocean which zones it, something of the effect of enchantment. The ship seems unreal; these strange costumes, gestures, and faces, but a shadowy tableau just emerged from the deep, which directly must receive back what it gave.

Perhaps it was some such influence, as above is attempted to be described, which, in Captain Delano's mind, heightened whatever, upon a staid scrutiny, might have seemed unusual; especially the conspicuous figures of four elderly grizzled negroes, their heads like black, doddered willow tops, who, in venerable contrast to the tumult below them, were couched, sphinx-like, one on the starboard cat-head, another on the larboard, and the remaining pair face to face on the opposite bulwarks above the main-chains. They each had bits of unstranded old junk in their hands, and, with a sort of stoical self-content, were picking the junk into oakum, a small heap of which lay by their sides. They accompanied the task with a continuous, low, monotonous chant; droning and druling away like so many gray-headed bag-pipers playing a funeral march.

The quarter-deck rose into an ample elevated poop, upon the forward verge of which, lifted, like the oakum-pickers, some eight feet above the general throng, sat along in a row, separated by regular spaces, the cross-legged figures of six other blacks; each with a rusty hatchet in his hand, which, with a bit of brick and a rag, he was engaged like a scullion in scouring; while between each two was a small stack of hatchets, their rusted edges turned forward awaiting a like operation. Though occasionally the four oakum-pickers would briefly address some person or persons in the crowd below, yet the six hatchet-polishers neither spoke to others, nor breathed a whisper among themselves, but sat intent upon their task, except at intervals, when, with the peculiar love in negroes of uniting industry with pastime, two and two they sideways clashed their hatchets together, like cymbals, with a barbarous din. All six, unlike the generality, had the raw aspect of unsophisticated Africans.

But that first comprehensive glance which took in those ten figures, with scores less conspicuous, rested but an instant upon them, as, impatient of the hubbub of voices, the visitor turned in quest of whosoever it might be that commanded the ship.

But as if not unwilling to let nature make known her own case among his suffering charge, or else in despair of restraining it for the time, the Spanish captain, a gentlemanly, reserved-looking, and rather young man to a stranger's eye, dressed with singular richness, but bearing plain traces of recent sleepless cares and disquietudes, stood passively by, leaning against the main-mast, at one moment casting a dreary, spiritless look upon his excited people, at the next an unhappy glance toward his visitor. By his side stood a black of small stature, in whose rude face, as occasionally, like a shepherd's dog, he mutely turned it up into the Spaniard's, sorrow and affection were equally blended.

Struggling through the throng, the American advanced to the Spaniard, assuring him of his sympathies, and offering to render whatever assistance might be in his power. To which the Spaniard returned for the present but grave and ceremonious acknowledgments, his national formality dusked by the saturnine mood of ill-health.

But losing no time in mere compliments, Captain Delano, returning to the gangway, had his basket of fish brought up; and as the wind still continued light, so that some hours at least must elapse ere the ship could be brought to the anchorage, he bade his men return to the sealer, and fetch back as much water as the whale-boat could carry, with whatever soft bread the steward might have, all the remaining pumpkins on board, with a box of sugar, and a dozen of his private bottles of cider.

Not many minutes after the boat's pushing off, to the vexation of all, the wind entirely died away, and the tide turning, began drifting back the ship helplessly seaward. But trusting this would not long last, Captain Delano sought, with good hopes, to cheer up the strangers, feeling no small satisfaction that, with persons in their condition, he could—thanks to his frequent voyages along the Spanish main—converse with some freedom in their native tongue.

While left alone with them, he was not long in observing some things tending to heighten his first impressions; but surprise was lost in pity, both for the Spaniards and blacks, alike evidently reduced from scarcity of water and provisions; while long-continued suffering seemed to have brought out the less good-natured qualities of the negroes, besides, at the same time, impairing the Spaniard's authority over them. But, under the circumstances, precisely this condition of things was to have been anticipated. In armies, navies, cities, or families, in nature herself, nothing more relaxes good order than misery. Still, Captain Delano was not without the idea, that had Benito Cereno been a man of greater energy, misrule would hardly have come to the present pass. But the debility, constitutional or induced by hardships, bodily and mental, of the Spanish captain, was too obvious to be overlooked. A prey to settled dejection, as if long mocked with hope he would not now indulge it, even when it had ceased to be a mock, the prospect of that day, or evening at furthest, lying at anchor, with plenty of water for his people, and a brother captain to counsel and befriend, seemed in no perceptible degree to encourage him. His mind appeared unstrung, if not still more seriously affected. Shut up in these oaken walls, chained to one dull round of command, whose unconditionality cloyed him, like some hypochondriac abbot he moved slowly about, at times suddenly pausing, starting, or staring, biting his lip, biting his fingernail, flushing, paling, twitching his beard, with other symptoms of an absent or moody mind. This distempered spirit was lodged, as before hinted, in as distempered a frame. He was rather tall, but seemed never to have been robust, and now with nervous suffering was almost worn to a skeleton. A tendency to some pulmonary complaint appeared to have been lately confirmed. His voice was like that of one with lungs half gone—hoarsely suppressed, a husky whisper. No wonder that, as in this state he tottered about, his private servant apprehensively followed him. Sometimes the negro gave his master his arm, or took his handkerchief out of his pocket for him; performing these and similar offices with that affectionate zeal which transmutes into something filial or fraternal acts in themselves but menial; and which has gained for the negro the repute of making the most pleasing body-servant in the world; one, too, whom a master need be on no stiffly superior terms with, but may treat with familiar trust; less a servant than a devoted companion.

Marking the noisy indocility of the blacks in general, as well as what seemed the sullen inefficiency of the whites it was not without humane satisfaction that Captain Delano witnessed the steady good conduct of Babo.

But the good conduct of Babo, hardly more than the ill-behavior of others, seemed to withdraw the half-lunatic Don Benito from his cloudy languor. Not that such precisely was the impression made by the Spaniard on the mind of his visitor. The Spaniard's individual unrest was, for the present, but noted as a conspicuous feature in the ship's general affliction. Still, Captain Delano was not a little concerned at what he could not help taking for the time to be Don Benito's unfriendly indifference towards himself. The Spaniard's manner, too, conveyed a sort of sour and gloomy disdain, which he seemed at no pains to disguise. But this the American in charity ascribed to the harassing effects of sickness, since, in former instances, he had noted that there are peculiar natures on whom prolonged physical suffering seems to cancel every social instinct of kindness; as if, forced to black bread themselves, they deemed it but equity that each person coming nigh them should, indirectly, by some slight or affront, be made to partake of their fare.

But ere long Captain Delano bethought him that, indulgent as he was at the first, in judging the Spaniard, he might not, after all, have exercised charity enough. At bottom it was Don Benito's reserve which displeased him; but the same reserve was shown towards all but his faithful personal attendant. Even the formal reports which, according to sea-usage, were, at stated times, made to him by some petty underling, either a white, mulatto or black, he hardly had patience enough to listen to, without betraying contemptuous aversion. His manner upon such occasions was, in its degree, not unlike that which might be supposed to have been his imperial countryman's, Charles V., just previous to the anchoritish retirement of that monarch from the throne.

This splenetic disrelish of his place was evinced in almost every function pertaining to it. Proud as he was moody, he condescended to no personal mandate. Whatever special orders were necessary, their delivery was delegated to his body-servant, who in turn transferred them to their ultimate destination, through runners, alert Spanish boys or slave boys, like pages or pilot-fish within easy call continually hovering round Don Benito. So that to have beheld this undemonstrative invalid gliding about, apathetic and mute, no landsman could have dreamed that in him was lodged a dictatorship beyond which, while at sea, there was no earthly appeal.

Thus, the Spaniard, regarded in his reserve, seemed the involuntary victim of mental disorder. But, in fact, his reserve might, in some degree, have proceeded from design. If so, then here was evinced the unhealthy climax of that icy though conscientious policy, more or less adopted by all commanders of large ships, which, except in signal emergencies, obliterates alike the manifestation of sway with every trace of sociality; transforming the man into a block, or rather into a loaded cannon, which, until there is call for thunder, has nothing to say.

Viewing him in this light, it seemed but a natural token of the perverse habit induced by a long course of such hard self-restraint, that, notwithstanding the present condition of his ship, the Spaniard should still persist in a demeanor, which, however harmless, or, it may be, appropriate, in a well-appointed vessel, such as the San Dominick might have been at the outset of the voyage, was anything but judicious now. But the Spaniard, perhaps, thought that it was with captains as with gods: reserve, under all events, must still be their cue. But probably this appearance of slumbering dominion might have been but an attempted disguise to conscious imbecility—not deep policy, but shallow device. But be all this as it might, whether Don Benito's manner was designed or not, the more Captain Delano noted its pervading reserve, the less he felt uneasiness at any particular manifestation of that reserve towards himself.

Neither were his thoughts taken up by the captain alone. Wonted to the quiet orderliness of the sealer's comfortable family of a crew, the noisy confusion of the San Dominick's suffering host repeatedly challenged his eye. Some prominent breaches, not only of discipline but of decency, were observed. These Captain Delano could not but ascribe, in the main, to the absence of those subordinate deck-officers to whom, along with higher duties, is intrusted what may be styled the police department of a populous ship. True, the old oakum-pickers appeared at times to act the part of monitorial constables to their countrymen, the blacks; but though occasionally succeeding in allaying trifling outbreaks now and then between man and man, they could do little or nothing toward establishing general quiet. The San Dominick was in the condition of a transatlantic emigrant ship, among whose multitude of living freight are some individuals, doubtless, as little troublesome as crates and bales; but the friendly remonstrances of such with their ruder companions are of not so much avail as the unfriendly arm of the mate. What the San Dominick wanted was, what the emigrant ship has, stern superior officers. But on these decks not so much as a fourth-mate was to be seen.

The visitor's curiosity was roused to learn the particulars of those mishaps which had brought about such absenteeism, with its consequences; because, though deriving some inkling of the voyage from the wails which at the first moment had greeted him, yet of the details no clear understanding had been had. The best account would, doubtless, be given by the captain. Yet at first the visitor was loth to ask it, unwilling to provoke some distant rebuff. But plucking up courage, he at last accosted Don Benito, renewing the expression of his benevolent interest, adding, that did he (Captain Delano) but know the particulars of the ship's misfortunes, he would, perhaps, be better able in the end to relieve them. Would Don Benito favor him with the whole story.

Don Benito faltered; then, like some somnambulist suddenly interfered with, vacantly stared at his visitor, and ended by looking down on the deck. He maintained this posture so long, that Captain Delano, almost equally disconcerted, and involuntarily almost as rude, turned suddenly from him, walking forward to accost one of the Spanish seamen for the desired information. But he had hardly gone five paces, when, with a sort of eagerness, Don Benito invited him back, regretting his momentary absence of mind, and professing readiness to gratify him.

While most part of the story was being given, the two captains stood on the after part of the main-deck, a privileged spot, no one being near but the servant.

"It is now a hundred and ninety days," began the Spaniard, in his husky whisper, "that this ship, well officered and well manned, with several cabin passengers—some fifty Spaniards in all—sailed from Buenos Ayres bound to Lima, with a general cargo, hardware, Paraguay tea and the like—and," pointing forward, "that parcel of negroes, now not more than a hundred and fifty, as you see, but then numbering over three hundred souls. Off Cape Horn we had heavy gales. In one moment, by night, three of my best officers, with fifteen sailors, were lost, with the main-yard; the spar snapping under them in the slings, as they sought, with heavers, to beat down the icy sail. To lighten the hull, the heavier sacks of mata were thrown into the sea, with most of the water-pipes lashed on deck at the time. And this last necessity it was, combined with the prolonged detentions afterwards experienced, which eventually brought about our chief causes of suffering. When—"

Here there was a sudden fainting attack of his cough, brought on, no doubt, by his mental distress. His servant sustained him, and drawing a cordial from his pocket placed it to his lips. He a little revived. But unwilling to leave him unsupported while yet imperfectly restored, the black with one arm still encircled his master, at the same time keeping his eye fixed on his face, as if to watch for the first sign of complete restoration, or relapse, as the event might prove.

The Spaniard proceeded, but brokenly and obscurely, as one in a dream.

—"Oh, my God! rather than pass through what I have, with joy I would have hailed the most terrible gales; but—"

His cough returned and with increased violence; this subsiding, with reddened lips and closed eyes he fell heavily against his supporter.

"His mind wanders. He was thinking of the plague that followed the gales," plaintively sighed the servant; "my poor, poor master!" wringing one hand, and with the other wiping the mouth. "But be patient, Señor," again turning to Captain Delano, "these fits do not last long; master will soon be himself."

Don Benito reviving, went on; but as this portion of the story was very brokenly delivered, the substance only will here be set down.

It appeared that after the ship had been many days tossed in storms off the Cape, the scurvy broke out, carrying off numbers of the whites and blacks. When at last they had worked round into the Pacific, their spars and sails were so damaged, and so inadequately handled by the surviving mariners, most of whom were become invalids, that, unable to lay her northerly course by the wind, which was powerful, the unmanageable ship, for successive days and nights, was blown northwestward, where the breeze suddenly deserted her, in unknown waters, to sultry calms. The absence of the water-pipes now proved as fatal to life as before their presence had menaced it. Induced, or at least aggravated, by the more than scanty allowance of water, a malignant fever followed the scurvy; with the excessive heat of the lengthened calm, making such short work of it as to sweep away, as by billows, whole families of the Africans, and a yet larger number, proportionably, of the Spaniards, including, by a luckless fatality, every remaining officer on board. Consequently, in the smart west winds eventually following the calm, the already rent sails, having to be simply dropped, not furled, at need, had been gradually reduced to the beggars' rags they were now. To procure substitutes for his lost sailors, as well as supplies of water and sails, the captain, at the earliest opportunity, had made for Baldivia, the southernmost civilized port of Chili and South America; but upon nearing the coast the thick weather had prevented him from so much as sighting that harbor. Since which period, almost without a crew, and almost without canvas and almost without water, and, at intervals, giving its added dead to the sea, the San Dominick had been battle-dored about by contrary winds, inveigled by currents, or grown weedy in calms. Like a man lost in woods, more than once she had doubled upon her own track.

"But throughout these calamities," huskily continued Don Benito, painfully turning in the half embrace of his servant, "I have to thank those negroes you see, who, though to your inexperienced eyes appearing unruly, have, indeed, conducted themselves with less of restlessness than even their owner could have thought possible under such circumstances."

Here he again fell faintly back. Again his mind wandered; but he rallied, and less obscurely proceeded.

"Yes, their owner was quite right in assuring me that no fetters would be needed with his blacks; so that while, as is wont in this transportation, those negroes have always remained upon deck—not thrust below, as in the Guineamen—they have, also, from the beginning, been freely permitted to range within given bounds at their pleasure."

Once more the faintness returned—his mind roved—but, recovering, he resumed:

"But it is Babo here to whom, under God, I owe not only my own preservation, but likewise to him, chiefly, the merit is due, of pacifying his more ignorant brethren, when at intervals tempted to murmurings."

"Ah, master," sighed the black, bowing his face, "don't speak of me; Babo is nothing; what Babo has done was but duty."

"Faithful fellow!" cried Captain Delano. "Don Benito, I envy you such a friend; slave I cannot call him."

As master and man stood before him, the black upholding the white, Captain Delano could not but bethink him of the beauty of that relationship which could present such a spectacle of fidelity on the one hand and confidence on the other. The scene was heightened by the contrast in dress, denoting their relative positions. The Spaniard wore a loose Chili jacket of dark velvet; white small-clothes and stockings, with silver buckles at the knee and instep; a high-crowned sombrero, of fine grass; a slender sword, silver mounted, hung from a knot in his sash—the last being an almost invariable adjunct, more for utility than ornament, of a South American gentleman's dress to this hour. Excepting when his occasional nervous contortions brought about disarray, there was a certain precision in his attire curiously at variance with the unsightly disorder around; especially in the belittered Ghetto, forward of the mainmast, wholly occupied by the blacks.

The servant wore nothing but wide trowsers, apparently, from their coarseness and patches, made out of some old topsail; they were clean, and confined at the waist by a bit of unstranded rope, which, with his composed, deprecatory air at times, made him look something like a begging friar of St. Francis.

However unsuitable for the time and place, at least in the blunt-thinking American's eyes, and however strangely surviving in the midst of all his afflictions, the toilette of Don Benito might not, in fashion at least, have gone beyond the style of the day among South Americans of his class. Though on the present voyage sailing from Buenos Ayres, he had avowed himself a native and resident of Chili, whose inhabitants had not so generally adopted the plain coat and once plebeian pantaloons; but, with a becoming modification, adhered to their provincial costume, picturesque as any in the world. Still, relatively to the pale history of the voyage, and his own pale face, there seemed something so incongruous in the Spaniard's apparel, as almost to suggest the image of an invalid courtier tottering about London streets in the time of the plague.

The portion of the narrative which, perhaps, most excited interest, as well as some surprise, considering the latitudes in question, was the long calms spoken of, and more particularly the ship's so long drifting about. Without communicating the opinion, of course, the American could not but impute at least part of the detentions both to clumsy seamanship and faulty navigation. Eyeing Don Benito's small, yellow hands, he easily inferred that the young captain had not got into command at the hawse-hole, but the cabin-window; and if so, why wonder at incompetence, in youth, sickness, and gentility united?

But drowning criticism in compassion, after a fresh repetition of his sympathies, Captain Delano, having heard out his story, not only engaged, as in the first place, to see Don Benito and his people supplied in their immediate bodily needs, but, also, now further promised to assist him in procuring a large permanent supply of water, as well as some sails and rigging; and, though it would involve no small embarrassment to himself, yet he would spare three of his best seamen for temporary deck officers; so that without delay the ship might proceed to Conception, there fully to refit for Lima, her destined port.

Such generosity was not without its effect, even upon the invalid. His face lighted up; eager and hectic, he met the honest glance of his visitor. With gratitude he seemed overcome.

"This excitement is bad for master," whispered the servant, taking his arm, and with soothing words gently drawing him aside.

When Don Benito returned, the American was pained to observe that his hopefulness, like the sudden kindling in his cheek, was but febrile and transient.

Ere long, with a joyless mien, looking up towards the poop, the host invited his guest to accompany him there, for the benefit of what little breath of wind might be stirring.

As, during the telling of the story, Captain Delano had once or twice started at the occasional cymballing of the hatchet-polishers, wondering why such an interruption should be allowed, especially in that part of the ship, and in the ears of an invalid; and moreover, as the hatchets had anything but an attractive look, and the handlers of them still less so, it was, therefore, to tell the truth, not without some lurking reluctance, or even shrinking, it may be, that Captain Delano, with apparent complaisance, acquiesced in his host's invitation. The more so, since, with an untimely caprice of punctilio, rendered distressing by his cadaverous aspect, Don Benito, with Castilian bows, solemnly insisted upon his guest's preceding him up the ladder leading to the elevation; where, one on each side of the last step, sat for armorial supporters and sentries two of the ominous file. Gingerly enough stepped good Captain Delano between them, and in the instant of leaving them behind, like one running the gauntlet, he felt an apprehensive twitch in the calves of his legs.

But when, facing about, he saw the whole file, like so many organ-grinders, still stupidly intent on their work, unmindful of everything beside, he could not but smile at his late fidgety panic.

Presently, while standing with his host, looking forward upon the decks below, he was struck by one of those instances of insubordination previously alluded to. Three black boys, with two Spanish boys, were sitting together on the hatches, scraping a rude wooden platter, in which some scanty mess had recently been cooked. Suddenly, one of the black boys, enraged at a word dropped by one of his white companions, seized a knife, and, though called to forbear by one of the oakum-pickers, struck the lad over the head, inflicting a gash from which blood flowed.

In amazement, Captain Delano inquired what this meant. To which the pale Don Benito dully muttered, that it was merely the sport of the lad.

"Pretty serious sport, truly," rejoined Captain Delano. "Had such a thing happened on board the Bachelor's Delight, instant punishment would have followed."

At these words the Spaniard turned upon the American one of his sudden, staring, half-lunatic looks; then, relapsing into his torpor, answered, "Doubtless, doubtless, Señor."

Is it, thought Captain Delano, that this hapless man is one of those paper captains I've known, who by policy wink at what by power they cannot put down? I know no sadder sight than a commander who has little of command but the name.

"I should think, Don Benito," he now said, glancing towards the oakum-picker who had sought to interfere with the boys, "that you would find it advantageous to keep all your blacks employed, especially the younger ones, no matter at what useless task, and no matter what happens to the ship. Why, even with my little band, I find such a course indispensable. I once kept a crew on my quarterdeck thrumming mats for my cabin, when, for three days, I had given up my ship—mats, men, and all—for a speedy loss, owing to the violence of a gale, in which we could do nothing but helplessly drive before it."

"Doubtless, doubtless," muttered Don Benito.

"But," continued Captain Delano, again glancing upon the oakum-pickers and then at the hatchet-polishers, near by, "I see you keep some, at least, of your host employed."

"Yes," was again the vacant response.

"Those old men there, shaking their pows from their pulpits," continued Captain Delano, pointing to the oakum-pickers, "seem to act the part of old dominies to the rest, little heeded as their admonitions are at times. Is this voluntary on their part, Don Benito, or have you appointed them shepherds to your flock of black sheep?"

"What posts they fill, I appointed them," rejoined the Spaniard, in an acrid tone, as if resenting some supposed satiric reflection.

"And these others, these Ashantee conjurors here," continued Captain

Delano, rather uneasily eyeing the brandished steel of the hatchet-polishers, where, in spots, it had been brought to a shine, "this seems a curious business they are at, Don Benito?"

"In the gales we met," answered the Spaniard, "what of our general cargo was not thrown overboard was much damaged by the brine. Since coming into calm weather, I have had several cases of knives and hatchets daily brought up for overhauling and cleaning."

"A prudent idea, Don Benito. You are part owner of ship and cargo, I presume; but none of the slaves, perhaps?"

"I am owner of all you see," impatiently returned Don Benito, "except the main company of blacks, who belonged to my late friend, Alexandro Aranda."

As he mentioned this name, his air was heart-broken; his knees shook; his servant supported him.

Thinking he divined the cause of such unusual emotion, to confirm his surmise, Captain Delano, after a pause, said: "And may I ask, Don Benito, whether—since awhile ago you spoke of some cabin passengers—the friend, whose loss so afflicts you, at the outset of the voyage accompanied his blacks?"

"Yes."

"But died of the fever?"

"Died of the fever. Oh, could I but—"

Again quivering, the Spaniard paused.

"Pardon me," said Captain Delano, lowly, "but I think that, by a sympathetic experience, I conjecture, Don Benito, what it is that gives the keener edge to your grief. It was once my hard fortune to lose, at sea, a dear friend, my own brother, then supercargo. Assured of the welfare of his spirit, its departure I could have borne like a man; but that honest eye, that honest hand—both of which had so often met mine—and that warm heart; all, all—like scraps to the dogs—to throw all to the sharks! It was then I vowed never to have for fellow-voyager a man I loved, unless, unbeknown to him, I had provided every requisite, in case of a fatality, for embalming his mortal part for interment on shore. Were your friend's remains now on board this ship, Don Benito, not thus strangely would the mention of his name affect you."

"On board this ship?" echoed the Spaniard. Then, with horrified gestures, as directed against some spectre, he unconsciously fell into the ready arms of his attendant, who, with a silent appeal toward Captain Delano, seemed beseeching him not again to broach a theme so unspeakably distressing to his master.

This poor fellow now, thought the pained American, is the victim of that sad superstition which associates goblins with the deserted body of man, as ghosts with an abandoned house. How unlike are we made! What to me, in like case, would have been a solemn satisfaction, the bare suggestion, even, terrifies the Spaniard into this trance. Poor Alexandro Aranda! what would you say could you here see your friend—who, on former voyages, when you, for months, were left behind, has, I dare say, often longed, and longed, for one peep at you—now transported with terror at the least thought of having you anyway nigh him.

At this moment, with a dreary grave-yard toll, betokening a flaw, the ship's forecastle bell, smote by one of the grizzled oakum-pickers, proclaimed ten o'clock, through the leaden calm; when Captain Delano's attention was caught by the moving figure of a gigantic black, emerging from the general crowd below, and slowly advancing towards the elevated poop. An iron collar was about his neck, from which depended a chain, thrice wound round his body; the terminating links padlocked together at a broad band of iron, his girdle.

"How like a mute Atufal moves," murmured the servant.

The black mounted the steps of the poop, and, like a brave prisoner, brought up to receive sentence, stood in unquailing muteness before Don Benito, now recovered from his attack.

At the first glimpse of his approach, Don Benito had started, a resentful shadow swept over his face; and, as with the sudden memory of bootless rage, his white lips glued together.

This is some mulish mutineer, thought Captain Delano, surveying, not without a mixture of admiration, the colossal form of the negro.

"See, he waits your question, master," said the servant.

Thus reminded, Don Benito, nervously averting his glance, as if shunning, by anticipation, some rebellious response, in a disconcerted voice, thus spoke:—

"Atufal, will you ask my pardon, now?"

The black was silent.

"Again, master," murmured the servant, with bitter upbraiding eyeing his countryman, "Again, master; he will bend to master yet."

"Answer," said Don Benito, still averting his glance, "say but the one word, *pardon*, and your chains shall be off."

Upon this, the black, slowly raising both arms, let them lifelessly fall, his links clanking, his head bowed; as much as to say, "no, I am content."

"Go," said Don Benito, with inkept and unknown emotion.

Deliberately as he had come, the black obeyed.

"Excuse me, Don Benito," said Captain Delano, "but this scene surprises me; what means it, pray?"

"It means that that negro alone, of all the band, has given me peculiar cause of offense. I have put him in chains; I—"

Here he paused; his hand to his head, as if there were a swimming there, or a sudden bewilderment of memory had come over him; but meeting his servant's kindly glance seemed reassured, and proceeded:—

"I could not scourge such a form. But I told him he must ask my pardon. As yet he has not. At my command, every two hours he stands before me."

"And how long has this been?"

"Some sixty days."

"And obedient in all else? And respectful?"

"Yes."

"Upon my conscience, then," exclaimed Captain Delano, impulsively, "he has a royal spirit in him, this fellow."

"He may have some right to it," bitterly returned Don Benito, "he says he was king in his own land."

"Yes," said the servant, entering a word, "those slits in Atufal's ears once held wedges of gold; but poor Babo here, in his own land, was only a poor slave; a black man's slave was Babo, who now is the white's."

Somewhat annoyed by these conversational familiarities, Captain Delano turned curiously upon the attendant, then glanced inquiringly at his master; but, as if long wonted to these little informalities, neither master nor man seemed to understand him.

"What, pray, was Atufal's offense, Don Benito?" asked Captain Delano; "if it was not something very serious, take a fool's advice, and, in view of his general docility, as well as in some natural respect for his spirit, remit him his penalty."

"No, no, master never will do that," here murmured the servant to himself, "proud Atufal must first ask master's pardon. The slave there carries the padlock, but master here carries the key."

His attention thus directed, Captain Delano now noticed for the first, that, suspended by a slender silken cord, from Don Benito's neck, hung a key. At once, from the servant's muttered syllables, divining the key's purpose, he smiled and said:—"So, Don Benito—padlock and key—significant symbols, truly."

Biting his lip, Don Benito faltered.

Though the remark of Captain Delano, a man of such native simplicity as to be incapable of satire or irony, had been dropped in playful allusion to the Spaniard's singularly evidenced lordship over the black; yet the hypochondriac seemed some way to have taken it as a malicious reflection upon his confessed inability thus far to break down, at least, on a verbal summons, the entrenched will of the slave. Deploring this supposed misconception, yet despairing of correcting it, Captain Delano shifted the subject; but finding his companion more than ever withdrawn, as if still sourly digesting the lees of the presumed affront above-mentioned, by-and-by Captain Delano likewise became less talkative, oppressed, against his own will, by what seemed the secret vindictiveness of the morbidly sensitive Spaniard. But the good sailor, himself of a quite contrary disposition, refrained, on his part, alike from the appearance as from the feeling of resentment, and if silent, was only so from contagion.

Presently the Spaniard, assisted by his servant somewhat discourteously crossed over from his guest; a procedure which, sensibly enough, might have been allowed to pass for idle caprice of ill-humor, had not master and man, lingering round the corner of the elevated skylight, began whispering together in low voices. This was unpleasing. And more; the moody air of the Spaniard, which at times had not been without a sort of valetudinarian stateliness, now seemed anything but dignified; while the menial familiarity of the servant lost its original charm of simple-hearted attachment.

In his embarrassment, the visitor turned his face to the other side of the ship. By so doing, his glance accidentally fell on a young Spanish sailor, a coil of rope in his hand, just stepped from the deck to the first round of the mizzen-rigging. Perhaps the man would not have been particularly noticed, were it not that, during his ascent to one of the yards, he, with a sort of covert intentness, kept his eye fixed on Captain Delano, from whom, presently, it passed, as if by a natural sequence, to the two whisperers.

His own attention thus redirected to that quarter, Captain Delano gave a slight start. From something in Don Benito's manner just then, it seemed as if the visitor had, at least partly, been the subject of the withdrawn consultation going on—a conjecture as little agreeable to the guest as it was little flattering to the host.

The singular alternations of courtesy and ill-breeding in the Spanish captain were unaccountable, except on one of two suppositions—innocent lunacy, or wicked imposture.

But the first idea, though it might naturally have occurred to an indifferent observer, and, in some respect, had not hitherto been wholly a stranger to Captain Delano's mind, yet, now that, in an incipient way, he began to regard the stranger's conduct something in the light of an intentional affront, of course the idea of lunacy was virtually vacated. But if not a lunatic, what then? Under the circumstances, would a gentleman, nay, any honest boor, act the part now acted by his host? The man was an imposter. Some low-born adventurer, masquerading as an oceanic grandee; yet so ignorant of the first requisites of mere gentlemanhood as to be betrayed into the present remarkable indecorum. That strange ceremoniousness, too, at other times evinced, seemed not uncharacteristic of one playing a part above his real level. Benito Cereno—Don Benito Cereno—a sounding name. One, too, at that period, not unknown, in the surname, to supercargoes and sea captains trading along the Spanish Main, as belonging to one of the most enterprising and extensive mercantile families in all those provinces; several members of it having titles; a sort of Castilian Rothschild, with a noble brother, or cousin, in every great trading town of South America. The alleged Don Benito was in early manhood, about twenty-nine or thirty. To assume a sort of roving cadetship in the maritime affairs of such a house, what more likely scheme for a young knave of talent and spirit? But the Spaniard was a pale invalid. Never mind. For even to the degree of simulating mortal disease, the craft of some tricksters had been known to attain. To think that, under the aspect of infantile weakness, the most savage energies might be couched—those velvets of the Spaniards but the silky paw of his fangs.

From no train of thought did these fancies come; not from within, but from without; suddenly, too, and in one throng, like hoar frost; yet as soon to vanish as the mild sun of Captain Delano's good-nature regained its meridian.

Glancing over once more towards his host—whose sideface, revealed above the skylight, was now turned towards him—he was struck by the profile, whose clearness of cut was refined by the thinness, incident to ill-health, as well as ennobled about the chin by the beard. Away with suspicion. He was a true off-shoot of a true hidalgo Cereno.

Relieved by these and other better thoughts, the visitor, lightly humming a tune, now began indifferently pacing the poop, so as not to betray to Don Benito that he had at all mistrusted incivility, much less duplicity; for such mistrust would yet be proved illusory, and by the event; though, for the present, the circumstance which had provoked that distrust remained unexplained. But when that little mystery should have been cleared up, Captain Delano thought he might extremely regret it, did he allow Don Benito to become aware that he had indulged in ungenerous surmises. In short, to the Spaniard's black-letter text, it was best, for awhile, to leave open margin.

Presently, his pale face twitching and overcast, the Spaniard, still supported by his attendant, moved over towards his guest, when, with even more than his usual embarrassment, and a strange sort of intriguing intonation in his husky whisper, the following conversation began:—

"Señor, may I ask how long you have lain at this isle?"

"Oh, but a day or two, Don Benito."

"And from what port are you last?"

"Canton."

"And there, Señor, you exchanged your sealskins for teas and silks, I think you said?"

"Yes. Silks, mostly."

"And the balance you took in specie, perhaps?"

Captain Delano, fidgeting a little, answered—

"Yes; some silver; not a very great deal, though."

"Ah—well. May I ask how many men have you, Señor?"

Captain Delano slightly started, but answered—

"About five-and-twenty, all told."

"And at present, Señor, all on board, I suppose?"

"All on board, Don Benito," replied the Captain, now with satisfaction.

"And will be to-night, Señor?"

At this last question, following so many pertinacious ones, for the soul of him Captain Delano could not but look very earnestly at the questioner, who, instead of meeting the glance, with every token of craven discomposure dropped his eyes to the deck; presenting an unworthy contrast to his servant, who, just then, was kneeling at his feet, adjusting a loose shoe-buckle; his disengaged face meantime, with humble curiosity, turned openly up into his master's downcast one.

The Spaniard, still with a guilty shuffle, repeated his question:

"And—and will be to-night, Señor?"

"Yes, for aught I know," returned Captain Delano—"but nay," rallying himself into fearless truth, "some of them talked of going off on another fishing party about midnight."

"Your ships generally go—go more or less armed, I believe, Señor?"

"Oh, a six-pounder or two, in case of emergency," was the intrepidly indifferent reply, "with a small stock of muskets, sealing-spears, and cutlasses, you know."

As he thus responded, Captain Delano again glanced at Don Benito, but the latter's eyes were averted; while abruptly and awkwardly shifting the subject, he made some peevish allusion to the calm, and then, without apology, once more, with his attendant, withdrew to the opposite bulwarks, where the whispering was resumed.

At this moment, and ere Captain Delano could cast a cool thought upon what had just passed, the young Spanish sailor, before mentioned, was seen descending from the rigging. In act of stooping over to spring inboard to the deck, his voluminous, unconfined frock, or shirt, of coarse woolen, much spotted with tar, opened out far down the chest, revealing a soiled under garment of what seemed the finest linen, edged, about the neck, with a narrow blue ribbon, sadly faded and worn. At this moment the young sailor's eye was again fixed on the whispers, and Captain Delano thought he observed a lurking significance in it, as if silent signs, of some Freemason sort, had that instant been interchanged.

This once more impelled his own glance in the direction of Don Benito, and, as before, he could not but infer that himself formed the subject of the conference. He paused. The sound of the hatchet-polishing fell on his ears. He cast another swift side-look at the two. They had the air of conspirators. In connection with the late questionings, and the incident of the young sailor, these things now begat such return of involuntary suspicion, that the singular guilelessness of the American could not endure it. Plucking up a gay and humorous expression, he crossed over to the two rapidly, saying:—"Ha, Don Benito, your black here seems high in your trust; a sort of privy-counselor, in fact."

Upon this, the servant looked up with a good-natured grin, but the master started as from a venomous bite. It was a moment or two before the Spaniard sufficiently recovered himself to reply; which he did, at last, with cold constraint:—"Yes, Señor, I have trust in Babo."

Here Babo, changing his previous grin of mere animal humor into an intelligent smile, not ungratefully eyed his master.

Finding that the Spaniard now stood silent and reserved, as if involuntarily, or purposely giving hint that his guest's proximity was inconvenient just then, Captain Delano, unwilling to appear uncivil even to incivility itself, made some trivial remark and moved off; again and again turning over in his mind the mysterious demeanor of Don Benito Cereno.

He had descended from the poop, and, wrapped in thought, was passing near a dark hatchway, leading down into the steerage, when, perceiving motion there, he looked to see what moved. The same instant there was a sparkle in the shadowy hatchway, and he saw one of the Spanish sailors, prowling there, hurriedly placing his hand in the bosom of his frock, as if hiding something. Before the man could have been certain who it was that was passing, he slunk below out of sight. But enough was seen of him to make it sure that he was the same young sailor before noticed in the rigging.

What was that which so sparkled? thought Captain Delano. It was no lamp—no match—no live coal. Could it have been a jewel? But how come sailors with jewels?—or with silk-trimmed under-shirts either? Has he been robbing the trunks of the dead cabin-passengers? But if so, he would hardly wear one of the stolen articles on board ship here. Ah, ah—if, now, that was, indeed, a secret sign I saw passing between this suspicious fellow and his captain awhile since; if I could only be certain that, in my uneasiness, my senses did not deceive me, then—

Here, passing from one suspicious thing to another, his mind revolved the strange questions put to him concerning his ship.

By a curious coincidence, as each point was recalled, the black wizards of Ashantee would strike up with their hatchets, as in ominous comment on the white stranger's thoughts. Pressed by such enigmas and portents, it would have been almost against nature, had not, even into the least distrustful heart, some ugly misgivings obtruded.

Observing the ship, now helplessly fallen into a current, with enchanted sails, drifting with increased rapidity seaward; and noting that, from a lately intercepted projection of the land, the sealer was hidden, the stout mariner began to quake at thoughts which he barely durst confess to himself. Above all, he began to feel a ghostly dread of Don Benito. And yet, when he roused himself, dilated his chest, felt himself strong on his legs, and coolly considered it—what did all these phantoms amount to?

Had the Spaniard any sinister scheme, it must have reference not so much to him (Captain Delano) as to his ship (the Bachelor's Delight). Hence the present drifting away of the one ship from the other, instead of favoring any such possible scheme, was, for the time, at least, opposed to it. Clearly any suspicion, combining such contradictions, must need be delusive. Beside, was it not absurd to think of a vessel in distress—a vessel by sickness almost dismanned of her crew—a vessel whose inmates were parched for water—was it not a thousand times absurd that such a craft should, at present, be of a piratical character; or her commander, either for himself or those under him, cherish any desire but for speedy relief and refreshment? But then, might not general distress, and thirst in particular, be affected? And might not that same undiminished Spanish crew, alleged to have perished off to a remnant, be at that very moment lurking in the hold? On heart-broken pretense of entreating a cup of cold water, fiends in human form had got into lonely dwellings, nor retired until a dark deed had been done. And among the Malay pirates, it was no unusual thing to lure ships after them into their treacherous harbors, or entice boarders from a declared enemy at sea, by the spectacle of thinly manned or vacant decks, beneath which prowled a hundred spears with yellow arms ready to upthrust them through the mats. Not that Captain Delano had entirely credited such things. He had heard of them—and now, as stories, they recurred. The present destination of the ship was the anchorage. There she would be near his own vessel. Upon gaining that vicinity, might not the San Dominick, like a slumbering volcano, suddenly let loose energies now hid?

He recalled the Spaniard's manner while telling his story. There was a gloomy hesitancy and subterfuge about it. It was just the manner of one making up his tale for evil purposes, as he goes. But if that story was not true, what was the truth? That the ship had unlawfully come into the Spaniard's possession? But in many of its details, especially in reference to the more calamitous parts, such as the fatalities among the seamen, the consequent prolonged beating about, the past sufferings from obstinate calms, and still continued suffering from thirst; in all these points, as well as others, Don Benito's story had corroborated not only the wailing ejaculations of the indiscriminate multitude, white and black, but likewise—what seemed impossible to be counterfeit—by the very expression and play of every human feature, which Captain Delano saw. If Don Benito's story was, throughout, an invention, then every soul on board, down to the youngest negress, was his carefully drilled recruit in the plot: an incredible inference. And yet, if there was ground for mistrusting his veracity, that inference was a legitimate one.

But those questions of the Spaniard. There, indeed, one might pause. Did they not seem put with much the same object with which the burglar or assassin, by day-time, reconnoitres the walls of a house? But, with ill purposes, to solicit such information openly of the chief person endangered, and so, in effect, setting him on his guard; how unlikely a procedure was that? Absurd, then, to suppose that those questions had been prompted by evil designs. Thus, the same conduct, which, in this instance, had raised the alarm, served to dispel it. In short, scarce any suspicion or uneasiness, however apparently reasonable at the time, which was not now, with equal apparent reason, dismissed.

At last he began to laugh at his former forebodings; and laugh at the strange ship for, in its aspect, someway siding with them, as it were; and laugh, too, at the odd-looking blacks, particularly those old scissors-grinders, the Ashantees; and those bed-ridden old knitting women, the oakum-pickers; and almost at the dark Spaniard himself, the central hobgoblin of all.

For the rest, whatever in a serious way seemed enigmatical, was now good-naturedly explained away by the thought that, for the most part, the poor invalid scarcely knew what he was about; either sulking in black vapors, or putting idle questions without sense or object. Evidently, for the present, the man was not fit to be intrusted with the ship. On some benevolent plea withdrawing the command from him, Captain Delano would yet have to send her to Conception, in charge of his second mate, a worthy person and good navigator—a plan not more convenient for the San Dominick than for Don Benito; for, relieved from all anxiety, keeping wholly to his cabin, the sick man, under the good nursing of his servant, would, probably, by the end of the passage, be in a measure restored to health, and with that he should also be restored to authority.

Such were the American's thoughts. They were tranquilizing. There was a difference between the idea of Don Benito's darkly pre-ordaining Captain Delano's fate, and Captain Delano's lightly arranging Don Benito's. Nevertheless, it was not without something of relief that the good seaman presently perceived his whale-boat in the distance. Its absence had been prolonged by unexpected detention at the sealer's side, as well as its returning trip lengthened by the continual recession of the goal.

The advancing speck was observed by the blacks. Their shouts attracted the attention of Don Benito, who, with a return of courtesy, approaching Captain Delano, expressed satisfaction at the coming of some supplies, slight and temporary as they must necessarily prove.

Captain Delano responded; but while doing so, his attention was drawn to something passing on the deck below: among the crowd climbing the landward bulwarks, anxiously watching the coming boat, two blacks, to all appearances accidentally incommoded by one of the sailors, violently pushed him aside, which the sailor someway resenting, they dashed him to the deck, despite the earnest cries of the oakum-pickers.

"Don Benito," said Captain Delano quickly, "do you see what is going on there? Look!"

But, seized by his cough, the Spaniard staggered, with both hands to his face, on the point of falling. Captain Delano would have supported him, but the servant was more alert, who, with one hand sustaining his master, with the other applied the cordial. Don Benito restored, the black withdrew his support, slipping aside a little, but dutifully remaining within call of a whisper. Such discretion was here evinced as quite wiped away, in the visitor's eyes, any blemish of impropriety which might have attached to the attendant, from the indecorous conferences before mentioned; showing, too, that if the servant were to blame, it might be more the master's fault than his own, since, when left to himself, he could conduct thus well.

His glance called away from the spectacle of disorder to the more pleasing one before him, Captain Delano could not avoid again congratulating his host upon possessing such a servant, who, though perhaps a little too forward now and then, must upon the whole be invaluable to one in the invalid's situation.

"Tell me, Don Benito," he added, with a smile—"I should like to have your man here, myself—what will you take for him? Would fifty doubloons be any object?"

"Master wouldn't part with Babo for a thousand doubloons," murmured the black, overhearing the offer, and taking it in earnest, and, with the strange vanity of a faithful slave, appreciated by his master, scorning to hear so paltry a valuation put upon him by a stranger. But Don Benito, apparently hardly yet completely restored, and again interrupted by his cough, made but some broken reply.

Soon his physical distress became so great, affecting his mind, too, apparently, that, as if to screen the sad spectacle, the servant gently conducted his master below.

Left to himself, the American, to while away the time till his boat should arrive, would have pleasantly accosted some one of the few Spanish seamen he saw; but recalling something that Don Benito had said touching their ill conduct, he refrained; as a shipmaster indisposed to countenance cowardice or unfaithfulness in seamen.

While, with these thoughts, standing with eye directed forward towards that handful of sailors, suddenly he thought that one or two of them returned the glance and with a sort of meaning. He rubbed his eyes, and looked again; but again seemed to see the same thing. Under a new form, but more obscure than any previous one, the old suspicions recurred, but, in the absence of Don Benito, with less of panic than before. Despite the bad account given of the sailors, Captain Delano resolved forthwith to accost one of them. Descending the poop, he made his way through the blacks, his movement drawing a queer cry from the oakum-pickers, prompted by whom, the negroes, twitching each other aside, divided before him; but, as if curious to see what was the object of this deliberate visit to their Ghetto, closing in behind, in tolerable order, followed the white stranger up. His progress thus proclaimed as by mounted kings-at-arms, and escorted as by a Caffre guard of honor, Captain Delano, assuming a good-humored, off-handed air, continued to advance; now and then saying a blithe word to the negroes, and his eye curiously surveying the white faces, here and there sparsely mixed in with the blacks, like stray white pawns venturously involved in the ranks of the chess-men opposed.

While thinking which of them to select for his purpose, he chanced to observe a sailor seated on the deck engaged in tarring the strap of a large block, a circle of blacks squatted round him inquisitively eyeing the process.

The mean employment of the man was in contrast with something superior in his figure. His hand, black with continually thrusting it into the tar-pot held for him by a negro, seemed not naturally allied to his face, a face which would have been a very fine one but for its haggardness. Whether this haggardness had aught to do with criminality, could not be determined; since, as intense heat and cold, though unlike, produce like sensations, so innocence and guilt, when, through casual association with mental pain, stamping any visible impress, use one seal—a hacked one.

Not again that this reflection occurred to Captain Delano at the time, charitable man as he was. Rather another idea. Because observing so singular a haggardness combined with a dark eye, averted as in trouble and shame, and then again recalling Don Benito's confessed ill opinion of his crew, insensibly he was operated upon by certain general notions which, while disconnecting pain and abashment from virtue, invariably link them with vice.

If, indeed, there be any wickedness on board this ship, thought Captain Delano, be sure that man there has fouled his hand in it, even as now he fouls it in the pitch. I don't like to accost him. I will speak to this other, this old Jack here on the windlass.

He advanced to an old Barcelona tar, in ragged red breeches and dirty night-cap, cheeks trenched and bronzed, whiskers dense as thorn hedges. Seated between two sleepy-looking Africans, this mariner, like his younger shipmate, was employed upon some rigging—splicing a cable—the sleepy-looking blacks performing the inferior function of holding the outer parts of the ropes for him.

Upon Captain Delano's approach, the man at once hung his head below its previous level; the one necessary for business. It appeared as if he desired to be thought absorbed, with more than common fidelity, in his task. Being addressed, he glanced up, but with what seemed a furtive, diffident air, which sat strangely enough on his weather-beaten visage, much as if a grizzly bear, instead of growling and biting, should simper and cast sheep's eyes. He was asked several questions concerning the voyage—questions purposely referring to several particulars in Don Benito's narrative, not previously corroborated by those impulsive cries greeting the visitor on first coming on board. The questions were briefly answered, confirming all that remained to be confirmed of the story. The negroes about the windlass joined in with the old sailor; but, as they became talkative, he by degrees became mute, and at length quite glum, seemed morosely unwilling to answer more questions, and yet, all the while, this ursine air was somehow mixed with his sheepish one.

Despairing of getting into unembarrassed talk with such a centaur, Captain Delano, after glancing round for a more promising countenance, but seeing none, spoke pleasantly to the blacks to make way for him; and so, amid various grins and grimaces, returned to the poop, feeling a little strange at first, he could hardly tell why, but upon the whole with regained confidence in Benito Cereno.

How plainly, thought he, did that old whiskerando yonder betray a consciousness of ill desert. No doubt, when he saw me coming, he dreaded lest I, apprised by his Captain of the crew's general misbehavior, came with sharp words for him, and so down with his head. And yet—and yet, now that I think of it, that very old fellow, if I err not, was one of those who seemed so earnestly eyeing me here awhile since. Ah, these currents spin one's head round almost as much as they do the ship. Ha, there now's a pleasant sort of sunny sight; quite sociable, too.

His attention had been drawn to a slumbering negress, partly disclosed through the lace-work of some rigging, lying, with youthful limbs carelessly disposed, under the lee of the bulwarks, like a doe in the shade of a woodland rock. Sprawling at her lapped breasts, was her wide-awake fawn, stark naked, its black little body half lifted from the deck, crosswise with its dam's; its hands, like two paws, clambering upon her; its mouth and nose ineffectually rooting to get at the mark; and meantime giving a vexatious half-grunt, blending with the composed snore of the negress.

The uncommon vigor of the child at length roused the mother. She started up, at a distance facing Captain Delano. But as if not at all concerned at the attitude in which she had been caught, delightedly she caught the child up, with maternal transports, covering it with kisses.

There's naked nature, now; pure tenderness and love, thought Captain Delano, well pleased.

This incident prompted him to remark the other negresses more particularly than before. He was gratified with their manners: like most uncivilized women, they seemed at once tender of heart and tough of constitution; equally ready to die for their infants or fight for them. Unsophisticated as leopardesses; loving as doves. Ah! thought Captain Delano, these, perhaps, are some of the very women whom Ledyard saw in Africa, and gave such a noble account of.

These natural sights somehow insensibly deepened his confidence and ease. At last he looked to see how his boat was getting on; but it was still pretty remote. He turned to see if Don Benito had returned; but he had not.

To change the scene, as well as to please himself with a leisurely observation of the coming boat, stepping over into the mizzen-chains, he clambered his way into the starboard quarter-gallery—one of those abandoned Venetian-looking water-balconies previously mentioned—retreats cut off from the deck. As his foot pressed the half-damp, half-dry sea-mosses matting the place, and a chance phantom cats-paw—an islet of breeze, unheralded, unfollowed—as this ghostly cats-paw came fanning his cheek; as his glance fell upon the row of small, round dead-lights—all closed like coppered eyes of the coffined—and the state-cabin door, once connecting with the gallery, even as the dead-lights had once looked out upon it, but now calked fast like a sarcophagus lid; and to a purple-black tarred-over, panel, threshold, and post; and he bethought him of the time when that state-cabin and this state-balcony had heard the voices of the Spanish king's officers, and the forms of the Lima viceroy's daughters had perhaps leaned where he stood—as these and other images flitted through his mind, as the cats-paw through the calm, gradually he felt rising a dreamy inquietude, like that of one who alone on the prairie feels unrest from the repose of the moon.

He leaned against the carved balustrade, again looking off toward his boat; but found his eye falling upon the ribbon grass, trailing along the ship's water-line, straight as a border of green box; and parterres of seaweed, broad ovals and crescents, floating nigh and far, with what seemed long formal alleys between, crossing the terraces of swells, and sweeping round as if leading to the grottoes below. And overhanging all was the balustrade by his arm, which, partly stained with pitch and partly embossed with moss, seemed the charred ruin of some summer-house in a grand garden long running to waste.

Trying to break one charm, he was but becharmed anew. Though upon the wide sea, he seemed in some far inland country; prisoner in some deserted château, left to stare at empty grounds, and peer out at vague roads, where never wagon or wayfarer passed.

But these enchantments were a little disenchanted as his eye fell on the corroded main-chains. Of an ancient style, massy and rusty in link, shackle and bolt, they seemed even more fit for the ship's present business than the one for which she had been built.

Presently he thought something moved nigh the chains. He rubbed his eyes, and looked hard. Groves of rigging were about the chains; and there, peering from behind a great stay, like an Indian from behind a hemlock, a Spanish sailor, a marlingspike in his hand, was seen, who made what seemed an imperfect gesture towards the balcony, but immediately, as if alarmed by some advancing step along the deck within, vanished into the recesses of the hempen forest, like a poacher.

What meant this? Something the man had sought to communicate, unbeknown to any one, even to his captain. Did the secret involve aught unfavorable to his captain? Were those previous misgivings of Captain Delano's about to be verified? Or, in his haunted mood at the moment, had some random, unintentional motion of the man, while busy with the stay, as if repairing it, been mistaken for a significant beckoning?

Not unbewildered, again he gazed off for his boat. But it was temporarily hidden by a rocky spur of the isle. As with some eagerness he bent forward, watching for the first shooting view of its beak, the balustrade gave way before him like charcoal. Had he not clutched an outreaching rope he would have fallen into the sea. The crash, though feeble, and the fall, though hollow, of the rotten fragments, must have been overheard. He glanced up. With sober curiosity peering down upon him was one of the old oakum-pickers, slipped from his perch to an outside boom; while below the old negro, and, invisible to him, reconnoitering from a port-hole like a fox from the mouth of its den, crouched the Spanish sailor again. From something suddenly suggested by the man's air, the mad idea now darted into Captain Delano's mind, that Don Benito's plea of indisposition, in withdrawing below, was but a pretense: that he was engaged there maturing his plot, of which the sailor, by some means gaining an inkling, had a mind to warn the stranger against; incited, it may be, by gratitude for a kind word on first boarding the ship. Was it from foreseeing some possible interference like this, that Don Benito had, beforehand, given such a bad character of his sailors, while praising the negroes; though, indeed, the former seemed as docile as the latter the contrary? The whites, too, by nature, were the shrewder race. A man with some evil design, would he not be likely to speak well of that stupidity which was blind to his depravity, and malign that intelligence from which it might be hidden? Not unlikely, perhaps. But if the whites had dark secrets concerning Don Benito, could then Don Benito be any way in complicity with the blacks? But they were too stupid. Besides, who ever heard of a white so far a renegade as to apostatize from his very species almost, by leaguing in against it with negroes? These difficulties recalled former ones. Lost in their mazes, Captain Delano, who had now regained the deck, was uneasily advancing along it, when he observed a new face; an aged sailor seated cross-legged near the main hatchway. His skin was shrunk up with wrinkles like a pelican's empty pouch; his hair frosted; his countenance grave and composed. His hands were full of ropes, which he was working into a large knot. Some blacks were about him obligingly dipping the strands for him, here and there, as the exigencies of the operation demanded.

Captain Delano crossed over to him, and stood in silence surveying the knot; his mind, by a not uncongenial transition, passing from its own entanglements to those of the hemp. For intricacy, such a knot he had never seen in an American ship, nor indeed any other. The old man looked like an Egyptian priest, making Gordian knots for the temple of Ammon. The knot seemed a combination of double-bowline-knot, treble-crown-knot, back-handed-well-knot, knot-in-and-out-knot, and jamming-knot.

At last, puzzled to comprehend the meaning of such a knot, Captain Delano addressed the knotter:—

"What are you knotting there, my man?"

"The knot," was the brief reply, without looking up.

"So it seems; but what is it for?"

"For some one else to undo," muttered back the old man, plying his fingers harder than ever, the knot being now nearly completed.

While Captain Delano stood watching him, suddenly the old man threw the knot towards him, saying in broken English—the first heard in the ship—something to this effect: "Undo it, cut it, quick." It was said lowly, but with such condensation of rapidity, that the long, slow words in Spanish, which had preceded and followed, almost operated as covers to the brief English between.

For a moment, knot in hand, and knot in head, Captain Delano stood mute; while, without further heeding him, the old man was now intent upon other ropes. Presently there was a slight stir behind Captain Delano. Turning, he saw the chained negro, Atufal, standing quietly there. The next moment the old sailor rose, muttering, and, followed by his subordinate negroes, removed to the forward part of the ship, where in the crowd he disappeared.

An elderly negro, in a clout like an infant's, and with a pepper and salt head, and a kind of attorney air, now approached Captain Delano. In tolerable Spanish, and with a good-natured, knowing wink, he informed him that the old knotter was simple-witted, but harmless; often playing his odd tricks. The negro concluded by begging the knot, for of course the stranger would not care to be troubled with it. Unconsciously, it was handed to him. With a sort of congé, the negro received it, and, turning his back, ferreted into it like a detective custom-house office after smuggled laces. Soon, with some African word, equivalent to pshaw, he tossed the knot overboard.

All this is very queer now, thought Captain Delano, with a qualmish sort of emotion; but, as one feeling incipient seasickness, he strove, by ignoring the symptoms, to get rid of the malady. Once more he looked off for his boat. To his delight, it was now again in view, leaving the rocky spur astern.

The sensation here experienced, after at first relieving his uneasiness, with unforeseen efficacy soon began to remove it. The less distant sight of that well-known boat—showing it, not as before, half blended with the haze, but with outline defined, so that its individuality, like a man's, was manifest; that boat, Rover by name, which, though now in strange seas, had often pressed the beach of Captain Delano's home, and, brought to its threshold for repairs, had familiarly lain there, as a Newfoundland dog; the sight of that household boat evoked a thousand trustful associations, which, contrasted with previous suspicions, filled him not only with lightsome confidence, but somehow with half humorous self-reproaches at his former lack of it.

"What, I, Amasa Delano—Jack of the Beach, as they called me when a lad—I, Amasa; the same that, duck-satchel in hand, used to paddle along the water-side to the schoolhouse made from the old hulk—I, little Jack of the Beach, that used to go berrying with cousin Nat and the rest; I to be murdered here at the ends of the earth, on board a haunted pirate-ship by a horrible Spaniard? Too nonsensical to think of! Who would murder Amasa Delano? His conscience is clean. There is some one above. Fie, fie, Jack of the Beach! you are a child indeed; a child of the second childhood, old boy; you are beginning to dote and drule, I'm afraid."

Light of heart and foot, he stepped aft, and there was met by Don Benito's servant, who, with a pleasing expression, responsive to his own present feelings, informed him that his master had recovered from the effects of his coughing fit, and had just ordered him to go present his compliments to his good guest, Don Amasa, and say that he (Don Benito) would soon have the happiness to rejoin him.

There now, do you mark that? again thought Captain Delano, walking the poop. What a donkey I was. This kind gentleman who here sends me his kind compliments, he, but ten minutes ago, dark-lantern in hand, was dodging round some old grind-stone in the hold, sharpening a hatchet for me, I thought. Well, well; these long calms have a morbid effect on the mind, I've often heard, though I never believed it before. Ha! glancing towards the boat; there's Rover; good dog; a white bone in her mouth. A pretty big bone though, seems to me.—What? Yes, she has fallen afoul of the bubbling tide-rip there. It sets her the other way, too, for the time. Patience.

It was now about noon, though, from the grayness of everything, it seemed to be getting towards dusk.

The calm was confirmed. In the far distance, away from the influence of land, the leaden ocean seemed laid out and leaded up, its course finished, soul gone, defunct. But the current from landward, where the ship was, increased; silently sweeping her further and further towards the tranced waters beyond.

Still, from his knowledge of those latitudes, cherishing hopes of a breeze, and a fair and fresh one, at any moment, Captain Delano, despite present prospects, buoyantly counted upon bringing the San Dominick safely to anchor ere night. The distance swept over was nothing; since, with a good wind, ten minutes' sailing would retrace more than sixty minutes, drifting. Meantime, one moment turning to mark "Rover" fighting the tide-rip, and the next to see Don Benito approaching, continued walking the poop.

Gradually he felt a vexation arising from the delay of his boat; this soon merged into uneasiness; and at last—his eye falling continually, as from a stage-box into the pit, upon the strange crowd before and below him, and, by-and-by, recognizing there the face—now composed to indifference—of the Spanish sailor who had seemed to beckon from the main-chains—something of his old trepidations returned.

Ah, thought he—gravely enough—this is like the ague: because it went off, it follows not that it won't come back.

Though ashamed of the relapse, he could not altogether subdue it; and so, exerting his good-nature to the utmost, insensibly he came to a compromise.

Yes, this is a strange craft; a strange history, too, and strange folks on board. But—nothing more.

By way of keeping his mind out of mischief till the boat should arrive, he tried to occupy it with turning over and over, in a purely speculative sort of way, some lesser peculiarities of the captain and crew. Among others, four curious points recurred:

First, the affair of the Spanish lad assailed with a knife by the slave boy; an act winked at by Don Benito. Second, the tyranny in Don Benito's treatment of Atufal, the black; as if a child should lead a bull of the Nile by the ring in his nose. Third, the trampling of the sailor by the two negroes; a piece of insolence passed over without so much as a reprimand. Fourth, the cringing submission to their master, of all the ship's underlings, mostly blacks; as if by the least inadvertence they feared to draw down his despotic displeasure.

Coupling these points, they seemed somewhat contradictory. But what then, thought Captain Delano, glancing towards his now nearing boat—what then? Why, Don Benito is a very capricious commander. But he is not the first of the sort I have seen; though it's true he rather exceeds any other. But as a nation—continued he in his reveries—these Spaniards are all an odd set; the very word Spaniard has a curious, conspirator, Guy-Fawkish twang to it. And yet, I dare say, Spaniards in the main are as good folks as any in Duxbury, Massachusetts. Ah good! At last "Rover" has come.

As, with its welcome freight, the boat touched the side, the oakum-pickers, with venerable gestures, sought to restrain the blacks, who, at the sight of three gurried water-casks in its bottom, and a pile of wilted pumpkins in its bow, hung over the bulwarks in disorderly raptures.

Don Benito, with his servant, now appeared; his coming, perhaps, hastened by hearing the noise. Of him Captain Delano sought permission to serve out the water, so that all might share alike, and none injure themselves by unfair excess. But sensible, and, on Don Benito's account, kind as this offer was, it was received with what seemed impatience; as if aware that he lacked energy as a commander, Don Benito, with the true jealousy of weakness, resented as an affront any interference. So, at least, Captain Delano inferred.

In another moment the casks were being hoisted in, when some of the eager negroes accidentally jostled Captain Delano, where he stood by the gangway; so that, unmindful of Don Benito, yielding to the impulse of the moment, with good-natured authority he bade the blacks stand back; to enforce his words making use of a half-mirthful, half-menacing gesture. Instantly the blacks paused, just where they were, each negro and negress suspended in his or her posture, exactly as the word had found them—for a few seconds continuing so—while, as between the responsive posts of a telegraph, an unknown syllable ran from man to man among the perched oakum-pickers. While the visitor's attention was fixed by this scene, suddenly the hatchet-polishers half rose, and a rapid cry came from Don Benito.

Thinking that at the signal of the Spaniard he was about to be massacred, Captain Delano would have sprung for his boat, but paused, as the oakum-pickers, dropping down into the crowd with earnest exclamations, forced every white and every negro back, at the same moment, with gestures friendly and familiar, almost jocose, bidding him, in substance, not be a fool. Simultaneously the hatchet-polishers resumed their seats, quietly as so many tailors, and at once, as if nothing had happened, the work of hoisting in the casks was resumed, whites and blacks singing at the tackle.

Captain Delano glanced towards Don Benito. As he saw his meagre form in the act of recovering itself from reclining in the servant's arms, into which the agitated invalid had fallen, he could not but marvel at the panic by which himself had been surprised, on the darting supposition that such a commander, who, upon a legitimate occasion, so trivial, too, as it now appeared, could lose all self-command, was, with energetic iniquity, going to bring about his murder.

The casks being on deck, Captain Delano was handed a number of jars and cups by one of the steward's aids, who, in the name of his captain, entreated him to do as he had proposed—dole out the water. He complied, with republican impartiality as to this republican element, which always seeks one level, serving the oldest white no better than the youngest black; excepting, indeed, poor Don Benito, whose condition, if not rank, demanded an extra allowance. To him, in the first place, Captain Delano presented a fair pitcher of the fluid; but, thirsting as he was for it, the Spaniard quaffed not a drop until after several grave bows and salutes. A reciprocation of courtesies which the sight-loving Africans hailed with clapping of hands.

Two of the less wilted pumpkins being reserved for the cabin table, the residue were minced up on the spot for the general regalement. But the soft bread, sugar, and bottled cider, Captain Delano would have given the whites alone, and in chief Don Benito; but the latter objected; which disinterestedness not a little pleased the American; and so mouthfuls all around were given alike to whites and blacks; excepting one bottle of cider, which Babo insisted upon setting aside for his master.

Here it may be observed that as, on the first visit of the boat, the American had not permitted his men to board the ship, neither did he now; being unwilling to add to the confusion of the decks.

Not influenced by the peculiar good-humor at present prevailing, and for the time oblivious of any but benevolent thoughts, Captain Delano, who, from recent indications, counted upon a breeze within an hour or two at furthest, dispatched the boat back to the sealer, with orders for all the hands that could be spared immediately to set about rafting casks to the watering-place and filling them. Likewise he bade word be carried to his chief officer, that if, against present expectation, the ship was not brought to anchor by sunset, he need be under no concern; for as there was to be a full moon that night, he (Captain Delano) would remain on board ready to play the pilot, come the wind soon or late.

As the two captains stood together, observing the departing boat—the servant, as it happened, having just spied a spot on his master's velvet sleeve, and silently engaged rubbing it out—the American expressed his regrets that the San Dominick had no boats; none, at least, but the unseaworthy old hulk of the long-boat, which, warped as a camel's skeleton in the desert, and almost as bleached, lay pot-wise inverted amidships, one side a little tipped, furnishing a subterraneous sort of den for family groups of the blacks, mostly women and small children; who, squatting on old mats below, or perched above in the dark dome, on the elevated seats, were described, some distance within, like a social circle of bats, sheltering in some friendly cave; at intervals, ebon flights of naked boys and girls, three or four years old, darting in and out of the den's mouth.

"Had you three or four boats now, Don Benito," said Captain Delano, "I think that, by tugging at the oars, your negroes here might help along matters some. Did you sail from port without boats, Don Benito?"

"They were stove in the gales, Señor."

"That was bad. Many men, too, you lost then. Boats and men. Those must have been hard gales, Don Benito."

"Past all speech," cringed the Spaniard.

"Tell me, Don Benito," continued his companion with increased interest, "Tell me, were these gales immediately off the pitch of Cape Horn?"

"Cape Horn?—who spoke of Cape Horn?"

"Yourself did, when giving me an account of your voyage," answered Captain Delano, with almost equal astonishment at this eating of his own words, even as he ever seemed eating his own heart, on the part of the Spaniard. "You yourself, Don Benito, spoke of Cape Horn," he emphatically repeated.

The Spaniard turned, in a sort of stooping posture, pausing an instant, as one about to make a plunging exchange of elements, as from air to water.

At this moment a messenger-boy, a white, hurried by, in the regular performance of his function carrying the last expired half hour forward to the forecastle, from the cabin time-piece, to have it struck at the ship's large bell.

"Master," said the servant, discontinuing his work on the coat sleeve, and addressing the rapt Spaniard with a sort of timid apprehensiveness, as one charged with a duty, the discharge of which, it was foreseen, would prove irksome to the very person who had imposed it, and for whose benefit it was intended, "master told me never mind where he was, or how engaged, always to remind him, to a minute, when shaving-time comes. Miguel has gone to strike the half-hour afternoon. It is *now* master. Will master go into the cuddy?"

"Ah—yes," answered the Spaniard, starting, as from dreams into realities; then turning upon Captain Delano, he said that ere long he would resume the conversation.

"Then if master means to talk more to Don Amasa," said the servant, "why not let Don Amasa sit by master in the cuddy, and master can talk, and Don Amasa can listen, while Babo here lathers and strops."

"Yes," said Captain Delano, not unpleased with this sociable plan, "yes, Don Benito, unless you had rather not, I will go with you."

"Be it so, Señor."

As the three passed aft, the American could not but think it another strange instance of his host's capriciousness, this being shaved with such uncommon punctuality in the middle of the day. But he deemed it more than likely that the servant's anxious fidelity had something to do with the matter; inasmuch as the timely interruption served to rally his master from the mood which had evidently been coming upon him.

The place called the cuddy was a light deck-cabin formed by the poop, a sort of attic to the large cabin below. Part of it had formerly been the quarters of the officers; but since their death all the partitionings had been thrown down, and the whole interior converted into one spacious and airy marine hall; for absence of fine furniture and picturesque disarray of odd appurtenances, somewhat answering to the wide, cluttered hall of some eccentric bachelor-squire in the country, who hangs his shooting-jacket and tobacco-pouch on deer antlers, and keeps his fishing-rod, tongs, and walking-stick in the same corner.

The similitude was heightened, if not originally suggested, by glimpses of the surrounding sea; since, in one aspect, the country and the ocean seem cousins-german.

The floor of the cuddy was matted. Overhead, four or five old muskets were stuck into horizontal holes along the beams. On one side was a claw-footed old table lashed to the deck; a thumbed missal on it, and over it a small, meagre crucifix attached to the bulk-head. Under the table lay a dented cutlass or two, with a hacked harpoon, among some melancholy old rigging, like a heap of poor friars' girdles. There were also two long, sharp-ribbed settees of Malacca cane, black with age, and uncomfortable to look at as inquisitors' racks, with a large, misshapen arm-chair, which, furnished with a rude barber's crotch at the back, working with a screw, seemed some grotesque engine of torment. A flag locker was in one corner, open, exposing various colored bunting, some rolled up, others half unrolled, still others tumbled. Opposite was a cumbrous washstand, of black mahogany, all of one block, with a pedestal, like a font, and over it a railed shelf, containing combs, brushes, and other implements of the toilet. A torn hammock of stained grass swung near; the sheets tossed, and the pillow wrinkled up like a brow, as if whoever slept here slept but illy, with alternate visitations of sad thoughts and bad dreams.

The further extremity of the cuddy, overhanging the ship's stern, was pierced with three openings, windows or port-holes, according as men or cannon might peer, socially or unsocially, out of them. At present neither men nor cannon were seen, though huge ring-bolts and other rusty iron fixtures of the wood-work hinted of twenty-four-pounders.

Glancing towards the hammock as he entered, Captain Delano said, "You sleep here, Don Benito?"

"Yes, Señor, since we got into mild weather."

"This seems a sort of dormitory, sitting-room, sail-loft, chapel, armory, and private closet all together, Don Benito," added Captain Delano, looking round.

"Yes, Señor; events have not been favorable to much order in my arrangements."

Here the servant, napkin on arm, made a motion as if waiting his master's good pleasure. Don Benito signified his readiness, when, seating him in the Malacca arm-chair, and for the guest's convenience drawing opposite one of the settees, the servant commenced operations by throwing back his master's collar and loosening his cravat.

There is something in the negro which, in a peculiar way, fits him for avocations about one's person. Most negroes are natural valets and hairdressers; taking to the comb and brush congenially as to the castanets, and flourishing them apparently with almost equal satisfaction. There is, too, a smooth tact about them in this employment, with a marvelous, noiseless, gliding briskness, not ungraceful in its way, singularly pleasing to behold, and still more so to be the manipulated subject of. And above all is the great gift of good-humor. Not the mere grin or laugh is here meant. Those were unsuitable. But a certain easy cheerfulness, harmonious in every glance and gesture; as though God had set the whole negro to some pleasant tune.

When to this is added the docility arising from the unaspiring contentment of a limited mind, and that susceptibility of bland attachment sometimes inhering in indisputable inferiors, one readily perceives why those hypochondriacs, Johnson and Byron—it may be, something like the hypochondriac Benito Cereno—took to their hearts, almost to the exclusion of the entire white race, their serving men, the negroes, Barber and Fletcher. But if there be that in the negro which exempts him from the inflicted sourness of the morbid or cynical mind, how, in his most prepossessing aspects, must he appear to a benevolent one? When at ease with respect to exterior things, Captain Delano's nature was not only benign, but familiarly and humorously so. At home, he had often taken rare satisfaction in sitting in his door, watching some free man of color at his work or play. If on a voyage he chanced to have a black sailor, invariably he was on chatty and halfgamesome terms with him. In fact, like most men of a good, blithe heart, Captain Delano took to negroes, not philanthropically, but genially, just as other men to Newfoundland dogs.

Hitherto, the circumstances in which he found the San Dominick had repressed the tendency. But in the cuddy, relieved from his former uneasiness, and, for various reasons, more sociably inclined than at any previous period of the day, and seeing the colored servant, napkin on arm, so debonair about his master, in a business so familiar as that of shaving, too, all his old weakness for negroes returned.

Among other things, he was amused with an odd instance of the African love of bright colors and fine shows, in the black's informally taking from the flag-locker a great piece of bunting of all hues, and lavishly tucking it under his master's chin for an apron.

The mode of shaving among the Spaniards is a little different from what it is with other nations. They have a basin, specifically called a barber's basin, which on one side is scooped out, so as accurately to receive the chin, against which it is closely held in lathering; which is done, not with a brush, but with soap dipped in the water of the basin and rubbed on the face.

In the present instance salt-water was used for lack of better; and the parts lathered were only the upper lip, and low down under the throat, all the rest being cultivated beard.

The preliminaries being somewhat novel to Captain Delano, he sat curiously eyeing them, so that no conversation took place, nor, for the present, did Don Benito appear disposed to renew any.

Setting down his basin, the negro searched among the razors, as for the sharpest, and having found it, gave it an additional edge by expertly strapping it on the firm, smooth, oily skin of his open palm; he then made a gesture as if to begin, but midway stood suspended for an instant, one hand elevating the razor, the other professionally dabbling among the bubbling suds on the Spaniard's lank neck. Not unaffected by the close sight of the gleaming steel, Don Benito nervously shuddered; his usual ghastliness was heightened by the lather, which lather, again, was intensified in its hue by the contrasting sootiness of the negro's body. Altogether the scene was somewhat peculiar, at least to Captain Delano, nor, as he saw the two thus postured, could he resist the vagary, that in the black he saw a headsman, and in the white a man at the block. But this was one of those antic conceits, appearing and vanishing in a breath, from which, perhaps, the best regulated mind is not always free.

Meantime the agitation of the Spaniard had a little loosened the bunting from around him, so that one broad fold swept curtain-like over the chair-arm to the floor, revealing, amid a profusion of armorial bars and ground-colors—black, blue, and yellow—a closed castle in a blood-red field diagonal with a lion rampant in a white.

"The castle and the lion," exclaimed Captain Delano—"why, Don Benito, this is the flag of Spain you use here. It's well it's only I, and not the King, that sees this," he added, with a smile, "but"—turning towards the black—"it's all one, I suppose, so the colors be gay;" which playful remark did not fail somewhat to tickle the negro.

"Now, master," he said, readjusting the flag, and pressing the head gently further back into the crotch of the chair; "now, master," and the steel glanced nigh the throat.

Again Don Benito faintly shuddered.

"You must not shake so, master. See, Don Amasa, master always shakes when I shave him. And yet master knows I never yet have drawn blood, though it's true, if master will shake so, I may some of these times. Now master," he continued. "And now, Don Amasa, please go on with your talk about the gale, and all that; master can hear, and, between times, master can answer."

"Ah yes, these gales," said Captain Delano; "but the more I think of your voyage, Don Benito, the more I wonder, not at the gales, terrible as they must have been, but at the disastrous interval following them. For here, by your account, have you been these two months and more getting from Cape Horn to St. Maria, a distance which I myself, with a good wind, have sailed in a few days. True, you had calms, and long ones, but to be becalmed for two months, that is, at least, unusual. Why, Don Benito, had almost any other gentleman told me such a story, I should have been half disposed to a little incredulity."

Here an involuntary expression came over the Spaniard, similar to that just before on the deck, and whether it was the start he gave, or a sudden gawky roll of the hull in the calm, or a momentary unsteadiness of the servant's hand, however it was, just then the razor drew blood, spots of which stained the creamy lather under the throat: immediately the black barber drew back his steel, and, remaining in his professional attitude, back to Captain Delano, and face to Don Benito, held up the trickling razor, saying, with a sort of half humorous sorrow, "See, master—you shook so—here's Babo's first blood."

No sword drawn before James the First of England, no assassination in that timid King's presence, could have produced a more terrified aspect than was now presented by Don Benito.

Poor fellow, thought Captain Delano, so nervous he can't even bear the sight of barber's blood; and this unstrung, sick man, is it credible that I should have imagined he meant to spill all my blood, who can't endure the sight of one little drop of his own? Surely, Amasa Delano, you have been beside yourself this day. Tell it not when you get home, sappy Amasa. Well, well, he looks like a murderer, doesn't he? More like as if himself were to be done for. Well, well, this day's experience shall be a good lesson.

Meantime, while these things were running through the honest seaman's mind, the servant had taken the napkin from his arm, and to Don Benito had said—"But answer Don Amasa, please, master, while I wipe this ugly stuff off the razor, and strop it again."

As he said the words, his face was turned half round, so as to be alike visible to the Spaniard and the American, and seemed, by its expression, to hint, that he was desirous, by getting his master to go on with the conversation, considerately to withdraw his attention from the recent annoying accident. As if glad to snatch the offered relief, Don Benito resumed, rehearsing to Captain Delano, that not only were the calms of unusual duration, but the ship had fallen in with obstinate currents; and other things he added, some of which were but repetitions of former statements, to explain how it came to pass that the passage from Cape Horn to St. Maria had been so exceedingly long; now and then mingling with his words, incidental praises, less qualified than before, to the blacks, for their general good conduct. These particulars were not given consecutively, the servant, at convenient times, using his razor, and so, between the intervals of shaving, the story and panegyric went on with more than usual huskiness.

To Captain Delano's imagination, now again not wholly at rest, there was something so hollow in the Spaniard's manner, with apparently some reciprocal hollowness in the servant's dusky comment of silence, that the idea flashed across him, that possibly master and man, for some unknown purpose, were acting out, both in word and deed, nay, to the very tremor of Don Benito's limbs, some juggling play before him. Neither did the suspicion of collusion lack apparent support, from the fact of those whispered conferences before mentioned. But then, what could be the object of enacting this play of the barber before him? At last, regarding the notion as a whimsy, insensibly suggested, perhaps, by the theatrical aspect of Don Benito in his harlequin ensign, Captain Delano speedily banished it.

The shaving over, the servant bestirred himself with a small bottle of scented waters, pouring a few drops on the head, and then diligently rubbing; the vehemence of the exercise causing the muscles of his face to twitch rather strangely.

His next operation was with comb, scissors, and brush; going round and round, smoothing a curl here, clipping an unruly whisker-hair there, giving a graceful sweep to the temple-lock, with other impromptu touches evincing the hand of a master; while, like any resigned gentleman in barber's hands, Don Benito bore all, much less uneasily, at least, than he had done the razoring; indeed, he sat so pale and rigid now, that the negro seemed a Nubian sculptor finishing off a white statue-head.

All being over at last, the standard of Spain removed, tumbled up, and tossed back into the flag-locker, the negro's warm breath blowing away any stray hair which might have lodged down his master's neck; collar and cravat readjusted; a speck of lint whisked off the velvet lapel; all this being done; backing off a little space, and pausing with an expression of subdued self-complacency, the servant for a moment surveyed his master, as, in toilet at least, the creature of his own tasteful hands.

Captain Delano playfully complimented him upon his achievement; at the same time congratulating Don Benito.

But neither sweet waters, nor shampooing, nor fidelity, nor sociality, delighted the Spaniard. Seeing him relapsing into forbidding gloom, and still remaining seated, Captain Delano, thinking that his presence was undesired just then, withdrew, on pretense of seeing whether, as he had prophesied, any signs of a breeze were visible.

Walking forward to the main-mast, he stood awhile thinking over the scene, and not without some undefined misgivings, when he heard a noise near the cuddy, and turning, saw the negro, his hand to his cheek. Advancing, Captain Delano perceived that the cheek was bleeding. He was about to ask the cause, when the negro's wailing soliloquy enlightened him.

"Ah, when will master get better from his sickness; only the sour heart that sour sickness breeds made him serve Babo so; cutting Babo with the razor, because, only by accident, Babo had given master one little scratch; and for the first time in so many a day, too. Ah, ah, ah," holding his hand to his face.

Is it possible, thought Captain Delano; was it to wreak in private his Spanish spite against this poor friend of his, that Don Benito, by his sullen manner, impelled me to withdraw? Ah, this slavery breeds ugly passions in man.—Poor fellow!

He was about to speak in sympathy to the negro, but with a timid reluctance he now re-entered the cuddy.

Presently master and man came forth; Don Benito leaning on his servant as if nothing had happened.

But a sort of love-quarrel, after all, thought Captain Delano.

He accosted Don Benito, and they slowly walked together. They had gone but a few paces, when the steward—a tall, rajah-looking mulatto, orientally set off with a pagoda turban formed by three or four Madras handkerchiefs wound about his head, tier on tier—approaching with a salam, announced lunch in the cabin.

On their way thither, the two captains were preceded by the mulatto, who, turning round as he advanced, with continual smiles and bows, ushered them on, a display of elegance which quite completed the insignificance of the small bareheaded Babo, who, as if not unconscious of inferiority, eyed askance the graceful steward. But in part, Captain Delano imputed his jealous watchfulness to that peculiar feeling which the full-blooded African entertains for the adulterated one. As for the steward, his manner, if not bespeaking much dignity or self-respect, yet evidenced his extreme desire to please; which is doubly meritorious, as at once Christian and Chesterfieldian.

Captain Delano observed with interest that while the complexion of the mulatto was hybrid, his physiognomy was European—classically so.

"Don Benito," whispered he, "I am glad to see this usher-of-the-golden-rod of yours; the sight refutes an ugly remark once made to me by a Barbadoes planter; that when a mulatto has a regular European face, look out for him; he is a devil. But see, your steward here has features more regular than King George's of England; and yet there he nods, and bows, and smiles; a king, indeed—the king of kind hearts and polite fellows. What a pleasant voice he has, too?"

"He has, Señor."

"But tell me, has he not, so far as you have known him, always proved a good, worthy fellow?" said Captain Delano, pausing, while with a final genuflexion the steward disappeared into the cabin; "come, for the reason just mentioned, I am curious to know."

"Francesco is a good man," somewhat sluggishly responded Don Benito, like a phlegmatic appreciator, who would neither find fault nor flatter.

"Ah, I thought so. For it were strange, indeed, and not very creditable to us white-skins, if a little of our blood mixed with the African's, should, far from improving the latter's quality, have the sad effect of pouring vitriolic acid into black broth; improving the hue, perhaps, but not the wholesomeness."

"Doubtless, doubtless, Señor, but"—glancing at Babo—"not to speak of negroes, your planter's remark I have heard applied to the Spanish and Indian intermixtures in our provinces. But I know nothing about the matter," he listlessly added.

And here they entered the cabin.

The lunch was a frugal one. Some of Captain Delano's fresh fish and pumpkins, biscuit and salt beef, the reserved bottle of cider, and the San Dominick's last bottle of Canary.

As they entered, Francesco, with two or three colored aids, was hovering over the table giving the last adjustments. Upon perceiving their master they withdrew, Francesco making a smiling congé, and the Spaniard, without condescending to notice it, fastidiously remarking to his companion that he relished not superfluous attendance.

Without companions, host and guest sat down, like a childless married couple, at opposite ends of the table, Don Benito waving Captain Delano to his place, and, weak as he was, insisting upon that gentleman being seated before himself.

The negro placed a rug under Don Benito's feet, and a cushion behind his back, and then stood behind, not his master's chair, but Captain Delano's. At first, this a little surprised the latter. But it was soon evident that, in taking his position, the black was still true to his master; since by facing him he could the more readily anticipate his slightest want.

"This is an uncommonly intelligent fellow of yours, Don Benito," whispered Captain Delano across the table.

"You say true, Señor."

During the repast, the guest again reverted to parts of Don Benito's story, begging further particulars here and there. He inquired how it was that the scurvy and fever should have committed such wholesale havoc upon the whites, while destroying less than half of the blacks. As if this question reproduced the whole scene of plague before the Spaniard's eyes, miserably reminding him of his solitude in a cabin where before he had had so many friends and officers round him, his hand shook, his face became hueless, broken words escaped; but directly the sane memory of the past seemed replaced by insane terrors of the present. With starting eyes he stared before him at vacancy. For nothing was to be seen but the hand of his servant pushing the Canary over towards him. At length a few sips served partially to restore him. He made random reference to the different constitution of races, enabling one to offer more resistance to certain maladies than another. The thought was new to his companion.

Presently Captain Delano, intending to say something to his host concerning the pecuniary part of the business he had undertaken for him, especially—since he was strictly accountable to his owners—with reference to the new suit of sails, and other things of that sort; and naturally preferring to conduct such affairs in private, was desirous that the servant should withdraw; imagining that Don Benito for a few minutes could dispense with his attendance. He, however, waited awhile; thinking that, as the conversation proceeded, Don Benito, without being prompted, would perceive the propriety of the step.

But it was otherwise. At last catching his host's eye, Captain Delano, with a slight backward gesture of his thumb, whispered, "Don Benito, pardon me, but there is an interference with the full expression of what I have to say to you."

Upon this the Spaniard changed countenance; which was imputed to his resenting the hint, as in some way a reflection upon his servant. After a moment's pause, he assured his guest that the black's remaining with them could be of no disservice; because since losing his officers he had made Babo (whose original office, it now appeared, had been captain of the slaves) not only his constant attendant and companion, but in all things his confidant.

After this, nothing more could be said; though, indeed, Captain Delano could hardly avoid some little tinge of irritation upon being left ungratified in so inconsiderable a wish, by one, too, for whom he intended such solid services. But it is only his querulousness, thought he; and so filling his glass he proceeded to business.

The price of the sails and other matters was fixed upon. But while this was being done, the American observed that, though his original offer of assistance had been hailed with hectic animation, yet now when it was reduced to a business transaction, indifference and apathy were betrayed. Don Benito, in fact, appeared to submit to hearing the details more out of regard to common propriety, than from any impression that weighty benefit to himself and his voyage was involved.

Soon, his manner became still more reserved. The effort was vain to seek to draw him into social talk. Gnawed by his splenetic mood, he sat twitching his beard, while to little purpose the hand of his servant, mute as that on the wall, slowly pushed over the Canary.

Lunch being over, they sat down on the cushioned transom; the servant placing a pillow behind his master. The long continuance of the calm had now affected the atmosphere. Don Benito sighed heavily, as if for breath.

"Why not adjourn to the cuddy," said Captain Delano; "there is more air there." But the host sat silent and motionless.

Meantime his servant knelt before him, with a large fan of feathers. And Francesco coming in on tiptoes, handed the negro a little cup of aromatic waters, with which at intervals he chafed his master's brow; smoothing the hair along the temples as a nurse does a child's. He spoke no word. He only rested his eye on his master's, as if, amid all Don Benito's distress, a little to refresh his spirit by the silent sight of fidelity.

Presently the ship's bell sounded two o'clock; and through the cabin windows a slight rippling of the sea was discerned; and from the desired direction.

"There," exclaimed Captain Delano, "I told you so, Don Benito, look!"

He had risen to his feet, speaking in a very animated tone, with a view the more to rouse his companion. But though the crimson curtain of the stern-window near him that moment fluttered against his pale cheek, Don Benito seemed to have even less welcome for the breeze than the calm.

Poor fellow, thought Captain Delano, bitter experience has taught him that one ripple does not make a wind, any more than one swallow a summer. But he is mistaken for once. I will get his ship in for him, and prove it.

Briefly alluding to his weak condition, he urged his host to remain quietly where he was, since he (Captain Delano) would with pleasure take upon himself the responsibility of making the best use of the wind.

Upon gaining the deck, Captain Delano started at the unexpected figure of Atufal, monumentally fixed at the threshold, like one of those sculptured porters of black marble guarding the porches of Egyptian tombs.

But this time the start was, perhaps, purely physical. Atufal's presence, singularly attesting docility even in sullenness, was contrasted with that of the hatchet-polishers, who in patience evinced their industry; while both spectacles showed, that lax as Don Benito's general authority might be, still, whenever he chose to exert it, no man so savage or colossal but must, more or less, bow.

Snatching a trumpet which hung from the bulwarks, with a free step Captain Delano advanced to the forward edge of the poop, issuing his orders in his best Spanish. The few sailors and many negroes, all equally pleased, obediently set about heading the ship towards the harbor.

While giving some directions about setting a lower stu'n'sail, suddenly Captain Delano heard a voice faithfully repeating his orders. Turning, he saw Babo, now for the time acting, under the pilot, his original part of captain of the slaves. This assistance proved valuable. Tattered sails and warped yards were soon brought into some trim. And no brace or halyard was pulled but to the blithe songs of the inspirited negroes.

Good fellows, thought Captain Delano, a little training would make fine sailors of them. Why see, the very women pull and sing too. These must be some of those Ashantee negresses that make such capital soldiers, I've heard. But who's at the helm. I must have a good hand there.

He went to see.

The San Dominick steered with a cumbrous tiller, with large horizontal pullies attached. At each pulley-end stood a subordinate black, and between them, at the tiller-head, the responsible post, a Spanish seaman, whose countenance evinced his due share in the general hopefulness and confidence at the coming of the breeze.

He proved the same man who had behaved with so shamefaced an air on the windlass.

"Ah,—it is you, my man," exclaimed Captain Delano—"well, no more sheep's-eyes now;—look straight forward and keep the ship so. Good hand, I trust? And want to get into the harbor, don't you?"

The man assented with an inward chuckle, grasping the tillerhead firmly. Upon this, unperceived by the American, the two blacks eyed the sailor intently.

Finding all right at the helm, the pilot went forward to the forecastle, to see how matters stood there.

The ship now had way enough to breast the current. With the approach of evening, the breeze would be sure to freshen.

Having done all that was needed for the present, Captain Delano, giving his last orders to the sailors, turned aft to report affairs to Don Benito in the cabin; perhaps additionally incited to rejoin him by the hope of snatching a moment's private chat while the servant was engaged upon deck.

From opposite sides, there were, beneath the poop, two approaches to the cabin; one further forward than the other, and consequently communicating with a longer passage. Marking the servant still above, Captain Delano, taking the nighest entrance—the one last named, and at whose porch Atufal still stood—hurried on his way, till, arrived at the cabin threshold, he paused an instant, a little to recover from his eagerness. Then, with the words of his intended business upon his lips, he entered. As he advanced toward the seated Spaniard, he heard another footstep, keeping time with his. From the opposite door, a salver in hand, the servant was likewise advancing.

"Confound the faithful fellow," thought Captain Delano; "what a vexatious coincidence."

Possibly, the vexation might have been something different, were it not for the brisk confidence inspired by the breeze. But even as it was, he felt a slight twinge, from a sudden indefinite association in his mind of Babo with Atufal.

"Don Benito," said he, "I give you joy; the breeze will hold, and will increase. By the way, your tall man and time-piece, Atufal, stands without. By your order, of course?"

Don Benito recoiled, as if at some bland satirical touch, delivered with such adroit garnish of apparent good breeding as to present no handle for retort.

He is like one flayed alive, thought Captain Delano; where may one touch him without causing a shrink?

The servant moved before his master, adjusting a cushion; recalled to civility, the Spaniard stiffly replied: "You are right. The slave appears where you saw him, according to my command; which is, that if at the given hour I am below, he must take his stand and abide my coming."

"Ah now, pardon me, but that is treating the poor fellow like an ex-king indeed. Ah, Don Benito," smiling, "for all the license you permit in some things, I fear lest, at bottom, you are a bitter hard master."

Again Don Benito shrank; and this time, as the good sailor thought, from a genuine twinge of his conscience.

Again conversation became constrained. In vain Captain Delano called attention to the now perceptible motion of the keel gently cleaving the sea; with lack-lustre eye, Don Benito returned words few and reserved.

By-and-by, the wind having steadily risen, and still blowing right into the harbor, bore the San Dominick swiftly on. Rounding a point of land, the sealer at distance came into open view.

Meantime Captain Delano had again repaired to the deck, remaining there sometime. Having at last altered the ship's course, so as to give the reef a wide berth, he returned for a few moments below.

I will cheer up my poor friend, this time, thought he.

"Better and better, Don Benito," he cried as he blithely reentered: "there will soon be an end to your cares, at least for awhile. For when, after a long, sad voyage, you know, the anchor drops into the haven, all its vast weight seems lifted from the captain's heart. We are getting on famously, Don Benito. My ship is in sight. Look through this side-light here; there she is; all a-taunt-o! The Bachelor's Delight, my good friend. Ah, how this wind braces one up. Come, you must take a cup of coffee with me this evening. My old steward will give you as fine a cup as ever any sultan tasted. What say you, Don Benito, will you?"

At first, the Spaniard glanced feverishly up, casting a longing look towards the sealer, while with mute concern his servant gazed into his face. Suddenly the old ague of coldness returned, and dropping back to his cushions he was silent.

"You do not answer. Come, all day you have been my host; would you have hospitality all on one side?"

"I cannot go," was the response.

"What? it will not fatigue you. The ships will lie together as near as they can, without swinging foul. It will be little more than stepping from deck to deck; which is but as from room to room. Come, come, you must not refuse me."

"I cannot go," decisively and repulsively repeated Don Benito.

Renouncing all but the last appearance of courtesy, with a sort of cadaverous sullenness, and biting his thin nails to the quick, he glanced, almost glared, at his guest, as if impatient that a stranger's presence should interfere with the full indulgence of his morbid hour. Meantime the sound of the parted waters came more and more gurglingly and merrily in at the windows; as reproaching him for his dark spleen; as telling him that, sulk as he might, and go mad with it, nature cared not a jot; since, whose fault was it, pray?

But the foul mood was now at its depth, as the fair wind at its height.

There was something in the man so far beyond any mere unsociality or sourness previously evinced, that even the forbearing good-nature of his guest could no longer endure it. Wholly at a loss to account for such demeanor, and deeming sickness with eccentricity, however extreme, no adequate excuse, well satisfied, too, that nothing in his own conduct could justify it, Captain Delano's pride began to be roused. Himself became reserved. But all seemed one to the Spaniard. Quitting him, therefore, Captain Delano once more went to the deck.

The ship was now within less than two miles of the sealer. The whale-boat was seen darting over the interval.

To be brief, the two vessels, thanks to the pilot's skill, ere long in neighborly style lay anchored together.

Before returning to his own vessel, Captain Delano had intended communicating to Don Benito the smaller details of the proposed services to be rendered. But, as it was, unwilling anew to subject himself to rebuffs, he resolved, now that he had seen the San Dominick safely moored, immediately to quit her, without further allusion to hospitality or business. Indefinitely postponing his ulterior plans, he would regulate his future actions according to future circumstances. His boat was ready to receive him; but his host still tarried below. Well, thought Captain Delano, if he has little breeding, the more need to show mine. He descended to the cabin to bid a ceremonious, and, it may be, tacitly rebukeful adieu. But to his great satisfaction, Don Benito, as if he began to feel the weight of that treatment with which his slighted guest had, not indecorously, retaliated upon him, now supported by his servant, rose to his feet, and grasping Captain Delano's hand, stood tremulous; too much agitated to speak. But the good augury hence drawn was suddenly dashed, by his resuming all his previous reserve, with augmented gloom, as, with half-averted eyes, he silently reseated himself on his cushions. With a corresponding return of his own chilled feelings, Captain Delano bowed and withdrew.

He was hardly midway in the narrow corridor, dim as a tunnel, leading from the cabin to the stairs, when a sound, as of the tolling for execution in some jail-yard, fell on his ears. It was the echo of the ship's flawed bell, striking the hour, drearily reverberated in this subterranean vault. Instantly, by a fatality not to be withstood, his mind, responsive to the portent, swarmed with superstitious suspicions. He paused. In images far swifter than these sentences, the minutest details of all his former distrusts swept through him.

Hitherto, credulous good-nature had been too ready to furnish excuses for reasonable fears. Why was the Spaniard, so superfluously punctilious at times, now heedless of common propriety in not accompanying to the side his departing guest? Did indisposition forbid? Indisposition had not forbidden more irksome exertion that day. His last equivocal demeanor recurred. He had risen to his feet, grasped his guest's hand, motioned toward his hat; then, in an instant, all was eclipsed in sinister muteness and gloom. Did this imply one brief, repentant relenting at the final moment, from some iniquitous plot, followed by remorseless return to it? His last glance seemed to express a calamitous, yet acquiescent farewell to Captain Delano forever. Why decline the invitation to visit the sealer that evening? Or was the Spaniard less hardened than the Jew, who refrained not from supping at the board of him whom the same night he meant to betray? What imported all those day-long enigmas and contradictions, except they were intended to mystify, preliminary to some stealthy blow? Atufal, the pretended rebel, but punctual shadow, that moment lurked by the threshold without. He seemed a sentry, and more. Who, by his own confession, had stationed him there? Was the negro now lying in wait?

The Spaniard behind—his creature before: to rush from darkness to light was the involuntary choice.

The next moment, with clenched jaw and hand, he passed Atufal, and stood unharmed in the light. As he saw his trim ship lying peacefully at anchor, and almost within ordinary call; as he saw his household boat, with familiar faces in it, patiently rising and falling on the short waves by the San Dominick's side; and then, glancing about the decks where he stood, saw the oakum-pickers still gravely plying their fingers; and heard the low, buzzing whistle and industrious hum of the hatchet-polishers, still bestirring themselves over their endless occupation; and more than all, as he saw the benign aspect of nature, taking her innocent repose in the evening; the screened sun in the quiet camp of the west shining out like the mild light from Abraham's tent; as charmed eye and ear took in all these, with the chained figure of the black, clenched jaw and hand relaxed. Once again he smiled at the phantoms which had mocked him, and felt something like a tinge of remorse, that, by harboring them even for a moment, he should, by implication, have betrayed an atheist doubt of the ever-watchful Providence above.

There was a few minutes' delay, while, in obedience to his orders, the boat was being hooked along to the gangway. During this interval, a sort of saddened satisfaction stole over Captain Delano, at thinking of the kindly offices he had that day discharged for a stranger. Ah, thought he, after good actions one's conscience is never ungrateful, however much so the benefited party may be.

Presently, his foot, in the first act of descent into the boat, pressed the first round of the side-ladder, his face presented inward upon the deck. In the same moment, he heard his name courteously sounded; and, to his pleased surprise, saw Don Benito advancing—an unwonted energy in his air, as if, at the last moment, intent upon making amends for his recent discourtesy. With instinctive good feeling, Captain Delano, withdrawing his foot, turned and reciprocally advanced. As he did so, the Spaniard's nervous eagerness increased, but his vital energy failed; so that, the better to support him, the servant, placing his master's hand on his naked shoulder, and gently holding it there, formed himself into a sort of crutch.

When the two captains met, the Spaniard again fervently took the hand of the American, at the same time casting an earnest glance into his eyes, but, as before, too much overcome to speak.

I have done him wrong, self-reproachfully thought Captain Delano; his apparent coldness has deceived me; in no instance has he meant to offend.

Meantime, as if fearful that the continuance of the scene might too much unstring his master, the servant seemed anxious to terminate it. And so, still presenting himself as a crutch, and walking between the two captains, he advanced with them towards the gangway; while still, as if full of kindly contrition, Don Benito would not let go the hand of Captain Delano, but retained it in his, across the black's body.

Soon they were standing by the side, looking over into the boat, whose crew turned up their curious eyes. Waiting a moment for the Spaniard to relinquish his hold, the now embarrassed Captain Delano lifted his foot, to overstep the threshold of the open gangway; but still Don Benito would not let go his hand. And yet, with an agitated tone, he said, "I can go no further; here I must bid you adieu. Adieu, my dear, dear Don Amasa. Go—go!" suddenly tearing his hand loose, "go, and God guard you better than me, my best friend."

Not unaffected, Captain Delano would now have lingered; but catching the meekly admonitory eye of the servant, with a hasty farewell he descended into his boat, followed by the continual adieus of Don Benito, standing rooted in the gangway.

Seating himself in the stern, Captain Delano, making a last salute, ordered the boat shoved off. The crew had their oars on end. The bowsmen pushed the boat a sufficient distance for the oars to be lengthwise dropped. The instant that was done, Don Benito sprang over the bulwarks, falling at the feet of Captain Delano; at the same time calling towards his ship, but in tones so frenzied, that none in the boat could understand him. But, as if not equally obtuse, three sailors, from three different and distant parts of the ship, splashed into the sea, swimming after their captain, as if intent upon his rescue.

The dismayed officer of the boat eagerly asked what this meant. To which, Captain Delano, turning a disdainful smile upon the unaccountable Spaniard, answered that, for his part, he neither knew nor cared; but it seemed as if Don Benito had taken it into his head to produce the impression among his people that the boat wanted to kidnap him. "Or else—give way for your lives," he wildly added, starting at a clattering hubbub in the ship, above which rang the tocsin of the hatchet-polishers; and seizing Don Benito by the throat he added, "this plotting pirate means murder!" Here, in apparent verification of the words, the servant, a dagger in his hand, was seen on the rail overhead, poised, in the act of leaping, as if with desperate fidelity to befriend his master to the last; while, seemingly to aid the black, the three white sailors were trying to clamber into the hampered bow. Meantime, the whole host of negroes, as if inflamed at the sight of their jeopardized captain, impended in one sooty avalanche over the bulwarks.

All this, with what preceded, and what followed, occurred with such involutions of rapidity, that past, present, and future seemed one.

Seeing the negro coming, Captain Delano had flung the Spaniard aside, almost in the very act of clutching him, and, by the unconscious recoil, shifting his place, with arms thrown up, so promptly grappled the servant in his descent, that with dagger presented at Captain Delano's heart, the black seemed of purpose to have leaped there as to his mark. But the weapon was wrenched away, and the assailant dashed down into the bottom of the boat, which now, with disentangled oars, began to speed through the sea.

At this juncture, the left hand of Captain Delano, on one side, again clutched the half-reclined Don Benito, heedless that he was in a speechless faint, while his right foot, on the other side, ground the prostrate negro; and his right arm pressed for added speed on the after oar, his eye bent forward, encouraging his men to their utmost.

But here, the officer of the boat, who had at last succeeded in beating off the towing sailors, and was now, with face turned aft, assisting the bowsman at his oar, suddenly called to Captain Delano, to see what the black was about; while a Portuguese oarsman shouted to him to give heed to what the Spaniard was saying.

Glancing down at his feet, Captain Delano saw the freed hand of the servant aiming with a second dagger—a small one, before concealed in his wool—with this he was snakishly writhing up from the boat's bottom, at the heart of his master, his countenance lividly vindictive, expressing the centred purpose of his soul; while the Spaniard, half-choked, was vainly shrinking way, with husky words, incoherent to all but the Portuguese.

That moment, across the long-benighted mind of Captain Delano, a flash of revelation swept, illuminating, in unanticipated clearness, his host's whole mysterious demeanor, with every enigmatic event of the day, as well as the entire past voyage of the San Dominick. He smote Babo's hand down, but his own heart smote him harder. With infinite pity he withdrew his hold from Don Benito. Not Captain Delano, but Don Benito, the black, in leaping into the boat, had intended to stab.

Both the black's hands were held, as, glancing up towards the San Dominick, Captain Delano, now with scales dropped from his eyes, saw the negroes, not in misrule, not in tumult, not as if frantically concerned for Don Benito, but with mask torn away, flourishing hatchets and knives, in ferocious piratical revolt. Like delirious black dervishes, the six Ashantees danced on the poop. Prevented by their foes from springing into the water, the Spanish boys were hurrying up to the topmost spars, while such of the few Spanish sailors, not already in the sea, less alert, were described, helplessly mixed in, on deck, with the blacks.

Meantime Captain Delano hailed his own vessel, ordering the ports up, and the guns run out. But by this time the cable of the San Dominick had been cut; and the fag-end, in lashing out, whipped away the canvas shroud about the beak, suddenly revealing, as the bleached hull swung round towards the open ocean, death for the figure-head, in a human skeleton; chalky comment on the chalked words below, "*Follow your leader.*"

At the sight, Don Benito, covering his face, wailed out: "'Tis he, Aranda! my murdered, unburied friend!"

Upon reaching the sealer, calling for ropes, Captain Delano bound the negro, who made no resistance, and had him hoisted to the deck. He would then have assisted the now almost helpless Don Benito up the side; but Don Benito, wan as he was, refused to move, or be moved, until the negro should have been first put below out of view. When, presently assured that it was done, he no more shrank from the ascent.

The boat was immediately dispatched back to pick up the three swimming sailors. Meantime, the guns were in readiness, though, owing to the San Dominick having glided somewhat astern of the sealer, only the aftermost one could be brought to bear. With this, they fired six times; thinking to cripple the fugitive ship by bringing down her spars. But only a few inconsiderable ropes were shot away. Soon the ship was beyond the gun's range, steering broad out of the bay; the blacks thickly clustering round the bowsprit, one moment with taunting cries towards the whites, the next with upthrown gestures hailing the now dusky moors of ocean—cawing crows escaped from the hand of the fowler.

The first impulse was to slip the cables and give chase. But, upon second thoughts, to pursue with whale-boat and yawl seemed more promising.

Upon inquiring of Don Benito what fire-arms they had on board the San Dominick, Captain Delano was answered that they had none that could be used; because, in the earlier stages of the mutiny, a cabin-passenger, since dead, had secretly put out of order the locks of what few muskets there were. But with all his remaining strength, Don Benito entreated the American not to give chase, either with ship or boat; for the negroes had already proved themselves such desperadoes, that, in case of a present assault, nothing but a total massacre of the whites could be looked for. But, regarding this warning as coming from one whose spirit had been crushed by misery the American did not give up his design.

The boats were got ready and armed. Captain Delano ordered his men into them. He was going himself when Don Benito grasped his arm.

"What! have you saved my life, Señor, and are you now going to throw away your own?"

The officers also, for reasons connected with their interests and those of the voyage, and a duty owing to the owners, strongly objected against their commander's going. Weighing their remonstrances a moment, Captain Delano felt bound to remain; appointing his chief mate—an athletic and resolute man, who had been a privateer's-man—to head the party. The more to encourage the sailors, they were told, that the Spanish captain considered his ship good as lost; that she and her cargo, including some gold and silver, were worth more than a thousand doubloons. Take her, and no small part should be theirs. The sailors replied with a shout.

The fugitives had now almost gained an offing. It was nearly night; but the moon was rising. After hard, prolonged pulling, the boats came up on the ship's quarters, at a suitable distance laying upon their oars to discharge their muskets. Having no bullets to return, the negroes sent their yells. But, upon the second volley, Indian-like, they hurtled their hatchets. One took off a sailor's fingers. Another struck the whale-boat's bow, cutting off the rope there, and remaining stuck in the gunwale like a woodman's axe. Snatching it, quivering from its lodgment, the mate hurled it back. The returned gauntlet now stuck in the ship's broken quarter-gallery, and so remained.

The negroes giving too hot a reception, the whites kept a more respectful distance. Hovering now just out of reach of the hurtling hatchets, they, with a view to the close encounter which must soon come, sought to decoy the blacks into entirely disarming themselves of their most murderous weapons in a hand-to-hand fight, by foolishly flinging them, as missiles, short of the mark, into the sea. But, ere long, perceiving the stratagem, the negroes desisted, though not before many of them had to replace their lost hatchets with handspikes; an exchange which, as counted upon, proved, in the end, favorable to the assailants.

Meantime, with a strong wind, the ship still clove the water; the boats alternately falling behind, and pulling up, to discharge fresh volleys.

The fire was mostly directed towards the stern, since there, chiefly, the negroes, at present, were clustering. But to kill or maim the negroes was not the object. To take them, with the ship, was the object. To do it, the ship must be boarded; which could not be done by boats while she was sailing so fast.

A thought now struck the mate. Observing the Spanish boys still aloft, high as they could get, he called to them to descend to the yards, and cut adrift the sails. It was done. About this time, owing to causes hereafter to be shown, two Spaniards, in the dress of sailors, and conspicuously showing themselves, were killed; not by volleys, but by deliberate marksman's shots; while, as it afterwards appeared, by one of the general discharges, Atufal, the black, and the Spaniard at the helm likewise were killed. What now, with the loss of the sails, and loss of leaders, the ship became unmanageable to the negroes.

With creaking masts, she came heavily round to the wind; the prow slowly swinging into view of the boats, its skeleton gleaming in the horizontal moonlight, and casting a gigantic ribbed shadow upon the water. One extended arm of the ghost seemed beckoning the whites to avenge it.

"Follow your leader!" cried the mate; and, one on each bow, the boats boarded. Sealing-spears and cutlasses crossed hatchets and hand-spikes. Huddled upon the long-boat amidships, the negresses raised a wailing chant, whose chorus was the clash of the steel.

For a time, the attack wavered; the negroes wedging themselves to beat it back; the half-repelled sailors, as yet unable to gain a footing, fighting as troopers in the saddle, one leg sideways flung over the bulwarks, and one without, plying their cutlasses like carters' whips. But in vain. They were almost overborne, when, rallying themselves into a squad as one man, with a huzza, they sprang inboard, where, entangled, they involuntarily separated again. For a few breaths' space, there was a vague, muffled, inner sound, as of submerged sword-fish rushing hither and thither through shoals of black-fish. Soon, in a reunited band, and joined by the Spanish seamen, the whites came to the surface, irresistibly driving the negroes toward the stern. But a barricade of casks and sacks, from side to side, had been thrown up by the mainmast. Here the negroes faced about, and though scorning peace or truce, yet fain would have had respite. But, without pause, overleaping the barrier, the unflagging sailors again closed. Exhausted, the blacks now fought in despair. Their red tongues lolled, wolf-like, from their black mouths. But the pale sailors' teeth were set; not a word was spoken; and, in five minutes more, the ship was won.

Nearly a score of the negroes were killed. Exclusive of those by the balls, many were mangled; their wounds—mostly inflicted by the long-edged sealing-spears, resembling those shaven ones of the English at Preston Pans, made by the poled scythes of the Highlanders. On the other side, none were killed, though several were wounded; some severely, including the mate. The surviving negroes were temporarily secured, and the ship, towed back into the harbor at midnight, once more lay anchored.

Omitting the incidents and arrangements ensuing, suffice it that, after two days spent in refitting, the ships sailed in company for Conception, in Chili, and thence for Lima, in Peru; where, before the vice-regal courts, the whole affair, from the beginning, underwent investigation.

Though, midway on the passage, the ill-fated Spaniard, relaxed from constraint, showed some signs of regaining health with free-will; yet, agreeably to his own foreboding, shortly before arriving at Lima, he relapsed, finally becoming so reduced as to be carried ashore in arms. Hearing of his story and plight, one of the many religious institutions of the City of Kings opened an hospitable refuge to him, where both physician and priest were his nurses, and a member of the order volunteered to be his one special guardian and consoler, by night and by day.

The following extracts, translated from one of the official Spanish documents, will, it is hoped, shed light on the preceding narrative, as well as, in the first place, reveal the true port of departure and true history of the San Dominick's voyage, down to the time of her touching at the island of St. Maria.

But, ere the extracts come, it may be well to preface them with a remark.

The document selected, from among many others, for partial translation, contains the deposition of Benito Cereno; the first taken in the case. Some disclosures therein were, at the time, held dubious for both learned and natural reasons. The tribunal inclined to the opinion that the deponent, not undisturbed in his mind by recent events, raved of some things which could never have happened. But subsequent depositions of the surviving sailors, bearing out the revelations of their captain in several of the strangest particulars, gave credence to the rest. So that the tribunal, in its final decision, rested its capital sentences upon statements which, had they lacked confirmation, it would have deemed it but duty to reject.

I, Don Jose de Abos and Padilla, His Majesty's Notary for the Royal Revenue, and Register of this Province, and Notary Public of the Holy Crusade of this Bishopric, etc.

Do certify and declare, as much as is requisite in law, that, in the criminal cause commenced the twenty-fourth of the month of September, in the year seventeen hundred and ninety-nine, against the negroes of the ship San Dominick, the following declaration before me was made:

Declaration of the first witness, Don Benito Cereno.

The same day, and month, and year, His Honor, Doctor Juan Martinez de Rozas, Councilor of the Royal Audience of this Kingdom, and learned in the law of this Intendency, ordered the captain of the ship San Dominick, Don Benito Cereno, to appear; which he did in his litter, attended by the monk Infelez; of whom he received the oath, which he took by God, our Lord, and a sign of the Cross; under which he promised to tell the truth of whatever he should know and should be asked;—and being interrogated agreeably to the tenor of the act commencing the process, he said, that on the twentieth of May last, he set sail with his ship from the port of Valparaiso, bound to that of Callao; loaded with the produce of the country beside thirty cases of hardware and one hundred and sixty blacks, of both sexes, mostly belonging to Don Alexandro Aranda, gentleman, of the city of Mendoza; that the crew of the ship consisted of thirty-six men, beside the persons who went as passengers; that the negroes were in part as follows:

[*Here, in the original, follows a list of some fifty names, descriptions, and ages, compiled from certain recovered documents of Aranda's, and also from recollections of the deponent, from which portions only are extracted.*]

—One, from about eighteen to nineteen years, named José, and this was the man who waited upon his master, Don Alexandro, and who speaks well the Spanish, having served him four or five years; . . . a mulatto, named Francesco, the cabin steward, of a good person and voice, having sung in the Valparaiso churches, native of the province of Buenos Ayres, aged about thirty-five years. . . . A smart negro, named Dago, who had been for many years a grave-digger among the Spaniards, aged forty-six years. . . . Four old negroes, born in Africa, from sixty to seventy, but sound, calkers by trade, whose names are as follows:—the first was named Muri, and he was killed (as was also his son named Diamelo); the second, Nacta; the third, Yola, likewise killed; the fourth, Ghofan; and six full-grown negroes, aged from thirty to forty-five, all raw, and born among the Ashantees—Matilu-qui, Yan, Lecbe, Mapenda, Yambaio, Akim; four of whom were killed; . . . a powerful negro named Atufal, who being supposed to have been a chief in Africa, his owner set great store by him. . . . And a small negro of Senegal, but some years among the Spaniards, aged about thirty, which negro's name was Babo; . . . that he does not remember the names of the others, but that still expecting the residue of Don Alexandro's papers will be found, will then take due account of them all, and remit to the court; . . . and thirty-nine women and children of all ages.

[The catalogue over, the deposition goes on.]

. . . That all the negroes slept upon deck, as is customary in this navigation, and none wore fetters, because the owner, his friend Aranda, told him that they were all tractable; . . . that on the seventh day after leaving port, at three o'clock in the morning, all the Spaniards being asleep except the two officers on the watch, who were the boatswain, Juan Robles, and the carpenter, Juan Bautista Gayete, and the helmsman and his boy, the negroes revolted suddenly, wounded dangerously the boatswain and the carpenter, and successively killed eighteen men of those who were sleeping upon deck, some with handspikes and hatchets, and others by throwing them alive overboard, after tying them; that of the Spaniards upon deck, they left about seven, as he thinks, alive and tied, to manœuvre the ship, and three or four more, who hid themselves, remained also alive. Although in the act of revolt the negroes made themselves masters of the hatchway, six or seven wounded went through it to the cockpit, without any hindrance on their part; that during the act of revolt, the mate and another person, whose name he does not recollect, attempted to come up through the hatchway, but being quickly wounded, were obliged to return to the cabin; that the deponent resolved at break of day to come up the companion-way, where the negro Babo was, being the ringleader, and Atufal, who assisted him, and having spoken to them, exhorted them to cease committing such atrocities, asking them, at the same time, what they wanted and intended to do, offering, himself, to obey their commands; that notwithstanding this, they threw, in his presence, three men, alive and tied, overboard; that they told the deponent to come up, and that they would not kill him; which having done, the negro Babo asked him whether there were in those seas any negro countries where they might be carried, and he answered them, No; that the negro Babo afterwards told him to carry them to Senegal, or to the neighboring islands of St. Nicholas; and he answered, that this was impossible, on account of the great distance, the necessity involved of rounding Cape Horn, the bad condition of the vessel, the want of provisions, sails, and water; but that the negro Babo replied to him he must carry them in any way; that they would do and conform themselves to everything the deponent should require as to eating and drinking; that after a long conference, being absolutely compelled to please them, for they threatened to kill all the whites if they were not, at all events, carried to Senegal, he told them that what was most wanting for the voyage was water; that they would go near the coast to take it, and thence they would proceed on their course; that the negro Babo agreed to it; and the deponent steered towards the intermediate ports, hoping to meet some Spanish or foreign vessel that would save them; that within ten or eleven days they saw the land, and continued their course by it in the vicinity of Nasca; that the deponent observed that the negroes were now restless and mutinous, because he did not effect the taking in of water, the negro Babo having required, with threats, that it should be done, without fail, the following day; he told him he saw plainly that the coast was steep, and the rivers designated in the maps were not to be found, with other reasons suitable to the circumstances; that the best way would be to go to the island of Santa Maria, where they might water easily, it being a solitary island, as the foreigners did; that the deponent did not go to Pisco, that was near, nor make any other port of the coast, because the negro Babo had intimated to him several times, that he would kill all the whites the very moment he should perceive any city, town, or settlement of any kind on the shores to which they should be carried: that having determined to go to the island of Santa Maria, as the deponent had planned, for the purpose of trying whether, on the passage or near the island itself, they could find any vessel that should favor them, or whether he could escape from it in a boat to the neighboring coast of Arruco, to adopt the necessary means he immediately changed his course, steering for the island; that the negroes Babo and Atufal held daily conferences, in which they discussed what was necessary for their design of returning to Senegal, whether they were to kill all the Spaniards, and particularly the deponent; that eight days after parting from the coast of Nasca, the deponent being on the watch a little after daybreak, and soon after the negroes had their meeting, the negro Babo came to the place where the deponent was, and told him that he had determined to kill his master, Don Alexandro Aranda, both because he and his companions could not otherwise be sure of their liberty, and that to keep the seamen in subjection, he wanted to prepare a warning of what road they should be made to take did they or any of them oppose him; and that, by means of the death of Don Alexandro, that warning would best be given; but, that what this last meant, the deponent did not at the time comprehend, nor could not, further than that the death of Don Alexandro was intended; and moreover the negro Babo proposed to the deponent to call the mate Raneds, who was sleeping in the cabin, before the thing was done, for fear, as the deponent understood it, that the mate, who was a good navigator, should be killed with Don Alexandro and the rest; that the deponent, who was the friend, from youth, of Don Alexandro, prayed and conjured, but all was useless; for the negro Babo answered him that the thing could not be prevented, and that all the Spaniards risked their death if they could attempt to frustrate his will in this matter, or any other; that, in this conflict, the deponent called the mate, Raneds, who was forced to go apart, and immediately the negro Babo commanded the Ashantee Martinqui and the Ashantee Lecbe to go and commit the murder; that those two went down with hatchets to the berth of Don Alexandro; that, yet half alive and mangled, they dragged him on deck; that they were going to throw him overboard in that state, but the negro Babo stopped them, bidding the murder be completed on the deck before him, which was done, when, by his orders, the body was carried below, forward; that nothing more was seen of it by the deponent for three days; . . . that Don Alonzo Sidonia, an old man, long resident at Valparaiso, and lately appointed to a civil office in Peru, whither he had taken passage, was at the time sleeping in the berth opposite Don Alexandro's; that awakening at his cries, surprised by them, and at the sight of the negroes with their bloody hatchets in their hands, he threw himself into the sea through a window which was near him, and was drowned, without it being in the power of the deponent to assist or take him up; . . . that a short time after killing Aranda, they brought upon deck his german-cousin, of middle-age, Don Francisco Masa, of Mendoza, and the young Don Joaquin, Marques de Aramboalaza, then lately from Spain, with his Spanish servant Ponce, and the three young clerks of Aranda, José Mozairi, Lorenzo Bargas, and Hermenegildo Gandix, all of Cadiz; that Don Joaquin and Hermenegildo Gandix, the negro Babo, for purposes hereafter to appear, preserved alive; but Don Francisco Masa, José Mozairi, and Lorenzo Bargas, with Ponce the servant, beside the boatswain, Juan Robles, the boatswain's mates, Manual Viscaya and Roderigo Hurta, and four of the sailors, the negro Babo ordered to be thrown alive into the sea, although they made no resistance, nor begged for anything else but mercy; that the boatswain, Juan Robles, who knew how to swim, kept the longest above water, making acts of contrition, and, in the last words he uttered, charged this deponent to cause mass to be said for his soul to our Lady of Succor: . . . that, during the three days which followed, the deponent, uncertain what fate had befallen the remains of Don Alexandro, frequently asked the negro Babo where they were, and, if still on board, whether they were to be preserved for interment ashore, entreating him so to order it; that the negro Babo answered nothing till the fourth day, when at sunrise, the deponent coming on deck, the negro Babo showed him a skeleton, which had been substituted for the ship's proper figure-head—the image of Christopher Colon, the discoverer of the New World; that the negro Babo asked him whose skeleton that was, and whether, from its whiteness, he should not think it a white's; that, upon discovering his face, the negro Babo, coming close, said words to this effect: "Keep faith with the blacks from here to Senegal, or you shall in spirit, as now in body, follow your leader," pointing to the prow; . . . that the same morning the negro Babo took by succession each Spaniard forward, and asked him whose skeleton that was, and whether, from its whiteness, he should not think it a white's; that each Spaniard covered his face; that then to each the negro Babo repeated the words in the first place said to the deponent; . . . that they (the Spaniards), being then assembled aft, the negro Babo harangued them, saying that he had now done all; that the deponent (as navigator for the negroes) might pursue his course, warning him and all of them that they should, soul and body, go the way of Don Alexandro, if he saw them (the Spaniards) speak or plot anything against them (the negroes)—a threat which was repeated every day; that, before the events last mentioned, they had tied the cook to throw him overboard, for it is not known what thing they heard him speak, but finally the negro Babo spared his life, at the request of the deponent; that a few days after, the deponent, endeavoring not to admit any means to preserve the lives of the remaining whites, spoke to the negroes of peace and tranquillity, and agreed to draw up a paper, signed by the deponent and the sailors who could write, as also by the negro Babo, for himself and all the blacks, in which the deponent obliged himself to carry them to Senegal, and they not to kill any more, and he formally to make over to them the ship, with the cargo, with which they were for that time satisfied and quieted. . . . But the next day, the more surely to guard against the sailors' escape, the negro Babo commanded all the boats to be destroyed but the long-boat, which was unseaworthy, and another, a cutter in good condition, which knowing it would yet be wanted for towing the water casks, he had it lowered down into the hold.

[*Various particulars of the prolonged and perplexed navigation ensuing here follow, with incidents of a calamitous calm, from which portion one passage is extracted, to wit:*]
—That on the fifth day of the calm, all on board suffering much from the heat, and want of water, and five having died in fits, and mad, the negroes became irritable, and for a chance gesture, which they deemed suspicious—

though it was harmless—made by the mate, Raneds, to the deponent in the act of handing a quadrant, they killed him; but that for this they afterwards were sorry, the mate being the only remaining navigator on board, except the deponent.

—That omitting other events, which daily happened, and which can only serve uselessly to recall past misfortunes and conflicts, after seventy-three days' navigation, reckoned from the time they sailed from Nasca, during which they navigated under a scanty allowance of water, and were afflicted with the calms before mentioned, they at last arrived at the island of Santa Maria, on the seventeenth of the month of August, at about six o'clock in the afternoon, at which hour they cast anchor very near the American ship, Bachelor's Delight, which lay in the same bay, commanded by the generous Captain Amasa Delano; but at six o'clock in the morning, they had already described the port, and the negroes became uneasy, as soon as at distance they saw the ship, not having expected to see one there; that the negro Babo pacified them, assuring them that no fear need be had; that straightway he ordered the figure on the bow to be covered with canvas, as for repairs, and had the decks a little set in order; that for a time the negro Babo and the negro Atufal conferred; that the negro Atufal was for sailing away, but the negro Babo would not, and, by himself, cast about what to do; that at last he came to the deponent, proposing to him to say and do all that the deponent declares to have said and done to the American captain;

that the negro Babo warned him that if he varied in the least, or uttered any word, or gave any look that should give the least intimation of the past events or present state, he would instantly kill him, with all his companions, showing a dagger, which he carried hid, saying something which, as he understood it, meant that that dagger would be alert as his eye; that the negro Babo then announced the plan to all his companions, which pleased them; that he then, the better to disguise the truth, devised many expedients, in some of them uniting deceit and defense; that of this sort was the device of the six Ashantees before named, who were his bravoes; that them he stationed on the break of the poop, as if to clean certain hatchets (in cases, which were part of the cargo), but in reality to use them, and distribute them at need, and at a given word he told them; that, among other devices, was the device of presenting Atufal, his right hand man, as chained, though in a moment the chains could be dropped; that in every particular he informed the deponent what part he was expected to enact in every device, and what story he was to tell on every occasion, always threatening him with instant death if he varied in the least: that, conscious that many of the negroes would be turbulent, the negro Babo appointed the four aged negroes, who were calkers, to keep what domestic order they could on the decks; that again and again he harangued the Spaniards and his companions, informing them of his intent, and of his devices, and of the invented story that this deponent was to tell; charging them lest any of them varied from that story; that these arrangements were made and matured during the interval of two or three hours, between their first sighting the ship and the arrival on board of Captain Amasa Delano; that this happened about half-past seven o'clock in the morning, Captain Amasa Delano coming in his boat, and all gladly receiving him; that the deponent, as well as he could force himself, acting then the part of principal owner, and a free captain of the ship, told Captain Amasa Delano, when called upon, that he came from Buenos Ayres, bound to Lima, with three hundred negroes; that off Cape Horn, and in a subsequent fever, many negroes had died; that also, by similar casualties, all the sea officers and the greatest part of the crew had died.

[*And so the deposition goes on, circumstantially recounting the fictitious story dictated to the deponent by Babo, and through the deponent imposed upon Captain Delano; and also recounting the friendly offers of Captain Delano, with other things, but all of which is here omitted. After the fictitious story, etc. the deposition proceeds:*]

—that the generous Captain Amasa Delano remained on board all the day, till he left the ship anchored at six o'clock in the evening, deponent speaking to him always of his pretended misfortunes, under the fore-mentioned principles, without having had it in his power to tell a single word, or give him the least hint, that he might know the truth and state of things; because the negro Babo, performing the office of an officious servant with all the appearance of submission of the humble slave, did not leave the deponent one moment; that this was in order to observe the deponent's actions and words, for the negro Babo understands well the Spanish; and besides, there were thereabout some others who were constantly on the watch, and likewise understood the Spanish; . . . that upon one occasion, while deponent was standing on the deck conversing with Amasa Delano, by a secret sign the negro Babo drew him (the deponent) aside, the act appearing as if originating with the deponent; that then, he being drawn aside, the negro Babo proposed to him to gain from Amasa Delano full particulars about his ship, and crew, and arms; that the deponent asked "For what?" that the negro Babo answered he might conceive; that, grieved at the prospect of what might overtake the generous Captain Amasa Delano, the deponent at first refused to ask the desired questions, and used every argument to induce the negro Babo to give up this new design; that the negro Babo showed the point of his dagger; that, after the information had been obtained the negro

Babo again drew him aside, telling him that that very night he (the deponent) would be captain of two ships, instead of one, for that, great part of the American's ship's crew being to be absent fishing, the six Ashantees, without any one else, would easily take it; that at this time he said other things to the same purpose; that no entreaties availed; that before Amasa Delano's coming on board, no hint had been given touching the capture of the American ship: that to prevent this project the deponent was powerless; . . . —that in some things his memory is confused, he cannot distinctly recall every event; . . . —that as soon as they had cast anchor at six of the clock in the evening, as has before been stated, the American Captain took leave, to return to his vessel; that upon a sudden impulse, which the deponent believes to have come from God and his angels, he, after the farewell had been said, followed the generous Captain Amasa Delano as far as the gunwale, where he stayed, under pretense of taking leave, until Amasa Delano should have been seated in his boat; that on shoving off, the deponent sprang from the gunwale into the boat, and fell into it, he knows not how, God guarding him; that—

[*Here, in the original, follows the account of what further happened at the escape, and how the San Dominick was retaken, and of the passage to the coast; including in the recital many expressions of "eternal gratitude" to the "generous Captain Amasa Delano." The deposition then proceeds with recapitulatory remarks, and a partial renumeration of the negroes, making record of their individual part in the past events, with a view to furnishing, according to command of the court, the data whereon to found the criminal sentences to be pronounced. From this portion is the following*;]

—That he believes that all the negroes, though not in the first place knowing to the design of revolt, when it was accomplished, approved it. . . . That the negro, José, eighteen years old, and in the personal service of Don Alexandro, was the one who communicated the information to the negro Babo, about the state of things in the cabin, before the revolt; that this is known, because, in the preceding midnight, he used to come from his berth, which was under his master's, in the cabin, to the deck where the ringleader and his associates were, and had secret conversations with the negro Babo, in which he was several times seen by the mate; that, one night, the mate drove him away twice; . . . that this same negro José was the one who, without being commanded to do so by the negro Babo, as Lecbe and Martinqui were, stabbed his master, Don Alexandro, after he had been dragged half-lifeless to the deck; . . . that the mulatto steward, Francesco, was of the first band of revolters, that he was, in all things, the creature and tool of the negro Babo; that, to make his court, he, just before a repast in the cabin, proposed, to the negro Babo, poisoning a dish for the generous Captain

Amasa Delano; this is known and believed, because the negroes have said it; but that the negro Babo, having another design, forbade Francesco; . . . that the Ashantee Lecbe was one of the worst of them; for that, on the day the ship was retaken, he assisted in the defense of her, with a hatchet in each hand, with one of which he wounded, in the breast, the chief mate of Amasa Delano, in the first act of boarding; this all knew; that, in sight of the deponent, Lecbe struck, with a hatchet, Don Francisco Masa, when, by the negro Babo's orders, he was carrying him to throw him overboard, alive, beside participating in the murder, before mentioned, of Don Alexandro Aranda, and others of the cabin-passengers; that, owing to the fury with which the Ashantees fought in the engagement with the boats, but this Lecbe and Yan survived; that Yan was bad as Lecbe; that Yan was the man who, by Babo's command, willingly prepared the skeleton of Don Alexandro, in a way the negroes afterwards told the deponent, but which he, so long as reason is left him, can never divulge; that Yan and Lecbe were the two who, in a calm by night, riveted the skeleton to the bow; this also the negroes told him; that the negro Babo was he who traced the inscription below it; that the negro Babo was the plotter from first to last; he ordered every murder, and was the helm and keel of the revolt; that Atufal was his lieutenant in all; but Atufal, with his own hand, committed no murder; nor did the negro Babo; . . . that Atufal was shot, being killed in the fight with the boats, ere boarding; . . . that the negresses, of age, were knowing to the revolt, and testified themselves satisfied at the death of their master, Don Alexandro; that, had the negroes not restrained them, they would have tortured to death, instead of simply killing, the Spaniards slain by command of the negro Babo; that the negresses used their utmost influence to have the deponent made away with; that, in the various acts of murder, they sang songs and danced—not gaily, but solemnly; and before the engagement with the boats, as well as during the action, they sang melancholy songs to the negroes, and that this melancholy tone was more inflaming than a different one would have been, and was so intended; that all this is believed, because the negroes have said it.

—that of the thirty-six men of the crew, exclusive of the passengers (all of whom are now dead), which the deponent had knowledge of, six only remained alive, with four cabin-boys and ship-boys, not included with the crew; . . . —that the negroes broke an arm of one of the cabin-boys and gave him strokes with hatchets.

[*Then follow various random disclosures referring to various periods of time. The following are extracted*;]

—That during the presence of Captain Amasa Delano on board, some attempts were made by the sailors, and one by Hermenegildo Gandix, to convey hints to him of the true state of affairs; but that these attempts were ineffectual, owing to fear of incurring death, and, furthermore, owing to the devices which offered contradictions to the true state of affairs, as well as owing to the generosity and piety of Amasa Delano incapable of sounding such wickedness; . . . that Luys Galgo, a sailor about sixty years of age, and formerly of the king's navy, was one of those who sought to convey tokens to Captain Amasa Delano; but his intent, though undiscovered, being suspected, he was, on a pretense, made to retire out of sight, and at last into the hold, and there was made away with. This the negroes have since said; . . . that one of the ship-boys feeling, from Captain Amasa Delano's presence, some hopes of release, and not having enough prudence, dropped some chance-word respecting his expectations, which being overheard and understood by a slave-boy with whom he was eating at the time, the latter struck him on the head with a knife, inflicting a bad wound, but of which the boy is now healing; that likewise, not long before the ship was brought to anchor, one of the seamen, steering at the time, endangered himself by letting the blacks remark some expression in his countenance, arising from a cause similar to the above; but this sailor, by his heedful after conduct, escaped; . . . that these statements are made to show the court that from the beginning to the end of the revolt, it was impossible for the deponent and his men to act otherwise than they did; . . . —that the third clerk, Hermenegildo Gandix, who before had been forced to live among the seamen, wearing a seaman's habit, and in all respects appearing to be one for the time; he, Gandix, was killed by a musket ball fired through mistake from the boats before boarding; having in his fright run up the mizzen-rigging, calling to the boats—"don't board," lest upon their boarding the negroes should kill him; that this inducing the Americans to believe he some way favored the cause of the negroes, they fired two balls at him, so that he fell wounded from the rigging, and was drowned in the sea; . . . —that the young Don Joaquin, Marques de Aramboalaza, like Hermenegildo Gandix, the third clerk, was degraded to the office and appearance of a common seaman; that upon one occasion when Don Joaquin shrank, the negro Babo commanded the Ashantee Lecbe to take tar and heat it, and pour it upon Don Joaquin's hands; . . . —that Don Joaquin was killed owing to another mistake of the Americans, but one impossible to be avoided, as upon the approach of the boats, Don Joaquin, with a hatchet tied edge out, and upright to his hand, was made by the negroes to appear on the bulwarks; whereupon, seen with arms in his hands and in a questionable attitude, he was shot for a renegade seaman; . . . —that on the person of Don Joaquin was found secreted a jewel, which, by papers that were discovered, proved to have been meant for the shrine of our Lady of Mercy in Lima; a votive offering, beforehand prepared and guarded, to attest his gratitude, when he should have landed in Peru, his last destination, for the safe conclusion of his entire voyage from

Spain; . . . —that the jewel, with the other effects of the late Don Joaquin, is in the custody of the brethren of the Hospital de Sacerdotes, awaiting the disposition of the honorable court; . . . —that, owing to the condition of the deponent, as well as the haste in which the boats departed for the attack, the Americans were not forewarned that there were, among the apparent crew, a passenger and one of the clerks disguised by the negro Babo; . . . —that, beside the negroes killed in the action, some were killed after the capture and re-anchoring at night, when shackled to the ring-bolts on deck; that these deaths were committed by the sailors, ere they could be prevented. That so soon as informed of it, Captain Amasa Delano used all his authority, and, in particular with his own hand, struck down Martinez Gola, who, having found a razor in the pocket of an old jacket of his, which one of the shackled negroes had on, was aiming it at the negro's throat; that the noble Captain Amasa Delano also wrenched from the hand of Bartholomew Barlo a dagger, secreted at the time of the massacre of the whites, with which he was in the act of stabbing a shackled negro, who, the same day, with another negro, had thrown him down and jumped upon him; . . . —that, for all the events, befalling through so long a time, during which the ship was in the hands of the negro Babo, he cannot here give account; but that, what he has said is the most substantial of what occurs to him at present, and is the truth under the oath which he has taken; which declaration he affirmed and ratified, after hearing it read to him.

He said that he is twenty-nine years of age, and broken in body and mind; that when finally dismissed by the court, he shall not return home to Chili, but betake himself to the monastery on Mount Agonia without; and signed with his honor, and crossed himself, and, for the time, departed as he came, in his litter, with the monk Infelez, to the Hospital de Sacerdotes.

BENITO CERENO

DOCTOR ROZAS

If the Deposition have served as the key to fit into the lock of the complications which precede it, then, as a vault whose door has been flung back, the San Dominick's hull lies open today.

Hitherto the nature of this narrative, besides rendering the intricacies in the beginning unavoidable, has more or less required that many things, instead of being set down in the order of occurrence, should be retrospectively, or irregularly given; this last is the case with the following passages, which will conclude the account:

During the long, mild voyage to Lima, there was, as before hinted, a period during which the sufferer a little recovered his health, or, at least in some degree, his tranquillity. Ere the decided relapse which came, the two captains had many cordial conversations—their fraternal unreserve in singular contrast with former withdrawments.

Again and again it was repeated, how hard it had been to enact the part forced on the Spaniard by Babo.

"Ah, my dear friend," Don Benito once said, "at those very times when you thought me so morose and ungrateful, nay, when, as you now admit, you half thought me plotting your murder, at those very times my heart was frozen; I could not look at you, thinking of what, both on board this ship and your own, hung, from other hands, over my kind benefactor. And as God lives, Don Amasa, I know not whether desire for my own safety alone could have nerved me to that leap into your boat, had it not been for the thought that, did you, unenlightened, return to your ship, you, my best friend, with all who might be with you, stolen upon, that night, in your hammocks, would never in this world have wakened again. Do but think how you walked this deck, how you sat in this cabin, every inch of ground mined into honey-combs under you. Had I dropped the least hint, made the least advance towards an understanding between us, death, explosive death—yours as mine—would have ended the scene."

"True, true," cried Captain Delano, starting, "you have saved my life, Don Benito, more than I yours; saved it, too, against my knowledge and will."

"Nay, my friend," rejoined the Spaniard, courteous even to the point of religion, "God charmed your life, but you saved mine. To think of some things you did—those smilings and chattings, rash pointings and gesturings. For less than these, they slew my mate, Raneds; but you had the Prince of Heaven's safe-conduct through all ambuscades."

"Yes, all is owing to Providence, I know: but the temper of my mind that morning was more than commonly pleasant, while the sight of so much suffering, more apparent than real, added to my good-nature, compassion, and charity, happily interweaving the three. Had it been otherwise, doubtless, as you hint, some of my interferences might have ended unhappily enough. Besides, those feelings I spoke of enabled me to get the better of momentary distrust, at times when acuteness might have cost me my life, without saving another's. Only at the end did my suspicions get the better of me, and you know how wide of the mark they then proved."

"Wide, indeed," said Don Benito, sadly; "you were with me all day; stood with me, sat with me, talked with me, looked at me, ate with me, drank with me; and yet, your last act was to clutch for a monster, not only an innocent man, but the most pitiable of all men. To such degree may malign machinations and deceptions impose. So far may even the best man err, in judging the conduct of one with the recesses of whose condition he is not acquainted. But you were forced to it; and you were in time undeceived. Would that, in both respects, it was so ever, and with all men."

"You generalize, Don Benito; and mournfully enough. But the past is passed; why moralize upon it? Forget it. See, yon bright sun has forgotten it all, and the blue sea, and the blue sky; these have turned over new leaves."

"Because they have no memory," he dejectedly replied; "because they are not human."

"But these mild trades that now fan your cheek, do they not come with a human-like healing to you? Warm friends, steadfast friends are the trades."

"With their steadfastness they but waft me to my tomb, Señor," was the foreboding response.

"You are saved," cried Captain Delano, more and more astonished and pained; "you are saved: what has cast such a shadow upon you?"

"The negro."

There was silence, while the moody man sat, slowly and unconsciously gathering his mantle about him, as if it were a pall.

There was no more conversation that day.

But if the Spaniard's melancholy sometimes ended in muteness upon topics like the above, there were others upon which he never spoke at all; on which, indeed, all his old reserves were piled. Pass over the worst, and, only to elucidate, let an item or two of these be cited. The dress, so precise and costly, worn by him on the day whose events have been narrated, had not willingly been put on. And that silver-mounted sword, apparent symbol of despotic command, was not, indeed, a sword, but the ghost of one. The scabbard, artificially stiffened, was empty.

As for the black—whose brain, not body, had schemed and led the revolt, with the plot—his slight frame, inadequate to that which it held, had at once yielded to the superior muscular strength of his captor, in the boat. Seeing all was over, he uttered no sound, and could not be forced to. His aspect seemed to say, since I cannot do deeds, I will not speak words. Put in irons in the hold, with the rest, he was carried to Lima. During the passage, Don Benito did not visit him. Nor then, nor at any time after, would he look at him. Before the tribunal he refused. When pressed by the judges he fainted. On the testimony of the sailors alone rested the legal identity of Babo.

Some months after, dragged to the gibbet at the tail of a mule, the black met his voiceless end. The body was burned to ashes; but for many days, the head, that hive of subtlety, fixed on a pole in the Plaza, met, unabashed, the gaze of the whites; and across the Plaza looked towards St. Bartholomew's church, in which vaults slept then, as now, the recovered bones of Aranda: and across the Rimac bridge looked towards the monastery, on Mount Agonia without; where, three months after being dismissed by the court, Benito Cereno, borne on the bier, did, indeed, follow his leader.

HERMAN MELVILLE
1819–91

After his father died, twelve-year-old Herman Melville left school and worked to help support his family. Stints as a bank clerk, a clerk in the family fur and cap business, a farmhand, and a teacher preceded his adventures as a seaman. At sea he discovered the hardships and the magic that were to spark his writing talent.

In 1839 he joined the crew of the *St. Lawrence*, which was transporting cotton to Liverpool. On his return to America, young Melville quickly signed articles as an ordinary seaman aboard the *Acushnet*, a new vessel bound for the whaling grounds of the Pacific. This signaled the beginning of a four-year odyssey that would give Melville experience on four different ships and a knowledge of the South Sea Islands to boot.

With Richard Tobias Greene, Melville deserted the *Acushnet* when it docked at Nukuhiva Island in the Marquesas Islands. Fleeing to the island's interior, they were captured by the Typees, reputed cannibals. Luck was with the deserters. The Typees treated them kindly, adopting Melville as a special favorite. He remained with them until he was rescued by an Australian whaler a month later.

That ship, the *Lucy Ann*, was no floating paradise. Melville joined a mutiny against the ship's incompetent captain, an action that led to his arrest and incarceration with the rest of the crew in Tahiti. After an easy escape he signed on the *Charles and Henry* as a harpooner. The subsequent voyage, though pleasant enough, was not notably successful in its mission, finding whales. Joining the frigate *United States*, Melville sailed back to Boston, where he landed on 3 October 1844.

Urged by family and friends to write down the yarns he began telling about his adventures in the South Seas, Melville produced a fictionalized account of experiences on Nukuhiva, appropriately titled *Typee: A Peep at Polynesian Life* (1846). The book, published first in England and then America, created enough of a stir to encourage Melville to write a sequel, *Omoo: A Narrative of Adventures in the South Seas* (1847), which contrasted the primitive and civilized cultures of Tahiti.

A third book about South Sea life, *Mardi: and a Voyage Thither* (1849), proved less successful than its predecessors. The romance *Redburn* (1849) had as its subject a sailor's journey of initiation. It recreated Melville's experience aboard the *St. Lawrence* a decade earlier.

White-Jacket; or, The World in a Man-of-War (1850), inspired by Melville's voyage in the *United States*, attacked some of the widespread abuses in the U.S. Navy at mid-century. While in that ship Melville witnessed the flogging of 163 sailors, who had often committed only minor offenses. *White-*

Jacket, distributed to members of Congress during the debates over this practice, presumably played a role in its banning.

In the summer of 1850 Melville met Nathaniel Hawthorne. Their friendship gave Melville a new perspective on the literary art and helped him to shape his work-in-progress. He subsequently dedicated that work, *Moby-Dick; or, The Whale* (1851) to Hawthorne; Hawthorne's *House of the Seven Gables* (1851) was inscribed to Melville.

Moby-Dick, Melville's masterpiece, was neither an unqualified popular nor a complete critical success in 1851. While Melville himself thought highly of the work, its place as one of the best works of American literature was recognized only in this century. His next novel, *Pierre; or, The Ambiguities* (1852), did not sell well, was not welcomed by critics, and was an artistic failure in Melville's own estimation.

Turning to short fiction, Melville penned some of his best work. Between 1853 and 1855 he published "Bartleby the Scrivener," "Benito Cereno," and "The Encantadas" in popular magazines. *Israel Potter: His Fifty Years of Exile*, a startling story including accounts of some of John Paul Jones' engagements, was published first serially in *Putnam's Monthly Magazine* before appearing as a book in 1855.

The Confidence Man: His Masquerade (1857), now considered Melville's minor masterpiece, was set on a Mississippi steamboat rather than an ocean-going vessel. It was the last piece of prose fiction the writer published in his lifetime, though he lived for thirty-four more years.

In debt, Melville took a mundane job in the New York customhouse in 1866, which he held for nineteen years, writing on the side. His later works include several volumes of verse—*Battle-Pieces and Aspects of the War* (1866), *Clarel* (1876), *John Marr and Other Sailors* (1888), and *Timoleon* (1891)—which have never struck a responsive chord in American audiences. The novella *Billy Budd, Foretopman* remained unpublished until 1924.

"Benito Cereno" was included in *The Piazza Tales* in 1856.

The Open Boat

BY STEPHEN CRANE

A Tale Intended to Be after the Fact: Being the Experience of Four Men from the Sunk Steamer COMMODORE

I

NONE OF THEM KNEW the color of the sky. Their eyes glanced level and were fastened upon the waves that swept toward them. These waves were of the hue of slate, save for the tops, which were of foaming white, and all of the men knew the colors of the sea. The horizon narrowed and widened, and dipped and rose, and at all times its edge was jagged with waves that seemed thrust up in points like rocks.

Many a man ought to have a bathtub larger than the boat which here rode upon the sea. These waves were most wrongfully and barbarously abrupt and tall, and each froth-top was a problem in small-boat navigation.

The cook squatted in the bottom, and looked with both eyes at the six inches of gunwale which separated him from the ocean. His sleeves were rolled over his fat forearms, and the two flaps of his unbuttoned vest dangled as he bent to bail out the boat. Often he said, "Gawd! that was a narrow clip." As he remarked it he invariably gazed eastward over the broken sea.

The oiler, steering with one of the two oars in the boat, sometimes raised himself suddenly to keep clear of water that swirled in over the stern. It was a thin little oar, and it seemed often ready to snap.

The correspondent, pulling at the other oar, watched the waves and wondered why he was there.

The injured captain, lying in the bow, was at this time buried in that profound dejection and indifference which comes, temporarily at least, to even the bravest and most enduring when, willy-nilly, the firm fails, the army loses, the ship goes down. The mind of the master of a vessel is rooted deep in the timbers of her, though he command for a day or a decade; and this captain had on him the stern impression of a scene in the grays of dawn of seven turned faces, and later a stump of a topmast with a white ball on it, that slashed to and fro at the waves, went low and lower, and down. Thereafter there was something strange in his voice. Although steady, it was deep with mourning, and of a quality beyond oration or tears.

"Keep'er a little more south, Billie," said he.

"A little more south, sir," said the oiler in the stern.

A seat in this boat was not unlike a seat upon a bucking broncho, and by the same token a broncho is not much smaller. The craft pranced and reared and plunged like an animal. As each wave came, and she rose for it, she seemed like a horse making at a fence outrageously high. The manner of her scramble over these walls of water is a mystic thing, and, moreover, at the top of them were ordinarily these problems in white water, the foam racing down from the summit of each wave requiring a new leap, and a leap from the air. Then, after scornfully bumping a crest, she would slide and race and splash down a long incline, and arrive bobbing and nodding in front of the next menace.

A singular disadvantage of the sea lies in the fact that after successfully surmounting one wave you discover that there is another behind it just as important and just as nervously anxious to do something effective in the way of swamping boats. In a ten-foot dinghy one can get an idea of the resources of the sea in the line of waves that is not probable to the average experience, which is never at sea in a dinghy. As each slaty wall of water approached, it shut all else from the view of the men in the boat, and it was not difficult to imagine that this particular wave was the final outburst of the ocean, the last effort of the grim water. There was a terrible grace in the move of the waves, and they came in silence, save for the snarling of the crests.

In the wan light the faces of the men must have been gray. Their eyes must have glinted in strange ways as they gazed steadily astern. Viewed from a balcony, the whole thing would, doubtless, have been weirdly picturesque. But the men in the boat had no time to see it, and if they had had leisure, there were other things to occupy their minds. The sun swung steadily up the sky, and they knew it was broad day because the color of the sea changed from slate to emerald-green streaked with amber lights, and the foam was like tumbling snow. The process of the breaking day was unknown to them. They were aware only of this effect upon the color of the waves that rolled toward them.

In disjointed sentences the cook and the correspondent argued as to the difference between a life-saving station and a house of refuge. The cook had said: "There's a house of refuge just north of the Mosquito Inlet Light, and as soon as they see us they'll come off in their boat and pick us up."

"As soon as who see us?" said the correspondent.

"The crew," said the cook.

"Houses of refuge don't have crews," said the correspondent. "As I understand them, they are only places where clothes and grub are stored for the benefit of shipwrecked people. They don't carry crews."

"Oh, yes, they do," said the cook.

"No, they don't," said the correspondent.

"Well, we're not there yet, anyhow," said the oiler, in the stern.

"Well," said the cook, "perhaps it's not a house of refuge that I'm thinking of as being near Mosquito Inlet Light; perhaps it's a life-saving station."

"We're not there yet," said the oiler in the stern.

II

As the boat bounced from the top of each wave the wind tore through the hair of the hatless men, and as the craft plopped her stern down again the spray slashed past them. The crest of each of these waves was a hill, from the top of which the men surveyed for a moment a broad tumultuous expanse, shining and wind-riven. It was probably splendid, it was probably glorious, this play of the free sea, wild with lights of emerald and white and amber.

"Bully good thing it's an on-shore wind," said the cook. "If not, where would we be? Wouldn't have a show."

"That's right," said the correspondent.

The busy oiler nodded his assent.

Then the captain, in the bow, chuckled in a way that expressed humor, contempt, tragedy, all in one. "Do you think we've got much of a show now, boys?" said he.

Whereupon the three were silent, save for a trifle of hemming and hawing. To express any particular optimism at this time they felt to be childish and stupid, but they all doubtless possessed this sense of the situation in their minds. A young man thinks doggedly at such times. On the other hand, the ethics of their condition was decidedly against any open suggestion of hopelessness. So they were silent.

"Oh, well," said the captain, soothing his children, "we'll get ashore all right."

But there was that in his tone which made them think; so the oiler quoth, "Yes! if this wind holds."

The cook was bailing. "Yes! if we don't catch hell in the surf."

Canton-flannel gulls flew near and far. Sometimes they sat down on the sea, near patches of brown seaweed that rolled over the waves with a movement like carpets on a line in a gale. The birds sat comfortably in groups, and they were envied by some in the dinghy, for the wrath of the sea was no more to them than it was to a covey of prairie chickens a thousand miles inland. Often they came very close and stared at the men with black bead-like eyes. At these times they were uncanny and sinister in their unblinking scrutiny, and the men hooted angrily at them, telling them to be gone. One came, and evidently decided to alight on the top of the captain's head. The bird flew parallel to the boat and did not circle, but made short sidelong jumps in the air in chicken fashion. His black eyes were wistfully fixed upon the captain's head. "Ugly brute," said the oiler to the bird. "You look as if you were made with a jackknife." The cook and the correspondent swore darkly at the creature. The captain naturally wished to knock it away with the end of the heavy painter, but he did not dare do it, because anything resembling an emphatic gesture would have capsized this freighted boat; and so, with his open hand, the captain gently and carefully waved the gull away. After it had been discouraged from the pursuit the captain breathed easier on account of his hair, and others breathed easier because the bird struck their minds at this time as being somehow gruesome and ominous.

In the meantime the oiler and the correspondent rowed; and also they rowed. They sat together in the same seat, and each rowed an oar. Then the oiler took both oars; then the correspondent took both oars, then the oiler; then the correspondent. They rowed and they rowed. The very ticklish part of the business was when the time came for the reclining one in the stern to take his turn at the oars. By the very last star of truth, it is easier to steal eggs from under a hen than it was to change seats in the dinghy. First the man in the stern slid his hand along the thwart and moved with care, as if he were of Sèvres. Then the man in the rowing-seat slid his hand along the other thwart. It was all done with the most extraordinary care. As the two sidled past each other, the whole party kept watchful eyes on the coming wave, and the captain cried: "Look out, now! Steady, there!"

The brown mats of seaweed that appeared from time to time were like islands, bits of earth. They were travelling, apparently, neither one way nor the other. They were, to all intents, stationary. They informed the men in the boat that it was making progress slowly toward the land.

The captain, rearing cautiously in the bow after the dinghy soared on a great swell, said that he had seen the lighthouse at Mosquito Inlet. Presently the cook remarked that he had seen it. The correspondent was at the oars then, and for some reason he too wished to look at the lighthouse; but his back was toward the far shore, and the waves were important, and for some time he could not seize an opportunity to turn his head. But at last there came a wave more gentle than the others, and when at the crest of it he swiftly scoured the western horizon.

"See it?" said the captain.

"No," said the correspondent, slowly; "I didn't see anything."

"Look again," said the captain. He pointed. "It's exactly in that direction."

At the top of another wave the correspondent did as he was bid, and this time his eyes chanced on a small, still thing on the edge of the swaying horizon. It was precisely like the point of a pin. It took an anxious eye to find a lighthouse so tiny.

"Think we'll make it, Captain?"

"If this wind holds and the boat don't swamp, we can't do much else," said the captain.

The little boat, lifted by each towering sea and splashed viciously by the crests, made progress that in the absence of seaweed was not apparent to those in her. She seemed just a wee thing wallowing, miraculously top up, at the mercy of five oceans. Occasionally a great spread of water, like white flames, swarmed into her.

"Bail her, cook," said the captain, serenely.

"All right, Captain," said the cheerful cook.

III

It would be difficult to describe the subtle brotherhood of men that was here established on the seas. No one said that it was so. No one mentioned it. But it dwelt in the boat, and each man felt it warm him. They were a captain, an oiler, a cook, and a correspondent, and they were friends—friends in a more curiously iron-bound degree than may be common. The hurt captain, lying against the water jar in the bow, spoke always in a low voice and calmly; but he could never command a more ready and swiftly obedient crew than the motley three of the dinghy. It was more than a mere recognition of what was best for the common safety. There was surely in it a quality that was personal and heart-felt. And after this devotion to the commander of the boat, there was this comradeship, that the correspondent, for instance, who had been taught to be cynical of men, knew even at the time was the best experience of his life. But no one said that it was so. No one mentioned it.

"I wish we had a sail," remarked the captain. "We might try my overcoat on the end of an oar, and give you two boys a chance to rest." So the cook and the correspondent held the mast and spread wide the overcoat; the oiler steered; and the little boat made good way with her new rig. Sometimes the oiler had to scull sharply to keep a sea from breaking into the boat, but otherwise sailing was a success.

Meanwhile the lighthouse had been growing slowly larger. It had now almost assumed color, and appeared like a little gray shadow on the sky. The man at the oars could not be prevented from turning his head rather often to try for a glimpse of this little gray shadow.

At last, from the top of each wave, the men in the tossing boat could see land. Even as the lighthouse was an upright shadow on the sky, this land seemed but a long black shadow on the sea. It certainly was thinner than paper. "We must be about opposite New Smyrna," said the cook, who had coasted this shore often in schooners. "Captain, by the way, I believe they abandoned that life-saving station there about a year ago."

"Did they?" said the captain.

The wind slowly died away. The cook and the correspondent were not now obliged to slave in order to hold high the oar. But the waves continued their old impetuous swooping at the dinghy, and the little craft, no longer underway, struggled woundily over them. The oiler or the correspondent took the oars again.

Shipwrecks are *apropos* of nothing. If men could only train for them and have them occur when the men had reached pink condition, there would be less drowning at sea. Of the four in the dinghy none had slept any time worth mentioning for two days and two nights previous to embarking in the dinghy, and in the excitement of clambering about the deck of a foundering ship they had also forgotten to eat heartily.

For these reasons, and for others, neither the oiler nor the correspondent was fond of rowing at this time. The correspondent wondered ingenuously how in the name of all that was sane could there be people who thought it amusing to row a boat. It was not an amusement; it was a diabolical punishment, and even a genius of mental aberrations could never conclude that it was anything but a horror to the muscles and a crime against the back. He mentioned to the boat in general how the amusement of rowing struck him, and the weary-faced oiler smiled in full sympathy. Previously to the foundering, by the way, the oiler had worked a double watch in the engine-room of the ship.

"Take her easy now, boys," said the captain. "Don't spend yourselves. If we have to run a surf you'll need all your strength, because we'll sure have to swim for it. Take your time."

Slowly the land arose from the sea. From a black line it became a line of black and a line of white—trees and sand. Finally the captain said that he could make out a house on the shore. "That's the house of refuge, sure," said the cook. "They'll see us before long, and come out after us."

The distant lighthouse reared high. "The keeper ought to be able to make us out now, if he's looking through a glass," said the captain. "He'll notify the life-saving people."

"None of those other boats could have got ashore to give word of this wreck," said the oiler, in a low voice, "else the life-boat would be out hunting us."

Slowly and beautifully the land loomed out of the sea. The wind came again. It had veered from the northeast to the southeast. Finally a new sound struck the ears of the men in the boat. It was the low thunder of the surf on the shore. "We'll never be able to make the lighthouse now," said the captain. "Swing her head a little more north, Billie."

"A little more north, sir," said the oiler.

Whereupon the little boat turned her nose once more down the wind, and all but the oarsman watched the shore grow. Under the influence of this expansion doubt and direful apprehension were leaving the minds of the men. The management of the boat was still most absorbing, but it could not prevent a quiet cheerfulness. In an hour, perhaps, they would be ashore.

Their backbones had become thoroughly used to balancing in the boat, and they now rode this wild colt of a dinghy like circus men. The correspondent thought that he had been drenched to the skin, but happening to feel in the top pocket of his coat, he found therein eight cigars. Four of them were soaked with sea-water; four were perfectly scatheless. After a search, somebody produced three dry matches; and thereupon the four waifs rode impudently in their little boat and, with an assurance of an impending rescue shining in their eyes, puffed at the big cigars, and judged well and ill of all men. Everybody took a drink of water.

IV

"Cook," remarked the captain, "there don't seem to be any signs of life about your house of refuge."

"No," replied the cook. "Funny they don't see us!"

A broad stretch of lowly coast lay before the eyes of the men. It was of low dunes topped with dark vegetation. The roar of the surf was plain, and sometimes they could see the white lip of a wave as it spun up the beach. A tiny house was blocked out black upon the sky. Southward, the slim lighthouse lifted its little gray length.

Tide, wind, and waves were swinging the dinghy northward. "Funny they don't see us," said the men.

The surf's roar was here dulled, but its tone was nevertheless thunderous and mighty. As the boat swam over the great rollers the men sat listening to this roar. "We'll swamp sure," said everybody.

It is fair to say here that there was not a life-saving station within twenty miles in either direction; but the men did not know this fact, and in consequence they made dark and opprobrious remarks concerning the eyesight of the nation's life-savers. Four scowling men sat in the dinghy and surpassed records in the invention of epithets.

"Funny they don't see us."

The light-heartedness of a former time had completely faded. To their sharpened minds it was easy to conjure pictures of all kinds of incompetency and blindness and, indeed, cowardice. There was the shore of the populous land, and it was bitter and bitter to them that from it came no sign.

"Well," said the captain, ultimately, "I suppose we'll have to make a try for ourselves. If we stay out here too long, we'll none of us have strength left to swim after the boat swamps."

And so the oiler, who was at the oars, turned the boat straight for the shore. There was a sudden tightening of muscles. There was some thinking.

"If we don't all get ashore," said the captain—"if we don't all get ashore, I suppose you fellows know where to send news of my finish?"

They then briefly exchanged some addresses and admonitions. As for the reflections of the men, there was a great deal of rage in them. Perchance they might be formulated thus: "If I am going to be drowned—if I am going to be drowned—if I am going to be drowned, why, in the name of the seven mad gods who rule the sea, was I allowed to come thus far and contemplate sand and trees? Was I brought here merely to have my nose dragged away as I was about to nibble the sacred cheese of life? It is preposterous. If this old ninny-woman, Fate, cannot do better than this, she should be deprived of the management of men's fortunes. She is an old hen who knows not her intention. If she has decided to drown me, why did she not do it in the beginning and save me all this trouble? The whole affair is absurd. . . . But no; she cannot mean to drown me. She dare not drown me. She cannot drown me. Not after all this work." Afterward the man might have had an impulse to shake his fist at the clouds. "Just you drown me, now, and then hear what I call you!"

The billows that came at this time were more formidable. They seemed always just about to break and roll over the little boat in a turmoil of foam. There was a preparatory and long growl in the speech of them. No mind unused to the sea would have concluded that the dinghy could ascend these sheer heights in time. The shore was still afar. The oiler was a wily surf-man. "Boys," he said swiftly, "she won't live three minutes more, and we're too far out to swim. Shall I take her to sea again, Captain?"

"Yes; go ahead!" said the captain.

This oiler, by a series of quick miracles and fast and steady oarsmanship, turned the boat in the middle of the surf and took her safely to sea again.

There was a considerable silence as the boat bumped over the furrowed sea to deeper water. Then somebody in gloom spoke: "Well, anyhow, they must have seen us from the shore by now."

The gulls went in slanting flight up the wind toward the gray, desolate east. A squall, marked by dingy clouds and clouds brick-red, like smoke from a burning building, appeared from the southeast.

"What do you think of those life-saving people? Ain't they peaches?"

"Funny they haven't seen us."

"Maybe they think we're out here for sport! Maybe they think we're fishin'. Maybe they think we're damned fools."

It was a long afternoon. A changed tide tried to force them southward, but wind and wave said northward. Far ahead, where coast-line, sea, and sky formed their mighty angle, there were little dots which seemed to indicate a city on the shore.

"St. Augustine?"

The captain shook his head. "Too near Mosquito Inlet."

And the oiler rowed, and then the correspondent rowed; then the oiler rowed. It was a weary business. The human back can become the seat of more aches and pains than are registered in books for the composite anatomy of a regiment. It is a limited area, but it can become the theater of innumerable muscular conflicts, tangles, wrenches, knots, and other comforts.

"Did you ever like to row, Billie?" asked the correspondent.

"No," said the oiler; "hang it!"

When one exchanged the rowing-seat for a place in the bottom of the boat, he suffered a bodily depression that caused him to be careless of everything save an obligation to wiggle one finger. There was cold sea-water swashing to and fro in the boat, and he lay in it. His head, pillowed on a thwart, was within an inch of the swirl of a wave-crest, and sometimes a particularly obstreperous sea came inboard and drenched him once more. But these matters did not annoy him. It is almost certain that if the boat had capsized he would have tumbled comfortably out upon the ocean as if he felt sure that it was a great soft mattress.

"Look! There's a man on the shore!"

"Where?"

"There! See 'im? See 'im?"

"Yes, sure! He's walking along."

"Now he's stopped. Look! He's facing us!"

"He's waving at us!"

"So he is! By thunder!"

"Ah, now we're all right! Now we're all right! There'll be a boat out here for us in half an hour."

"He's going on. He's running. He's going up to that house there."

The remote beach seemed lower than the sea, and it required a searching glance to discern the little black figure. The captain saw a floating stick, and they rowed to it. A bath towel was by some weird chance in the boat, and, tying this on the stick, the captain waved it. The oarsman did not dare turn his head, so he was obliged to ask questions.

"What's he doing now?"

"He's standing still again. He's looking, I think. . . . There he goes again—toward the house. . . . Now he's stopped again."

"Is he waving at us?"

"No, not now; he was, though."

"Look! There comes another man!"

"He's running."

"Look at him go, would you!"

"Why, he's on a bicycle. Now he's met the other man. They're both waving at us. Look!"

"There comes something up the beach."

"What the devil is that thing?"

"Why, it looks like a boat."

"Why, certainly, it's a boat."

"No; it's on wheels."

"Yes, so it is. Well, that must be the life-boat. They drag them along shore on a wagon."

"That's the life-boat, sure."

"No, by God, it's—it's an omnibus."

"I tell you it's a life-boat."

"It is not! It's an omnibus. I can see it plain. See? One of these big hotel omnibuses."

"By thunder, you're right. It's an omnibus, sure as fate. What do you suppose they are doing with an omnibus? Maybe they are going around collecting the life-crew, hey?"

"That's it, likely. Look! There's a fellow waving a little black flag. He's standing on the steps of the omnibus. There come those other two fellows. Now they're all talking together. Look at the fellow with the flag. Maybe he ain't waving it!"

"That ain't a flag, is it? That's his coat. Why, certainly, that's his coat."

"So it is; it's his coat. He's taken it off and is waving it around his head. But would you look at him swing it!"

"Oh, say, there isn't any life-saving station there. That's just a winter-resort hotel omnibus that has brought over some of the boarders to see us drown."

"What's that idiot with the coat mean? What's he signaling, anyhow?"

"It looks as if he were trying to tell us to go north. There must be a life-saving station up there."

"No; he thinks we're fishing. Just giving us a merry hand. See? Ah, there, Willie!"

"Well, I wish I could make something out of those signals. What do you suppose he means?"

"He don't mean anything; he's just playing."

"Well, if he'd just signal us to try the surf again, or to go to sea and wait, or go north, or go south, or go to hell, there would be some reason in it. But look at him! He just stands there and keeps his coat revolving like a wheel. The ass!"

"There come more people."

"Now there's quite a mob. Look! Isn't that a boat?"

"Where? Oh, I see where you mean. No, that's no boat."

"That fellow is still waving his coat."

"He must think we like to see him do that. Why don't he quit it? It don't mean anything."

"I don't know. I think he is trying to make us go north. It must be that there's a life-saving station there somewhere."

"Say, he ain't tired yet. Look at 'im wave!"

"Wonder how long he can keep that up. He's been revolving his coat ever since he caught sight of us. He's an idiot. Why aren't they getting men to bring a boat out? A fishing-boat—one of those big yawls—could come out here all right. Why don't he do something?"

"Oh, it's all right now."

"They'll have a boat out here for us in less than no time, now that they've seen us."

A faint yellow tone came into the sky over the low land. The shadows on the sea slowly deepened. The wind bore coldness with it, and the men began to shiver.

"Holy smoke!" said one, allowing his voice to express his impious mood, "if we keep on monkeying out here! If we've got to flounder out here all night!"

"Oh, we'll never have to stay here all night! Don't you worry. They've seen us now, and it won't be long before they'll come chasing out after us."

The shore grew dusky. The man waving a coat blended gradually into this gloom, and it swallowed in the same manner the omnibus and the group of people. The spray, when it dashed uproariously over the side, made the voyagers shrink and swear like men who were being branded.

"I'd like to catch the chump who waved the coat. I feel like socking him one, just for luck."

"Why? What did he do?"

"Oh, nothing, but then he seemed so damned cheerful."

In the meantime the oiler rowed, and then the correspondent rowed, and then the oiler rowed. Gray-faced and bowed forward, they mechanically, turn by turn, plied the leaden oars. The form of the lighthouse had vanished from the southern horizon, but finally a pale star appeared, just lifting from the sea. The streaked saffron in the west passed before the all-merging darkness, and the sea to the east was black. The land had vanished, and was expressed only by the low and drear thunder of the surf.

"If I am going to be drowned—if I am going to be drowned—if I am going to be drowned, why, in the name of the seven mad gods who rule the sea, was I allowed to come thus far and contemplate sand and trees? Was I brought here merely to have my nose dragged away as I was about to nibble the sacred cheese of life?"

The patient captain, drooped over the water-jar, was sometimes obliged to speak to the oarsman.

"Keep her head up! Keep her head up!"

"Keep her head up, sir." The voices were weary and low.

This was surely a quiet evening. All save the oarsman lay heavily and listlessly in the boat's bottom. As for him, his eyes were just capable of noting the tall black waves that swept forward in a most sinister silence, save for an occasional subdued growl of a crest.

The cook's head was on a thwart, and he looked without interest at the water under his nose. He was deep in other scenes. Finally he spoke. "Billie," he murmured, dreamfully, "what kind of pie do you like best?"

V

"Pie!" said the oiler and the correspondent, agitatedly. "Don't talk about those things, blast you!"

"Well," said the cook, "I was just thinking about ham sandwiches, and—"

A night on the sea in an open boat is a long night. As darkness settled finally, the shine of the light, lifting from the sea in the south, changed to full gold. On the northern horizon a new light appeared, a small bluish gleam on the edge of the waters. These two lights were the furniture of the world. Otherwise there was nothing but waves.

Two men huddled in the stern, and distances were so magnificent in the dinghy that the rower was enabled to keep his feet partly warm by thrusting them under his companions. Their legs indeed extended far under the rowing-seat until they touched the feet of the captain forward. Sometimes, despite the efforts of the tired oarsman, a wave came piling into the boat, an icy wave of the night, and the chilling water soaked them anew. They would twist their bodies for a moment and groan, and sleep the dead sleep once more, while the water in the boat gurgled about them as the craft rocked.

The plan of the oiler and the correspondent was for one to row until he lost the ability, and then arouse the other from his seawater couch in the bottom of the boat.

The oiler plied the oars until his head drooped forward and the overpowering sleep blinded him; and he rowed yet afterward. Then he touched a man in the bottom of the boat, and called his name. "Will you spell me for a little while?" he said meekly.

"Sure, Billie," said the correspondent, awaking and dragging himself to a sitting position. They exchanged places carefully, and the oiler, cuddling down in the sea-water at the cook's side, seemed to go to sleep instantly.

The particular violence of the sea had ceased. The waves came without snarling. The obligation of the man at the oars was to keep the boat headed so that the tilt of the rollers would not capsize her, and to preserve her from filling when the crests rushed past. The black waves were silent and hard to be seen in the darkness. Often one was almost upon the boat before the oarsman was aware.

In a low voice the correspondent addressed the captain. He was not sure that the captain was awake, although this iron man seemed to be always awake. "Captain, shall I keep her making for that light north, sir?"

The same steady voice answered him. "Yes. Keep it about two points off the port bow."

The cook had tied a life-belt around himself in order to get even the warmth which this clumsy cork contrivance could donate, and he seemed almost stove-like when a rower, whose teeth invariably chattered wildly as soon as he ceased his labor, dropped down to sleep.

The correspondent, as he rowed, looked down at the two men sleeping underfoot. The cook's arm was around the oiler's shoulders, and, with their fragmentary clothing and haggard faces, they were the babes of the sea—a grotesque rendering of the old babes in the wood.

Later he must have grown stupid at his work, for suddenly there was a growling of water, and a crest came with a roar and a swash into the boat, and it was a wonder that it did not set the cook afloat in his life-belt. The cook continued to sleep, but the oiler sat up, blinking his eyes and shaking with the new cold.

"Oh, I'm awful sorry, Billie," said the correspondent, contritely.

"That's all right, old boy," said the oiler, and lay down again and was asleep.

Presently it seemed that even the captain dozed, and the correspondent thought that he was the one man afloat on all the ocean. The wind had a voice as it came over the waves, and it was sadder than the end.

There was a long, loud swishing astern of the boat, and a gleaming trail of phosphorescence, like blue flame, was furrowed on the black waters. It might have been made by a monstrous knife.

Then there came a stillness, while the correspondent breathed with open mouth and looked at the sea.

Suddenly there was another swish and another long flash of bluish light, and this time it was alongside the boat, and might almost have been reached with an oar. The correspondent saw an enormous fin speed like a shadow through the water, hurling the crystalline spray and leaving the long glowing trail.

The correspondent looked over his shoulder at the captain. His face was hidden, and he seemed to be asleep. He looked at the babes of the sea. They certainly were asleep. So, being bereft of sympathy, he leaned a little way to one side and swore softly into the sea.

But the thing did not then leave the vicinity of the boat. Ahead or astern, on one side or the other, at intervals long or short, fled the long sparkling streak, and there was to be heard the *whirroo* of the dark fin. The speed and power of the thing was greatly to be admired. It cut the water like a gigantic and keen projectile.

The presence of this biding thing did not affect the man with the same horror that it would if he had been a picnicker. He simply looked at the sea dully and swore in an undertone.

Nevertheless, it is true that he did not wish to be alone with the thing. He wished one of his companions to awake by chance and keep him company with it. But the captain hung motionless over the water-jar, and the oiler and the cook in the bottom of the boat were plunged in slumber.

VI

"If I am going to be drowned—if I am going to be drowned—if I am going to be drowned, why, in the name of the seven mad gods who rule the sea, was I allowed to come thus far and contemplate sand and trees?"

During this dismal night, it may be remarked that a man would conclude that it was really the intention of the seven mad gods to drown him, despite the abominable injustice of it. For it was certainly an abominable injustice to drown a man who had worked so hard, so hard. The man felt it would be a crime most unnatural. Other people had drowned at sea since galleys swarmed with painted sails, but still—

When it occurs to a man that nature does not regard him as important, and that she feels she would not maim the universe by disposing of him, he at first wishes to throw bricks at the temple, and he hates deeply the fact that there are no bricks and no temples. Any visible expression of nature would surely be pelleted with his jeers.

Then, if there be no tangible thing to hoot, he feels, perhaps, the desire to confront a personification and indulge in pleas, bowed to one knee, and with hands supplicant, saying, "Yes, but I love myself."

A high cold star on a winter's night is the word he feels that she says to him. Thereafter he knows the pathos of his situation.

The men in the dinghy had not discussed these matters, but each had, no doubt, reflected upon them in silence and according to his mind. There was seldom any expression upon their faces save the general one of complete weariness. Speech was devoted to the business of the boat.

To chime the notes of his emotion, a verse mysteriously entered the correspondent's head. He had even forgotten that he had forgotten this verse, but it suddenly was in his mind.

A soldier of the Legion lay dying in Algiers;
There was lack of woman's nursing,
    there was dearth of woman's tears;
But a comrade stood beside him,
    and he took the comrade's hand,
And he said, "I never more shall see
    my own, my native land."

In his childhood the correspondent had been made acquainted with the fact that a soldier of the Legion lay dying in Algiers, but he had never regarded it as important. Myriads of his schoolfellows had informed him of the soldier's plight, but the dinning had naturally ended by making him perfectly indifferent. He had never considered it his affair that a soldier of the Legion lay dying in Algiers, nor had it appeared to him as a matter for sorrow. It was less to him than the breaking of a pencil's point.

Now, however, it quaintly came to him as a human, living thing. It was no longer merely a picture of a few throes in the breast of a poet, meanwhile drinking tea and warming his feet at the grate; it was an actuality—stern, mournful, and fine.

The correspondent plainly saw the soldier. He lay on the sand with his feet out straight and still. While his pale left hand was upon his chest in an attempt to thwart the going of his life, the blood came between his fingers. In the far Algerian distance, a city of low square forms was set against a sky that was faint with the last sunset hues. The correspondent, plying the oars and dreaming of the slow and slower movements of the lips of the soldier, was moved by a profound and perfectly impersonal comprehension. He was sorry for the soldier of the Legion who lay dying in Algiers.

The thing which had followed the boat and waited had evidently grown bored at the delay. There was no longer to be heard the slash of the cutwater, and there was no longer the flame of the long trail. The light in the north still glimmered, but it was apparently no nearer to the boat. Sometimes the boom of the surf rang in the correspondent's ears, and he turned the craft seaward then and rowed harder. Southward, some one had evidently built a watch-fire on the beach. It was too low and too far to be seen, but it made a shimmering, roseate reflection upon the bluff in back of it, and this could be discerned from the boat. The wind came stronger, and sometimes a wave suddenly raged out like a mountain-cat, and there was to be seen the sheen and sparkle of a broken crest.

The captain, in the bow, moved on his water-jar and sat erect. "Pretty long night," he observed to the correspondent. He looked at the shore. "Those life-saving people take their time."

"Did you see that shark playing around?"

"Yes, I saw him. He was a big fellow, all right."

"Wish I had known you were awake."

Later the correspondent spoke into the bottom of the boat. "Billie!" There was a slow and gradual disentanglement. "Billie, will you spell me?"

"Sure," said the oiler.

As soon as the correspondent touched the cold, comfortable seawater in the bottom of the boat and had huddled close to the cook's life-belt he was deep in sleep, despite the fact that his teeth played all the popular airs. This sleep was so good to him that it was but a moment before he heard a voice call his name in a tone that demonstrated the last stages of exhaustion. "Will you spell me?"

"Sure, Billie."

The light in the north had mysteriously vanished, but the correspondent took his course from the wide-awake captain.

Later in the night they took the boat farther out to sea, and the captain directed the cook to take one oar at the stern and keep the boat facing the seas. He was to call out if he should hear the thunder of the surf. This plan enabled the oiler and the correspondent to get respite together. "We'll give those boys a chance to get into shape again," said the captain. They curled down and, after a few preliminary chatterings and trembles, slept once more the dead sleep. Neither knew they had bequeathed to the cook the company of another shark, or perhaps the same shark.

As the boat caroused on the waves, spray occasionally bumped over the side and gave them a fresh soaking, but this had no power to break their repose. The ominous slash of the wind and the water affected them as it would have affected mummies.

"Boys," said the cook, with the notes of every reluctance in his voice, "she's drifted in pretty close. I guess one of you had better take her to sea again." The correspondent, aroused, heard the crash of the toppled crests.

As he was rowing, the captain gave him some whiskey-and-water, and this steadied the chills out of him. "If I ever get ashore and anybody shows me even a photograph of an oar—"

At last there was a short conversation.

"Billie! . . . Billie, will you spell me?"

"Sure," said the oiler.

VII

When the correspondent again opened his eyes, the sea and the sky were each of the gray hue of the dawning. Later, carmine and gold was painted upon the waters. The morning appeared finally, in its splendor, with a sky of pure blue, and the sunlight flamed on the tips of the waves.

On the distant dunes were set many little black cottages, and a tall white windmill reared above them. No man, nor dog, nor bicycle appeared on the beach. The cottages might have formed a deserted village.

The voyagers scanned the shore. A conference was held in the boat. "Well," said the captain, "if no help is coming, we might better try a run through the surf right away. If we stay out here much longer we will be too weak to do anything for ourselves at all." The others silently acquiesced in this reasoning. The boat was headed for the beach. The correspondent wondered if none ever ascended the tall wind-tower, and if then they never looked seaward. This tower was a giant, standing with its back to the plight of the ants. It represented in a degree, to the correspondent, the serenity of nature amid the struggles of the individual—nature in the wind, and nature in the vision of men. She did not seem cruel to him then, nor beneficent, nor treacherous, nor wise. But she was indifferent, flatly indifferent. It is, perhaps, plausible that a man in this situation, impressed with the unconcern of the universe, should see the innumerable flaws of his life, and have them taste wickedly in his mind, and wish for another chance. A distinction between right and wrong seems absurdly clear to him, then, in this new ignorance of the grave-edge, and he understands that if he were given another opportunity he would mend his conduct and his words, and be better and brighter during an introduction or at a tea.

"Now, boys," said the captain, "she is going to swamp sure. All we can do is to work her in as far as possible, and then when she swamps, pile out and scramble for the beach. Keep cool now, and don't jump until she swamps sure."

The oiler took the oars. Over his shoulders he scanned the surf. "Captain," he said, "I think I'd better bring her about and keep her head-on to the seas and back her in."

"All right, Billie," said the captain. "Back her in." The oiler swung the boat then, and, seated in the stern, the cook and the correspondent were obliged to look over their shoulders to contemplate the lonely and indifferent shore.

The monstrous inshore rollers heaved the boat high until the men were again enabled to see the white sheets of water scudding up the slanted beach. "We won't get in very close," said the captain. Each time a man could wrest his attention from the rollers, he turned his glance toward the shore, and in the expression of the eyes during this contemplation there was a singular quality. The correspondent, observing the others, knew that they were not afraid, but the full meaning of their glances was shrouded.

As for himself, he was too tired to grapple fundamentally with the fact. He tried to coerce his mind into thinking of it, but the mind was dominated at this time by the muscles, and the muscles said they did not care. It merely occurred to him that if he should drown it would be a shame.

There were no hurried words, no pallor, no plain agitation. The men simply looked at the shore. "Now, remember to get well clear of the boat when you jump," said the captain.

Seaward the crest of a roller suddenly fell with a thunderous crash, and the long white comber came roaring down upon the boat.

"Steady now," said the captain. The men were silent. They turned their eyes from the shore to the comber and waited. The boat slid up the incline, leaped at the furious top, bounced over it, and swung down the long back of the wave. Some water had been shipped, and the cook bailed it out.

But the next crest crashed also. The tumbling, boiling flood of white water caught the boat and whirled it almost perpendicular. Water swarmed in from all sides. The correspondent had his hands on the gunwale at this time, and when the water entered at that place he swiftly withdrew his fingers, as if he objected to wetting them.

The little boat, drunken with this weight of water, reeled and snuggled deeper into the sea.

"Bail her out, cook! Bail her out!" said the captain.

"All right, Captain," said the cook.

"Now, boys, the next one will do for us sure," said the oiler. "Mind to jump clear of the boat."

The third wave moved forward, huge, furious, implacable. It fairly swallowed the dinghy, and almost simultaneously the men tumbled into the sea. A piece of life-belt had lain in the bottom of the boat, and as the correspondent went overboard he held this to his chest with his left hand.

The January water was icy, and reflected immediately that it was colder than he had expected to find it off the coast of Florida. This appeared to his dazed mind as a fact important enough to be noted at the time. The coldness of the water was sad; it was tragic. This fact was somehow mixed and confused with his opinion of his own situation, so that it seemed almost a proper reason for tears. The water was cold.

When he came to the surface he was conscious of little but the noisy water. Afterward he saw his companions in the sea. The oiler was ahead in the race. He was swimming strongly and rapidly. Off to the correspondent's left, the cook's great white and corked back bulged out of the water, and in the rear the captain was hanging with his one good hand to the keel of the overturned dinghy.

There is a certain immovable quality to a shore, and the correspondent wondered at it amid the confusion of the sea.

It seemed also very attractive; but the correspondent knew that it was a long journey, and he paddled leisurely. The piece of life-preserver lay under him, and sometimes he whirled down the incline of a wave as if he were on a hand-sled.

But finally he arrived at a place in the sea where travel was beset with difficulty. He did not pause swimming to inquire what manner of current had caught him, but there his progress ceased. The shore was set before him like a bit of scenery on a stage, and he looked at it and understood with his eyes each detail of it.

As the cook passed, much farther to the left, the captain was calling to him, "Turn over on your back, cook! Turn over on your back and use the oar."

"All right, sir." The cook turned on his back, and, paddling with an oar, went ahead as if he were a canoe.

Presently the boat also passed to the left of the correspondent, with the captain clinging with one hand to the keel. He would have appeared like a man raising himself to look over a board fence if it were not for the extraordinary gymnastics of the boat. The correspondent marvelled that the captain could still hold to it.

They passed on nearer to shore—the oiler, the cook, the captain—and following them went the water-jar, bouncing gaily over the seas.

The correspondent remained in the grip of this strange new enemy, a current. The shore, with its white slope of sand and its green bluff topped with little silent cottages, was spread like a picture before him. It was very near to him then, but he was impressed as one who, in a gallery, looks at a scene from Brittany or Algiers.

He thought: "I am going to drown? Can it be possible? Can it be possible? Can it be possible?" Perhaps an individual must consider his own death to be the final phenomenon of nature.

But later a wave perhaps whirled him out of this small deadly current, for he found suddenly that he could again make progress toward the shore. Later still he was aware that the captain, clinging with one hand to the keel of the dinghy, had his face turned away from the shore and toward him, and was calling his name. "Come to the boat! Come to the boat!"

In his struggle to reach the captain and the boat, he reflected that when one gets properly wearied drowning must really be a comfortable arrangement—a cessation of hostilities accompanied by a large degree of relief; and he was glad of it, for the main thing in his mind for some moments had been horror of the temporary agony; he did not wish to be hurt.

Presently he saw a man running along the shore. He was undressing with most remarkable speed. Coat, trousers, shirt, everything flew magically off him.

"Come to the boat!" called the captain.

"All right, Captain." As the correspondent paddled, he saw the captain let himself down to bottom and leave the boat. Then the correspondent performed his one little marvel of the voyage. A large wave caught him and flung him with ease and supreme speed completely over the boat and far beyond it. It struck him even then as an event in gymnastics and a true miracle of the sea. An overturned boat in the surf is not a plaything to a swimming man.

The correspondent arrived in water that reached only to his waist, but his condition did not enable him to stand for more than a moment. Each wave knocked him into a heap, and the undertow pulled at him.

Then he saw the man who had been running and undressing, and undressing and running, come bounding into the water. He dragged ashore the cook, and then waded toward the captain; but the captain waved him away and sent him to the correspondent. He was naked—naked as a tree in winter; but a halo was about his head, and he shone like a saint. He gave a strong pull, and a long drag, and a bully heave at the correspondent's hand. The correspondent, schooled in the minor formulae, said, "Thanks, old man." But suddenly the man cried, "What's that?" He pointed a swift finger. The correspondent said, "Go."

In the shallows, face downward, lay the oiler. His forehead touched sand that was periodically, between each wave, clear of the sea.

The correspondent did not know all that transpired afterward. When he achieved safe ground he fell, striking the sand with each particular part of his body. It was as if he had dropped from a roof, but the thud was grateful to him.

It seems that instantly the beach was populated with men with blankets, clothes, and flasks, and women with coffee-pots and all the remedies sacred to their minds. The welcome of the land to the men from the sea was warm and generous; but a still and dripping shape was carried slowly up the beach, and the land's welcome for it could only be the different and sinister hospitality of the grave.

When it came night, the white waves paced to and fro in the moonlight, and the wind brought the sound of the great sea's voice to the men on the shore, and they felt that they could then be interpreters.

STEPHEN CRANE
1871–1900

Stephen Crane, the youngest of a Methodist minister's fourteen children, was born in Newark but lived in a succession of New Jersey and New York towns before his father died in 1880.

A born writer, Crane gained early experience writing vacation news for his older brother Townley, who owned a news service in Asbury Park, New Jersey. While in college—he spent a single term each at Lafayette College and Syracuse University—Crane sold stories to the *Detroit Free Press*. However, he was never successful at routine reportage; his facts were bereft of the sense impressions that gave life to his work. Consequently, when he left college he was unable to satisfy editors who might have employed him full-time as a reporter. Reduced to doing free-lance work, he placed individual feature stories wherever he could, primarily in the New York *Tribune*, employment that proved neither lucrative nor satisfying. He lived in poverty for several years.

By 1891 Crane had written a draft of *Maggie: A Girl of the Streets*; when he was unable to secure a publisher for the novel even after revisions, he borrowed money from a brother and published the book himself. It did not sell, but it caught the attention of Hamlin Garland, who was so impressed that he helped young Crane find buyers for his stories.

The naturalism and impressionistic technique of *The Red Badge of Courage* (1895) did attract the public, whose warm acceptance of this book made Stephen Crane's reputation; thereafter *Maggie* found a publisher.

Crane's reporting of the Spanish-American and Greco-Turkish wars gave him material for several books, including *The Open Boat and Other Tales* (1898). The title story, reprinted here, was inspired by Crane's experience in a shipwreck off the Florida coast.

Youth

BY JOSEPH CONRAD

THIS COULD HAVE OCCURRED nowhere but in England, where men and sea interpenetrate, so to speak—the sea entering into the life of most men, and the men knowing something or everything about the sea, in the way of amusement, of travel, or of breadwinning.

We were sitting round a mahogany table that reflected the bottle, the claret-glasses, and our faces as we leaned on our elbows. There was a director of companies, an accountant, a lawyer, Marlow, and myself. The director had been a *Conway* boy, the accountant had served four years at sea, the lawyer—a fine crusted Tory, High Churchman, the best of old fellows, the soul of honour—had been chief officer in the P. & O. service in the good old days when mail-boats were square-rigged at least on two masts, and used to come down the China Sea before a fair monsoon with stun'-sails set alow and aloft. We all began life in the merchant service. Between the five of us there was the strong bond of the sea, and also the fellowship of the craft, which no amount of enthusiasm for yachting, cruising, and so on can give, since one is only the amusement of life and the other is life itself.

Marlow (at least I think that is how he spelt his name) told the story, or rather the chronicle, of a voyage:—

"Yes, I have seen a little of the Eastern seas; but what I remember best is my first voyage there. You fellows know there are those voyages that seem ordered for the illustration of life, that might stand for a symbol of existence. You fight, work, sweat, nearly kill yourself, sometimes do kill yourself, trying to accomplish something—and you can't. Not from any fault of yours. You simply can do nothing, neither great nor little—not a thing in the world—not even marry an old maid, or get a wretched 600-ton cargo of coal to its port of destination.

"It was altogether a memorable affair. It was my first voyage to the East, and my first voyage as second mate; it was also my skipper's first command. You'll admit it was time. He was sixty if a day; a little man, with a broad, not very straight back, with bowed shoulders and one leg more bandy than the other, he had that queer twisted-about appearance you see so often in men who work in the fields. He had a nutcracker face—chin and nose trying to come together over a sunken mouth—and it was framed in iron-gray fluffy hair, that looked like a chin-strap of cotton-wool sprinkled with coal-dust. And he had blue eyes in that old face of his, which were amazingly like a boy's, with that candid expression some quite common men preserve to the end of their days by a rare internal gift of simplicity of heart and rectitude of soul. What induced him to accept me was a wonder. I had come out of a crack Australian clipper, where I had been third officer, and he seemed to have a prejudice against crack clippers as aristocratic and high-toned. He said to me, 'You know, in this ship you will have to work.' I said I had to work in every ship I had ever been in. 'Ah, but this is different, and you gentlemen out of them big ships; . . . but there! I dare say you will do. Join to-morrow.'

"I joined to-morrow. It was twenty-two years ago; and I was just twenty. How time passes! It was one of the happiest days of my life. Fancy! Second mate for the first time—a really responsible officer! I wouldn't have thrown up my new billet for a fortune. The mate looked me over carefully. He was also an old chap, but of another stamp. He had a Roman nose, a snow-white, long beard, and his name was Mahon, but he insisted that it should be pronounced Mann. He was well connected; yet there was something wrong with his luck, and he had never got on.

"As to the captain, he had been for years in coasters, then in the Mediterranean, and last in the West Indian trade. He had never been round the Capes. He could just write a kind of sketchy hand, and didn't care for writing at all. Both were thorough good seamen of course, and between those two old chaps I felt like a small boy between two grandfathers.

"The ship also was old. Her name was the *Judea*. Queer name, isn't it? She belonged to a man Wilmer, Wilcox—some name like that; but he has been bankrupt and dead these twenty years or more, and his name don't matter. She had been laid up in Shadwell basin for ever so long. You may imagine her state. She was all rust, dust, grime—soot aloft, dirt on deck. To me it was like coming out of a palace into a ruined cottage. She was about 400 tons, had a primitive windlass, wooden latches to the doors, not a bit of brass about her, and a big square stern. There was on it, below her name in big letters, a lot of scrollwork, with the gilt off, and some sort of a coat of arms, with the motto 'Do or Die' underneath. I remember it took my fancy immensely. There was a touch of romance in it, something that made me love the old thing—something that appealed to my youth!

"We left London in ballast—sand ballast—to load a cargo of coal in a northern port for Bankok. Bankok! I thrilled. I had been six years at sea, but had only seen Melbourne and Sydney, very good places, charming places in their way—but Bankok!

"We worked out of the Thames under canvas, with a North Sea pilot on board. His name was Jermyn, and he dodged all day long about the galley drying his handkerchief before the stove. Apparently he never slept. He was a dismal man, with a perpetual tear sparkling at the end of his nose, who either had been in trouble, or was in trouble, or expected to be in trouble— couldn't be happy unless something went wrong. He mistrusted my youth, my common-sense, and my seamanship, and made a point of showing it in a hundred little ways. I dare say he was right. It seems to me I knew very little then, and I know not much more now; but I cherish a hate for that Jermyn to this day.

"We were a week working up as far as Yarmouth Roads, and then we got into a gale—the famous October gale of twenty-two years ago. It was wind, lightning, sleet, snow, and a terrific sea. We were flying light, and you may imagine how bad it was when I tell you we had smashed bulwarks and a flooded deck. On the second night she shifted her ballast into the lee bow, and by that time we had been blown off somewhere on the Dogger Bank. There was nothing for it but go below with shovels and try to right her, and there we were in that vast hold, gloomy like a cavern, the tallow dips stuck and flickering on the beams, the gale howling above, the ship tossing about like mad on her side; there we all were, Jermyn, the captain, every one, hardly able to keep our feet, engaged on that gravedigger's work, and trying to toss shovelfuls of wet sand up to windward. At every tumble of the ship you could see vaguely in the dim light men falling down with a great flour- ish of shovels. One of the ship's boys (we had two), impressed by the weird- ness of the scene, wept as if his heart would break. We could hear him blub- bering somewhere in the shadows.

"On the third day the gale died out, and by and by a north-country tug picked us up. We took sixteen days in all to get from London to the Tyne! When we got into dock we had lost our turn for loading, and they hauled us off to a tier where we remained for a month. Mrs. Beard (the captain's name was Beard) came from Colchester to see the old man. She lived on board. The crew of runners had left, and there remained only the officers, one boy and the steward, a mulatto who answered to the name of Abraham. Mrs. Beard was an old woman, with a face all wrinkled and ruddy like a winter apple, and the figure of a young girl. She caught sight of me once, sewing on a button, and insisted on having my shirts to repair. This was something different from the captains' wives I had known on board crack clippers. When I brought her the shirts, she said: 'And the socks? They want mending, I am sure, and John's—Captain Beard's—things are all in order now. I would be glad of something to do.' Bless the old woman. She overhauled my outfit for me, and meantime I read for the first time *Sartor Resartus* and Burnaby's *Ride to Khiva*. I didn't understand much of the first then; but I remember I preferred the soldier to the philosopher at the time; a preference which life has only confirmed. One was a man, and the other was either more—or less. However, they are both dead and Mrs. Beard is dead, and youth, strength, genius, thoughts, achievements, simple hearts— all die. . . . No matter.

"They loaded us at last. We shipped a crew. Eight able seamen and two boys. We hauled off one evening to the buoys at the dock-gates, ready to go out, and with a fair prospect of beginning the voyage next day. Mrs. Beard was to start for home by a late train. When the ship was fast we went to tea. We sat rather silent through the meal—Mahon, the old couple, and I. I finished first, and slipped away for a smoke, my cabin being in a deck-house just against the poop. It was high water, blowing fresh with a drizzle; the double dock-gates were opened, and the steam-colliers were going in and out in the darkness with their lights burning bright, a great plashing of propellers, rattling of winches, and a lot of hailing on the pierheads. I watched the procession of head-lights gliding high and of green lights gliding low in the night, when suddenly a red gleam flashed at me, vanished, came into view again, and remained. The fore-end of a steamer loomed up close. I shouted down the cabin, 'Come up, quick!' and then heard a startled voice saying afar in the dark, 'Stop her, sir.' A bell jingled. Another voice cried warningly, 'We are going right into that barque, sir.' The answer to this was a gruff 'All right,' and the next thing was a heavy crash as the steamer struck a glancing blow with the bluff of her bow about our fore-rigging. There was a moment of confusion, yelling, and running about. Steam roared. Then somebody was heard saying, 'All clear, sir.' . . . 'Are you all right?' asked the gruff voice. I had jumped forward to see the damage, and hailed back, 'I think so.' 'Easy astern,' said the gruff voice. A bell jingled. 'What steamer is that?' screamed Mahon. By that time she was no more to us than a bulky shadow manœuvring a little way off. They shouted at us some name—a woman's name, Miranda or Melissa—or some such thing. 'This means another month in this beastly hole,' said Mahon to me, as we peered with lamps about the splintered bulwarks and broken braces. 'But where's the captain?'

"We had not heard or seen anything of him all that time. We went aft to look. A doleful voice arose hailing somewhere in the middle of the dock, '*Judea* ahoy!' . . . How the devil did he get there? . . . 'Hallo!' we shouted. 'I am adrift in our boat without oars,' he cried. A belated water-man offered his services, and Mahon struck a bargain with him for half-a-crown to tow our skipper alongside; but it was Mrs. Beard that came up the ladder first. They had been floating about the dock in that mizzly cold rain for nearly an hour. I was never so surprised in my life.

"It appears that when he heard my shout 'Come up' he understood at once what was the matter, caught up his wife, ran on deck, and across, and down into our boat, which was fast to the ladder. Not bad for a sixty-year-old. Just imagine that old fellow saving heroically in his arms that old woman —the woman of his life. He set her down on a thwart, and was ready to climb back on board when the painter came adrift somehow, and away they went together. Of course in the confusion we did not hear him shouting. He looked abashed. She said cheerfully, 'I suppose it does not matter my losing the train now?' 'No, Jenny—you go below and get warm,' he growled. Then to us: 'A sailor has no business with a wife—I say. There I was, out of the ship. Well, no harm done this time. Let's go and look at what that fool of a steamer smashed.'

"It wasn't much, but it delayed us three weeks. At the end of that time, the captain being engaged with his agents, I carried Mrs. Beard's bag to the railway-station and put her all comfy into a third-class carriage. She lowered the window to say, 'You are a good young man. If you see John—Captain Beard—without his muffler at night, just remind him from me to keep his throat well wrapped up.' 'Certainly, Mrs. Beard,' I said. 'You are a good young man; I noticed how attentive you are to John—to Captain—' The train pulled out suddenly; I took my cap off to the old woman: I never saw her again. . . . Pass the bottle.

"We went to sea next day. When we made that start for Bankok we had been already three months out of London. We had expected to be a fortnight or so—at the outside.

"It was January, and the weather was beautiful—the beautiful sunny winter weather that has more charm than in the summer-time, because it is unexpected, and crisp, and you know it won't, it can't, last long. It's like a windfall, like a god-send, like an unexpected piece of luck.

"It lasted all down the North Sea, all down Channel; and it lasted till we were three hundred miles or so to the westward of the Lizards: then the wind went round to the sou'west and began to pipe up. In two days it blew a gale. The *Judea*, hove to, wallowed on the Atlantic like an old candle-box. It blew day after day: it blew with spite, without interval, without mercy, without rest. The world was nothing but an immensity of great foaming waves rushing at us, under a sky low enough to touch with the hand and dirty like a smoked ceiling. In the stormy space surrounding us there was as much flying spray as air. Day after day and night after night there was nothing round the ship but the howl of the wind, the tumult of the sea, the noise of water pouring over her deck. There was no rest for her and no rest for us. She tossed, she pitched, she stood on her head, she sat on her tail, she rolled, she groaned, and we had to hold on while on deck and cling to our bunks when below, in a constant effort of body and worry of mind.

"One night Mahon spoke through the small window of my berth. It opened right into my very bed, and I was lying there sleepless, in my boots, feeling as though I had not slept for years, and could not if I tried. He said excitedly—

"'You got the sounding-rod in here, Marlow? I can't get the pumps to suck. By God! It's no child's play.'

"I gave him the sounding-rod and lay down again, trying to think of various things—but I thought only of the pumps. When I came on deck they were still at it, and my watch relieved at the pumps. By the light of the lantern brought on deck to examine the sounding-rod I caught a glimpse of their weary, serious faces. We pumped all the four hours. We pumped all night, all day, all the week—watch and watch. She was working herself loose, and leaked badly—not enough to drown us at once, but enough to kill us with the work at the pumps. And while we pumped the ship was going from us piecemeal: the bulwarks went, the stanchions were torn out, the ventilators smashed, the cabin-door burst in. There was not a dry spot in the ship. She was being gutted bit by bit. The long-boat changed, as if by magic, into matchwood where she stood in her gripes. I had lashed her myself, and was rather proud of my handiwork, which had withstood so long the malice of the sea. And we pumped. And there was no break in the weather. The sea was white like a sheet of foam, like a caldron of boiling milk; there was not a break in the clouds, no—not the size of a man's hand—no, not for so much as ten seconds. There was for us no sky, there were for us no stars, no sun, no universe—nothing but angry clouds and an infuriated sea. We pumped watch and watch, for dear life; and it seemed to last for months, for years, for all eternity, as though we had been dead and gone to a hell for sailors. We forgot the day of the week, the name of the month, what year it was, and whether we had ever been ashore. The sails blew away, she lay broadside on under a weather-cloth, the ocean poured over her, and we did not care. We turned those handles, and had the eyes of idiots. As soon as we had crawled on deck I used to take a round turn with a rope about the men, the pumps, and the mainmast, and we turned, we turned incessantly, with the water to our waists, to our necks, over our heads. It was all one. We had forgotten how it felt to be dry.

"And there was somewhere in me the thought: By Jove! this is the deuce of an adventure—something you read about; and it is my first voyage as second mate—and I am only twenty—and here I am lasting it out as well as any of these men, and keeping my chaps up to the mark. I was pleased. I would not have given up the experience for worlds. I had moments of exultation. Whenever the old dismantled craft pitched heavily with her counter high in the air, she seemed to me to throw up, like an appeal, like a defiance, like a cry to the clouds without mercy, the words written on her stern: 'Judea, London. Do or Die.'

"O youth! The strength of it, the faith of it, the imagination of it! To me she was not an old rattle-trap carting about the world a lot of coal for a freight—to me she was the endeavour, the test, the trial of life. I think of her with pleasure, with affection, with regret—as you would think of someone dead you have loved. I shall never forget her. . . . Pass the bottle.

"One night when tied to the mast, as I explained, we were pumping on, deafened with the wind, and without spirit enough in us to wish ourselves dead, a heavy sea crashed aboard and swept clean over us. As soon as I got my breath I shouted, as in duty bound, 'Keep on, boys!' when suddenly I felt something hard floating on deck strike the calf of my leg. I made a grab at it and missed. It was so dark we could not see each other's faces within a foot—you understand.

"After that thump the ship kept quiet for a while, and the thing, whatever it was, struck my leg again. This time I caught it—and it was a saucepan. At first, being stupid with fatigue and thinking of nothing but the pumps, I did not understand what I had in my hand. Suddenly it dawned upon me, and I shouted, 'Boys, the house on deck is gone. Leave this, and let's look for the cook.'

"There was a deck-house forward, which contained the galley, the cook's berth, and the quarters of the crew. As we had expected for days to see it swept away, the hands had been ordered to sleep in the cabin—the only safe place in the ship. The steward, Abraham, however, persisted in clinging to his berth, stupidly, like a mule—from sheer fright I believe, like an animal that won't leave a stable falling in an earthquake. So we went to look for him. It was chancing death, since once out of our lashings we were as exposed as if on a raft. But we went. The house was shattered as if a shell had exploded inside. Most of it had gone overboard—stove, men's quarters, and their property, all was gone; but two posts, holding a portion of the bulkhead to which Abraham's bunk was attached, remained as if by a miracle. We groped in the ruins and came upon this, and there he was, sitting in his bunk, surrounded by foam and wreckage, jabbering cheerfully to himself. He was out of his mind; completely and for ever mad, with this sudden shock coming upon the fag-end of his endurance. We snatched him up, lugged him aft, and pitched him head-first down the cabin companion. You understand there was no time to carry him down with infinite precautions and wait to see how he got on. Those below would pick him up at the bottom of the stairs all right. We were in a hurry to go back to the pumps. That business could not wait. A bad leak is an inhuman thing.

"One would think that the sole purpose of that fiendish gale had been to make a lunatic of that poor devil of a mulatto. It eased before morning, and next day the sky cleared, and as the sea went down the leak took up. When it came to bending a fresh set of sails the crew demanded to put back—and really there was nothing else to do. Boats gone, decks swept clean, cabin gutted, men without a stitch but what they stood in, stores spoiled, ship strained. We put her head for home, and—would you believe it? The wind came east right in our teeth. It blew fresh, it blew continuously. We had to beat up every inch of the way, but she did not leak so badly, the water keeping comparatively smooth. Two hours' pumping in every four is no joke—but it kept her afloat as far as Falmouth.

"The good people there live on casualties of the sea, and no doubt were glad to see us. A hungry crowd of shipwrights sharpened their chisels at the sight of that carcass of a ship. And, by Jove! they had pretty pickings off us before they were done. I fancy the owner was already in a tight place. There were delays. Then it was decided to take part of the cargo out and caulk her topsides. This was done, the repairs finished, cargo reshipped; a new crew came on board, and we went out—for Bankok. At the end of a week we were back again. The crew said they weren't going to Bankok—a hundred and fifty days' passage—in a something hooker that wanted pumping eight hours out of the twenty-four; and the nautical papers inserted again the little paragraph: 'Judea. Barque. Tyne to Bankok; coals; put back to Falmouth leaky and with crew refusing duty.'

"There were more delays—more tinkering. The owner came down for a day, and said she was as right as a little fiddle. Poor old Captain Beard looked like the ghost of a Geordie skipper—through the worry and humiliation of it. Remember he was sixty, and it was his first command. Mahon said it was a foolish business, and would end badly. I loved the ship more than ever, and wanted awfully to get to Bankok. To Bankok! Magic name, blessed name. Mesopotamia wasn't a patch on it. Remember I was twenty, and it was my first second-mate's billet, and the East was waiting for me.

"We went out and anchored in the outer roads with a fresh crew—the third. She leaked worse than ever. It was as if those confounded shipwrights had actually made a hole in her. This time we did not even go outside. The crew simply refused to man the windlass.

"They towed us back to the inner harbour, and we became a fixture, a feature, an institution of the place. People pointed us out to visitors as "That 'ere barque that's going to Bankok—has been here six months—put back three times.' On holidays the small boys pulling about in boats would hail, 'Judea, ahoy!' and if a head showed above the rail shouted, 'Where you bound to?—Bankok?' and jeered. We were only three on board. The poor old skipper mooned in the cabin. Mahon undertook the cooking, and unexpectedly developed all a Frenchman's genius for preparing nice little messes. I looked languidly after the rigging. We became citizens of Falmouth. Every shopkeeper knew us. At the barber's or tobacconist's they asked familiarly, 'Do you think you will ever get to Bankok?' Meantime the owner, the underwriters, and the charterers squabbled amongst themselves in London, and our pay went on. . . . Pass the bottle.

"It was horrid. Morally it was worse than pumping for life. It seemed as though we had been forgotten by the world, belonged to nobody, would go nowhere; it seemed that, as if bewitched, we would have to live for ever and ever in that inner harbour, a derision and a byword to generations of long-shore loafers and dishonest boatmen. I obtained three months' pay and a five days' leave, and made a rush for London. It took me a day to get there and pretty well another to come back—but three months' pay went all the same. I don't know what I did with it. I went to a music-hall, I believe, lunched, dined, and supped in a swell place in Regent Street, and was back in time, with nothing but a complete set of Byron's works and a new railway rug to show for three months' work. The boatman who pulled me off to the ship said: 'Hallo! I thought you had left the old thing. *She* will never get to Bankok.' 'That's all *you* know about it,' I said scornfully—but I didn't like that prophecy at all.

"Suddenly a man, some kind of agent to somebody, appeared with full powers. He had grog-blossoms all over his face, an indomitable energy, and was a jolly soul. We leaped into life again. A hulk came alongside, took our cargo, and then we went into dry dock to get our copper stripped. No wonder she leaked. The poor thing, strained beyond endurance by the gale, had, as if in disgust, spat out all the oakum of her lower seams. She was re-caulked, new coppered, and made as tight as a bottle. We went back to the hulk and reshipped our cargo.

"Then, on a fine moonlight night, all the rats left the ship.

"We had been infested with them. They had destroyed our sails, consumed more stores than the crew, affably shared our beds and our dangers, and now, when the ship was made seaworthy, concluded to clear out. I called Mahon to enjoy the spectacle. Rat after rat appeared on our rail, took a last look over his shoulder, and leaped with a hollow thud into the empty hulk. We tried to count them, but soon lost the tale. Mahon said: 'Well, well! don't talk to me about the intelligence of rats. They ought to have left before, when we had that narrow squeak from foundering. There you have the proof how silly is the superstition about them. They leave a good ship for an old rotten hulk, where there is nothing to eat, too, the fools! . . . I don't believe they know what is safe or what is good for them, any more than you or I.'

"And after some more talk we agreed that the wisdom of rats had been grossly overrated, being in fact no greater than that of men.

"The story of the ship was known, by this, all up the Channel from

Land's End to the Forelands, and we could get no crew on the south coast. They sent us one all complete from Liverpool, and we left once more—for Bankok.

"We had fair breezes, smooth water right into the tropics, and the old *Judea* lumbered along in the sunshine. When she went eight knots everything cracked aloft, and we tied our caps to our heads; but mostly she strolled on at the rate of three miles an hour. What could you expect? She was tired—that old ship. Her youth was where mine is—where yours is— you fellows who listen to this yarn; and what friend would throw your years and your weariness in your face? We didn't grumble at her. To us aft, at least, it seemed as though we had been born in her, reared in her, had lived in her for ages, had never known any other ship. I would just as soon have abused the old village church at home for not being a cathedral.

"And for me there was also my youth to make me patient. There was all the East before me, and all life, and the thought that I had been tried in that ship and had come out pretty well. And I thought of men of old who, centuries ago, went that road in ships that sailed no better, to the land of palms, and spices, and yellow sands, and of brown nations ruled by kings more cruel than Nero the Roman, and more splendid than Solomon the Jew. The old barque lumbered on, heavy with her age and the burden of her cargo, while I lived the life of youth in ignorance and hope. She lumbered on through an interminable procession of days; and the fresh gilding flashed back at the setting sun, seemed to cry out over the darkening sea the words painted on her stern, '*Judea*, London. Do or Die.'

"Then we entered the Indian Ocean and steered northerly for Java Head. The winds were light. Weeks slipped by. She crawled on, do or die, and people at home began to think of posting us as overdue.

"One Saturday evening, I being off duty, the men asked me to give them an extra bucket of water or so—for washing clothes. As I did not wish to screw on the fresh-water pump so late, I went forward whistling, and with a key in my hand to unlock the forepeak scuttle, intending to serve the water out of a spare tank we kept there.

"The smell down below was as unexpected as it was frightful. One would have thought hundreds of paraffin-lamps had been flaring and smoking in that hole for days. I was glad to get out. The man with me coughed and said, 'Funny smell, sir.' I answered negligently, 'It's good for the health, they say,' and walked aft.

"The first thing I did was to put my head down the square of the midship ventilator. As I lifted the lid a visible breath, something like a thin fog, a puff of faint haze, rose from the opening. The ascending air was hot, and had a heavy, sooty, paraffiny smell. I gave one sniff, and put down the lid gently. It was no use choking myself. The cargo was on fire.

"Next day she began to smoke in earnest. You see it was to be expected, for though the coal was of a safe kind, that cargo had been so handled, so broken up with handling, that it looked more like smithy coal than anything else. Then it had been wetted—more than once. It rained all the time we were taking it back from the hulk, and now with this long passage it got heated, and there was another case of spontaneous combustion.

"The captain called us into the cabin. He had a chart spread on the table, and looked unhappy. He said, 'The coast of West Australia is near, but I mean to proceed to our destination. It is the hurricane month, too; but we will just keep her head for Bankok, and fight the fire. No more putting back anywhere, if we all get roasted. We will try first to stifle this 'ere damned combustion by want of air.'

"We tried. We battened down everything, and still she smoked. The smoke kept coming out through imperceptible crevices; it forced itself through bulkheads and covers; it oozed here and there and everywhere in slender threads, in an invisible film, in an incomprehensible manner. It made its way into the cabin, into the forecastle; it poisoned the sheltered places on the deck, it could be sniffed as high as the mainyard. It was clear that if the smoke came out the air came in. This was disheartening. This combustion refused to be stifled.

"We resolved to try water, and took the hatches off. Enormous volumes of smoke, whitish, yellowish, thick, greasy, misty, choking, ascended as high as the trucks. All hands cleared out aft. Then the poisonous cloud blew away, and we went back to work in a smoke that was no thicker now than that of an ordinary factory chimney.

"We rigged the force-pump, got the hose along, and by and by it burst. Well, it was as old as the ship—a prehistoric hose, and past repair. Then we pumped with the feeble head-pump, drew water with buckets, and in this way managed in time to pour lots of Indian Ocean into the main hatch. The bright stream flashed in sunshine, fell into a layer of white crawling smoke, and vanished on the black surface of coal. Steam ascended mingling with the smoke. We poured salt water as into a barrel without a bottom. It was our fate to pump in that ship, to pump out of her, to pump into her; and after keeping water out of her to save ourselves from being drowned, we frantically poured water into her to save ourselves from being burnt.

"And she crawled on, do or die, in the serene weather. The sky was a miracle of purity, a miracle of azure. The sea was polished, was blue, was pellucid, was sparkling like a precious stone, extending on all sides, all round to the horizon—as if the whole terrestrial globe had been one jewel, one colossal sapphire, a single gem fashioned into a planet. And on the lustre of the great calm waters the *Judea* glided imperceptibly, enveloped in languid and unclean vapours, in a lazy cloud that drifted to leeward, light and slow; a pestiferous cloud defiling the splendour of sea and sky.

"All this time of course we saw no fire. The cargo smouldered at the bottom somewhere. Once Mahon, as we were working side by side, said to me with a queer smile: 'Now, if she only would spring a tidy leak—like that time when we first left the Channel—it would put a stopper on this fire. Wouldn't it?' I remarked irrelevantly, 'Do you remember the rats?'

"We fought the fire and sailed the ship too as carefully as though nothing had been the matter. The steward cooked and attended on us. Of the other twelve men, eight worked while four rested. Everyone took his turn, captain included. There was equality, and if not exactly fraternity, then a deal of good feeling. Sometimes a man, as he dashed a bucketful of water down the hatchway, would yell out, 'Hurrah for Bankok!' and the rest laughed. But generally we were taciturn and serious—and thirsty. Oh! how thirsty! And we had to be careful with the water. Strict allowance. The ship smoked, the sun blazed. . . . Pass the bottle.

"We tried everything. We even made an attempt to dig down to the fire. No good, of course. No man could remain more than a minute below. Mahon, who went first, fainted there, and the man who went to fetch him out did likewise. We lugged them out on deck. Then I leaped down to show how easily it could be done. They had learned wisdom by that time, and contented themselves by fishing for me with a chain-hook tied to a broom-handle, I believe. I did not offer to go and fetch up my shovel, which was left down below.

"Things began to look bad. We put the long-boat into the water. The second boat was ready to swing out. We had also another, a 14-foot thing, on davits aft, where it was quite safe.

"Then, behold, the smoke suddenly decreased. We redoubled our efforts to flood the bottom of the ship. In two days there was no smoke at all. Everybody was on the broad grin. This was on a Friday. On Saturday no work, but sailing the ship, of course, was done. The men washed their clothes and their faces for the first time in a fortnight, and had a special dinner given them. They spoke of spontaneous combustion with contempt, and implied *they* were the boys to put out combustions. Somehow we all felt as though we each had inherited a large fortune. But a beastly smell of burning hung about the ship. Captain Beard had hollow eyes and sunken cheeks. I had never noticed so much before how twisted and bowed he was. He and Mahon prowled soberly about hatches and ventilators, sniffing. It struck me suddenly poor Mahon was a very, very old chap. As to me, I was as pleased and proud as though I had helped to win a great naval battle. O! Youth!

"The night was fine. In the morning a homeward-bound ship passed us hull down—the first we had seen for months; but we were nearing the land at last, Java Head being about 190 miles off, and nearly due north.

"Next day it was my watch on deck from eight to twelve. At breakfast the captain observed, 'It's wonderful how that smell hangs about the cabin.' About ten, the mate being on the poop, I stepped down on the main-deck for a moment. The carpenter's bench stood abaft the mainmast: I leaned against it sucking at my pipe, and the carpenter, a young chap, came to talk to me. He remarked, 'I think we have done very well, haven't we?' and then I perceived with annoyance the fool was trying to tilt the bench. I said curtly, 'Don't, Chips,' and immediately became aware of a queer sensation, of an absurd delusion—I seemed somehow to be in the air. I heard all round me like a pent-up breath released—as if a thousand giants simultaneously had said Phoo!—and felt a dull concussion which made my ribs ache suddenly. No doubt about it—I was in the air, and my body was describing a short parabola. But short as it was, I had the time to think several thoughts in, as far as I can remember, the following order: This can't be the carpenter—What is it?—Some accident—Submarine volcano?—Coals, gas!—By Jove! we are being blown up—Everybody's dead—I am falling into the after-hatch—I see fire in it.

"The coal-dust suspended in the air of the hold had glowed dull-red at the moment of the explosion. In the twinkling of an eye, in an infinitesimal fraction of a second since the first tilt of the bench, I was sprawling full length on the cargo. I picked myself up and scrambled out. It was quick like a rebound. The deck was a wilderness of smashed timber, lying crosswise like trees in a wood after a hurricane; an immense curtain of soiled rags waved gently before me—it was the main-sail blown to strips. I thought, The masts will be toppling over directly; and to get out of the way bolted on all-fours towards the poop-ladder. The first person I saw was Mahon, with eyes like saucers, his mouth open, and the long white hair standing straight on end round his head like a silver halo. He was just about to go down when the sight of the main-deck stirring, heaving up, and changing into splinters before his eyes, petrified him on the top step. I stared at him in unbelief, and he stared at me with a queer kind of shocked curiosity. I did not know that I had no hair, no eyebrows, no eyelashes, that my young moustache was burnt off, that my face was black, one cheek laid open, my nose cut, and my chin bleeding. I had lost my cap, one of my slippers, and my shirt was torn to rags. Of all this I was not aware. I was amazed to see the ship still afloat, the poop-deck whole—and, most of all, to see anybody alive. Also the peace of the sky and the serenity of the sea were distinctly surprising. I suppose I expected to see them convulsed with horror. . . . Pass the bottle.

"There was a voice hailing the ship from somewhere—in the air, in the sky—I couldn't tell. Presently I saw the captain—and he was mad. He asked me eagerly, 'Where's the cabin-table?' and to hear such a question was a frightful shock. I had just been blown up, you understand, and vibrated with that experience—I wasn't quite sure whether I was alive. Mahon began to stamp with both feet and yelled at him, 'Good God! don't you see the deck's blown out of her?' I found my voice, and stammered out as if conscious of some gross neglect of duty, 'I don't know where the cabin-table is.' It was like an absurd dream.

"Do you know what he wanted next? Well, he wanted to trim the yards. Very placidly, and as if lost in thought, he insisted on having the foreyard squared. 'I don't know if there's anybody alive,' said Mahon, almost tearfully. 'Surely,' he said, gently, 'there will be enough left to square the foreyard.'

"The old chap, it seems, was in his own berth winding up the chronometers, when the shock sent him spinning. Immediately it occurred to him—as he said afterwards—that the ship had struck something, and he ran out into the cabin. There, he saw, the cabin-table had vanished somewhere. The deck being blown up, it had fallen down into the lazarette of course. Where we had our breakfast that morning he saw only a great hole in the floor. This appeared to him so awfully mysterious, and impressed him so immensely, that what he saw and heard after he got on deck were mere trifles in comparison. And, mark, he noticed directly the wheel deserted and his barque off her course—and his only thought was to get that miserable, stripped, undecked, smouldering shell of a ship back again with her head pointing at her port of destination. Bankok! That's what he was after. I tell you this quiet, bowed, bandy-legged, almost deformed little man was immense in the singleness of his idea and in his placid ignorance of our agitation. He motioned us forward with a commanding gesture, and went to take the wheel himself.

"Yes; that was the first thing we did—trim the yards of that wreck! No one was killed, or even disabled, but everyone was more or less hurt. You should have seen them! Some were in rags, with black faces, like coal-heavers, like sweeps, and had bullet heads that seemed closely cropped, but were in fact singed to the skin. Others, of the watch below, awakened by being shot out from their collapsing bunks, shivered incessantly, and kept on groaning even as we went about our work. But they all worked. That crew of Liverpool hard cases had in them the right stuff. It's my experience they always have. It is the sea that gives it—the vastness, the loneliness surrounding their dark stolid souls. Ah! Well! we stumbled, we crept, we fell, we barked our shins on the wreckage, we hauled. The masts stood, but we did not know how much they might be charred down below. It was nearly calm, but a long swell ran from the west and made her roll. They might go at any moment. We looked at them with apprehension. One could not foresee which way they would fall.

"Then we retreated aft and looked about us. The deck was a tangle of planks on edge, of planks on end, of splinters, of ruined woodwork. The masts rose from that chaos like big trees above a matted undergrowth. The interstices of that mass of wreckage were full of something whitish, sluggish, stirring—of something that was like a greasy fog. The smoke of the invisible fire was coming up again, was trailing, like a poisonous thick mist in some valley choked with dead wood. Already lazy wisps were beginning to curl upwards amongst the mass of splinters. Here and there a piece of timber, stuck upright, resembled a post. Half of a fife-rail had been shot through the foresail, and the sky made a patch of glorious blue in the ignobly soiled canvas. A portion of several boards holding together had fallen across the rail, and one end protruded overboard, like a gangway leading upon nothing, like a gangway leading over the deep sea, leading to death—as if inviting us to walk the plank at once and be done with our ridiculous troubles. And still the air, the sky—a ghost, something invisible was hailing the ship.

"Someone had the sense to look over, and there was the helmsman, who had impulsively jumped overboard, anxious to come back. He yelled and swam lustily like a merman, keeping up with the ship. We threw him a rope, and presently he stood amongst us streaming with water and very crestfallen. The captain had surrendered the wheel, and apart, elbow on rail and chin in hand, gazed at the sea wistfully. We asked ourselves, What next? I thought, Now, this is something like. This is great. I wonder what will happen. O youth!

"Suddenly Mahon sighted a steamer far astern. Captain Beard said, 'We may do something with her yet.' We hoisted two flags, which said in the international language of the sea, 'On fire. Want immediate assistance.' The steamer grew bigger rapidly, and by and by spoke with two flags on her foremast, 'I am coming to your assistance.'

"In half an hour she was abreast, to windward, within hail, and rolling slightly, with her engines stopped. We lost our composure, and yelled all together with excitement, 'We've been blown up.' A man in a white helmet, on the bridge, cried, 'Yes! All right! all right!' and he nodded his head, and smiled, and made soothing motions with his hand as though at a lot of frightened children. One of the boats dropped in the water, and walked towards us upon the sea with her long oars. Four Calashes pulled a swinging stroke. This was my first sight of Malay seamen. I've known them since, but what struck me then was their unconcern: they came alongside, and even the bowman standing up and holding to our main-chains with the boat-hook did not deign to lift his head for a glance. I thought people who had been blown up deserved more attention.

"A little man, dry like a chip and agile like a monkey, clambered up. It was the mate of the steamer. He gave one look, and cried, 'O boys—you had better quit.'

"We were silent. He talked apart with the captain for a time—seemed to argue with him. Then they went away together to the steamer.

"When our skipper came back we learned that the steamer was the *Somerville*, Captain Nash, from West Australia to Singapore *via* Batavia with mails, and that the agreement was she should tow us to Anjer or Batavia, if possible, where we could extinguish the fire by scuttling, and then proceed on our voyage—to Bankok! The old man seemed excited. 'We will do it yet,' he said to Mahon, fiercely. He shook his fist at the sky. Nobody else said a word.

"At noon the steamer began to tow. She went ahead slim and high, and what was left of the *Judea* followed at the end of seventy fathom of tow-rope—followed her swiftly like a cloud of smoke with mastheads protruding above. We went aloft to furl the sails. We coughed on the yards, and were careful about the bunts. Do you see the lot of us there, putting a neat furl on the sails of that ship doomed to arrive nowhere? There was not a man who didn't think that at any moment the masts would topple over. From aloft we could not see the ship for smoke, and they worked carefully, passing the gaskets with even turns. 'Harbour furl—aloft there!' cried Mahon from below.

"You understand this? I don't think one of those chaps expected to get down in the usual way. When we did I heard them saying to each other, 'Well, I thought we would come down overboard, in a lump—sticks and all—blame me if I didn't.' 'That's what I was thinking to myself,' would answer wearily another battered and bandaged scarecrow. And, mind, these were men without the drilled-in habit of obedience. To an onlooker they would be a lot of profane scallywags without a redeeming point. What made them do it—what made them obey me when I, thinking consciously how fine it was, made them drop the bunt of the foresail twice to try and do it better? What? They had no professional reputation—no examples, no praise. It wasn't a sense of duty; they all knew well enough how to shirk, and laze, and dodge—when they had a mind to it—and mostly they had. Was it the two pounds ten-a-month that sent them there? They didn't think their pay half good enough. No; it was something in them, something inborn and subtle and everlasting. I don't say positively that the crew of a French or German merchantman wouldn't have done it, but I doubt whether it would have been done in the same way. There was a completeness in it, something solid like a principle, and masterful like an instinct—a disclosure of something secret—of that hidden something, that gift of good or evil that makes racial difference, that shapes the fate of nations.

"It was that night at ten that, for the first time since we had been fighting it, we. saw the fire. The speed of the towing had fanned the smouldering destruction. A blue gleam appeared forward, shining below the wreck of the deck. It wavered in patches, it seemed to stir and creep like the light of a glowworm. I saw it first, and told Mahon. 'Then the game's up,' he said. 'We had better stop this towing, or she will burst out suddenly fore and aft before we can clear out.' We set up a yell; rang bells to attract their attention; they towed on. At last Mahon and I had to crawl forward and cut the rope with an axe. There was no time to cast off the lashings. Red tongues could be seen licking the wilderness of splinters under our feet as we made our way back to the poop.

"Of course they very soon found out in the steamer that the rope was gone. She gave a loud blast of her whistle, her lights were seen sweeping in a wide circle, she came up ranging close alongside, and stopped. We were all in a tight group on the poop looking at her. Every man had saved a little bundle or a bag. Suddenly a conical flame with a twisted top shot up forward and threw upon the black sea a circle of light, with the two vessels side by side and heaving gently in its centre. Captain Beard had been sitting on the gratings still and mute for hours, but now he rose slowly and advanced in front of us, to the mizzen-shrouds. Captain Nash hailed: 'Come along! Look sharp. I have mail-bags on board. I will take you and your boats to Singapore.'

"'Thank you! No!' said our skipper. 'We must see the last of the ship.'

"'I can't stand by any longer,' shouted the other. 'Mails—you know.'

"'Ay! ay! We are all right.'

"'Very well! I'll report you in Singapore. . . . Good-bye!'

"He waved his hand. Our men dropped their bundles quietly. The steamer moved ahead, and passing out of the circle of light, vanished at once from our sight, dazzled by the fire which burned fiercely. And then I knew that I would see the East first as commander of a small boat. I thought it fine; and the fidelity to the old ship was fine. We should see the last of her. Oh, the glamour of youth! Oh, the fire of it, more dazzling than the flames of the burning ship, throwing a magic light on the wide earth, leaping audaciously to the sky, presently to be quenched by time, more cruel, more pitiless, more bitter than the sea—and like the flames of the burning ship surrounded by an impenetrable night.

"The old man warned us in his gentle and inflexible way that it was part of our duty to save for the underwriters as much as we could of the ship's gear. Accordingly we went to work aft, while she blazed forward to give us plenty of light. We lugged out a lot of rubbish. What didn't we save? An old barometer fixed with an absurd quantity of screws nearly cost me my life: a sudden rush of smoke came upon me, and I just got away in time. There were various stores, bolts of canvas, coils of rope; the poop looked like a marine bazaar, and the boats were lumbered to the gunwales. One would have thought the old man wanted to take as much as he could of his first command with him. He was very, very quiet, but off his balance evidently. Would you believe it? He wanted to take a length of old stream-cable and a kedge-anchor with him in the long-boat. We said, 'Ay, ay, sir,' deferentially, and on the quiet let the things slip overboard. The heavy medicine-chest went that way, two bags of green coffee, tins of paint—fancy, paint!—a whole lot of things. Then I was ordered with two hands into the boats to make a stowage and get them ready against the time it would be proper for us to leave the ship.

"We put everything straight, stepped the long-boat's mast for our skipper, who was to take charge of her, and I was not sorry to sit down for a moment. My face felt raw, every limb ached as if broken, I was aware of all my ribs, and would have sworn to a twist in the backbone. The boats, fast astern, lay in a deep shadow, and all around I could see the circle of the sea lighted by the fire. A gigantic flame arose forward straight and clear. It flared fierce, with noises like the whirr of wings, with rumbles as of thunder. There were cracks, detonations, and from the cone of flame the sparks flew upwards, as man is born to trouble, to leaky ships, and to ships that burn.

"What bothered me was that the ship, lying broadside to the swell and to such wind as there was—a mere breath—the boats would not keep astern where they were safe, but persisted, in a pig-headed way boats have, in getting under the counter and then swinging alongside. They were knocking about dangerously and coming near the flame, while the ship rolled on them, and, of course, there was always the danger of the masts going over the side at any moment. I and my two boat-keepers kept them off as best we could, with oars and boat-hooks; but to be constantly at it became exasperating, since there was no reason why we should not leave at once. We could not see those on board, nor could we imagine what caused the delay. The boat-keepers were swearing feebly, and I had not only my share of the work but also had to keep at it two men who showed a constant inclination to lay themselves down and let things slide.

"At last I hailed, 'On deck there,' and someone looked over. 'We're ready here,' I said. The head disappeared, and very soon popped up again. 'The captain says, All right, sir, and to keep the boats well clear of the ship.'

"Half an hour passed. Suddenly there was a frightful racket, rattle, clanking of chain, hiss of water, and millions of sparks flew up into the shivering column of smoke that stood leaning slightly above the ship. The cat-heads had burned away, and the two red-hot anchors had gone to the bottom, tearing out after them two hundred fathom of red-hot chain. The ship trembled, the mass of flame swayed as if ready to collapse, and the fore top-gallant-mast fell. It darted down like an arrow of fire, shot under, and instantly leaping up within an oar's-length of the boats, floated quietly, very black on the luminous sea. I hailed the deck again. After some time a man in an unexpectedly cheerful but also muffled tone, as though he had been trying to speak with his mouth shut, informed me, 'Coming directly, sir,' and vanished. For a long time I heard nothing but the whirr and roar of the fire. There were also whistling sounds. The boats jumped, tugged at the painters, ran at each other playfully, knocked their sides together, or, do what we would, swung in a bunch against the ship's side. I couldn't stand it any longer, and swarming up a rope, clambered aboard over the stern.

"It was as bright as day. Coming up like this, the sheet of fire facing me was a terrifying sight, and the heat seemed hardly bearable at first. On a settee cushion dragged out of the cabin Captain Beard, his legs drawn up and one arm under his head, slept with the light playing on him. Do you know what the rest were busy about? They were sitting on deck right aft, round an open case, eating bread and cheese and drinking bottled stout.

"On the background of flames twisting in fierce tongues above their heads they seemed at home like salamanders, and looked like a band of desperate pirates. The fire sparkled in the whites of their eyes, gleamed on patches of white skin seen through the torn shirts. Each had the marks as of a battle about him—bandaged heads, tied-up arms, a strip of dirty rag round a knee—and each man had a bottle between his legs and a chunk of cheese in his hand. Mahon got up. With his handsome and disreputable head, his hooked profile, his long white beard, and with an uncorked bottle in his hand, he resembled one of those reckless sea-robbers of old making merry amidst violence and disaster. 'The last meal on board,' he explained solemnly. 'We had nothing to eat all day, and it was no use leaving all this.' He flourished the bottle and indicated the sleeping skipper. 'He said he couldn't swallow anything, so I got him to lie down,' he went on; and as I stared, 'I don't know whether you are aware, young fellow, the man had no sleep to speak of for days—and there will be dam' little sleep in the boats.' 'There will be no boats by and by if you fool about much longer,' I said, indignantly. I walked up to the skipper and shook him by the shoulder. At last he opened his eyes, but did not move. 'Time to leave her, sir,' I said quietly.

"He got up painfully, looked at the flames, at the sea sparkling round the ship, and black, black as ink farther away; he looked at the stars shining dim through a thin veil of smoke in a sky black, black as Erebus.

"'Youngest first,' he said.

"And the ordinary seaman, wiping his mouth with the back of his hand, got up, clambered over the taffrail, and vanished. Others followed. One, on the point of going over, stopped short to drain his bottle, and with a great swing of his arm flung it at the fire. 'Take this!' he cried.

"The skipper lingered disconsolately, and we left him to commune alone for a while with his first command. Then I went up again and brought him away at last. It was time. The ironwork on the poop was hot to the touch.

"Then the painter of the long-boat was cut, and the three boats, tied together, drifted clear of the ship. It was just sixteen hours after the explosion when we abandoned her. Mahon had charge of the second boat, and I had the smallest—the 14-foot thing. The long-boat would have taken the lot of us; but the skipper said we must save as much property as we could—for the underwriters—and so I got my first command. I had two men with me, a bag of biscuits, a few tins of meat, and a breaker of water. I was ordered to keep close to the long-boat, that in case of bad weather we might be taken into her.

"And do you know that I thought? I thought I would part company as soon as I could. I wanted to have my first command all to myself. I wasn't going to sail in a squadron if there were a chance for independent cruising. I would make land by myself. I would beat the other boats. Youth! All youth! The silly, charming, beautiful youth.

"But we did not make a start at once. We must see the last of the ship. And so the boats drifted about that night, heaving and setting on the swell. The men dozed, waked, sighed, groaned. I looked at the burning ship.

"Between the darkness of earth and heaven she was burning fiercely upon a disc of purple sea shot by the blood-red play of gleams; upon a disc of water glittering and sinister. A high, clear flame, an immense and lonely flame, ascended from the ocean, and from its summit the black smoke poured continuously at the sky. She burned furiously; mournful and imposing like a funeral pile kindled in the night, surrounded by the sea, watched over by the stars. A magnificent death had come like a grace, like a gift, like a reward to that old ship at the end of her laborious days. The surrender of her weary ghost to the keeping of stars and sea was stirring like the sight of a glorious triumph. The masts fell just before daybreak, and for a moment there was a burst and turmoil of sparks that seemed to fill with flying fire the night patient and watchful, the vast night lying silent upon the sea. At daylight she was only a charred shell, floating still under a cloud of smoke and bearing a glowing mass of coal within.

"Then the oars were got out, and the boats forming in a line moved round her remains as if in procession—the long-boat leading. As we pulled across her stern a slim dart of fire shot out viciously at us, and suddenly she went down, head first, in a great hiss of steam. The unconsumed stern was the last to sink; but the paint had gone, had cracked, had peeled off, and there were no letters, there was no word, no stubborn device that was like her soul, to flash at the rising sun her creed and her name.

"We made our way north. A breeze sprang up, and about noon all the boats came together for the last time. I had no mast or sail in mine, but I made a mast out of a spare oar and hoisted a boat-awning for a sail, with a boat-hook for a yard. She was certainly overmasted, but I had the satisfaction of knowing that with the wind aft I could beat the other two. I had to wait for them. Then we all had a look at the captain's chart, and, after a sociable meal of hard bread and water, got our last instructions. These were simple: steer north, and keep together as much as possible. 'Be careful with that jury-rig, Marlow,' said the captain; and Mahon, as I sailed proudly past his boat, wrinkled his curved nose and hailed, 'You will sail that ship of yours under water, if you don't look out, young fellow.' He was a malicious old man—and may the deep sea where he sleeps now rock him gently, rock him tenderly to the end of time!

"Before sunset a thick rain-squall passed over the two boats, which were far astern, and that was the last I saw of them for a time. Next day I sat steering my cockle-shell—my first command—with nothing but water and sky around me. I did sight in the afternoon the upper sails of a ship far away, but said nothing, and my men did not notice her. You see I was afraid she might be homeward bound, and I had no mind to turn back from the portals of the East. I was steering for Java—another blessed name—like Bankok, you know. I steered many days.

"I need not tell you what it is to be knocking about in an open boat. I remember nights and days of calm, when we pulled, we pulled, and the boat seemed to stand still, as if bewitched within the circle of the sea horizon. I remember the heat, the deluge of rain-squalls that kept us baling for dear life (but filled our water-cask), and I remember sixteen hours on end with a mouth dry as a cinder and a steering-oar over the stern to keep my first command head on to a breaking sea. I did not know how good a man I was till then. I remember the drawn faces, the dejected figures of my two men, and I remember my youth and the feeling that will never come back any more—the feeling that I could last for ever, outlast the sea, the earth, and all men; the deceitful feeling that lures us on to joys, to perils, to love, to vain effort—to death; the triumphant conviction of strength, the heat of life in the handful of dust, the glow in the heart that with every year grows dim, grows cold, grows small, and expires—and expires, too soon, too soon—before life itself.

"And this is how I see the East. I have seen its secret places and have looked into its very soul; but now I see it always from a small boat, a high outline of mountains, blue and afar in the morning; like faint mist at noon; a jagged wall of purple at sunset. I have the feel of the oar in my hand, the vision of a scorching blue sea in my eyes. And I see a bay, a wide bay, smooth as glass and polished like ice, shimmering in the dark. A red light burns far off upon the gloom of the land, and the night is soft and warm. We drag at the oars with aching arms, and suddenly a puff of wind, a puff faint and tepid and laden with strange odours of blossoms, of aromatic wood, comes out of the still night—the first sigh of the East on my face. That I can never forget. It was impalpable and enslaving, like a charm, like a whispered promise of mysterious delight.

"We had been pulling this finishing spell for eleven hours. Two pulled, and he whose turn it was to rest sat at the tiller. We had made out the red light in that bay and steered for it, guessing it must mark some small coasting port. We passed two vessels, outlandish and high-sterned, sleeping at anchor, and, approaching the light, now very dim, ran the boat's nose against the end of a jutting wharf. We were blind with fatigue. My men dropped the oars and fell off the thwarts as if dead. I made fast to a pile. A current rippled softly. The scented obscurity of the shore was grouped into vast masses, a density of colossal clumps of vegetation, probably—mute and fantastic shapes. And at their foot the semicircle of a beach gleamed faintly, like an illusion. There was not a light, not a stir, not a sound. The mysterious East faced me, perfumed like a flower, silent like death, dark like a grave.

"And I sat weary beyond expression, exulting like a conqueror, sleepless and entranced as if before a profound, a fateful enigma.

"A splashing of oars, a measured dip reverberating on the level of water, intensified by the silence of the shore into loud claps, made me jump up. A boat, a European boat, was coming in. I invoked the name of the dead; I hailed: *Judea* ahoy! A thin shout answered.

"It was the captain. I had beaten the flagship by three hours, and I was glad to hear the old man's voice again, tremulous and tired. 'Is it you, Marlow?' 'Mind the end of that jetty, sir,' I cried.

"He approached cautiously, and brought up with the deep-sea lead-line which we had saved—for the underwriters. I eased my painter and fell alongside. He sat, a broken figure at the stern, wet with dew, his hand clasped in his lap. His men were asleep already. 'I had a terrible time of it,' he murmured. 'Mahon is behind—not very far.' We conversed in whispers, in low whispers, as if afraid to wake up the land. Guns, thunder, earthquakes would not have awakened the men just then.

"Looking round as we talked, I saw away at sea a bright light travelling in the night. 'There's a steamer passing the bay,' I said. She was not passing, she was entering, and she even came close and anchored. 'I wish,' said the old man, 'you would find out whether she is English. Perhaps they could give us a passage somewhere.' He seemed nervously anxious. So by dint of punching and kicking I started one of my men into a state of somnambulism, and giving him an oar, took another and pulled towards the lights of the steamer.

"There was a murmur of voices in her, metallic hollow clangs of the engine-room, footsteps on the deck. Her ports shone, round like dilated eyes. Shapes moved about, and there was a shadowy man high up on the bridge. He heard my oars.

"And then, before I could open my lips, the East spoke to me, but it was in a Western voice. A torrent of words was poured into the enigmatical, the fateful silence; outlandish, angry words, mixed with words and even whole sentences of good English, less strange but even more surprising. The voice swore and cursed violently; it riddled the solemn peace of the bay by a volley of abuse. It began by calling me Pig, and from that went crescendo into unmentionable adjectives—in English. The man up there raged aloud in two languages, and with a sincerity in his fury that almost convinced me I had, in some way, sinned against the harmony of the universe. I could hardly see him, but began to think he would work himself into a fit.

"Suddenly he ceased, and I could hear him snorting and blowing like a porpoise. I said—

"'What steamer is this, pray?'

"'Eh? What's this? And who are you?'

"'Castaway crew of an English barque burnt at sea. We came here to-night. I am the second mate. The captain is in the long-boat, and wishes to know if you would give us a passage somewhere.'

"'Oh, my goodness! I say. . . . This is the *Celestial* from Singapore on her return trip. I'll arrange with your captain in the morning, . . . and, . . . I say, . . . did you hear me just now?'

"'I should think the whole bay heard you.'

"'I thought you were a shore-boat. Now, look here—this infernal lazy scoundrel of a caretaker has gone to sleep again—curse him. The light is out, and I nearly ran foul of the end of this damned jetty. This is the third time he plays me this trick. Now, I ask you, can anybody stand this kind of thing? It's enough to drive a man out of his mind. I'll report him. . . . I'll get the Assistant Resident to give him the sack, by. . . ! See—there's no light. It's out, isn't it? I take you to witness the light's out. There should be a light, you know. A red light on the—'

"'There was a light,' I said mildly.

"'But it's out, man! What's the use of talking like this? You can see for yourself it's out—don't you? If you had to take a valuable steamer along this God-forsaken coast you would want a light, too. I'll kick him from end to end of his miserable wharf. You'll see if I don't. I will—'

"'So I may tell my captain you'll take us?' I broke in.

"'Yes, I'll take you. Good-night,' he said, brusquely.

"I pulled back, made fast again to the jetty, and then went to sleep at last. I had faced the silence of the East. I had heard some of its language. But when I opened my eyes again the silence was as complete as though it had never been broken. I was lying in a flood of light, and the sky had never looked so far, so high, before. I opened my eyes and lay without moving.

"And then I saw the men of the East—they were looking at me. The whole length of the jetty was full of people. I saw brown, bronze, yellow faces, the black eyes, the glitter, the colour of an Eastern crowd. And all these beings stared without a murmur, without a sigh, without a movement. They stared down at the boats, at the sleeping men who at night had come to them from the sea. Nothing moved. The fronds of palms stood still against the sky. Not a branch stirred along the shore, and the brown roofs of hidden houses peeped through the green foliage, through the big leaves that hung shining and still like leaves forged of heavy metal. This was the East of the ancient navigators, so old, so mysterious, resplendent and sombre, living and unchanged, full of danger and promise. And these were the men. I sat up suddenly. A wave of movement passed through the crowd from end to end, passed along the heads, swayed the bodies, ran along the jetty like a ripple on the water, like a breath of wind on a field—and all was still again. I see it now—the wide sweep of the bay, the glittering sands, the wealth of green infinite and varied, the sea blue like the sea of a dream, the crowd of attentive faces, the blaze of vivid colour—the water reflecting it all, the curve of the shore, the jetty, the high-sterned outlandish craft floating still, and the three boats with the tired men from the West sleeping, unconscious of the land and the people and of the violence of sunshine. They slept thrown across the thwarts, curled on bottom-boards, in the careless attitudes of death. The head of the old skipper, leaning back in the stern of the long-boat, had fallen on his breast, and he looked as though he would never wake. Farther out old Mahon's face was upturned to the sky, with the long white beard spread out on his breast, as though he had been shot where he sat at the tiller; and a man, all in a heap in the bows of the boat, slept with both arms embracing the stem-head and with his cheek laid on the gun-wale. The East looked at them without a sound.

"I have known its fascination since; I have seen the mysterious shores, the still water, the lands of brown nations, where a stealthy Nemesis lies in wait, pursues, overtakes so many of the conquering race, who are proud of their wisdom, of their knowledge, of their strength. But for me all the East is contained in that vision of my youth. It is all in that moment when I opened my young eyes on it. I came upon it from a tussle with the sea—and I was young—and I saw it looking at me. And this is all that is left of it! Only a moment; a moment of strength, of romance, of glamour—of youth! . . . A flick of sunshine upon a strange shore, the time to remember, the time for a sigh, and—good-bye!—Night—Good-bye . . . !"

He drank.

"Ah! The good old time—the good old time. Youth and the sea. Glamour and the sea! The good, strong sea, the salt, bitter sea, that could whisper to you and roar at you and knock your breath out of you."

He drank again.

"By all that's wonderful it is the sea, I believe, the sea itself—or is it youth alone? Who can tell? But you here—you all had something out of life: money, love—whatever one gets on shore—and, tell me, wasn't that the best time, that time when we were young at sea; young and had nothing, on the sea that gives nothing, except hard knocks—and sometimes a chance to feel your strength—that only—what you all regret?"

And we all nodded at him: the man of finance, the man of accounts, the man of law, we all nodded at him over the polished table that like a still sheet of brown water reflected our faces, lined, wrinkled; our faces marked by toil, by deceptions, by success, by love; our weary eyes looking still, looking always, looking anxiously for something out of life, that while it is expected is already gone—has passed unseen, in a sigh, in a flash—together with the youth, with the strength, with the romance of illusions.

The Secret Sharer

BY JOSEPH CONRAD

One

ON MY RIGHT HAND there were lines of fishing stakes resembling a mysterious system of half-submerged bamboo fences, incomprehensible in its division of the domain of tropical fishes, and crazy of aspect as if abandoned forever by some nomad tribe of fishermen now gone to the other end of the ocean; for there was no sign of human habitation as far as the eye could reach. To the left a group of barren islets, suggesting ruins of stone walls, towers, and blockhouses, had its foundations set in a blue sea that itself looked solid, so still and stable did it lie below my feet; even the track of light from the westering sun shone smoothly, without that animated glitter which tells of an imperceptible ripple. And when I turned my head to take a parting glance at the tug which had just left us anchored outside the bar, I saw the straight line of the flat shore joined to the stable sea, edge to edge, with a perfect and unmarked closeness, in one leveled floor half brown, half blue under the enormous dome of the sky. Corresponding in their insignificance to the islets of the sea, two small clumps of trees, one on each side of the only fault in the impeccable joint, marked the mouth of the river Meinam we had just left on the first preparatory stage of our homeward journey; and, far back on the inland level, a larger and loftier mass, the grove surrounding the great Paknam pagoda, was the only thing on which the eye could rest from the vain task of exploring the monotonous sweep of the horizon. Here and there gleams as of a few scattered pieces of silver marked the windings of the great river; and on the nearest of them, just within the bar, the tug steaming right into the land became lost to my sight, hull and funnel and masts, as though the impassive earth had swallowed her up without an effort, without a tremor. My eye followed the light cloud of her smoke, now here, now there, above the plain, according to the devious curves of the stream, but always fainter and farther away, till I lost it at last behind the miter-shaped hill of the great pagoda. And then I was left alone with my ship, anchored at the head of the Gulf of Siam.

She floated at the starting point of a long journey, very still in an immense stillness, the shadows of her spars flung far to the eastward by the setting sun. At that moment I was alone on her decks. There was not a sound in her—and around us nothing moved, nothing lived, not a canoe on the water, not a bird in the air, not a cloud in the sky. In this breath-less pause at the threshold of a long passage we seemed to be measuring our fitness for a long and arduous enterprise, the appointed task of both our existences to be carried out, far from all human eyes, with only sky and sea for spectators and for judges.

There must have been some glare in the air to interfere with one's sight, because it was only just before the sun left us that my roaming eyes made out beyond the highest ridges of the principal islet of the group something which did away with the solemnity of perfect solitude. The tide of darkness flowed on swiftly; and with tropical suddenness a swarm of stars came out above the shadowy earth, while I lingered yet, my hand resting lightly on my ship's rail as if on the shoulder of a trusted friend. But, with all that multitude of celestial bodies staring down at one, the comfort of quiet com-munion with her was gone for good. And there were also disturbing sounds by this time—voices, footsteps forward; the steward flitted along the main-deck, a busily ministering spirit; a hand bell tinkled urgently under the poop deck. . . .

I found my two officers waiting for me near the supper table, in the lighted cuddy. We sat down at once, and as I helped the chief mate, I said:

"Are you aware that there is a ship anchored inside the islands? I saw her mastheads above the ridge as the sun went down."

He raised sharply his simple face, overcharged by a terrible growth of whisker, and emitted his usual ejaculations: "Bless my soul, sir! You don't say so!"

My second mate was a round-cheeked, silent young man, grave beyond his years, I thought; but as our eyes happened to meet I detected a slight quiver on his lips. I looked down at once. It was not my part to encourage sneering on board my ship. It must be said, too, that I knew very little of my officers. In consequence of certain events of no particular significance, ex-cept to myself, I had been appointed to the command only a fortnight be-fore. Neither did I know much of the hands forward. All these people had been together for eighteen months or so, and my position was that of the only stranger on board. I mention this because it has some bearing on what is to follow. But what I felt most was my being a stranger to the ship; and if all the truth must be told, I was somewhat of a stranger to myself. The youngest man on board (barring the second mate), and untried as yet by a position of the fullest responsibility, I was willing to take the adequacy of the others for granted. They had simply to be equal to their tasks; but I wondered how far I should turn out faithful to that ideal conception of one's own personality every man sets up for himself secretly.

Meantime the chief mate, with an almost visible effect of collaboration on the part of his round eyes and frightful whiskers, was trying to evolve a theory of the anchored ship. His dominant trait was to take all things into earnest consideration. He was of a painstaking turn of mind. As he used to say, he "liked to account to himself" for practically everything that came in his way, down to a miserable scorpion he had found in his cabin a week before. The why and the wherefore of that scorpion—how it got on board and came to select his room rather than the pantry (which was a dark place and more what a scorpion would be partial to), and how on earth it managed to drown itself in the inkwell of his writing desk—had exercised him infinitely. The ship within the islands was much more easily accounted for; and just as we were about to rise from table he made his pronouncement. She was, he doubted not, a ship from home lately arrived. Probably she drew too much water to cross the bar except at the top of spring tides. Therefore she went into that natural harbor to wait for a few days in preference to remaining in an open roadstead.

"That's so," confirmed the second mate, suddenly, in his slightly hoarse voice. "She draws over twenty feet. She's the Liverpool ship *Sephora* with a cargo of coal. Hundred and twenty-three days from Cardiff."

We looked at him in surprise.

"The tugboat skipper told me when he came on board for your letters, sir," explained the young man. "He expects to take her up the river the day after tomorrow."

After thus overwhelming us with the extent of his information he slipped out of the cabin. The mate observed regretfully that he "could not account for that young fellow's whims." What prevented him telling us all about it at once, he wanted to know.

I detained him as he was making a move. For the last two days the crew had had plenty of hard work, and the night before they had very little sleep. I felt painfully that I—a stranger—was doing something unusual when I directed him to let all hands turn in without setting an anchor watch. I proposed to keep on deck myself till one o'clock or thereabouts. I would get the second mate to relieve me at that hour.

"He will turn out the cook and the steward at four," I concluded, "and then give you a call. Of course at the slightest sign of any sort of wind we'll have the hands up and make a start at once."

He concealed his astonishment. "Very well, sir." Outside the cuddy he put his head in the second mate's door to inform him of my unheard-of caprice to take a five hours' anchor watch on myself. I heard the other raise his voice incredulously—"What? The Captain himself?" Then a few more murmurs, a door closed, then another. A few moments later I went on deck.

My strangeness, which had made me sleepless, had prompted that unconventional arrangement, as if I had expected in those solitary hours of the night to get on terms with the ship of which I knew nothing, manned by men of whom I knew very little more. Fast alongside a wharf, littered like any ship in port with a tangle of unrelated things, invaded by unrelated shore people, I had hardly seen her yet properly. Now, as she lay cleared for sea, the stretch of her main-deck seemed to me very fine under the stars. Very fine, very roomy for her size, and very inviting. I descended the poop and paced the waist, my mind picturing to myself the coming passage through the Malay Archipelago, down the Indian Ocean, and up the Atlantic. All its phases were familiar enough to me, every characteristic, all the alternatives which were likely to face me on the high seas—everything! . . . except the novel responsibility of command. But I took heart from the reasonable thought that the ship was like other ships, the men like other men, and that the sea was not likely to keep any special surprises expressly for my discomfiture.

Arrived at that comforting conclusion, I bethought myself of a cigar and went below to get it. All was still down there. Everybody at the after end of the ship was sleeping profoundly. I came out again on the quarterdeck, agreeably at ease in my sleeping suit on that warm breathless night, barefooted, a glowing cigar in my teeth, and, going forward, I was met by the profound silence of the fore end of the ship. Only as I passed the door of the forecastle I heard a deep, quiet, trustful sigh of some sleeper inside. And suddenly I rejoiced in the great security of the sea as compared with the unrest of the land, in my choice of that untempted life presenting no disquieting problems, invested with an elementary moral beauty by the absolute straightforwardness of its appeal and by the singleness of its purpose.

The riding light in the forerigging burned with a clear, untroubled, as if symbolic, flame, confident and bright in the mysterious shades of the night. Passing on my way aft along the other side of the ship, I observed that the rope side ladder, put over, no doubt, for the master of the tug when he came to fetch away our letters, had not been hauled in as it should have been. I became annoyed at this, for exactitude in some small matters is the very soul of discipline. Then I reflected that I had myself peremptorily dismissed my officers from duty, and by my own act had prevented the anchor watch being formally set and things properly attended to. I asked myself whether it was wise ever to interfere with the established routine of duties even from the kindest of motives. My action might have made me appear eccentric. Goodness only knew how that absurdly whiskered mate would "account" for my conduct, and what the whole ship thought of that informality of their new captain. I was vexed with myself.

Not from compunction certainly, but, as it were mechanically, I proceeded to get the ladder in myself. Now a side ladder of that sort is a light affair and comes in easily, yet my vigorous tug, which should have brought it flying on board, merely recoiled upon my body in a totally unexpected jerk. What the devil! . . . I was so astounded by the immovableness of that ladder that I remained stockstill, trying to account for it to myself like that imbecile mate of mine. In the end, of course, I put my head over the rail.

The side of the ship made an opaque belt of shadow on the darkling glassy shimmer of the sea. But I saw at once something elongated and pale floating very close to the ladder. Before I could form a guess a faint flash of phosphorescent light, which seemed to issue suddenly from the naked body of a man, flickered in the sleeping water with the elusive, silent play of summer lightning in a night sky. With a gasp I saw revealed to my stare a pair of feet, the long legs, a broad livid back immersed right up to the neck in a greenish cadaverous glow. One hand, awash, clutched the bottom rung of the ladder. He was complete but for the head. A headless corpse! The cigar dropped out of my gaping mouth with a tiny plop and a short hiss quite audible in the absolute stillness of all things under heaven. At that I suppose he raised up his face, a dimly pale oval in the shadow of the ship's side. But even then I could only barely make out down there the shape of his black-haired head. However, it was enough for the horrid, frost-bound sensation which had gripped me about the chest to pass off. The moment of vain exclamations was past, too. I only climbed on the spare spar and leaned over the rail as far as I could, to bring my eyes nearer to that mystery floating alongside.

As he hung by the ladder, like a resting swimmer, the sea lightning played about his limbs at every stir; and he appeared in it ghastly, silvery, fishlike. He remained as mute as a fish, too. He made no motion to get out of the water, either. It was inconceivable that he should not attempt to come on board, and strangely troubling to suspect that perhaps he did not want to. And my first words were prompted by just that troubled incertitude.

"What's the matter?" I asked in my ordinary tone, speaking down to the face upturned exactly under mine.

"Cramp," it answered, no louder. Then slightly anxious, "I say, no need to call anyone."

"I was not going to," I said.

"Are you alone on deck?"

"Yes."

I had somehow the impression that he was on the point of letting go the ladder to swim away beyond my ken—mysterious as he came. But, for the moment, this being appearing as if he had risen from the bottom of the sea (it was certainly the nearest land to the ship) wanted only to know the time. I told him. And he, down there, tentatively:

"I suppose your captain's turned in?"

"I am sure he isn't," I said.

He seemed to struggle with himself, for I heard something like the low, bitter murmur of doubt. "What's the good?" His next words came out with a hesitating effort.

"Look here, my man. Could you call him out quietly?"

I thought the time had come to declare myself.

"*I* am the captain."

I heard a "By Jove!" whispered at the level of the water. The phosphorescence flashed in the swirl of the water all about his limbs, his other hand seized the ladder.

"My name's Leggatt."

The voice was calm and resolute. A good voice. The self-possession of that man had somehow induced a corresponding state in myself. It was very quietly that I remarked:

"You must be a good swimmer."

"Yes. I've been in the water practically since nine o'clock. The question for me now is whether I am to let go this ladder and go on swimming till I sink from exhaustion, or—to come on board here."

I felt this was no mere formula of desperate speech, but a real alternative in the view of a strong soul. I should have gathered from this that he was young; indeed, it is only the young who are ever confronted by such clear issues. But at the time it was pure intuition on my part. A mysterious communication was established already between us two—in the face of that silent, darkened tropical sea. I was young, too; young enough to make no comment. The man in the water began suddenly to climb up the ladder, and I hastened away from the rail to fetch some clothes.

Before entering the cabin I stood still, listening in the lobby at the foot of the stairs. A faint snore came through the closed door of the chief mate's room. The second mate's door was on the hook, but the darkness in there was absolutely soundless. He, too, was young and could sleep like a stone. Remained the steward, but he was not likely to wake up before he was called. I got a sleeping suit out of my room and, coming back on deck, saw the naked man from the sea sitting on the main hatch, glimmering white in the darkness, his elbows on his knees and his head in his hands. In a moment he had concealed his damp body in a sleeping suit of the same gray-stripe pattern as the one I was wearing and followed me like my double on the poop. Together we moved right aft, barefooted, silent.

"What is it?" I asked in a deadened voice, taking the lighted lamp out of the binnacle, and raising it to his face.

"An ugly business."

He had rather regular features; a good mouth; light eyes under somewhat heavy, dark eyebrows; a smooth, square forehead; no growth on his cheeks; a small, brown mustache, and a well-shaped, round chin. His expression was concentrated, meditative, under the inspecting light of the lamp I held up to his face; such as a man thinking hard in solitude might wear. My sleeping suit was just right for his size. A well-knit young fellow of twenty-five at most. He caught his lower lip with the edge of white, even teeth.

"Yes," I said, replacing the lamp in the binnacle. The warm, heavy tropical night closed upon his head again.

"There's a ship over there," he murmured.

"Yes, I know. The *Sephora*. Did you know of us?"

"Hadn't the slightest idea. I am the mate of her—" He paused and corrected himself. "I should say I *was*."

"Aha! Something wrong?"

"Yes. Very wrong indeed. I've killed a man."

"What do you mean? Just now?"

"No, on the passage. Weeks ago. Thirty-nine south. When I say a man—"

"Fit of temper," I suggested, confidently.

The shadowy, dark head, like mine, seemed to nod imperceptibly above the ghostly gray of my sleeping suit. It was, in the night, as though I had been faced by my own reflection in the depths of a somber and immense mirror.

"A pretty thing to have to own up to for a Conway boy," murmured my double, distinctly.

"You're a Conway boy?"

"I am," he said, as if startled. Then, slowly . . . "Perhaps you too—"

It was so; but being a couple of years older I had left before he joined. After a quick interchange of dates a silence fell; and I thought suddenly of my absurd mate with his terrific whiskers and the "Bless my soul—you don't say so" type of intellect. My double gave me an inkling of his thoughts by saying: "My father's a parson in Norfolk. Do you see me before a judge and jury on that charge? For myself I can't see the necessity. There are fellows that an angel from heaven—And I am not that. He was one of those creatures that are just simmering all the time with a silly sort of wickedness. Miserable devils that have no business to live at all. He wouldn't do his duty and wouldn't let anybody else do theirs. But what's the good of talking! You know well enough the sort of ill-conditioned snarling cur—"

He appealed to me as if our experiences had been as identical as our clothes. And I knew well enough the pestiferous danger of such a character where there are no means of legal repression. And I knew well enough also that my double there was no homicidal ruffian. I did not think of asking him for details, and he told me the story roughly in brusque, disconnected sentences. I needed no more. I saw it all going on as though I were myself inside that other sleeping suit.

"It happened while we were setting a reefed foresail, at dusk. Reefed foresail! You understand the sort of weather. The only sail we had left to keep the ship running; so you may guess what it had been like for days. Anxious sort of job, that. He gave me some of his cursed insolence at the sheet. I tell you I was overdone with this terrific weather that seemed to have no end to it. Terrific, I tell you—and a deep ship. I believe the fellow himself was half crazed with funk. It was no time for gentlemanly reproof, so I turned round and felled him like an ox. He up and at me. We closed just as an awful sea made for the ship. All hands saw it coming and took to the rigging, but I had him by the throat, and went on shaking him like a rat, the men above us yelling, 'Look out! look out!' Then a crash as if the sky had fallen on my head. They say that for over ten minutes hardly anything was to be seen of the ship—just the three masts and a bit of the forecastle head and of the poop all awash driving along in a smother of foam. It was a miracle that they found us, jammed together behind the forebitts. It's clear that I meant business, because I was holding him by the throat still when they picked us up. He was black in the face. It was too much for them. It seems they rushed us aft together, gripped as we were, screaming 'Murder!' like a lot of lunatics, and broke into the cuddy. And the ship running for her life, touch and go all the time, any minute her last in a sea fit to turn your hair gray only a-looking at it. I understand that the skipper, too, started raving like the rest of them. The man had been deprived of sleep for more than a week, and to have this sprung on him at the height of a furious gale nearly drove him out of his mind. I wonder they didn't fling me overboard after getting the carcass of their precious shipmate out of my fingers. They had rather a job to separate us, I've been told. A sufficiently fierce story to make an old judge and a respectable jury sit up a bit. The first thing I heard when I came to myself was the maddening howling of that endless gale, and on that the voice of the old man. He was hanging on to my bunk, staring into my face out of his sou'wester.

"'Mr. Leggatt, you have killed a man. You can act no longer as chief mate of this ship.'"

His care to subdue his voice made it sound monotonous. He rested a hand on the end of the skylight to steady himself with, and all that time did not stir a limb, so far as I could see. "Nice little tale for a quiet tea party," he concluded in the same tone.

One of my hands, too, rested on the end of the skylight; neither did I stir a limb, so far as I knew. We stood less than a foot from each other. It occurred to me that if old "Bless my soul—you don't say so" were to put his head up the companion and catch sight of us, he would think he was seeing double, or imagine himself come upon a scene of weird witchcraft; the strange captain having a quiet confabulation by the wheel with his own gray ghost. I became very much concerned to prevent anything of the sort. I heard the other's soothing undertone.

"My father's a parson in Norfolk," it said. Evidently he had forgotten he had told me this important fact before. Truly a nice little tale.

"You had better slip down into my stateroom now," I said, moving off stealthily. My double followed my movements; our bare feet made no sound; I let him in, closed the door with care, and, after giving a call to the second mate, returned on deck for my relief.

"Not much sign of any wind yet," I remarked when he approached.

"No, sir. Not much," he assented, sleepily, in his hoarse voice, with just enough deference, no more, and barely suppressing a yawn.

"Well, that's all you have to look out for. You have got your orders."

"Yes, sir."

I paced a turn or two on the poop and saw him take up his position face forward with his elbow in the ratlines of the mizzen rigging before I went below. The mate's faint snoring was still going on peacefully. The cuddy lamp was burning over the table on which stood a vase with flowers, a polite attention from the ship's provision merchant—the last flowers we should see for the next three months at the very least. Two bunches of bananas hung from the beam symmetrically, one on each side of the rudder casing. Everything was as before in the ship—except that two of her captain's sleeping suits were simultaneously in use, one motionless in the cuddy, the other keeping very still in the captain's stateroom.

It must be explained here that my cabin had the form of the capital letter L, the door being within the angle and opening into the short part of the letter. A couch was to the left, the bed place to the right; my writing desk and the chronometers' table faced the door. But anyone opening it, unless he stepped right inside, had no view of what I call the long (or vertical) part of the letter. It contained some lockers surmounted by a bookcase; and a few clothes, a thick jacket or two, caps, oilskin coat, and such like, hung on hooks. There was at the bottom of that part a door opening into my bathroom, which could be entered also directly from the saloon. But that way was never used.

The mysterious arrival had discovered the advantage of this particular shape. Entering my room, lighted strongly by a big bulkhead lamp swung on gimbals above my writing desk, I did not see him anywhere till he stepped out quietly from behind the coats hung in the recessed part.

"I heard somebody moving about, and went in there at once," he whispered.

I, too, spoke under my breath.

"Nobody is likely to come in here without knocking and getting permission."

He nodded. His face was thin and the sunburn faded, as though he had been ill. And no wonder. He had been, I heard presently, kept under arrest in his cabin for nearly seven weeks. But there was nothing sickly in his eyes or in his expression. He was not a bit like me, really; yet, as we stood leaning over my bed place, whispering side by side, with our dark heads together and our backs to the door, anybody bold enough to open it stealthily would have been treated to the uncanny sight of a double captain busy talking in whispers with his other self.

"But all this doesn't tell me how you came to hang on to our side ladder," I inquired, in the hardly audible murmurs we used, after he had told me something more of the proceedings on board the *Sephora* once the bad weather was over.

"When we sighted Java Head I had had time to think all those matters out several times over. I had six weeks of doing nothing else, and with only an hour or so every evening for a tramp on the quarter-deck."

He whispered, his arms folded on the side of my bed place, staring through the open port. And I could imagine perfectly the manner of this thinking out—a stubborn if not a steadfast operation; something of which I should have been perfectly incapable.

"I reckoned it would be dark before we closed with the land," he continued, so low that I had to strain my hearing near as we were to each other, shoulder touching shoulder almost. "So I asked to speak to the old man. He always seemed very sick when he came to see me—as if he could not look me in the face. You know, that foresail saved the ship. She was too deep to have run long under bare poles. And it was I that managed to set it for him. Anyway, he came. When I had him in my cabin—he stood by the door looking at me as if I had the halter round my neck already—I asked him right away to leave my cabin door unlocked at night while the ship was going through Sunda Straits. There would be the Java coast within two or three miles, off Angier Point. I wanted nothing more. I've had a prize for swimming my second year in the Conway."

"I can believe it," I breathed out.

"God only knows why they locked me in every night. To see some of their faces you'd have thought they were afraid I'd go about at night strangling people. Am I a murdering brute? Do I look it? By Jove! If I had been he wouldn't have trusted himself like that into my room. You'll say I might have chucked him aside and bolted out, there and then—it was dark already. Well, no. And for the same reason I wouldn't think of trying to smash the door. There would have been a rush to stop me at the noise, and I did not mean to get into a confounded scrimmage. Somebody else might have got killed—for I would not have broken out only to get chucked back, and I did not want any more of that work. He refused, looking more sick than ever. He was afraid of the men, and also of that old second mate of his who had been sailing with him for years—a gray-headed old humbug; and his steward, too, had been with him devil knows how long—seventeen years or more—a dogmatic sort of loafer who hated me like poison, just because I was the chief mate. No chief mate ever made more than one voyage in the *Sephora*, you know. Those two old chaps ran the ship. Devil only knows what the skipper wasn't afraid of (all his nerve went to pieces altogether in that hellish spell of bad weather we had)—of what the law would do to him—of his wife, perhaps. Oh, yes! she's on board. Though I don't think she would have meddled. She would have been only too glad to have me out of the ship in any way. The 'brand of Cain' business, don't you see. That's all right. I was ready enough to go off wandering on the face of the earth—and that was price enough to pay for an Abel of that sort. Anyhow, he wouldn't listen to me. 'This thing must take its course. I represent the law here.' He was shaking like a leaf. 'So you won't?' 'No!' 'Then I hope you will be able to sleep on that,' I said, and turned my back on him. 'I wonder that *you* can,' cries he, and locks the door.

"Well after that, I couldn't. Not very well. That was three weeks ago. We have had a slow passage through the Java Sea; drifted about Carimata for ten days. When we anchored here they thought, I suppose, it was all right. The nearest land (and that's five miles) is the ship's destination; the consul would soon set about catching me; and there would have been no object in bolting to these islets there. I don't suppose there's a drop of water on them. I don't know how it was, but tonight that steward, after bringing me my supper, went out to let me eat it, and left the door unlocked. And I ate it— all there was, too. After I had finished I strolled out on the quarterdeck. I don't know that I meant to do anything. A breath of fresh air was all I wanted, I believe. Then a sudden temptation came over me. I kicked off my slippers and was in the water before I had made up my mind fairly. Somebody heard the splash and they raised an awful hullabaloo. 'He's gone! Lower the boats! He's committed suicide! No, he's swimming.' Certainly I was swimming. It's not so easy for a swimmer like me to commit suicide by drowning. I landed on the nearest islet before the boat left the ship's side. I heard them pulling about in the dark, hailing, and so on, but after a bit they gave up. Everything quieted down and the anchorage became as still as death. I sat down on a stone and began to think. I felt certain they would start searching for me at daylight. There was no place to hide on those stony things—and if there had been, what would have been the good? But now I was clear of that ship, I was not going back. So after a while I took off all my clothes, tied them up in a bundle with a stone inside, and dropped them in the deep water on the outer side of that islet. That was suicide enough for me. Let them think what they liked, but I didn't mean to drown myself. I meant to swim till I sank—but that's not the same thing. I struck out for another of these little islands, and it was from that one that I first saw your riding light. Something to swim for. I went on easily, and on the way I came upon a flat rock a foot or two above water. In the daytime, I dare say, you might make it out with a glass from your poop. I scrambled up on it and rested myself for a bit. Then I made another start. That last spell must have been over a mile."

His whisper was getting fainter and fainter, and all the time he stared straight out through the porthole, in which there was not even a star to be seen. I had not interrupted him. There was something that made comment impossible in his narrative, or perhaps in himself; a sort of feeling, a quality, which I can't find a name for. And when he ceased, all I found was a futile whisper: "So you swam for our light?"

"Yes—straight for it. It was something to swim for. I couldn't see any stars low down, because the coast was in the way, and I couldn't see the land, either. The water was like glass. One might have been swimming in a confounded thousand-feet-deep cistern with no place for scrambling out anywhere; but what I didn't like was the notion of swimming round and round like a crazed bullock before I gave out; and as I didn't mean to go back . . . No. Do you see me being hauled back, stark naked, off one of these little islands by the scruff of the neck and fighting like a wild beast? Somebody would have got killed for certain, and I did not want any of that. So I went on. Then your ladder—"

"Why didn't you hail the ship?" I asked, a little louder.

He touched my shoulder lightly. Lazy footsteps came right over our heads and stopped. The second mate had crossed from the other side of the poop and might have been hanging over the rail for all we knew.

"He couldn't hear us talking—could he?" My double breathed into my very ear, anxiously.

His anxiety was an answer, a sufficient answer, to the question I had put to him. An answer containing all the difficulty of that situation. I closed the porthole quietly, to make sure. A louder word might have been overheard.

"Who's that?" he whispered then.

"My second mate. But I don't know much more of the fellow than you do."

And I told him a little about myself. I had been appointed to take charge while I least expected anything of the sort, not quite a fortnight ago. I didn't know either the ship or the people. Hadn't had the time in port to look about me or size anybody up. And as to the crew, all they knew was that I was appointed to take the ship home. For the rest, I was almost as much of a stranger on board as himself, I said. And at the moment I felt it most acutely. I felt that it would take very little to make me a suspect person in the eyes of the ship's company.

He turned about meantime; and we, the two strangers in the ship, faced each other in identical attitudes.

"Your ladder—" he murmured, after a silence. "Who'd have thought of finding a ladder hanging over at night in a ship anchored out here! I felt just then a very unpleasant faintness. After the life I've been leading for nine weeks, anybody would have got out of condition. I wasn't capable of swimming round as far as your rudder chains. And, lo and behold! there was a ladder to get hold of. After I gripped it I said to myself, 'What's the good?' When I saw a man's head looking over I thought I would swim away presently and leave him shouting—in whatever language it was. I didn't mind being looked at. I—I liked it. And then you speaking to me so quietly—as if you had expected me—made me hold on a little longer. It had been a confounded lonely time—I don't mean while swimming. I was glad to talk a little to somebody that didn't belong to the *Sephora*. As to asking for the captain, that was a mere impulse. It could have been no use, with all the ship knowing about me and the other people pretty certain to be round here in the morning. I don't know—I wanted to be seen, to talk with somebody, before I went on. I don't know what I would have said. . . . 'Fine night, isn't it?' or something of the sort."

"Do you think they will be round here presently?" I asked with some incredulity.

"Quite likely," he said, faintly.

He looked extremely haggard all of a sudden. His head rolled on his shoulders.

"H'm. We shall see then. Meantime get into that bed," I whispered. "Want help? There."

It was a rather high bed place with a set of drawers underneath. This amazing swimmer really needed the lift I gave him by seizing his leg. He tumbled in, rolled over on his back, and flung one arm across his eyes. And then, with his face nearly hidden, he must have looked exactly as I used to look in that bed. I gazed upon my other self for a while before drawing across carefully the two green serge curtains which ran on a brass rod. I thought for a moment of pinning them together for greater safety, but I sat down on the couch, and once there I felt unwilling to rise and hunt for a pin. I would do it in a moment. I was extremely tired, in a peculiarly intimate way by the strain of stealthiness, by the effort of whispering and the general secrecy of this excitement. It was three o'clock by now and I had been on my feet since nine, but I was not sleepy; I could not have gone to sleep.

I sat there, fagged out, looking at the curtains, trying to clear my mind of the confused sensation of being in two places at once, and greatly bothered by an exasperating knocking in my head. It was a relief to discover suddenly that it was not in my head at all, but on the outside of the door. Before I could collect myself the words "Come in" were out of my mouth, and the steward entered with a tray, bringing in my morning coffee. I had slept, after all, and I was so frightened that I shouted, "This way! I am here, steward," as though he had been miles away. He put down the tray on the table next the couch and only then said, very quietly, "I can see you are here, sir." I felt him give me a keen look, but I dared not meet his eyes just then. He must have wondered why I had drawn the curtains of my bed before going to sleep on the couch. He went out, hooking the door open as usual.

I heard the crew washing decks above me. I knew I would have been told at once if there had been any wind. Calm, I thought, and I was doubly vexed. Indeed, I felt dual more than ever. The steward reappeared suddenly in the doorway. I jumped up from the couch so quickly that he gave a start.

"What do you want here?"

"Close your port, sir—they are washing decks."

"It is closed," I said, reddening.

"Very well, sir." But he did not move from the doorway and returned my stare in an extraordinary, equivocal manner for a time. Then his eyes wavered, all his expression changed, and in a voice unusually gentle, almost coaxingly:

"May I come in to take the empty cup away, sir?"

"Of course!" I turned my back on him while he popped in and out. Then I unhooked and closed the door and even pushed the bolt. This sort of thing could not go on very long. The cabin was as hot as an oven, too. I took a peep at my double, and discovered that he had not moved, his arm was still over his eyes; but his chest heaved; his hair was wet; his chin glistened with perspiration. I reached over him and opened the port.

"I must show myself on deck," I reflected.

Of course, theoretically, I could do what I liked, with no one to say nay to me within the whole circle of the horizon; but to lock my cabin door and take the key away I did not dare. Directly I put my head out of the companion I saw the group of my two officers, the second mate barefooted, the chief mate in long India-rubber boots, near the break of the poop, and the steward halfway down the poop ladder talking to them eagerly. He happened to catch sight of me and dived, the second ran down on the main-deck shouting some order or other, and the chief mate came to meet me, touching his cap.

There was a sort of curiosity in his eye that I did not like. I don't know whether the steward had told them that I was "queer" only, or downright drunk, but I know the man meant to have a good look at me. I watched him coming with a smile which, as he got into point-blank range, took effect and froze his very whiskers. I did not give him time to open his lips.

"Square the yards by lifts and braces before the hands go to breakfast."

It was the first particular order I had given on board that ship; and I stayed on deck to see it executed, too. I had felt the need of asserting myself without loss of time. That sneering young cub got taken down a peg or two on that occasion, and I also seized the opportunity of having a good look at the face of every foremast man as they filed past me to go to the after braces. At breakfast time, eating nothing myself, I presided with such frigid dignity that the two mates were only too glad to escape from the cabin as soon as decency permitted; and all the time the dual working of my mind distracted me almost to the point of insanity. I was constantly watching myself, my secret self, as dependent on my actions as my own personality, sleeping in that bed, behind that door which faced me as I sat at the head of the table. It was very much like being mad, only it was worse because one was aware of it.

I had to shake him for a solid minute, but when at last he opened his eyes it was in the full possession of his senses, with an inquiring look.

"All's well so far," I whispered. "Now you must vanish into the bathroom."

He did so, as noiseless as a ghost, and then I rang for the steward, and facing him boldly, directed him to tidy up my stateroom while I was having my bath—"and be quick about it." As my tone admitted of no excuses, he said, "Yes, sir," and ran off to fetch his dustpan and brushes. I took a bath and did most of my dressing, splashing, and whistling softly for the steward's edification, while the secret sharer of my life stood drawn up bolt upright in that little space, his face looking very sunken in daylight, his eyelids lowered under the stern, dark line of his eyebrows drawn together by a slight frown.

When I left him there to go back to my room the steward was finishing dusting. I sent for the mate and engaged him in some insignificant conversation. It was, as it were, trifling with the terrific character of his whiskers; but my object was to give him an opportunity for a good look at my cabin. And then I could at last shut, with a clear conscience, the door of my stateroom and get my double back into the recessed part. There was nothing else for it. He had to sit still on a small folding stool, half smothered by the heavy coats hanging there. We listened to the steward going into the bathroom out of the saloon, filling the water bottles there, scrubbing the bath, setting things to rights, whisk, bang, clatter—out again into the saloon—turn the key—click. Such was my scheme for keeping my second self invisible. Nothing better could be contrived under the circumstances. And there we sat; I at my writing desk ready to appear busy with some papers, he behind me out of sight of the door. It would not have been prudent to talk in daytime; and I could not have stood the excitement of that queer sense of whispering to myself. Now and then, glancing over my shoulder, I saw him far back there, sitting rigidly on the low stool, his bare feet close together, his arms folded, his head hanging on his breast—and perfectly still. Anybody would have taken him for me.

I was fascinated by it myself. Every moment I had to glance over my shoulder. I was looking at him when a voice outside the door said:

"Beg pardon, sir."

"Well!" . . . I kept my eyes on him, and so when the voice outside the door announced, "There's a ship's boat coming our way, sir," I saw him give a start—the first movement he had made for hours. But he did not raise his bowed head.

"All right. Get the ladder over."

I hesitated. Should I whisper something to him? But what? His immobility seemed to have been never disturbed. What could I tell him he did not know already? . . . Finally I went on deck.

Two

The skipper of the *Sephora* had a thin red whisker all round his face, and the sort of complexion that goes with hair of that color; also the particular, rather smeary shade of blue in the eyes. He was not exactly a showy figure; his shoulders were high, his stature but middling—one leg slightly more bandy than the other. He shook hands, looking vaguely around. A spiritless tenacity was his main characteristic, I judged. I behaved with a politeness which seemed to disconcert him. Perhaps he was shy. He mumbled to me as if he were ashamed of what he was saying; gave his name (it was something like Archbold—but at this distance of years I hardly am sure), his ship's name, and a few other particulars of that sort, in the manner of a criminal making a reluctant and doleful confession. He had had terrible weather on the passage out—terrible—terrible—wife aboard, too.

By this time we were seated in the cabin and the steward brought in a tray with a bottle and glasses. "Thanks! No." Never took liquor. Would have some water, though. He drank two tumblerfuls. Terrible thirsty work. Ever since daylight had been exploring the islands round his ship.

"What was that for—fun?" I asked, with an appearance of polite interest.

"No!" He sighed. "Painful duty."

As he persisted in his mumbling and I wanted my double to hear every word, I hit upon the notion of informing him that I regretted to say I was hard of hearing.

"Such a young man, too!" he nodded, keeping his smeary blue, unintelligent eyes fastened upon me. "What was the cause of it—some disease?" he inquired, without the least sympathy and as if he thought that, if so, I'd got no more than I deserved.

"Yes; disease," I admitted in a cheerful tone which seemed to shock him. But my point was gained, because he had to raise his voice to give me his tale. It is not worth while to record that version. It was just over two months since all this had happened, and he had thought so much about it that he seemed completely muddled as to its bearings, but still immensely impressed.

"What would you think of such a thing happening on board your own ship? I've had the *Sephora* for these fifteen years. I am a well-known shipmaster."

He was densely distressed—and perhaps I should have sympathized with him if I had been able to detach my mental vision from the unsuspected sharer of my cabin as though he were my second self. There he was on the other side of the bulkhead, four or five feet from us, no more, as we sat in the saloon. I looked politely at Captain Archbold (if that was his name), but it was the other I saw, in a gray sleeping suit, seated on a low stool, his bare feet close together, his arms folded, and every word said between us falling into the ears of his dark head bowed on his chest.

"I have been at sea now, man and boy, for seven-and-thirty years, and I've never heard of such a thing happening in an English ship. And that it should be my ship. Wife on board, too."

I was hardly listening to him.

"Don't you think," I said, "that the heavy sea which, you told me, came aboard just then might have killed the man? I have seen the sheer weight of a sea kill a man very neatly, by simply breaking his neck."

"Good God!" he uttered, impressively, fixing his smeary blue eyes on me. "The sea! No man killed by the sea ever looked like that." He seemed positively scandalized at my suggestion. And as I gazed at him certainly not prepared for anything original on his part, he advanced his head close to mine and thrust his tongue out at me so suddenly that I couldn't help starting back.

After scoring over my calmness in this graphic way he nodded wisely. If I had seen the sight, he assured me, I would never forget it as long as I lived. The weather was too bad to give the corpse a proper sea burial. So next day at dawn they took it up on the poop, covering its face with a bit of bunting; he read a short prayer, and then, just as it was, in its oilskins and long boots, they launched it amongst those mountainous seas that seemed ready every moment to swallow up the ship herself and the terrified lives on board of her.

"That reefed foresail saved you," I threw in.

"Under God—it did," he exclaimed fervently. "It was by a special mercy, I firmly believe, that it stood some of those hurricane squalls."

"It was the setting of that sail which—" I began.

"God's own hand in it," he interrupted me. "Nothing less could have done it. I don't mind telling you that I hardly dared give the order. It seemed impossible that we could touch anything without losing it, and then our last hope would have been gone."

The terror of that gale was on him yet. I let him go on for a bit, then said, casually—as if returning to a minor subject:

"You were very anxious to give up your mate to the shore people, I believe?"

He was. To the law. His obscure tenacity on that point had in it something incomprehensible and a little awful; something, as it were, mystical, quite apart from his anxiety that he should not be suspected of "countenancing any doings of that sort." Seven-and-thirty virtuous years at sea, of which over twenty of immaculate command, and the last fifteen in the *Sephora*, seemed to have laid him under some pitiless obligation.

"And you know," he went on, groping shame-facedly amongst his feelings, "I did not engage that young fellow. His people had some interest with my owners. I was in a way forced to take him on. He looked very smart, very gentlemanly, and all that. But do you know—I never liked him, somehow. I am a plain man. You see, he wasn't exactly the sort for the chief mate of a ship like the *Sephora*."

I had become so connected in thoughts and impressions with the secret sharer of my cabin that I felt as if I, personally, were being given to understand that I, too, was not the sort that would have done for the chief mate of a ship like the *Sephora*. I had no doubt of it in my mind.

"Not at all the style of man. You understand," he insisted, superfluously, looking hard at me.

I smiled urbanely. He seemed at a loss for a while.

"I suppose I must report a suicide."

"Beg pardon?"

"Sui-cide! That's what I'll have to write to my owners directly I get in."

"Unless you manage to recover him before tomorrow," I assented, dispassionately. . . . "I mean, alive."

He mumbled something which I really did not catch, and I turned my ear to him in a puzzled manner. He fairly bawled:

"The land—I say, the mainland is at least seven miles off my anchorage."

"About that."

My lack of excitement, of curiosity, of surprise, of any sort of pronounced interest, began to arouse his distrust. But except for the felicitous pretense of deafness I had not tried to pretend anything. I had felt utterly incapable of playing the part of ignorance properly, and therefore was afraid to try. It is also certain that he had brought some ready-made suspicions with him, and that he viewed my politeness as a strange and unnatural phenomenon. And yet how else could I have received him? Not heartily! That was impossible for psychological reasons, which I need not state here. My only object was to keep off his inquiries. Surlily? Yes, but surliness might have provoked a point-blank question. From its novelty to him and from its nature, punctilious courtesy was the manner best calculated to restrain the man. But there was the danger of his breaking through my defense bluntly. I could not, I think, have met him by a direct lie, also for psychological (not moral) reasons. If he had only known how afraid I was of his putting my feeling of identity with the other to the test! But, strangely enough—(I thought of it only afterwards)—I believe that he was not a little disconcerted by the reverse side of that weird situation, by something in me that reminded him of the man he was seeking—suggested a mysterious similitude to the young fellow he had distrusted and disliked from the first.

However that might have been, the silence was not very prolonged. He took another oblique step.

"I reckon I had no more than a two-mile pull to your ship. Not a bit more."

"And quite enough, too, in this awful heat," I said.

Another pause full of mistrust followed. Necessity, they say, is mother of invention, but fear, too, is not barren of ingenious suggestions. And I was afraid he would ask me point-blank for news of my other self.

"Nice little saloon, isn't it?" I remarked, as if noticing for the first time the way his eyes roamed from one closed door to the other. "And very well fitted out, too. Here, for instance," I continued, reaching over the back of my seat negligently and flinging the door open, "is my bathroom."

He made an eager movement, but hardly gave it a glance. I got up, shut the door of the bathroom, and invited him to have a look round, as if I were very proud of my accommodation. He had to rise and be shown round, but he went through the business without any raptures whatever.

"And now we'll have a look at my stateroom," I declared, in a voice as loud as I dared to make it, crossing the cabin to the starboard side with purposely heavy steps.

He followed me in and gazed around. My intelligent double had vanished. I played my part.

"Very convenient—isn't it?"

"Very nice. Very comf . . ." He didn't finish and went out brusquely as if to escape from some unrighteous wiles of mine. But it was not to be. I had been too frightened not to feel vengeful; I felt I had him on the run, and I meant to keep him on the run. My polite insistence must have had some-

THE SECRET SHARER   549

thing menacing in it, because he gave in suddenly. And I did not let him off
a single item; mate's room, pantry, storerooms, the very sail locker which
was also under the poop—he had to look into them all. When at last I
showed him out on the quarter-deck he drew a long, spiritless sigh, and
mumbled dismally that he must really be going back to his ship now. I desired my mate, who had joined us, to see to the captain's boat.

The man of whiskers gave a blast on the whistle which he used to wear
hanging round his neck, and yelled, "*Sephora's* away!" My double down
there in my cabin must have heard, and certainly could not feel more relieved than I. Four fellows came running out from somewhere forward and
went over the side, while my own men, appearing on deck too, lined the
rail. I escorted my visitor to the gangway ceremoniously, and nearly overdid
it. He was a tenacious beast. On the very ladder he lingered, and in that
unique, guiltily conscientious manner of sticking to the point:

"I say . . . you . . . you don't think that—"

I covered his voice loudly:

"Certainly not. . . . I am delighted. Good-by."

I had an idea of what he meant to say, and just saved myself by the privilege of defective hearing. He was too shaken generally to insist, but my
mate, close witness of that parting, looked mystified and his face took on a
thoughtful cast. As I did not want to appear as if I wished to avoid all communication with my officers, he had the opportunity to address me.

"Seems a very nice man. His boat's crew told our chaps a very extraordinary story, if what I am told by the steward is true. I suppose you had it
from the captain, sir?"

"Yes. I had a story from the captain."

"A very horrible affair—isn't it, sir?"

"It is."

"Beats all these tales we hear about murders in Yankee ships."

"I don't think it beats them. I don't think it resembles them in the least."

"Bless my soul—you don't say so! But of course I've no acquaintance
whatever with American ships, not I, so I couldn't go against your knowledge. It's horrible enough for me. . . . But the queerest part is that those
fellows seemed to have some idea the man was hidden aboard here. They
had really. Did you ever hear of such a thing?"

"Preposterous—isn't it?"

We were walking to and fro athwart the quarter-deck. No one of the
crew forward could be seen (the day was Sunday), and the mate pursued:

"There was some little dispute about it. Our chaps took offense. 'As if we
would harbor a thing like that,' they said. 'Wouldn't you like to look for him
in our coalhole?' Quite a tiff. But they made it up in the end. I suppose he
did drown himself. Don't you, sir?"

"I don't suppose anything."

"You have no doubt in the matter, sir?"

"None whatever."

I left him suddenly. I felt I was producing a bad impression, but with my double down there it was most trying to be on deck. And it was almost as trying to be below. Altogether a nerve-trying situation. But on the whole I felt less torn in two when I was with him. There was no one in the whole ship whom I dared take into my confidence. Since the hands had got to know his story, it would have been impossible to pass him off for anyone else, and an accidental discovery was to be dreaded now more than ever. . . .

The steward being engaged in laying the table for dinner, we could talk only with our eyes when I first went down. Later in the afternoon we had a cautious try at whispering. The Sunday quietness of the ship was against us; the stillness of air and water around her was against us; the elements, the men were against us—everything was against us in our secret partnership; time itself—for this could not go on forever. The very trust in Providence was, I suppose, denied to his guilt. Shall I confess that this thought cast me down very much? And as to the chapter of accidents which counts for so much in the book of success, I could only hope that it was closed. For what favorable accident could be expected?

"Did you hear everything?" were my first words as soon as we took up our position side by side, leaning over my bed place.

He had. And the proof of it was his earnest whisper, "The man told you he hardly dared to give the order."

I understood the reference to be to that saving foresail.

"Yes. He was afraid of it being lost in the setting."

"I assure you he never gave the order. He may think he did, but he never gave it. He stood there with me on the break of the poop after the main topsail blew away, and whimpered about our last hope—positively whimpered about it and nothing else—and the night coming on! To hear one's skipper go on like that in such weather was enough to drive any fellow out of his mind. It worked me up into a sort of desperation. I just took it into my own hands and went away from him, boiling, and—But what's the use telling you? *You* know! . . . Do you think that if I had not been pretty fierce with them I should have got the men to do anything? Not I! The bo's'n perhaps? Perhaps! It wasn't a heavy sea—it was a sea gone mad! I suppose the end of the world will be something like that; and a man may have the heart to see it coming once and be done with it—but to have to face it day after day—I don't blame anybody. I was precious little better than the rest. Only—I was an officer of that old coal wagon, anyhow—"

"I quite understand," I conveyed that sincere assurance into his ear. He was out of breath with whispering; I could hear him pant slightly. It was all very simple. The same strung-up force which had given twenty-four men a chance, at least, for their lives, had, in a sort of recoil, crushed an unworthy mutinous existence.

But I had no leisure to weigh the merits of the matter—footsteps in the saloon, a heavy knock. "There's enough wind to get under way with, sir." Here was the call of a new claim upon my thoughts and even upon my feelings.

"Turn the hands up," I cried through the door. "I'll be on deck directly."

I was going out the make the acquaintance of my ship. Before I left the cabin our eyes met—the eyes of the only two strangers on board. I pointed to the recessed part where the little campstool awaited him and laid my finger on my lips. He made a gesture—somewhat vague—a little mysterious, accompanied by a faint smile, as if of regret.

This is not the place to enlarge upon the sensations of a man who feels for the first time a ship move under his feet to his own independent word. In my case they were not unalloyed. I was not wholly alone with my command; for there was that stranger in my cabin. Or rather, I was not completely and wholly with her. Part of me was absent. That mental feeling of being in two places at once affected me physically as if the mood of secrecy had penetrated my very soul. Before an hour had elapsed since the ship had begun to move, having occasion to ask the mate (he stood by my side) to take a compass bearing of the pagoda, I caught myself reaching up to his ear in whispers. I say I caught myself, but enough had escaped to startle the man. I can't describe it otherwise than by saying that he shied. A grave, preoccupied manner, as though he were in possession of some perplexing intelligence, did not leave him henceforth. A little later I moved away from the rail to look at the compass with such a stealthy gait that the helmsman noticed it—and I could not help noticing the unusual roundness of his eyes. These are trifling instances, though it's to no commander's advantage to be suspected of ludicrous eccentricities. But I was also more seriously affected. There are to a seaman certain words, gestures, that should in given conditions come as naturally, as instinctively as the winking of a menaced eye. A certain order should spring on to his lips without thinking; a certain sign should get itself made, so to speak, without reflection. But all unconscious alertness had abandoned me. I had to make an effort of will to recall myself back (from the cabin) to the conditions of the moment. I felt that I was appearing an irresolute commander to those people who were watching me more or less critically.

And, besides, there were the scares. On the second day out, for instance, coming off the deck in the afternoon (I had straw slippers on my bare feet) I stopped at the open pantry door and spoke to the steward. He was doing something there with his back to me. At the sound of my voice he nearly jumped out of his skin, as the saying is, and incidentally broke a cup.

"What on earth's the matter with you?" I asked, astonished.

He was extremely confused. "Beg your pardon, sir. I made sure you were in your cabin."

"You see I wasn't."

"No, sir. I could have sworn I had heard you moving in there not a moment ago. It's most extraordinary . . . very sorry, sir."

I passed on with an inward shudder. I was so identified with my secret double that I did not even mention the fact in those scanty, fearful whispers we exchanged. I suppose he had made some slight noise of some kind or other. It would have been miraculous if he hadn't at one time or another. And yet, haggard as he appeared, he looked always perfectly self-controlled, more than calm—almost invulnerable. On my suggestion he remained almost entirely in the bathroom, which, upon the whole, was the safest place. There could be really no shadow of an excuse for anyone ever wanting to go in there, once the steward had done with it. It was a very tiny place. Sometimes he reclined on the floor, his legs bent, his head sustained on one elbow. At others I would find him on the campstool, sitting in his gray sleeping suit and with his cropped dark hair like a patient, unmoved convict. At night I would smuggle him into my bed place, and we would whisper together, with the regular footfalls of the officer of the watch passing and repassing over our heads. It was an infinitely miserable time. It was lucky that some tins of fine preserves were stowed in a locker in my stateroom; hard bread I could always get hold of; and so he lived on stewed chicken, pâté de foie gras, asparagus, cooked oysters, sardines—on all sorts of abominable sham delicacies out of tins. My early-morning coffee he always drank; and it was all I dared do for him in that respect.

Every day there was the horrible maneuvering to go through so that my room and then the bathroom should be done in the usual way. I came to hate the sight of the steward, to abhor the voice of that harmless man. I felt that it was he who would bring on the disaster of discovery. It hung like a sword over our heads.

The fourth day out, I think (we were then working down the east side of the Gulf of Siam, tack for tack, in light winds and smooth water)—the fourth day, I say, of this miserable juggling with the unavoidable, as we sat at our evening meal, that man, whose slightest movement I dreaded, after putting down the dishes ran up on deck busily. This could not be dangerous. Presently he came down again; and then it appeared that he had remembered a coat of mine which I had thrown over a rail to dry after having been wetted in a shower which had passed over the ship in the afternoon. Sitting stolidly at the head of the table I became terrified at the sight of the garment on his arm. Of course he made for my door. There was no time to lose.

"Steward," I thundered. My nerves were so shaken that I could not govern my voice and conceal my agitation. This was the sort of thing that made my terrifically whiskered mate tap his forehead with his forefinger. I had detected him using that gesture while talking on deck with a confidential air to the carpenter. It was too far to hear a word, but I had no doubt that this pantomime could only refer to the strange new captain.

"Yes, sir," the pale-faced steward turned resignedly to me. It was this maddening course of being shouted at, checked without rhyme or reason, arbitrarily chased out of my cabin, suddenly called into it, sent flying out of his pantry on incomprehensible errands, that accounted for the growing wretchedness of his expression.

"Where are you with that coat?"

"To your room, sir."

"Is there another shower coming?"

"I'm sure I don't know, sir. Shall I go up again and see, sir?"

"No! never mind."

My object was attained, as of course my other self in there would have heard everything that passed. During this interlude my two officers never raised their eyes off their respective plates; but the lip of that confounded cub, the second mate, quivered visibly.

I expected the steward to hook my coat on and come out at once. He was very slow about it; but I dominated my nervousness sufficiently not to shout after him. Suddenly I became aware (it could be heard plainly enough) that the fellow for some reason or other was opening the door of the bathroom. It was the end. The place was literally not big enough to swing a cat in. My voice died in my throat and I went stony all over. I expected to a hear a yell of surprise and terror, and made a movement, but had not the strength to get on my legs. Everything remained still. Had my second self taken the poor wretch by the throat? I don't know what I could have done next moment if I had not seen the steward come out of my room, close the door, and then stand quietly by the sideboard.

"Saved," I thought. "But, no! Lost! Gone! He was gone!"

I laid my knife and fork down and leaned back in my chair. My head swam. After a while, when sufficiently recovered to speak in a steady voice, I instructed my mate to put the ship round at eight o'clock himself.

"I won't come on deck," I went on. "I think I'll turn in, and unless the wind shifts I don't want to be disturbed before midnight. I feel a bit seedy."

"You did look middling bad a little while ago," the chief mate remarked without showing any great concern.

They both went out, and I stared at the steward clearing the table. There was nothing to be read on that wretched man's face. But why did he avoid my eyes, I asked myself. Then I thought I should like to hear the sound of his voice.

"Steward!"

"Sir!" Startled as usual.

"Where did you hang up that coat?"

"In the bathroom, sir." The usual anxious tone. "It's not quite dry yet, sir."

For some time longer I sat in the cuddy. Had my double vanished as he had come? But of his coming there was an explanation, whereas his disappearance would be inexplicable. . . . I went slowly into my dark room, shut the door, lighted the lamp, and for a time dared not turn round. When at last I did I saw him standing bolt-upright in the narrow recessed part. It would not be true to say I had a shock, but an irresistible doubt of his bodily existence flitted through my mind. Can it be, I asked myself, that he is not visible to other eyes than mine? It was like being haunted. Motionless, with a grave face, he raised his hands slightly at me in a gesture which meant clearly, "Heavens! what a narrow escape!" Narrow indeed. I think I had come creeping quietly as near insanity as any man who has not actually gone over the border. That gesture restrained me, so to speak.

The mate with the terrific whiskers was now putting the ship on the other tack. In the moment of profound silence which follows upon the hands going to their stations I heard on the poop his raised voice: "Hard alee!" and the distant shout of the order repeated on the main-deck. The sails, in that light breeze, made but a faint fluttering noise. It ceased. The ship was coming round slowly: I held my breath in the renewed stillness of expectation; one wouldn't have thought that there was a single living soul on her decks. A sudden brisk shout, "Mainsail haul!" broke the spell, and in the noisy cries and rush overhead of the men running away with the main brace we two, down in my cabin, came together in our usual position by the bed place.

He did not wait for my question. "I heard him fumbling here and just managed to squat myself down in the bath," he whispered to me. "The fellow only opened the door and put his arm in to hang the coat up. All the same—"

"I never thought of that," I whispered back, even more appalled than before at the closeness of the shave, and marveling at that something unyielding in his character which was carrying him through so finely. There was no agitation in his whisper. Whoever was being driven distracted, it was not he. He was sane. And the proof of his sanity was continued when he took up the whispering again.

"It would never do for me to come to life again."

It was something that a ghost might have said. But what he was alluding to was his old captain's reluctant admission of the theory of suicide. It would obviously serve his turn—if I had understood at all the view which seemed to govern the unalterable purpose of his action.

"You must maroon me as soon as ever you can get amongst these islands off the Cambodge shore," he went on.

"Maroon you! We are not living in a boy's adventure tale," I protested. His scornful whispering took me up.

"We aren't indeed! There's nothing of a boy's tale in this. But there's nothing else for it. I want no more. You don't suppose I am afraid of what can be done to me? Prison or gallows or whatever they may please. But you don't see me coming back to explain such things to an old fellow in a wig and twelve respectable tradesmen, do you? What can they know whether I am guilty or not—or of *what* I am guilty, either? That's my affair. What does the Bible say? 'Driven off the face of the earth.' Very well, I am off the face of the earth now. As I came at night so I shall go."

"Impossible!" I murmured. "You can't."

"Can't? . . . Not naked like a soul on the Day of Judgment. I shall freeze on to this sleeping suit. The Last Day is not yet—and . . . you have understood thoroughly. Didn't you?"

I felt suddenly ashamed of myself. I may say truly that I understood—and my hesitation in letting that man swim away from my ship's side had been a mere sham sentiment, a sort of cowardice.

"It can't be done now till next night," I breathed out. "The ship is on the off-shore tack and the wind may fail us."

"As long as I know that you understand," he whispered. "But of course you do. It's a great satisfaction to have got somebody to understand. You seem to have been there on purpose." And in the same whisper, as if we two whenever we talked had to say things to each other which were not fit for the world to hear, he added, "It's very wonderful."

We remained side by side talking in our secret way—but sometimes silent or just exchanging a whispered word or two at long intervals. And as usual he stared through the port. A breath of wind came now and again into our faces. The ship might have been moored in dock, so gently and on an even keel she slipped through the water, that did not murmur even at our passage, shadowy and silent like a phantom sea.

At midnight I went on deck, and to my mate's great surprise put the ship round on the other tack. His terrible whiskers flitted round me in silent criticism. I certainly should not have done it if it had been only a question of getting out of that sleepy gulf as quickly as possible. I believe he told the second mate, who relieved him, that it was a great want of judgment. The other only yawned. That intolerable cub shuffled about so sleepily and lolled against the rails in such a slack, improper fashion that I came down on him sharply.

"Aren't you properly awake yet?"

"Yes, sir! I am awake."

"Well, then, be good enough to hold yourself as if you were. And keep a lookout. If there's any current we'll be closing with some islands before daylight."

The east side of the gulf is fringed with islands, some solitary, others in groups. On the blue background of the high coast they seem to float, on silvery patches of calm water, arid and gray, or dark green and rounded like clumps of evergreen bushes, with the larger ones, a mile or two long, showing the outlines of ridges, ribs of gray rock under the dank mantle of matted leafage. Unknown to trade, to travel, almost to geography, the manner of life they harbor is an unsolved secret. There must be villages—settlements of fishermen at least—on the largest of them, and some communication with the world is probably kept up by native craft. But all that forenoon, as we headed for them, fanned along by the faintest of breezes, I saw no sign of man or canoe in the field of the telescope I kept on pointing at the scattered group.

At noon I gave no orders for a change of course, and the mate's whiskers became much concerned and seemed to be offering themselves unduly to my notice. At last I said:

"I am going to stand right in. Quite in—as far as I can take her."

The stare of extreme surprise imparted an air of ferocity also to his eyes, and he looked truly terrific for a moment.

"We're not doing well in the middle of the gulf," I continued, casually. "I am going to look for the land breezes tonight."

"Bless my soul! Do you mean, sir, in the dark amongst the lot of all them islands and reefs and shoals?"

"Well—if there are any regular land breezes at all on this coast one must get close inshore to find them, mustn't one?"

"Bless my soul!" he exclaimed again under his breath. All that afternoon he wore a dreamy, contemplative appearance which in him was a mark of perplexity. After dinner I went into my stateroom as if I meant to take some rest. There we two bent our dark heads over a half-unrolled chart lying on my bed.

"There," I said. "It's got to be Koh-ring. I've been looking at it ever since sunrise. It has got two hills and a low point. It must be inhabited. And on the coast opposite there is what looks like the mouth of a biggish river—with some towns, no doubt, not far up. It's the best chance for you that I can see."

"Anything. Koh-ring let it be."

He looked thoughtfully at the chart as if surveying chances and distances from a lofty height—and following with his eyes his own figure wandering on the blank land of Cochin-China, and then passing off that piece of paper clean out of sight into uncharted regions. And it was as if the ship had two captains to plan her course for her. I had been so worried and restless running up and down that I had not had the patience to dress that day. I had remained in my sleeping suit, with straw slippers and a soft floppy hat. The closeness of the heat in the gulf had been most oppressive, and the crew were used to seeing me wandering in that airy attire.

"She will clear the south point as she heads now," I whispered into his ear. "Goodness only knows when, though, but certainly after dark. I'll edge her in to half a mile, as far as I may be able to judge in the dark—"

"Be careful," he murmured, warningly—and I realized suddenly that all my future, the only future for which I was fit, would perhaps go irretrievably to pieces in any mishap to my first command.

I could not stop a moment longer in the room. I motioned him to get out of sight and made my way on the poop. That unplayful cub had the watch. I walked up and down for a while thinking things out, then beckoned him over.

"Send a couple of hands to open the two quarter-deck ports," I said, mildly.

He actually had the impudence, or else so forgot himself in his wonder at such an incomprehensible order, as to repeat:

"Open the quarter-deck ports! What for, sir?"

"The only reason you need concern yourself about is because I tell you to do so. Have them open wide and fastened properly."

He reddened and went off, but I believe made some jeering remark to the carpenter as to the sensible practice of ventilating a ship's quarter-deck. I know he popped into the mate's cabin to impart the fact to him because the whiskers came on deck, as it were by chance, and stole glances at me from below—for signs of lunacy or drunkenness, I suppose.

A little before supper, feeling more restless than ever, I rejoined, for a moment, my second self. And to find him sitting so quietly was surprising, like something against nature, inhuman.

I developed my plan in a hurried whisper.

"I shall stand in as close as I dare and then put her round. I will presently find means to smuggle you out of here into the sail locker, which communicates with the lobby. But there is an opening, a sort of square for hauling the sails out, which gives straight on the quarter-deck and which is never closed in fine weather, so as to give air to the sails. When the ship's way is deadened in stays and all the hands are aft at the main braces, you will have a clear road to slip out and get overboard through the open quarter-deck port. I've had them both fastened up. Use a rope's end to lower yourself into the water so as to avoid a splash—you know. It could be heard and cause some beastly complication."

He kept silent for a while, then whispered, "I understand."

"I won't be there to see you go," I began with an effort. "The rest . . . I only hope I have understood, too."

"You have. From first to last"—and for the first time there seemed to be a faltering, something strained in his whisper. He caught hold of my arm, but the ringing of the supper bell made me start. He didn't though; he only released his grip.

After supper I didn't come below again till well past eight o'clock. The faint, steady breeze was loaded with dew; and the wet, darkened sails held all there was of propelling power in it. The night, clear and starry, sparkled darkly, and the opaque, lightless patches shifting slowly against the low stars were the drifting islets. On the port bow there was a big one more distant and shadowily imposing by the great space of sky it eclipsed.

On opening the door I had a back view of my very own self looking at a chart. He had come out of the recess and was standing near the table.

"Quite dark enough," I whispered.

He stepped back and leaned against my bed with a level, quiet glance. I sat on the couch. We had nothing to say to each other. Over our heads the officer of the watch moved here and there. Then I heard him move quickly. I knew what that meant. He was making for the companion; and presently his voice was outside my door.

"We are drawing in pretty fast, sir. Land looks rather close."

"Very well," I answered. "I am coming on deck directly."

I waited till he was gone out of the cuddy, then rose. My double moved too. The time had come to exchange our last whispers, for neither of us was ever to hear each other's natural voice.

"Look here!" I opened a drawer and took out three sovereigns. "Take this anyhow. I've got six and I'd give you the lot, only I must keep a little money to buy some fruit and vegetables for the crew from native boats as we go through Sunda Straits."

He shook his head.

"Take it," I urged him, whispering desperately. "No one can tell what—"

He smiled and slapped meaningly the only pocket of the sleeping jacket. It was not safe, certainly. But I produced a large old silk handkerchief of mine, and tying the three pieces of gold in a corner, pressed it on him. He was touched, I suppose, because he took it at last and tied it quickly round his waist under the jacket, on his bare skin.

Our eyes met; several seconds elapsed, till, our glances still mingled I extended my hand and turned the lamp out. Then I passed through the cuddy, leaving the door of my room wide open. . . . "Steward!"

He was still lingering in the pantry in the greatness of his zeal, giving a rub-up to a plated cruet stand the last thing before going to bed. Being careful not to wake up the mate, whose room was opposite, I spoke in an undertone.

He looked round anxiously. "Sir!"

"Can you get me a little hot water from the galley?"

"I am afraid, sir, the galley fire's been out for some time now."

"Go and see."

He flew up the stairs.

"Now," I whispered, loudly, into the saloon—too loudly, perhaps, but I was afraid I couldn't make a sound. He was by my side in an instant—the double captain slipped past the stairs—through a tiny dark passage . . . a sliding door. We were in the sail locker, scrambling on our knees over the sails. A sudden thought struck me. I saw myself wandering barefooted, bareheaded, the sun beating on my dark poll. I snatched off my floppy hat and tried hurriedly in the dark to ram it on my other self. He dodged and fended off silently. I wonder what he thought had come to me before he understood and suddenly desisted. Our hands met gropingly, lingered united in a steady, motionless clasp for a second. . . . No word was breathed by either of us when they separated.

I was standing quietly by the pantry door when the steward returned.

"Sorry, sir. Kettle barely warm. Shall I light the spirit lamp?"

"Never mind."

I came out on deck slowly. It was now a matter of conscience to shave the land as close as possible—for now he must go overboard whenever the ship was put in stays. Must! There could be no going back for him. After a moment I walked over to leeward and my heart flew into my mouth at the nearness of the land on the bow. Under any other circumstances I would not have held on a minute longer. The second mate had followed me anxiously.

I looked on till I felt I could command my voice.

"She will weather," I said then in a quiet tone.

"Are you going to try that, sir?" he stammered out incredulously.

I took no notice of him and raised my tone just enough to be heard by the helmsman.

"Keep her good full."

"Good full, sir."

The wind fanned my cheek, the sails slept, the world was silent. The strain of watching the dark loom of the land grow bigger and denser was too much for me. I had shut my eyes—because the ship must go closer. She must! The stillness was intolerable. Were we standing still?

When I opened my eyes the second view started my heart with a thump. The black southern hill of Koh-ring seemed to hang right over the ship like a towering fragment of the everlasting night. On that enormous mass of blackness there was not a gleam to be seen, not a sound to be heard. It was gliding irresistibly towards us and yet seemed already within reach of the hand. I saw the vague figures of the watch grouped in the waist, gazing in awed silence.

"Are you going on, sir?" inquired an unsteady voice at my elbow.

I ignored it. I had to go on.

"Keep her full. Don't check her way. That won't do now," I said, warningly.

"I can't see the sails very well," the helmsman answered me, in strange, quavering tones.

Was she close enough? Already she was, I won't say in the shadow of the land, but in the very blackness of it, already swallowed up as it were, gone too close to be recalled, gone from me altogether.

"Give the mate a call," I said to the young man who stood at my elbow as still as death. "And turn all hands up."

My tone had a borrowed loudness reverberated from the height of the land. Several voices cried out together: "We are all on deck, sir."

Then stillness again, with the great shadow gliding closer, towering higher, without a light, without a sound. Such a hush had fallen on the ship that she might have been a bark of the dead floating in slowly under the very gate of Erebus.

"My God! Where are we?"

It was the mate moaning at my elbow. He was thunderstruck, and as it were deprived of the moral support of his whiskers. He clapped his hands and absolutely cried out, "Lost!"

"Be quiet," I said, sternly.

He lowered his tone, but I saw the shadowy gesture of his despair. "What are we doing here?"

"Looking for the land wind."

He made as if to tear his hair, and addressed me recklessly.

"She will never get out. You have done it, sir. I knew it'd end in something like this. She will never weather, and you are too close now to stay. She'll drift ashore before she's round. O my God!"

I caught his arm as he was raising it to batter his poor devoted head, and shook it violently.

"She's ashore already," he wailed, trying to tear himself away.

"Is she? . . . Keep good full there!"

"Good full, sir," cried the helmsman in a frightened, thin, childlike voice.

I hadn't let go the mate's arm and went on shaking it. "Ready about, do you hear? You go forward"—shake—"and stop there"—shake—"and hold your noise"—shake—"and see these head-sheets properly overhauled" —shake, shake—shake.

And all the time I dared not look towards the land lest my heart should fail me. I released my grip at last and he ran forward as if fleeing for dear life.

I wondered what my double there in the sail locker thought of this commotion. He was able to hear everything—and perhaps he was able to understand why, on my conscience, it had to be thus close—no less. My first order "Hard alee!" re-echoed ominously under the towering shadow of Koh-ring as if I had shouted in a mountain gorge. And then I watched the land intently. In that smooth water and light wind it was impossible to feel the ship coming-to. No! I could not feel her. And my second self was making now ready to ship out and lower himself overboard. Perhaps he was gone already . . . ?

The great black mass brooding over our very mastheads began to pivot away from the ship's side silently. And now I forgot the secret stranger ready to depart, and remembered only that I was a total stranger to the ship. I did not know her. Would she do it? How was she to be handled?

I swung the mainyard and waited helplessly. She was perhaps stopped, and her very fate hung in the balance, with the black mass of Koh-ring like the gate of the everlasting night towering over her taffrail. What would she do now? Had she way on her yet? I stepped to the side swiftly, and on the shadowy water I could see nothing except a faint phosphorescent flash revealing the glassy smoothness of the sleeping surface. It was impossible to tell—and I had not learned yet the feel of my ship. Was she moving? What I needed was something easily seen, a piece of paper, which I could throw overboard and watch. I had nothing on me. To run down for it I didn't dare. There was no time. All at once my strained, yearning stare distinguished a white object floating within a yard of the ship's side. White on the black water. A phosphorescent flash passed under it. What was that thing? . . . I recognized my own floppy hat. It must have fallen off his head . . . and he didn't bother. Now I had what I wanted—the saving mark for my eyes. But I hardly thought of my other self, now gone from the ship, to be hidden forever from all friendly faces, to be a fugitive and a vagabond on the earth, with no brand of the curse on his sane forehead to stay a slaying hand . . . too proud to explain.

And I watched the hat—the expression of my sudden pity for his mere flesh. It had been meant to save his homeless head from the dangers of the sun. And now—behold—it was saving the ship, by serving me for a mark to help out the ignorance of my strangeness. Ha! It was drifting forward, warning me just in time that the ship had gathered sternway.

"Shift the helm," I said in a low voice to the seaman standing still like a statue.

The man's eyes glistened wildly in the binnacle light as he jumped round to the other side and spun round the wheel.

I walked to the break of the poop. On the overshadowed deck all hands stood by the forebraces waiting for my order. The stars ahead seemed to be gliding from right to left. And all was so still in the world that I heard the quiet remark, "She's round," passed in a tone of intense relief between two seamen.

"Let go and haul."

The foreyards ran round with a great noise, amidst cheery cries. And now the frightful whiskers made themselves heard giving various orders. Already the ship was drawing ahead. And I was alone with her. Nothing! no one in the world should stand now between us, throwing a shadow on the way of silent knowledge and mute affection, the perfect communion of a seaman with his first command.

Walking to the taffrail, I was in time to make out, on the very edge of a darkness thrown by a towering black mass like the very gateway of Erebus —yes, I was in time to catch an evanescent glimpse of my white hat left behind to mark the spot where the secret sharer of my cabin and of my thoughts, as though he were my second self, had lowered himself into the water to take his punishment: a free man, a proud swimmer striking out for a new destiny.

JOSEPH CONRAD
1857–1924

Nothing in Jósef Teodor Konrad Walecz Korzeniowski's early life portended his future as a writer of English sea fiction. He was born in the landlocked territory of the Polish Ukraine and did not even catch a glimpse of the sea until he was seventeen. When he did it was very nearly love at first sight; within two years he had committed himself to be an apprentice on the *Mont-Blanc*, a vessel bound for Martinique. The effort to master English was made several years later.

After various smuggling and gambling adventures and an unhappy love affair in 1877–78, Conrad shot himself in the chest. The suicide attempt was unsuccessful, and he soon joined the English merchant marine. After receiving his master's certificate in 1886, he commanded two vessels, the *Otago* and SS *Roide Belges*, before retiring from sea duty altogether in 1894.

He began writing while at sea. His first story, "The Black Mate," appeared in 1886. His first novel, *Almayer's Folly*, which was not completed until 1894, was begun in 1892–93, when he was serving as first mate on a ship sailing from London to Adelaide.

Conrad had difficulty obtaining regular commands, so when *Almayer's Folly* was warmly received he forsook the sailor's life and pursued a long and distinguished career as a writer of fiction. One of his notable early works is *The Nigger of the Narcissus* (1897). Far more than an action story touched by the exotic, its theme is the profound riddle of human contact.

In *Lord Jim* (1900) Conrad brilliantly uses multiple points of view and intermediate narrators to create an artistic *tour de force*. The complex narrative technique is an integral part of the fabric of the novel, which examines the neglect of duty by a sensitive young sailor who looks for a way to atone for his failure.

The novella *Heart of Darkness* (1902), one of the most widely read of Conrad's tales, echoes the nightmarish atmosphere of a steamboat trip the author made up the Congo in 1890. It was a journey that made him apprehensive of the evil lurking along the river and left him seriously ill.

The novella *Typhoon* (1903) and the novel *Nostromo* (1904), both about the sea, were followed by two political works, *The Secret Agent* (1907) and *Under Western Eyes* (1911). The master storyteller also published, among other works, *Chance* (1913), *Victory* (1915), *The Shadow-Line* (1917), and *The Rover* (1922) before his death in 1924.

While his writing did not bring instant critical or financial success, it has worn well, and his eminent place in English letters is now secure. Conrad's fiction, firmly rooted in personal experience, transcends the particular and speaks to a universal audience, an achievement that has won him readers and sustained his stature as one of the towering figures in sea fiction.

Youth, a novella that has always been particularly attractive to American readers, was first published in *Youth: A Narrative, and Two Other Stories* (1903). *The Secret Sharer* was first published in 1910.

Acknowledgments

Guy de Maupassant: "At Sea," copyright 1923 and renewed 1951 by Alfred A. Knopf, Inc. Reprinted from *The Collected Novels and Stories of Guy de Maupassant*, translated by Ernest Boyd, by permission of the publisher.

Lord Dunsany: "Story of Land and Sea," copyright 1916 by Elkin Matthews. Reprinted from *Tales of Wonder* by Elkin Matthews.

William Faulkner: "Turnabout," copyright 1932 and renewed 1960 by Curtis Publishing House. Reprinted from *Collected Stories of William Faulkner* by permission of Random House, Inc.

F. Scott Fitzgerald: "The Rough Crossing," copyright 1951 by Charles Scribner's Sons; copyright renewed. Reprinted from *The Stories of F. Scott Fitzgerald*, edited by Malcolm Cowley, by permission of Charles Scribner's Sons.

C. S. Forester: "Night Stalk," copyright 1942 by The Curtis Publishing Company. Copyright renewed 1970 by Dorothy E. Forester. Reprinted from *Gold from Crete: Ten Stories* by C. S. Forester, by permission of Little, Brown and Company.

E. M. Forster: "The Story of the Siren," copyright 1928 by Harcourt, Brace, Inc.; renewed 1956 by E. M. Forster. Reprinted from *The Eternal Moment and Other Stories* by E. M. Forster, by permission of Harcourt Brace Jovanovich, Inc.

Ernest Hemingway: "After the Storm," copyright 1932 by Ernest Hemingway; copyright renewed 1960. Reprinted from *Winner Take Nothing*, copyright 1933 by Charles Scribner's Sons. Copyright renewed 1961 by Mary Hemingway, by permission of Charles Scribner's Sons.

W. Somerset Maugham: "Red," copyright 1921 by Asia Publishing Company. Reprinted from *The Trembling of a Leaf* by W. Somerset Maugham, by permission of Doubleday & Company, Inc., and executors of the estate of the late W. Somerset Maugham and William Heineman Limited.

Nicholas Monsarrat: "HMS *Marlborough* Will Enter Harbour," copyright 1947 by Nicholas Monsarrat. Reprinted from *Depends on What You Mean by Love*, by permission of Mrs. Ann Monsarrat and Curtis Brown, Ltd.

John W. Thomason, Jr.: "Mutiny," copyright 1929 by Charles Scribner's Sons. Copyright renewed 1957 by Leda B. Thomason. Reprinted from . . . *And a Few Marines*, by permission of Charles Scribner's Sons.

H. M. Tomlinson: "The Derelict," copyright 1927. Reprinted by permission of H. Charles Tomlinson.

Arthur T. Quiller-Couch: "The Roll-Call of the Reef," copyright 1896 by Arthur T. Quiller-Couch. Reprinted from *Selected Stories by "Q"* (1921) by permission of Monro Pennefather & Co.

John Updike: "Lifeguard," copyright 1961 by John Updike. Reprinted from *Pigeon Feathers and Other Stories*, by permission of Alfred A. Knopf, Inc. Originally appeared in *The New Yorker*.

The **Naval Institute Press** is the book-publishing arm of the U.S. Naval Institute, a private, nonprofit professional society for members of the sea services and civilians who share an interest in naval and maritime affairs. Established in 1873 at the U.S. Naval Academy in Annapolis, Maryland, where its offices remain today, the Naval Institute has more than 100,000 members worldwide.

Members of the Naval Institute receive the influential monthly magazine *Proceedings* and discounts on fine nautical prints, ship and aircraft photos, and subscriptions to the quarterly *Naval History* magazine. They also have access to the transcripts of the Institute's Oral History Program and get discounted admission to any of the Institute-sponsored seminars regularly offered around the country.

The Naval Institute's book-publishing program, begun in 1898 with basic guides to naval practices, has broadened its scope in recent years to include books of more general interest. Now the Naval Institute Press publishes more than forty new titles each year, ranging from how-to books on boating and navigation to battle histories, biographies, ship and aircraft guides, and novels. Institute members receive discounts on the Press's more than 375 books.

Full-time students are eligible for special half-price membership rates. Life memberships are also available.

For a free catalog describing the Naval Institute Press books currently available, and for further information about U.S. Naval Institute membership, please write to:

Membership & Communications Department
U.S. Naval Institute
Annapolis, Maryland 21402

Or call, toll-free, (800) 233-USNI. In Maryland, call (301) 224-3378.

DATE DUE
